BROTHERS
AND OTHERS
IN LAW

Brothers in Law
Friends at Court
Sober as a Judge

HENRY CECIL

THE COMPANION BOOK CLUB

Made and printed in Great Britain
for The Companion Book Club (Odhams Press Ltd.)
by C. Tinling & Co. Limited
Liverpool, London and Prescot
S.960.1R.P.

To Francis Younghusband
With all good wishes

from Henry Cecil

January 1966

Autographed

80/0

BROTHERS
AND OTHERS
IN LAW

"A blessed companion is a book"—JERROLD

CONTENTS

★

THIS Companion Book Club edition contains fourteen scenes, taken from the Boulting Brothers production *Brothers in Law*, which show Richard Attenborough as Henry, Ian Carmichael as Roger Thursby, Terry-Thomas as Mr Green, Jill Adams as Sally, Miles Malleson as Mr Grimes, Raymond Huntley as Mr Tatlock, Eric Barker as Alec and Olive Sloane as Mrs Newent. The film was produced by John Boulting and directed by Roy Boulting. *Brothers in Law* was adapted for the screen by Frank Harvey, Jeffrey Dell and Roy Boulting. Released by British Lion Films.

These illustrations will be found facing pages 32, 33, 64, 65, 128, 129, 160 and 161.

BROTHERS IN LAW

A*

CHAPTER ONE

CALL TO THE BAR

"GEORGE SMITH is acquitted by the jury at Assizes of a criminal offence. 'You are discharged,' the judge says to him, and then adds: 'You were very lucky in your jury.' Mr Smith issues a writ against the judge claiming damages for slander. What are the first steps likely to be taken in Mr Smith's action after the service of the writ?"

ROGER THURSBY looked round the hall where he was about to answer this last question in his Bar Final Examination. He was fairly well satisfied with his answers to the other questions and he had done most of them quickly. So he had plenty of time for the last. He looked at the pictures of past eminent judges on the walls. Surely, he thought, no judge would behave like the one in the question. He saw sternness in some of the faces, but no trace of the meanness which seemed to him implicit in the remark made by the judge to the prisoner. The jury had acquitted the man. Presumed innocent even before the verdict, he could not be thought less so after he had been found Not Guilty. Yet, after his acquittal, the judge, merely to gratify his own personal feelings, had strongly suggested that he was guilty. And the prisoner could not hit back. Or could he? That was the question. Well, there was plenty of time to answer it. How nice it was to be at the end of all his examinations. Roger was not an over-confident young man, but he knew that he had done well enough to pass at any rate. And soon he would be a barrister. Only twenty-one and a barrister. It was a great thought. There were not many young men who could be called to the Bar today at the age of twenty-one. A distant cousin of his had been called on his twenty-first birthday. But that was long before the days of military service. Roger had had to do a lot of work, and to give up quite a good deal, to be called before he was twenty-two. But he'd done it in the end. He had eaten all his dinners and had been pleased that this curious and pleasant custom was still retained as an essential qualification for admission to the English Bar. It must have been nicer still in the old days, he thought, when association in the Inns of Court with men of law and dinners with them in the evening took the place of examinations. He had enjoyed the dinners, meeting all sorts of different young men and women in the process. He had liked the sometimes quaint procedure and had been rather proud to drink a toast from a loving cup to the "pious, glorious and immortal memory of Good Queen Bess". And he had passed all his examinations, except this last, the Final. And now that was over, all but the last question. Well, the answer was simple enough.

"The judge," he wrote, "would, by the Treasury Solicitor, enter an appearance to the writ, possibly under protest, and would then apply to stay or dismiss the proceedings as an abuse of the process of the Court." He paused and thought for a moment. Would it be too dangerous? Well, it wouldn't be fair to plough him for it. Here goes. And he wrote: "Although I think the judge's application would be successful, as anything said by a judge in Court, however unfair or ill-advised, must be absolutely privileged if it in any way relates to the proceedings, all the same I think that the words 'abuse of the process of the Court' should have stuck in that judge's throat."

*   *   *

"I do hereby call you to the Bar and do publish you barrister." The Treasurer of Roger's Inn had said the magic words and shaken hands with him, and Roger was a barrister. His optimism during the Final had been justified. Indeed, he had been placed in the first class, which he had not expected. And now here he was standing with the other newly-called young men and women. The actual ceremony was finished and the Treasurer was about to deliver a short homily to them before they sat down to dinner, the first dinner he would eat in his Inn as a barrister. Possibly one day he would be doing what the Treasurer was doing. He'd better listen to what he was going to say.

"Some years ago," began the Treasurer, "more than I now like to think, I was called to the Bar by a most learned Master of the Bench of this Honourable Society. He spoke to us as I am now speaking to you. What he said was excellent, but I am bound to admit that there can be too much of an excellent thing—even, for example, of the admirable sherry with which this Honourable Society still provides us. Now I am not suggesting for one moment that the length of the address and the sherry had anything to do with one another—but the fact remains that he kept us standing —and waiting for our dinner—as you are now, for the best part of half an hour. Whether it was due to this I know not, but the custom of making this address thereafter fell into desuetude and has only just been revived. This brings me at once to the quality which I strongly commend to you as the second most important quality to be cultivated by you in your career. I will deal with the first in a moment. The second is brevity. Don't confuse quantity with quality. Say little and say it well. One might think that I was giving advice to a newly-appointed judge, but it is almost as important for counsel to know when to hold his tongue as for a judge. But the first quality, without which no barrister ought to succeed, is a fearless integrity. That quality needs no explanation. Fearless integrity. You will nearly always know instinctively what is the right thing to do. Do it. Finally, I commend to you the quality of good fellowship—'strive mightily but eat and drink as friends.' Which seems to me to be a good note on which to end this address. I wish all of you the success you deserve; I feel sure you will have it and I hope that thought will not depress too many of you."

And, after Grace had been said, judges, barristers and students sat down to dinner.

CHAPTER TWO

THE BEGINNING

"For my next song," said the baritone from abroad, "I have chosen a German one. I shall sing it in the original language but, to help you follow it, I will first give you a fairly literal translation. 'In the woods the birds sing and the other animals make their personal noises. But I sit by the disused well and weep. Where there once was up-drip now there is down-drip'."

"Drip's the word," whispered Roger to Sally. "Can't we slip out before he makes *his* personal noises?"

"Be quiet," said Sally.

He had to endure that song and the next, which was called —Roger thought most reasonably—"Torment", and then he managed to persuade Sally to leave.

"It really is too bad," he said when they were safely outside the hall. "We're supposed to be celebrating my 'call' and you have to drag me there. Anyway, we're out now. Let's *go* and celebrate. I can do with some down-drip."

"We've missed Mother," said Sally.

"Was she going to sing too?"

"You don't imagine I'd have made you come otherwise. I told you about it."

"I believe you did, now I come to think of it—but my mind's been so full up with my 'call' that I haven't been taking in much else. Have we really missed your mother?"

"Don't sound so pleased. She hasn't a bad voice at all."

"I'm sure it's lovely. Like you are. But, oh, Sally, I can't

13

think of anything except that I'm a barrister, a real live one. I've been one for twenty-four hours. I could defend you for murder or shoplifting. I could get you a divorce or appear at your inquest. Am I being very silly? Anyway," he went on, without giving Sally a chance to answer, "I haven't talked about it all the time. I did ask you to marry me, didn't I?"

"In a sort of way, I suppose—in the intervals."

"Why did you say 'no'?"

"It wasn't a definite 'no'."

"It wasn't a definite 'yes'."

"I suppose you'll be wanting everything 'yes' or 'no' now. You lawyers! Let me tell you one thing. You'll have to keep your law for the Courts. I'm not just going to be black or white. I'll be grey when I please."

"I love you in grey. What'll you wear when you come to hear my first case?"

"First catch your fish," said Sally. "Besides," she added, "you said you'd thought of asking Joyce to marry you."

"That was an alternative. Not both at the same time."

"Look," said Sally. "You keep your beautiful legal mind for your unfortunate clients—if you get any."

"I'm sorry, Sally. I didn't mean to be flippant—at least—I did. I am sorry, Sally. I don't know what to say. D'you think I'll ever grow up?"

"Well, twenty-one isn't all that old. Come on, cheer up. Now we *will* go and celebrate. I didn't mean to be beastly."

A few minutes later they were drinking.

"Here's to Roger Thursby, barrister-at-law."

"Here's to Roger Thursby, Esquire, Q.C."

"Here's to Mr. Justice Thursby."

"Here's to us."

When they parted later that evening Roger was very, very happy, though he was still uncertain whether it should be Sally or Joy. But he forgot them both when he went to sleep and all his dreams were of judges and barristers, beautiful clients and criminals. Sometimes they got a bit mixed up, but, even if they had not, they would not have borne much resemblance to the real thing.

The next day he kept an appointment at No. 1 Temple Court, the chambers of Mr Kendall Grimes, a junior of many years' standing with a substantial practice, to whom he had been given an introduction. His appointment was for 9.30 and he arrived ten minutes early and introduced himself to Mr Grimes' clerk, Alec Blake.

"Good morning, sir," said Alec pleasantly. "I'm glad you've

come early. Gives me a chance to put you in the picture. Don't suppose you know anything about the Temple, sir?"

"I don't," said Roger. "Not a thing."

"Well, there's lots to learn, sir."

He might have added, as Roger soon appreciated, that the first thing to learn on going into chambers in the Temple is the importance of the clerk.

"One thing, if I may say at once, sir," went on Alec, "is always to be on the spot. Stay in chambers late. Come early. You never know what may happen."

As he made this last remark Alec sucked his teeth, and gave Roger a knowing look. It was not that there was anything in his teeth to suck, but it was a method, not entirely unknown in the Temple, of indicating that the sucker knew a thing or two. Roger shivered slightly. It was to him as cleaning windows is to some people and much as he came to like Alec he could never reconcile himself to this particular sound. On this, his introduction to it, he was too thrilled at his first contact with chambers in the Temple to be as affected by it as he became later. At that moment the telephone rang.

"Excuse me, sir," said Alec as he answered it. "Hullo. Yes. Mr Grimes' clerk speaking. Oh—Albert. Look, old boy, we can't do it, really we can't. Must be thirty-three. What's that? Yes, of course, I know they've a leader. I'm only asking for the junior's fee. I ought to ask for the leader's by rights. Letting you off lightly. What! Now really, old boy, it's a bit late to come that one. I dare say you don't like the two-thirds rule—but it hasn't gone yet. What's that? If we weren't on the telephone I'd tell you what you could do with that Report. No, I can't send him in for twenty-five. All right, I *won't*, if you like. Now look, old boy, what about a coffee and we'll talk it over. See you over the way? About half-eleven? O.K."

Alec turned to Roger.

"Sorry, sir. One of the things we have to do," and he gave a loud suck. Roger tried to look as though he didn't mind the suck and had understood something of what had happened, whereas he had not the faintest idea what it was all about, and he didn't like the suck at all.

"It's most interesting," he said. "Is that Mr Grimes by any chance?" he went on, pointing to a photograph of someone in uniform which was hanging on the wall above Alec's table.

"It is, sir," said Alec. "He doesn't like my keeping it there, as a matter of fact, but I put my foot down. There were quite a number of people who stayed at home in 1914. He was in it from the start. Don't see why *I* shouldn't say so, even if *he* won't. Anyway, it's my photo and I can put it where I like. It's amazing, really, sir. You'd never think of him as a soldier. You wait and you'll see what I mean. But he went in just as a private, just as a private, sir—no pulling strings for our Mr Grimes, and how d'you think he ended up?"

"How?" asked Roger.

"As a sergeant-major, sir. If I hadn't seen him myself—I was a boy in the Temple then, sir—I wouldn't have believed it. Amazing. You'll see what I mean, sir. Mentioned twice in despatches he was, sir."

"Jolly good," said Roger.

The telephone rang again and just as Alec was answering it there was a noise on the staircase rather like a small express train coming up it and a second later Mr Grimes burst into the room, panting. Roger at first thought there had been an accident but he soon found out that this was Mr Grimes' normal method of entrance. Mr Grimes looked, panting, at Alec for a moment.

"It's Mr Brookes," whispered Alec, putting his hand over the mouthpiece.

Mr Grimes nodded and then noticed Roger. He did not know whether he was a client or the prospective pupil or another barrister's clerk. So he gave him a "Good morning" which would do for any of them and bolted into his room, which was next to the clerk's room.

Alec finished his conversation with Mr Brookes. "Yes, sir. I'll have him there, sir. Don't you worry, sir. That's very nice of you, sir." He turned from the telephone, obviously pleased at what Mr Brookes had said and, with one last violent suck, winked at Roger plainly indicating that there were no flies on Mr Alec Blake. Then with a: "He'll see you in a moment, sir," he went hurriedly into Mr Grimes' room.

Roger started to collate his first impressions of a barrister's chambers, with a view to telling Sally and Joy and his mother. It was exciting to be about to start his career, though a barrister's chambers looked very different from what he had imagined. It was not that they were clean. They weren't. Nor did he yet know that the lavatory was old-fashioned and that there was no hot water, unless you used a gas ring. He was as yet unaware that the system of cleaning was for a lady called a laundress to come in every morning, make herself a cup of tea and go on to the next set of chambers. It was just that he couldn't imagine, say, Crippen, being defended by anyone who worked in No. 1 Temple Court, which, it will be understood, was not one of the new buildings in the Temple. And Mr Grimes looked indeed very different from his idea of a busy barrister. He was tallish, thin, quite bald, except for two large tufts of coal-black hair which stood up obstinately on either side of the bald expanse and which equally obstinately refused to change their colour with the years. At the time Roger first saw him he also had bushy side whiskers which came half-way down his cheek on one side and not quite half-way down on the other. They, too, were obstinately black. Roger subsequently learned that he had once worn a drooping black moustache but that one day he had shaved it off and, like the disappointed witch in the fairy tale, it was never seen again.

There were other things, too, which Roger had yet to learn about Mr Grimes—that he was unmarried and lived near the Essex marshes with an old and feeble housekeeper who looked after him when he was not looking after her, that he kept bees, to which he was devoted, that his work, his bees, and his housekeeper appeared to be his only interests in life, that every morning he sat meekly in the driving-seat of a very fast car and drove it anything but meekly to the Temple, and that, on reaching the Temple, he jumped out as though his life depended on it and rushed to his chambers, with the result which Roger had just witnessed. His sight appeared to be extremely good, and it was said that the large horn-rimmed glasses which he wore in Court contained plain glass and were used by him simply because he found them useful for taking off when cross-examining a witness. Roger never discovered whether this rumour was based on fact or not, but he was quite satisfied that the story that Mr Grimes once appeared before the judge in chambers with each tuft of hair full of bees was entirely apocryphal.

Roger was still wondering at what he had just heard from Alec and seen in Mr Grimes' room when Alec came out and conducted him into Mr Grimes' room.

"This is Mr Thursby, sir."

Mr Grimes held out his hand. "How are ye, my dear fellow?" he said. "How are ye?" He had a rather high-pitched sing-song way of speaking. "So ye've come to the Bar, have ye? That's the way. Have a chair, my dear fellow. That's right, that's right."

"Mr Milroy said you might have a vacancy for a pupil," said Roger. "Do you think you might be able to take me?"

"Do I think we might be able to take ye, my dear fellow? Well, my dear fellow, we might, you know, we might. Have ye been called?"

"Yes."

"Who proposed ye?"

"Well, my mother knows Mr Milroy. He's a Bencher of my Inn, and he introduced me to Mr Sanderson."

"When were ye called, my dear fellow?"

"The day before yesterday, as a matter of fact."

"Just out of the egg, my dear fellow, just out of the egg. D'ye think ye're going to like it?"

"I'm sure I shall, but, of course, I don't really know much about it yet. I suppose the more important question really is whether it will like me."

"Quite right, my dear fellow, quite right. Yes, I think we can take ye, I think we can take ye. When would ye like to start?"

"Straight away, if I may."

"Of course ye may, my dear fellow, of course ye may. Take these papers and have a look at them. Alec will show ye where the pupils' room is. Ye'll find a couple of others there. They'll tell ye how the wheels go round. Now, off ye go, my dear fellow. Ask me anything you want to. Good-bye, my dear fellow—good-bye, bye, bye." And Mr Grimes showed Roger to the door.

"All right, sir?" said Alec.

"Mr Grimes said I could start at once," said Roger.

"Very well, sir. That's the pupils' room over there. I'll show you in. I hope you'll be happy here, sir."

They started to go together towards the pupils' room door when Alec stopped for a moment.

"Oh, sir, would you make out two cheques, please. One for a hundred guineas for Mr Grimes and one for me for ten."

"Now?"

"No—any time, sir, thank you."

At that moment, Alec was sent for hurriedly by Mr Grimes.

"Would you mind showing yourself in, sir?" said Alec to Roger. "I'm so sorry, sir," and Alec rushed away.

Roger opened the door of the pupils' room and walked in. "My name's Thursby," he said. "I'm a new pupil."

"How are ye, my dear fellow, how are ye?" said a man of about thirty-three, giving a very creditable imitation of Mr Grimes.

CHAPTER THREE

FIRST DAY IN COURT

THERE were two others in the room.

"Let me introduce everyone," said the speaker in his normal voice. "I'm Henry Blagrove. I live here. Professionally, you know. Expect you saw my name on the door. Been there seven years. Tell you more about myself later. You'll learn about me, if nothing else, while you're here. This is Peter Hallfield. He's been a pupil six whole months. A confident young man. Though, between you and me, I can't think why. And this is Charles Hepplewhite. He's just finishing. Another month, isn't it?"

"How d'you do?" said Roger generally. "What do I do next, please?"

"Ye'll soon learn, my dear fellow, ye'll soon learn," said Henry. "It's up to these chaps to say where you're to sit. Nothing to do with me. I just come in here and waste your time when I've nothing to do of my own. Which, I may tell you in confidence, is pretty often."

"Would this do?" said Charles, indicating part of a table in the middle of the room. "Here's a chair."

"Thank you very much," said Roger. He sat down and put on the table the papers which Mr Grimes had given him. On the outside was written: "Pennythwaite *v.* The Drum Bottling Co. (1948) Ltd. Instructions to Counsel to advise. 3 guas. Leather-head, Frank and Compton, 4, Cockburn Buildings, E.C.4. Plaintiff's Solicitors."

Henry looked over Roger's shoulder at the brief.

"Oh, that," he said. "You'll have some fun with that when you can understand it. Which is more than the Court of Appeal could. It's been twice to them and once to the House of Lords. All on a point of pleading. Now we're back where we started. Fortunately the Plaintiff's got legal aid and the Defendants are in liquidation. I don't suppose you understand what I'm talking about."

"Quite frankly," said Roger, "since I arrived here I haven't understood a thing."

"Then you've got a chance," said Henry. "It's people like Peter here who come to grief because they don't know a thing either but they think they do. I've done my best for him. Still do, as you can see, but it's a losing battle."

"Henry," said Peter, "just because you're the most hopeless failure at the Bar and ought to have left it years ago, there's no need to be persistently offensive. He doesn't mean it, by the way," he added to Roger. "He just says things because he likes the sound of them. Does the same in Court. It amuses the judges, but they usually decide against him."

"Too true," said Henry. "They ought to keep someone like me in every set of chambers as an awful warning."

"Of what?" asked Roger.

"Of the result of talking too much and working too little."

Roger soon learned all about Henry Blagrove, and one of the first things he found out was that Henry knew himself as well as any man can; that he knew, for example, that he could have succeeded at the Bar but probably never would. He was right n saying that he worked too little. He was incredibly lazy and, though sometimes he would do a great deal of work in one particular case, he would avoid hard work whenever possible. He loved the life and fortunately, or unfortunately, he had just enough work to enable him to stay at the Bar. He had a keen sense of humour and fun, he was highly intelligent, cheerful and generous, but he had no inclination for the sustained hard work which he knew was necessary to success. He had very keen perception and his judgment was excellent. He had very nearly a woman's intuition and knew almost at once which way a judge's mind was working—which occasionally was more than the judge did himself. He was indeed a tremendous asset to those of Mr Grimes' pupils who were sensible enough to listen to him. He had learned very quickly the secrets of success at the Bar; he had learned the tricks of the trade; he knew the ethics; he was popular with his fellow barristers, he never broke the rules. And he was a first-class mimic, though from force of habit he was inclined to imitate Mr Grimes too often. Working so close to him he found it difficult not to do so, and was far too lazy to resist the temptation. Roger did not, of course, learn all Henry's qualities at this first meeting, but one thing he found out very quickly. Henry loved to talk.

"What would you like to know to begin with?" he asked Roger, shortly after their introduction.

"There's so much. I don't know where to begin."

"It really is rather extraordinary," said Henry, "that here you are, a fully-fledged barrister, licensed to lose anyone's case for him and you haven't had an hour of practical experience. Now a medical student has to watch a lot of butchery before he qualifies to dig for his first appendix. Yet your kind old Uncle George could send you a brief tomorrow. By the way, have you an Uncle George?"

"I'm afraid not. I don't think I know any solicitors."

"Well, it doesn't really matter, because the ones you know are seldom much use. Whenever you meet a solicitor and he learns you're at the Bar, he'll murmur something about all his work being conveyancing or litigation not much coming his way. Still, at your present stage it's just as well. When you go into Court for the first time you'll have a nice white wig and a little theoretical knowledge, but, for the rest, you'll be supported by the love of your parents and the admiration of your girl friends. Which last, no doubt, you will do a good deal to cultivate, telling them the most thrilling stories of what you said to the judge and the judge said to you. You don't mind me lecturing like this, I suppose?"

"I'm most grateful."

"I wish you'd shut up for a moment," said Charles. "I strongly suspect I'm going to be left in front of Nettlefold and I've hardly looked at the thing."

Before Roger could begin to understand the meaning of this remark, he heard similar noises to those which he had heard when Mr Grimes had entered chambers.

"Heigh-ho," said Charles. "We're off."

The next moment the door opened and Alec rushed in. Without a word he picked up the papers in front of Charles and rushed off again saying, as he went out: "Court six first and then the Official Referee."

"Come on," said Charles, "we're in this procession. You'd better make up your mind from the beginning what position you'll take up. Grimeyboy will run all the way with Alec trotting behind him. Peter, when he comes, usually goes a short head behind Alec. I walk. What'll you do?"

"Which would you advise?" said Roger to Henry. But before he could answer, Mr Grimes rushed past—while talking they had gone into the clerk's room—put a hand on Roger and said:

"Come on, my dear fellow, come on. Now ye'll see what it's all about." And down the stairs he rushed, pursued by Alec and the pupils. On this occasion Roger felt he had better keep up with his master. He caught up with him just before he crossed the Strand.

"Should I wear my robes, d'you think?" he asked.

"Oh—yes, my dear fellow. Always wear your robes. That's the way to get known. Have ye got them with ye?"

"I've left them in chambers, I'm afraid."

"Go back for them, my dear fellow. Ye've plenty of time," said Mr Grimes as he rushed across the Strand with Alec hard on his heels.

Roger went hastily back to chambers to collect the bag containing his robes. It was a sack-like affair of royal blue cloth with his initials embroidered on it in white and it contained a wig in a box with "Roger Thursby Esq." painted on the lid in gold letters, three pairs of white bands and a gown. When he had ordered them he had thought that he would prefer a red to a blue bag. The assistant had coughed deferentially.

"I'm afraid that will come a little later, sir," he had said. "You start with a blue one."

"What are the red ones for?"

"Well, sir, in a sort of way you get presented with a red bag, though it'll cost you a guinea."

"What do you mean?"

"Well, a leader, sir, a Q.C., will give you one for doing well in a case in which he leads you. Then you give his clerk a guinea.

21

I've never been able to think why. He doesn't pay for the bag. I hope you'll get one all right, sir."

"Supposing I don't?"

The assistant had coughed. "Well, sir," he had said, "there are people who never get a red bag, but between you and me, sir, if you don't get one in your first seven years, you won't have made much headway."

Roger found his robes and hurried across to the robing room. Mr Grimes had already gone, but he found Henry there.

"It's easy to get lost," he said. "I thought I'd come and guide you. It's a bit hectic this morning."

"That's awfully kind of you," said Roger and robed himself as quickly as he could. "Have you any idea what I'm going to hear?" he asked.

"Well, I believe the thing before Nettlefold is a running down case and then there's a building reference before the Official Referee. Normally you'll at least be able to look at the briefs before you go into Court."

Henry led Roger to Queen's Bench Court 6, where they were just in time to see the judge arrive. Then Henry returned to chambers.

"Fisher against Mollet," called the associate, the bewigged official sitting below the judge, and Mr Grimes at once got up.

"May it please your Ludship," he began. He was one of the few counsel who still used that pronunciation of Lordship. "I appear in this case for the plaintiff with my learned friend Mr Hepplewhite. My learned friend Mr Ferret appears for the defendant. Me Lud, this is a claim for damages for personal injuries."

"A running down case, is it, Mr Grimes?" asked the judge.

"Yes, me Lud, on the Watford by-pass. My client was driving very slowly along the main road when the defendant suddenly came out of a side turning with no warning at all and there was a collision."

"Why was your client going at such a slow speed? It is unusual on that road, to say the least of it."

"Oh, me Lud, he was in no particular hurry and, if I may say so, driving most carefully."

"So you say, Mr Grimes. But if he was going so slowly, one wonders why he couldn't stop before the collision. But I suppose we'd better wait until it comes out in the evidence. Is the special damage agreed?"

"Yes, me Lud, except for one item."

"What is the agreed amount?"

"One hundred and twenty-five pounds, me Lud. That is for repairs to the car and loss of wages."

"What is the item not agreed?"

"A pair of trousers, me Lud. I can't think why my learned friend won't admit it."

"Let me see," said the judge. "You're claiming £7 10s. They were new, I suppose?"

"Oh, yes, me Lud."

"You want to fight the pair of trousers, do you, Mr Ferret?" asked the judge.

"Well, my Lord, no bill has been produced nor have the trousers."

"Well, I hope we're not going to spend too much time on them," said the judge. "If we do, one side or the other would be able to buy a whole suit with the amount expended in costs."

"Oh, me Lud, I shall be very short about them. But if my learned friend wants me to prove the trousers, I'll have to prove them. I don't see why my client should make him a present of them."

"I gather they wouldn't be much use now, Mr Grimes. Now, don't let's waste any more time. Is there a plan?"

"Yes, me Lud."

"Thank you. Is there an agreed medical report?"

"Yes, me Lud."

"Thank you. Very well—perhaps you'll call your first witness. I'll read the report in due course."

So began the first accident case which Roger had ever seen tried. After the second witness had been called, Roger noticed Alec hovering close to the row in which Mr Grimes and he were sitting. Suddenly, Mr Grimes whispered to him.

"Come and sit this side of me, my dear fellow."

Roger did as he was told. This brought Mr Grimes nearer to the end of the row. A moment later he had exchanged seats with Charles who now sat next to Roger. A moment later Mr Grimes was gone. There was a slight sound from the breeze caused by his gown as he rushed away through the door of the Court, followed by Alec.

"Ought I to follow him?" whispered Roger to Charles.

"Do what you something well like, my dear chap," said Charles with unexpected asperity. "I'm left with this ruddy thing and I haven't read half of it."

"Yes, Mr, Mr—er, Hepplewhite," said the judge, "do you wish to re-examine?"

Charles got to his feet and cleared his throat—a sure sign in an advocate of nervousness, varying from the slight to the verge-of-tears variety. In Charles' case it was between the two. He no longer wanted to cry, only to run away. It is indeed somewhat of an ordeal for a young man in his first year at the Bar to be left with a case in the High Court. The fact that he has only looked at the brief and does not know it thoroughly does not make very much difference to the way he conducts it, but it certainly does not increase his self-confidence.

"If you please, my Lord." He cleared his throat again and began: "My learned friend has asked you whether you hooted. Are you quite sure that you did?"

Mr Ferret immediately got up, looked sorrowfully at Charles, said to the judge: "Really, my Lord!" and sat down.

Roger, who had a vivid imagination, wondered what on earth he himself would do. Obviously the judge and Mr Ferret knew what was happening though the glances they exchanged conveyed nothing to Roger. He felt very sorry for Charles and hoped that he'd never find himself in the same position. The judge looked in a kindly manner at the white wig of Charles and said:

"Mr Ferret thinks that was rather a leading question, Mr Hepplewhite. I'm afraid I'm inclined to agree."

A leading question, of course, thought Roger. But what on earth does one ask instead? Would "Did you hoot?" be a leading question. Perhaps it would be better to say, "Did you or did you not hoot?" A moment later Roger experienced a thrill of pleasure.

"Did you or did you not hoot?" asked Charles.

"He has already said that he's not really sure," said the judge. "Can you carry it much further than that?"

"If your Lordship pleases," said Charles and sat down.

"Don't you want to ask him anything about the trousers, Mr Hepplewhite?"

"The trousers, my Lord?" said Charles unhappily. The judge appeared to have made it plain at the outset that he did not want to hear too much about the trousers. And now here he was inviting him to go into the matter. The fact was that the plaintiff had been somewhat knocked about in cross-examination over the trousers. The judge was not sure that he had done himself justice in his answers to Mr Ferret. The witness was a nervous young man and had been rather over-persuaded to agree to things to which the judge was not at all satisfied he intended to agree. A few well-directed questions in re-examination might have restored the position. But Charles was quite incapable of asking them.

"The trousers, my Lord?" he said again.

What on earth would I ask? thought Roger. This is a pretty nerve-racking game. I wonder if I ought to have gone on the Stock Exchange.

Seeing that Charles was quite incapable of dealing with the matter, the judge himself proceeded to ask the necessary questions and a few others too, some of them leading. Mr Ferret grimaced. He couldn't stop the judge asking leading questions and he saw what was going to happen. Until Mr Grimes returned, the judge was in effect going to conduct the case on behalf of the plaintiff and by the time Mr Grimes did return, he would have got so used to it that he might have become unconsciously in the plaintiff's favour. Justice is a funny thing. It can never be perfect. Roger learned in due course that sometimes the poorer counsel wins a case just because he's so bad that the judge has to step in. So what seemed unfair to the one side becomes unfair to the other.

After the running down case had been going on for some little time, Roger felt someone touch his arm. It was Alec.

"Have you seen Mr Hallfield anywhere?" he asked anxiously.

"I haven't, I'm afraid," said Roger.

"Well, would you come with me, please, sir," said Alec. "It's rather urgent."

Roger went clumsily in front of Charles, brushing some of his papers to the floor in the process, got out of counsel's row and was soon trotting after Alec through what seemed like endless corridors. He wanted to ask Alec all sorts of questions but the pace was too fast. Eventually they reached a Court.

"In here, sir," said Alec.

Mr Grimes was on his feet addressing the Official Referee.

"If your Honour pleases," he said, "I submit that in meal or in malt the onus of proof is on the defendant."

"Why meal or malt, Mr Grimes?" said Sir Hugo Cramp, the Official Referee.

"If your Honour pleases," said Mr Grimes with a deferential smile.

"Yes, but why, Mr Grimes? You're always saying in meal or in malt, and I can't think why, I really can't."

"Just a phrase, your Honour, just a phrase."

"Well, you've said it three times in half an hour. I made a note of it."

Indeed, that was the only note that Sir Hugo had so far made. The stage for making notes had not yet arrived and he hoped that it never would—except for doodling and the like and making notes of Mr Grimes' stock expression. The case ought to be settled. So should all building references. And in Sir Hugo's Court they nearly always were. It was a good thing for everyone. It saved the parties expense and Sir Hugo time, and it resulted in the next litigants' cases coming on earlier for trial—or settlement.

"Take a note, my dear fellow," whispered Mr Grimes to Roger.

"What in?" asked Roger.

"A notebook, my dear fellow—I'm sorry, your Honour. I was

25

just arranging with my learned friend Mr—Mr Thorburn——"

"Yes, yes," said Sir Hugo, "but these devilling arrangements should be made beforehand. I take it that I'm going to be deprived of the pleasure of hearing your further argument, Mr Grimes."

"Only for a very short time, your Honour. I'm on my feet before Mr Justice Nettlefold."

Sir Hugo removed his spectacles and looked at Mr Grimes with a puzzled air for a moment, "Oh, of course," he said. "The prophetic present. Well, I mustn't keep you, Mr Grimes. Very good of you to have come at all and I'm sure your learned junior will fill your place admirably while you are away."

"It's very good of your Honour," said Mr Grimes and with a few whispered words to Roger—"Ye'll be all right, my dear fellow, just tell him the tale, just tell him the tale," Mr Grimes was gone.

It had all happened so quickly that Roger had difficulty in realizing that he, Roger Thursby Esq., barrister-at-law, aged twenty-one, called to the Bar two days previously, had been left in Court to represent one side or the other (he did not know which) in a building dispute before a judge called an Official Referee, of whom he had only vaguely heard. He looked round the Court. There was not a face he knew. Something inside his head began to go round and round and the Official Referee's face started to approach him with alarming swiftness. He realized that he must pull himself together or faint. Sir Hugo addressed him:

"Now that the wind has dropped, Mr Truefold, would you continue your learned leader's submission?" Roger wished he had fainted. He rose unsteadily, and looked blankly in front of him.

"Your learned leader was saying," went on Sir Hugo who, without intending to be unkind, enjoyed this sort of scene immensely, "let me see—what was he saying? Something about malt, I believe. Strange, in a building dispute. Ah—no, I remember—he was submitting that the onus was on the other side. No doubt you would like to elaborate the submission?"

Roger continued to look blankly in front of him. It was not that the power of speech had left him, but he simply did not know what to say. He had sufficient presence of mind to realize that, if he started, "Your Honour" and then paused, the Official Referee would, after waiting a decent interval, say, "Yes, Mr Truefold?" and then he would either have to repeat, "Your Honour" or lapse into silence again. It was better not to break it at all unless and until he could think of one sentence which meant something.

The only sentence he could think of was: "I want to go home," and that wouldn't do at all. It flashed through his mind that he could pretend to faint and he cursed himself for having resisted a moment before the genuine impulse to do so. But he had a natural inclination to tell the truth. This was sometimes embarrassing in his relations with Sally and Joy, but they were a long way from his mind at this particular moment. He remained standing and staring and thinking for the thoughts which would not come.

"Come, Mr Trueband," said Sir Hugo affably, "it's quite calm now. Shall we proceed?"

There was nothing for it. "Your Honour," he began—and then came the inevitable pause. Sir Hugo looked enquiringly at him, and so did counsel on the other side and, indeed, nearly everyone in the Court.

The pause had already passed the stage at which it became unbearable when Sir Hugo duly came in with the expected "Yes, Mr Truefold?" to which Roger replied with the only words he had so far learned: "Your Honour," and again there was that terrible pause. Eventually Sir Hugo broke it with: "I suppose you say that the defendants, having admitted that the work was done and that it has not been paid for, it is for them to show that parts of it have not been properly done?"

With relief which he could not conceal, Roger added a word to his repertoire. "Yes, Your Honour," he said, and getting bolder —"I do." Then, "Your Honour," he added, in case the emphasis sounded rude.

"An admirable submission, Mr Truelove," said Sir Hugo, "and very succinctly put. But," and he paused and frowned for a moment. "But," he went on, "isn't it for the plaintiff in the first instance to give evidence that he has performed his contract—and can he do that without showing that the work was properly done?"

Roger's boldness vanished. The only truthful answer he could make would have been: "I don't know." But that wouldn't do. So he adopted his first line of defence, of standing and staring, keeping a "Your Honour" in reserve for use if necessary.

"You can't very well rely," went on Sir Hugo, "on the maxim *omnia rite*, etc.—incidentally, I never can remember exactly how it goes."

"*Omnia rite ac sollemniter esse acta præsumuntur*," said Roger, thanking his patron saint for making him learn that legal maxim for his Bar examinations.

"Thank you, Mr Tredgold," said Sir Hugo, "thank you very much. But you can't rely on that maxim in a case such as the present, can you?"

27

At any rate, there was an answer to that which made sense.

"I suppose not, Your Honour."

"Or *can* you, perhaps?" went on Sir Hugo. "I'm not sure. Perhaps you could refer me to one or two of the authorities on the point."

At this juncture, Roger's opponent could not resist getting up and saying:

"Surely, Your Honour, there is no presumption in law that a builder always does the right thing. If there were any presumption I should have thought it would have been the other way about."

"Well, to whom does the presumption apply, do you think?" said Sir Hugo, mercifully directing his question to Roger's opponent. "To Official Referees, perhaps?"

At that moment Alec came into Court, although Roger did not see him Mr. Grimes had managed to take over the reins from Charles in the running down case, not without a little obstruction from Mr Justice Nettlefold who disliked Mr Grimes' habit of chopping and changing and who, besides, was now running cheerfully along with the plaintiff. "Mr Hepplewhite is deputizing very satisfactorily for you, Mr Grimes," the judge said quite untruthfully—except in the sense that, as the judge was doing all the work for the plaintiff, it was quite satisfactory from that gentleman's point of view. However, eventually the judge allowed himself to be persuaded and Mr Grimes took over. The plaintiff did not do quite so well after that. This was no fault of Mr Grimes. It is just the way things happen. Once Alec had seen Mr Grimes safely into Court before Mr Justice Nettlefold he returned to the Official Referee's Court to see what was happening there, ready to send the junior clerk—who had now come over with him— sprinting round to fetch Mr Grimes if disaster seemed imminent.

"Anyway," went on Sir Hugo, "isn't there anything to be done in this case? Is there a Scott Schedule, Mr Truebland?" and he turned pleasantly and enquiringly to Roger. Roger was still standing and the relief when the Official Referee started to address his opponent was so great that he had begun to feel the warm blood moving through his veins again. But at the mention of "Scott Schedule" it froze again. What on earth was a Scott Schedule? He thought of Sir Walter Scott and Scott the explorer. He thought of Scotland. Perhaps Sir Hugo had said Scotch Schedule. Just as people sometimes have an insane urge to throw themselves in front of tube trains, Roger suddenly had an urge to say: "No, Your Honour, but I think there's an Irish stew." That would be the end of his career at the Bar. Short and inglorious. But over. No more standing and staring and freezing and boiling. Which is worse, a cold sweat or a hot sweat? All these thoughts crammed themselves confusedly into his mind as he stood miserably waiting. Then he heard a voice from the ceiling of the Court:

"A Scott Schedule, Your Honour?" it said.

He knew that it was his voice really, but he did not feel himself speak and he never knew his voice sounded like that.

"Yes, Mr Trueglove. Is there one? Or perhaps Mr Grimes ran away with it."

Roger endeavoured to smile, but it was very difficult. After what seemed an age his opponent came to his rescue.

"I'm afraid there isn't, Your Honour," he said.

"And why not?" asked Sir Hugo. "How am I expected to try this case without a Scott Schedule? How many items are there in dispute?"

"About fifty, Your Honour."

"Fifty," Sir Hugo almost screamed. "This is intolerable."

"It's the plaintiff's responsibility," said Roger's opponent. "He has the carriage of the proceedings."

"I don't care whose responsibility it is," said Sir Hugo feigning an indignation which he did not in the least feel. It was a first-class opportunity for browbeating the parties into settling the case. "It's quite outrageous. You and your opponent had better put your heads together. I shall rise now for ten minutes and after that time I expect to be told that you and he are well on the way to a compromise. This is an expensive court, you know." He frowned for a moment and then looked cheerfully at counsel "It doesn't matter to me in the least," he went on, "whether you settle or not. If I don't try this case, I shall try another. I'm just thinking of the parties."

Roger looked enquiringly at his opponent, who gave him a faintly perceptible wink.

"And in any event, I'm not going to try it without a Scott Schedule. The case will have to be adjourned anyway, but I'll give you a chance to settle it first."

Sir Hugo rose, bowed to counsel and withdrew to his room. As soon as Alec had seen what was happening he had sent his junior at full speed to fetch Mr Grimes. Meantime, Roger's opponent, a man named Featherstone, turned to him and said:

"Well, my boy, there we are. What shall we do about it? I'll give you a hundred and fifty. Not a penny more. You'd better take it, or you'll only have the costs to pay. You know what the old boy's like about costs. No Scott Schedule, indeed," and Mr Featherstone rubbed his hands. "No Scott Schedule, my dear boy. What d'you think of that?" and he laughed heartily.

"Would you very much mind telling me what a Scott Schedule is, please?" asked Roger.

"Haven't the faintest idea, my dear boy. Never come to this Court if I can help it. But it's something the old boy wants. No Scott Schedule, that's bad, isn't it? Well, what about it? Will you take a hundred and fifty?"

"I think I'd better wait till Mr Grimes comes back," said Roger.

"Wait till he comes back? We'll be here all night. He's probably on his way to the House of Lords at the moment, just giving a friendly look in to the Court of Appeal on his way. He won't be back. Not on your life. No Scott Schedule, now I ask you!"

At that moment Roger heard with a mixture of relief and distaste a sound he recognized. It was Alec giving a loud suck.

"Mr Grimes will be here in a minute. I've sent for him."

"What'd I better do?" whispered Roger.

"Just hang on, sir," said Alec. "Don't agree to anything." Alec emphasized this last remark in the usual way.

Roger turned to his opponent.

"Mr Grimes is on his way."

"I've heard that one before. Well—I hope he won't keep us all night. P'raps he's gone to fetch the Scott Schedule. You're a pupil, I suppose?"

"Yes."

"How d'you like it?"

"I only started today. I find it a bit hair-raising, I'm afraid."

"You'll soon get used to it with old Grimes. I wish he'd be quick. I'd like to go and have a cup of coffee. D'you know where he is as a matter of fact?"

"He's doing an accident case before Mr Justice Nettlefold."

"Is he, by Jove? Well—*he* won't let him go."

At that moment in Queen's Bench Court 6 Mr Grimes became aware that his junior clerk was making urgent signs to him. He was in the middle of cross-examining a witness.

"I had no chance of avoiding the crash," said the witness.

"So that's what ye say, is it? We shall see," said Mr Grimes. "We shall see."

"I wish you wouldn't make these comments," said the judge. "I know they don't mean anything and that we may never see and that, as there isn't a jury, it doesn't much matter whether we do see or we don't, but cross-examination should be used for asking questions and asking questions only. You can make your comments when you address me."

"If your Ludship pleases. So ye couldn't avoid the accident, couldn't ye?"

"No."

"Why didn't ye put on your brakes?"

"I did."

"Oh, ye did, did ye? Then why didn't ye stop?"

"I did."

"Oh, ye did, did ye? Then why did the accident happen?"

"Because the plaintiff ran into me."

"Oh, he ran into ye, did he? I suggest ye ran into him."

"It was the other way round. The damage to the cars shows it."

"Oh, it does, does it? We shall see," said Mr Grimes. "We shall see."

"Mr Grimes," began the judge, but he was too late. Mr Grimes was on his way out.

A minute later he came, panting, into the Official Referee's Court.

"At last," said Featherstone.

"I'm so sorry, my dear fellow," said Mr Grimes. "So sorry to have kept ye. Now, what's it all about?"

"The old boy wants us to settle."

"Oh, he does, does he? Well, that's simple enough, my dear fellow. You just pay and it's all over."

"I'll pay you something."

"That's very good of ye, my dear fellow, very good of ye. Ye've had all the work done and ye'll pay something! Ye wouldn't like us to build another house for ye as well?"

"Well, you'll need to, I should think. This one's falling down already."

"Is it really, my dear fellow? Funny your clients are still living in it then."

"Come on, let's go outside. We've got to settle it somehow. The old boy isn't going to try it."

The upshot of it all was that eventually the defendant agreed to pay Mr Grimes' client £300 and all his costs, and there was then a rush back to the other case, where they arrived just in time to find the judge rising for lunch.

"Come on, my dear fellow," said Mr Grimes. "Come and get a bite while there's time. So good of ye to have helped me. Thank ye so much." He led Roger at a fast trot to the restaurant in the crypt at the Law Courts. There Mr Grimes helped himself to a plate of meat and salad, asked for a cup of coffee and took it to a marble-topped table which was no different from any others, except that it bore a notice: "The seats at this table, are reserved for Counsel from 12 o'clock until 2 o'clock."

Roger felt very important sitting at such a table and even the ordinary nature of the food and the noise made by Mr Grimes in getting rid of his as fast as possible did not spoil his pleasure.

Between the bites and swallows, Mr Grimes asked Roger if he thought he'd learned anything and how he liked his first morn-

31

ing. Before Roger could reply, he went on to criticize Queen's Bench Judges, Official Referees and his opponents in each of the cases, finally ending up his criticisms with the pronouncement:

"But there you are, my dear fellow, they will do these things, they will do these things."

Five minutes later they were off again, this time at only a very fast walking pace. They went to a place known as the "Bear Garden" where Mr Grimes had a summons to dispose of before a judicial officer called a Master. It was to be heard by Master Tiptree. Before they went into the Master's room, Mr Grimes was joined by Alec and the clerk from the solicitors instructing him. Mr Grimes greeted the clerk most affably and then proceeded to say something to him in a low voice. Roger could only catch that it began with:

"I don't mind telling you, my dear fellow——" but what he didn't mind telling him, Roger never heard. Fortunately they did not have to wait long and soon they were in front of Master Tiptree. Roger knew from his Bar examination that various applications in the course of an action were made to a Master, but he only had a slight theoretical knowledge of such matters. A Master appearing in a question in an examination paper is very different from an actual live one sitting in his room.

"This is an application for discovery of specific documents, Master," began Mr Grimes.

"Where's the affidavit?" asked the Master.

"Oh, Master, before we come to the affidavit, I'd like to tell you something about the action."

"I dare say you would, Mr Grimes, but I want to see the affidavit."

"If you please, Master."

Mr Grimes obtained a sheet of paper from the solicitor's clerk and handed it to the Master.

He glanced at it, threw it back at Mr Grimes and said: "What d'you call that, Mr Grimes?"

Mr Grimes looked at the offending document. "I'm so sorry, Master. It's the wrong affidavit."

"I am only too well aware of that, Mr Grimes. I want the right one."

"Here it is, Master. I'm so sorry."

Mr Grimes handed another affidavit to the Master, who read it quickly.

"This won't do, Mr Grimes. It doesn't say the alleged missing document relates to the matters in question."

"Oh, but Master, if you'll be good enough to look at the pleadings, you'll see it must be material."

"I do hereby call you to the Bar and do publish you barrister."

An appointment at the chambers of Mr Kendall Grimes.

"Now, off ye go, my dear fellow. Take these papers and have a look at them. Alec will show ye where the pupils' room is."

"Oh, sir," said Alec, "would you make out two cheques, please. One for a hundred guineas for Mr Grimes and one for me for ten."

"I dare say, Mr Grimes, but Order 31, Rule 19A is quite definite and has not been complied with."

"Oh, but Master——"

"It's no good saying, 'Oh, but Master,' Mr Grimes. You know as well as I do your affidavit is defective. D'you want an adjournment or shall I dismiss the summons?"

Mr Grimes' opponent then intervened.

"Master, I ask you to refuse an adjournment and dismiss the summons."

"I dare say you do, but I'm not going to. You can have the costs thrown away."

"But Master——"

"I've made up my mind. You can go to the judge if you don't like it. Now Mr Grimes, have you made up your mind?"

"Yes, please, Master. I ask for an adjournment to put the affidavit in order."

"Very well."

The Master started to write out his Order.

Mr Grimes whispered to Roger: "Just stay and take the Order, my dear fellow," and without another word he was off towards Mr Justice Nettlefold's Court.

The Master wrote for a few moments. When he looked up he saw that Mr Grimes had gone.

"Pupil?" he asked Roger.

"Yes, Master."

"How long?"

"Today."

"Order 31, Rule 19A mean anything to you?"

"Not a thing, Master."

"I should look it up when you get back to chambers, if I were you. It's the only way to learn the practice. You can't learn it in a vacuum. But if you look up everything that happens, you'll get a reasonable knowledge of it in time."

"Thank you very much, Master."

"Not at all. Good luck to you."

Roger left the Master's room with the solicitor's clerk. "Never heard Master Tiptree so agreeable," said the clerk. "He threw a book at me once."

With difficulty Roger found his way back to the Court. The judge was giving judgment in favour of Mr Grimes' client. No sooner was it over than there was a frantic dash back to chambers, where Mr Grimes had several conferences.

Charles and Roger went into the pupils' room together. Henry was there reading *The Times*.

"Where's Peter?" asked Charles.

"He went off to the Old Bailey," said Henry. "Said building cases weren't in his line. Gosh!" he went on. "You don't mean to tell me Thursby got landed with it instead?"

"He did," said Charles, "but he's still breathing."

"Poor fellow," said Henry. "Tell me about it in your own unexpurgated Billingsgate."

Roger told him.

"Well, well, well," said Henry. "He wins one case and settles the other and, knowing Grimeyboy, his client won't have lost on the deal. What I say is *fiat justitia ruat Grimes*, or, as the poet says,

'So justice be done,
Let Grimeyboy run'."

CHAPTER FOUR

AT HOME

Mrs Thursby, Roger's widowed mother, was, she hoped, making a cake when Roger arrived home after his first day as a pupil.

"Darling, how nice," she said. "You can give it a stir. I want to go and try on a new dress. Aunt Ethel sent it me. She's only worn it once. Just keep on stirring. I'm sure it'll be all right. Anyway, we can always give it to Mrs Rhodes. Oh, no, she doesn't come any more. Let me see, who is it now——"

"Mother, darling," said Roger, "I've had my first day in the Temple."

"Of course, darling, how silly of me. Did you enjoy it? I won't be a moment. Just keep on stirring."

And Mrs Thursby went to her bedroom. She was a young forty-eight. She had lost her husband soon after Roger was born. For some reason that neither she nor Roger, after he grew up, could understand, she had never married again. She was attractive and kind and plenty of men have no objection to butterfly minds. Roger's father, who had been a man of the highest intelligence and intellectual capacity, had adored her. So did Roger.

He stirred the mixture in the pudding bowl and as he did so he went over in his mind all that had happened during the day. Now that he was safely home it gave him a considerable thrill to think he had actually spoken in Court. He must tell his mother, though she wouldn't really take in the significance. But he must tell Sally and Joy. Which first? He stopped stirring and went to the telephone. It was Joy's turn really, he supposed.

"Joy—yes, it's me. Are you free this evening? I've quite a lot to tell you. Oh—what a shame. Can't you come and have a drink first? Yes, do, that'll be lovely. Come straight over. See you in ten minutes."

He went back to the kitchen.

"Roger," called his mother, "do come and look."

He went to her bedroom.

"It's lovely, isn't it? And I did need one so badly. I can wear it for the Fotheringays. Don't you like it?"

"I do, darling. D'you know I spoke in Court today?"

"Did you really, darling? How very nice. What exactly did you say? Don't you like the way the skirt seems to come from nowhere?"

"It suits you to a T."

"D'you really think so?"

"Of course I do. I didn't actually say very much."

"No, of course not. They couldn't expect very much to begin with. I expect you'll say more tomorrow."

"Joy's coming round for a drink. You don't mind?"

"Of course not. I think she's a sweet girl. It makes me look thinner, doesn't it?"

At last Joy arrived and Roger was able to tell someone all about his first day.

"I think you're wonderful," said Joy. "I should love to come and hear you. When can I?"

"Well, of course, I don't know exactly when I shall be speaking again."

"Was it a murder case?"

"Well—no, as a matter of fact."

"Breach of promise?"

"As a matter of fact, it was a building dispute."

"It sounds terribly dull. Weren't you bored?"

The one thing Roger had not been was bored.

"You see, things which don't sound of interest to the layman are very interesting to lawyers."

"I don't think I should terribly care to hear a building dispute. All about houses and things. Still, I suppose you have to start somewhere. Must take time to work up to a murder case."

"Joy, dear, you don't work up to a murder case."

"But surely, Roger, you're wrong. I've always understood you start with silly things like debt collecting and business cases, like your building dispute, I suppose, and eventually work your way into real cases like murder and blackmail and divorce and so on. Anyway, what did you say? Did you make the jury cry? It must have been very clever of you if you did with a building dispute.

35

But then you are so clever, Roger, that I wouldn't put it past you."

"They don't have juries with Official Referees."

"Sounds like football."

"Well, it isn't. An Official Referee is a judge. You call him 'Your Honour'. He's very important. This one was called Sir Hugo Cramp."

"Well, what did you say to him?"

"Well, among other things—I quoted a legal maxim to him. He thanked me very much."

"Did it win you your case?"

"Well, it wasn't exactly my case." He paused for a moment. Then very seriously he said:

"Joy, d'you think I'll ever be any good? I was terribly frightened."

"You frightened? I can't believe it. You're pulling my leg."

"I'm not. Really, Joy, I'm not."

"What's frightening about it? You just get up and say what you want and then sit down."

"And suppose you don't know what to say?"

"Then don't get up."

"But I had to."

"But I don't see why. It's a free country. Anyway, next time make certain what you want to say, get up and say it and sit down."

"You make it sound very simple."

"Well, Uncle Alfred's a solicitor. Which reminds me—I suppose he might send you a brief one day. Would you like that, Roger?"

"Oh, Joy, it would be wonderful."

"What would you do if I get Uncle Alfred to send you a brief?"

"What would you like me to do?"

"There's something I'd like you not to do."

"What?"

"Not see Sally."

"Oh," said Roger, unhappily. "D'you think that's quite fair?"

"It's just as you like. I'm sure Uncle Alfred has got lots of young men to send briefs to. He'll bear up."

"But, Joy, dear, it's so difficult. And it wouldn't be fair to Sally."

"That's right, dear—always the little unselfish one, thinking of other people. You're too good for this world."

"Who are *you* going out with, anyway?"

"A friend of mine."

"So I gathered. Do I know him?"

"Who said it was a him?"

"I did. Who is it?"

36

"D'you want to know all that much?"

"Not if you don't want to tell me."

"Then why ask me?"

"Oh, Joy—don't let's quarrel. It's my first day at the Bar. And I want you to share it with me."

"I'd love to share it with you—but not with you and Sally."

"I rang you before her."

"You went out with her last night."

"How d'you know?"

"Now I know you did. Oh, Roger, why can't we just be married and live happily ever after?"

"We're so young, Joy. We don't any of us know our minds yet. I'd marry you both if I could."

"Thanks very much. P'raps you'd like power to add to our number. It's George Utterson as a matter of fact."

"That oaf."

"He's not in the least an oaf. He's going to be Prime Minister one of these days. *He's* not frightened to talk in public. I heard him at a meeting the other day. He was grand. They applauded like anything." She stopped for a moment. Then much more softly she said: "Oh, Roger, if you'd give up Sally—I'd never see him again. I wouldn't even see him tonight."

CHAPTER FIVE

AROUND AND ABOUT THE LAW

THE next day was calmer at No. 1 Temple Court. Mr Grimes was in chambers all day and, except for rushing out for his lunch and rushing back again, his presence in chambers was only noticed by the procession of clients who came for conferences and by the occasional sound of "Good-bye, my dear fellow, bye, bye, bye" as he saw one or two of the more valued clients to the door. In consequence, Roger was able to ask Henry a number of questions.

"Tomorrow," said Henry, "is an important day. I'm in Court. I have to appear before His Honour Judge Boyle at a County Court. P'raps you'd like to come with me. You won't see anything of County Courts with Grimeyboy."

"D'you think Mr Grimes would mind?" asked Roger.

"Grimes, not Mr Grimes," said Henry. "I meant to tell you about that before. Once you're called you call everyone at the Bar by his surname."

"Even a Q.C.?"

"Everyone. Even an ex-Attorney-General. The newest recruit to the profession will call the most distinguished of all plain Smith or whatever it is. And, while I'm about it, you might as well know how to talk to a judge—out of Court, I mean, or if you write to him. How would you address Mr Justice Blank if you ran into him in the Strand?"

"Well, I'd obviously be wrong. How should I?"

"Judge. "So sorry, Judge," or "do look where you're going, Judge." If he's in the Court of Appeal, call him Lord Justice."

"And what about an Official Referee?"

"To be quite honest, I've never spoken to one—after his appointment. I suppose you could say 'Official Referee,' but it's rather a mouthful. 'Your Honour' must be wrong. I don't care for 'Sir Hugo' or 'sir.' No, you've got me there. The best advice is not to talk to them. There are only four anyway, so you should be all right. Now, what else can I do for you?"

"Sure you don't mind?"

"My dear boy, I'm only too delighted. Otherwise I'd have to look at these papers. I tell you, I'm bone idle. I'm delighted to have a good excuse for not working."

"Well, yesterday I heard the clerk talking to someone on the telephone about something called the two-thirds rule. Something to do with fees, I gathered. Can you tell me what it is?"

"Indeed I can. I feel quite strongly on the subject. We had some pronouncements from a Committee on the subject quite recently. Up till a few years before the war if you or I or Grimes or any junior—you know that barristers are either juniors or Q.C.'s, and that a Q.C. has to have a junior?"

"That's just about all I do know."

"Well, as I was saying, up till a few years before the war, if a junior was led by a Q.C. the junior had to receive two-thirds of the fee charged by the Q.C. So if you were lucky and led by Carson or F. E. Smith or someone like that, you might get a fee of 666 guineas for doing a case you'd have been perfectly prepared to do for a hundred, or even less. Doesn't sound very logical, you say?"

"I don't say anything," said Roger. "I'm listening. I must say, though, I like the sound of 666 guineas. Have you ever had that?"

"I have not, I regret to say. Well, a few years before the war it was agreed that the two-thirds rule should only apply to a fee of 150 guineas or less. Above that it was to be a matter of arrangement."

"No more 666," said Roger, sadly.

"Well, some solicitors were prepared to stick to the old rule.

Of course some didn't. But there's worse to come. The Committee I mentioned has suggested that the rule should be abolished altogether. The point about the rule is this. By and large, barristers are not overpaid. Indeed much of their work is underpaid. This two-thirds rule is the cream which, when added to the skim milk, makes milk of a reasonable quality. The Committee, while recognizing that barristers are not paid too much, have said something like this: 'This two-thirds rule increases the cost of litigation. If it's abolished, barristers will have nothing to make up for the lowness of their other fees, but none the less let's abolish it and good luck to you all'."

"What's going to happen?"

"If you ask me, nothing, but we shall see, my dear fellow, we shall see."

At that moment Alec came into the room, took away the papers which were in front of Roger and replaced them with a large bundle.

"Mr Grimes thinks you'd better look at these," he said and went out again. The brief he left was about six to eight inches thick. Roger looked at it for a moment.

"D'you think I'll ever be able to cope with anything of this kind?" he asked. "It makes me despair just to look at it."

"Well," said Henry, "it all depends. If you take to the job and are good enough for it, you'll be able to tackle anything in due course. But it'll take time. Let's hope you only get little stuff to begin with. Otherwise you could come a nasty cropper. When I started I made the most awful bloomer with a case. The solicitors took it away from me in the end, but not before I'd done a lot of damage. Think of a medical student being allowed to play at pulling out a patient's appendix and grabbing hold of the wrong thing! I don't even know now whether I was stopped in time. As I said before, it's funny that we're allowed to do it. It's true that the public can't come to us direct as they can to doctors. But there are plenty of Uncle Georges in the world of solicitors—father Georges even—and, of course, brother Georges—their wretched clients don't know that it's your first brief."

"But," said Roger, "one has to start some time. Every professional man has to have his first case, whether it's a doctor, accountant or a barrister."

"Yes," said Henry, "that's true enough, but all professional men, except barristers, have had practical experience first. If a barrister couldn't address the Court until he's had, say, a year as a pupil, that'd be reasonable. Jolly good experience for you yesterday, but what about the poor client?"

"I hope he wasn't there," said Roger.

"Of course," said Henry, "Peter ought to have been doing it, but he wouldn't really have been any better than you. Worse, probably. He'd have talked nonsense; you only said nothing. Neither of you ought to have been allowed to do it, but there you are, my dear fellow, they will do these things, they will do these things."

"Was I what you call 'devilling'?" asked Roger.

"Well," said Henry, "if looking unhappy and saying nothing can be called devilling, you were."

"I suppose," said Roger, "that that's what Gilbert was referring to when he said:

'Pocket a fee with a grin on your face
When you haven't been there to attend to the case'."

"Yes," said Henry, "but it isn't entirely fair to the Bar to put it just like that. A chap can't be in two places at once and he can't tell when he first accepts a brief in a case that it's going to clash with any other. So there are times when he's got to get help from someone else. All I say is that pupils shouldn't be allowed to give it. Your case is certainly an extreme one and I don't suppose it has happened before or will happen again, but the principle is just the same. No offence to you, but during the whole of your year you won't be capable of handling a defended case in the High Court efficiently, even if you've read it thoroughly."

"Then why didn't Grimes ask you to help him?" asked Roger.

"Well," said Henry, "that could be a long story, but I'll make it a short one. In a nutshell, I've got too big for my boots and I won't devil a brief unless I do the whole thing, or at any rate get half the fee."

"Look," said Roger, "I don't mean to be rude, but you tell me an awful lot. How am I to know you're right?"

"Good for you," said Henry. "You can't know. And you're quite right to ask. Go on asking. Don't take anything for granted, not even Grimeyboy. In a month or two you'll think everything he says and does is right."

"Isn't it?"

"It doesn't matter whether it is or it isn't, you'll think it is. Almost every pupil swears by his master. And it's often quite a long time before he realizes that his written work was bad, that he was only a very moderate lawyer and a poor advocate. I'm not saying any of that about Grimeyboy. It wouldn't in fact be true. But the point is, you must judge for yourself. Ask 'why' the whole time. Oh, hullo, Peter. How's the Old Bailey? You know that Thursby had to devil for you yesterday?"

"Thanks very much," said Peter. "I'll give you half my fee.

40

Quite a good assault case, as a matter of fact. I'd have been sorry to have missed that. Oh, and there's a good one in the Court of Criminal Appeal tomorrow, I'm told."

"D'you think I could go?" asked Roger.

"You certainly could," said Henry, "and if you want to become like Peter, I should. But if you're wise you'll get on with your work here. Popping off to the Old Bailey or the Court of Criminal Appeal to get a cheap thrill won't teach you anything."

"I may decide to go to the Criminal Bar," said Peter.

"If I were you, I should," said Henry. "Now I must go and work for once."

Henry went to his room and Roger started to open a set of papers.

"Don't feel much like work this morning," said Peter. "Had a bit of a night last night. What are you reading?"

"I haven't started really," said Roger. "This is something called Biggs and Pieman."

"Oh, that's quite amusing. Pieman's the M.P., you know. It'll never come into Court. It's a sort of woman scorned action. Neither side can afford to fight it. Wish they would. It'd be great fun. She's a very attractive woman. I saw her in the clerk's room before she saw Grimeyboy."

"What's it about?"

"Well—it's a claim for money lent. To judge from the letters, Mrs Biggs and Mr Pieman used to see more of one another than they ought to have done—seeing that there was a Mr Biggs. Well, Pieman apparently needed money to start him on his political career and Mrs B. provided it. How much of it was Mr B.'s I don't know. Later on when the good ship Pieman was firmly launched he broke it off with Mrs B. She was very angry and asked for her money back. He wouldn't pay. So she sued him. He says it's a gift."

"When is it coming on for trial?"

"I tell you, it isn't. Mr B. doesn't know anything about it, but if it came into Court he soon would. There are things in those letters most husbands wouldn't approve of. You read them. They're grand fun. She wanted to know if the action could be heard *in camera*. Of course it couldn't. So it's only a question of who'll give in first. Wouldn't do Pieman any good for his constituency to know that he'd been financed by another man's wife. Wouldn't do her any good for her husband to know she's been so very kind to Mr P. Now, what else is there?"

Peter looked casually at the briefs lying on the table. He picked up one, opened it and read a little, put it back in its red tape and sighed.

"How can anyone be expected to get up any enthusiasm for drawing-pins? Consignments of drawing-pins. I ask you."

He picked up another set of papers.

"This isn't much better," he said. "It's about wallpaper. I wish he'd have a breach of promise or an enticement action. He hardly ever does a divorce case. Had one the other day, though. Not bad at all. Cruelty case."

He paused for a moment, trying to recollect some of the more lurid details.

"D'you know, he used to tie her up to a chair and then make faces at her. Now, what would he get out of that?"

"I can't think," said Roger, but he said it in a tone which caused Peter to say:

"Sorry, old boy. Don't want to interrupt. Think I'll go down to the Old Bailey. Where's Charles?"

"I haven't seen him this morning."

"Oh, of course. He's got a judgment summons somewhere."

"What's that?"

"Oh—a summons for debt, you know. I'm not quite sure actually, but you get an Order sending them to prison if they don't pay, or something."

"I thought that was abolished years ago."

"So did I, old boy, but it's something like that. You ask Henry. He knows all the answers. Pity he's got no guts. Might have done well. Well, so long, old boy. May not see you again till tomorrow. Depends what they've on at the Old Bailey. I'll take my robes. Might get a docker."

"A what?"

"Dock brief. You know, surely. I did before I was called. Any prisoner who's got a couple of guineas and the clerk's fee can choose any counsel sitting in Court. So if you just go and sit there you may get a brief. Look hard at the prisoner and hope you hypnotize him into choosing you. Henry's got a good story about dock briefs."

"What's that?"

"Well, I might as well tell you first. Don't often get in in front of Henry. Well, there was an old lag down at the Bailey. He'd been there dozens of times, knew the ropes. Well, he was up one day for something and decided he'd like to have counsel to defend him. So he brought out his money and they took him up into the dock before the Recorder.

" 'Can I have a dock brief, please, my Lord?' he asked, very politely.

" 'Has he two pounds four shillings and sixpence?' asked the Recorder. The clerk informed the Recorder that the money was there.

42

" 'Very well,' said the Recorder. 'Choose whom you like,' and he pointed to the two rows of counsel sitting in Court. Some were very young, like me, and couldn't have had any experience. Others were very old and moth-eaten. At least one had a hearing aid.

" 'What!' said the old lag in horror. 'One of those?'

"The Recorder looked at the two rows of counsel and then said rather mournfully: 'Yes, I'm afraid so. That's all we have in stock at the moment'."

"Well," said Roger, "I wish you luck. But if you did get a brief, would you know what to do with it?"

"As much as anyone else, old boy. Just get up and spout to the jury. Can't come to much harm. They're all guilty. So it doesn't really matter what happens. Feather in your cap if you get them off. Inevitable if they're convicted."

"I wonder they bother to try them," said Roger.

"Must go through the motions, old boy," said Peter. "And anyway, where would the legal profession be? Justice must not only be done but must appear to be done and, may I add, must be paid for being done. Bye, bye, old boy. Hope you like Mrs Biggs' letters. Some of them are a bit hot. I tried a bit on one of my girl friends. Went down very well. Breach of copyright, I suppose. But who cares? So long."

For the next hour Roger was left alone and he devoted himself to the study of *Biggs (married woman)* v. *Pieman*. He found it enthralling—not so much in the way that Peter did, but because he felt so important to be looking into the intimate affairs of other people and, in particular, people of some prominence. Here he was, only just called to the Bar, and he knew things about a Member of Parliament which hardly anyone else knew. And then, supposing by one of those extraordinary coincidences that do take place, he happened to meet Mr Biggs! He might be a member of his uncle's club. And suppose his uncle introduced him and they had dinner together. He'd have to listen while Biggs extolled the virtues of his wife.

"A sweet little woman, though I say it myself who shouldn't," Mr Biggs might say.

"I don't know whether you should or you shouldn't," Roger would think to himself. "Fortunately you didn't say good little woman." Mr Biggs would go on:

"Pretty as a picture—but I'd trust her with anyone. It's not everyone who can say that, these days."

"Indeed not," Roger would think. "Not with accuracy, anyway."

At that moment, Mr Grimes came into the pupils' room.

43

"How are ye, my dear fellow? What are ye looking at? Oh, dear, dear, dear. That kettle of fish. Well, the fellows will be fellows and the girls will be girls. They will do these things, they will do these things."

"D'you think the action will come into Court?"

"Oh, dear me no, my dear fellow. We can't have that, can we? Dear, dear, dear. Our husband doesn't know of our goings on and we don't want him to. We don't want him to, my dear fellow."

"Then why did she bring the action?"

"Just a try on, my dear fellow, just a try on. He might have paid up. You can never tell, my dear fellow, you can never tell. There's only one motto I know of that's any good. 'Never go to law,' my dear ₁ellow, 'never go to law'. And then where should *we* be, my dear fellow? We shouldn't, should we? So it's just as well they will do these things, isn't it, my dear fellow, just as well."

Then Alec came in.

"Can you see Mr Wince, sir? He was just passing and wanted to have a word with you about Cooling and Mallet."

Mr Grimes immediately left the pupils' room. It was not far enough to run but he went as fast as he could. Roger imagined that he would be pretty good at getting to the bathroom first in a boarding house.

"And how's Mr Wince?" Roger heard him say. "How's Mr Wince to-day? Come along in, my dear fellow, come along in," and then Mr Grimes' door closed and Roger heard no more. He wondered what Mr Wince wanted. What was Cooling and Mallet about? He looked on his table. What a piece of luck. There it was. He quickly tied up the bundle he had been reading and opened Cooling and Mallet. At that moment Alec came in.

"Mr Grimes wants these, I'm afraid, sir," he said and took them away.

Roger went back to the sins of Mr Pieman and Mrs Biggs. Even at his age he found it a little sad to see how the attitude between men and women can change. The letters, which in the early correspondence started and ended so very, very affectionately, full of all the foolish-looking but (to them) sweet-sounding endearments of lovers, gradually cooled off. "My dearest, sweetest turnip, how I adore you" became "Dear Mr Pieman, if I do not receive a cheque by return I shall place the matter in other hands." Is it really possible that I could ever hate the sight of Joy or Sally as undoubtedly Mr Pieman now hates the sight of Mrs Biggs? Perhaps it only happens, he thought, when the relationship has

44

been that of husband and wife, or worse. At twenty-one these things are a little difficult to understand.

Roger had an hour more with Mr Pieman and Mrs Biggs when Charles returned. The Court he had attended was some way away, but he was still hot and flushed.

"Hullo," said Roger. "How did you get on? I hear you've been doing a judgment something or other. I wish you'd tell me about it."

"I wish you'd asked me that yesterday. Then I might have had to look it up. As it is, I have lost my one and only client."

"I'm so sorry. What happened?" asked Roger sympathetically.

"I'd learned the ruddy thing by heart. There wasn't a thing I didn't know." He broke off. "It really is too bad."

"Do tell me, unless you'd rather not."

"I think I'd like to get it off my chest. I was doing a j.s.—a judgment summons. That's an application to send to prison a person who hasn't paid a judgment debt, but you can only succeed if you can prove he has had the means to pay the debt or at any rate part of it since the judgment. The debtor has to attend and my job was to cross-examine him for all I was worth to show that he could have paid. I went to the Court with my client and I told him the sort of questions I was going to ask and he seemed very impressed. 'That'll shake him,' he said several times. I was really feeling confident. And what d'you think happened? The case was called on and the chap didn't turn up. Well, that was bad enough, but it was after that that the trouble really began. After all, I can't know everything, can I, and I *had* read that brief. If the chap had been there I'd have knocked him to bits. But he wasn't. 'Well,' said the judge, 'what do you want me to do?' Well, I ought to have looked it up, I suppose, but I hadn't. I'd no idea what I wanted him to do. Fortunately my client knew more than I did. 'Have him fined,' he whispered. 'Would Your Honour fine him?' I said.

" 'Your client wants his money, I suppose,' said the judge. 'What good will fining him do?'

"I had no idea. Again my client prompted me. 'If he doesn't pay, he goes to prison.'

"I repeated this to the judge.

" 'But surely that isn't right,' said the judge. 'You've got to prove means before he goes to prison.'

" 'Not in the case of a fine,' whispered my client.

" 'Not in the case of a fine, Your Honour,' I repeated, like the good parrot I had become.

"I was already beginning to feel extremely small, particularly after the exhibition I'd given to my client in the train as to what

45

I was going to do with this judgment debtor. Here I was, just repeating what he was feeding me with. But even that wouldn't have been so bad if it had been right.

" 'Nonsense,' said the judge. 'You can't commit a man for non-payment of a fine unless you can prove he has the means to pay. Do you know what is meant by an argument in a circle?'

" 'I think so, Your Honour,' I said.

" 'A good example,' said the judge, 'is the law relating to judgment summonses. If a judgment debt isn't paid, the debtor can only be sent to prison if you can prove he has had the means to pay. Usually you can't do that unless he's present to be cross-examined about his means. If he doesn't obey the summons to appear, he can be fined, but you can't do anything about the fine unless you can prove he has the means to pay it. But he doesn't come. So you can't ask him questions or prove anything. So you're back where you started. Of course, if he's got any goods on which distress can be levied, it's different, but then you'd have tried execution and wouldn't have bothered about a judgment summons in that case.'

"Meantime I'm standing there, getting red in the face.

" 'Well, Mr Hepplewhite, what would you like me to do?'

"Someone in the row—a barrister or solicitor—whispered to me. 'Ask for a 271.'

"Again I did as suggested.

" 'What on earth's that?' asked the judge.

"Well, what could I say? The chap next to me might have been pulling my leg. I didn't know. I didn't know anything. So I said so. You can hardly blame the judge.

" 'Really,' he said. 'This is too bad. Summons dismissed.'

"My client said something to me about looking up the rules another time and added that he wouldn't be coming back my way. On the way home I started looking it up—and, blow me, if there isn't a thing called a 271. The chap was quite right. It was the only thing to do. Even the judge didn't know it. It's certainly a lesson to look up the rules another time. But it takes it out of you, a thing like that."

"It must have been awful," said Roger. "But you can't look up everything before you go into Court," he went on. "How d'you know what to look up?"

"Well, I suppose," said Charles, "if you have a judgment summons, you ought to look up the rules which govern them. And I suppose, too, one ought to visualize the possibility of a man not turning up and find out what you can do then. I shan't forget 271 in a hurry. I feel like writing to the judge about it. After all, he ought to have known it."

46

"What is a 271?" asked Roger.

"It's an authority to arrest the debtor and bring him before the Court if he doesn't pay a fine within the time he's been given to pay it. So it isn't an argument in a circle. You can get the debtor there. Funny the judge didn't know."

"I suppose there are things judges don't know," said Roger. "Henry's got a case in a County Court tomorrow. D'you think it would be a good thing if I went with him? He said I could."

"I should. You'll learn a lot from Henry. And, apart from that, he'll tell you stories on the way. He's got an unending fund of them. And they'll all be new to *you*. I expect that's one of the reasons he asked you to come."

Roger spent the rest of the day reading the papers in *Biggs* v. *Pieman* and the case about drawing-pins. The evening he spent with Sally.

"It's amazing to think what's going on and no one knows it. I saw a case today about a Member of Parliament."

"Who?"

"Oh, I couldn't tell you that. One of the first things Grimes told me was that anything I learn I must treat with confidence."

"Then why did you tell me about the case at all?"

"You couldn't possibly identify the parties."

"What's it about then?"

"Well, I suppose there can't be any harm in that. There are over six hundred M.P.'s and an infinite variety of married women."

So Roger told her the facts as well as he remembered them.

"Humph!" said Sally. "It *is* quite interesting. Sounds like old Pieman. I wouldn't put it past him."

"What did you say?" said Rogers, so horrified that he was unable to stop himself from asking the question, or from showing in his voice the surprise he felt.

"Roger—it is—it's old Pieman. Mother will be thrilled."

"Sally, you're not to."

"Then it is. How extraordinary."

"The other thing I was looking at," said Roger, lamely, "was about drawing-pins."

"It's much too late now, Roger. I know all about it."

"Sally, you mustn't tell anyone. Promise you won't."

"You didn't tell me in confidence, Roger."

"But I learned it in confidence."

"Then you shouldn't have told me in the first instance. Now, let's think who I've seen about with old Pieman."

"Sally, you mustn't. How was I to know you knew him?"

"How were you to know I didn't."

47

"I never thought for a moment—oh, Sally, please promise you won't tell anyone. I've done the most terrible thing."

"I know who it is," said Sally. "A very smart woman—now what's her name? Let me think."

"Please, Sally, please. I'm sure it isn't, anyway."

"How can you possibly tell? I know, Anstruther, that's the name, Mollie Anstruther."

"No," said Roger.

"Roger," said Sally, "I'm sorry to have to tell you this—I do it more in sorrow than in anger and all for your own good—but it'll hurt you more than it hurts me all the same—you're an ass —an unmitigated ass. Why on earth did you say 'no' when I mentioned Mollie Anstruther? That eliminates one possibility. Now I can try to think of someone else. I thought that was the sort of trick barristers played on other people."

"Well, I didn't think it would be fair on the woman to let you think it was her."

"Then it must be Dorothy Biggs. I've often seen them about together."

Roger said nothing for a moment. Then:

"How on earth could I tell you'd guess?" he said miserably.

"What'll you do if I promise not to tell anyone?"

"I'll be more careful in future."

"Is that all? You'll do that anyway, I hope."

"There won't be any necessity. If you go telling people about it, it'll quite likely become known that it came out through me and then I shall be disbarred. After three days, too. I'm in your hands, Sally."

"Don't be silly," said Sally. "Of course I shan't tell anyone."

"You're a darling. I don't know what I should do without you."

"Well, you'd have told someone else, I suppose."

"Yes, I suppose I should. I am an ass. You're quite right, Sally. How lucky it was you."

"Well," said Sally thoughtfully, "Joy might not have known the parties—but if she had—I'm sure she'd have done just what I did. Wouldn't she, Roger?"

"Yes," said Roger, uncomfortably, "I'm sure she would."

"Well, that's settled," said Sally brightly. "Now you're going to tell me about the drawing-pins."

"They were in confidence, Sally. You might have sat on one of them."

"Too true," said Sally. "And does this mean that you're never going to tell me anything?"

"Of course not. I can tell you anything that happens in Court.

48

And I can tell you about the people in chambers. Old Grimes is an extraordinary person. But he's got the most tremendous practice. And I gather his clients swear by him."

"From what you told me yesterday on the phone, I thought you did most of his work for him."

"I didn't put it as high as that. Oh, by the way, tomorrow I'm going to a County Court with an awfully nice chap called Henry Blagrove. He's quite brilliant, I think, but I haven't heard him in Court yet."

"What's a County Court? Where they fine you for not having dog licences?"

"Oh, no. It's a Court for trying small civil cases—breaches of contracts, debts, accident cases and so on. And they have things called judgment summonses there. D'you know, they still send people to prison for not paying debts. I must say I thought that had been abolished after Pickwick Papers."

"Are there debtors' prisons still then?"

"I don't think so. They go to ordinary prisons, I think. As a matter of fact, I don't believe many people actually go to prison. About a thousand a year, I was told."

"I must ask Mother," said Sally. "She sings at prisons sometimes."

"That is good of her," said Roger. "She must go down awfully well. They like almost anything there—I mean, I mean——"

"Explain it to Mother," said Sally, "here she is."

Mrs Mannering came into the room a moment later.

"How are you, Roger? How nice of you to take tickets for Friday. I'm sure you can't afford it, as a poor struggling barrister."

"I've been looking forward to hearing you," said Roger. "I was only saying so to Sally a moment ago."

"How sweet of you. Walter Burr's going to accompany me. I've made him promise not to say a word. He's a brilliant accompanist but he's suddenly got the idea that he's a comedian too. And he always tries to introduce the songs and do a comic turn at the same time. Seems catching in the musical profession at the moment. Oh, who do you think gave me a lift home, wasn't it kind? Walter Pieman—the M.P., you know. I met him at Hilda's."

Roger and Sally said nothing for a moment. Then Sally said:

"It only goes to show, doesn't it?"

"Goes to show what?" said her mother.

"That M.P.'s have their uses."

The next day Roger met Henry at a tube station on the way to the County Court.

"I see you've a red bag," said Roger. "Have you had it long?"

"I was lucky," said Henry. "I got a brief with a leader in my

49

second year and somehow or other it produced this. Lucky. It's much lighter than carrying a suitcase, particularly if you've got a lot of books to take."

"But why a suitcase?"

"Well—after a few years some people don't like to be seen with a blue bag. So they use a suitcase instead."

"Who gave you yours?"

"Mostyn, as a matter of fact."

"I say, that's awfully good, isn't it? He's one of the biggest leaders now, isn't he?"

"Well, he's made a lot of headway in the last year or two. Yes, I was lucky. Curiously enough, I actually earned it. I worked like hell."

"Don't people always earn them?"

"As often as not it's done between the clerks. George meets Ernest in the 'Cock.' 'D'you think you could get young Bolster a red bag, Ernie?' he says over the third pint. 'I'll try, old boy,' says Ernest. And if Ernest tries the answer is probably 'yes.' It's a funny custom. The only people who make anything out of it really are the people who make the bags. But it's a sort of milestone in a chap's career. The day he gets his red bag. You certainly won't find your way to the Woolsack without one."

They discussed the other milestones in a career at the Bar; then they talked about County Courts.

"What's this judge like?" asked Roger.

"Well, fortunately," said Henry, "there aren't any others like him today. I don't mean by that that he's a bad judge. He isn't. But he's very inconsiderate. Furthermore, he's peppery, pompous and conceited, but he's quite a good judge for all that, though not as good as he thinks he is. Incidentally, one of the funniest things I ever heard happened in front of him. Like to hear?"

"That's one of the reasons I've come," said Roger.

"Charles told you that, I suppose," said Henry, and they both laughed.

There were three main characters in the story which Henry told Roger. The first was a barrister called Galloway, a well-intentioned, very serious and literally-minded man. The second was a former County Court judge called Musgrave.

"He's dead now," said Henry. "He was a nice old boy and quite a good judge when he tried a case, but he was a wicked old man and wouldn't sit after lunch. There aren't any others like him today, either."

"What d'you mean?" asked Roger.

"What I say. He wouldn't sit after lunch. He spent part of the morning either making people settle cases or adjourning them for one reason or another and finally he tried what was left and rose at lunch-time. Very rarely he came back after lunch, but usually he made some excuse for postponing any case which hadn't finished by lunch-time until another day. I liked him, but he certainly was naughty. Well, one day Galloway had a case in front of Musgrave. It was an accident case which would have been likely to occupy a considerable part of the day. The judge had a medical referee sitting beside him to advise. When I say sitting, well, it was arranged that he should sit. The only question in the case was whether a man's illness had been caused by the accident, but a good deal of evidence would have had to be given about it. Before the judge sat he sent for the doctors who were being called on each side and told them to have a word with the medical referee. After they'd had a chat for ten minutes or so, the judge went in to see them himself. Five minutes later he came into Court, sat down and announced that there would be judgment in the case for the defendants with costs.

" 'But——' said the unfortunate Galloway, who was appearing for the plaintiff.

" 'But what?' said the judge, quite severely.

" 'But——' repeated Galloway.

" 'If that's all you have to say, Mr Galloway, I'll have the next case called,' and this was duly done.

"Well, of course, the plaintiff wasn't going to take that lying down. His case had never been tried. The judge had no doubt acted upon what the doctors had told him behind closed doors. It was a complete denial of justice. So the plaintiff appealed to the Court of Appeal and Galloway started to tell their Lordships all about it. He hadn't gone very far with the story before the president of the Court, Lord Justice Brand, said:

" 'It's very difficult to believe that this really happened. Naturally, I'm not doubting your word, Mr Galloway, but how can it have happened as you say without your saying something to the judge?'

" 'I did say something, my Lord.'

" 'Oh—what was that?'

" '*But*, my Lord.'

" 'Yes, Mr Galloway?'

" '*But*, my Lord.'

" 'But what, Mr Galloway?'

" 'Just *but*, my Lord.'

" 'I'm afraid I'm out of my depth,' said another Lord Justice. 'Are you still addressing us, Mr Galloway?'

" 'Yes, my Lord.'

" 'Then what did you mean when you said "but" to my brother?'

" 'That was what I said, my Lord.'

" 'I know you did, twice. But why?'

" 'I couldn't think of anything else to say, my Lord.'

" 'Now, look,' said Lord Justice Brand. 'Let us get this straight. You didn't say "but" to us——?'

" 'Oh, yes, he did,' said Lord Justice Rowe.

" 'I know, I know,' said Lord Justice Brand. 'Please let me finish. The "but" you said to us was the "but" you said to the learned County Court judge, or to put it more accurately, it was another "but" but the same word. "But" is what you said to the County Court judge.'

" 'Yes, my Lord,' said Galloway.

"Lord Justice Brand sat back in his chair triumphantly.

" 'But,' said Lord Justice Rowe, 'if I may be forgiven the use of the word, but is that all you said to the learned judge?'

" 'Yes, my Lord, just "but". '

" 'But it doesn't mean anything.'

" 'I didn't get a chance to say anything more, my Lord, and I was too flabbergasted.'

" 'Really, Mr Galloway,' said Lord Justice Brand. 'When I was at the Bar, I considered it to be my duty in the interests of my client to stand up to the judge and, if necessary, to be rude to him, yes, to be rude to him. I cannot believe that counsel of your experience would allow a thing like that to happen unchallenged.'

"In the end, of course, they allowed the appeal and sent the case back to the County Court to be properly heard before another judge, but not before poor Galloway's mildness had been further criticized.

"A week later he had an accident case before Boyle—the judge you're going to meet. Galloway was appearing for the plaintiff. He got up and started to open the case to the jury, explaining to them where the accident happened and so on. He was just saying:

" 'Now, members of the jury, at that juncture the defendant's car without any warning of any kind whatsoever——' when the judge interrupted:

" 'Mr Galloway, might I have a plan, please?'

" 'Be quiet,' said Galloway and continued to address the jury. 'And without any warning of any kind whatsoever——'

"Just as the Court of Appeal could not believe what was said to have happened in Musgrave's Court, Boyle couldn't believe he'd heard Galloway aright. Galloway was a polite man and his behaviour was normally impeccable.

" 'I really can't follow this without a plan,' said Boyle.

" 'Will you be quiet,' said Galloway and started to go on address-

52

ing the jury. But not for long. This time the judge had no doubt what had been said.

" 'Have you taken leave of your senses, Mr Galloway?' he said angrily. 'How dare you speak to me like that!'

" 'Well, your Honour,' said Galloway. 'I was told last week by the Court of Appeal that it was my duty to be rude to the judge.' "

CHAPTER SIX

HIS HONOUR JUDGE BOYLE

They arrived at the Court in plenty of time and went straight to the robing-room. It was crowded with solicitors and counsel.

"Hullo, Henry, are we against one another?" said a middle-aged barrister.

"I don't know. I'm in—now what's the name of it? Wait a minute, I can never remember."

He opened his bag and got out the brief. "Oh, yes, of course, Swift and Edgerley."

"Yes, that's me," said the other. "We've got a hope. We're about last. He's got some judgment summonses, half a dozen possession cases and three other actions before ours. Any use asking him to let us go?"

"Not a chance," said Henry. "But all the same I should think we'd better try. The old so-and-so will never let anyone get away before lunch. I think he likes an audience really, to hear his wise remarks and his quotations from Birkenhead's famous judgment. Is anyone else going to have a crack at it? Let's get in before he sits and see what the form is."

Counsel's and solicitors' row made an impressive sight for His Honour Judge Boyle as he walked on to the Bench. Henry was right in thinking that he liked an audience. The judge moved in and sat down slowly. He was a heavy man and not young. The first thing he did was to look at the pencils. He obviously did not approve of them. He tapped on his desk for the clerk to speak to him.

"Take these beastly things away," he said, "and get me some decent ones. I can't use those. How many more times have I got to say so?"

"I'm sorry, your Honour," said the clerk.

"It's not your fault," grunted the judge. "It's what they send us. I've complained about it dozens of times. They'll expect me to write with my thumbnail next."

The clerk sent out for some more pencils.

A solicitor got up: "Might I mention to your Honour," he began.

"No, not yet," said the judge irritably.

The solicitor sat down with a sigh.

"Cheerful mood today," whispered one member of the Bar to another.

"The old idiot. I'd like to chuck the lot at him."

"If people want to talk they must go outside," said the judge.

"Charming," said Henry, but quietly enough.

The new pencils were brought. The judge tried them. "I suppose they'll have to do," he said eventually. "They're better than the last. Thank you, Mr Jones."

"Shall I call the first application, your Honour?"

"Yes, please."

"Mrs Turner," called the clerk, and a small woman went into the witness box. She was making an application for some money to be paid out to her from a fund in Court. She was a widow whose husband had been killed some years before in an accident and the Court controlled her use of the damages she had been awarded.

"Well," said the judge, after glancing at the papers in front of him, "what do you want £10 for?"

He asked her as though she were a beggar at the back door when she was, in fact, the owner of the fund in Court. It was her money, but the Court had the paternal duty of seeing that she did not expend it too foolishly. The judge's manner was not in the least paternal.

"Please, your Worship," the woman began——

"She's had it," whispered a solicitor, "calling him your worship."

"It's a first payment for a television set."

The judge's eyes gleamed. His remarks about television and other abominations of the modern age had frequently been reported in the Press.

"A television set," he growled. "What on earth d'you want with one of those things? Read a good book and get it from the library. Cost you nothing."

"Please, your Worship, I can't read, not really."

"What on earth have we been paying taxes for all these years? It's disgraceful."

"Please, your Worship, I'm nearly blind."

"Oh, I'm sorry," said the judge. He thought for a moment and then added in a more kindly tone: "But is a television set much use to you then? Why not have a wireless instead?"

"Oh, I have a wireless, your Worship."

"I see."

The judge hesitated.

"You think you'll get some pleasure out of a television set, do you?"

"Oh, yes, your Worship. Mrs Crane across the road has one and she can't see a thing."

"Perhaps it's an advantage then," said the judge. "Yes, very well, Mrs Turner. You shall have your television set. Ten pounds I think you want. Very well. Can you pay the instalments all right? Good. They'll give you your money in the office. I hope your sight improves."

"Might I now mention to your Honour," began the solicitor who had tried before, hoping that the shock which the judge had just received might have put him in a more receptive mood.

"Certainly not," said the judge just as fiercely as before, but not quite for the same reason. He was visualizing Mrs Turner's life without her husband and without much sight. "And probably she hasn't much to think with either," he was pondering, "though p'raps it's as well," when the solicitor had interrupted.

"Mr Copplestone," called the clerk, and a young man went into the witness box. The judge glared at him. He had already glanced at his application.

"A motor bicycle," he said. "One of those horrible things. Why don't you use a pedal cycle or walk? Much better for you and safer. You'll go and kill yourself."

"I'm getting married," ventured the young man.

"You'll kill your wife too," said the judge.

"I'm twenty-one next month," said the young man, "and we wanted the bike for our honeymoon."

This was a young man who had been awarded damages when he was a small boy. At the age of twenty-one he would be entitled to all of it, but until then the Court had control.

"Why can't you wait?" asked the judge. He knew he couldn't keep the young man away from a motor bicycle for long, but he did not want to be a party to the transaction.

"We don't want to, your Honour."

"I dare say you don't. Have you your parents' permission?"

"To have the bike, your Honour?"

"No, of course not. No one asks parents' permission for anything these days. You just go and do it. No—to marry, I mean. Still need it for that."

"Can I speak?" said a man from the back of the Court.

"Silence," called the usher.

"But it's all wrong," shouted the man.

55

"Silence," called the usher even louder.

"Let that man be brought forward," commanded the judge. He required no bringing forward and came hastily to the witness box.

"Who are you?" asked the judge.

"I'm his father," said the man. "And I think it's a shame."

"You've already interrupted the proceedings twice and if you speak like that I shall deal with you for contempt of Court. You'll either speak properly or not at all. Now, what is it you want to say?"

"I say, give the boy his bike. Why spoil the young people's pleasure? You only get married once."

"Unfortunately," said the judge, unable to resist the temptation, "that today is not always the case, though I hope it will be in this instance. But if I let him have this horrible machine one of them at least will probably be killed."

"They can't afford a car," said the man. "And they don't want to go for a honeymoon by bus or train. They want to be with each other. And I say they ought to be. My old woman and I went walking, but then we didn't have the luck to have had an accident and get the damages. Though it doesn't look as though that's going to be much good to him."

"Will you be quiet," said the judge.

"Why doesn't the Registrar do these?" whispered Henry to his opponent.

"Because the old fool likes doing them. He ought to do them in chambers, anyway. Pompous old idiot. Doesn't care two hoots how much time he takes up or how much he inconveniences everyone."

The judge finished his applications, having very grudgingly given the young man his money. He realized that it would not be fair in this instance to refuse it.

"Now, does anyone want to mention any of the cases?"

The solicitor had a third attempt.

"Any member of the Bar," asked the judge, ignoring the solicitor.

Henry's opponent got up.

"Your Honour is always so exceedingly considerate that I'm prompted to ask leave to mention the last case in your Honour's list," he said.

"Let me see," said the judge, "Swift and Edgerley, is that it?"

"Yes, your Honour. My learned friend, Mr Blagrove, and I were wondering whether your Honour would give any indication of whether that case is likely to be heard today. I would not have mentioned the matter but your Honour is always so exceedingly helpful in these matters and as there are seven cases in front of us——" he paused and waited to see what effect his piece of hypocrisy had had.

"One does one's best, Mr Tate," said the judge, "but, as you know, it's very difficult with such heavy lists. Would it be a convenience to you if I said that I would not hear your case before the luncheon adjournment?"

"No bloody use at all," said Tate in an undertone to Henry. "Thank you very much, your Honour," he went on. "That is most kind of your Honour. Perhaps we might have leave to mention the matter again after the adjournment."

"Certainly, Mr Tate."

"If your Honour pleases," beamed Mr Tate. "The old so-and-so," he added to Henry, "he knows bloody well we can't get back to the Temple from here."

"Any other applications from the Bar?" asked the judge. There was no response.

"Now, Mr Bloat, what is your application?"

"Would your Honour release my case too until after lunch?"

"If I release every case I shall have nothing to do. Are there any other applications?"

"But, your Honour——" began Mr Bloat.

"What is it, Mr Bloat?" said the judge angrily. "It's quite impossible for me to help the parties in these matters if they don't accept my decision when I've given it. I do the best I can."

"I think you're brilliant," said Henry to Tate when they were in the robing-room again. "It would stick in my gullet to talk to the old boy like that."

"When you're my age," said Tate, "you'll never mind saying 'please' to anyone if it'll get you anywhere or anything—even if you think you oughtn't to have had had to ask for it—indeed, even if it's your own. It costs nothing and sometimes it gets something. At any rate we can have a smoke and plenty of time for lunch. He only rises for half an hour."

"But you perjured your immortal soul in the process."

"If you feel so strongly on the subject, my boy," said Tate, "you should have got up and disagreed when I said the old fool was so exceedingly helpful. See how far that would have got us! Anyway by keeping silent you adopted my lie and cannot now be heard to complain of it. Estopped, my boy, that's what you are. And when you get before St Peter, he'll have you for that. 'You told a lie to His Honour Judge Boyle,' he'll say. You'll start to deny it. 'We can't have that,' he'll say. 'You told a lie to Judge Boyle all right. Good for you. Come inside'."

Eventually Henry's case was heard and he and Roger left the Court together.

"What sort of a clerk is Alec?" Roger asked him.

"Alec has, in my view," said Henry, "only one fault. This," and Henry imitated Alec sucking his teeth so successfully that Roger winced. "Cheer up—you'll have to get used to that," said Henry, and did it again. "Some people," he went on, "would say that he had two other faults. He doesn't drink or smoke. But that's a matter of opinion."

"Clerks seem to be most frightfully important," said Roger.

"Well, you've noticed something. They are. A top-class man will always get on, but a second-rater could be made or marred by his clerk."

"How does a clerk begin?"

"Usually as a boy in the Temple, at a very small wage. Then, if he's no good, he goes to something else. If he does take to it, he becomes a junior and then, if he's lucky, a senior clerk. D'you know, Alec was making a thousand a year when he was not much older than you are, and a thousand was a thousand in those days."

"It's extraordinary. Of course, the method of paying them beats me. I must say I like the idea of having my clerk paid by the clients. Is there any other profession in the world where it happens?"

"I don't know of one—except, of course, that they're really paid by commission and there are plenty of commission jobs. But they are rather different, I suppose. Yes, it is a curious arrangement that every time I have a conference my clerk gets five bob and the client pays him. But, of course, until you've got a practice you'll have to pay him a salary. And they're inclined to take the shillings in the guineas now as well from everyone."

"What do they make these days?

"Depends entirely on the chambers. But a clerk in a really good set of chambers might make two or three thousand a year, I suppose. And he's never read a law-book in his life, though he's carried a good few. All the same, the work he does is jolly important and the wheels wouldn't go round without him. Getting briefs, fixing up the fees and arranging it so that you're not in too many places at the same time. It takes a bit of doing. An intelligent and experienced clerk earns his keep all right."

"What I like," said Roger, "is the sort of relationship which seems to exist between them and us."

"Quite right!" said Henry. "It's quite different from any other. There's an intimacy and understanding between a barrister and his clerk which, as far as I know, doesn't exist in any other job. And neither side ever takes advantage of it. But Heaven preserve me from a bad clerk. Alec does me proud—indeed, he'd do me much better if I'd let him, and I don't mind his little habit as much as you seem to." And Henry repeated it several times until he saw that it really upset Roger. "Sorry, old boy," he said. "I didn't know you took it to heart so. I'll try to remember," and he just checked himself from repeating the process.

Shortly afterwards they parted. Henry went home and Roger went back to chambers. When he arrived there, he was greeted by Alec.

"There's a brief been sent down to you, sir, for next Friday."

"For me?"

"Yes, sir. I thought you might know about it. The solicitors are something Merivale. Someone you know, I expect?"

"Gosh," said Roger. "Joy's uncle already."

CHAPTER SEVEN

FIRST BRIEF

IT was a divorce case. Roger picked it up lovingly. It looked so beautiful in its fresh pink tape with "Mr Roger Thursby" typed neatly on it and almost as important, the fee—the fee that someone was going to pay him for his services. Seven whole guineas. He had never earned as much before in his life, though he had once earned a few guineas by tutoring a boy advertised as "Backward (nothing mental)." He was a nice boy with a fiercely obstinate disposition and determined to learn nothing that his parents wanted him taught. He could recognize almost any bird or flower and many tunes from classical music. His parents were not musical, so he used to turn on the Third Programme. Funny, thought Roger, how one train of thought leads to another. Why should I be thinking of Christopher because someone's sent me a brief? A brief. His very own. Mr Roger Thursby. Five and two, total seven. And at the bottom "Thornton, Merivale & Co., 7 Butts Buildings, E.C.4. Solicitors for the Petitioner." The Petitioner. The life and happiness of one man or one woman had been entrusted to him. Man or woman, which was it? The outside of the brief, which was entitled "In the High Court of Justice Probate, Divorce and Admiralty Division (Divorce). Newent E. *v.* Newent K. R.," did not disclose whether the petitioner was to be a beautiful blonde. Perhaps it was an actress—Sally's mother might know her —no, that wouldn't do—it was Joy's uncle who'd sent the brief. What a pity it wasn't Sally's. He'd no business to think that. It was most ungrateful. How kind it was of Joy and she was really very pretty. Or was it a man, an admiral, perhaps, or a general or even a Member of Parliament? Well, he could soon find out. He opened the brief. E. stood for Ethel. His first petitioner was a woman. Poor thing! What a brute of a husband! Now she had Roger to protect her. It was Roger Galahad Thursby who looked eagerly at the rest of the papers. At the age of twenty-one Roger found that rescuing ladies (in the imagination) occupied quite a portion of his idle moments. At that age the pictures of such events rather embarrassed him. He preferred her to be fully clothed. Roger started to read the brief and was a little disappointed to find that all that Mr Newent had done was to leave his wife—and, as far as could be ascertained, not even for another woman. Roger made the best of it, however, and soon imagined himself giving his client words of encouragement and consolation which would stem the poor girl's grief. Even this idea was slightly shaken when he found that the poor girl was forty-five and that she was what is called "asking for the discretion of the Court." But Roger steeled himself to the task. He was broadminded. He did not in fact approve of infidelity. He had attended several weddings and had always been impressed by the words of the marriage service. He had difficulty in reconciling them with the number of divorces which now take place. But now he was face to face with an unfaithful wife—on paper anyway, and he would soon see her. He could not help feeling a thrill at the prospect. He had never to his knowledge met an—an adulteress before. It was rather a terrible word. The newspapers often covered it up. They talked of misconduct and infidelity. Adulteress sounded much worse. And then he remembered the great words on the subject. "He that is without sin among you——" Yes, Roger would speak to this poor, fallen woman in a kindly, understanding way. She would never realize he was only twenty-one. He would speak with such an air of knowledge, such a wealth of understanding, that she would probably cry. And he would say: "Madam, you and I have only just met—but I think I know what you have been through." He paused in his thoughts. What next? Ah, yes, more sinned against than sinning. The lonely, slighted wife, devoted to a husband who neglected her for his business and his billiards. There she was alone at home, waiting, waiting—an easy prey for the handsome seducer. Yes, more sinned against than sinning, that was it. He read through the whole brief, the correspondence, the petition and the discretion statement. This last document was the one in which Mrs Newent disclosed how she came to sin and humbly asked the Court—not to forgive her—but to grant a decree of divorce just the same. Mr Newent apparently was quite willing to be divorced and had not even entered an appearance to the petition. This was a pity, thought Roger. It was difficult to make an impassioned speech against someone who wouldn't fight. And it was very clear that Mr Newent wasn't going to fight. His last letter to Ethel went as follows:

Dear Ethel,

It is no good asking me to return. I told you when I left that this is final and it is. I had one year of happiness with you and five years of the other thing. You cared much more for your beastly boarding house and some of the boarders than you did for me, though I shall be surprised if you make more of a success of that business than you did of our marriage. "Service with a smile" you used to put in your advertisements. Having regard to the charges you made and the little value you gave for them, I should have expected service to be with a smile, not to say a broad grin. If you don't treat your guests better than you treated me you'll lose them too. Most of them, that is. But then some people never learn. I have. And I'm not coming back to "Sans Repos"—which is what it ought to be called. But you wouldn't understand. You can understand this, though, that I'm not coming back—no never—whether you divorce me or whether you don't. I hope you will because I'd like to be free. Not that I've met anyone else. I'll be darn careful about the next one, believe me. But if I can't be free, at any rate I'll be happy. I don't wish you any harm, Ethel. Maybe there is some man who'd be happy with you, but it's not

Yours
Kenneth

This letter had been written in reply to a very short one by Ethel which had simply said:

I'm writing for the last time to know whether you propose to return to me. If you do not I shall take such action as I may be advised.

The material parts of the discretion statement were as follows:

After I had been married to my husband for some years he ceased to take any interest in my business of a boarding house proprietress, although he knew when we married that I was very keen on my business and wanted to continue with it after marriage. He had agreed to this, but nevertheless he was always asking me to give it up and make a home for him. At last he refused even to look after the accounts, and one of the boarders, who had been with us for some years and who did a little accounting in his spare time, very kindly started to do them for me. As a result of this I got to know this gentleman, a Mr Storrington, rather well. One night he asked

61

me to go to a dance with him, and, as at the time my husband was staying with his parents (one of whom was ill), I did not think there would be any harm in it. We went to a dance and unfortunately I had rather too much to drink. I am not a teetotaller, but very rarely drink intoxicating liquor. During the evening I had several drinks and though I felt all right during the dance, when we left I felt dizzy and faint. Mr Storrington very kindly offered to help me to my bedroom and somehow or other he came in and adultery took place. I felt very ashamed the next morning and told Mr Storrington that it must never happen again or he would have to leave. Mr Storrington promised that it would not occur again. Since my husband left me I have seen more and more of Mr Storrington and an affection has developed between us and, if this Court sees fit to grant me a decree of divorce, I wish to marry Mr Storrington and he is willing to marry me. Although Mr Storrington and I are living in the same house on affectionate terms adultery has not occurred between us except as aforesaid, nor have I committed any act of adultery with any other person. To the best of my knowledge and belief my husband was and is wholly unaware of my adultery.

It was a pity in some ways, thought Roger at first, that Mr Storrington was still about the place. For it meant that the petitioner already had a companion and friend. But Roger soon adjusted himself to the new situation, and decided that the poor little woman who had never known happiness with her husband should be given a new and happy life with her new husband, and it would be Roger who would be responsible for giving it her. After he had been through the papers several times Roger asked if he could see Mr Grimes, and eventually Alec managed to sandwich him in between two conferences.

"Well, my dear fellow, what can I do for ye?"

Roger mentioned that he'd had a brief for the petitioner in an undefended divorce. Might he ask a few questions about it?

"Of course, my dear fellow, of course. But ye won't have any trouble, my dear fellow. Not like it was in the old days. That was a very different cup of tea, a very different cup of tea, my dear fellow. Nowadays it's like shelling peas, my dear chap. In one door and out the other before you can say 'knife'."

"This is what they call a discretion case. Does that make any difference?"

"Oh, that's all right, my dear fellow, just tell the judge the tale, tell the judge the tale."

"As a matter of fact my client committed adultery before her husband left her. Does that make any difference?"

"Did he know of it, my dear fellow?"

"Oh—no."

"Then that's all right then, my dear fellow. What the eye sees not, the heart grieves not."

"I just wondered if it was desertion for a man to leave his wife if she'd committed adultery."

"Oh, yes, my dear fellow, so long as he doesn't know, that's desertion all right. You look up *Herod and Herod*. That'll tell you all about it. And there are some later cases in the Court of Appeal. Now is there anything else I can do for you, my dear fellow?"

"No, thank you very much. It's most kind of you."

"Not at all, my dear fellow. Very glad you've had your first brief. Had to wait much longer in my day. But everything's faster these days. I don't know what we're coming to. Judges on the Bench that haven't been called twenty years. I don't know, my dear fellow, I don't know. But there it is, they will do these things, they will do these things. Good-bye, my dear fellow, good-bye, bye, bye."

Roger went back to the pupils' room, very pleased with life. But, easy though his task was going to be, he wouldn't leave anything to chance. First he would master the facts, then the law and then—then—glorious moment—he would have a conference with his client.

"Hear you've got an undefended," said Peter. "I think they're a bore."

"Have you done one?" asked Charles.

"No, but I've heard hundreds. Simple as pie—but an awful bore. No, give me something a bit meatier for my first brief."

"Haven't you had one, then?" said Roger.

"As a matter of fact," said Peter, "it's not a terribly good thing to have a brief too early in one's career. Might come an awful cropper. Of course an undefended's different. But I just don't care for the sound of them. Shouldn't want my friends to send me one of those. If that's all the use they've got for me I'd rather they went somewhere else."

" 'Said the fox' " said Charles, " 'adding to his wife, "they always give me indigestion, anyway." ' "

"I don't know what you're talking about," said Peter. "Anyway I can't afford to waste my time here. I'm going down to the Bailey."

"Hope you get that dock brief," said Charles. "That'll be a start."

"Well done," said Charles when Peter had left. "Who sent it you?"

"Uncle of a girl friend."

63

"Good show. I never seem to be lucky that way. Are you going to have a conference?"

"I suppose so. It's marked on the brief—two guineas."

"That doesn't mean a thing, as a matter of fact. They pay it whether you have one or not."

"How odd," said Roger.

"I suppose it's the same with every job. There are always things which are difficult to explain to people who aren't in it."

"I suppose there are. But I think I ought to have a conference, anyway."

"Is it sticky then?"

"Oh, I don't think so. I spoke to Grimes and he said it was all right. But I think I ought to ask her a few questions."

"When'll you have it?"

"I don't know. What ought I to do about it? Speak to Alec?"

"Yes, I should think so. I've never had one yet."

"You've never had a conference?"

"No, as I told you, we haven't all got girl friends with solicitor uncles."

"I am lucky."

"I should say you are. That'll make up for what happened on your first day. Very different going into a Court knowing all about it—with your own case too. What's it about?"

Roger told him and then went to arrange with Alec for a conference.

"You usually see them outside the Court, sir," said Alec, "but I can get them down here if you'd like."

"Yes, I think so, please," said Roger feeling very daring at giving orders to his clerk. Outside the Court did not seem to be the real thing.

After that he went to the Bar Library and read the case of *Herod* v. *Herod* and several other later cases in which it had been approved. It seemed clear enough. Then he looked up every other point of law he could think of. He went back to chambers with a note of what he had read. Then he went home.

His mother was out. So he went straight to the telephone to thank Joy. "It's terribly good of your uncle, Joy."

"He's a dear old boy and if I give him a nice kiss, he'll do quite a lot for me. Shall I give him lots more kisses, Roger?"

"Oh, please, Joy."

"What'll you give me then?"

"We'll go and dine."

"Lovely. Where? When?"

"Well, I haven't had the cheque yet. I wonder when they send it."

64

"I've been a real live barrister for twenty-four hours, Sally. I could defend you for murder or shoplifting. Am I being very silly?"

Roger's blood froze again. "Whatever *is* a Scott Schedule?"

Henry was a tremendous asset to those of Mr Grimes' pupils who were sensible enough to listen to him. He had learned the tricks of the trade; he knew the ethics. And he loved to talk.

"I'd better give him another kiss, don't you think? I like talking about kisses to you, Roger. Don't you?"

"Of course I do, Joy, it is sweet of you. I can't thank you enough."

"Oh, yes, you can. And I'll expect you to try."

"Of course I will."

"Promise."

"Of course."

"Roger, darling—how lovely. I'll go and see uncle tonight and we'll dine tomorrow. I'll lend you the money if the cheque hasn't come."

"Oh—I couldn't let you. But I can try mother."

As soon as he'd finished talking to Joy, blushing slightly he telephoned Sally.

"Oh, Roger, I am glad. What's it about?"

"Well, I'd rather like to talk to you about it, if I might. It's not the sort of thing I can mention on the telephone."

"Well, when would you like?"

"You couldn't come round now? I expect Mother's got enough food."

"I'd love it."

As soon as Sally had arrived Roger showed her the lovely brief, but he covered up the names with his hand.

"You can't possibly know the people in this case and it must be all right for me to tell you if you don't know their names. Even they wouldn't mean anything to you."

"All right," said Sally, "if you say so."

"D'you mind if I tell you about the case as though I were addressing the judge?" he asked.

"Of course not."

"May it please your Lordship," began Roger, "my client who is a lady of mature years——"

"Stop," said Sally, "that won't do. How old is she?"

"Forty-five."

"Well—she'd hit you over the head with her umbrella for that —out of Court if not in. Why mention her age, anyway?"

"I think it's important in this case. You see, Sally, there are things in this case which you and I wouldn't talk about normally —I mean—I know everyone does nowadays, but you're different. I do want you to understand that when I talk about—talk about this woman's—this woman's—er—behaviour—it's only because it's in the case."

"Strictly professionally," said Sally. "I suppose you're trying to tell me she's committed adultery."

"Yes," said Roger, "I am, Sally, I'm afraid."

"That's all right, Roger, it's not your fault; she did it, not you."

"Quite," said Roger. "I'm so glad you understand. Now may I go on?"

"Please."

"May it please your Lordship, my client who is no longer young——'

"No," said Sally, "if you must say anything about it, and I can't yet see why you should, say what her age is. She may not like that, but she'd prefer it to any of your phrases."

"Oh, all right. My client who is forty-five is bringing this petition on the grounds of desertion. As your Lordship probably knows desertion is a matrimonial offence and consists of——"

"Just a moment, Roger," interrupted Sally, "I don't know anything about Courts and judges, but I suppose there have been a good many cases of desertion before yours."

"Oh, Lord, yes."

"Well—don't you think the judge might know what is meant by it then?"

"I said 'as your Lordship probably knows——' "

"D'you think he'd like the 'probably'? Some judges are pretty touchy, I believe."

"All right then. As your Lordship knows——"

"Well, if he knows, why tell him?" said Sally.

"I'm sure I've read that they say things like that, Sally."

"I expect that's when the judge *doesn't* know, Roger, and it's a polite way of telling him. If it's something that he must know and you know he must know it seems a bit odd to me telling him at all. You might just as well tell him that the case is brought under English law. I suppose every case is, unless it's a special one."

"I say, you know, Sally, I do think you're marvellous. You ought to have gone to the Bar. You're going to be the most awful help to me. Oh—I could kiss you."

Sally said nothing. Roger did nothing.

"Just another of your phrases, I suppose. Well, it's better than saying I'm of mature years. Though I expect I shall be before —now where were we?" she went on hurriedly.

"How would *you* start, Sally?"

"Well, I suppose, I'd say that it was a petition for divorce on the ground of desertion and then say shortly what the facts were."

"When would you mention the discretion?"

"What discretion?"

Roger explained what was meant by a discretion statement and told Sally what was in it.

"But I don't understand," said Sally.

"But I thought I'd made it clear. Where a petitioner has committed adultery he or she has got to file——"

"Oh, no, I understand all that. What I don't understand is what the husband has done wrong."

"He left her and wouldn't come back."

"Yes, but she'd committed adultery."

"But he didn't know of it. It's all quite clear. It's in *Herod and Herod*. I read it this afternoon."

"Are you sure you didn't misread it, Roger dear? After all you are fairly new to the game and I expect some of these things are difficult to understand——"

"Now, look, Sally. I think you're awfully clever and all that, and you're going to be an awful lot of use to me, if you will, but when I say the law's so and so you've got to accept it from me. I've looked it up."

"But Roger, I'm sorry to seem so dense. Do try and make me understand it. I gather the law disapproves of adultery."

"Of course."

"I suppose the law agrees that it's a breach of the marriage vows or whatever the law calls them to commit adultery?"

"Certainly."

"So if a wife commits adultery the husband is entitled to leave her."

"Quite."

"Well, that's what happened in your case."

"He didn't know."

"But surely, Roger, that can't make any difference."

"Well, it does."

"I still can't believe it," said Sally. "Look. Marriage starts with a husband and wife living together, doesn't it?"

"Yes."

"And if one leaves the other it's desertion."

"Exactly. That's what's happened here. He's left her."

"Not so fast, Roger. Is a wife entitled to have her husband living with her if she commits adultery?"

"No," began Roger—and then seeing where this admission was leading him to, he went on: "Well, it depends. If the husband finds out he can leave her."

"And are you really saying that if the husband doesn't find out—if the lady's clever enough to conceal it from him—then she has the right that he should go on living with her?"

"That," said Roger, "is the law of England."

"I'm sorry," said Sally, "you know and I don't. You've just looked it up. You've taken all your Bar examinations. But I just can't believe it. You're saying that, provided a man or woman is a good enough liar, he or she can commit adultery as much as they like?"

"It sounds odd put that way, I agree," said Roger.

"Well, isn't that what you were saying?"

Roger thought for a moment.

"I suppose it is really. I must say it does sound strange the way you put it. I didn't think of it like that, and I'm sure there's nothing in the cases I looked at about it. I think I'd better look at them again. I say, Sally, you really are a wonder. I could—didn't I hear mother?"

"You should know by now, Roger," said Sally.

"Oh, no, it's the people next door."

"Yes, Roger. You were saying?"

"Where was I now? Oh, yes—well, when do you think I should mention this discretion business?"

"Wouldn't it be a good thing to go and hear one or two undefended divorces yourself first, so that you can see when it's normally done?"

"How right you are. I will."

"May I come and hear you do yours, Roger?"

"Of course—that is—well——"

"Well, of course, if I'll make you nervous, Roger——"

"It's not exactly that, Sally. You see—as a matter of fact—it's like this really—of course I'd love you to be there—but, as a matter of fact, well—Joy's uncle sent me the brief actually."

"Well," said Sally, "that was very nice of him—and her, but why should that make any difference? Or have they taken the whole Court for the occasion?"

"No, of course not, but I expect Joy would like to be there—and I thought, I mean, mightn't it be a bit embarrassing? For both of you, I mean. And as it was Joy's uncle who sent the brief——"

"And Joy who helped you to prepare it?"

"That isn't fair, Sally. I won't ask you another time if you're going to throw it in my teeth."

"I simply asked if I could come to hear you. I'm not throwing anything in your teeth. Joy and I won't tear each other's eyes out, you know. We'd be sent to prison if we did. Which of us would you defend, Roger, if we were? You couldn't do both, could you?"

"I think that's a horrible question," said Roger.

CHAPTER EIGHT

FIRST CONFERENCE

Two days later Roger had his first conference. Peter and Charles went into Henry's room so that he could have the pupils' room for the purpose.

Mrs Newent came with Mr Smith, a managing clerk from Messrs Thornton, Merivale & Co., who introduced himself and his client to Roger. He invited them to sit down. They did so. Mrs Newent was attractive in a cheap sort of way, rather over-dressed and too much make-up. She had very shapely legs with sheer nylon stockings and she showed Roger much too much of them both. His eyes followed their movements, which were fairly frequent, as a rabbit's eyes follow a snake. From time to time with an effort he would look at the ceiling or out of the window or at the bookshelves, but it was no use. Back they had to come. He had never been so close to such things before. They revolted but fascinated him, and he simply could not help himself. He cleared his throat preparatorily to opening the proceedings. But Mrs Newent got in first.

"You're very young, if I may say so," she said. She did not mean that she was in the least dismayed. Several of her friends had had divorces. One had to go through the formalities and that was all. Indeed, it was very nice to be represented by a pleasant-looking young man who couldn't keep his eyes off one's legs.

"It must be an awful responsibility," she added.

Roger coughed. 'That's what we're here for," he said eventually.

"I'm so glad," said Mrs Newent, and recrossed her legs. "I feel sort of safe with you."

Even at that early stage and even with his inexperience, Roger began to wonder whether the discretion statements constituted the full and frank disclosure which such statements are supposed to be. He remembered, too, that the statement said quite a number of things about the husband and the dance and so forth, but when it came to the adultery it was disposed of in a very few words. The reason for Mr Storrington going into her bedroom was slurred over in the words, "Somehow or other he came in."

"Now," went on Mrs Newent, "was there something you wanted to ask me?"

By this time Roger had looked again at the cases and it certainly seemed as if what he had told Sally was right. It appeared that, in spite of Sally's doubts, the law was that, provided the adulteress was clever enough, she had the right that her husband should go on living with her. But there was just the point that it was for her to prove that her husband knew nothing about it. Roger quite rightly wanted to be sure of this.

"It's about your discretion statement," he began.

"Mr Smith here wrote that out," said Mrs Newent. "I only signed it, you know. That's right, isn't it, Mr Smith?"

"I wrote it out on your instructions, Mrs Newent."

"Instructions? I don't remember giving any instructions."

"It's what you told me, I mean."

"Oh, yes. What long words you lawyers use. If you'd said that at first I'd have understood."

"I take it the statement is true, Mrs Newent?" asked Roger.

"True?" said Mrs Newent, recrossing her legs. "Of course. Mr Smith wouldn't have written it down otherwise, would he?"

"There was only the once and you'd had a little too much to drink."

"That's right. Gin and frenches all the evening. I felt on top of the world."

"I thought you became dizzy and faint."

"That's right."

"After you felt on top of the world you became dizzy and faint?" asked Roger.

"That's right," said Mrs Newent. "You are a clever young man. I'm glad I've got you. D'you mind if I have a cigarette?"

"Of course not," said Roger and offered her one and lit it for her. She guided his hand to the cigarette, much to his discomfort.

"I think you ought to do very well," she said. "I shall remember you appeared for me when I see your name in the papers."

Roger blushed and coughed and tried to look at the ceiling.

"Now, there's another thing," he said. "Are you quite sure that your husband knew nothing about this and suspected nothing?" For answer Mrs Newent put her first finger to the side of her nose and winked.

"Are you sure?" repeated Roger.

"Not a notion," said Mrs Newent. "We were discretion itself, if you'll pardon my using the word."

"But," said Roger, "it only happened once and then you were faint and dizzy. How can you have been discretion itself if you were faint and dizzy?"

"Come now, young man," said Mrs Newent. "I'm not sure you're as clever as I thought. I go to a dance. Right?"

"Yes," said Roger.

"I drink too much. Right?"

"Yes," said Roger.

70

"I go out into the cold air and as every judge knows—I should hope—it hits me for six. Right?"

"You became faint and dizzy."

"Exactly. So he helps me home. Now I'm home. I'm still faint and dizzy at the bottom of the stairs. Can't get up by myself. Right?"

"Yes."

"He helps me up the stairs. We get to my room. Still faint and dizzy. With me?"

"Yes."

"Like the perfect gentleman he is he sees me into my bedroom. All clear so far?"

"Yes."

"Right. Well, when we get into the bedroom we take a liking to each other—see, and I become less faint and dizzy. But it was too late then."

"How do you know your husband knows nothing about it?"

"Because he wasn't there and no one could have told him. As soon as we took a liking to one another I sent Bert out of the room to his own room, making enough noise that people in the next room would have heard him go away within a minute or two of his coming in. Then he comes back like a mouse. Didn't even hear him come in myself. Didn't hear him go, either. I was asleep then. But I know he was ever so careful."

"When your husband came back, did he seem to suspect anything?"

"Not a thing. He was just the same as ever. Cold as an iceberg. A woman's got to get a bit of warmth from someone, hasn't she?"

"But it was only once?"

"It was only once," replied Mrs Newent with emphasis. "Because I know what's nice," she added, "that doesn't mean to say I don't know what's wrong. And with all the other boarders around you've got to be careful. People talk. Now what else d'you want to ask me? I'm getting a bit tired of this cross-questioning. I thought you were on my side."

"Of course I'm on your side," said Roger, "but I have to ask you these questions."

"Well, I can't think why," said Mrs Newent. "It's all plain and straightforward. I want a divorce, Mr Newent wants a divorce, what more d'you want? I don't know why there's all this palaver, anyway."

"We don't have divorce by consent in this country," said Roger.

"Well—who says it's by consent? He left me, didn't he? That's

71

desertion, isn't it? Then you have this ridiculous business about discretion. I wouldn't have told you if I'd known there'd be all this fuss. Was I faint and dizzy? When did I stop being faint and dizzy? And if not, why not? You wouldn't have known if I hadn't told you and there wouldn't have been all this nonsense. I'll know better another time. I thought one could trust one's lawyer."

"We have a duty to the Court," said Mr Smith.

"Fiddlesticks," said Mrs Newent. "A lot of old fools sitting up there, what do they care? They're half asleep, anyway. I went with my friend the other day. No fuss about hers. All over in five minutes. She didn't put in any discretion statement either, not on your sweet life. She couldn't have remembered for one thing. I'm too honest, that's my trouble. And what do I get for it? Asked a lot of intimate questions. I'd be ashamed if I were a man. It's not as though I'd done anything really wrong."

"But I thought you said——" began Roger.

"All right, Mr Clever, not as wrong as all that. There are worse things. Murder, for instance, or blackmail. All right, I was wrong to let him in my room that night. All right. I've told you. There it is in black and white. You've got my ruddy discretion statement and I hope it chokes you both—and the judge. Now, is there anything else you want?"

The conference was very different from the one Roger had visualized and he was glad when it ended. He felt slightly sick. Mrs Newent was not quite the sort of maiden he would care to rescue, even fully clothed.

CHAPTER NINE

JOYCE

THAT evening he dined with Joy. He had not had the cheque from the solicitors, but his mother had lent him the money.

"Of course, darling," she had said. "It'll be an investment, really. You'll be able to keep me soon. Won't that be lovely? And I shan't have to look to Aunt Ethel for a new dress. I do think you're clever, darling."

"It was Joy really, Mother."

"But I'm sure the solicitors wouldn't have sent it to you if they hadn't heard of your reputation. I shall tell everyone about you. Fancy making a name for yourself in a week. But then I knew you would. It's your father in you. Not me, I'm afraid. Now that it's all right, I don't mind telling you, I've always been a little frightened that you might be a fool like me. I'm so glad you're not, darling. Shall we get a bottle of champagne and celebrate. We can pay for it next month."

"That'd be lovely, darling, but I must go out with Joy tonight."

"Oh, of course."

"And you mustn't start talking about my having made a name for myself. I haven't done anything of the sort. I've been sent my first brief by the uncle of a girl friend and it's just an undefended divorce. I haven't even done it yet. I might make an awful mess of it."

"Oh, no you won't, not you."

"Well, I hope not, but—oh, darling, I'm appearing for the most awful woman. I'm so glad you're not like her."

"Thank you, darling. So am I, if she's all that awful."

"She's really terrible. It makes me feel uncomfortable to meet her. And the things she says. D'you know I felt quite sick after I'd had a conference with her. Don't tell anyone else. I suppose one's got to get used to that sort of thing, but I hope I don't get many more like her. I'll be glad when it's over. Would you like to come and hear it?"

"Darling, of course. When is it?"

"To-morrow."

"You must tell me how to get there. Or will you take me?"

"Well, darling—you know I'd love to take you—but don't you think it would look a bit obvious if we went in together? Rather like showing off. Besides, I don't want it to look as if it were my first brief. You do understand, don't you?"

"Of course, darling. I won't come at all, if you'd rather not."

"No, I'd love you to."

"I shan't make you nervous?"

"Oh, no—once it's started, I shall be all right."

"Well, you must tell me where it is. One of those places with blue lamps outside them, is it?"

"Mother, darling, those are police stations."

"That's right. Well, there's a Court next to them sometimes, isn't there?"

"Mother, this is the High Court of Justice, Probate, Divorce and Admiralty Division. It's in the Law Courts in the Strand. It's the most important legal place there is, except the House of Lords and Privy Council."

"Well, you mustn't be cross with me, darling. I don't know anything about the law. And what did you say about Admiralty? I thought yours was a divorce case. Does an admiral try it? I must say, he'd look rather sweet with his cocked hat."

"No, it's the Divorce Division, but that's linked up with Admiralty and Probate for historical reasons. But it won't be an admiral in a cocked hat. It'll be a judge in a wig and gown. And I'll be in mine too. I'll tell you how to get there and which Court it's in. Now I really must fly or I'll be late for Joy. Thank you so much for the money."

Joy was all ready for him, looking very pretty indeed. They went to a Soho restaurant.

"This is going to be a lovely evening," said Joy on the way. "I'm so proud of you, Roger. I know you're going to do terribly well. Uncle Alfred's very impressed too. He says there's an awful shortage of young men at the Bar and you're just what he's looking for. You mustn't say I told you, but if you do this case all right, he's going to send you a lot more."

"Oh—Joy, it sounds too good to be true."

"I gave him such a nice kiss for it. Right in the middle of his forehead. Funny, that's where he likes it. It's not my idea. But then an uncle's different. Oh, here we are. It's going to be a lovely evening, Roger."

She squeezed his arm.

"Two, sir?" said the waiter. "Over here, sir, if you please. Will this suit you, sir? Thank you, sir. And what about a little aperitif before dinner? Dry Martini, glass of sherry, anything you like, sir?"

"Do you think I should, Joy? I shall want a clear head in the morning."

"Of course, silly. It won't hurt you at all. Buck you up. Stop you feeling nervous. I'll have a Dry Martini, please. You do the same, Roger. It'll be good for you."

So they each had a Dry Martini and with their dinner they had a bottle of wine and by the middle of dinner, Roger, egged on by Joy, could see himself persuading judges, convincing juries and generally making a big name for himself at the Bar.

"Then you'll become a Q.C., Roger. I'm sure you'll be the youngest ever."

"D'you really think so?"

"Of course I do. But then I expect you'll forget all about little me."

"How can you say such a thing? It'll all be due to you really."

"Then you won't drop me like an old sock when you're successful?"

"I'm not like that, Joy."

"No, Roger, but you'll have so many people around you. I'm not very big, Roger. Sally's much taller."

"Don't let's talk about Sally."

Even older men can imagine a lot and forget a lot under the influence of a few drinks. At twenty-one all sorts of things can happen. To Roger, Joy seemed prettier than she'd ever been, really lovely, so that when she eventually said softly, looking down at her coffee:

"Roger, will you be a little loving to me tonight?" he was able to answer without any effort:

"Joy, darling, you know I will."

"Roger, darling."

Everything felt strangely unreal to Roger and it was very pleasant. He was going to be a great man and he had the prettiest girl in the world opposite him. Life was very good, very good indeed. Then he thought of his case in the morning. Perhaps it would be reported in the papers. Oh, no, of course it couldn't be, except for the judge's judgment. Thinking of the case he suddenly thought of his client, Mrs Newent. It gave him a slightly unpleasant shock but, when he mentioned her, Joy helped him by saying:

"But in a great career you're bound to come across nasty people. Someone had to defend Crippen, didn't they?"

"Of course. How silly of me."

They got up from the table. Roger felt slightly wobbly on his feet. Suddenly he thought of his client again. "Faint and dizzy." Well, he didn't feel faint or dizzy, but he did feel as though everything was very easy to do. A lack of restraint, that's what it was. Had he misjudged Mrs Newent? Perhaps she wasn't used to drink and it had done something to her. He could understand it now. He had never really wanted to kiss Joy before. But when she put herself in his arms in the taxi, there was no difficulty about it at all.

"Darling, you're wonderful," he said.

"Roger, I love you."

"I love you, Joy."

"Oh, Roger, I'm so happy."

CHAPTER TEN

THE DIVORCE COURT

THE next morning Roger woke with a slight headache. There was a ring on the telephone. He got out of bed and answered it. It was Sally.

"Just to wish you good luck, Roger. I shall be there, but you needn't take any notice of me."

"Oh, thank you, Sally. Thank you very much for ringing."

He went back to bed for a few minutes. What had he said to Joy the night before? What hadn't he said? Oh, dear, how difficult it all was. And they'd both be there. Well, he mustn't think of that now. He must concentrate on his case. He had found out that you don't normally address the judge in an undefended divorce case before calling your evidence. Henry had told him and he'd been to hear some cases, as Sally had suggested. They certainly sounded simple enough.

He got to chambers early and found Henry there already.

"Who are you in front of?" Henry asked.

"Judge Crane."

"Oh, that's good. You'll be all right in front of him. Bit of luck for you you're not before Judge Ryman. He's sitting today. He can be very difficult. He actually tries all his cases. It can be very awkward. Personally, I think he's right, but I'm in a decided minority. I think it's for Parliament to change the law if people want divorce made easier. But very few people agree with me. I expect I'm wrong, but there it is. Glad you're not in front of Ryman. That would have been a bit tough for your first case."

At ten minutes past ten Roger, feeling rather self-conscious, walked across the Strand carrying his blue bag. He was on the way to the robing-room. At the entrance to the Law Courts he met his mother.

"Not late, you see, darling," she said. "Can you tell me where I go?"

"Would you mind very much asking an attendant? I've got to go and robe and I don't want to be late. We're sixth in the list, but you can never tell. Some of the people in the first five cases might not be there."

He felt a little like he did in his first days at a public school when he was terrified his mother would call him by his Christian name.

He robed and went to the Court. He found Mrs Newent outside. She did not at first recognize him in his wig. She had recovered from her fit of anger in chambers and, feeling a little nervous herself, wanted someone to be nice to her.

"You look sweet," she said.

Roger blushed and coughed.

"I don't think we'll have to wait very long," he said.

"It's going to be all right, isn't it?" said Mrs Newent.

"Oh, yes, I think so," said Roger with reasonable confidence. Now that it was so near to the beginning of the battle, he was glad to think that Judge Crane was an easy judge. How nice of Henry to tell him. What a good chap he was. It made all the difference. He did in fact feel a little weak at the knees. He walked into the Court and at once saw Joy sitting at one end and Sally at the other. They were both attractively dressed. He tried not to let them see he had noticed them. His mother was sitting in the middle of a row. Counsel's row was almost full, but he was just able to get a seat at the end. A few minutes later the judge came in. The associate got up and called:

"Foster against Foster," and then handed the papers in the case to the judge. Counsel got up and the case began.

"May it please your Lordship, this is a husband's petition on the grounds of desertion. Mr Foster, please."

A man went into the witness box and took the oath. The following dialogue took place:

COUNSEL: "Is your full name Ernest Edward Foster?"

THE WITNESS: "Yes."

COUNSEL: "Where do you now live, Mr Foster?"

THE WITNESS: "Apple Tree Lodge, Buckley, Essex."

COUNSEL: "And were you married on the 14th day of June 1930 to Elizabeth Foster, whose maiden name was Hadlow at the Register Office for the District of Bilcombe in the County of Surrey?"

THE WITNESS: "Yes."

COUNSEL: "And there are no children of the marriage?"

THE WITNESS: "No."

COUNSEL: "And after the marriage did you live at various places with your wife and finally at Apple Tree Lodge where you now are?"

THE WITNESS: "Yes."

COUNSEL: "Now I think your marriage was quite happy at first, but after that did relations between you and your wife become strained?"

THE WITNESS: "Yes."

COUNSEL: "And were there disagreements and quarrels and so forth?"

THE WITNESS: "Yes."

COUNSEL: "And finally on the 14th June 1946 did she leave you?"

THE WITNESS: "Yes."

COUNSEL: "Did she say anything before she left?"

THE WITNESS: "No."

COUNSEL: "Nothing at all?"

THE WITNESS: "No."

COUNSEL: "Didn't she say anything about never coming back to you again?"

JUDGE CRANE: "I think that's a little leading, Mr Fox."

COUNSEL: "I'm sorry, my Lord. Did she or did she not say anything about not coming back to you again?"

THE WITNESS: "She did."

COUNSEL: "What did she say?"

THE WITNESS: "That she wouldn't come back."

COUNSEL: "And has she ever come back?"

THE WITNESS: "No."

COUNSEL: "Now, will you look at these two letters. There are copies for my Lord. (*Letters handed to Witness.*) Are those letters in your wife's handwriting?"

THE WITNESS: "Yes."

COUNSEL: "Your Lordship will see that in them she repeats that she will never come back to the petitioner again."

JUDGE CRANE: "Yes, I see."

COUNSEL: "Now may he see the acknowledgment of service? (*Document handed to the Witness.*) Do you see a signature you recognize at the bottom of that document?"

THE WITNESS: "Yes."

COUNSEL: "Whose is it?"

THE WITNESS: "My wife's."

COUNSEL: "Thank you, Mr Foster. My Lord, if your Lordship is satisfied on the evidence I ask for a decree nisi."

JUDGE CRANE: "Very well, Mr Fox. Decree nisi."

The next case was called. The dialogue was very much the same, except that that case was, like Roger's, a discretion case. The petitioner was a man and, in addition to evidence very similar to that which had been given in the last case, the following passage occurred:

COUNSEL: "May the witness see his discretion statement? (*The document is shown to the Witness.*) Now, Mr Brown, do you see a signature at the bottom of that document which you recognize?"

THE WITNESS: "Yes."

COUNSEL: "Whose is it?"

THE WITNESS: "Mine."

COUNSEL: "Before you signed that document, did you read it through carefully?"

THE WITNESS: "I did."

COUNSEL: "Are the contents true?"

THE WITNESS: "They are."

COUNSEL: "And have you committed adultery with anyone else or on any other occasions than are mentioned in that statement?"

THE WITNESS: "No."

COUNSEL: "Thank you, Mr Brown. My Lord, upon that evidence, I respectfully submit that this is a case in which your Lordship can properly exercise your discretion in favour of the petitioner

78

and if your Lordship is satisfied, I ask you to do so and to pronounce a decree nisi."

JUDGE CRANE: "Very well. I exercise my discretion in favour of the petitioner and grant a decree nisi."

It was all very short, thought Roger. He would like, if he could, to make rather more of his case, if possible. He didn't want trouble, but this was, if anything, too easy. Mrs Newent, on the other hand, was very satisfied. This, she told herself, was exactly and precisely what the doctor had ordered. Her confidence now almost completely restored, she began to wonder where she and Mr Storrington should go and have a celebration that night. Just at that moment another associate came in and spoke to his colleague sitting below Judge Crane.

The latter, after a whispered conversation with him, stood up and spoke to the judge in an undertone. Then he announced:

"The following cases will be taken before His Honour Judge Ryman in Probate Divorce and Admiralty Court 4. Will the parties and their witnesses please proceed to that Court at once. Speed and Speed, Newent and Newent, Laver and Laver."

As Roger got up to go counsel next to him said:

"Bad luck, old boy. Glad it isn't me."

Roger felt his inside leave him for the floor. Why had he said to himself that he'd like to make a little more of his case? This was fate's revenge. He wondered what Ryman was like. Oh, well, there was nothing for it. And anyway he would see him try one case first, that was something. Fortunately Mrs Newent was quite unaware that there had been any change in her fortunes. She assumed that much the same happened in every Court. Roger started on his way to Court 4, with the managing clerk from her solicitors, and followed by Mrs Newent, his mother, Joy and Sally, who walked along together.

"So glad you could come," said Joy.

"I'd have hated to disappoint you," said Sally.

Roger went into the Court where Judge Ryman was sitting. After a short delay the associate called:

"Speed against Speed."

Counsel next to Roger stood up and put his client, a woman, into the witness box. Roger looked at the judge. He noticed nothing particularly forbidding about his appearance and was grateful for that. Mrs Speed was petitioning for a divorce on the ground of cruelty. After counsel had asked the preliminary questions about the marriage, he started to ask about the history of the married life.

"Did he ever hit you?" he asked.

"Really," said the judge, "the Court of Appeal and the learned

President have said more than once that leading questions should not be asked. This is a petition on the ground of cruelty. Please don't lead on any essential matters."

"If your Lordship pleases. Well, Mrs Speed, did he or did he not hit you?"

"Really," said the judge, "that's just as bad."

"With great respect, my Lord," said counsel, who was a fierce little man with more ferocity than sense or knowledge. "That was not a leading question. She could have said 'yes' or 'no'."

"I'm sorry to disagree, Mr Brunt," said the judge. 'The witness could have answered 'yes' or 'no' to your first question, but it was none the less leading. So is this one."

"Well, my Lord, I've often asked this kind of question at the Old Bailey without objection."

"I'm afraid I'm only concerned with this Court, Mr Brunt."

"My Lord, I wish to be heard on this point."

"By all means, Mr Brunt, if you think it of any value. You can always go to the Court of Appeal, you know, if you object to my ruling."

"Think of the expense, my Lord. My client wants a divorce, not a visit to all the Courts in the country."

"Please behave yourself, Mr Brunt. I can only say that if your client wants a divorce she must give her evidence without the assistance of leading questions. That is particularly the case in a matter such as the present one where, no doubt, the bulk of the evidence will be that of your client herself. I have to make up my mind whether I believe her or not. That's difficult enough anyway in most undefended cases. It's impossible if she only answers 'yes' or 'no'."

"Very well, my Lord. I have made my protest," said Mr Brunt.

"Now, Mrs Speed, how often did these assaults take place?"

"Mr Brunt," said the judge, "I'm sorry to have to interrupt you again so soon, but that is not only a leading question, it is a double question and a most improper one in view of my ruling. The witness has not yet said that her husband did hit her."

"Well, madam," said Mr Brunt in a voice in which he did not conceal the annoyance, "did he hit you?"

"Really, Mr Brunt," said the judge. "There must be a limit to all this."

"Really, my Lord," said Mr Brunt angrily. "Your Lordship told me to ask the question and then your Lordship complains when I do ask it. I agree that there must be a limit."

"Mr Brunt, that was a most improper observation. I must ask you to apologize for it."

Mr Brunt hesitated, made a quick appreciation, decided he had gone too far, though in his view not without extreme provocation, and said:

"I apologize, my Lord, but it is very difficult to know what questions to ask in front of your Lordship."

"Well, please try, Mr Brunt," said the judge. "Only don't make them leading questions. If you would like me to suggest one, I will."

"That would be most kind of your Lordship."

"Perhaps you'd better ask her how her husband treated her after the first few months of married life."

"Thank you, my Lord, I will."

Meantime, Roger, who was not altogether able to make up his mind whether Mr Brunt or the judge was in the right, realized that what Henry had said had been only too true. He prayed that he would be able to avoid leading questions. It's very difficult if you don't really know what they are. Roger did not yet appreciate that the context or circumstances in which a question is asked may make it leading and that the question, "Did he or did he not do so-and-so" may, according to the circumstances, be a grossly leading question or not a leading question at all.

"He treated me like a slave," said the witness.

"In what way?" asked Mr Brunt.

"In every way."

"Would you be a little more explicit, please madam," said Mr Brunt. "Enumerate some of the ways."

"En—enu—enum——?" said the witness, puzzled.

"Give some examples," paraphrased Mr Brunt.

"It was always happening."

"What was always happening, Mrs Speed?" asked the judge.

"Him treating me like that, your Honour."

"Yes, but how did he treat you?" asked the judge.

"Oh, terrible."

"Yes, but we weren't there, Mrs Speed. You must tell us what he did," said the judge.

"It was all the time."

"But what was all the time?" said the judge.

"What he did."

"But what was it?" said the judge.

"Everything."

"Tell me one thing he did," said the judge.

"There were so many."

"Then it should be easy to tell me one," said the judge.

"It's a long time ago."

"Well, Mr Brunt, you must see if you can elicit anything from

81

the witness. I've tried, but with no success, I'm afraid," said the judge.

"Madam," said Mr Brunt, "what did your husband do to you?"

"It was that time at Christmas," said Mrs Speed.

"What happened at Christmas?" said Mr Brunt.

"No, it was Easter," said Mrs Speed. "You've got me all flummoxed."

"Well, what happened at Easter?" asked Mr Brunt.

"You want me to tell the judge?"

"That's what I've been asking you to do for the last five minutes," said Mr Brunt.

"I didn't half tell him off," said Mrs Speed, "but I don't think he heard me."

"How long was this case supposed to take?" asked the judge.

"Fifteen minutes, my Lord," said the associate.

"Well, it's taken nearly that to get this witness's name and address, which is about all we have got so far, Mr Brunt, would you like me to stand the case over to be started afresh another day before another judge? At this rate it will need at least an hour."

"If your Lordship had let me ask the questions as I wanted to," said Mr Brunt, "it might have been over by now."

"Equally," said the judge, "if I'd let you give the evidence. I thought possibly, Mr Brunt, you'd *like* the case to be stood over and heard *de novo* by another judge."

"Yes," said Mr Brunt, "I think perhaps I'll accept your Lordship's kind suggestions."

The case was accordingly adjourned and Roger, now on the high diving-board, waited for the word to go.

"Newent against Newent," called the associate.

"May it please your Lordship, this is a wife's petition on the ground of desertion. I should tell your Lordship that it's a discretion case. Mrs Newent, please."

"Are you putting in the discretion statement now, Mr Thursby?" asked the judge.

Do I or don't I, thought Roger. I don't know. Why hadn't I asked? Here I am, stuck before I started and mother's here and Joy and Sally. Oh, hell, why didn't I watch what they usually do?

The judge noticed the pause and Roger's white wig and said pleasantly: "That's the usual course, Mr Thursby, unless there's some special reason for not doing so."

"Very well, my Lord," said Roger gratefully. "I'll put it in now."

"Very well, Mr Thursby, thank you," said the judge.

That was better. It **was** good to be called Mr Thursby and now he was on an even keel again.

Mrs Newent was sworn and was asked by Roger the usual preliminary questions.

"And now, Mrs Newent, will you tell his Lordship how your married life went?" asked Roger.

"It was all right at first," she said, "but after that he started picking on me, said I paid more attention to my boarders than to him."

"And did you?" intervened the judge.

"Not more than was necessary, my Lord. There's a lot of work to do running a boarding house."

"Yes, Mr Thursby?" said the judge.

"And what happened in the end?" asked Roger.

"He left me," said Mrs Newent.

It seemed very little to ask, thought Roger, but what more is there? Oh, yes, the letters.

"After he left you, did he write to you, or did you write to him?" asked Roger and then added, "Or not," in case it was a leading question.

The judge smiled.

"That wouldn't really cure it, Mr Thursby," he said, "if it needed a cure, but fortunately it didn't."

"Thank you, my Lord," said Roger.

"I wrote to him once or twice," said Mrs Newent.

"What did you say in your letters?" asked Roger.

"Has notice to produce been given?" asked the judge.

"I don't know, my Lord," said Roger.

"Well, perhaps you'd ask your client then."

"Has notice to produce been given?" said Roger.

"Pardon?" said Mrs Newent.

"No, your solicitor client, Mr Thursby," said the judge.

"I'm sorry, my Lord," said Roger suddenly realizing what he'd done. He turned to Mr Smith and asked him if notice to produce had been given.

"Of course. It says so in the brief, doesn't it?" said Mr Smith. He was an experienced managing clerk and did not like what was happening.

"Yes, my Lord," said Roger.

"Very well," said the judge. "You can ask what was in the letters."

"What was in the letters?" asked Roger.

"I don't really remember," said Mrs Newent.

"So much for them," said the judge. "But what about the letters from the husband? Were there any?"

"Yes, my Lord," said Roger.

"Well, you can put those to her," said the judge.

"Did you receive these letters from your husband, Mrs Newent?" asked Roger, and then started to open his mouth to say "or not" and just checked himself in time. He must remember to ask Henry about leading questions.

"Yes," said Mrs Newent, "these are in his handwriting."

The letters were handed to the judge and he read them.

"Yes, Mr Thursby?"

"Has he returned to you, Mrs Newent?"

"No."

"Or offered to return?" asked the judge.

"No."

"Or to make a home for you?"

"No."

For some reason that he could never make out, Roger then proceeded to sit down, as though the case was over. The judge seemed to realize what had happened and quietly said: "Discretion, Mr Thursby?"

Roger jumped up, blushing.

"I'm sorry, my Lord. Mrs Newent, would you look at your discretion statement."

He asked her the necessary questions about the statement, ending with:

"Have you ever committed adultery except as stated in your statement?"

"No," said Mrs Newent firmly.

"What else, if anything, has taken place between you and the man named in your statement?" asked the judge.

"What else?" repeated Mrs Newent, a little nervously.

The judge nodded.

"Nothing."

"But you say you are living on affectionate terms in the same house. Has he suggested further acts of adultery to you?"

"No, my Lord."

"Why not?"

Mrs Newent was totally at a loss to answer the question.

"You're living in the same house and you want to get married. Presumably you're still attracted to one another. You've committed adultery once, so neither of you have any conscientious objection to doing so. I could understand your refusing, but I don't quite understand his not asking you."

"Oh, I see what you mean, my Lord. Yes, he did ask me."

"But you refused?"

"Yes."

"Because you thought it wrong?"

"Yes, my Lord."

"Thank you, Mrs Newent," said the judge. "There's only one other question I want to ask you. How long was it after your admitted act of adultery that your husband left you?"

"About a couple of months, my Lord."

"Thank you, Mrs Newent," said the judge.

Suddenly Roger thought he scented danger.

"Are you sure your husband never knew of your adultery, Mrs Newent?" he asked.

"Well," said the judge, "that is, I'm afraid, a leading question, but, now it's asked, she'd better answer it."

"Quite sure," said Mrs Newent firmly. "He never knew or suspected a thing."

"Did you treat your husband in exactly the same way, after your adultery with Mr Storrington, as before?"

"How d'you mean, my Lord, the same way?"

"Well, for instance, you say that you were ashamed the next morning. Your shame might have resulted in your treating your husband rather differently, don't you think?"

"I don't really know, my Lord."

"You continued to share the same room?"

"The same room, my Lord, but not the same bed. We hadn't for some time."

"Yes, Mr Thursby," said the judge. "Any further questions?"

Roger thought for a moment. He could not think of anything else to ask.

"No, thank you, my Lord," he said. There was then a pause while Roger made up his mind what to do next. You ask for a decree, don't you, he said to himself. That's it, I think. Or is there anything else first? I'm not sure. Oh, well——

"Upon that evidence, my Lord——"

"Acknowledgment of service, Mr Thursby?"

"I'm sorry, my Lord."

Of course, he would forget that. That made at least two things he'd forgotten, but thank Heaven the case was almost over. In a moment or so he would be outside the Court. It had been pretty bad, but it could have been worse. The witness identified her husband's signature on the document acknowledging receipt of the petition and then she left the witness box.

"Yes, Mr Thursby?" said the judge.

"Upon that evidence, my Lord, I ask your Lordship to exercise your discretion and grant a decree nisi with costs."

There, he'd said it and his first case was about to be over. Not much credit winning an undefended case, but still—what was that? What was the judge saying?

"It's not quite as simple as that, Mr Thursby." What on earth was he talking about? Surely he knew about *Herod and Herod*.

"You see, Mr Thursby," went on the judge, "your client committed adultery before her husband left her."

"Yes, my Lord," began Roger with no clear realization of what he was going to say, "but—but——" very tentatively he started to say, "Her—Herod——"

"But is it quite clear," went on the judge, "that *Herod and Herod* applies to a case where adultery is committed *before* the other spouse leaves? It strikes me as a bit odd that a wife who commits adultery should still have the right to the consortium of her husband, provided she's a good enough liar."

Good Heavens, thought Roger, that's exactly what Sally said.

"How can you desert someone who hasn't the right to be lived with?" went on the judge.

"My Lord," began Roger, but it was much too difficult. He wanted to say something about *Herod*'s case, but had no idea how to put it. As if reading his thoughts, the judge continued:

"I know there's a passage in *Herod* which helps you, but is it more than a dictum? We'd better look at it, hadn't we?"

The judge sent for that case and for some others. After reading several passages aloud and talking to Roger, who was almost unable to say anything except, "Yes, my Lord," or "No, my Lord," the judge eventually said:

"Well, Mr Thursby, much as I regret it, you have convinced me that the principle must be the same in each case, although with the greatest respect to the judges concerned, I cannot think that it is the law of this country that the adulterer who can lie well enough is entitled to the consortium of the other spouse, and that it is only the less efficient liar who loses the right to be lived with."

Roger was now extremely pleased. The judge had said—quite untruthfully—that Roger had convinced him. They were words to be treasured. And so he'd won his case after all. And there *had* been a struggle, which made victory all the sweeter.

"Then, my Lord," began Roger, "I ask——"

"But I'm afraid," went on the judge, "that isn't the end of the matter. *Herod* and all the other cases make it quite plain that it is for the petitioner to prove that the adultery has not caused the desertion. That's so, is it not, Mr Thursby?"

"Yes, my Lord."

"Well—have you proved it?"

"The evidence is, my Lord, that the husband did not know of it."

"I agree that is the evidence and though I was not much impressed by your client, I'll assume for the moment that he didn't know. But is that enough?"

Roger was now completely out of his depth. There was nothing he could say.

"I don't know whether you're prepared to argue the point today," said the judge. "If not, I'll give you an adjournment to enable you to do so on a later occasion."

"That's very good of your Lordship," said Roger, having no idea what the point was.

"The point is this, Mr Thursby. I know that you can show me cases where it has been said on high authority that, if a husband or wife does not know of or suspect the other's adultery, that adultery cannot be said to have caused the desertion. But, with the greatest respect to the learned judges who have said this, is it correct? There are many things which a husband or wife who has been unfaithful may do or refrain from doing as a result of being unfaithful, and any one or more of those acts or omissions may cause the other spouse to leave. In such a case surely the petitioner would not have proved that the adultery had not caused the desertion, even though it was not known or suspected. Now, Mr Thursby, d'you think you're in a position to argue that point today?"

Whether I shall ever be, thought Roger, is most uncertain, but one thing is quite certain, I can't do it now. I must get help.

"I should be most grateful for an adjournment, my Lord," he said.

"You shall have it," said the judge. "It isn't at all an easy point. Adjourned for fourteen days if that's convenient for you and many thanks for your help today."

CHAPTER ELEVEN

POST MORTEM

THE judge went on with the next case and Roger, very hot and very red in the face, gathered up his papers and went out of the Court. There he was joined by Mrs Newent.

"What's all that in aid of?" she asked. "Why haven't I got my divorce? What's happened?"

"It's a little difficult to explain," said Roger.

"There's nothing difficult about it at all," said Mrs Newent. "It's what comes of having schoolboys to do one's case for one. I ought to have known from the start. How old are you, anyway?"

The humiliation was so great that Roger could have burst into tears. He felt like throwing his brief at Mrs Newent, running to the Embankment and jumping into the Thames. What was the good of anything? He wished the earth would swallow him up.

"Well, how old are you?" persisted Mrs Newent. Even at that stage of his misery Roger remembered for an instant the image he had built up of Mrs Newent before he met her, the poor girl abandoned by her callous husband. Now he was all on the side of Mr Newent. He wondered how he had stood her for as long as he had.

"Lost your voice?" said Mrs Newent. "Not very much to lose anyway," she added.

This at last spurred Roger into action.

"If you're not satisfied with the way I am doing your case, madam," he said, with as much dignity as red-faced twenty-one could muster, "you can ask your solicitors to instruct someone else to continue it. I do not propose to stand here listening to your abuse. Good morning."

He left Mrs Newent with Mr Smith and went hurriedly to the robing-room. He still felt it was the end of the world. But, as he went, he went over in his mind the way the case had gone before Judge Ryman. What had he done wrong? Well, he had made mistakes once or twice, but they wouldn't have made any difference, surely? He had persuaded the judge that *Herod and Herod* applied—well, if he hadn't persuaded him, he'd at any rate mentioned *Herod* and the judge had gone into the matter. The judge had decided the first point of law in his favour. How on earth could he have imagined the second point would arise? Would anyone else have thought of it? Besides, the judge had thanked him for his help. He knew quite well he hadn't given any help, but the judge must think well of him to say it. But then the word "schoolboys" started ringing in his ears again and he again had an urge to jump into the Thames.

"Warm, isn't it, sir?" said the attendant who helped him off with his gown.

"Yes," said Roger. "Very warm. Thank you."

As he disrobed, he prayed that neither his mother, nor Sally nor Joy would be at the entrance to the Courts when he got out. He wanted to go and lock himself up somewhere out of sight of everyone. So this was the mighty Roger Thursby Esq., Q.C.! Called a schoolboy by his own client! He looked through the window of the door of the robing-room to see if the coast was clear. It seemed to be. So he went out hurriedly and rushed across the Strand in almost as fast a time as Mr Grimes usually put up. He went back to chambers.

"Get on all right, sir?" asked Alec.

"I don't know. It's been adjourned."

"When to?"

"Fourteen days, I think."

"Why was that, sir? Witness missing?"

"No—I think he wants some point argued further."

"I understand, sir," said Alec, an expression into which Roger read a wealth of meaning which was not in fact there. As he started to go into his room, Henry came into the clerks' room.

"Hullo," he said. "How did you get on?"

And then before Roger could reply, he went on:

"Like to come and have a chat with me about it?"

Roger gratefully accepted and went into Henry's room, where he told him as best he could what had happened in Court.

"My dear chap," said Henry, "I think you did damned well. Much better than I should have done at your age. I shouldn't have been able to open my mouth. Jolly good show. There's nothing to be depressed about. And you seemed to have got on with old Ryman all right. He enjoys an argument. All right, we'll give it him."

"I shall never be able to argue," said Roger miserably. "I've made a mess of it. I'm hopeless."

"My dear old boy," said Henry, "if you could have seen me coming away from my first County Court cases almost sobbing, you wouldn't worry half so much. I used to lose cases which quite definitely ought to have been won. All the way home I used to try to convince myself that there was nothing else that I could have done, but I knew darned well there was. As far as I can see, you did everything you could and you've got an adjournment to get ready for the argument. That's very much better than I did in my first case."

"I can't think you did worse," said Roger.

"I did indeed," said Henry. "Mark you, it'll happen to you too. Or you'll be extraordinarily lucky if it doesn't. My only point is, it hasn't happened this time. Your case is still on its feet. You can win it yet. Or maybe in the Court of Appeal, if necessary."

"Me in the Court of Appeal?" said Roger.

"Why not?" said Henry. "They'll be very nice to you."

"They'll need to be," said Roger. "But what was your first case?"

"Just a simple little accident case. Absolutely plain sailing. One just couldn't lose it. The defendant's driver had turned down a street which had stalls in the road and had then hit one of the stalls, damaged it and some of the stock. After the accident he said he was sorry but he'd misjudged the distance. Said that to a policeman. So there couldn't be any doubt about it. He was prosecuted for careless driving and fined. It was a sitter. The only question was the amount of damages and there I'd got evidence to prove everything up to the hilt. It was given to me because it was reckoned it was a case that couldn't be lost. The only reason the defendants were fighting it was because the insurance company doubted the amount of the damage. And, as I've told you, I could prove every penny of the damages and I did. The judge was quite satisfied about the damages. Oh, yes, it was the perfect case for a beginner. Excellent experience and no one could come to any harm. You couldn't lose it."

Henry paused for a moment. "I lost it all right," he went on. "I lost that perfect, unanswerable, copybook case. I lost it. The defendant's driver does a man twelve pounds worth of damage and what does the plaintiff get for it? The privilege of paying about twenty pounds costs in addition to bearing the whole of his own loss. And why? Because he briefed *me*. That's why. Simple enough."

"But how did you come to lose it?"

"You may well ask. I'll tell you. No one actually saw the collision. The plaintiff heard a bang, looked round and saw his stall on the ground with the lorry half over it and half the stock ruined. Counsel for the defendant objected to the evidence of what the defendant's driver said to the policeman on the ground that the driver wasn't the agent of the defendant to make admissions. I didn't know what that meant but the judge said it was quite right and wouldn't allow that bit of evidence to be given. I wasn't so worried because, after all, the lorry had run into the stall, hadn't it? At the end of my case counsel for the defendant got up and calmly submitted that his client had no case to answer. No one had seen the accident, the driver might have had to swerve to avoid a child or a cyclist or anything. It was for the plaintiff to prove that the accident was due to the negligence of the defendant's driver. Well, although it was my first case, I thought I'd done rather well, because I'd brought down a case to quote to the judge if necessary. It was called *Ellor and Selfridge* and in it the Court held that where a motorist knocked somebody down on the pavement that was *prima facie* evidence of negligence as motor cars don't usually go on pavements. It was, therefore, for the motorist to show how he got there.

" 'What do you say to that?' said the judge to my opponent.

" 'The answer to that is quite simple,' was the reply. 'In *Ellor and Selfridge* the accident was on the pavement. I agree that lorries do not usually go on pavements, but here the accident was on the roadway. Lorries do go on roadways. It's the only place they do go. After the accident the lorry was still on the roadway. I don't complain about the plaintiff having a stall on the roadway, but he has it there at his risk. If an accident happens to it while it's in the roadway, he's got to prove that the accident was due to someone's fault. The mere fact that the accident happened doesn't prove that. As I said, it might have been due to some emergency.'

" 'Well, what do you say to that?' said the judge to me. I stammered and stuttered and got very red in the face. I said everything I could think of. I knew that if I could ever get the driver into the witness box I was bound to win because he would have to admit that there wasn't any emergency and that all that had happened was that he'd misjudged the distance. The thought that the defendant was going to get away with it was horrible. I did not become hysterical, but I felt like it. I said the same thing over and over again. The one thing I did *not* say was that if a lorry runs into a stationary stall on the highway, such an accident is normally caused by the fault of the lorry driver and it is therefore for him to explain how the accident happened, just as much as if the accident had happened on the pavement. The same would apply to an empty car which was standing stationary in broad daylight in the street. If it's run into it's obviously for the person who runs into it to explain how it happened. But I didn't say any of this, or think of it, till I was half-way back to the Temple. I just talked nonsense until suddenly the judge said:

" 'Yes, I've got your point, Mr Blagrove. Do you want to add anything?'

"Well, of course, I sat down on that and the judge proceeded to give judgment against me.

" 'Ask for leave to appeal,' said the solicitor's clerk behind me. "I did as I was told.

" 'No,' said the judge, 'it's a plain case. I'm sorry for the plaintiff, but I can't let my judgment be blinded by sympathy. Leave to appeal refused.'

"Well, you should have seen the plaintiff outside the Court after that. He was hopping mad at first. I don't blame him. And then he said something which I've never forgotten—he said it just as I was leaving him. He'd calmed down by then.

" 'Hadn't you better do a bit more studying, boy, before you do your next case?' he said.

"He said it in quite a kindly tone. That made it worse. 'I can't think,' he went on, 'the law's such an ass as all that.' Well, of course, it isn't, but I was. And when I suddenly realized in the train on the way home what I ought to have said, I felt like jumping out on to the line, I can tell you. Then, of course, I started to explain to myself that it wouldn't have made any difference. One always ends up that way, but I knew it would really."

"I must say, it's a relief to hear that," said Roger, and he then told Henry what Mrs Newent had said.

"Of course, it is pretty dreadful for her to be represented by me," he went on, "when one comes to think of it. And I do look so young, too."

"Well, you know my views on that," said Henry. "I don't think anyone should be allowed to address a Court until he's read for a year in chambers. But that isn't the case. And I'm quite sure you did as well as anyone with a first brief could have done. And you can still win, you know."

"You've cheered me up no end," said Roger. "I suppose everyone feels like this to begin with."

"Of course they do. We'll look up the point together if you like. I've nothing to do. Let's go and have lunch and then go to the Bar Library."

Roger felt much better at the end of the day, but on the way home he wondered what his mother and Joy and Sally had thought of him. He found a note from Sally when he got home.

Well done, it said. *Can I come and see you?*

She ought to have been doing the case, thought Roger. She'd have told Mrs Newent a thing or two if she'd spoken to her like that. But then Mrs Newent wouldn't have spoken to her like that. There wouldn't have been any need to.

"You were simply perfect," said his mother. "I was so proud of you. You were quite the best-looking in the row."

"How did you think I got on though?"

"Well, of course, darling, I don't know anything about law, but the judge seemed to do all the talking really. I suppose that's what he's there for."

"I did say something, Mother, and, if you remember, the judge thanked me in the end."

"Yes, I thought the judge awfully nice. I really would have liked to ask him to tea."

"Mother," said Roger in horror. "You mustn't do anything of the sort. Promise you won't?"

"Of course, I won't, if you'd rather I didn't. But I would just like to drop him a note to thank him for being so sweet to you."

Roger was very, very fond of his mother and he would never have cheerfully throttled her, but it was about the last straw. That's all she'd seen. The judge being sweet to him. And the worst of it was that it was no doubt true. The judge had been sweet to him and he looked like a schoolboy. All the good work done by Henry for a moment seemed to have been wasted. He was back where he started. But then he realized that his mother might write to the judge. So he had to say something.

"Mother," he said, "you must promise not to do that either. The case is still going on. It would be most improper. You might get sent to prison and I might get disbarred."

Just for the moment the idea of getting disbarred didn't seem too bad. He would go abroad and do whatever one does there.

"I was only joking, darling," said his mother. "You mustn't take everything so seriously. What a nice woman Mrs Newent seemed. I was so sorry for her."

"Mrs Newent," said Roger deliberately, "is a bitch."

"Roger!" said his mother. "If that's the sort of language you are going to be taught at the Bar, I'm not sure that it's a good thing I let you start. Really, you quite took my breath away. It's not at all a nice word to use."

"It's the only word," said Roger, "with which to describe Mrs Newent."

"I can't think why you say that," said his mother. "Of course I didn't hear or understand half of what was said, but as far as I could make out, her husband had run off with one of the boarders. No, don't try and explain it, darling, I hate these legal technicalities and the sordid things that some husbands do. Not like your father, Roger. He was a very fine man. I thought you looked just like his pictures as a boy when I saw you in Court."

"Thank you, darling," said Roger. "I'm so glad you were pleased. Now I must use the phone."

He telephoned Joy.

"Roger, Roger darling. I was *so* thrilled. You were wonderful. I want to come right round now and kiss you, I'm so pleased. I never dreamed you'd be anything like that. You were quite perfect. And the judge thanking you at the end and everything. I'm so happy for you, I just don't know what to do. You'll have people coming to you to do their cases for them from everywhere. I'm sure Uncle Alfred will be terribly bucked. Oh, Roger—you are so clever. How do you do it?"

Knowing in his heart what the truth of the matter was, Roger did not take as readily to this eulogy as a young man might have been expected to do.

"Thank you very much, Joy. I don't think it was as good as all that, really."

"Oh, but Roger, it was, it was. And, d'you know, the woman sitting next to me asked if I knew who you were. I said you were one of the most brilliant of the younger men."

"Oh, you shouldn't have, Joy, really. What did she say?"

"Well, I didn't actually catch what she said. She had to speak awfully quietly, as you know, or we'd have been turned out. But I know she was impressed. Probably she's got a case coming on and she might even bring it to you. She was quite good-looking, Roger—but I shan't be jealous—not after last night."

Oh, Lord! thought Roger. Last night. She hadn't forgotten. No, she wouldn't. But after all, I must be fair. She did get me the brief—this bloody, bloody brief, he suddenly said to himself. No, I must control myself. I wonder what Uncle Alfred thinks about it all.

At that moment Uncle Alfred, that is, Alfred Merivale, senior partner in Thornton, Merivale & Co., was having a word with his managing clerk, Mr Smith, who had been in Court with Roger.

"Don't make such a fuss, George," he was saying. "We'll just take in a leader next time."

"Who's going to pay for it, sir?"

"Well, you aren't. So why should you worry?"

"Mrs Newent won't. She's livid, sir. Says it's our fault."

"You are a miserable devil, George. I don't know how I've stood you for so long. Still we've got to have someone with a long face in the office. It's good for funerals and people drawing wills, I suppose. How d'you say the young man did?"

"He was quite hopeless, sir. I've seen some pretty good messes made of cases in the past, but that beat anything. My sympathies were all with the client, I can tell you. If I'd had someone appearing for me like that I think I'd have gone mad."

"No one is appearing for you, George. And the case isn't over, anyway. Has he got a good presence, d'you think? You can't expect him to *say* anything yet."

"Really, sir," said George. "I do think you ought to study the client a bit more. That case might have been lost today."

"Well, it wasn't, George, it wasn't. I believe you'd have been pleased if it had been. No, I think I did make a slight mistake, but fortunately it's not too late to mend. We ought to have had someone to lead him in the first instance. After all, it was a discretion case and occasionally they go wrong. Yes, I ought to have thought of that. But it's so seldom, that I'm afraid I took a chance on it. And no harm's been done, George, no harm at all. On the contrary, I've learned a lesson. We must give him someone to lead him each time to begin with."

"Why on earth d'you want to have him at all, sir?" grumbled George.

"If a very old great uncle chooses to pander to his very sweet little great niece—at his own expense, George—at his own expense, what the devil does it matter to you? It won't cost the client a penny more and the young man will get a nice lot of experience and quite a few guineas." He paused for a moment and thought. "Yes, George," he went on, "you're quite right to be down on me for taking a chance with this case, but all's well that ends well and only good has come of it. He's very young at the moment. D'you think we'll ever be able to send him into Court by himself?"

"He's quite well built," said George. "He could carry the books if the clerk's missing."

Meantime, Joy was continuing to compliment Roger on his magnificent performance and she went on so long and so ecstatically that in the end Roger almost began to wonder if he had been so bad after all.

"I can't manage just now, Joy, dear—but could we meet for a drink or a walk or something about nine?"

"Where, darling?"

"The Pot-hole?"

"I'll be there, darling. Oh, Roger, I am so happy for you."

A few minutes later he telephoned Sally.

"Thank you for your note, Sally. It was very sweet of you. Could I come and see you?"

"Of course. Mother's out at present. Excellent opportunity."

He went round at once. She opened the door to him.

"Glad you're still in one piece," she said.

"What d'you mean?" said Roger. He was still under the influence of Joy's remarks.

"Well, you did have a pretty rough time, didn't you? I thought you took it very well, I'd have wanted to run away."

"You think I was rotten, I suppose," said Roger, a trifle sulkily.

"Oh, Roger, don't be silly. I tell you, I don't know how you stood there at all. It was dreadful for you. Personally, I don't think it should be allowed."

The spell was broken.

"That's what Henry says," said Roger.

"Who's Henry?"

"Henry Blagrove. A chap in Grimes' chambers. I've told you about him, surely?"

"Oh, that one, the nice one. Yes, you have. Well, I'm glad someone else agrees with me. I shall get quite swollen-headed soon."

"You mean about what the judge said?"

"I must say I was rather pleased, after our little talk. But really, Roger, I thought you took it splendidly. I thought you were going to break down once, but you didn't."

"Really, Sally, there is a limit, you know."

"Be honest, Roger. Didn't you feel like dropping your brief and running for it?"

Roger laughed.

"Why are you always so right, Sally? I've never known anyone like you—not any girl, anyway. Henry's rather like you as a matter of fact—except—except——"

He didn't finish the sentence.

"Except what, Roger?"

"Oh, nothing—forget it."

"Except that he's kinder, Roger? Was that it?"

Roger said nothing. She was right again.

"But you see, Roger," said Sally rather sadly, "Henry doesn't happen to be in love with you."

"Oh, Sally," said Roger, "I wish I knew if I loved you, I really do. Why don't you tell me if I do? You're always right. I'll believe you if you tell me."

"I don't want to be right this time, Roger," said Sally.

Neither of them spoke for a time after that. Roger broke the silence with:

"D'you think I'll ever improve, Sally?"

"D'you want to know what I really think?"

"Yes, of course," he said quickly and then: "No—I'm not sure if I do." He thought for a moment. "Better get it over," he went on, "let's have it. I can always sort football coupons."

"Roger," said Sally slowly, "I think you're going to be a great man."

"Sally, you don't, you don't really?" he said, fantastically excited, and then he suddenly choked. He'd have wept if he'd tried to say another word.

"But," Sally went on quite calmly, "there's a long way to go yet and you'll have to work terribly hard. You'll have a lot of disappointments, particularly because you're so young and don't understand anything yet. But you will, you will—and, barring accidents, you'll go to the top. I shall be quite pleased I once knew you?"

"Oh, Sally," he said and burst into tears.

He went down on his knees and put his head in her lap. She stroked it gently.

"I love you, Sally, I love you. I know I do."

"You don't, Roger, dear, though I love to hear you say it—and I'll always remember that you did——" She stopped for a moment as though deliberately pigeon-holing the memory—then she went on. "Roger dear, dearest Roger, you don't love anyone at the moment—except Roger."

They remained for a little while in silence.

"Am I as bad as that?" he asked eventually. "Just a selfish cad not minding who I hurt?"

"No, of course not," she said more brightly. "But you're young and ambitious and you like a good time, too. And that's all there is to it. And why shouldn't you be like that? It's perfectly natural. Now, dry your eyes and give me a nice kiss. I won't read anything into it."

CHAPTER TWELVE

CONFERENCE WITH MR MERIVALE

THE next day Mr Merivale himself made an appointment to see Roger.

"Good morning, young man," he said after they had been introduced. "I'm very grateful to you for all the work you've put into this rather troublesome little case of Newent."

"Oh, thank you, Mr Merivale. I haven't done much good at present, I'm afraid."

"Well," said Mr Merivale, "he's a difficult judge, she's a difficult client and it's not as simple a matter as I once thought. That's my fault, not yours. Quite frankly, young man, I think it was unfair of me to ask you to take the responsibility."

"Oh, not at all. It was very good of you to send me the brief. I'm sorry I haven't done better with it. I imagine you'd like to give it to someone else now."

"By no means," said Mr Merivale, "by no manner of means at all. I cannot think what could have put such an idea into your head." He hesitated a moment and then said: "You didn't see my clerk after the first hearing, I suppose?"

"No, I'm afraid I left in rather a hurry. Mrs Newent was rather offensive to me."

"Well, that's all right then—I mean, I suppose she was a bit excited, but she shouldn't have been rude. But that's quite all right now. She quite understands the position and of course she wants you to go on with the case, of course she does. Be a fool if she didn't. I hear from my clerk that you put up a very stout performance—'for the ashes of your fathers and the temples of your gods'."

"I beg your pardon?" said Roger.

"Horatius, my boy. 'And how can man die better than facing fearful odds—for the ashes of his fathers, etc., etc.' Not that I'm suggesting you died, my boy. Far from it. Put up an excellent performance, excellent. Wish I'd been there to see it myself. I'll come next time, though, I really will."

"I'm glad Mr Smith was pleased," said Roger.

"Mr Smith was very pleased indeed," said Mr Merivale. "And I may tell you, young man, that Mr Smith is not a man who is easily pleased. Far from it. Far from it. Particularly where counsel are concerned. No, I had a long talk with Mr Smith about you and I hope that in consequence we've going to see a lot more of you, my boy. We need young men like you these days. Fighters, that's what we want. Like your Mr Grimes, for instance. There are not many of them today. And there's a fighter for you. Never knows when he's beaten. D'you know, I've seen that man stand up in the Court of Appeal with the whole Court against him—all three of them—and battle with them for days. Another man would have sat down the first day."

"And did he win, Mr Merivale?"

"No, my boy, I can't say that he won that particular case. But he went on three days and no one could have done more. Birkenhead himself couldn't have won it. Yes, that's the man for my money—my client's money, that is—a man who'll stand up to it, a man who's not frightened to tell the whole Court they're wrong—courteously, of course. But firmly and definitely and again and again, if necessary, until they almost have to throw him out by force. If a man's a fighter, I'll back him to the end. But they're very difficult to find today. Look at Marshall Hall, now, my boy. There was a fighter for you. Hardly knew a scrap of law, but it didn't matter. He'd thunder at the jury until they daren't convict his client. He'd never give up until the verdict had been returned. And, as often as not, it was in his client's favour. Of course, he couldn't win all his cases—no one could. Don't forget that, my boy, when you lose some. But fight, my boy, fight all the time. You don't mind an old man giving you a bit of advice, my boy?"

"I'm most grateful. I think it's very kind of you to take the trouble."

"Now look," went on Mr Merivale. "This case of Newent. Between you and me, it's a tough 'un. It was bad of me not to realize it before. But we all make mistakes. That's how we learn. Now, I want you to do me a favour, my boy, a personal favour."

"Why, certainly, Mr Merivale, of course I will."

"It's just this. Newent's a case where in my considered opinion —my considered opinion, and of course I've been at it now for a good many years—Newent's a case where I think two heads will be better than one. I remember the late Lord Atkin saying that to me in his junior days—we used to brief him, you know—yes, and Mr Scrutton, as he then was—oh, yes, and others too. I flatter myself I've always known how to choose counsel—that's why I was so pleased to hear of you, my boy. I remember Atkin saying: 'Merivale,' he said, 'two of these,' and he tapped his head, 'are better than one.'

" 'Mr Atkin,' I said, 'there aren't two like yours in the world.'

" 'Well, then,' he said, 'get a leader with one as like it as you can find.' He was a great man, a very great man, but d'you see, he decided in that particular case that two heads were better than one. You'd never have thought it possible that a man with his brain could want help from anyone, but, 'this is a case for a leader, Mr Merivale,' he said, and so a leader we had. And I'm going to make so bold in this case, young man, although I haven't the head of an Atkin—but just a few more years of experience than you perhaps, eh? I'm going to make so bold as to suggest that we have a leader in this case. Now, sir," he added, "now, sir, would you have any serious objections to our taking that course? If you have, say so, and it shan't be done. Mr Smith and I have absolute confidence in you, sir, absolute confidence. Those in fact were Mr Smith's very words. 'Would you trust him again in Court, Mr Smith?' I asked. 'I would,' said Mr Smith, and he added—and mark this—'with something very heavy indeed.' One doesn't often get remarks like that out of Mr Smith, I can tell you. And I don't mind adding, I was pleased, my boy, because I hadn't heard you myself. Now, what d'you say, my boy—you've only to say the word and we'll drop the idea altogether—but would you take a very old man's advice and—just as a favour to him—we get conceited, we old men, you know, and we like to think we're always right—would you, just to tickle my vanity—would you agree to our taking in a leader?"

"But, of course, Mr Merivale," said Roger, who now had visions of a red bag, "but, of course, I shall be only too pleased. As a matter of fact the judge said it was a difficult point—and now I come to think of it, Lord Atkin himself has said something about the matter."

"Has he now?" said Mr Merivale. "Has he indeed? Now that's most interesting. I shall study that with the greatest interest. Well, I'm delighted to hear you approve of the idea, my boy, delighted. And now all we've got to do is to choose our leader."

He held up his hand.

"No, my boy, I know what you're going to say. It isn't etiquette for you to suggest a name? I wouldn't dream of infringing the rules, wouldn't dream of it. Just a few words with your clerk and hey presto. I shall think of the name that's escaped me for the moment. Now, my boy, I think that's all I've got to ask you at present, and I'm most grateful to you for seeing me at such short notice. It was most kind."

"Not at all, Mr Merivale."

"Well, good-bye, Mr—Mr Thursby—good-bye, and I shall ook forward to attending a consultation with you and—and—now what was the name I was trying to think of?" and opening the door he went into the clerks' room. A few minutes later he came back again.

"Forgive my intruding again. I was just wondering"—he coughed and hesitated—"I was just wondering," he said again. "I've got a young great niece called Joyce—I believe you've met her—I was just wondering whether you'd care to dine with us next Friday—not a party, you know—quite informal—but Joy happens to be coming and with my daughter, who looks after me, it would make up the numbers. I hope you don't think it's a presumption on my part."

"Of course not, Mr Merivale. It's most kind of you. I shall love to come. Oh, and I don't know if this is the right thing to say, but would you please thank Mr Smith for the kind remarks he made about me.'

"I shall not forget, my boy, I shall not forget. Mr Smith shall be told."

And Mr Merivale left.

CHAPTER THIRTEEN

CONSULTATION

"WELL, George," said Mr Merivale when he was back in his office, "that's settled. The young man took it very well."

"So should I take it very well," said George, "if someone told me I was going to be paid two or three times as much for doing nothing. Who are you going to have?"

"Plaistowe, I think," said Mr Merivale, "if he can take it."

"And what's that going to cost you?"

"I don't know and I don't care. When you're an old man like me, you may find other ways of getting pleasure, though to look at you, George, one would think that you'll be looking for something as unpleasant as possible, but I know what I like and if I can pay for it, why shouldn't I have it?"

"I don't like to see money chucked away, sir. Plaistowe will want at least thirty. That means you'll have to pay that bright young specimen of yours twenty, sir. Really, sir, it goes against the grain to give him anything at all—but twenty really is the limit. Why, we could have got any of the best juniors at the Divorce Bar to do it for fifteen at the most, sir."

"I sometimes wonder why you trouble to call me 'sir', George. It normally is a sign of respect which I find in your case is lamentably lacking. I won't say that's always been so. Forty years ago you used to behave yourself quite well. You were a little frightened of me, I think. But now all you say to yourself is—'the old fool won't be here much longer, doesn't much matter what I do say. Anyway, I'm much too much use to the firm for them to fire me. I'm part of the furniture—which is solid, meant to last, and ugly'."

"I've the greatest respect for you, sir, but I hate to see you making a fool of yourself."

"Well, I'm not. If I choose to spend fifty pounds or whatever it is on giving my niece a bracelet I can do so without asking you, can't I? Well, that's all I'm doing. Only she'll like this much more than a bracelet. Now don't let's have any more nonsense about it. Fix up a consultation with Plaistowe as soon as we know he can take it. I should say you'd better not have the client there in the first instance. He can see her later if he wants to. You'd better attend it as you saw what happened in Court."

"I did indeed, sir," said George. "I shall have great pleasure in telling Mr Plaistowe all about it."

"Now, George, you're to behave yourself. It's not young Thursby's fault. It's mine, if you like. Well, you've taken it out of me, don't try to take it out of him, too. Come to think of it, I'll come with you to see fair play. I'm not going to have him bully-ragged. Joy would be very cross indeed and she'd be fully justified."

"P'raps you'd like to go by yourself, sir," said George.

"Now, George, don't sulk. Of course you must be there to put Plaistowe in the picture. I'm only coming to see that you don't make it too lurid."

"As you please, sir," said George. "I'm only an unadmitted managing clerk and I know my place."

"Whose fault is it you're not a partner? You could have had your articles years ago."

"I knew my place then and I know it now. I don't believe in all this partner business. My job's a managing clerk, I know it and I can do it, and that's how it's going to stay."

"By all means, George, but as that's how you want it, don't grizzle."

A few days later a consultation was arranged with Plaistowe, a busy common law silk who did a certain amount of divorce work and was known to be exceptionally able. His fees were extremely moderate for a man of his ability and in consequence he was very much in demand. Before the consultation began Plaistowe asked to see Roger. They shook hands.

"How are you, my dear chap? I don't think we've met before. You're in Grimes' chambers, I believe?"

"I'm his pupil, as a matter of fact," said Roger. "I've only been there just over a week."

"Got away to a flying start, eh? Good for you. I thought I'd just have a word with you about this before we saw the clients. I gather the lady's not here today. But she's given all her evidence —unless we want something more out of her—so that's all to the good. I gather we don't care for her very much."

"No," said Roger.

They talked about the case for a short time and then Mr Merivale and Mr Smith were shown in.

"How are you, Mr Merivale? It's a long time since we met. Not since I took silk, I believe."

"Ah, I don't very often come to the Temple nowadays, Mr Plaistowe, but in this case Mr Smith—whom, of course, you know, particularly wanted me to come. So, as I have to do what I'm told, here I am and very pleased to see you again."

Plaistowe shook hands with Mr Smith and they all sat down.

"I gather our client's a bit of a so-and-so," said Plaistowe. "D'you think the judge believed her?" Plaistowe looked first at Roger and then at Mr Smith. Roger cleared his throat.

"I think probably Mr Smith will know that better than me—with all his experience."

Mr Merivale looked at Mr Smith with something of an air of triumph, which seemed to say, "Not quite such a fool as you thought, eh, George?"

"He won't believe her where he can help it, sir," said Mr Smith. "But I don't think he's going to down us on that. He doesn't like the nearness of the adultery to the desertion, and he's not satisfied that the mere fact that the husband didn't know is enough. Would you agree with me, sir?" and he turned to Roger.

"It sounded rather like it," said Roger.

"Well, do we want any more evidence from our client? What d'you say, Mr Merivale?" asked Plaistowe.

"I think you'd better put that to Mr Smith. I'm really only here as I've said because he asked me to come. I don't really know much about it, except that your learned junior has so far done admirably, as Mr Smith will confirm."

Plaistowe caught Mr Smith's eye and quickly said:

"I'm quite sure he will. Well, what d'you say, Mr Smith? Is there any point in trying to get any more out of our client?"

"Quite candidly," said Mr Smith, "the less we see of that lady in the witness box—or indeed anywhere else—the better. He caught her out in a thumping lie and although he hasn't said anything about it at the moment, knowing Judge Ryman, I'm pretty sure it's in safe keeping."

"Then you think just argue the point of law that there must be desertion if there's no knowledge of the adultery?"

"Yes, sir," said Mr Smith, "that's my opinion, but, of course, Mr Thursby here may have different views. From what I gathered during his address to the judge, as far as I was able——"

"Yes, Mr Thursby," interrupted Mr Merivale, "and what is your opinion? My recollection is that, when I saw you in chambers, you were of precisely the same opinion as Mr Smith has just expressed, though Mr Smith won't mind my saying that I thought you put it rather better."

"I wouldn't say that at all," said Roger, "but for what it is worth, that is my opinion."

"I'm glad you confirm Mr Smith's view," said Mr Merivale. "It's always satisfactory to the lowly solicitor when counsel agrees with him. Alas, it is not so often, I fear."

"You're too modest," said Plaistowe. "I nearly always agree with solicitors—when they're right."

CHAPTER FOURTEEN

SALLY

SALLY's mother lay on a couch with her eyes closed. Sally came into the room but her mother took no apparent notice. Sally sat down and opened a paper and rustled it. Her mother's eyes remained closed. After waiting a few minutes, Sally said quite softly:

"Mother, darling, are you with Brahms?"

There was no answer and the eyes remained closed. So Sally went on reading. After a few minutes Mrs Mannering opened her eyes.

"No, Schubert, darling," she said. "What is it you want?"

"Could you bear to be separated for a moment?" asked Sally.

"He turned me out," said her mother. "Said he had an appointment with someone or other. I forget the name. No. I remember. George Sand."

"That was Chopin, Mother."

"My darling Sally, you must allow me to dream whom I choose. It was George Sand. As a matter of fact he said she was leaving Chopin."

"Dates, Mother."

"There are no dates in dreams, darling, not in mine anyway. But you look serious. What is it?"

"D'you think I'd be silly to change my job, Mother?"

"You're in love with that young man, aren't you?" replied her mother.

"Terribly."

"How will changing your job help?"

"I thought—I thought," began Sally and for once spoke with less confidence and started to blush as she said it:

"I thought of going into a solicitor's office."

"I see," said her mother, and thought for a moment.

"That certainly makes sense." She paused again. "But is it any good, Sally? Have you any chance?"

"Oh, Mother, darling, I just don't know. Not at the moment, certainly, not a hope at the moment. But you can't be absolutely sure. And I'd wait for years and years if need be."

"You'd be very good for him," said her mother. "You'd make a nice pair. But he's terribly young, of course. Still, he'll grow. Of course, you're not all that old, though I agree that every one of your twenty-one years is equal to two of his. But that's usually so with girls."

"I'm sure he's not really fond of Joy," said Sally. "She's much prettier than I am, of course, but she's such a little ass, he couldn't be."

"I don't believe that's a criterion," said her mother. "There are lots of sweet little asses in the world, male and female, and highly intelligent people fall in love with them, marry them and live happily with them ever after."

"I suppose that's right," said Sally, "but I'm not really worried about Joy. Except for one thing."

"What's that?"

"She might buy him."

"What a horrible thing to say. You can't love a man who'll hand himself over to the highest bidder."

"He wouldn't know he was doing it. As you say, he's terribly young. He's very impressionable and—and very ambitious. If Joy can get her uncle to feed him with briefs——"

"Sally, this is really becoming unpleasant. You are actually proposing to start an auction. I realized it was something to do with Roger, of course, but I didn't realize you were seriously thinking of going into the market yourself."

"Well—that's why I wanted to talk to you. Do you really think it's dreadful? If Joy didn't brief him, I wouldn't. But if she does, why shouldn't I? Why should she have such a huge advantage? Why, out of mere gratitude he might feel he had to marry her. That really is dreadful, if you like."

"And suppose you send him bigger and better briefs than Joy —suppose you outbid her at every turn, two for each of her one, ten guineas where she sends five, the Court of Appeal when she sends him to the County Court, the House of Lords when she sends him to the Court of Appeal——"

"Don't, Mother," said Sally, "there's no need to make it sound beastlier than it is. All right, it is beastly if you like. But I wouldn't let him marry me out of gratitude. I should know and I wouldn't. He did sort of ask me to marry him once, but I wouldn't say 'Yes' then as I know he wasn't sure. I'll only marry him if he really wants me—but oh, Mother darling, I do want him to."

"You certainly have got it badly, Sally."

"You let Father accompany you, Mother, and it was torture. Wasn't that bidding for him?"

"You have a point there, Sally. That odious creature Nellie —what was her name? Thank Heaven—I've forgotten it. She used to let him play and she had a voice like an angel. What could I do? I wasn't in her class. But my wrong wouldn't make your wrong right."

"But you weren't wrong, Mother darling. You were right. Look how happy you were—it can't have been wrong. He'd have been most unhappy with Nellie what's-her-name. You'll admit that, won't you? And you had all those years of happiness together and you produced a most efficient, intelligent, not too bad-looking—and entirely miserable little girl. I'm going to do it, Mother darling. You did and I'm going to. It's sweet of you to make things so clear to me. Now you can go back to Brahms, sorry, Schubert."

She lifted her mother's legs on to the sofa again.

"Back you go," she said. "P'raps he's tired of George Sand by now."

The same afternoon Sally obtained a secretarial job with Messrs Moodie and Sharpe to start in a fortnight's time when she had completed her period of notice with her employers.

"Have you any experience of legal work, Miss Mannering?" asked Mr Sharpe, the partner who saw her, after she'd given satisfactory proof of her shorthand and typing ability.

"Not really," said Sally, "but I've been to the Courts once and I've got a friend who's a barrister."

"Oh, who's that?"

"Oh, you wouldn't know him. He's only a pupil. Just started. He's with a Mr Grimes."

"Oh, I know *him* well. We brief him sometimes, as a matter of fact. That's very interesting. And why do you want to come to a solicitor's office?"

"I like the law and, who knows, I might become a solicitor myself in the end, if I were good enough."

"And then you could send briefs to your friend—Mr—Mr—I don't think you mentioned the name?"

Sally blushed slightly.

"It's Thursby, as a matter of fact," she said. "Roger Thursby."

"You needn't feel embarrassed, Miss Mannering. It's quite a normal thing. I advised a client of mine to send his daughter to be articled to a solicitor. She was going to marry a barrister. A jolly good partnership, I thought, unless they went in for more productive schemes. Even then they can sometimes be combined. Oh—no—you mustn't flatter yourself that you're the first to think of that."

"Thank you for being so frank, Mr—er—Mr Sharpe."

"Thank you, Miss Mannering, and would you like to start today fortnight? Good. You'll be working for me. My secretary's leaving to get married. No, not a barrister. Oh, by the way, I ought to warn you that I'm on the conveyancing side. I don't do any litigation."

"I see," said Sally. "All the same, I'd like to come, please."

"Excellent. I think we should suit each other very well. And don't worry too much about the conveyancing. I have a most understanding partner. But he won't send briefs to people who aren't any good. Has an old-fashioned notion about studying the interests of the client. Oh, there is just one other thing. I hope you won't mind or feel offended. It's purely a formality. I'd just like you to meet my wife first."

"I see," said Sally.

"It's much better that way," said Mr Sharpe. "She'll pass you without a doubt."

"Indeed," said Sally.

"She has an almost pathological aversion to blondes. That's all I meant, I assure you."

CHAPTER FIFTEEN

NEWENT *v.* NEWENT

IN due course Mrs Newent's petition came on again for hearing. This time Roger was in a state of the happiest excitement. He was going to sit behind a Q.C. And he had only been called a little over a month. He wouldn't have to open his mouth in Court, but he'd be one of the counsel in the case, he was getting an enormous fee of twenty guineas, nearly three times as much as was marked on his original brief. He even wondered for a moment if he'd get both the seven and the twenty guineas, but he dismissed the thought as unworthy. Since the consultation he had spent many hours looking up authorities and he eventually had delivered a voluminous note to Plaistowe.

"Not at all bad, my dear chap. Difficult to believe you've only just been called."

"I had a bit of help from a man in my chambers called Blagrove."

"I see. Henry doing some work for a change. Never mind. Tell him I've marked it Beta plus. That'll shake him."

Mrs Newent came to the Court to watch. Her anger had been assuaged by Mr Merivale and she was quite pleased at the idea of being represented by a Q.C. That would be something to talk about afterwards, particularly to her friend who'd only had a junior.

At 10.20 Roger was duly installed in Court waiting for his leader to arrive. Suddenly his inside dropped to the ground, just as it had done when the case had been transferred from Judge Crane to Judge Ryman. He had seen Alec and Plaistowe's clerk deep in conversation together. Then to his horror they approached Mr Merivale and asked him to come outside. Roger had by this time seen enough of the Bar to know that even a Q.C. cannot be in two places at once. And if, for example, a case in a higher Court in which Plaistowe happened to be involved had unexpectedly not finished he might have to stay on and finish it. Suddenly Roger remembered having seen Plaistowe's name in *The Times* a few days before in a case in the House of Lords. He broke into a sweat. He was going to have to do it again. He hadn't even thought of the possibility. He had at any rate seen the cases, but it was hopeless for him to try and argue with a judge like Ryman. This time neither Sally nor Joy nor his mother were present, but their absence gave him no consolation. The Court was crowded and it would be awful; even if it had been empty it would have been just as bad. He had been so happy at the thought of sitting back and hearing how the case should be conducted and now he was going to have to do it himself—and, of course, he'd lose it. At that moment in his misery Alec came into Court, reached in front of him, said: "Excuse me, sir," and took away his brief. Fear was now replaced by utter gloom. They were going to take the brief away from him. Not that he could blame them, but that's what was going to happen. They'd already done it. How terribly humiliating! As if he hadn't had enough already. The fates were being very unkind. What would he say to Sally and Joy? He'd look such a fool. Oh, well—there was always sorting football coupons. He was interrupted in these miserable thoughts by Alec, who replaced the brief in front of him. On it he saw that what had once been marked as twenty guineas was now thirty-three. All the conference between the clerks had been about was an increase in the fee. Plaistowe's clerk thought that fifty guineas would be more appropriate to the occasion than thirty. So Roger had to have thirty-three whether he liked it or not. He sang to himself:

"What was once down-drip is now up-drip." He could have wept for joy—and nearly did. A few minutes later Plaistowe arrived and Roger's happiness was complete.

Then the judge sat and the case was called on. Plaistowe got up.

"May it please your Lordship, this petition in which I now appear with my learned friend, Mr Thursby——" Those words sounded very good to Roger. What a pity Sally couldn't have heard them. And Joy too, of course. After all, it was entirely through her that it had happened at all. And he'd have liked his mother there, too, though she wouldn't have appreciated the importance of the occasion. But he mustn't think of things like that. He must see how Plaistowe dealt with the case.

"Yes, I remember, Mr Plaistowe. It was adjourned for further argument. I'm very glad to have your help in the matter, though this remark is not intended as any disparagement of your learned junior."

"Thank you, my Lord."

Plaistowe then went on to recall the facts to the judge's mind and then to argue on the point of law. He quoted every case which had any possible bearing on the matter. He laid particular emphasis on the passages which supported his contentions, and eventually when he could do no more, he sat down.

Judge Ryman arranged the papers in front of him and proceeded to give judgment. Among other things he said this:

"I am bound in this Court to hold contrary to my own belief that it is at present the law of England that a man or woman who commits adultery remains entitled to the comfort and society of the other spouse so long as the adultery is sufficiently well concealed. But although I am bound to hold in this Court that adultery does not automatically prevent desertion, the petitioner must prove that the deserting party would have deserted anyway and that the adultery had nothing whatever to do with it. In my opinion, where the parties are living together, the acts or omissions or words of an adulterous spouse may, without amounting to neglect or misconduct, set in motion a train of events which breaks up the marriage. The wife returning from her lover may, as a result of a guilty conscience, say something to her husband or may even look at him in a way which starts an altercation. That altercation may lead to further disagreements and eventually the innocent spouse may leave the other. How can it then be said that just because the deserting spouse did not know of or suspect the adultery, the adultery had nothing to do with the desertion? In a case where the adultery was many years previously and there had been a long history of a happy marriage with children being born thereafter, no doubt it could be said that, when twenty years later the wife left her husband, her desertion had nothing to do with the very remote act of adultery. But conversely when the act of adultery is close to the desertion, I should have thought that it would be very difficult indeed for a petitioner to satisfy a Court that the adultery did not cause the desertion. In the present case the adultery *was* very close to the desertion. It may be that it caused it. I do not say it did. I do not know. And that means that the petitioner has certainly not proved to my satisfaction that her adultery had nothing to do with it. In the result, I hold that desertion has not been proved and the petition must be dismissed."

Well, thank Heaven, thought Roger, it wasn't my fault this time.

"Well, Mrs Newent," said Plaistowe outside the Court. "We shall have to consider whether to advise you to appeal. My personal opinion is that the judge is right, but, on the whole, I think that the Court of Appeal will take a different view."

"That's all Greek to me," said Mrs Newent. "And I didn't understand what the judge was saying either. But I've lost my case, have I?"

"You have at the moment."

"And I'm still married to that so-and-so?"

"Yes."

"Well, all I can say is, I wish him joy of it. I've had enough of the law. *He* can try next time. I don't know what all the fuss is about. My friend got her divorce all right. So why shouldn't I? It isn't justice."

"I'm extremely sorry, Mrs Newent," began Plaistowe.

"Not half as sorry as I am," said Mrs Newent. "Cost me a pretty penny and what have I got for it? Nothing."

She looked round for a moment as though trying to see whom she could blame. Her eye came to Roger.

"If you ask me," she went on, "it's all come about by employing schoolboys to do my case. If I'd had a proper barrister in the first instance this would never have happened."

"You've no right to talk like that," said Plaistowe.

"No right, haven't I? It's a free country and I can say what I like. Of course you all stand together. You would. But if you want my opinion you're all a bloody lot of twisters and that's straight."

"Come along, my dear chap," said Plaistowe to Roger. "Goodbye, Mr Merivale, Mr Smith. Let me know if I can be of any further help to you."

And so ended Roger's first case with a leader. He was secretly glad that Mrs Newent had started to abuse Plaistowe in much the same way as she had abused him, and that Plaistowe's reaction had been similar to his own. He wondered if Plaistowe would send him a red bag. He did not expect one, but it was nice to think of the possibility.

CHAPTER SIXTEEN

WRAP IT UP

It remained a possibility for a time, but not for very long. Plaistowe did in fact consider it but decided that it would be a bad precedent and possibly not very good for Roger, though he thought him a pleasant and potentially able young man.

After the tumult and the shouting about *Newent and Newent* had died down and Roger had told everyone about it, he returned to the normal life of a pupil with Mr Grimes. He looked at untold numbers of briefs. He went regularly into Court, he made notes in Court which sometimes Mr Grimes actually looked at. He turned up points of law in the Bar Library, he started to prepare those technical legal documents called pleadings as an exercise and then looked to see how Mr Grimes did them himself; he went and had coffee at Grooms, he lunched in the Crypt, in counsel's room in the Law Courts and very occasionally in hall. He often went to the "Bear Garden" and he followed Mr Grimes about as fast as he could and he asked Henry innumerable questions. Sometimes he had that terrible sinking feeling in the stomach when he was in Court with Mr Grimes and saw Alec hovering about waiting to pounce on his master to drag him to some other Court, leaving perhaps Roger to hold the fort while he was away.

But this did not actually happen for some months after his first day, though the fear of it was often there. Among other things he frequently went to the hearing of applications to adjourn cases. Mr Grimes often had to make such an application and one day, when it seemed as though he might be held up in the Privy Council and that no one else would be available, Roger was asked by Alec to be prepared to apply to the judge in charge of the non-jury list for a case to be stood out of the list. The application was consented to by the other side, but that did not necessarily mean that it would be granted. If cases about to come on for trial could be taken out of the list at will the lists would get into hopeless disorder. Some judges are fairly easy about granting applications which are consented to. Some are not so easy. Some are very difficult, particularly when the reason for the adjournment is simply that the parties are not ready. As usual Roger consulted Henry on the subject.

"Who is the judge?"

"Bingham, I think."

"That's bad. He's the worst. You must wrap it up."

"What's that mean?"

"Have you never heard of old Swift?"

"Only by name really. What about him?"

"I'll tell you. He was a judge with an attractive accent all of his own, though with a north country bias and a rather slow way of speaking. He would pronounce 'Mister' rather like 'Mistah' and 'o' in 'of' rather like 'u' in 'up.' He was a very popular judge, though he was very much master in his own Court. No one could take liberties with Swift. He could be very awkward if he wanted to and he was naughty sometimes. He could also be very helpful if he wanted to be, particularly to a young man. He had an amusing sense of humour. The story goes that one day Swift was hearing applications for adjournments when a young man called Croft with a very white wig got up and asked leave to mention the case of *Smith* against *Brown.*

" 'What is your application, Mistah Cruft?' said Swift.

" 'It's by consent, my Lord, to take the case out of the list for fourteen days, my Lord.'

" 'On what grounds, Mistah Cruft?' said Swift.

" 'Oh, my Lord, I don't think the parties are quite——'

"Before he could say any more Swift intervened.

" 'Wrap it up, Mistah Cruft,' he said.

" 'I beg your pardon, my Lord?' said young Croft, completely mystified.

" 'Wrap it up,' repeated Swift.

"Croft just looked miserable—I believe you know the feeling

—and thereupon Swift said rather sternly, but with a twinkle in his eye:

" 'Sit down, Mistah Cruft, and listen to Mistah Andrew Pain. You have an application, I believe, Mistah Andrew Pain?'

" 'Yes, my Lord—in the case of *Hatchett and Bellows* which is No. 1357 in the non-jury list.'

" 'What is your application?'

" 'To stand the case out for a month, my Lord.'

" 'And the grounds?'

" 'Oh, my Lord, the action is for breach of an oral contract. One of the witnesses to the making of the contract is in Brazil and can't be back for at least three weeks. At the time the case was set down it was not known by anyone that he would have to go there, but unfortunately only recently the witness' aged mother who is staying in Brazil became ill and he had to go to her. Then, my Lord, another reason for the adjournment is that through no fault of the parties or their solicitors some of the documents in the case were burnt. They are vital documents and the solicitors are trying to reach agreement as to what they contained. Then, my Lord, another witness, or I should say a possible witness, has suddenly left his address and we haven't been able to trace him yet. Finally, my Lord, one of the partners in the firm of solicitors instructing me has unfortunately just gone into hospital for appendicitis and the managing clerk who was attending to the matter has gone to another firm.'

" 'Mistah Cruft,' said Swift.

"Pain was still on his feet and his application not yet disposed of, so Croft, who was, of course, sitting down, thought he might have misheard and remained seated.

" 'Mistah Cruft,' said Swift loudly and sternly.

"Croft rose trembling to his feet.

" 'Mistah Cruft, did you hear Mr Andrew Pain's application?'

" 'Yes, my Lord.'

" 'That's what I call wrapping it up,' said Swift."

CHAPTER SEVENTEEN

CRIMINAL PROCEEDINGS

OCCASIONALLY, though not very often, Mr Grimes appeared in a Criminal Court and Roger, of course, went with him. Peter always went on these occasions because, as he said, that was more in his line. On one such occasion Mr Grimes had a big conspiracy case in which he was prosecuting on behalf of a large company. Such cases always start in the Magistrate's Court and the day before the first hearing Roger mentioned it to Henry.

"I wonder if you'll be before old Meadowes," said Henry. "I hope so. He's an amusing old bird sometimes."

"Come on," said Roger. "Let's have it—I can go to the Bar Library when you've told me."

"Well, Meadowes had an old hand up in front of him who rather liked going to prison in the winter. He had a pretty hard life and he found prison more comfortable in the cold weather. So, regularly every October he'd commit some crime worth six months, do his stretch and come out in the spring. Well, one day this old boy came up in front of Meadowes. He pleaded guilty as usual, said he had nothing to say and waited for the usual six months.

" 'Three months imprisonment,' said Meadowes.

"The old boy thought he must have misheard.

" 'What's that?' he said.

" 'Three months imprisonment,' repeated the clerk.

" 'But that's all wrong, your Worship. I always get six months for this.'

" 'Take him away,' said the clerk.

"The old boy clung to the bars of the dock.

" 'But please, your Worship, make it six. I always get six for this, straight I do.'

"A policeman started to remove him from the dock.

" 'Leave me alone, you something something,' said the old man. 'I have my rights.'

" 'Now, look,' said Meadowes, who thought he had better take a hand, 'if you don't behave yourself, I shan't send you to prison at all!' "

At that moment Alec came into the room.

"Mr Grimes would like to see you, sir," he said to Roger.

"How are ye, my dear fellow," said Mr Grimes when Roger arrived. "Now look, my dear fellow, will ye very kindly keep this case in the Magistrate's Court back till I arrive tomorrow. It'll be quite all right, my dear fellow. I've spoken to Brunner who's on the other side and he's agreeable. All ye have to do is to tell the clerk before the magistrate sits, and then wait till I come. If by accident it's called on before I come, just ask the magistrate to keep it back."

"You will be there, I suppose?" said Roger, who had learned a good deal now by experience.

"Of course I'll be there, my dear fellow, of course I'll be there. What are ye thinking of? Of course I'll be there. Dear, dear, dear

—not be there, who ever heard of such a thing, dear, dear, dear."

"Suppose it is called on and the magistrate won't keep it back?"

"Just tell him the tale, my dear fellow, just tell him the tale."

"But what tale?"

"Look, my dear fellow," said Mr Grimes, "if ye don't want to do it, ye needn't. I can get Hallfield to do it. But I thought ye might like it, my dear fellow, I thought ye might like it."

"Oh, I should very much."

"That's right, my dear fellow, that's the way, that's the way Ye have seen the papers, have ye?"

"I've looked at them, but not very thoroughly."

"Well, ye'd better look at them again now, my dear fellow. Ye'll find lots of tales to tell from them, my dear fellow. Oh, dear, yes. It's a fine kettle of fish. Taking machinery from under their very noses. I don't know what we're coming to, my dear fellow, I really don't. They'll be stealing houses next and factories. They took half the contents of one in this case. And from under their very noses, under their very noses. I don't know, my dear fellow, but there it is. They will do these things, they will do these things."

Roger took the papers away. The case was about a large conspiracy to steal. Roger wondered if he'd ever be able to master a brief of that size, though he had more confidence in being able to do so than he had three months previously.

The next day he went to the Magistrate's Court in plenty of time and saw the clerk before the magistrate sat.

"That's a bit awkward," said the clerk. "The lists are in a complete mess today. He's taking some summonses after the charges but there aren't many of them and they won't last long. Can't you start it?"

"I'd rather not," said Roger.

"I thought that's how you got experience at the Bar," said the clerk. "When I was practising as a solicitor they used to play it on me like blazes. Sometimes I'd get the most awful damn fools appearing for part of the case when I'd briefed someone quite good. But it's jolly good experience for the young chaps who come down. Not such a pleasant experience for the solicitor sometimes, or easy to explain to the client."

"Yes, it must be difficult, I agree. D'you think you'll be able to keep this case back, though?" asked Roger anxiously. "I'm sure the solicitor will be furious if I do it. I'm only a pupil, you know."

"Splendid," said the clerk. "I suppose it's the nasty part of my nature coming out. I love to see it happening to other people.

Watch the client squirm while you make a mess of it—not that you'd make a mess of it, I'm sure, Mr—Mr——"

"Thursby's my name," said Roger, "and I can be guaranteed to make a complete mess of it. So if that's what you want, call the case and you'll have a whale of a time."

Roger was surprised at his own self-confidence. The clerk laughed.

"Well, that's the first time I've heard counsel talk like that. Good for you, if I may say so, and if you don't mind an older man, albeit a solicitor, saying this—if you stick to that attitude of mind you'll have a darned good chance of getting on. It's these smart alecs and know-alls who come croppers. Good for you. Very glad to have met you. I'll keep the old boy back even if he starts dancing round the room."

"That's awfully good of you," said Roger. "I'm most grateful. Sorry to have done you out of a good laugh though. One day p'raps I'll have a brief of my own and then you'll be able to make up for it."

It was the first time Roger had been to a magistrate's court and he watched the proceedings with interest. First came the overnight charges, the drunks, the prostitutes, the suspected persons, and so forth.

"Were you drunk and incapable?"

"Yes."

"Facts, officer."

Facts stated.

"Anything known?"

"Not for this, your Worship."

"Anything to say?"

Nothing.

"Ten shillings, please."

And so on to the next case. The speed at which the magistrate got through his work astounded Roger and, after a morning at his Court, he thought that, if as he supposed, every Court had much the same amount to do, it was a great tribute to the care and ability of London magistrates that so few people complain of their cases not being properly heard. But he wondered what would happen if there were a concerted scheme on the part of the public to plead Not Guilty. It would cause chaos. As it was, most of those charged or summoned pleaded Guilty. It seems a pity all the same, he thought, that criminal cases have to be tried at such a rate. He had started to work out in his mind what the cost to the country of a few extra magistrates and courts would be, when his attention was distracted from this calculation by the case of Cora. She was a demure-looking person and when she went into the dock she looked modestly down at her feet. The charge

115

was read out and she was asked if she pleaded Guilty or Not Guilty. She started to say "Guilty" when she looked up and saw who the magistrate was. Metropolitan Courts have at least two magistrates, sometimes sitting alternate days, sometimes in separate Courts on the same day. She had arrived late and thought that someone else would be sitting.

"Oh, no," she said, "Not Guilty. Not Guilty at all. I should say not," and she added under her breath something which the gaoler could hear but the magistrate, who was old and slightly deaf, could not. What she said was: "Not with you there, you old stinker."

"What was that?" asked the magistrate.

"I didn't quite catch, your Worship," said the gaoler, after a slight cough.

"Didn't know it was me, was that it?" asked the magistrate.

"Something like that, your Worship," coughed the gaoler.

"Oh, I only wanted the sense, thank you," said the magistrate. "Very well. Take the oath, officer."

Roger discovered the reason for the sudden change in Cora's attitude. Most magistrates fine prostitutes forty shillings and that's the end of the matter. They pay this about once a fortnight and the amount is only a trifle out of their considerable earnings. That is the maximum penalty that can be imposed. But there is power under an old Act—some six hundred years old—to call upon them to find sureties for their good behaviour with the alternative of a term of imprisonment. No prostitute can find such sureties, whether she is on her own or run by a man. If she is on her own, she would not normally know any who would stand as surety; if she is controlled by a man, the man who controls her would not mind losing his twenty-five pounds or whatever it was when the condition of the recognizance was broken, as, of course, it would be—but he does not want to advertise his relationship to the girl. In consequence in almost every instance of a prostitute being called upon to find sureties for her good behaviour, she goes to prison instead. Mr Meadowes was wont to adopt this course and, as often as not, prostitutes who were to appear before him simply did not turn up, but came on another day when there was another magistrate. Cora had made a mistake. As soon as she saw it she changed her plea to "Not Guilty" just in time. Roger wondered whether the police would be able to establish, as they had to, that people who had been solicited by Cora had been annoyed. It could not be altogether an easy task, he thought, as none of the men solicited would be likely to give evidence. In Cora's case the material evidence was as follows:

POLICE OFFICER: "At the corner of Regent Street I saw the

accused approach a man. She smiled at him and said something. He walked away hurriedly. Five minutes later at about the same spot she approached another man. He spoke to her for a minute and then went away. He appeared annoyed. A few minutes later she approached another man. He apparently saw her coming and avoided her. I then arrested the accused. She said, 'Take your hands off me, you filthy stinker. Why don't you go after some of the French girls. They drop you too much, I suppose.' At the police station she was charged and said: 'You're all a lot of stinking so-and-so's'."

THE CLERK (TO CORA): "Do you want to ask the officer any questions?"

CORA: "I'll say. That first man you say I spoke to, how d'you know I didn't know him."

POLICE OFFICER: "He didn't appear to know you. He walked off hurriedly."

CORA: "He may not have liked me."

MAGISTRATE: "Next question."

CORA: "You say the next man was annoyed, how do you know?"

POLICE OFFICER: "He seemed annoyed."

MAGISTRATE: "How did he show his annoyance?"

POLICE OFFICER: "He just seemed annoyed, your Worship."

CORA: "What at?"

POLICE OFFICER: "Because you solicited him."

CORA: "How do you know that?"

POLICE OFFICER: "There couldn't have been any other reason."

CORA: "I might have asked him for a light."

POLICE OFFICER: "He didn't put his hand in his pocket."

CORA: "Well, of course, he wouldn't if he didn't have a match, would he? You didn't hear what I said, did you?"

POLICE OFFICER: "No, but you smiled at him."

CORA: "Is that a crime? Don't you smile at anyone?"

MAGISTRATE: "You needn't answer that question."

CORA: "Well, I want him to."

MAGISTRATE: "I don't. Next question."

CORA: "That's all, your Worship, except that it's all lies what the officer says."

MAGISTRATE: "Is what you have said true, officer?"

POLICE OFFICER: "Yes, your Worship. That's the case, your Worship."

CLERK (TO CORA): "Now, do you wish to give evidence on oath or make a statement from where you are?"

CORA: "I'll stay where I am, thank you. I was just waiting for a girl friend. I didn't speak or look at anyone. The officer may have mistaken me for someone else. That man I was supposed to have spoken to, he spoke to me first. He asked me the time. I suppose he had an appointment and was late. That's why he hurried off. That's all I've got to say."

The magistrate found the case proved and, on Cora admitting her previous convictions, which were read out, he ordered her to find two sureties for her good behaviour in the sum of twenty-five pounds each or go to prison for six months.

"It's a stinking shame," shouted Cora before she was removed from the dock, to which she clung for a short time. "Why don't you have your stinking name put up outside your stinking Court?"

Roger was rather disturbed by these cases. The Galahad in him became very prominent. Couldn't something be done for these girls? he asked himself. He wished he could help. He couldn't very well offer to be surety himself. For one thing he wasn't worth twenty-five pounds and for another he didn't think it would look well. But he made a mental resolution that if and when he had the power or opportunity, he would do all he could to help these wretched creatures, many of whom are born into the world without a reasonable chance. A morning at such a Court for a kind and thoughtful young man of twenty-one is a very moving experience. And so Roger found it. He must tell Sally.

The charges went on and Roger became even more worried at the speed with which they were disposed of and at the reliance the magistrate seemed to place on the evidence of the police. But after all, he said to himself, he ought to know. He's been there long enough. But how does he know a policeman's telling the truth and that the other chap isn't? I should find it jolly difficult sometimes. And just at that moment the magistrate dismissed a charge.

"Quite right to bring it, officer," he said, "but I think there's a doubt. You may go," he said to the prisoner.

When Roger saw the smile on the prisoner's face as he left the Court he was not at all sure that his first fears were justified. But how difficult it must be to decide so many cases rightly. And so quickly. He decided to speak to Sally about that too. "The tempo's too fast," he would say. Her mother would appreciate that.

The charges were finished and the summonses began. They were all petty motoring offences.

"You're charged with leaving your motor car on such and such a day at such and such a place, so as to cause an obstruction. Are you Guilty or Not Guilty?"

"Guilty."

"How long, officer?"

"One hour, thirty-five minutes."

"Anything known?"

118

"Fined ten shillings for obstruction at Marlborough Street Magistrates' Court on 3rd June, 1947."

"Anything to say?"

"I'm very sorry, but I didn't realize it was as long. There was nowhere else to leave it."

"I know the difficulties, but they must be overcome or the streets would be impassable. Pay forty shillings, please."

Then came a few pleas of Not Guilty.

The car hadn't been there as long as the officer said. It hadn't caused any obstruction. Why hadn't the officer taken the number of the other cars there? They were causing more obstruction. Some of the defendants were angry, some pained and some resigned to their fate, but they were all found guilty that day.

One lady who was fined said: "I'd like you to know that I entirely disagree with your decision."

"You can appeal, if you wish, madam."

"I think you twisted what I said. It isn't fair."

"That will be all, thank you, madam." He might have been bowing her out of a shop. She tossed her head and left and Roger could imagine her telling all her friends of the grave injustice she had suffered at the hands of Mr Meadowes. The fact remained that she had left her car in a busy street at a busy time of day when her car and any other vehicles which were left were bound to cause an obstruction. The fact also remained that she was fined no more than any of the others. But, of course, it was a grave injustice and the law is most unfair.

The summonses were finished and for once Roger did not feel alarmed as he did normally when the possibility of deputizing for Grimes drew near. The few kind remarks from the clerk made all the difference. Charles had told him of an experience he'd once had at a magistrate's court in the country. He had got to the Court early and he had had a long and pleasant talk with a man whom he believed to be the clerk to the justices. This gave Charles tremendous confidence, until the justices came in and he found that his friend was the usher and the clerk himself extremely fierce. Roger had made no such mistake. His friend was definitely the clerk.

"Well," said Mr Meadowes, "what are we waiting for?"

The clerk whispered to him: "Grimes isn't here yet. There's only a youngster holding for him. D'you mind waiting a few minutes? He won't be any time. It's a heavy case."

"All the more reason for getting on with it. Why can't he call the first witness? He can always be recalled if necessary. I won't let him be bounced. But we'll never get through these lists if we don't get on."

"I rather told him you'd wait."

"Well, now you'd better rather tell him I won't," said Mr
Meadowes. "Cheer up," he added. "I shan't eat him, you know."

"But I rather promised."

"Well, this'll teach you not to. Never make promises myself.
Bad habit. Thundering bad."

The clerk thought he saw an opening.

"D'you think so, really? We sometimes get some of our clients
to make promises and occasionally they keep them. That does a
lot of good."

"Well, you're not doing any," said Mr Meadowes. "I'm going
to start this case, promises or no promises. Now, will you tell them
to get on with it or shall I?"

The clerk looked apologetically at Roger and nodded to the
gaoler to bring in the prisoners. There was still no Mr Grimes.
His solicitor rushed out to a telephone box.

"Where on earth is Mr Grimes?" he shouted down the mouthpiece.

"The senior's out, sir," said a voice.

"I don't care where he is. Where's Mr Grimes? The case has
been called on."

"I'm afraid I don't know much about it, sir."

"Give me patience," said the solicitor.

At that moment a taxi drew up and out jumped Mr Grimes
and Alec. The solicitor could see this from the telephone box
and at once replaced the receiver. He rushed up to Grimes who
was hurrying into the Court.

"The case has been called on," he said excitedly.

"That's all right, my dear fellow," said Mr Grimes. "Here we
are and now we shan't have to wait. So pleased to see ye, so pleased
to see ye."

And Mr Grimes dashed into the Court, panting more from
habit than exertion, the distance from the taxi being much too
short to put any real strain on the lungs. He slipped into counsel's
row, bowed to the magistrate, whispered: "Thank ye so much,
my dear fellow," to Roger and proceeded to address the magistrate.

"It's very good of your Worship to have waited," he began.

"I didn't," said Mr Meadowes. "Too much to do."

"If your Worship pleases," said Mr Grimes and then opened
the case to the magistrate. As Roger listened his admiration for
Mr Grimes increased. He made everything crystal clear, every
detail was in its right place, the story was unfolded efficiently,
clearly and with overwhelming conviction. "Will I ever be able
to do it like that?" thought Roger. "I can't believe it possible."

As Henry had said, almost every pupil at the Bar thinks that his master does everything perfectly. Just as almost every jury-man thinks a judge's summing up is brilliant. The point, of course, is, as Roger later learned, that, seldom having heard anything done professionally before, they have no standard to judge by. Mr Grimes' opening was certainly a perfectly proper, sound opening, but there was nothing spectacular about it and it was child's play to any experienced advocate who had mastered his facts.

The case went on for two hours and was adjourned for a week. It was some time before the hearing was completed, although the magistrate set aside several special days for it. Meantime, the men and women charged with the various crimes alleged had the prosecution hanging over their heads and some of them were in custody. That seemed to Roger rather hard on them if they were not guilty, though having heard what Mr Grimes had said about them, he could not conceive that any of them was innocent or would be acquitted. All the same, he thought, mightn't a few more magistrates and Courts be an advantage? He asked Henry about it.

"It's the Treasury," said Henry. "Of course it's their job to fight every bit of expenditure especially at this time when the country has been crippled by two wars and public expenditure is enormous. Every suggestion of an extra judge or extra magis-trate is fought by them tooth and nail. But you mustn't forget they've got other claims on them from every quarter. They have to satisfy the most important. We naturally think the administration of justice is most important. But what about health and education? Are they less? Who's to judge? I can't. But of course, I agree that there ought to be extra magistrates. I shouldn't have thought any-one would have disagreed. But when you say it'll only cost so many thousands of pounds a year, that doesn't mean a thing until you add up all the other thousands of pounds you've got to spend and see where they're all to come from."

CHAPTER EIGHTEEN

BRIEF DELIVERED

"I'D like you to meet Sally," said Roger to Henry one day.

"I'd love to meet her," said Henry. "She sounds out of the ordinary."

At that moment Alec came in.

"Thornton, Merivale wants you to lead Mr Thursby in a bank-ruptcy matter, sir," he said to Henry. "Will that be all right?"

"Who are they?" said Henry. "Never been to me before that I can remember."

"They're clients of Mr Thursby, sir."

"Oh, Uncle Alfred, of course," said Henry. "Well, that sounds very nice. Thank you, Alec."

Alec went out and Henry turned to Roger.

"Is this your doing, old boy?" he asked.

"I know absolutely nothing about it," he said. "I'm as surprised as you are."

"Oh, come now," said Henry. "You mustn't be surprised at someone sending me a brief. I do get them occasionally, you know. Even a new client sometimes puts his head in the door."

"I'm sorry," said Roger. "I didn't mean it that way. But it's jolly lucky for me. I'm so glad you can take it. Will I be a nuisance? I know nothing about bankruptcy."

"You'll learn," said Henry. "Particularly if you fail at the Bar. I wonder when it's for. Hope it doesn't clash with Ascot."

"Are you a racing man, then?"

"Oh, gracious no, but there are such lovely things to be seen at Ascot, some with two legs and some with four, and the whole atmosphere appeals to me. It's the only meeting I go to. Like to come? If you've got any sense, you'll say 'no.' You stick to your work. You've a hell of a lot to learn. But I'll take you if you want —and Sally too, if you'd like."

"I think that's most unfair," said Roger. "Why did you have to ask me—and Sally? You know I'd love it. I hope the bank-ruptcy case prevents it. Anyway, what would Grimes say?"

"Grimes? He'd say, 'Dear, dear, dear, going to Ascot are we? Going to the races instead of getting on with our work, are we? Dear, dear, dear. Have a good time, my dear fellow, have a good time. Good-bye, bye, bye'."

"Well, I shall consult Sally on the subject," said Roger.

As he said that, the junior clerk came into the room and said that Roger was wanted on the telephone by a Miss Burnett. He went to the telephone.

"Hullo, Joy," said Roger.

"Oh, Roger, Uncle Alfred told me he was sending you another brief—and I just wondered if you'd got it."

"Oh, yes, Joy. I don't know if it's come yet, but I've just this moment heard about it."

Joy was in her uncle's office at the time and it had all been arranged in her presence so that it was not exactly a coincidence that she telephoned when she did. She believed in striking while the iron was hot and she thought that Roger had a conscience.

"I'm so pleased for you," said Joy. "You are doing well. It seems ages since I saw you. I was wondering——" and she paused to give Roger an opportunity to do what any decent man, who'd had a brief from a girl, would do.

"So was I," said Roger, with as much enthusiasm as he could muster. "I'd love to take you out one night soon if you're free."

"Any night, Roger. I'd put anything else off if it clashed."

At that moment there was a knock on the clerks' door. The junior opened the door and in came Sally. Roger was just saying:

"Well, let me see, how would to-morrow do?" when he noticed her.

Sally had a brief in her hand.

"That would be lovely, Roger. Where and when?"

"Oh," said Roger most uncomfortably. "Anywhere at all."

"Will you call for me, then?"

"Yes, certainly."

"About seven?"

"Yes."

"You sound awfully distrait all of a sudden. Is it another client?"

"I'd like to think so," said Roger.

"How lovely," said Joy, "if it is."

A remark which embarrassed Roger very much indeed.

He managed to finish the conversation with Joy and then turned to find Sally talking to the clerk.

"I've brought these papers down for Mr Blagrove," she was saying. "Mr Sharpe would be glad if he could have them back quickly. Hullo, Roger."

"What on earth are you doing here?"

"My people have just sent a brief down to Mr Blagrove. No one else was available, so they asked me to bring it. Funny, isn't it?"

"I didn't know you did any litigation."

"Oh, the firm does, but not the partner I work for. But this *is* from him. It's an opinion about a landlord and tenant matter. Mr Sharpe thought he'd like to try your Mr Blagrove. Have *you* had any more briefs lately?"

"I have, as a matter of fact."

"From the same source?"

Roger blushed. He could not help it. "Yes, if you want to know, but we oughtn't to chat here. It'll disturb the clerks. Come in and meet Henry."

"Won't I be taking up too much of your time? Briefs and telephone conversations and things," she added.

"Henry would love to meet you. Do come in."

He took her to Henry's room and introduced them.

"I've heard so much about you," said Sally, "though you're not quite what I expected. That isn't meant to be rude. On the contrary, as a matter of fact."

"Well, you're exactly what I expected, and knowing the source of my information, you couldn't ask for more than that, could you?" said Henry.

"I should like to think that," said Sally. "So this is where you decide how not to ask leading questions and whether to put the prisoner in the box and if the judge is likely to be prejudiced if you plead the Statute of Limitations?"

"You seem to know an awful lot about it," said Henry.

"I've been with solicitors for three months. I've brought you a brief."

"Me—you mean Roger."

"I don't, my firm's pretty careful who it briefs. I hope I shan't have my neck wrung for suggesting you. It'll be Roger's fault. But he thinks you've the wisdom of a Lord Chief Justice and the power of advocacy of a Carson and he's managed to put it across to me. He doesn't always succeed."

"Well, I hope it's something I can do. Your neck would be very much on my conscience. I'll certainly give it more than usual attention. Dispatch will oblige, I suppose!"

"Expedition specially requested," said Sally "is the form we use in our office when the papers have been overlooked for a week and the client is howling for that opinion we promised him."

"Well—I've nothing to do—so—oh, yes, I have, though. Roger's getting me all my work."

"I see," said Sally. "How nice. Does he get a commission? Or give one perhaps? Now I must go or I'll be shot. We've a lot to do in my office. Good-bye, so glad to have met you at last. Good-bye, Roger. We must meet some time out of working hours—if you have a spare moment."

The truth of the matter was that for quite a little time Roger had been neglecting both Joy and Sally. He had been devoting himself almost entirely to work. Now he found it a little disconcerting to be subjected to this two-pronged attack. He saw Sally out and went back to Henry.

"Roger," said Henry, "if at any time you should commit yourself irrevocably to Uncle Alfred's niece, would you consider it a breach of good faith if I asked your friend Sally out to dinner?"

CHAPTER NINETEEN

THE OLD BAILEY

IN due course the conspiracy case came on for trial at the Old Bailey. It was likely to take a fortnight or three weeks and in consequence to interfere a good deal with Mr Grimes' other work. Roger had considerable qualms. He felt sure he would be left to do part of it. Peter, on the other hand, would have been delighted to be left with it. It was his ambition to stand up at the Old Bailey and say something, and he had the doubtful advantage that he would never realize how badly he had said it. He said to Roger that, if Grimeyboy went away in the middle, he thought that, as he was senior to Roger, he ought to have the chance of taking over before him.

"Of course," said Roger and hoped that was how it would be.

"Since you came here," said Peter, "he hardly ever seems to use me. I don't think he likes me somehow."

I wonder if that is it, thought Roger, or if I really am better.

It was an interesting day for Roger when he went for the first time to the Old Bailey. He was surprised at the smallness of the Courts. But the solemnity was there all right. He tried to visualize the murderers and other criminals who had stood in the dock. This was the Court in which, Henry had told him, five black-mailers had once stood to receive their sentences from the then Lord Chief Justice. The Lord Chief Justice awarded the first man he sentenced eight years' penal servitude (as it was then called), the second ten years, the third twelve. It must have been obvious to the fifth man, the ringleader, what the judge was working up to, and slowly and methodically he worked up to it.

"And as this is the worst case of its kind I have ever tried," he began in sentencing the ringleader, "the sentence of the Court is that you be kept in penal servitude for life."

"I'm told," Henry had said, "that it was an artistic, though not a pleasant performance."

This, too, was the Court where the man who was said to have been a sort of Jekyll and Hyde had stood to receive his sentence.

"Counsel has argued eloquently on your behalf," said the judge, "that you are really two people, one very good and the other very bad. As to that, all I can say is that both of you must go to prison."

Roger would have been spared some unnecessary worry if he had known that Mr Grimes had given his personal undertaking to be present the whole time throughout the case, and Alec had charged a fee to compensate for the results of complying with such an undertaking. Mr Grimes was there all the time, and Roger had the advantage of seeing him hold innumerable conferences on other matters with solicitors and managing clerks in the corridors of the Old Bailey. In the middle of a case involving theft of machinery, he discussed among other things a libel action brought by a politician, a claim for damages for being caught up in a sausage machine, an action by a householder against his next-door neighbour for nuisance by barking dogs, a claim for breach of contract on the sale of fertilizers, an action for breach of promise, some bankruptcy proceedings, an appeal to the Privy Council and a host of other things. A temperamental recording machine which decided not to record from time to time would have produced some surprising results if it had been placed by the side of Mr Grimes eating a sandwich on a bench in the Old Bailey, while client after client came and told his tale of woe, received expert advice and went away rejoicing. And Mr Grimes never put a foot wrong. A lesser man might have confused one case with another. But not he. Mr Grimes treated each client as though he were his only client and as though his case were his only case.

"Yes, my dear fellow. Don't ye worry, my dear fellow, that's quite all right. Just write and tell them the tale, my dear fellow. Good-bye, bye, bye."

"Dear, dear, dear. You don't say, my dear fellow, dear, dear, dear, you don't say. Well, we'll soon put a stop to those goings on. Ye wait, my dear fellow, ye'll see. It'll be quite all right, quite all right. Good-bye, bye, bye." And so on and so on, punctuated by bites of sandwich. Do this, don't do that, try for this but take that if necessary, apply to the judge, go to the Master, issue a writ, pay into Court, appeal, don't appeal, it's a toss up, my dear fellow, we can but try; dear, dear, dear, they will do these things, my dear fellow, they will do these things.

And so back into Court, stomach full of ill-bitten, undigested sandwich, head, Roger would have thought, full of dogs, sausages and fertilizers—but not at all. Mr Grimes examined a difficult witness as though he had been doing nothing else but think about his evidence. Roger was astonished at the number of watertight compartments there must be in a busy barrister's mind. But then, I suppose, he said to himself, it's exactly the same with everyone's job. I don't imagine a surgeon often takes out the wrong part because he's confused two cases or that a doctor, visiting a case of measles, enquires about the big toe, which belongs next door.

The case went on day after day. Roger took voluminous notes, Peter took a few, and from time to time when he found that his services were not going to be required, wandered into the other Courts where something more interesting might be happening. Once while Peter was away, the judge said:

"Excuse me a moment, Mr Grimes. A prisoner wants a dock defence."

"Put up Arthur Green," said the clerk and Mr Green was brought up into the dock.

"You may choose whom you wish," said the judge.

"That one, please, my Lord," said Mr Green, and pointed to Mr Grimes.

"I'm afraid Mr Grimes is engaged on a case," said the judge.

"I thought you said I could choose whom I wish, my Lord," said Mr Green. "I want him."

"I'm sorry," said the judge. "Mr Grimes can't be in two Courts at once."

"I don't want him in two Courts at once, my Lord," said Mr Green. "Just in mine."

"Now, don't waste time," said the judge. "You can't have him, though no doubt Mr Grimes is suitably flattered. Now, choose someone else."

"Oh, well, I'll have him," and Mr Green pointed to counsel defending the chief conspirator.

"I'm sorry," said the judge. "He's engaged too."

"I thought you said——" began the man.

"I know, I know," said the judge. "But you can't have someone who's engaged on a case."

"How am I to know who's engaged on a case and who isn't, my Lord? Perhaps you could ask the gentlemen who aren't for hire to cover up their flags, my Lord."

"Now, don't be impertinent," said the judge quite genially. "I'm sorry about this. Perhaps those members of the Bar who are not engaged in the case would be good enough to stand up."

Three old, three middle-aged and three young men sprang to their feet with alacrity. This was a race in which youth had no advantage over age. Indeed a middle-aged man was first, though he ricked his back in the process. Roger remained seated.

"Get up, my dear fellow," said Mr Grimes. "Ye never know. Good experience for ye."

So Roger got up a little time after the others, just as Mr Green had come to much the same conclusion as the old lag in Henry's story. The apparent reluctance which Roger had to join the race appealed to Mr Green.

"Him, my Lord, please," said Mr Green, pointing to Roger.

"Mr—Mr——" began the judge, and then made a noise, half grunt, half swallow, three consonants and a couple of vowels. It was a work of art and had been cultivated by him over the years. It really sounded like a name and though no one could say what it was, no one could say what it was not. Whether a name began with a vowel or a consonant or a diphthong, the sound made by the judge was not unlike it, and, as he looked hard at its owner during the process, it never failed.

"Will you undertake this defence, please?" said the judge.

"If your Lordship pleases."

Roger wondered what was the next move.

"Go and see him," volunteered his next-door neighbour.

"Now?" asked Roger.

"Of course."

"Where do I see him?"

"In the cells. Bow to the judge and go into the dock and down the stairs. Quick. The old boy's waiting for you."

Roger looked up and saw that his informant was right. "Don't disturb yourself unduly," said the judge. "This case is going to last for weeks, anyway. What difference does an extra half hour make?"

Roger blushed. "I'm so sorry, my Lord," he said.

The judge gave him a friendly smile.

Roger walked into the dock rather self-consciously and went down the stairs which led from inside it to the cells below. He was shown to a room in which he could interview Mr Green who was promptly brought to him.

"Afternoon, sir," said Mr Green.

"Good afternoon," said Roger.

"Funny weather for the time of year," said Mr Green. "Felt like thunder this morning."

"Yes, it did," said Roger.

"But there," said Mr Green, "they will do these things."

"What!" said Roger.

"He defended me twenty years ago," said Mr Green. "I haven't forgotten. Nearly got me off too. If it hadn't been for the old judge he would have too. Dear, dear, dear. Now we're starting to look back. And that won't do. We must look forward, mustn't we? This your first case?"

"Not quite," said Roger.

"That's all right," said Mr Green. "I'll tell you what to do. It's easy, dead easy. I'd have done it myself but it looks better to have a mouthpiece. Can you sing?" he added.

"I don't know quite what that's got to do with it," said Roger.

"Ah!" said Mr Green knowingly, "but you haven't been at it as long as I have. There's a lot of things you don't understand now, aren't there?"

128

"My Lord, in this case I appear for the petitioner, a lady of impeccable virtue." Roger rehearses for his impending divorce case, but——Mrs Newent has asked for the discretion of the court.

"What's all that in aid of?" Mrs Newent asked. "Why haven't I got my divorce?" "It's a little difficult to explain," said Roger.

"Yes," said Roger. "I'm afraid there are."

"Well, now that's agreed—can you sing?"

"No, I can't, as a matter of fact."

"Never mind," said Mr Green. "As long as I know one way or the other. Can't take any chances. Forewarned is forearmed. Many a mickle makes a muckle. It's an ill wind and so on and so forth. I'm not keeping you, I hope?"

"I'm here to defend you," said Roger. "My time's your time. My services, such as they are, are at your disposal."

"That's a pretty speech," said Mr Green. "Can you make lots of those?"

Roger did not answer.

"All right," said Mr Green. "You win. Cut the cackle and come to the hosses. Now, I'll tell you what we'll do. I've got it all laid on."

"But what are you charged with?" asked Roger.

"Oh, that!" said Mr Green scornfully. "It's almost an insult. But I suppose it's like everything else these days. Going down. You've only got to deration butter and all the places serve margarine."

"I don't understand," said Roger.

"Now, look," said Mr Green. "Have you ever seen an indictment before?"

Roger had not and said so. He would have admitted it anyway, but he made the admission a second before he realized that it was a pretty odd system under which a young man who had never seen an indictment could be employed to defend somebody who was charged upon one. Roger had read the charges in Mr Grimes' conspiracy case, but for some reason he had never actually seen the indictment or a copy of it.

"Well, now, look—this is an indictment—or it's supposed to be."

He produced a typewritten foolscap document. All over it were pencil remarks made by himself.

"I call it an impertinence," went on Mr Green. "Do you know that I was once charged on an indictment containing thirty-three counts? Thirty-three. Now that's not bad, eh?"

"What happened?" asked Roger.

"Never mind what happened. That's not the point. But it's treating a chap with respect to bring in thirty-three counts. Shows you're frightened you might miss him here and there. Can't afford to take chances with him. I've had twenty-five, twenty and never less than ten or twelve. Oh, yes, I once had seven. And now look at this—I ask you—is it fair? Is it reasonable? I'm not so young as I was, I'm entitled to a bit of respect, aren't I? One count— one solitary, miserable count. They must think I've come down in the world. It hurts. That's what it does. If you've got a nice lot of counts to deal with, you've got something to fight. But this—this—it takes all the stuffing out of a man. I tell you—I had a good mind to plead Guilty and be done with it. One count! Two can play at that game. If they won't do the right thing, why should I? I've never pleaded Guilty in my life, but I tell you, I came as near doing it this time as I ever did. And then I remembered it was Ascot next week. So that wouldn't do. But if it hadn't been, I tell you—I'd have cut the ground from under their feet. Guilty, I should have said. That would have shaken them. There they are —counsel, solicitors, police, witnesses, judge, jury, ushers, flowers, herbs, spectators—everyone—and I say Guilty. I bet the clerk wouldn't have believed it. What was that? he'd have said. I'd have had a game with him. Not Guilty, I should have said. Oh, I thought you said Guilty, he'd have said. Yes, I'd have said, I did. Well, which is it, he'd have said, Guilty or Not Guilty. You choose, I should have said. I hate these parlour games. One of these days a judge will say—they look at TV all right, oh, yes, they do, whatever they say—one of these days a judge will say—will the next prisoner sign in, please?"

"Now, look, Mr Green," said Roger. "I know I'm very new to the Bar, but you're paying me to help you. Hadn't you better tell me about the case? I love to hear your views on these other matters, but after all, if you want to go to Ascot next week the case is more important."

"You'll do well, sir," said Mr Green. "You think of essentials. Ascot it is. I've never missed an Ascot yet—except when—well now I'm going back into past history. Dear, dear, dear. Now, let's get down to brass tacks. No beating about the bush. All fair and above board. In for a penny, in for a pound. Who laughs last, laughs loudest. You can't sing, I think you said?"

"Mr Green," said Roger, "this is a little difficult to say and please don't think I'm meaning to be offensive, but have you ever thought of pleading—that is—I mean—I hope you'll understand—putting up a defence of—of—insanity?"

"Cheer up," said Mr Green. "I always do this to begin with. Don't let it get you down. Helps me find out what sort of a chap you are. Now look. There's only one count against me. There's nothing in it at all. We're as good as out in the road already—only we're not. But don't you worry, we shall be. Now, d'you see what it says here?"

He showed Roger the indictment.

"Obtaining money by false pretences with intent to defraud. Well, it's ridiculous, that's what it is. It's laughable. It won't stick. They'll never wear it. Are you agreed upon your verdict? We are. Do you find the prisoner Arthur Green Guilty or Not

Guilty? Not Guilty. Not Guilty, and is that the verdict of you all? It is. And out we go. Shame I couldn't get bail or I wouldn't have been inside at all."

"Really," said Roger. "Time's getting on. You must tell me the facts. Have you a copy of the depositions?"

"That's a fair question. And here's a fair answer. Yes."

"Can I see them, please?"

"Don't you think they might put you off?"

"Mr Green, if you're not mad and want me to defend you, you must let me see the depositions."

"At last," said Mr Green. "Say it louder next time. I'm not sorry I chose you, but you're making me work. Don't you understand, young man, that at your game you've got to be able to shout down the other side, the judge, the jury and all? And what hope have you got if you can't shout me down? Eh? None at all. It's taken me ten minutes to get you annoyed even. Come on, get tough, let's see some rough stuff. Tear 'em to pieces."

"All right," said Roger. "P'raps you'd tell me what it's all about in as few words as possible, please."

"Apart from the 'please' that was all right. Good. I'll tell you. It's simple as pie. I'm charged with obtaining money by false pretences. How much money? Twenty pounds. A beggarly twenty pounds. How did I get it? By selling toffee. That's right, toffee. I get the money, they get the toffee. What's wrong with that?"

"Nothing as far as I can see—if they get enough toffee."

"That's quick of you. Enough toffee. Well, as a matter of fact, they didn't, but they're not charging me with that. Look—you see—all it says is 'by falsely pretending that a letter signed G. St Clair Smith was a genuine reference when in fact it was written by the accused himself'. That's all, positively all. It's laughable."

"Well—there is a Mr St Clair Smith then and he wrote it?"

"Be reasonable," said Mr Green. "Fair's fair and all that. But how would I get as far as this if there was a Mr Smith—St Clair or not?"

"Then there isn't anyone?"

"No idea. There may be for all I know," said Mr Green.

"Then who wrote the reference?"

"Who do you think?"

"Well," said Roger, "if you ask me to be frank, I think you did."

"Don't be bashful about it," said Mr Green. "Of course I did. Who else could have done—except Mr Smith, of course, and we're not sure about him, are we?"

"Well," said Roger, "if you wrote yourself a reference and pretended that it was written by Mr Smith, what's your defence?"

"They had the toffee, of course."

"But not enough?"

"They don't complain that it wasn't enough here. They just say about the reference."

"Yes, I see," said Roger. "But you had twenty pounds from them, didn't you?"

"Certainly."

"How much toffee did they get?"

"At least a quarter of what they ordered. More like a third."

"But you got the full price?"

"That's right."

"Well, I'm bound to say it sounds pretty fishy to me," said Roger.

"Of course it does. If it didn't sound fishy, I shouldn't be here, should I? I'll tell you something else. It was fishy. But that doesn't mean it was a crime. Oh, dear, no. It's a postal business I run. Cash with order, I say. Fair enough? And in my first letter I always offer a reference. What's more, I give them a reference whether they want it or not."

"You mean," said Roger, "you write yourself a reference under another name?"

"I mean," said Mr Green, "precisely that. But this chap, like most of them, has too sweet a tooth, that's his trouble. He wants his toffee. So he doesn't bother about a reference and just sends his money."

"Then I can't see why on earth you're charged if that's the only false pretence alleged. They've got to prove they relied on it and if they hadn't had it they couldn't have relied on it."

"Smart boy," said Mr Green. "You saw the point."

"Yes," said Roger. "But you did send a reference."

"You bet I did," said Mr Green. "I always do."

"And he must have had it before he sent the money," said Roger, "or the case wouldn't have gone on like this. You must let me see the depositions."

"All right," said Mr Green. "As you are so pressing," and he handed them to Roger, who read them for a few minutes.

"Well, it's quite plain from these that he had the reference first," said Roger. "I knew he must have done."

"Well, he didn't," said Mr Green. "The quickness of the hand deceives the eye. I can prove he didn't."

"How?"

"Elementary, my dear—I beg your pardon, sir. I shouldn't have done that. But it is too, too simple. Shall I explain?"

"Please do," said Roger.

"How d'you catch mice?" said Mr Green.

"Now really——" began Roger.

"With bait," went on Mr Green. "I send my little reference on the 24th but I actually date it the 20th. What happens? Complaints are made by the public about my toffee. Not enough of it. Stale, bad, rotten toffee, and so on. Now, for one reason or another I didn't want the police prying into my affairs, looking at my books (if any), and so on and so forth. So, after I've had the money, I send this nice little reference in pretty obviously disguised handwriting. Aha, say they, we've got him. Handwriting experts and all that. His handwriting. And the date? Just before the customer sent the money. We've got him, they say. The customer doesn't want much persuading that he had the reference before he sent the money, particularly when the police point out the date. 'You must have done,' they say. 'So I must,' says he. So they don't bother to look into my affairs except quite casually. A false reference is good enough for them. Saves them a lot of trouble. He's in the bag, they say. But, you see, he isn't. That's just where he isn't. Proof of posting isn't proof of delivery, eh? But it's proof of *non*-delivery. I get a receipt for my letter. And here it is. Shows I sent the letter after he sent the money. I tell you he had too sweet a tooth. They all have. Of course, when they come and see me and show me Mr St Clair Smith's letter I pretend I haven't seen it before, but I look nice and uncomfortable when I say it and what with the date on it, my other letter and the handwriting expert, they're happy as sandboys.

" 'Did you believe it to be a genuine reference, Mr Sweet Tooth?'

" 'I did.'

" 'If you had not believed it was a genuine reference, would you have sent the money?'

" 'I would not.'

" 'Thank you, Mr Sweet Tooth.' "

"Are you sure," said Roger, "that you only sent one letter to him at about that time?"

"Ah," said Mr Green. "I'm not so bad at choosing counsel after all. And you're not such a—now what am I saying? That's the one question you've got to ask. 'Did you have any letter from the defendant?' I prefer that to 'prisoner,' but I don't really mind if you forget—'did you have any letter from the defendant at about the time you received the reference?'' Well, he'll have to say 'no'— but that's the one point you've got to be careful of. Once you've held him down to that, we're home. Out comes the receipt for posting and I can go and lose all the money I haven't paid you at Ascot. Right?"

"I see the point," said Roger. "I must think about it."

Later that day when Roger returned to the Temple after completing his conference with Mr Green, he consulted Henry on the matter.

133

"You can never tell," said Henry. "If the chap admits that no other letters were sent to him at that time it looks like a winner. But don't you be too sure about getting that admission. And if you get the admission don't go on pressing him about it. That's a mistake beginners often make. They get the admission they need and they're so pleased about it they go on asking questions about it and before they know where they are, if the witness hasn't actually withdrawn the admission, he's what you might call blurred it, by adding words like, 'Well, I'm not not quite sure' or 'perhaps I'm wrong' and 'now I come to think of it there may have been another letter.' Economy in cross-examinations is very necessary."

"Thanks very much," said Roger. "Yes, I see. I am grateful. Now, another thing. It won't arise in this case because I haven't any witnesses except the prisoner. But I always thought counsel wasn't supposed to see witnesses and I saw one or two counsel with a lot of people round them. I didn't hear what they were saying, but I should have thought some of them probably were witnesses."

"Well," said Henry, "a good deal of latitude is allowed to counsel for the defence in criminal cases, but you're quite right in thinking that, generally speaking, counsel shouldn't talk to the witnesses except his own client or expert witnesses. But it's a matter for counsel's discretion, and in an exceptional case he certainly can. But don't you try to pretend to yourself that a case is exceptional when it isn't. We don't want you to get like old Ian McTavish, though I'm sure you won't."

"Who was he?"

"He was a lovable old man, whom everyone liked, but he was an old rascal. The story goes that his opponent in a fraud case at a County Court found the old boy in the consultation-room surrounded by witnesses, saying:

"'Now then, boys, all together. "We relied upon the representations".'"

CHAPTER TWENTY

DOCK BRIEF

ROGER had a difficult decision to make the day before the case of Mr Green came on for trial at the Old Bailey. Should he ask Sally, Joy and his mother, or alternatively one or more and which of them? He would dearly have liked his triumph—if it was to be one—witnessed, but on the other hand, suppose things went wrong and he made a fool of himself again? Eventually he decided to ask Sally her opinion.

"Roger," she said, "I should love to hear you, I really should. But d'you know, if I were you, I should wait until you've got more confidence. It's always possible the thought of one of us—never mind which—will distract or worry you. Then again—you might actually start to act for our benefit and that would be really bad. I'm doing myself out of a lot in saying this, because I'm sure my Mr Sharpe would let me go if I wanted to."

"*Your* Mr Sharpe?"

"Roger," said Sally, "you're not jealous?"

"Of course not," said Roger.

"No, I was afraid I must be mistaken."

"Surely you don't want me to be jealous?"

"Oh, Roger, you are young. Never mind. Forget it. Will you ask Joy to go to the Old Bailey?"

"Of course not," said Roger. "I nearly always take your advice. I've never known you wrong yet."

"Dear Roger, you're so sweet—and unformed."

"You think I'm an awful ass."

"I don't think anything of the sort. F. E. Smith was unformed once and all the others. You've lots of time. And d'you know—I think you've come on, even in the last six months."

"Do you really? You're not just trying to be nice?"

"Have you ever known me? No, I'd really like to come to the Old Bailey to see the difference. I'm sure it'll be considerable."

"Do come, Sally—I'd love you to be there."

"Don't tempt me, Roger. It isn't fair. You tell me all about it when it's over."

That evening Roger had an appointment to dine with Mr Merivale.

"My dear Roger," said Mr Merivale. "How very nice to see you. Very good of you to give me the time. You won't be able to go out in the evening much longer. Nose to the grindstone, my boy. But that's the Bar. Either too much work or too little. How are things going?"

"As a matter of fact," said Roger, "I've got a brief at the Old Bailey tomorrow."

"Dear me," said Mr Merivale. "For the prosecution or defence?"

"Defence."

"Pleading Guilty?"

"Oh, no. I hope to get him off."

"That's the way, my boy. Be a fighter. Ah, here's Joy. She'll have to give me a report on you. In case we have any big criminal cases."

"Oh, what's all this?" said Joy.

"I've got a case at the Old Bailey tomorrow."

"Oh, how lovely," said Joy.

"And you're going to report it for me," said Mr Merivale. "I shall send you both in my car."

"Oh, uncle—you are sweet," said Joy and gave him a kiss.

"It's most kind of you," said Roger, who did not see how he could possibly get out of it.

Roger did not tell his mother about the case. He decided to wait until it was over. It would be more effective and she'd be more likely to listen. On the day before the trial she was particularly difficult.

"Oh dear, oh dear," she kept on saying. "I'll forget my own name next."

Roger was quite used to this sort of thing, but he asked politely: "What is it, Mother darling?"

"If I knew, my pet, would I be asking? But there's something I've forgotten that I've got to do. And terrible things will happen if I don't do it."

"What terrible things?"

"My dear, darling Roger, how should I know until they happen? Then it'll be too late. Of course if I could think what it was I had to do, they wouldn't happen. Be an angel and think for me. You know I don't do it very well."

"I expect you've got to do something for Aunt Ethel."

"No, I think it's more important than Aunt Ethel."

"It must be serious then," said Roger. "I've got something important to do tomorrow too, but I'll tell you that later."

"Another examination, Roger darling? Surely not?"

"Now Mother, really! You know I'm qualified. You've seen me in Court."

"But you could still have examinations. Doctors do. The one who helped me with you said he wanted to be a gynæcologist. I was very flattered."

The next day Mr Merivale sent Joy in his car to fetch Roger and take them both to the Temple and thence to the Old Bailey.

"Oh, Roger, I'm so excited," said Joy. "Now you really are starting. I'm sure no one as young as you has ever had a case at the Old Bailey. Oh, Roger—I do love you—and you do love me, don't you, Roger? It's at times like these when I feel it so terribly."

She squeezed his hand. He squeezed hers.

"If I don't sound very affectionate, Joy, it's because I'm thinking about the case. A man may go to prison because of me—or be free because of me. It's a dreadful responsibility."

"I'm so proud of you, Roger," whispered Joy.

That morning Mr Sharpe sent for Sally.

"Sally," he said, "I wonder if you'd do me a small favour?"

"Of course," said Sally.

"There's a young man I know—or know of, I should say," he began.

"No, thank you," said Sally. "It's very kind of you all the same."

"Now, how on earth d'you know what I'm going to say? I know a lot of young men—a very large number. I go to a boys' club among other things."

"I hope none of them are where you're about to suggest I should go."

Sally had told Mr Sharpe some days previously about Roger's case.

"Well, sorry," said Mr Sharpe, "if it can't be *volens*, it'll have to be *nolens volens*. As your study of the law of contract will have told you, an employee is bound to obey all reasonable orders of his or her employer."

"Very good, sir," said Sally.

"You will proceed," said Mr Sharpe, "to the Old Bailey with all convenient haste. You will there make enquiry as to where a gentleman called Arthur Green is being tried and you will go to that Court, mentioning my name if necessary, in order to get you in—and bring me a complete report of the case. Go along now. You know you're dying to."

"But it won't be fair," said Sally. "I've stopped him taking Joy."

"Good thing too," said Mr Sharpe. "I never did like the sound of that girl. You know the motto. Anyway, you can't help yourself, you're under orders. Get the sack if you don't. Then who'll give you your articles?"

"What was that?" said Sally.

"I said it," said Mr Sharpe.

"Oh, oh——" said Sally about as excited as Roger had been when she told him he was going to be a great man. "Oh—oh—I could kiss you."

"I'm afraid," said Mr Sharpe, "that my wife would not approve of that even from a brunette. Pity. I should have liked the experience."

"You are good. Why are you so nice to me?" said Sally.

"I'm not particularly nice to you. I like people as a whole. As for you—I think you've got more brains for a girl of twenty-one than I've ever heard of. You'll end up President of the Law Society —unless you go and get married or something. And even then—

which reminds me—I believe I've just given you a job of work. Off with you. And a full report, mind you—not only the mistakes."

Before he went to Court Roger had a final word with Henry while Joy stayed in the car.

"It's quite definite, isn't it, that I only get one speech," Roger said, "and that's after I've called the prisoner?"

"Quite definite," said Henry, "and make it a good one."

Roger rejoined Joy and they drove to the Old Bailey, almost in silence, Roger becoming more and more nervous, like a runner before a race. They arrived at the Court and he took Joy through the main entrance. He decided to show her into Court before he robed. Ordinary spectators are supposed to go to the public gallery, but members of the legal profession can usually obtain admission for their friends to the body of the Court, unless the event is a very popular one. But the attendant at the entrance to the Court checks and sometimes stops the people who enter or try to do so.

"What do you want?" he asked politely but suspiciously of Roger.

"I'm Counsel," said Roger with as much assurance as he could manage.

"Oh," said the man, plainly taken aback. "I'm sorry, sir. I didn't——" He didn't finish the sentence.

Roger showed Joy in and then went up to the robing-room. When he came back to the Court it was twenty past ten. His case was first in the list. Nearly zero hour. As he came into the Court a police officer came up to him.

"Are you Mr Thursby by any chance?" he asked.

Roger said he was.

"Your client wants to see you at once, sir," he said.

He went hurriedly into the dock and down the stairs, wondering what it could be. Had he been more experienced he would not have been in the least surprised. Later he found out that old offenders, particularly those charged with fraud, often ask to see their counsel before and during the case and send them voluminous notes throughout the hearing. They are usually irrelevant and nearly always repetitive.

"Good morning," said Mr Green. "I hope you slept well."

"What is it?" said Roger. "There's only a few minutes before the case starts."

"Now, don't get fidgety," said Mr Green. "When you've done this as often as I have you'll be quite calm and steady. Look at me. My teeth aren't chattering, are they?"

"No."

"I'm not shaking like a leaf, am I?"

"No," said Roger, irritable with nervousness.

"Now would you not say that I was in very good shape?" asked Mr Green.

"What has this got to do with it?" said Roger. "I thought you wanted to see me about the case."

"Look," said Mr Green, "you're my counsel aren't you?"

"Yes."

"Well, I can ask my counsel questions, can't I?"

"Yes."

"Well, I'm asking one. Would you consider that I was in very good shape? It's important, you know. If you thought I wasn't, you might want an adjournment. It's I who've got to go in the witness box and lie like a trooper, not you."

"But you're not going to commit perjury?" said Roger, anxiously.

"Just a manner of speaking," said Mr Green. "I shall tell them much more truth than I gave them toffee. Now, how am I? Is my tie straight?"

"Really!" said Roger, and then said very seriously: "You will tell the truth, won't you?"

"What d'you take me for?" said Mr Green. "Anyone would think I was a crook. You'll hurt my feelings if you're not careful. And then where shall we be? Now, what about the tie? Does it cover the stud all right?"

"This is ridiculous," said Roger.

"Come, come, sir," said Mr Green. "I'm playing the leading part in this show. You may think you are till it comes to going to gaol. Then you'll cheerfully yield pride of place to me. True, isn't it? You wouldn't go to gaol instead of me, would you?"

"No," said Roger.

"Right, then, I'm the leading actor, and you don't send him on to the stage looking anyhow. He has a dresser, doesn't he? Couldn't afford one as well as you. So I thought you wouldn't mind giving me the once-over. Hair all right?"

"Quite," said Roger. That was easy. There was none.

"Trouser creases all right?"

"Very good."

"Pity I haven't got that gold tooth. I flogged it during my last stretch. Got some jam for it. D'you like jam?"

"I'm going back into Court," said Roger, "or I shan't be there when the judge comes in."

"Don't be cross," said Mr Green. "You'll never do any good if you're cross. Give me a nice smile. Come on. That's better. Now take it easy. It's going to be perfectly all right. Next time I see you it won't be here. Won't be at Ascot, I'm afraid. Can't get into the Royal Enclosure any more. Even Mr St Clair Smith couldn't get me in."

139

At that moment a warder came into the room.

"The judge is just going to sit, sir," he said.

"Good luck," said Mr Green. "Chin up, head high, no heel taps, all's fair in love and war, dark the dawn when day is nigh, faint heart never won—oh—he's gone." He turned to the warder:

"I almost threw that one back," he said, "but you should have seen the one that got away."

Roger only just had time to get into the Court before the knocks heralding the arrival of the judge. The judge took his seat, and Roger, having bowed low, sat down and looked across at the jury who were to try Mr Green. As he did so two ladies came into Court and were shown to the seats behind counsel. But for the sight which met his eyes Roger might have noticed them. They were Sally and her mother. They had met outside the Court.

"What on earth are you doing, Mother?" Sally had said.

"Well, I thought, as you weren't going, I would. Now I see that I might have done some more practising. Well, as I'm here I might as well stay. Which way do we go in? I promise not to sing."

The sight which had so shaken Roger was that of *his* mother sitting in the front row of the jury. At the last moment she had remembered what it was she had had to do. She sat cheerfully in the jury box looking interestedly at everything in the Court. Her eye travelled from the judge to the seats for counsel.

"That one looks a bit young," she said to herself as she looked along the line. "Quite like Roger really. Yes, very. I must tell him. Quite a striking likeness. Good gracious, it *is* Roger. Well, really, he might have told me. I wonder if he'll speak. Should I smile at him or won't he like it? Why shouldn't I? After all, I'm his mother."

She beamed at her son, and waved her hand slightly.

Roger went red in the face. He adored his mother and hated to hurt her feelings, but it was very difficult to smile. And, of course, he couldn't wave. He turned round to see if people had noticed his mother waving to him. On his right was Joy where he had put her. On his left were Sally and her mother. He only had a moment to consider whose double dealing—as it must have appeared—was the worse, his or Sally's. But bringing her mother was really too bad. But now what was he to do about his own mother? The jury were about to be sworn. When was he to tell the judge? And in what language? How awful to have to get up and say, "The lady's my mother," like Strephon in *Iolanthe.* "I suppose I'd better do it at once," he said to himself, and very unhappily rose and looked at the judge, who simply

140

shook his head at him and waved him to sit down. He did not feel he could speak to his next-door neighbour. It sounded too absurd. Being called by his Christian name at school was nothing. Oh, dear, this is a nice way to start. Will I ever recover? he thought. Now they were swearing the jury. He must do something. He got up again. The judge looked at him angrily. Even a layman should know that the swearing of the jury must not be interrupted. Applications could be made after they had been sworn. Here was a member of the Bar not only getting up when he ought to have waited, but getting up again after he'd been told to sit down. He really must be taught a lesson.

"Yes, what is it?" he snapped to Roger. "If you don't know the rules ask someone who does. I've told you to wait once."

Roger remained standing, waiting to speak.

"Will you please sit down," said the judge.

"My Lord, I want to mention——" began Roger.

"I've told you to wait," said the judge. All right, if the young man wanted it he should have it. He turned his body slightly towards counsel's seats.

"In this Court," he said, "where I have had the honour to preside for a good many years I have never yet seen counsel behave in this shocking manner. Justice could not be administered at all unless directions from the Bench were observed by the Bar. Until this moment, I have never known——"

Roger had had as much as he could stand and subsided, his face scarlet.

"Thank you," said the judge. "Thank you very much. I am very much obliged. Now perhaps the swearing of the jury can be continued."

Although the jury could in this particular case have all been sworn at once, it is the practice at the Old Bailey to swear them separately. In due course it became Mrs Thursby's turn. It must be right to object. His client had been told that he must object when the jurors came to the Book to be sworn. Now was the time. He had a good mind to leave his mother on the jury. But then he supposed he'd be disbarred. Fearless integrity, the Treasurer of his Inn had said. That was all very well for him. He'd never had his mother on the jury. Well, he must do it, but there's nothing fearless about it, he said to himself. I'm terrified. He got up again. The judge could not have believed it possible. He was a choleric man, equally capable of bestowing immense and undeserved praise in fantastically flattering terms and of—figuratively—spitting like two cats. This time the cats had it.

"I do not know your name," he began, thinking hard for the most offensive words he could find, "but that," he went on, "in view of your extraordinary behaviour I do not find altogether surprising. Will you now do me the personal favour of resuming your seat. Otherwise I shall be under the painful duty of reporting you to your Benchers before whom it cannot have been very long ago that you appeared to be called to the Bar."

As Roger still remained on his feet, waiting to speak, but not liking to interrupt the judge, from whom words poured steadily at him in a vitriolic stream, the judge said: "I order you to sit down."

Roger did as he was told and, from where he sat, said loudly and clearly—as though it were the last cry of a man about to be executed:

"I object to the next juror. She's my mother."

There was an immediate and thrilling silence. It was broken by Mr Green.

"I don't, my Lord. In fact I like the look of the lady."

"You be quiet," said the judge, and thought for several seconds. During the time he had had the honour to preside in that Court he had seldom had to think for so long before making a decision. Eventually he tapped his desk with a pencil and asked the clerk for Roger's name. Then he spoke:

"Mr Thursby," he began.

Roger did not know whether to get up or not. He'd been ordered to sit down. It would be contempt of Court to get up. Yet somehow when the judge was addressing him it seemed all wrong to remain seated. He did not know what to do until his next-door neighbour whispered:

"Get up. The old fool's going to apologize."

Roger took the advice and was relieved to find that he was not immediately ordered to sit down—indeed if the judge had told two warders to throw him to the ground he would not have been altogether surprised.

"Mr Thursby," repeated the judge in dulcet tones after Roger had risen, "I owe you a very humble apology, and I hope you will see fit to accept it. I am extremely sorry. By my haste I have placed you in a position which would have been horribly embarrassing for any member of the Bar and which for one of— if I may say so without offence—your limited experience must have been almost beyond bearing. You dealt with the situation with a courage and a patience which I shall long remember."

A lump came into Roger's throat, and it was all he could do to prevent himself from breaking down. He tried to say:

"Thank you, my Lord," but very little was heard of it and he sat down and looked at his knees. The judge then turned to Mrs Thursby.

"You had better leave the jury box, madam. I owe you an apology too, and I should like to say that you have every reason for being proud of your son."

To someone like Peter this would have been simply splendid. But it made Roger feel distinctly sick. And then he thought of all the people listening to him. Sally, Joy, Sally's mother and his own. Not to mention all the rest of those in Court. He felt as he had felt after boxing at school and being roundly trounced by a bigger boy, when the headmaster came up to him and said in a loud voice:

"Plucky boy."

It sent shivers down his back. He wondered if this sort of thing happened to everyone. They couldn't often have barristers' mothers on the jury at all, let alone in cases where their sons were engaged. Another juryman was sworn. The judge scribbled a note which the usher brought to Roger. It said:

So very sorry. I shall be so pleased if you will bring your mother to see me during the adjournment. S.K.

Roger did not know whether to answer it in writing or by bowing. He asked his neighbour.

"What do I do with this?"

"Just bow and grin."

He did as he was told. The judge smiled back at him. The jury had now been sworn and were informed of the charge against the prisoner. They were told he had pleaded Not Guilty and that it was for them to say whether he was Guilty or not.

Counsel for the prosecution opened the case quite shortly and called as his first witness the man who had bought the toffee. His name was Blake. He was duly asked about his purchase from Mr Green and about the false reference.

"Would you have sent the money if you had not believed this document to be a genuine reference?"

"No."

The moment arrived for Roger to cross-examine.

"You remember seeing the reference, I suppose?" he asked.

"Certainly."

"Did you have any other letters about the same time?"

"Letters? Yes, of course."

"From the defendant, I mean?"

"From the defendant? Only the one offering me the toffee."

"How long was that before you received the reference?"

"Two or three weeks."

"Quite sure?"

"Yes, I think so."

143

That's what Henry meant, thought Roger. I shouldn't have asked that last question.

"Two to three weeks?" repeated Roger.

"Yes," said Mr Blake.

This time Roger left it alone.

"Now, Mr Blake, you say you received the reference before you sent the money. Are you quite sure of that?"

"Certainly. Look at the date. The 20th. I sent the money on the 23rd. I must have received the reference on the 21st."

"Got the envelope by any chance?"

"I don't keep envelopes."

"So you're relying on your memory entirely?"

"Certainly not entirely. On the date on the reference as well."

"So that if it hadn't had that date on it you wouldn't have known whether you sent the money before or after you received the reference?"

"I certainly would have. I sent it after I had the reference—what's the point of being offered a reference if you don't wait for it?"

"Does this in any way shake your recollection?" asked Roger holding up the receipt for posting to be handed to the witness. Mr Blake looked at it.

"Well?" he said.

"Does that shake your recollection at all?" asked Roger.

"Not in the least," said the witness. "It's just a receipt for posting a letter."

"To you."

"What of it?"

"It was given to the prisoner."

"How do I know?"

"What is this document?" asked the judge. "Let me look at it."

It was handed to the judge who looked at it closely. "This is dated the 24th," he said. "It shows that a letter was posted to you on that date by someone."

"Yes, my Lord," said the witness.

"Well," said the judge, "it apparently came into the possession of the prisoner and if it was issued to him by the post office it shows that he posted a letter to you on the 24th."

"Yes, my Lord," said Mr Blake.

"Well—you've said that he only sent you one letter and that was two or three weeks before you received the reference."

"Possibly I was wrong, my Lord."

"Possibly anything," said the judge, "but what counsel very properly puts to you is this. If that receipt was issued to the prisoner are you still prepared to swear positively that you received the reference before you sent the money?"

"I must have, my Lord."

"Then how is this receipt to be accounted for?"

"I can't tell you that, my Lord, unless I had another letter rom the prisoner. I suppose I might have."

"But you can't remember one?"

"I can't say that I do, my Lord. Possibly, my Lord, the prisoner got it from someone else."

"Whom do you suggest?"

"I have no idea, my Lord. All I know is that I was offered a reference and, if I'm offered a reference, I'm sure I wouldn't send the money without getting it first. I know something about this mail order business."

"You mean you've been cheated before?" said Roger all too quickly.

"Steady," said Mr Green.

"Be quiet and behave yourself," said the judge. "Your case is being conducted admirably. It is a model of what such a cross-examination should be. Perhaps, Mr Thursby," he added, "that last question could be rephrased."

"Have you in the past been cheated?"

"I have."

"Toffee?" asked Roger with a flash of inspiration.

"Yes, as a matter of fact," said the witness.

"You've a sweet tooth?" asked Roger.

"Well, I have as a matter of fact."

"You like toffee, apparently?"

"I don't see why I should be ashamed of it," said Mr Blake.

"No one's suggesting you should be," said the judge. "Counsel only wishes to establish the fact that you are fond of toffee."

"Well, I am," said Mr Blake, "and I don't mind admitting it."

"P'raps you decided not to bother about a reference on this occasion and chanced sending the money?"

The witness did not answer.

"Well," said the judge, "what do you say to that?"

"I suppose it's possible," said Mr Blake, "but I don't think so."

"It could have happened?" said the judge.

"I suppose so," said Mr Blake reluctantly.

Eventually the case for the prosecution closed.

"Yes, Mr Thursby," said the judge pleasantly. "Are you going to open your case to the jury?"

What is this? thought Roger. He's inviting me to make two speeches. But I can't do that, surely. Henry said I couldn't, and

I'm sure that's what it said in the book. But here he is inviting me to do so. It'll look rude if I don't accept his offer. He's being so nice to me. I mustn't offend him. P'raps it's a sort of consolation prize. Oh—well, here goes.

"If your Lordship pleases," said Roger. "May it please your Lordship, members of the jury, the evidence for the prosecution has been completed and it now becomes my duty to open the defence."

How professional it sounded, thought Roger, as he said it. At that moment the judge suddenly realized that he might have misled Roger.

"Forgive me, Mr Thursby," he said, "but I assume that you are calling evidence in addition to the prisoner?"

"Oh, no, my Lord."

"Well then," said the judge, "you can't have two speeches, you know. You address the jury afterwards."

Well, I knew that, thought Roger. What's he want to make a ruddy fool of me for? Everybody will think I don't know a thing. Well, they're quite right but I don't want it advertised every moment. All right, here goes again.

"If your Lordship pleases. Mr Green, will you go into the witness box, please?"

"Certainly," said Mr Green. "With pleasure," and he came out of the dock, and went into the box to be sworn. Roger asked him the necessary questions about himself and then asked:

"Who wrote the reference which was sent to Mr Blake?"

"I did."

"When did you send it?"

"On the 24th February."

"Do you identify the receipt for posting?"

"I do."

"Did you write any other letter to Mr Blake except this reference and the original letter which he has produced?"

"I did not."

"Did you obtain that receipt for posting from someone else or is it in respect of the reference?"

"It's in respect of the reference."

"Thank you," said Roger and sat down. Counsel for the prosecution then cross-examined.

"Let me follow this," he said. "Do I rightly understand your evidence to be this? You offered to supply toffee to Mr Blake, and offered to send him a reference. He does not wait for the reference but sends the money. After you have received the money you send him a reference which you have written out yourself in a false name. Is that your story?"

146

"That," said Mr Green, "is not only my story but it happens to be true. I hope you don't mind."

"Don't be impertinent," said the judge.

"I'm very sorry, my Lord," said Mr Green. "I don't intend to be impertinent but I have a little way of talking sometimes which makes people think that I do. Perhaps I'd better apologize in advance for any false impressions I may——"

"Be quiet," said the judge, "you're not doing yourself any good by making these silly speeches. Behave yourself and answer the questions."

"Well, then," said counsel, "will you be good enough to tell my Lord and the jury why you thought it necessary after you'd received the money to send the reference?"

"For good measure," said Mr Green. "After all," he went on, "I'd offered a reference. Why shouldn't he have one? I thought it might make him happier."

"Really," said counsel, "I completely fail to understand you."

"Ah," said Mr Green, "there are more things in heaven and earth, Horatio, than are dreamt of——"

"Now, look," interrupted the judge, "I shan't warn you again. If I have any more nonsense from you I shall stand this case over to next session."

"I hope your Lordship won't do that," said Mr Green. "I may get another judge and I like being tried by your Lordship. There's nothing like a fair trial, I say."

"Well, behave yourself," said the judge, not altogether displeased.

"Makes you feel good, even if you aren't," went on Mr Green. "I'm so sorry, my Lord," he added quickly.

"Mr Thursby," said the judge, "I must really ask you to control your client. I shan't warn him again."

"If your Lordship pleases," said Roger, not knowing how on earth he was to comply with the direction.

Fortunately Mr Green was a little less irrepressible for the rest of his evidence.

"Now," said prosecuting counsel, "is this the language you used about yourself in this admittedly false reference? 'I have known Mr Arthur Green for many many years'."

"Quite true," said Mr Green. "I had."

"Wait," said counsel. "Does it go on like this? 'And during that period I can say that I have given him credit for thousands of pounds.' Was that true?"

"Well, I've trusted him all my life," said Mr Green, "and he's never let me down."

"Has he ever been worth thousands of pounds?"

147

"He's worth more than that to me," said Mr Green.

"Did the reference go on like this?" asked counsel. " 'In my view he is in a very substantial way of business and can be trusted for any amount. Knowing him as I do I cannot well say less.' Were you in a very substantial way of business?"

"Well, it's a comparative term. I was getting a lot of orders."

"By sending false references?"

"Oh, dear, no—I always sent the references afterwards. I told you already."

"I cannot see the object."

"I'm sorry," said Mr Green. "I've done my best to explain and got into trouble with his Lordship in trying to do so."

"Do you say this was an honest transaction?"

"Certainly. I got the money and he got the toffee."

"Not all he ordered."

"There's nothing about that in the indictment," said Mr Green.

"Never mind about the indictment," said counsel.

"But I do. That's what I'm being tried on, isn't it? It says I obtained goods by giving a false reference. Well, I didn't. Isn't that the end of the case?"

"Don't ask me questions," said counsel, "and kindly answer mine. Did not Mr Blake get less toffee than he paid for?"

"That's possible," said Mr Green. "I had a very bad man doing the packing at that time. He made away with a lot of toffee. Must have had a sweet tooth too. So it's quite possible Mr Blake got too little. But that wasn't my fault. I can't stand over the man who's doing the packing all the time, can I? I've got other work to do. And I'd no reason to distrust him at the time."

"Who was this man?"

"Well, the name he gave to me was Brown—without an 'e'— but, of course, it might have been an alias."

"Did you get a reference with him?"

"I don't much care for references," said Mr Green. "You see ——" he added and waved his hand expressively.

"Are you sure there ever was a Mr Brown?"

"Of course," said Mr Green. "I can describe him if you like. Aged about thirty-five, middling height, brown hair, turned his toes in as he walked, small moustache—though, of course, he might have shaved it off now. Fond of toffee," he added.

Prosecuting counsel paused.

"Yes, Mr Thackeray?" said the judge. "Any more questions?"

"I suggest," said counsel, "that you sent the reference before you received the money."

For answer Mr Green just waved the receipt.

"Will you answer my question?" asked counsel angrily.

148

"Well, Mr Thackeray," said the judge, "it is a pretty good answer, isn't it? Can you really do much more with this case? After all, it is for you to prove your case with reasonable certainty. No one likes false references—I don't suppose the jury do any more than you—but you've got to prove it was received before your client sent the money."

"There is the evidence of Mr Blake," said counsel.

"I know," said the judge, "but how far can that take you in a criminal trial? He was by no means certain about it—and here is the receipt. That is a genuine document, anyway. What the truth of this transaction is, I don't pretend to know, but the prisoner's quite right when he says he's being tried on this indictment which simply alleges one false pretence. I can't, of course, say there's no evidence—but it may be that the jury will say they have heard enough already."

"My Lord, the question of attempting to obtain by false pretences could arise."

"Surely not," said the judge. "How can he attempt to obtain money which he has already received?"

The judge turned towards the jury.

"Members of the jury," he said, "once the case for the prosecution is closed it is open for you at any stage to say you've heard enough and that you're not satisfied that the prisoner's guilt has been proved. You may think his methods of carrying on business are pretty odd—you may think that a little more investigation might have been made by the police into those methods—and such investigations can still be made. But there is only one charge against the prisoner and that has to be proved to your satisfaction. Perhaps you'd like to have a word with each other."

The jury did as they were told and three minutes later they stopped the case and returned a verdict of Not Guilty.

"Thank you," said Mr Green when the judge discharged him. "May I say something, my Lord?" he asked.

"Well, what is it?" asked the judge.

"I should like to thank you for a very fair trial, my Lord."

The judge said nothing, but he did not in the least object.

"Would I be out of order," went on Mr Green, "in inviting everyone to some mild form of celebration?"

"Be quiet," snapped the judge. "I've a good mind to send you to prison for contempt of Court."

"Oh, that's different," said Mr Green. "I'd better go."

And he left the dock. He went straight to Roger, shook hands with him and whispered:

"What did I tell you? Can you sing now?"

Roger said nothing.

"Would you like my card?" said Mr Green. "In case I can be of any help to you in the future?"

"Good-bye," said Roger.

"Good-bye," said Mr Green, and started to go. Then he came back.

"Oh, if at any time you should want any toffee——" he said, and went again.

CHAPTER TWENTY-ONE

A JEWEL OF A HUSBAND

THE judge rose for lunch immediately afterwards and Roger, as he had been bidden, took his mother to see him in his room.

"What do I call him?" she asked. "I've never met a judge before. I don't want to do the wrong thing. I'd hate to disgrace you."

"You call him 'Sir Stuart,'" said Roger. "I call him 'Judge,' I think."

They went to the judge's room.

"I would like to congratulate you again," he said to Roger's mother, "on the very brilliant beginning your son has made. He will go a very long way and you should be very proud of him."

"Thank you very much," she said. "I'm so glad he was able to be of some use."

"Mother's never been to the Old Bailey before," said Roger quickly.

"No," said Mrs Thursby. "I found it most interesting, and the flowers and herbs and things give it such a friendly, cosy air. Even the prisoner can't mind too much in such a charming atmosphere. It's more like a garden party really."

"I'm not sure," said the judge, "that our invitations are always as welcome."

"As a matter of fact," said Mrs Thursby. "I nearly mislaid mine and it was only by chance that I got here at all. Would you have been very angry if I hadn't come?"

"I'm afraid my mother doesn't quite appreciate the seriousness of a jury summons, Judge," said Roger hurriedly. "I'll make sure she knows next time. If I'd known this time, it wouldn't have happened. It was a dreadful shock for me when I saw her in the jury box."

"Well, all's well that ends well," said the judge. "Is this your first visit to the Old Bailey?" he added

"I've been coming here with Grimes for several days. I'm his pupil, Judge," said Roger.

"Indeed?" said the judge. "A remarkably fine piece of cross-examination for a pupil. Quite the best I've heard."

"Thank you very much indeed," said Roger, "and thank you, too, for being so nice to me."

"I'm not sure about that," said the judge, "but I'll try to make up for what happened earlier if you'll come and see me at the end of the day. I'll send these flowers to your mother." He indicated the bouquet which went into Court with him. "That is, if she'd do me the honour of accepting them."

"Oh, Sir Stuart, that is most kind," said Mrs Thursby. "I shall be thrilled. I've never had flowers from a judge before. Oh, yes, I did once now I come to think of it. My husband knew one of the judges who gave licences and things to public houses. He sent me some carnations. I suppose you do that too."

"Licensing justices," said the judge, not entirely pleased at the comparison. "No, that is rather different. Well, I'm very glad to have met you and once again I congratulate you upon your son," and he got up to indicate that the interview was at an end.

None too soon, thought Roger. I wonder what else mother might have said. He took her out to lunch, then she went home and he returned to Court.

The first case he heard after lunch was a plea of Guilty by a woman who had run away from her husband and married some-one else. She was charged with bigamy and obtaining credit by fraud from a boarding house where they'd spent their bigamous honeymoon. The judge sent the man to prison and then pro-ceeded to deal with the woman. He was informed that her husband was prepared to take her back again.

"You're a very wicked woman," he said to the weeping prisoner. "You have a jewel of a husband——" he stopped in the middle. "Let him come forward," he added.

A moment later the prisoner's husband went into the witness box.

"A jewel of a husband," repeated the judge. "Now, Mr Grant," he said, looking in the most friendly manner at the husband, "I understand you're prepared to take your wife back in spite of everything. Magnificent. That is so, isn't it?"

"My heart's full," said the man.

"Quite so," said the judge. "He very properly says that his heart is full. Most proper. A jewel of a husband. But you are pre-pared to take her back?"

"My heart's full," repeated the husband.

"Quite so," said the judge still beaming at him. "We all understand that. Very natural. But you are prepared to take her back?"

The man did not answer for a moment.

The judge's brow started to cloud ever so slightly.

"You are prepared to take her back?" he repeated.

"My heart's——" began the man.

"Yes, yes, I know. Very proper. But you are prepared to take her back?"

"Full," said the man.

"Mr Grant," said the judge in less kindly tones. "Would you be good enough to answer my question?"

"Very difficult, my Lord," said the man. "My heart's full."

"Look here," said the judge, his patience rapidly becoming exhausted, "are you prepared to take her back or not?"

"If you say so, my Lord," said the man.

"It's not for me to say one way or the other. She's your wife and it's for you to make up your mind. If you don't take her back I shall probably send her to prison."

"How long for?" said the man.

"Don't ask me questions," said the judge.

The man remained silent.

"Well, which is it to be?" said the judge. "We can't wait all night for you."

Still no answer.

"Well?" the judge almost shouted.

Roger reflected that the case had now progressed some way from the "jewel of a husband" stage.

"I don't think six months would do her any harm," said the man, "and it would give me time to think."

"Now look," said the judge, "when you married this woman you took her for better or worse."

"It seems to have been worse," said the man.

"Will you be quiet while I'm speaking," said the judge angrily. "Have you never heard of charity?"

"Charity," said the man, "begins at home. She left home."

"I'm not going to argue with you," said the judge. "If you lack all decent feeling, I can't give it to you, but, if you don't forgive her, it may be on your conscience for the rest of your life."

"What about her conscience?" said the man. "How would you like your wife to go running off with the lodger?"

"Take that man away," said the judge, and the husband left the witness box.

"Now, Margaret Grant, I'm not going to send you to prison. Dry your eyes and listen. You've behaved very stupidly—yes—and wickedly, but the exact circumstances of your married life are known only to you, and the man who was just standing in the witness box."

The woman opened her mouth as though to speak.

"Yes, what is it?" asked the judge. "You want to say something?"

"Only this, my Lord," faltered the woman.

"Yes?" said the judge in a kind, encouraging tone.

"He's a jewel of a husband, my Lord."

I'm glad I stayed, thought Roger.

CHAPTER TWENTY-TWO

OFFER OF A BRIEF

ROGER left the Old Bailey feeling happier than at any time since he was called to the Bar. He had defended his first prisoner and he had got him off. The judge had praised him and congratulated him on his cross-examination. It was almost unbelievable. Mr Green no doubt had friends and perhaps he would send them to him. He could almost hear people saying already: "He must have a chance, Thursby's defending him."

He went back to chambers very elated, and at once went to Henry.

"Well, how did you get on?"

"I got him off."

"Well done you. Jolly good. Tell me all about it."

Roger told him everything.

"One thing perhaps," said Henry, "I ought to warn you about."

"Oh?"

"Compliments from the Bench. You'll get them, you know, and you'll feel hugely pleased and think you've made your name and all that. For example, if you go to the Old Bailey again you will hear the old boy say: 'Members of the jury, you have just heard what in my opinion is a model of a speech from counsel for the prisoner. Since I have had the honour to preside at this Court——' and so on and so forth. I'm sorry to have to tell you, old boy," went on Henry, "that it don't mean a thing. Indeed, when that stops happening from that particular quarter it means that you really have made a little headway."

"Oh," said Roger, a little disappointed. "Then wasn't my cross-examination any good then?"

"I didn't hear it, but from what you tell me I should say it was very good. All I'm warning you about is not to be too elated when a judge plasters you with good things. There *are* compliments from the Bench which are greatly to be valued. But they are rare—and at your present stage you don't know which is which. You don't mind my telling you all this?"

"Of course not."

"I'm only doing it because no one told me. And it was the most frightful disappointment to me after His Honour Judge Smoothe had lauded me to the skies—and incidentally decided against me—to find that clients weren't queueing up to brief me. Later on, if you look around any Court presided over by a judge who indulges in fulsome praise of counsel, you'll see looks being exchanged between experienced counsel and solicitors. The best judges and those whose praise is worth having don't do it. But cheer up. You got him off and that's the chief thing. Now I suppose you're going to celebrate with Sally. Or could I hope that it's Joy?"

"Quite frankly, I hadn't thought," said Roger. "Oh—hell," he added. "I'm in for a spot of trouble there. But I won't worry you with it."

"Look," said Henry, "perhaps I shouldn't ask this, but would you very much mind if I did ask Sally to come out some time? I'll understand perfectly if you object."

"Of course not," said Roger. "I think it jolly decent of you to want to."

"I'm not sure that that's what I'd call it," said Henry, "but I'll try to behave."

When Roger got home that evening he at once telephoned Sally. What had she thought of him? He was dying to know.

"Hello, Sally," he said.

"Hello, Roger," she said somewhat coldly.

He couldn't help that. He must know what she thought.

"Sally, what did you think? I'm longing to know. Was I any better?"

"As a liar, d'you mean?" said Sally. "Yes, I think you've made quite remarkable progress in a very short time."

"Oh, Sally—you must let me explain. You mean about Joy being there?"

"And you're so quick too."

"Sally—you must let me explain. I'd no idea when I spoke to you that Joy was coming. Really I hadn't."

"She just happened to come, I suppose? What with your mother being on the jury, the day was pretty full of coincidences for you."

"Oh, Sally, please listen. I had to take her."

"Oh, it wasn't a coincidence? You just changed your mind about taking her, was that it? Well, I suppose everyone's entitled to change his mind."

"Which reminds me," said Roger. "What were you doing there? It was you who advised me not to have anyone there. And you not only come but you bring your mother too. The whole blooming outfit."

"Don't you call my mother an outfit," said Sally.

"Look," said Roger, "can't we meet and get things straight?"

So they met and everything was explained as far as it could be.

"It looks as though Joy's uncle is going to be pretty useful to you," said Sally.

"It does, doesn't it?" said Roger brightly.

"And what other Herculean tasks d'you imagine he'll impose on you in return. Marrying Joy, d'you think?"

"Oh, don't, Sally. It isn't fair. I wouldn't be human if I didn't want to get on."

"There are ways and ways of getting on. If you're in love with Joy, all right, splendid. Another excellent coincidence. Go ahead, marry her and let her uncle keep you."

"You're being beastly."

"Plain, if you like," said Sally. "If, on the other hand, you're not in love with Joy—well—what was the word you used—beastly, wasn't it? Oh, Roger dear, can't you get on without making up to Joy in order to get work out of her uncle?"

"It sounds awful putting it that way."

"Well, how would you put it—if you're not in love with her? And if you go on doing it long enough you'll find you have to marry the girl."

"I'm much too young to marry, anyway," said Roger, "and I haven't any money."

"That's what I mean. If Joy's uncle provides the income—you can't very decently marry someone else on it—when you do marry."

"I can't very well refuse the briefs."

"If you stop taking Joy out, they'll stop too."

Roger thought for a moment.

"You are right, Sally," he said. "At least I suppose so. You'd say it was rather like those men who—well, you know what I mean."

"Oh, I wouldn't put it quite like that," said Sally. "But it does seem a bit mean."

"All right," said Roger, "I'll stop. I'll tell Joy straight out that I'll never marry her. Then if her uncle still keeps on sending me briefs, that's his affair, isn't it? After all, the time may come when he briefs me for my own sake."

"We'll drink to that," said Sally.

And they did.

"Roger," said his mother that evening.

"Yes, darling?"

"How long d'you think it'll be before you're earning real money? I mean, flowers are all very nice, but they don't pay the bills."

"Oh, Mother—I'm afraid it may be an awful long time. I hope not, but it is a slow job, I'm afraid, unless one's awfully lucky."

"What d'you mean by slow?" said Mrs Thursby. "You wouldn't be likely to have two hundred pounds to spare next Thursday?"

"Mother—what do you mean?"

"Oh, well—never mind," said Mrs Thursby. "It doesn't matter."

"Why, Mother darling, what is it?"

"I did rather a stupid thing, I'm afraid. I lent Elsie some money —to pay her bootmakers I thought she said. It seemed an awful lot for shoes, but still she's always so well turned out I thought she couldn't have paid them for some years. But it was her Scots accent. It was really her bookmakers. And now she's lost some more and can't pay me back when she promised. Oh, well—it only means the gas and telephone may be a bit cut off."

"The telephone!" said Roger in horror.

"Well, we didn't always have them."

"But I might have something frightfully urgent. Alec might want to get hold of me."

"Oh, well, never mind. P'raps they'll forget to cut ours off. They must have a lot of others to deal with. Then if they do, we can always get an electric cooker. I've sometimes wondered whether I wouldn't prefer one."

"But the telephone, Mother. We must find the money for that. How much do you owe altogether?"

"I never had much head for figures, but if Elsie had sent that two hundred pounds back it would be quite all right."

"You didn't lend her two hundred pounds, Mother?"

"Well, she seemed to want it so badly. And I'd just had my quarterly cheque. It was to come back in a month. And d'you know she said she'd add another fifty pounds. That was very nice of her, I thought. I'm sure she meant to. I'd trust her anywhere, if you know what I mean."

"Backing horses is just lunacy," said Roger.

"Not according to Elsie. She said it was only a temporary setback. She said she made a large profit every year."

"So does everyone," said Roger. "That's why bookmakers smoke fat cigars. Oh, well—I suppose we'll manage somehow or other. But it is a bit of a blow."

The telephone rang.

"Hullo, oh, hullo, Joy—yes—what—can't you say it on the

156

telephone? It can't be as secret as all that. Oh, all right. I'll be along." He turned to his mother.

"Joy's got something she must tell me. I suppose I shall have to go. Shan't be long."

Roger decided to take advantage of the occasion and break the news to Joy as he'd agreed with Sally. Just as well to get it over. He went straight to her rooms. She was waiting on the doorstep.

"Oh, Roger, I thought you were never coming. Oh, Roger darling, I thought you were wonderful, getting that funny little man off and the judge apologizing to you and everything."

"It wasn't too bad," said Roger modestly. "But one mustn't let things like that go to one's head. Henry said it didn't really mean a thing."

"Well," said Joy, "see if this means a thing."

"What is it?"

"It's so terrific you won't believe it. Oh, I am a lucky girl. You know the big sausage people—Baggallys?"

"Yes, of course."

"Well, apparently somebody's been copying their sausages or something and they're bringing a huge action. I believe it's called a patent action." She pronounced it like patent in patent shoes.

"Patent," corrected Roger. He wouldn't have known it had a short "a" if Henry hadn't told him.

"Well?" said Roger puzzled.

"Well, Uncle Alfred is their solicitor, and he's going to send a brief in it to you."

"Me?" said Roger. "But it's ridiculous. I don't know anything about patents. Even if I did I couldn't do a case of that size."

"You won't be all by yourself," said Joy. "There are three other counsel in it besides you. There's, let me see, Sir George Pratt—Uncle Alfred says he's the chief man on the subject—and then there are two others and then there's you. So you'll get some help, you see. Oh, and Uncle Alfred's coming round to explain it to you himself. That's why you had to come at once. He'll be here in a moment."

No doubt Roger ought to have acted at once on what might be called the Sally plan. But he could hardly be blamed for just waiting to see what Uncle Alfred said first. Anyway, there wasn't enough time to say to Joy what he had intended to say. He'd have to wrap it up a bit. And that takes time. And then Uncle Alfred arrived.

"My dear Roger, you must forgive this informality—but I hope that, now that I might say you're almost one of the family you will forgive me. Now, my dear boy," he went on without giving Roger a chance to interrupt, "I want your help, your personal help. And I want to have a word with you before taking official action. I don't know whether Joy has told you that we've quite an important action for Baggallys. Now—I don't want you to think I'm not satisfied with the counsel we've so far briefed in the case. I am indeed. But I can't help feeling that in a case of this kind an outside view from one of the younger generation would be a help. We've all eaten sausages for so long that we may have got into a rut with our ideas. So, to cut a long story short, I want you—as a personal favour to me—to accept a junior brief in the matter. I must apologize for not mentioning it to you at an earlier stage, but, to be quite candid, it was Mr Smith's idea and he only had it quite recently."

"Well, it's most awfully kind of you, Mr Merivale."

"And there is one other matter. And I hope you'll forgive my mentioning that to you personally too. I know that counsel and solicitors don't discuss fees together. As far as you and I are concerned it's done for nothing. It's the clerk who deals with the fees. But this is rather an embarrassing situation and that's why I'd be grateful for your help. You see, my firm's an old-fashioned one. We haven't moved forward like some of the others. Now, of course you're aware, my dear boy, of the two-thirds rule. Well, my firm have always stuck to that, even when the Bar Council agreed with the Law Society that we needn't. So that, for example, Sir George has got three thousand guineas on his brief. Wincaster two thousand and Soames one thousand three hundred and thirty-three. Now quite frankly, my dear boy, we can't run to more than, say, four hundred for your brief. Not that you wouldn't be worth more, but we couldn't run to it. Now when Mr Smith approaches your clerk on the matter, your clerk who's used to our old-fashioned ways will expect two-thirds of one thousand three hundred and thirty-three, and it would be most embarrassing for Mr Smith. So what I want to know, my dear boy, is whether you will very kindly have a word with your clerk in advance and ask him to accept four hundred on the brief—that's, of course, if you're willing yourself—and only if you're willing—I realize that it's rather a lot to ask, but I thought as a personal favour to me you might possibly be prepared to consider it. Of course, there'll be refreshers—about a hundred a day I should think—and I suppose the case ought to last about six weeks. So your total fees in the matter ought to be between three and four thousand pounds. That's, of course, in the Court below. It's bound to go to the Court of Appeal and probably to the House of Lords. Now, my boy, will you do it? I'm not pressing you at all—but it would be a kindness."

Roger looked out of the window.

"It's terribly good of you," he said. "May I think it over?"

"I beg your pardon?" said Mr Merivale. "My hearing isn't quite as good as it was. I didn't quite catch what you said."

"May I think it over?" repeated Roger.

Mr Merivale put his hand through his hair several times. "I only do this, young man," he said, "when I am surprised to the point of being astounded."

"I want to ask advice," said Roger.

"Advice?" said Mr Merivale. "Advice is it? Well, my advice to you, young man, is that you should consult the nearest brain specialist. And another piece of advice is this: if you don't seize all the opportunities you're given at the Bar you won't get very far. I don't believe that there is any young man at the Bar who would have said what you did. Admittedly you have a very fine practice. But there must be days when you don't receive a brief marked four hundred guineas. Of course, the one thousand guinea briefs help to make up for it, but if what I'm told is true, there aren't as many of those as there used to be. And dock briefs— or should I say one dock brief at the Old Bailey—hardly seems to take their place. But no doubt you know best. May I take it then that you're too busy to accept the instructions? Or is that you would consider it undignified to accept less than two-thirds of Mr Soames' fee?"

Roger looked out of the window again and then blood suddenly rushed to his head. He had had the experience before and he had it again several times later in his career. When blood rushes like that to a man's head he may win a V.C., commit suicide, marry the girl or say something he will regret or be proud of for the rest of his life. Roger did not know whether he would be proud or sorry, but he knew he must say it. When blood rushes like that to the head there is indeed no option. The thing has to be done or said. There is one course and one course only which has to be taken, whatever the cost. Through the window Roger could see a prostitute leaning against some railings.

"Yes, Mr Merivale," he said. "Undignified. That's the word."

CHAPTER TWENTY-THREE

HENRY'S CASE

THREE months later Henry was dining with Sally.

"You're the nicest man I know," she said.

"You know what I think of you," he said, "and that by itself shows I'm not. I knew what would happen if I took you out to dinner. When you first briefed me in order to be near Roger I knew that, unless I took a very firm hold of myself, I should fall in love with you. So far from taking hold of myself I asked Roger if he'd mind. And here we are."

"Yes," said Sally, "here we are. And there's nothing to be done about it."

"P'raps it's as well," said Henry. "I shouldn't think very much of myself if you cared for me. As it is, it's all right. The only person who's in trouble is me. I must admit I rather like it."

"I'm in trouble too," said Sally.

"Ah, but you were before I met you. So I've no responsibility for that."

"How is he doing? You think he'll get on, don't you?"

"I'm quite sure he will. He works like a black and he never believes anything anyone says to him until he's seen it's right. He's a certainty. How long it'll take before he really gets going, I don't know. But once it starts it'll come with a rush. And you'll see he'll develop. He's got all the right instincts. A certain degree of priggishness may be an advantage to begin with at the Bar."

"Tell me another thing—you needn't if you don't want to. Have I a chance?"

"You tell me and I'll tell you," said Henry.

"Don't be flippant, please."

"I was not being flippant, I assure you. It's much worse at thirty-three than it is at twenty-one. I know. I've had both. You only know what it's like at twenty-one."

"It's terrible, Henry. Do please tell me. I'd believe almost anything you tell me. But I shan't believe you if you say "no." Since he gave up Joy I thought something might have happened. But it hasn't."

"Poor Joy," said Henry. "She overdid it."

"That isn't an answer, Henry. Or is it intended to be the kindest way? You are kind, Henry. I'd trust you anywhere. Who'd think of asking an interested party like you?"

"It is a compliment, I agree. No, I've often tried to think what's the answer to your question. And the only one I can give is 'yes.' "

"D'you mean it, Henry?"

"Of course I do. But you mustn't be too optimistic; he's much too wrapped up in his work. He thinks of very little else. He hasn't had a brief since he broke with Joy, but he might have a large practice if one judged from the amount of work he does. He's still terribly young, but he's developing. And, of course, he'll fall in love. And it could be with you. He'll be a blithering idiot, if he doesn't."

'Sweating it out' at the Old Bailey in the hope of getting a dock brief,
Roger is unexpectedly chosen by the loquacious Mr Green.

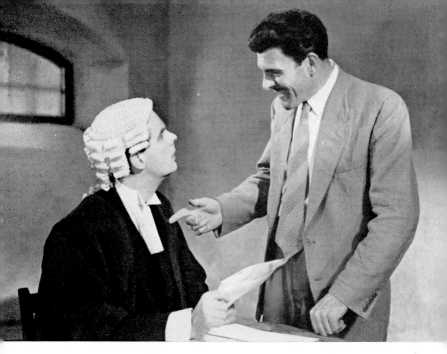

"Cheer up," said Mr Green. "We're as good as out in the road already—only we're not. But don't you worry, we shall be."

"Dear Henry—how lovely to be with you. You're the nicest man I know."

"No chance of promotion?" said Henry.

Sally shook her head. "I doubt it," she said.

"Oh, well," said Henry. "No case is ever lost till judgment is given, and even then there can be an appeal."

CHAPTER TWENTY-FOUR

THE STIGMA

ROGER's year was nearly at an end when one day Alec came into the pupils' room. Peter had left by this time and there were two new pupils. Roger was now the senior.

"I've got you a brief, sir," said Alec.

"Oh, Alec, how splendid," said Roger. "What is it?"

"It's only a judgment summons," said Alec, "but you never know what it may lead to."

"Thank you very much," said Roger and seized the papers eagerly. He found that he was in the comparatively unusual position of being briefed for the judgment debtor. Usually it is only the judgment creditor who is represented. For fairly obvious reasons. The debtor has no money to spare on engaging solicitors, let alone counsel. As always, Roger had a chat with Henry about it and in consequence he took Henry's advice and went to the County Court where the case was to be heard in order to see how the judge there, Judge Perkins, treated judgment summonses.

"They vary so tremendously," Henry had said. "Some judges don't seem to require any evidence of means worth speaking of and make committal orders right and left. Others hardly ever make them. I must say I think the whole thing's a bit out of date."

At one County Court which Roger had visited the dialogue during the hearing of judgment summonses had usually been like this:

CLERK: "British Loan Company against Brown."

SOLICITOR: "I appear for the judgment creditor, your Honour."

JUDGE: "Well, Mr Brown, have you any offer to make?"

BROWN: "I'm very sorry I've got into arrears, your Honour, but——"

JUDGE: "Never mind about that for the moment. Have you any offer to make?"

BROWN: "Well, it's so difficult, your Honour, with the wife ill and being out of work myself——"

JUDGE: "I'll go into all of that if necessary, but tell me first if you have any offer of any kind to make. This debt has got to be paid, you know."

BROWN: "I might manage ten shillings a week, your Honour."

JUDGE: "What do you say, Mr Worcester?"

SOLICITOR: "I'll take that with a committal order, your Honour."

JUDGE: "Very well, then. Committal order for fourteen days, suspended so long as two pounds a month is paid. Now, do you know what that means, Mr Brown?"

BROWN: "I have to pay two pounds a month."

JUDGE: "It means rather more than that, Mr Brown. It means that as long as you do pay two pounds a month all will be well—but, if you don't, then the bailiff will come and arrest you and take you to prison for fourteen days."

BROWN: "But suppose I can't pay, your Honour?"

JUDGE: "I've told you what will happen if you don't pay. You should have thought of that before you borrowed the money. Call the next case, please."

But Judge Perkins dealt with them differently. The first which Roger heard him dispose of was:

CLERK: "James Brothers against Smith."

SOLICITOR: "I appear for the judgment creditor, your Honour."

JUDGE: "Any offer to make, Mr Smith?"

SMITH: "A pound a month, your Honour."

JUDGE: "What do you say, Mr Bray?"

SOLICITOR: "If your Honour will reinforce it with a committal order——"

JUDGE: "You know perfectly well, Mr Bray, that I can't do that without evidence of means."

SOLICITOR: "But he's offered a pound a month, your Honour."

JUDGE: "That is simply a promise for the future. To my mind it is no evidence whatever that he has the money now or has had it in the past. Question him about his means if you wish."

The solicitor questioned Mr Smith about his means but without much effect, and eventually the judge simply made an order for him to pay one pound per month, with no penalty attached for non-payment.

The dialogue in the next one was as follows:

SOLICITOR: "Now Mr Davies, what do you earn?"

DAVIES: "It varies."

SOLICITOR: "What does it average?"

DAVIES: "Oh—seven to eight pounds."

SOLICITOR: "What about overtime?"

DAVIES: "I don't do a lot."

SOLICITOR: "How much on an average?"

DAVIES: "I don't know."

SOLICITOR: "You must have some idea. If necessary, you know, your firm can be brought here to prove what you do earn."

DAVIES: "Last week I didn't do any overtime at all."

SOLICITOR: "What about the week before?"

DAVIES: "I forget."

JUDGE: "Mr Davies, you must try to remember. You must know roughly what you average for overtime each week."

DAVIES: "Some weeks I don't do any."

JUDGE: "Mr Davies, if you persist in avoiding an answer to the question, I shall assume that you earn seven to eight pounds a week overtime."

DAVIES: "It's nothing like as much as that."

JUDGE: "How much is it, then?"

DAVIES: "Not more than two to three pounds."

JUDGE: "Very well then. Your average earnings are about ten pounds a week."

SOLICITOR: "Possibly more?"

DAVIES: "Not more."

SOLICITOR: "Whom d'you have to keep out of your ten pounds."

DAVIES: "My wife."

SOLICITOR: "Does she do any work?"

DAVIES: "She does a bit."

SOLICITOR: "How much does she earn?"

DAVIES: "I've no idea."

SOLICITOR: "You must have some idea."

DAVIES: "We don't discuss it. It's her business."

JUDGE: "No doubt it is, but I should have thought you might have taken sufficient interest in her affairs to know about how much she earned." (*Pause.*) "Well, don't you?"

DAVIES: "She gets a few pounds, I dare say."

SOLICITOR: "What is your rent?"

DAVIES: "Has this anything to do with the case?"

JUDGE: "It certainly has."

DAVIES: "I don't pay rent. I'm buying the house through a building society—at least the wife is. I just guarantee the payments."

SOLICITOR: "How much are they?"

DAVIES: "Eight pounds three shillings and four pence a month."

SOLICITOR: "Have you any other debts?"

DAVIES: "That's my affair."

JUDGE: "You will answer the question. Have you any other debts?"

DAVIES: "Not that I know of."

SOLICITOR: "Why haven't you paid anything off this judgment?"

DAVIES: "Because it isn't justice. He hit me first."

163

JUDGE: "That matter has already been decided. There is a judgment against you. How much a month do you offer?"

DAVIES: "Five shillings."

JUDGE: "You're just trifling with the Court. Is there anything else you want to say before I make an order?"

DAVIES: "It doesn't seem much use."

JUDGE: "Mr Davies, you will be detained until the rising of the Court and I shall then consider whether to fine you or send you to prison for contempt of Court. Meanwhile, I shall deal with this summons. You will be committed to prison for six weeks and the order will be suspended so long as you pay five pounds per month."

DAVIES: "I can't do it."

JUDGE: "Then you know the alternative. I am quite satisfied that you could have paid off the whole of this debt by now and have deliberately refrained from doing so."

In the next case before Judge Perkins the debtor admitted that he went in for football pools in a small way. The judge immediately made a committal order.

"You can't gamble with your creditor's money," he said. "It's not my concern whether you bet or not in the ordinary way, but if you could send half a crown a week to the pool promoters you could have sent it to the plaintiff, and you ought to have done so. Committal order for twenty-one days suspended so long as one pound per month is paid."

The next case was an even worse one. The debt was due to a wine merchant and the debtor admitted that he had been going to greyhound racing regularly ever since.

"This is quite outrageous," said the judge. "You will be committed to prison for six weeks and I shall suspend the order for seven days only. If the whole amount is not paid within that time, the order for your imprisonment will be effective."

"But I can't pay twenty-five pounds in seven days," said the alarmed debtor.

"Then you will spend six weeks in prison," said the judge. "I have no sympathy whatever with you. You buy drink on credit, don't pay for it and spend the money you could have used to pay for it on going to the races."

Roger went back to chambers feeling that he knew Judge Perkins' methods of dealing with judgment summonses fairly well. A day or two later he had a conference with his client, a cheerful gentleman called Starling. He came with his wife, who was also cheerful and was, in addition, an attractive young woman. They were brought by their solicitor, Mr Fergus Trent, who was an old friend of theirs.

164

"Well, here we are," said Mr Starling. "When's the party?"

"Next Tuesday."

"That's awkward. 'Fraid we shan't be able to come. It's Lingfield that day."

"D'you mean the races?" said Roger, a little alarmed.

"Don't be so prim and proper," said Mrs Starling. "Don't tell me you've never had a little flutter."

"Well, just on the Derby, you know. I've never been to a race meeting, as a matter of fact, only to point-to-points."

"Well, you ought to, old boy," said Mr Starling. "Do you a power of good. Champagne and brandy to begin with. Take a lovely girl with you. And you'll be on top of the world. I just take my wife. She's still pretty high in the handicap."

"I say, you know," said Roger, "this is rather serious. I don't know if you realize it."

"Serious, old boy? I'll say it is."

"I'm glad you appreciate that," said Roger.

"I meant if we couldn't go to Lingfield," said Mr Starling. "We always do well there."

"Look," said Roger, "this judge sends people to prison."

Mrs Starling laughed.

"Don't try and frighten us," she said, "that stopped a long time ago."

"But he does really. What was this debt for?"

"Repairs to a car, old boy. Had a nasty smash in the Watford by-pass. Between you and me I was a bit pickled. But I got through the tests all right. And Sheila was a brick. Said she'd been with me all the evening—when she knew in fact that I'd been out with some of the boys. I told you she was class, didn't I? Real thoroughbred. Never have to ride her in blinkers."

"The other way round sometimes, darling," said his wife.

"I'm afraid I don't follow all this," said Roger, "but you're going to be in great difficulty before this particular judge. Let me see. The debt's forty pounds. Judgment was obtained three months ago. Now can you honestly swear you've lost nothing on horses since then?"

"Come again," said Mr Starling.

Roger repeated the question.

"Old boy," said Mr Starling, "I can honestly swear, cross my heart and all that—I can honestly swear that we haven't *won* a penny. Otherwise, we'd have paid."

"How much have you lost?"

"Is that fair, old boy? Don't rub it in. Why, Sheila actually sold a couple of dresses. Talk of taking the clothes off your back."

"Mr Starling," said Roger, "I'm afraid this is going to be rather

165

a shock or you. I know this judge, Judge Perkins, and unless you can pay the whole of that forty pounds within a week from Tuesday next, he'll send you to prison for six weeks."

"You're not serious, old boy?"

"I am, absolutely."

"But that's terrible. I couldn't possibly go to gaol. It's Sheila's birthday in a fortnight, and we're having a party to celebrate."

"What with?" asked Roger.

"Oh, we can always raise a fiver or so."

"Well, you'd better raise eight fivers," said Roger.

"That's a different thing altogether, old boy. Just can't be done."

"Then you'll go to prison."

"But I'll lose my job."

"Haven't you any furniture you can sell?"

"All on h.p., old boy. Only just started to pay for it."

"Car?"

"Still in the Watford by-pass, I should think."

"I thought you had it repaired?"

"That was the other fellow's."

"Mr Thursby," intervened Mr Trent, "please don't think me impertinent, but are you quite sure about this particular judge?"

"Absolutely," said Roger. "I was down there last Thursday and he sent a chap to gaol for six weeks because he'd been gambling. Only gave him seven days to pay."

"Oh, well," said Mr Trent, "I'm afraid there's nothing for it."

"Come, come," said Mrs Starling, *"you're* not going to let us down, Fergie. Frank just can't go to gaol. I won't have it, I tell you. I'll speak to the judge myself and explain."

"I'm afraid that wouldn't do any good, Mrs Starling," said Roger.

"That's not very complimentary," said Mrs Starling. "I once got a bookie to give me five to one when he was showing four to one on his board."

"I told you she was class," put in Mr Starling.

"I'm afraid judges aren't like bookies."

"Apparently he'll skin me just the same," said Mr Starling.

"No," said the solicitor mournfully. "I'm afraid there's nothing for it."

"Well, we can try," said Roger.

"Try what?" said the solicitor.

"See if I can persuade the judge to give more time."

"D'you think you'll succeed?"

"Quite frankly—I don't, but one can never be sure till it's happened."

"No," said the solicitor even more gloomily. "There's nothing for it. I shall have to lend you ten pounds. It goes against the grain, but I shall have to. I wouldn't do it for you, Frank, but I've always had a soft spot for Sheila. So there we are. Thank you very much all the same, Mr Thursby. Sorry we shan't have the pleasure of seeing you at the County Court."

"I'm afraid I don't quite understand," said Roger.

He was quite prepared for anyone to withdraw instructions from him at any time, but in the first place he couldn't think what he had done to merit it yet, and secondly the solicitor's attitude was quite friendly. He was completely out of his depth.

"No alternative," said Mr Trent.

"But ten pounds isn't any good," said Roger. "He'll need forty pounds and possibly some costs as well."

"We'll just have to go bankrupt."

Roger thought for a moment.

"But," he said rather tentatively, "don't you have to owe fifty pounds in order to go bankrupt?"

"Quite so," said Mr Trent. "Our friend only owes forty pounds. Quite correct. It costs ten pounds to go bankrupt. I lend him ten pounds. He then owes fifty pounds and has the funds necessary to enable him to go bankrupt."

"Anyway," said Mr Starling, "I could rustle up some other debts if you really want them. I didn't know they'd be a help."

"Will you excuse me a moment?" said Roger.

He left the room and went hurriedly to Henry.

"Look, Henry. Can you tell me something in a hurry?"

He then stated what had happened.

"Well, is that all right?" he asked. "Will it work? What happens about the judgment summons if he goes bankrupt?"

"Yes, that's quite O.K.," said Henry. "Once a receiving order in bankruptcy is made against a man that's the end of the judgment summons. Incidentally he does not need to owe £50. Anyone who's unable to pay his debts, whatever they are, can file his own bankruptcy petition. But he does need £10 to do it."

"And anyone can avoid going to prison under a judgment summons by going bankrupt?"

"Quite correct," said Henry.

"Then why doesn't everyone do that?"

"Several reasons. Some people can't raise the ten pounds to go bankrupt."

"So that a man with ten pounds can avoid going to prison and a man without can't?"

"Right again. Then people who are in business on their own account, or have furniture or property of their own, don't want to go bankrupt as it means the end of their business and the selling up of their property."

"But if you're in a job and haven't any property, there isn't any snag about it?"

"Not normally, unless you don't like the stigma of bankruptcy."

"I'd prefer the stigma of bankruptcy to that of gaol."

"I quite agree," said Henry. "Of course quite a number of judgment debtors don't go bankrupt because they don't know that they can get out of their difficulties that way. But I gather your client does, now."

Roger thanked Henry and went hurriedly back to his clients.

"I'm so sorry to have left you. I just went to make sure that there are no snags about Mr Trent's suggestion. I gather you've got a job, Mr Starling?"

"That's right. It's called a job, but between you and me, old boy, it's grossly underpaid."

"And your furniture's all on hire purchase. Well, then, Mr Trent's idea seems an excellent one provided you don't mind the stigma of bankruptcy."

"What's that?" said Mrs Starling.

"The stigma," repeated Roger.

"Hold everything," said Mrs Starling. "Could we use your telephone?"

"Why, certainly," said Roger, puzzled.

"What is it, old girl?" said Mr Starling.

" 'The Stigma.' It's running in the 3.30. We've just got time."

"Good show," said Mr Starling. "Gosh—wouldn't we have been wild if we'd missed that? Could I use the phone, old boy? Won't be a jiffy. How much, old girl, d'you think? Half a quid each way?"

"Make it a quid, sweetheart," said Mrs Starling. "Then we'll have the doings to go to Lingfield."

"O.K.," said Mr Starling. "Which way do I go?"

Roger showed him, and came back to his room whilst Mr Starling was making his investment.

"That's two pounds you've put on, is it?" he asked Mrs Starling.

"Yes," she said. "Wish I could have made it a fiver. You don't have things like that happening every day. It's bound to win."

"D'you know anything about the horse?"

"Anything about it?" said Mrs Starling. "What more d'you want? With a name like that it couldn't lose."

Suddenly Mr Starling dashed in, almost like Mr Grimes.

"Look, old girl," he said, "there's an apprentice called Thursby riding it. Dare we risk a fiver?"

"Gosh, yes," said his wife.

168

"O.K., old girl."

And Mr Starling rushed back to the telephone.

"That's a bit of luck," said Mrs Starling. "You haven't a paper, I suppose?"

"I've a *Times*," said Roger.

"Thanks awfully."

She looked for the sporting page.

"It's in the twenty-to-one others. That'll mean one hundred and twenty-five pounds. How many runners are there? One, two, three, four——" she went on counting up to seventeen.

"Gosh, I wonder if he ought to do it on the tote. Some of it anyway. They might pay a hundred to one. Would you excuse me?"

She rushed to the door and almost collided with her husband coming back.

"Did you do any on the tote?" she asked excitedly. "It's in the twenty-to-one others."

"Relax, old girl," said Mr Starling. "Three quid each way on the tote. Two at S.P. O.K.?"

For answer, Mrs Starling kissed him.

"Oh, darling, I'm so happy. We'll celebrate to-night. Who'd have thought it? 'The Stigma' with Thursby up."

"And he gets a seven-pound allowance, old girl."

"Can he get down to the weight?"

She took *The Times* and looked at the sporting page again.

"Yes—easily. It's in the bag."

"Please forgive me, Mr Thursby. I don't suppose you understand this sort of thing. It means a great deal to us."

"As far as I can see," said Roger, feeling much older than twenty-one, "you've just backed a horse and stand to lose ten pounds, a sum which you're about to borrow from Mr Trent in order to go bankrupt."

"Old boy," said Mr Starling, "it does sound a trifle odd put that way, but Fergie understands. We put him on a good thing once. I say, old girl, you didn't happen to see if there's anything to double it with, did you? Quick, let's have a look."

He took *The Times* from her, and started reading out the names of horses.

"My godfathers," he shouted, "excuse me. 'Jolly Roger' in the 4.30. I'll see if I can get a half-quid each way double. Forgive me, old boy, I saw the name on the brief. Won't be a jiffy."

He rushed out of the door and nearly crashed into Mr Grimes, who was about to make a telephone call from the clerks' room.

"So sorry, old boy," said Mr Starling. "Terribly urgent." And took the receiver away from him.

Mr Grimes said nothing. For once he could not think of anything to say. Mr Starling might be a solicitor for aught he knew.

"Hullo, hullo——" said Mr Starling frantically. "Is that Vulgans? This is Frank Starling—Boozer. Are they off for the 3.30 yet? Oh, they are—damn—oh, well, can I hold for the result? Thanks so much." He turned to Mr Grimes.

"Damned shame, old man," he said. "They're off."

"Dear, dear, dear," said Mr Grimes.

"Well, we'll get the result first anyway," went on Mr Starling. "Then we can put half the winnings on the next, can't we, old boy? That's better really than a double. Make sure we have a fat win, anyway. Not much in your line I gather, old man?"

"Oh, well, my dear fellow," said Mr Grimes, "it keeps the telephone operator busy, if nothing else."

"I'm terribly sorry, old boy—what's that, what? Who between? It's a photo finish. Who? But of course you can say. No—that's too ridiculous. Excuse me a moment, old man. Don't hang up."

Mr Starling rushed back to the pupils' room.

"It's a photo finish," he announced excitedly.

"Who between?" asked his wife.

"Wouldn't say."

"But that's absurd. They'll always tell you if you ask them. Excuse me."

"You ask them, old girl."

Mr and Mrs Starling rushed out of the room to the telephone in time to hear the last of Mr Grimes' remarks to Alec.

"I don't know what we're coming to, I really don't."

Meantime Roger looked at the solicitor whose expression had hardly changed and who sat still, looking mournful.

"Odd," said Roger, "very odd."

"Not when you've known them as I long as have," said Mr Trent. "They'd gamble their souls away if anyone would lay the odds. I'll bet—now look what they've got me doing. Until I met Frank I didn't know one end of a racehorse from the other. And now I can even understand the sporting edition of the evening papers. I actually read the stop press—to see how much they've lost."

At that moment the door burst open and Mr and Mrs Starling rushed into the room.

"We've won, we've won, we've won," they shouted, and proceeded to dance together round the room.

" 'The Stigma' with Thursby up," they shouted. "Good old 'Stigma,' good old Thursby. Here, where's that silly piece of blue paper?"

He picked up the judgment summons which had been in front of Roger and tore it into small pieces.

The solicitor appeared quite unmoved.

"I'm glad they've won, anyway," Roger said to him. Mr and Mrs Starling were too occupied in making frenzied calculations on Roger's *Times* to be spoken to. "Aren't you?" he added.

"If you'd seen this happen as often as I have," said Mr Trent, "you wouldn't move a muscle. They'll spend it all in a week and then we'll be back where we started. Still, it's saved me ten pounds for the moment. But only for the moment," he added sadly.

Mr and Mrs Starling continued with their calculations for a little time and then started to make suggestions to Roger for every kind of celebration. After just over a quarter of an hour of this Mr Starling suddenly said:

"Ought to be able to get the tote prices now, old girl. Would you excuse me?" He went out to telephone again. Meanwhile, Roger started looking at the sporting page of *The Times*. He glanced idly at the information about the meeting. A few minutes later the door opened slowly and a very dejected Mr Starling walked in. As soon as his wife saw him, she knew.

"What's happened, sweetheart?" she said anxiously. "Objection?"

"Yes, confound it," said her husband. "By the stewards. Upheld. Upheld, now I ask you."

"That's extraordinary," said Roger. "D'you know, I've just happened to see that the senior steward's name is Perkins."

"Don't see anything funny in that, old man," said Mr Starling gloomily.

"Well," said Mr Trent, "I said it was only for the moment." He looked at his watch.

"Now we've missed the Bankruptcy Court. Never mind, we can do that to-morrow."

Sadly Mr and Mrs Starling and their solicitor left Roger. When they had gone, Roger said to Henry that he thought Judge Perkins must be quite a good judge.

CHAPTER TWENTY-FIVE

THE END OF THE BEGINNING

By the time Roger had almost finished his pupillage he had certainly acquired a good deal of knowledge and experience and his confidence was correspondingly increased. He had earned the magnificent sum of sixty guineas. (It had, of course, cost his mother one hundred and ten guineas to enable him to do so.) He had opened his mouth sufficiently often in Court that he had long since ceased to hear his voice echoing above him. Although he still felt intensely nervous when left, or about to be left, by Mr Grimes to do part of a case in the High Court and although, as Henry had prophesied, he was still quite unfit to conduct a whole case there, he was in a very different condition from that in which he had started. He had learned a great deal from Mr Grimes and almost as much from Henry.

In a Magistrate's Court or a County Court he started to feel fairly comfortable and, although likely to be defeated there by more experienced advocates, he did not make nearly as many mistakes as most beginners make. He had taken Henry's and Charles' experiences to heart. A few days before his time was up Henry said to him:

"I'm sure that Grimeyboy will ask you to stay on here, if you want to. You're going to be very useful to him."

"D'you really think so?"

"I've no doubt about it. There's another side to the question, though. How useful will he be to you? Well, you'll get a lot of experience and plenty of work. But unfortunately all his work is in the High Court and what you want is somewhere where there's plenty of smaller stuff about. Alec, no doubt, would do his best for you, but to get a County Court practice going in chambers where there isn't any small work is a pretty tough proposition. I think you'd do it in the end, but it'll be slow."

"Then, what's your suggestion?"

"Well," said Henry, "something phenomenal has happened. I'm going to move."

"You?"

"Yes. I've suddenly decided to try and do a bit more work. Sally's behind it, of course. I don't suppose it will last long. But she's persuaded me I ought to get out of this rut."

"Where are you going?"

"Well, I know Mountview pretty well and his chambers are simply bursting with work. He said he'd like to have me there if I'd come. And I'm going."

"I shall miss you," said Roger. "Can I come across and ask you anything when I want to?"

"You can come across altogether, if you want."

"Move with you, d'you mean?"

"I do. I suppose you'll ask me what I advise. Well——" began Henry.

"I'm not going to do anything of the sort. If that's a firm offer, I'll accept. I know a good thing when I see it, even at my stage."

He thought for a moment.

"It is good of you," he added. "D'you think Grimeyboy will mind?"

"Grimeyboy never minds anything," said Henry. "He takes everything as it comes. He's always been the same and always will be. Dear, dear, dear. I don't know what things are coming to. They will do these things, my dear fellow, they will do these things."

On the day on which his pupillage ended, Roger and Henry and Sally dined together. Roger was in high spirits.

"I don't know where I should be but for you two," he said. "Floating in the Thames, I should imagine, if I hadn't been picked up by now. D'you know I actually addressed the L.C.J. the other day?"

"What did you say?" asked Sally.

"Well," said Roger, "as a matter of fact it was—'if your Lordship pleases.' "

"I hope he took it well," said Henry.

"He said, 'So be it,' " said Roger. "I thought that was very decent of him. Now let's have a drink. And what shall we drink to? The future? Everyone's future, that is. I know what I want mine to be."

"And I know mine," said Henry.

"Me, too," said Sally.

"I wonder," said Roger, "whether any of us will get what we want."

"We shall see, my dear fellow, we shall see," said Henry.

FRIENDS AT COURT

CHAPTER ONE

A QUESTION OF SILK

ROGER THURSBY was counsel for the defendant. The plaintiff was in the witness box. After Roger had cross-examined him for half an hour the judge asked the witness if he would like to sit down.

"Thank you, my Lord," said the plaintiff, and sat down. But he would have preferred to run out of the Court, down the street, and into his mother's arms, or, at any rate, to someone kind and comforting. Even those who tell the truth in the witness box can have an uncomfortable time there, but the plaintiff had not even a clear conscience to cheer him. He wished he'd never started the action. He'd been warned that there were difficulties. Difficulties! That was a mild word. And now here was one of the ablest counsel at the junior Bar knocking him round the ring till everything was in a haze. If only he could go down for the count. At any rate it would be over then. He asked for a glass of water. That gave him a moment's breathing space—but only a moment, for the obliging usher brought it all too soon.

"He needs something a bit stronger," said Roger's opponent, in an undertone. And then, as the witness braced himself for the next blow, temporary relief came to him in a manner he had not anticipated. For, just as Roger said:

"Come, Mr Frail, you don't really mean that, do you?" the judge intervened by saying:

"Just one moment, Mr Thursby, please," The witness wondered if the judge was going to say—as he had said once before—in quiet but ominous tones: "Mr Frail, I don't think you're doing yourself justice." But the judge did not say that or anything like it. Instead, he began:

"Mr Leonard Seaforth Jones," and, before the witness could even start to wonder what Mr Leonard Seaforth Jones had to do with the case, he went on: "Her Majesty having been pleased to appoint you one of her counsel learned in the law, will you kindly take your place within the Bar."

Mr Jones, ordinarily very large and even larger in the regalia of his full-bottomed wig and Q.C.'s ceremonial dress, prized himself with some little difficulty along the front row of counsel's seats until he was approximately in the middle of the row, and bowed low to the judge. He then turned to his right and bowed to a Q.C. who was standing at that end of the row, then to another Q.C. at the other end and finally he turned round and bowed to the junior Bar. He was just about opposite Roger when he did this, and he and Roger exchanged winks. Then Mr Jones turned round, faced the judge, and sat down.

"Do you move, Mr Jones?" said the judge.

For answer, Mr Jones stood up, bowed again and then went, still with some difficulty, along the row and out at the other end, to wait patiently for his colleagues. When they had all gone through the necessary motions in that Court, they would all go to the next Court, where the same process would be repeated. And so on.

The witness eventually became aware that his torture was being interrupted by the final ceremony in the taking of silk.

"Miss Drusilla Manville, Her Majesty having been pleased to appoint you one of her counsel learned in the law, will you kindly take your place within the Bar." An extremely pretty woman, who could not have been more than thirty-five, went through the formalities. As she bowed to Roger, her full-bottomed wig looking curiously old as it hung down her young face, he whispered: "It suits you very well, if I may say so."

"Thank you, sir," she said, as she turned to face the judge again.

Roger suddenly remembered that his mother was in Court and would be wondering what on earth was happening. He scribbled a note, which he sent to her by a junior clerk: "I'll tell you all about it afterwards."

Ten minutes later he rose to resume his cross-examination of the plaintiff. But by this time the unhappy man had regained his composure sufficiently to indicate that he would like his seconds to throw in the towel.

"When they reach the glass-of-water stage," Roger told one of his pupils later, "there's at least an even chance that the end is near."

Roger had been called to the Bar just over twelve years and in that time he had made almost as much progress as it is possible for a junior to make. During the ceremony of taking silk, another of the new Q.C.'s, when bowing to Roger, had said:

"You next year?"

Roger shook his head, but not very convincingly, either to the questioner or to himself. He had, in fact, been thinking of applying for silk for some little time. But it was not a decision to be made in a hurry. The work that he had to do as a junior was of several kinds. He did a great deal of paper work, writing opinions and drafting the technical legal documents required in litigation. Then, quite as important, he acted as midwife, wet-nurse and doctor to a delicate baby case until it became strong and healthy or, almost as often, strangled it at birth, saying a few words of comfort to the parents.

"Much better to tell you now why you won't win than to explain later why you didn't."

"But are you quite sure, Mr Thursby? You won't mind my saying that our neighbour, who's a lawyer himself, said that he thought we'd be bound to win and it was he who told me to come to you."

"Well," Roger had said, "I can't deny that I think part of his advice was excellent."

The other side of Roger's practice as a junior was the conduct of cases in Court, when sometimes he would be opposed by a Q.C. and sometimes by another junior. Occasionally, if the case appeared to be an interesting one, his mother came to listen. And so it happened that, for the first time, she saw part of the ceremony of taking silk.

That night, in trying to explain the ceremony to his mother, Roger also discussed with her his own future. "Discussed" is perhaps not quite the correct word. Roger had inherited his father's brains. He was devoted to his mother, but devotion could not blind him to the fact that her intelligence was strictly limited. Nevertheless he nearly always talked over his problems with her. He never analysed his reasons for doing this, but there were really two. First, the discussion was often more or less a monologue by Roger and in any event it helped him to come to a decision. Secondly, they both liked the feeling that, whatever the problem, it was apparently shared between them.

"You see, Mother," he said, "a man may do awfully well as a junior because his paper work is first-class and he's good enough, though not spectacular, in Court. If he takes silk, he has to give up his paper work and may be a complete failure as a silk."

"Well, dear, why not just become a Queen's Counsel and give up this idea of taking silk?"

"Mother, how often have I got to tell you it's the same thing?"

"Then really, dear, I don't know what you're worrying about. If it were something different, you'd have to choose between the two, but, as they're both the same, it can't make any difference, can it, dear? Or have I got something wrong?"

"When you become a Queen's Counsel you have a silk gown, Mother. That's why it's called 'taking silk'. Don't you remember? I really have told you before."

"I know, dear. I really will try to remember this time."

The next day Mrs Thursby was talking to a friend. "My dear," she said, "Roger said something to me last night about taking silk."

"I'm so glad," said her friend, "because now you'll be able to tell me what it means."

"Well," said Mrs Thursby, with some confidence, "it means this." She stopped for a moment. "This is what it means," she went on, with slightly less confidence, "I'll tell you." Again she stopped.

"I'm able to tell you," she went on, after the pause, "because Roger explained it all most carefully to me."

There was another pause.

"When you're at the Bar," she continued eventually, but as though she were repeating a lesson she had not quite learned, "when you're at the Bar either you're a barrister—or you're not." There was a moment's silence while Mrs Thursby's friend tried hard to look enlightened. "That doesn't sound quite right," said Mrs Thursby.

"Well, I did wonder," said her friend.

"Because," went on Mrs Thursby, 'if you're at the Bar you *are* a barrister, aren't you? I wonder what Roger meant, because I'm sure he said that, and it sounded so right when he said it."

"I expect that's because he *is* a barrister," said her friend. "They're so convincing even when what they say is wrong."

"Yes, I know," said Mrs Thursby, "but I'm sure Roger wouldn't tell me anything wrong. Just give me a moment, dear. I'm sure it'll come to me."

Her friend gave her several moments. Suddenly Mrs Thursby's face lighted up.

"I remember," she said, "there are only two kinds of barrister. That's what I meant. When you're at the Bar you're either one kind or the other. D'you see, dear?"

"You mean—like with apples—either Cox's or Blenheims."

"Oh—no," said Mrs Thursby. "There are lots of kinds of apples. More like grapes—either muscats or the others."

"And which kind is Roger?"

"I'm afraid," said Mrs Thursby, "that's what I've forgotten."

It was perhaps rather too much for Mrs Thursby to remember that barristers are divided into juniors and Queen's Counsel, and that, as a general rule, the work of a Queen's Counsel is mostly confined to appearing in Court. Roger had explained to her years before, in fact soon after he was called, that being a junior did not necessarily mean that you were young or inexperienced. "Some of the juniors in the Chancery Division have beards, Mother," he had told her.

"Your father had a beard once, Roger," his mother had replied. "I'll find the photograph."

"And some juniors become judges without ever taking silk, you know," Roger had continued, while his mother was searching in a drawer.

"Here it is," she had said a moment later. "It was red—until he shaved it off—but, of course, the colour doesn't show there."

About nine months after he had talked about silk to his mother, Roger talked very seriously to his clerk on the subject. Donald

Pirbright had been his clerk for over eleven years. Roger had served his year's pupillage with a Mr Grimes and had then gone to other chambers. The clerk in the new chambers was Donald and, during the eleven years, there had grown up between Roger and his clerk the usual indefinable but close relationship which exists between a barrister and his clerk. Donald was an excellent clerk and, like all excellent clerks, he had his idiosyncrasies; they are not called faults in the Temple. When Roger arrived at his chambers in the morning, Donald would call him "sir." In the afternoon, after a visit or two to one of his favourite haunts, he would be more likely to say "sir, sir," or even "sir, sir, sir," and by the evening, as often as not, he called him "Roger." The discussion about silk was in the late afternoon.

"Well," said Roger, "what about it? Do I or don't I?"

"Next year," said Donald.

"What's the point of waiting? Bullet and Angel are applying."

"Sir, sir. Please don't mention Mr Bullet and Mr Angel. Not in the same breath as yourself, sir. Sir, really. Bullet and Angel. Sir, sir, sir."

"Bullet's not at all bad," said Roger.

"Bullet," said Donald, "*Mr* Bullet, I beg his pardon, is bloody hopeless."

"Anyway, he'll get it."

"Sir, sir, sir, don't come that one on me. Of course he'll get it. He's an M.P. They get it automatically."

"But why should I wait, anyway?" asked Roger. "What's the advantage of waiting? Or are you frightened?"

"Now, sir," said Donald, as sternly as his recent visits to 'The Feathers' would allow, "now, sir, my clerk's fees don't mean a thing. You know that. I'm surprised at you, sir. I really am."

Every time that Roger received a fee his clerk received one too. It is not certain who invented the practice, but Roger had thought more than once that there should be a statue in the Temple to the man who had thought of the brilliant idea which resulted in a barrister's clerk being paid not by his employer but by the client. The clerks might perhaps subscribe to a second statue, nestling under the shadow of the first, to the band of heroes among the clerks who, after the 1939-45 war, successfully established the practice by which a barrister pays the shillings in his guineas to the clerk. The idea was not a new one, but it was only after the war that there was a concerted attack on the Bar by the clerks, who, without a shot fired, achieved their object. When barristers and clerks were re-united after the war they naturally discussed their respective adventures during the war and then, as it were by a pre-arranged signal, in every set of chambers the clerk would say in an almost off-hand way:

"Oh, by the way, sir, we now have the shillings in the guineas."
A pause.

"That all right with you, sir? They're all doing it, sir."

Victory was complete almost immediately. A few waverers wandered uncertainly and self-consciously about the Temple for a week or two, but they soon felt that they were being regarded as outcasts and within a very short time:

"Oh, Bernard, I've been thinking about that matter you mentioned the other day."

"Matter, sir, matter?"

"You know—the shillings in the guineas."

"Oh—that, sir."

A pause.

"Well, sir?"

"All right, Bernard, I give in."

"Thank you very much, sir. They're all doing it, really, sir."

And they all were. And are.

When Donald said that his clerk's fees didn't mean a thing, he really meant it. Naturally he would have been sorry for himself as well as for Roger if, when he took silk, his practice declined and with it the clerk's fees and the shillings. But thoughts of that possibility were not uppermost in his mind and he was thinking almost entirely of Roger's interests.

"Well, why on earth d'you want me to wait, then? I'm working sixteen hours a day, week-ends included. I don't get time for a thing. I've about had enough. I haven't even had time to get married."

"Sir, sir, sir," said Donald. "That's nothing to do with time. Find the lady and you'll find the time."

"But I haven't time to find the lady. If I'm working for you all night and all day, how can I? No, really, Donald, it's not good enough. And anyway, you still haven't said what there is to wait for. I'm making ten thousand a year. If you think I won't get on as a silk at all, for Heaven's sake say so. I shan't take any notice, but do say so."

"Get on, sir, get on? Of course, you'll get on. I'll tell you something else, sir. You won't be a silk for more than five or six years—that's if you want to go up. I'm not sure if I'd come with you myself if you go on the Bench. We'd have to ask Henry—Mr Blagrove."

Henry Blagrove was the head of Roger's chambers. He was seven or eight years older than Roger and was as indolent by nature as Roger was energetic. But his charming and determined wife, Sally, had spurred him into a little more activity and he had eventually taken silk. He was extremely able and, as a silk, he had just about the size practice he wanted. Sally was a solicitor, but she had given up practice to have babies and Roger was godfather of their first. Theirs was a very happy set of chambers. If Roger became a High Court judge, Donald could have gone with him as clerk or stayed with Henry, and it was a difficult choice to make. However, that was a long way ahead at the moment.

"Well, if I'm going to get on as a silk, why not now? Tell me that."

"All right, sir, if that's how you want it—now it shall be. All the same, I'd have liked to have seen another year's junior work behind you."

"You wouldn't have to do it, Donald," said Roger. "You can play golf and take your wife out, while I sit sweating at home. Now we'll reverse the process. I can sit twiddling my thumbs while you search the highways and by-ways to find me a brief."

"Search the highways, my foot," said Donald.

"That's really all I wanted to know," said Roger. "P'raps you'd turn up the Law List and tell me all the people I've got to write to. How many d'you think there'll be?"

Roger now had the task of writing to every practising junior on his circuit, who was senior to him in call, to inform him of his intention to apply to the Lord Chancellor for the purpose of taking silk, so that they could apply also if they wanted to do so. It was a task to which he looked forward. It meant that he had made up his mind. It was a risk undoubtedly, but it was worth it. The only question now was whether the Lord Chancellor would give it him first time. He was certainly young—thirty-three—but there was no doubt about the size and quality of his practice. He did not think that he would receive—as some promising juniors had received in the past—a polite note with "next time" on it. Anyway, if he did, the decision would have been made for him. That night he wrote a letter to the Permanent Secretary to the Lord Chancellor:

I shall be grateful if you will place before the Lord Chancellor this my application to be considered for appointment as one of Her Majesty's Counsel.

He showed it to his mother.

"How many Q.C.'s are there, dear?" she asked.

"I don't know—altogether, I suppose, about three to four hundred, but I should say that only about half of them practise."

"The Queen must have a lot of cases to need all those counsel." Roger did his best to explain.

"You make it all sound very clear," said his mother.

"Good," said Roger.

"But I'm afraid," she went on, "I still don't understand. All the

183

same, I'm glad you'll be one of them. But don't ask her too many questions."

Some little time was to elapse before the Lord Chancellor's decision would be known and meantime Roger carried on with his ordinary work. But he did so in a much happier frame of mind. He could see the way ahead and there would be some time in it for other things besides law. He was very cheerful when he lunched next day at the Inn he used for the purpose. He usually sat with the same people, though he could never quite think why. Probably it was habit. They had been his neighbours when he first lunched in that Hall some years before and it seemed rude to sit elsewhere. In any event, lunch did not take long. The conversation during it was usually on the same lines. Arnold Carruthers, who sat opposite him, was a barrister of a good many years' experience. He found it helped him to discuss his professional problems with other people and almost invariably he would begin, as soon as he decently could—and sometimes before:

"Look, I'm an actress of uncertain age and not much talent. I get knocked down by a 'bus. What's it worth? I couldn't act much before the accident. Can't act at all now."

Sometimes it would be a point of law. "Look, the Court of Appeal in *Lea and Moore* seem to have said that you can't try a case in the County Court by consent unless it first started in the High Court. I'm referring, of course, to cases which are outside the normal jurisdiction. But they only looked at Section 43. They never once referred to Section 65. Now, I think——" And Carruthers would elaborate his point and try to obtain the opinions of those around him. If he was lucky someone would point out that a new Act did away with the effect of the decision.

Another of Roger's neighbours had a very small practice, a reasonable private income and a fund of undergraduate stories. He began on this occasion with: "D'you know this one? There was a girl with a rather short skirt standing in a 'bus. The conductor gave her a ticket, but she dropped it. 'Will it matter?' she asked the conductor. Have you heard it by the way?"

"Only once or twice," said his immediate neighbour, "and not for a very long time."

"Well, I don't suppose Thursby knows it. He's never heard any of them."

"No, I haven't, as a matter of fact," said Roger politely, "but it'll probably be above my head."

"Oh, no—not this one. Well—the conductor turned to the girl and said——"

At that moment Carruthers arrived.

"Look, so sorry to butt in, but I've got rather a teaser. D'you

184

mind? I'm a stable boy at a well-known racing stable——"

"Got anything for the Derby?"

"No, look, this is serious——"

"Then the girl said: 'But how shall I know if it's the right ticket?' Then the conductor turned to the girl and said——"

"And while I'm out exercising a horse which I haven't ridden before——"

"Hullo, Roger, they tell me you're applying for silk."

"But I've only just posted the letter——"

"Good news travels fast."

"Then the girl turned to a passenger and said: 'I wonder if you'd mind——' "

"Now this horse was well known to the trainer to be difficult, but I didn't know it. Now, while I'm on this brute——"

"Good news! If I get it first time, I expect I'll be in the bread line."

"Rubbish—I hear Forsythe's applied."

"Is there anything confidential you don't know?"

"Confidential be blowed. I bet you've written to at least thirty people on your circuit."

"More, if you want to know."

"Well, you can't expect them all to keep quiet about it."

"Then the girl said——"

"As I fell on the ground the trainer arrived and cursed me. What he actually said was——"

And so on and so forth, what the girl said, how the conductor turned, why the stable boy fell, what the trainer called him, interspersed with the latest gossip and a few polite enquiries. And lunch in Hall was over.

CHAPTER TWO

RETROSPECT

THAT evening Roger walked home from chambers. He thought first about the past, about his call nearly thirteen years before, his first miserable efforts in Court, the agonies he had gone through. How kind Henry Blagrove had been. He was sure he would never have got on but for Henry. It was not simply the encouragement Henry had given him, but he had shown him the only way to learn how to succeed at the Bar. I wonder if I've taught my pupils half as much as Henry taught me? Never accept anything without knowing why, Henry had always told him. Whether it's a matter of law or practice, you must know the principle behind it. When a judge says: "But you can't do that," find out why you can't do it, and very occasionally, in looking up to see why you can't do it, you'll find you can and that the judge was wrong. Yes, he owed nearly everything to Henry. He was glad that Henry owed something to him too—Sally. Roger found it difficult to remember himself and his girl friends without squirming. Who, outside of Dornford Yates, would have behaved as I did—or, indeed, as they did? Sally and Joy had both adored Roger. Roger at twenty-one, good-looking, ambitious, slightly priggish, wholly inexperienced was, to Roger at thirty-three, a somewhat nauseating spectacle. But he braced himself to the effort of looking back. And after all he had been very young. He thought of Joy, pretty and empty-headed. Well, perhaps not as empty as all that. She had sent her uncle to brief him, Uncle Alfred, that pompous elderly solicitor whom he had eventually insulted by refusing a three thousand guinea brief. How on earth had I the nerve? Three thousand guineas and we were very short of money at the time. But it would have meant marrying Joy. How right he had been. And as for Sally, who had more intelligence than any woman he had ever known, Sally adoring, rather lovely and rather sad. I wonder why I never wanted to marry her? I suppose because I just didn't want to marry at all. Anyway, my loss, if it was one, was Henry's gain. He fell for Sally and eventually she capitulated. They were very happy. I am pleased about that, he thought. If it hadn't been for me, Henry would never have met her. That's something I've done for him. All the same, I could do with a home now. I wonder if I'll get one. I'll certainly get more spare time soon, at least I hope so. Well, I'm not going to waste it. Why on earth do I lunch with Carruthers and Co? I joined Henry's Inn in addition to my own and I have to go and listen to that tripe. There were plenty of other people in Hall who seldom talked shop and never told dirty stories. I can't very well move somewhere else when I take silk. Oh—well I suppose I'm used to it by now. But that girl in the 'bus went on for ever. I don't even remember the end now. Perhaps I never heard it. I expect it was as old as the hills, anyway. His stories aren't just chestnuts—more like *marrons glacés*. Anyway, what am I worrying about? I'm going to take silk, marry and have a home. Life begins at thirty-three.

CHAPTER THREE

SLOGRAVE, PLUMB & CO.

"So Donald's letting you apply," said Henry the next day. "That's very decent of him. Of course, it'll ruin me, but don't let that worry you."

"If I get any of your leavings, I shall be lucky," said Roger.

"Leavings? I haven't returned a brief this year, but don't let it get you down. As a matter of fact, I'll exist quite well on *your* returns. You wait and see."

"I haven't got silk yet."

"You will. It's a foregone conclusion with your practice. Donald's a very lucky man. All he wants now is a junior who can take on your practice. D'you think Axford will hold it?"

Axford was older than Roger, but had not been in the chambers as long. He had started as a solicitor and then read for the Bar.

"I think he ought to keep some of it. He's a good lawyer and works like a black."

At that moment Donald came into the room. "Slograve, Plumb have just been on the 'phone. Want to come and see you at once. I said O.K."

"All right," said Roger. "Any excuse for not getting on with some work."

"It was Plumb himself. He sounded rather worried."

"He's always gloomy. When you start a case he's worried to death that the witnesses won't come up to scratch and, if they do, that the judge won't. Then, if you win the case, he's terrified it'll go to the Court of Appeal and, if you win there, he has sleepless nights thinking of the House of Lords allowing the appeal. Then, when the Lords dismiss the appeal with costs, he's on tenterhooks that the other side won't have the money to pay. And when they've paid in full, he's pretty sure to point out that the amount he's had to charge his client is more than they've got out of the other side. And if you point out to him that he could have charged a bit less, that worries him more than anything—because it happens to be true."

"I like your Mr Plumb," said Henry. "There's a richness about his gloom which I enjoy. One can almost pinch it as Mr Squeers pinched young Wackford. 'There's oiliness for you.' Don't forget me if they want a leader, Donald. Oh—by the way, I backed your confounded horse on Saturday."

Donald owned two racehorses. He called one "Conference" and the other "Consultation". He had bought them from a trainer for whom Roger had done a case.

"I didn't tell you to, sir. If you want to win on my horses, you wait till I give the word."

"Sally and I are going to Alexandra Park on Saturday. Have you got anything for us?"

"I'll come back and see you when I've seen Mr Plumb in, sir. Conference is coughing at the moment. Consultation looks extremely well. The only trouble with that horse is that it doesn't like jockeys. Once it's thrown its jockey it goes like the wind. Almost flies you might say. I thought of suggesting to the Jockey Club they might try some riderless races. Have some corn beyond the winning-post. That'd stop them. Oh—there's the bell. I expect that's old Plumb. Excuse me, sir."

"I'll go to my room," said Roger.

A few minutes later Mr Plumb was shown in to him. He had a red face and a bald head, and whether it was hot or not he was con-tinually wiping it with a handkerchief. He sat down rather pon-derously, wiped imaginary sweat from his forehead, sighed, frowned and then spoke. He had a voice reminiscent of that of the Radio Doctor but lacking its cheerfulness.

"It's very lucky indeed," he said in the gloomiest possible tones, "very lucky indeed you're not in Court, Mr Thursby. It's a great relief." He wiped his forehead again. "I don't know what I should have done. There's no one else in the Temple I could go to."

"That's very good of you to say so," said Roger, "but I'm sure there is."

"But there isn't, Mr Thursby, there really isn't. That's what's so worrying. You may take silk one day and then where shall we be?"

"And, of course, I might be knocked down by a 'bus," said Roger gently.

Mr Plumb said nothing.

"Well—I'll take all the care of myself I can," said Roger. "And we'll hope for the best."

"Mr Thursby," began Mr Plumb, and then stopped.

"Yes?" said Roger.

Mr Plumb hesitated.

"Well," said Roger cheerfully, "what's it all about?"

Mr Plumb again hesitated. He appeared to be in two minds as to what he wanted to say. Eventually one of his minds forged ahead, and he spoke:

"Well, Mr Thursby, I act for the proprietors of a seaside hotel. The Glorious at Westlea. It's a most respectable place, I assure you, terribly respectable. I've known Mr and Mrs Glacier—they own the place—for many years. They are very good clients, very good clients indeed." As he said this, Mr Plumb looked so mournful that Roger really wondered whether he was going to burst into tears.

"They buy hotels all over the place and, I may tell you in confidence, the conveyancing is worth a very considerable sum, a very considerable sum indeed."

Mr Plumb looked gloomier than ever.

"And what's happened? Have they stopped conveying?"

Mr Plumb wiped his forehead and was silent for a moment. Then his other mind came to the front and took command.

"Mr Thursby," he said, "my firm briefs you because I believe you to be without question easily the best junior at the Common Law Bar. I hope you will forgive my speaking plainly."

"No one could object to such plainness, however undeserved," said Roger.

"The plainness is to come, Mr Thursby. Because of our opinion of you, my partner and I accept your little bouts of facetiousness with as much goodwill as we can muster. But neither of us has much of a sense of humour, Mr Thursby. I know it is not fashionable to say so, but we have not. We are gloomy men, Mr Thursby, gloomy men."

"I'm so sorry," murmured Roger.

"Thank you," said Mr Plumb, "and would I be out of order if I asked you to add to your many kindnesses by not laughing at me too obviously too often? I'm consulting you about a most serious matter, very serious indeed and while I shall quite understand if in the circumstances you ask me to leave your chambers, if you do not take that course I shall be grateful if you will at any rate conceal your amusement. No doubt sometimes you may indulge in a quip which, owing to my lack of humour, will go over my head and out of the window and maybe will rocket into the satellites. Pray do so, if you wish, so long as you are reasonably certain I shall not notice it."

"I'm so sorry," said Roger. "I really am. Please don't take any notice of my flippancy. I apologize for it. It's very rude. I must confess, though, that, however serious a case, a light touch every now and then helps things along. I have even heard a judge make a joke in sending a man to prison."

"And may I ask," said Mr Plumb, "did it send the fellow roaring with laughter to the cells?"

"A fair comment, Mr Plumb, and not one I should expect from anyone without a sense of humour. I think, if I may say so, you have one somewhere around."

"It is of course possible," said Mr Plumb with the utmost gloom. "It is of course possible." And he wiped his forehead.

"But to continue about my clients," he went on. "Mr and Mrs Glacier are Swiss by birth but they are naturalized. They have lived here a considerable time. They started with very little capital and have worked up a magnificent business—magnificent. It is all very depressing."

Roger restrained himself from asking what was depressing about that.

"Mr Thursby, solicitors have their feelings. I know that people are inclined to regard lawyers as soulless bloodsuckers—but Slograve, Plumb are at any rate not without a soul."

A little rhyme insisted on inserting itself in Roger's thoughts:

'High-minded but dumb
Slograve Plumb'

but he kept it to himself.

"I won't deny," continued Mr Plumb, "that the loss of their business would not mean a lot to us. It would. A very great deal."

I convey, you convey, he conveys, went through Roger's mind.

"Indeed, such a loss could be a very serious blow to our business."

Would that I may convey, would that you may convey, would that they (and in particular Mr and Mrs Glacier) may convey. May they convey, let them convey—consult Roger Thursby and they *shall* convey.

"But at the moment I am thinking not so much of our firm as of these two people. A man and a woman. My clients."

Meet to be conveyed, considered Roger.

"Ruin, Mr Thursby. A life's work gone. Gaol. Naturalization cancelled. Back to Switzerland."

How will they be conveyed? resisted Roger. Instead: "How does it all arise?" he asked.

"It's absurd really," said Mr Plumb, "quite absurd. But, like so many serious matters, it arises from a small one. The licensing laws. The requirements with which licensees have to comply are very considerable and sometimes onerous, very onerous indeed. For example, there is no objection to a licensee giving a friend a drink after hours if he chooses. But who is a friend?"

"Who is my neighbour?" asked Roger.

"Precisely. An equally difficult question. A landlord of a hotel should be a friend to his guests."

"It's a prosecution for a breach of the licensing laws?" queried Roger.

"If that were all," said Mr Plumb, "I should not have troubled you with the matter. That would be serious, but nothing more. It is far worse than that."

He wiped his forehead several times. Roger was tempted to ask him if he would like a glass of water, but he refrained.

"You can imagine the shock it was to me when my clients came to me only this morning—you'll see I've wasted no time in coming to you—when they came to me and said they had been charged with bribery of the police. Bribery of the police. A conviction for that and they're finished in this country, apart from the fact that they'd probably go to prison. Mr Thursby, I don't ask you to take my word for it, but Mr and Mrs Glacier are charming and respectable people."

And require a lot of conveyancing, added Roger to himself.

"I cannot for one moment think them guilty, but there it is, they're charged—under the Prevention of Corruption Act. Now, I believe in acting under counsel's advice from the word go—not, I may say, because that relieves us of legal responsibility, but because—provided you go to the right counsel—it pays—it pays us, it pays the client."

And the client pays counsel, said Roger—again to himself. But he knew Mr Plumb was right, And, indeed, he encouraged his clients to come to him at an early stage. Many an action has been won or lost by the preliminary steps which have been taken long before it ever came into Court.

"Now I might have gone to Mr Erswell of the Criminal Bar— a very sound man, if I may say so. But I wanted something better than that. Erswell is, if I may say so, excellent in Court, admirable at putting his case—when it's been prepared for him in an adequate brief—before judge or jury. But I have a feeling that this matter requires rather more imagination in its handling. So I've come to you and I hope—I earnestly hope you'll be able to help us."

"I'll certainly do my best, Mr Plumb," said Roger. "Perhaps you'll tell me the facts."

"I'd prefer to call them allegations, Mr Thursby. They are these. There have been rather late parties at the Glorious from time to time and apparently neighbours objected to the noise. I need hardly say that the parties were entirely respectable, but admittedly they were late and admittedly you cannot have a party without a noise. Apparently complaints were made to the police and, in consequence, somehow or other plain-clothes detectives attended on one or two occasions. A few weeks ago an inspector and a sergeant from the local police station called on Mr and Mrs Glacier and informed them that they would be proceeded against for breach of the licensing laws. It is alleged that at that interview and again at a subsequent interview Mr and Mrs Glacier attempted to bribe the officers by handing them, on the first occasion, twenty pounds in one pound notes and, on the second occasion, twenty-five pounds. It is alleged that the money was handed to the police to persuade them either to stop the prosecution or to make the offence appear to be a very trivial one."

"I can understand your anxiety, Mr Plumb," said Roger. "What do your clients say about it? Do they admit giving the money?"

"Most certainly not," said Mr Plumb. "And I may tell you, Mr Thursby, that I believe them."

"Well," said Roger, "I haven't met either of them and I haven't yet heard them tell their story, but I'll tell you quite frankly I shall be very surprised if their story is true. Now, please don't get excited, Mr Plumb."

For Mr Plumb had started to brush his forehead very vigorously indeed.

"I'm not in the least excited," said Mr Plumb, his red face redder and his handerkchief doing overtime. "I'm not in the least excited, but am I to understand that you are calling my clients liars?"

"Certainly not," said Roger, "not yet. I tell you, I haven't seen them or heard them tell their story. Of course, I can't form a judgment on them yet. But just consider what it means if they're telling the truth. It means that an inspector and a sergeant—with very likely as many years of good character behind them as your clients—have put their heads together for no known reason to pretend that they have received money from your clients."

"You're not suggesting, Mr Thursby, that the police never tell lies and never trump up cases?"

"No," said Roger. "It does happen occasionally, but there has to be a reason for it. And don't forget this. Those pound notes— forty-five of them, I think you said, are going to be produced at the trial. And I'll tell you who'll produce them."

"The inspector and the sergeant, I presume?"

"Certainly not. Possibly even the local Chief Constable, and at least the Superintendent. After your clients handed these notes to the police officers—I mean after they *didn't* hand them to the police officers, these police officers on two separate occasions handed two separate bundles of notes to a superior officer. Now, of course, the Superintendent or the Chief Constable might be in the swindle, but I imagine you'll agree that that's going a bit far. So that, apparently, just in order to do down your clients, the inspector and sergeant laid their hands on forty-five pound notes and took them to the Superintendent or some superior officer, with a fraudulent story that your clients had tried to bribe them. Now it's one thing to invent a story. It's another to invent forty-five pound notes. They have to be obtained and they were obtained. Quite a lot of money, you know, for police officers to have. Much too dangerous to have drawn them from a bank or the post office. They must have kept them under the bed."

The movement of Mr Plumb's hand had slowed down a bit.

"Mr Thursby," he said, "you shake me. But I still can't believe it. I'm sure there's some explanation."

"I think perhaps," said Roger, "you'd better bring your clients to see me and we'll hear what it is. I'm in Court all day tomorrow but I expect Donald can fix a conference after 4.30."

CHAPTER FOUR

MR GRIMES

ROGER was in Court the next day dealing with a contract for the supply of machinery to Peru. The case was expected to last a long time. His opponent was Mr Grimes. The judge was Mr Justice Chance.

"How are ye, my dear fellow?" said Mr Grimes to Roger outside the Court. "A little bird tells me ye've applied for silk. Good for you, my dear fellow, good for you. But——" and Mr Grimes shook his head, "things aren't what they used to be, my dear fellow, not what they used to be. Ye'll find it a bit of a teaser, my dear fellow. Silks are two a penny, my dear chap, two a penny."

"I'm going to charge twopence," said Roger.

"That's the way, my dear fellow, that's the way, but I don't know what we're coming to. D'ye know, I've had a dozen letters from fellows on my circuit—they were only called yesterday—I don't know what they think will happen to them, but there it is, my dear fellow, they will do these things, they will do these things. Now, what about this case of ours, my dear fellow, my clients aren't at all inclined to settle it, ye know."

"Nor are mine," said Roger.

"Stubborn, my dear fellow, stubborn," said Mr Grimes.

"It's dogged as does it," said Roger.

"I beg your pardon?" said Mr Grimes.

"Nothing," said Roger. "But why should you want to settle? You've an unanswerable case and a hopeless opponent. What more could anyone want?"

"I can't understand your chaps fighting it, my dear fellow, I really can't," said Mr Grimes.

"Nor can I," said Roger. "But it's lucky some of them will. Between you and me they're only doing it to keep me in practice."

"Ye will pull my leg, my dear fellow, ye will pull my leg," said Mr Grimes. "But all the same, my dear fellow, I think ye'd be wise to make me an offer. I think ye'd be wise."

"If you'd said that twelve years ago I should have put my head on the block and invited you to chop it off."

"Was it as much as twelve years ago, my dear fellow, was it really?"

"Well, you haven't changed. As young and bustling as ever. What's your record from the Temple to the Bear Garden?"

Mr Grimes never walked if he could trot and never trotted if he could run. Age had slowed him down a little, but only a little. The policeman on duty outside the Law Courts seldom needed to hold up the traffic for Mr Grimes; he was across the Strand almost before they'd seen him. It would have been an exceptionally skilled motorist who could have caught him. But he always complained bitterly: "When they've killed a judge, my dear fellow," he used to say, "they'll put a bridge up or a subway. Till then one just has to take a chance. Good-bye, my dear fellow, so nice to have seen ye— good-bye, bye, bye."

The "byes" floated across the Strand as Mr Grimes dodged a 'bus, slipped behind a lorry, glared at a cyclist and cannoned into a pedestrian on the other side. "So sorry, my dear fellow, it's these ——" but by this time he was up the stairs leading to the Bear Garden and the pedestrian never learned what "these" were.

"Oh, I don't know," said Mr Grimes to Roger, "one can't quite do what one used to do, you know, one can't quite do it."

"Well, you seem to," said Roger. "I don't notice the slightest difference."

"That's very kind of ye, my dear fellow, very kind of ye. Now, what about this case? Ye really ought to make an offer."

"I said you hadn't changed," said Roger. "No, I think we'll see what old Chance thinks of the preliminary point. If he's against us on it, I might offer you something. Not much, mind you."

"That's all right, my dear fellow, my people don't want to settle. Ye have a fight, my dear fellow, and see where it gets ye."

As Roger said nothing and was about to go into Court Mr Grimes added: "Why don't ye offer something, my dear fellow?"

"You seem in a bad way," said Roger. "Let's see. You're claiming five thousand pounds. I'll offer you two hundred and fifty."

"Two hundred and fifty pounds, my dear fellow, two hundred and fifty pounds?" Mr Grimes almost screamed. "That won't even pay the costs."

"I don't suppose it will," said Roger, "but it'll be something towards them."

"If that's all ye've got to say," said Mr Grimes, "we'd better go into Court."

"I was just going," said Roger, "when you stopped me."

"Why not make it one thousand pounds, my dear fellow? I might persuade my people to take it."

"I'll make it guineas," said Roger.

"A thousand guineas?"

"Oh—no . . . two-fifty."

"It's ridiculous, my dear fellow. I tell ye it will only just pay the brief fee."

"That'd be something."

"The judge'll be coming in, my dear fellow, shall we ask him to stay out for a bit?"

"All right," said Roger, who recognized the white flag when he saw it. He called for Donald.

"See if you can keep the judge back for a bit. It looks as though this is going to be settled."

"I'll try, sir," said Donald, "but you know what this judge is like."

Roger did know, and so did everyone else. Chance J. had a sweet smile and a melodious voice. He never raised it, he seldom said a harsh word to anyone. It is said that on one occasion he smiled so pleasantly at the prisoner he was about to sentence that the poor fellow couldn't believe it when he got ten years. He even appealed on the ground that it must have been a mistake. Chance J. always sat at 10.30 a.m. He had done it for years and proposed to go on doing so. He expected everyone else to do the same. He expected every case to be ready at the appointed time. If counsel was late he found his case struck out or at least put to the bottom of the list. And what made it worse, Chance J. was so nice about it.

"A traffic accident, Mr Peabody?" he had been known to say. "I'm so very sorry. It must have been very difficult for you. No doubt you'll come by train next time. Much more reliable. I've had your case put to the bottom of the list. I doubt whether it will be heard today. I'm so very sorry. Please explain the matter to your client. I'm sure he'll understand. Yes, Mr Blank, I'll take your application for an adjournment now. It is refused. Thank you so much."

However, Donald went hastily off to find Mr Justice Chance's clerk. They were old friends, played cricket together and had stood each other drinks at every bar within three hundred yards of the Law Courts.

"Hello, old boy, what can I do for you?"

"Keep the old —— back for a bit." The —— was in fact unspoken. That was out of respect for the Bench. You just looked the word, gave a momentary pause and the decencies were observed.

"Have a heart," said the judge's clerk. "I couldn't even keep him back for the Attorney. 'I'll start the next case,' he said when I asked him. 'There isn't one,' I said. 'This is supposed to take all day.' 'Well, go and draw one from someone else. I'm sitting at 10.30.'"

"Doesn't he ever remember he was at the Bar?"

"Now you've said something. Between you and me, I told him myself. 'James,' he said, 'I used to wait hours when I was at the Bar. I didn't like it, but I had to. Now I'm not going to wait any more.' But he said it all so nicely there was nothing I could say. Really, I daren't ask him, old boy. I'd do it for you if I'd do it for anyone. It'd be no good if I did. He'd simply give me a sweet smile. 'Shall we go in, James?' he'd say."

So at 10.30 a.m. precisely Roger's and Mr Grimes' case was duly called on immediately after Mr Justice Chance had taken his seat. Mr Grimes was whispering furiously to his clients, as the associate said:

"*Green, Rawhide and Smithers* against *Confucios.*"

Mr Grimes rose: "I wonder whether your Ludship would grant me a few minutes' indulgence?"

The judge smiled sweetly. "Indulgence, Mr Grimes?" he said most amiably.

"Just a few minutes, me Lud. Your Ludship may not be troubled with the case."

"But it's no trouble, Mr Grimes. That's what I'm here for."

"But, me Lud," began Mr Grimes unhappily.

"That's all right, Mr Grimes," said the judge. "Pray open the case. It has a South American flavour, if one may judge from the Defendants' name. Oil, Mr Grimes?"

"Machinery, me Lud."

"Ah, machinery. You'll have to treat me very gently, Mr Grimes. Nice simple language, please. Is there a model in Court? I see something down there which——"

The judge put on his glasses.

"Oh—no, I'm sorry," he added.

It was Mr Grimes' client.

"Now, I think we've wasted enough time, Mr Grimes. Shall we get on?" and he gave Mr Grimes the kind of beaming smile he had given the prisoner who had got the ten years. "Now, please, Mr Grimes," he went on without the slightest show of irritation—indeed still smiling—as Mr Grimes turned round and started murmuring feverishly to his client. "Please, Mr Grimes, conferences afterwards. At one o'clock, shall we say?"

"I'll take five hundred pounds," whispered Mr Grimes to Roger.

"Sorry," said Roger. "Two fifty."

"Guineas," said Mr Grimes.

"Certainly," said Roger.

"Mr Grimes," said the judge, "can you hear me?"

"Oh, me Lud, I beg your Ludship's pardon, but I'm glad to tell your Ludship that your Ludship will not be troubled—that me learned friend and I have come to terms."

"A close thing, Mr Grimes," said the judge. "Do you want any order from me?"

"I suggest, my Lord," said Roger, "that the action should be stayed on terms endorsed on counsel's brief."

"I think I should have a judgment, me Lud," said Mr Grimes.

196

"Dear, dear," said the judge. "I thought I was told that the parties had come to terms. Either they have or they haven't. That's right, isn't it, Mr Grimes?"

"Oh—yes, me Lud."

"Mr Thursby?"

"Certainly, my Lord."

"I'm so glad we're agreed," said the judge. "Now, perhaps Mr Grimes would kindly open the case or tell me the agreed terms."

"Won't you agree to a judgment, my dear fellow," whispered Mr Grimes to Roger.

"I don't mind," said Roger.

A few minutes later Mr Justice Chance started the hearing of the next case and Roger and Mr Grimes left the Court.

"Tell me," said Roger when they were outside, "why did you crack like that? You hadn't such a bad case."

"Ye're quite right, my dear fellow, I *hadn't* such a bad case at all—yesterday. But that agent fellow suddenly turned round and went back on his proof. So what could I do, my dear fellow, but still there it is, my dear fellow, they will do these things."

CHAPTER FIVE

MR AND MRS GLACIER

WITH a long case out of the way, Roger was able to go back to chambers, and Mr Plumb was informed that he could have an earlier conference if he wished it. He jumped at the opportunity and telephoned his clients, Mr and Mrs Glacier, to meet him at Roger's chambers They all arrived just before 3 p.m. and Mr Plumb asked to see Roger alone before he introduced him to the clients.

"How are you, Mr Plumb? Do sit down."

"Very good of you to see us so soon," said Mr Plumb mournfully as he sat down. "I must say I'm more than ever glad I came to you in the first instance." And he wiped his forehead. He waited a moment or two before speaking, and then: "Mr Thursby, you were quite right, quite right," he said.

"About what?"

"About the money. I put it to my clients just as you put it to me—about the actual notes being produced by the Chief Constable or the Superintendent or someone—and after a bit they asked if they could have a word together outside my room. When they came back they admitted that what they'd told me hadn't been true. It's most unsettling, Mr Thursby, most disturbing. But what's my duty? I

197

don't pretend I don't want to keep them as clients—as I told you the conveyancing——"

"Quite," said Roger.

"But if you tell me to throw them out, I will," said Mr Plumb. "Slograve, Plumb have their reputation to think of. That comes first. We've never broken the rules yet."

"Well, Mr Plumb, in a civil case I think that a solicitor or a barrister is fully justified in throwing out a client who deliberately lies to him. Often in a criminal case, but that isn't always quite so easy."

"Mr Thursby, there seems to be a slight misunderstanding," said Mr Plumb, mopping his completely dry brow. "I don't want to throw them out. I want to know if I've got to."

"I was coming to that," said Roger. "The mere fact that a client tells you a lie certainly doesn't make it necessary for you to refuse to act for him, particularly if he corrects it himself. But, subject to certain general rules, each case has to be judged by itself."

"General rules, you say? Such as?"

"Well, I expect you know them as well as I do. Have you never been asked—how can you appear for someone whom you know to be guilty?"

"Yes," said Mr Plumb, "I have been asked that—more than once."

"And how d'you answer it?"

"Well, Mr Thursby, to be quite candid, I change the subject. I find it much too difficult. You see, Mr Thursby, my firm doesn't do much criminal work, but, in every case we've handled, I've known the defendant to be guilty, and I feel a little awkward about it, particularly as we got two of them off."

"D'you mean that your clients admitted to you that they were guilty?"

"Oh, dear me no, Mr Thursby, dear me no. Then it would have been quite simple. We'd just have pleaded guilty. But not a bit of it. They swore blind they were innocent and what's worse they got away with it. In one case the magistrate swallowed it and in another case the jury."

"I take it you didn't see them commit the crime yourself, Mr Plumb?"

"I beg your pardon, Mr Thursby? I don't quite follow."

Roger repeated the question.

"See them do it myself? Of course not. What a question, if I may say so, Mr Thursby."

"Well," said Roger, "if you didn't see them commit the crime and they denied to you that they'd committed it, how did you *know* they'd committed it?"

198

"Well—it was quite obvious in each case. The evidence was overwhelming."

"Apparently the jury and the magistrate didn't think so. They're the people to judge, aren't they, not you? You say you *knew* your clients were guilty, but you didn't, you know, you only *thought* it. The judges of the matter thought otherwise. So, as Dr Johnson once said, you were wrong and they were right."

"I think I see what you're getting at, Mr Thursby."

"You mustn't put forward what you *know* to be a false case but, subject to that, you must put forward whatever your client's case is, whether you believe in it or not."

"You make me feel a good deal better, Mr Thursby," said Mr Plumb, mopping his brow as though he felt a good deal worse.

'When you come to think of it, Mr Plumb," went on Roger, "hardly anyone would be defended if his lawyer had to believe in his innocence. If it's any comfort to you, in the few criminal cases I've had I haven't believed in my client's innocence yet."

"You don't say."

"I do—at least that's not quite accurate. When I was a very young man I was much more inclined to believe what I was told and I did once appear for a motorist in whose innocence I passionately believed. She was very pretty, so I may have been prejudiced. It wasn't a very serious matter. She was fined forty shillings. I felt like paying it myself."

"Well, Mr Thursby, I'd better say at once that I do not—and shall not—feel like going to gaol for Mr and Mrs Glacier—not for all the conveyancing in the world."

"Hadn't we better have them in?" said Roger, "or was there something else you wanted to tell me first?"

"Well, there was, but on the whole I think you'd better get it from them yourself. I wasn't very successful in the first instance."

Roger rang the bell and Donald showed Mr and Mrs Glacier into his room. Mr Plumb introduced them. Mr Glacier was a small bearded man with a slight foreign accent. He had an extremely good command of English but, every now and then, he would use a perfectly correct expression in a manner which suggested that he was uncertain whether it was right. It might well have been an affectation. Mrs Glacier had obviously been very attractive when young. Her knowledge of English was not as good as her husband's —except as regards bridge terminology; she knew all the words necessary to be able to play the game regularly from 3 to 6 p.m.

"Mr and Mrs Glacier," said Roger, 'I'm sure you'll understand that I'm only here to help you, but I cannot emphasize too strongly the necessity for your telling me the truth and the whole truth. If you don't, I may make things infinitely worse for you."

"The truth," said Mr Glacier. "Ah—who knows it?"

"You and your wife do in this case."

"Is the world round or flat?" asked Mr Glacier. "Is the moon made of green cheese?" Mr Glacier paused to see if he had made an impression. Apparently he had. There was silence.

"At one time it was popularly supposed that the world was flat. If a boy at school had said it was round he would not have been telling the truth, as it was then known. Who knows—tomorrow the world may be flat."

"It may indeed," said Mr Plumb sadly.

"And green cheese," continued Mr Glacier, "is it impossible that it was once believed that the moon *was* made of green cheese? The truth—pah!" said Mr Glacier. "When you English lawyers talk of the truth you make me——" and he looked round the room as though for a spittoon.

"Mr Glacier," said Roger, "I have not the time at the moment for a discussion as to the meaning of truth, but let us assume the earth once was flat and now is round, and that the moon was once made of green cheese and now is made of—— I don't think you mentioned what the moon is now made of?"

"Brass," said Mr Glacier.

"Brass?" queried Mr Plumb.

"No one has been there yet and brought away a—what is the word?—a sample. It could be. Or perhaps I should say you cannot prove it is not."

"Scientists could," said Roger.

"Scientists," said Mr Glacier with an air of triumph, "the best scientists of the day once were convinced that the earth was flat."

"Very well, brass it shall be," said Roger. "And now shall we get down to the matter in question? All this arose because I wanted you to understand that you may do yourselves a great deal of harm by not telling me the unvarnished——"

"Brass," put in Mrs Glacier.

"The inside of Holloway Prison is, I believe," said Roger, "no more comfortable than that of Wormwood Scrubs. Bribery of the police is a very serious charge. Anyone convicted of it is very likely to go to prison. Mr Glacier would start at Wormwood Scrubs and Mrs Glacier at Holloway. I'm sorry to put it so crudely, but, unless you treat this matter seriously, you may be sorry later."

"Very well, sir," said Mr Glacier, "put your questions. I will endeavour to answer them with a—how do you say?—a candour that will surprise us both."

"You are both charged," said Roger, looking at the summonses which Mr Plumb had given him, "with two offences. It is said that on the 14th December Mr Glacier gave twenty pounds to Inspector

Worcester as an inducement to persuade him to withdraw the licensing prosecution or to give false evidence. I understand that you did in fact give the inspector twenty pounds on that occasion."

"No," said Mr Glacier.

"But Mr Plumb tells me——" began Roger.

"No," repeated Mr Glacier.

Roger looked at Mrs Glacier.

"I pass too," she said.

"Mr Plumb," said Roger, "I thought you told me——"

"Ask them again," said Mr Plumb.

"Did you not give the inspector twenty pounds?" repeated Roger.

"I did not," said Mr Glacier.

"Either on the 14th December or on any other day?"

"On no occasion did I hand the inspector twenty pounds. My wife will confirm this."

Roger looked at Mr Plumb, who sat quite calmly, only very occasionally mopping his brow.

"Ask him again," said Mr Plumb.

"Really," said Roger, "I confess I'm getting a little tired of this. Mr Plumb originally informed me that you denied giving any money to the police, but after I had pointed out to him that the actual notes would be produced in Court he told me that you had admitted you had given the money."

"Can I rely on the money we gave being produced in Court?" asked Mr Glacier.

"I thought you said you hadn't given any."

"Can I rely on the money we gave being produced in Court?" repeated Mr Glacier.

"You certainly can," said Roger rather crossly.

"I venture most respectfully to disagree," said Mr Glacier. "The money we gave will not be produced in Court—most assuredly it will not be. You may corroborate me, my peach."

"I collaborate," said Mrs Glacier.

"Ask me again the question," said Mr Glacier.

"Did you give the inspector twenty pounds?"

"No," said Mr Glacier. "Definitely not."

A sudden light dawned on Roger.

"How much did you give?"

"Thirty pounds," beamed Mr Glacier.

"That was the first call," put in Mrs Glacier.

"Correct, my angel," said Mr Glacier.

"The second time you're supposed to have given twenty-five pounds," said Roger. "How much was it then?"

"Thirty-five pounds," said Mr Glacier, with obvious enjoyment.

"I suppose there's no corroboration of your story?" said Roger.

"I collaborate," said Mrs Glacier.

"Yes," said Roger, "but I'm afraid you're an interested party. You're charged with the offence."

"But it's the truth," said Mr Glacier, adding, after a slight pause, "this time."

"Quite," said Roger, 'but how is one to know? And if I believe you—and it doesn't matter whether I do or I don't—will the jury believe you unless there's something to show that you're telling the truth and the police officers aren't?"

"The jury," said Mr Glacier, "will not know of—how shall I say?—the way we first put it to Mr Plumb."

"That's certainly an advantage," said Roger.

"I'm afraid," said Mr Plumb, "that I'm a little out of my depth. Mr and Mrs Glacier are charged with giving money to the police. They admit it. What defence is it that they gave more than is charged against them?"

"I'll come to that in a moment." said Roger, "First of all, I wanted to see whether we'd be likely to establish that you had paid more than is alleged in the summonses."

"Suppose you can? What then?" said Mr Plumb.

"I rather fancy," said Roger, "that the police would be much more interested in prosecuting their own black sheep than in securing a conviction against Mr and Mrs Glacier."

"You're not suggesting we should tell the police what our clients have admitted to us?" said Mr Plumb, wiping his forehead vigorously.

"I certainly am," said Roger, "if it has any chance of being believed and quite likely if it hasn't."

"Do I understand," said Mr Glacier, "that you intend to betray our—what is the word?—our confidences to the police?"

"Of course not," said Roger. "Until I know a lot more I don't know what I'm going to advise you. But if I advise you to instruct us to tell the police and you don't want us to do so, of course we shan't tell them. What you tell us is in confidence and if you don't want to take my advice you needn't. Is that plain, Mr Glacier?"

"Then would you explain why you should want at all to tell our case to the police? You will forgive me, Mr Thursby. I am not any longer talking of the earth being round or flat or the moon being made of green cheese or brass or cobalt or anything at all. What I am saying is nothing to do with the moon. Is that plain, sir?"

"Entirely."

"Well, sir, I do not read many detective stories, nor do I read of very many cases in Court, but in my fifty-seven years I have read something of crime and I do not remember any case where a man's own lawyer has gone to the police—how do you say?—like a lamb to the slaughter—or perhaps I should say has led his client like a lamb to the slaughter."

"Don't let's worry about detective stories or other cases, Mr Glacier, though, as a matter of fact, there are quite a number of cases where a solicitor has gone to the police with his client to make a confession."

"I do not propose to make a confession. Why should I present it to them as you say on a plate—like a piece of cake?"

"As I've said before," said Roger, "until I know the full facts I can't say what I'm going to advise you, but, as you're so worried about this particular point, let me deal with it. Supposing I do advise you to go to the police and say what has happened, how will it hurt you?" ·

"Mon Dieu! The earth *is* flat," said Mr Glacier. "He asks how it will hurt me. You hear that, my cabbage. The moon *is* made of green cheese."

"I collaborate," said Mrs Glacier.

"Now listen," said Roger patiently. "Let's assume that you don't tell the police anything, what will happen? Both police officers will give evidence that you gave them twenty pounds on the first occasion and twenty-five pounds on the second occasion. Upon that evidence the magistrates are bound to commit you for trial at the Assizes. When it comes to your trial the same thing will happen. The officers will give their story in evidence. If you don't give evidence in your own defence you will obviously be convicted. There'll be nothing to contradict the police evidence, and so the jury will believe them. Do you follow so far?"

Mr Glacier nodded in assent. Mr Plumb paused with his handkerchief in mid-air. He was puzzled and fascinated.

"If, on the other hand, you do give evidence," went on Roger, "you will then have to say what you've told me now. If it's got to come out then, how does it hurt you for it to come out earlier?"

This time Mr Plumb nodded in assent. But the effect on Mr Glacier was electric. He looked agonizingly upwards, he tugged at his beard several times, stood up, sat down, stood up again and threw out his arms, sat down and buried his head in his hands. Then he looked imploringly as for comfort to his wife.

"I collaborate," she said.

"What's the trouble?" asked Roger.

"The world is not flat—it is not round—it is triangular—it is going round very fast indeed—now it is going to stop and we shall all be thrown off." He cupped his hand to his ear. "D'you hear those rumblings?" he asked. "We shall be blown off any minute now."

Mr Plumb, who had followed Roger's explanation of the situation with complete understanding and some pleasure, now began to mop his forehead vigorously again.

"Mr Glacier," said Roger, "I can only imagine that you're troubled at having to tell the truth to the jury."

"Troubled?" said Mr Glacier. "That is a good word. Troubled! It is we who rot in gaol, sir, not you or the amiable Mr Plumb—it is we, your clients. If we want to tell the truth to the jury, do we need a lawyer—two lawyers? Please do not think I mind the money. I like money, yes. But I pay your fees willingly if there is some point. But if all you say is go and lift up your chin so that it can be conveniently punched, or place your body in a position where it can be conveniently kicked—well, sir—I can do that without your assistance. I need no help to fall into the river. It is kind of you to offer to give me—how do you say?—a send off, but I can jump— and quite as far and as deep as you can push me—if I want to, sir— but—I do not want to, sir—*I do not want* to, sir. Do I make that plain?"

"I suppose," said Roger quite calmly, "that your idea is that we should invent a good story for you to tell."

"What else is a lawyer for? When the truth is good, what need have I of a lawyer? I go to a lawyer when the truth is—how do you say?—inconvenient."

"Well," said Roger, "there may be some countries where lawyers behave like that. And there may be one or two over here who'd do it for you, but not many, and they'd be kicked out pretty quick if they were found out."

"There are not many such?" asked Mr Glacier.

"Very few," said Roger.

"You have their addresses perhaps?" said Mr Glacier.

"I have not," said Roger. "I think perhaps, Mr Plumb, the time has come——"

Mr Plumb said gloomily: "I'm afraid Mr Glacier doesn't understand our ways. You see, Mr Glacier, although lawyers in this country have to help their clients, they have to do it honestly."

"But, of course," said Mr Glacier. "That is all I was asking."

Mr Plumb and Roger tried hard to explain to Mr Glacier what are the duties and responsibilities of lawyers in this country. Roger even repeated part of his earlier advice to Mr Plumb. Mr Glacier tried hard to follow.

"But let me ask you something," he said after a little time. "You wish your client to win the day, do you not?"

"But by proper methods," interposed Mr Plumb.

"Quite so. But you want to do the best for him?"

"Certainly."

"Well, gentlemen, let us suppose you have a client charged with

204

murder and you think he has committed the crime. No—I have quite understood this afternoon's lesson—you only *think* he has committed it, you do not *know* it. Now, thinking he has committed it—do you say to him, as you said to me, now tell us the truth? If you are right in thinking him culpable—I mean guilty, of course—he will, will he not, have to admit the crime when he tells you the truth? And, if he tells you that he is guilty, I understand now from you that he will have to say the same to the judge and jury. Is that best for him, gentlemen? Is it even good for him? How hard do you try to persuade your client to tell the truth when you believe the truth will—what is the word?—will condemn him?"

"Mr Glacier," said Roger, "this is a very interesting discussion on the ethics of the legal profession, but I'm afraid I haven't time for very much more. If you want me to continue to advise you in your particular case, I will do so—provided you now understand and will stick to the rules. I must make it plain, though, that if you don't I reserve the right to throw up the case in the middle."

"I have read of that, now I come to think of it," said Mr Glacier. "I am interested to know what it means. I am sorry to have shocked you so much, gentlemen. I confess that you have shocked me. But I think I am, as you say, over it now and I would like you to proceed, if you please."

"Well, then," said Roger, 'I'd like you to tell me in your own words how you came to pay this money, what was said when you paid it, where you got the actual money from and whether there's any means of proving that you paid sixty-five pounds and not forty-five pounds."

Mr Glacier hesitated for a moment. "As to proof—beyond my wife's and my own word—I shall have to think, but the rest I can answer now. We run a small club at the Glorious; our daughter is the secretary. The unfortunate matter of drinks after hours strictly concerns the club rather than the hotel. Our daughter, who is young and—you will forgive a father's pride—beautiful, has just become fiancée—engaged—unofficially. To someone of importance. It is perhaps not necessary at the moment to mention his name. If she had been prosecuted, it would have been most unfortunate—it might even have prevented the marriage—one cannot say where these things end. We were therefore extremely worried about the matter and, at the time the officers disclosed themselves at the party, the situation was in fact mentioned to them. No hint, I assure you, gentlemen, of money. We just happened to mention how unfortunate it would be if Melanie were charged. You can imagine then how pleased we were to find when the inspector and sergeant came to serve us with the licensing summonses that there was no summons for Melanie. We were overjoyed and we said so. The officers said they were only doing their duty and that Melanie did not— how did they say?—did not come into it. Now, the office in which we interviewed the police contains my safe where, during the day, a fair amount of cash is kept. I felt so pleased—so grateful that, without really thinking anything about it, I opened it, took out a bundle of notes and asked the inspector to accept it with our most distinguished compliments."

"You say a bundle of notes. How d'you know there were thirty?"

"When I—how do you say?—balanced the cash."

"You could have made a mistake."

"Certainly not. Impossible. There is a check for everything. It balanced except for thirty pounds."

"What did the inspector say?"

"He said it was very kind of us but we were to remember he had only been doing his duty."

"How did you come to give the next lot?"

"The inspector came again with the sergeant to prepare a plan of the premises for the Court proceedings. They chatted to us. It was all very friendly. They or I mentioned our daughter. Again we said how grateful we were. Again they said they were only doing their duty. Again I went to the safe. This time I knew it was thirty-five pounds I took out. There was a packet of twenty-five pounds and I took another packet of ten pounds."

"Why?"

"Why does one do anything? I felt grateful. We are not poor. And then, too, I thought perhaps it was expected of me. The officers stayed rather longer than was necessary."

"How did you account for the money in your books?"

"Entertainment expenses."

"Well, I should like to see your books for the day and I'd like your accountant to go through the slips or checks for that day and let me have a report. What I want to find out is if there's any possible corroboration in your books and papers that the extra ten pounds passed each time."

"To be quite frank with you, sir. I do not think there can be."

"All the same I'd like it done, please," said Roger. "I'm bound to say I find difficulty in accepting what Mr Glacier says in its entirety—he will forgive me in the circumstances for saying so, I hope. If the officers were dishonest, I can't see why they should have put in a charge at all if they'd been given the money like that. They could just have kept it and no one would have been any the wiser. But suppose that what Mr Glacier says isn't entirely accurate. Suppose he did try to bribe the officers—it *is* possible that a dishonest policeman would try to get the best out of both worlds—by reporting the matter to his superior and keeping ten pounds on the way. He would argue to himself that Mr Glacier would probably deny everything—as indeed he did at first—and would have done so up to the trial, if Mr Plumb and I hadn't intervened. He would feel quite satisfied that at any rate Mr Glacier would never dare to say he had given more than the forty-five pounds mentioned in the summonses. Of course, after he had been convicted he might tell everything, but it would be too late then. No one would believe him. So, from a dishonest officer's point of view, it was pretty well a certainty. If we'd got some corroboration and went to the police, I believe there'd be a very good chance of their chasing their own people instead of you. And if they didn't, as I've pointed out, you'd have lost nothing. For better or worse, your story's coming out in the end. Bring it out now and it may do you more good. I think it's worth trying anyway, but we do want something more than your word if we can get it. Mark you, in any event the fact that we tell the police the story at all is fairly strong and will make them think a bit."

"So you advise?" said Mr Plumb.

"First of all, get someone on to the books at once. There must be no delay at all. Then, in a couple of days I'd advise Mr and Mrs Glacier to authorize you, Mr Plumb, to go straight to the Chief Constable of the County and tell him everything—not in confidence, mind you. Openly. Tell him he can use it as much as he likes."

"Is that necessary, Mr Thursby?" queried Mr Plumb.

"In my view, yes. In fact, in criminal matters there can be no such thing as without prejudice or the like and, although I've no doubt the Chief Constable would respect your confidence as far as he properly could—which incidentally might not be possible—you can't go to a Chief Constable and say—between you and me, old boy, and you won't let it go any further, but I've murdered my grandmother—although he'd keep it in confidence if he could— you've nothing to gain from his so doing and you may have something to gain from keeping it quite open. For example, we can tell the jury all about it if they go on with the prosecution. But the object, of course, is, with luck, to stop the prosecution. If we fail in that, as far as I can see, we'll only have done ourselves a bit of good. But it's up to Mr and Mrs Glacier. If they don't like the idea that's an end of it."

"Mr Thursby," said Mr Glacier, "I am beginning to entertain a great respect for you if I may say so. I like the idea."

"I collaborate," said Mrs Glacier.

CHAPTER SIX

THE ANCIENT MARINER

On his way home that evening, rather earlier than usual, Roger was stopped by one of the ancient mariners of the Temple. Their ages vary from something over forty to something under ninety. It is very difficult to get away from any of them, but no one likes to hurt their feelings. So they ply a flourishing trade. If Roger saw any of them far enough off and he considered himself unobserved, he would slip through an arch into another of the Temple's courts; but there are not many long approaches in the Temple and usually he, like everyone else except the really rude men of the Temple, had to submit to the inevitable. There is seldom anything sad about these ancient warriors. Few of them have ever had any practice and must have had independent means to enable them to continue at the Bar. None of them would recognize himself as one of their number and they are completely oblivious of the fact that their victims are wriggling and squirming to get away. Of course, sometimes they meet each other. That is excellent. All they want to do is talk, and they both talk and neither listens and a good time is had by all.

"Haven't seen you for a long time, old boy," said Roger's captor. "Done any sketching lately?"

"Not really had much time, as a matter of fact."

"Ah, you're one of the busy ones—though between you and me I haven't met anyone who isn't. Everyone rushing off to or from a conference or consultation. Strictly between ourselves, old boy, I often suspect the conference is at the Cock and the consultation in the imagination. Not in your case, of course."

"I'm going home, as a matter of fact."

"And the best place, too. My home's here. Come up and have a glass of sherry and a yarn."

"Well, as a matter of fact——"

"Come along, old boy—take your mind off all those briefs. Come on—it's only just up here." He led the polite and unresisting Roger to his residential chambers.

"I like living over the shop, I must say. Saves an awful lot of time. I bet it takes you at least three-quarters of an hour to get home." Roger conceded that it did.

"There you are, you see. Takes me exactly three minutes. Have a chair. I'll get a couple of glasses."

Roger waited patiently and wondered how long he would have to endure the punishment. He would refuse a second glass That was definite.

"Here we are, old boy. Hope you'll like it. Rather a good line I've got from El Vino. I know the manager there rather well and he always lets me have anything rather special. Well—here's luck."

They sipped the sherry.

"Not bad, eh?"

"Very good. Very good indeed."

"I had Mervyn here the other day. Said it was the best he'd ever had. He ought to know. He was weaned on sherry. Well, what's the news? Who's going for silk? No one's written to me yet. As a matter of fact, they don't always, you know. I've seen a name or two in the paper—junior to me by years—but not so much as by your leave or with your leave. Oh, well—it's a sign of the times. Mind you, I don't believe anyone's applied just because they've had a note from someone else saying he is. Still I like these old courtesies. But courtesy's out of date, I suppose. Like me."

"Nonsense," said Roger. "Didn't you have that robbery appeal in the Court of Criminal Appeal the other day?"

"Yes."

"Jolly good," said Roger, glad that he was right. "You were successful, I gather?"

The ancient mariner's face fell slightly. "As a matter of fact I was for the Crown, old boy, and they allowed the appeal. Between you and me I still don't know what they were talking about. Said I oughtn't to have asked one prisoner where he met the other."

"Where was it?"

"In gaol, of course. How was I to know? Anyway, he only answered 'In Devonshire, sir,' and I don't suppose the jury knew it was Dartmoor."

"Bad luck," said Roger, "but, as old Grimes would say—they will do these things, they will do these things."

"Amazing man, old Grimes. Goes on for ever. Just as good as ever. Now *he* never has time for a sherry. But, of course, he hasn't. I don't know how he gets through it all. What you doing tonight? Theatre or something?"

"As a matter of fact, I've got a spot of work."

The ancient mariner winked. "I know, old boy," he said. "I could do with some myself."

CHAPTER SEVEN

CRABTREE

ROGER was in Court all the next morning trying to convince the Court of Appeal that one of its previous decisions had been made *per incuriam* or, as the layman might put it, by a slip of the tongue. He had little success. It is not particularly easy to convince a single judge that his tongue has slipped. It is naturally even more difficult to convince three judges that all their three tongues have slipped and all at approximately the same moment. During a lull in the proceedings, while his opponent was being asked a question, Roger—in a flash of genius—decided that, if one of the Lords Justices should be made a peer, his motto should be "*Per incuriam nihil*," which, Roger thought, might be translated for the benefit of members of his family who knew no Latin as "Always conscious of our bloomers."

He was interrupted in these thoughts by the Lord Justice in question:

"Well, Mr Thursby," he said, "I can't speak for my brethren, but personally I have no doubt about the matter."

"My Lord," said Roger, with a glance at the clock, "I hope that after lunch I shall have the opportunity first, of infusing some doubt in your Lordship's mind and then, of satisfying your Lordship that my argument is sound."

"You will require an extremely effective lunch," said the Lord Justice.

"I'm afraid," said Roger, "I shall be lunching on a summons for interrogatories."

"I hope," said another Lord Justice, "you won't seek to administer any interrogatories to us on our previous decision."

"Oh, my Lord," said Roger, "no one is bound to answer any interrogatory which might incriminate him."

And on that note the Court adjourned for lunch and Roger, with Donald, went hurriedly to the Bear Garden to do his summons.

"Who's against us?" he asked Donald on the way.

"Now keep calm, sir," said Donald. 'It's Crabtree."

"Oh—no," said Roger, "No—please not . . . anything but that."

"Can't you agree it with him?" asked Donald.

"I'll certainly try," said Roger, "but I can never understand what he says."

Miles Crabtree was an extremely nice fellow and everyone liked him, but he suffered from a most serious defect which made it difficult to understand why he ever received a brief. He was practically incapable of saying one complete sentence by itself. His cross-examination of a witness would usually run something like this:

"Now, Mr Sanders,"—and here he would point his finger at the witness and frown slightly in a rather learned manner—which at first terrified an untruthful witness and which was calculated to make any witness feel that some really difficult question was going to be asked; well, it was going to be difficult, but not in the way the

witness thought. . . . "Now, Mr Sanders, I want to ask you about
—but so that your Lordship can follow the question would you
be kind enough to turn to page 3 of the correspondence. Your
Lordship will see there—in any event it's in the pleadings—would
your Lordship look at page 2 of the defence—now, Mr Sanders,
with regard to the meeting on the 20th January, but before I come
to that would you be so good as to explain why—I don't want to
trap you in any way—perhaps my learned friend would let the
witness have a copy of the correspondence—would you be good
enough to explain why—no, it's no good looking for assistance at
the back of the Court, and I want a straight answer Yes or No to
this question—your Lordship has found the passage? I don't want
to be told afterwards you didn't understand the question Mr Sanders,
so I'll make it quite plain and if you've any doubt will you please
say so now—will you kindly wait, sir, until I've formulated the
question—you needn't think I'm going to be browbeaten as you
browbeat my client—will you kindly give me your attention, sir.
Have you—and tell me directly one way or the other—did you or
did you not at that meeting in January—no, not the one in January
—I'm so sorry, my Lord. I got confused with the correspondence—
if your Lordship will turn to page 36—the last sentence but one—
no, your Lordship is perfectly right—there is no page 36—there
must be some mistake—oh, no—I have it, my Lord, it's page 26.
And now, sir, I think you've had long enough, quite long enough,
to answer the question. Will you kindly do so?"

"I'm afraid I haven't followed the question," says the witness.

"So you haven't followed the question, haven't you?" begins
Crabtree.

"I'm afraid I haven't either," says the judge.

"Oh—I'm so sorry, my Lord. Your Lordship is very patient. If
I may refer your Lordship to page 36—no, page 26 of the correspondence—your Lordship will see there——"

"Mr Crabtree," says the judge, "I think it would be better if you
just asked the witness a question—just one to begin with. I'll do my
best to follow."

"Your Lordship is very good. Very well, then, Mr Sanders—you
remember that meeting, the one I was referring to, not the one in
January—that was a mistake on my part—the one in February, the
meeting which is referred to in the correspondence. You know the
one I'm talking about, there's no mistake about it, is there? Now,
at that meeting there were three of you present. You, Mrs Bole, Mr
and Mrs Meadowes—no, that makes four, I'm sorry. There were
four people present and what I want to ask you, Mr Sanders, is did
any of you at that meeting—any one or more of you, I mean you or
Mrs Bole or Mr and Mrs Meadowes—I think there was no one else

present—that's been admitted—your Lordship will see that in the particulars delivered on the 14th January last—no, I'm sorry, my Lord, it's in the defence itself under paragraph 7—oh, no, my Lord, I'm so very sorry—it *is* in the particulars of the 14th January after all —I had them in the wrong order in my bundle—I'm so sorry, my Lord. Now, Mr Sanders, this is very important, I shall make a note of your answer—did you, or Mrs Bole or Mr and Mrs Meadowes— any one of you, I mean—say anything like this—I don't mean the actual words—no one expects you to remember the exact words of a conversation all that time ago, but anything of the kind, I mean. I'm waiting for your answer, Mr Sanders."

"Did who say what?" intervenes the judge.

"Oh, my Lord," says Crabtree, "I'm so sorry. I thought I'd asked the witness. Well, Mr Sanders, so that there may be no doubt at all about it I'll ask you again."

And so on and on goes Crabtree, the most patient of judges eventually wishing that either he or Crabtree had never been born.

It was not, therefore, very surprising that Roger should be dismayed at the thought of having Crabtree as an opponent. He had altogether fifty minutes in which to deal with the summons before Master Tiptree, and another one before Master Peabody and, if possible, to get something to eat. But, he reflected with some comfort, thank Heaven there'll be an end of all this if I get silk. He prayed that the Lord Chancellor would give it to him.

"Hullo, my dear fellow," said Crabtree, as Roger came into the Bear Garden—so called because a lot of shouting goes on—though nothing like as much as there used to be.

The noise is comprised of:

First Attendant (in loud voice): First call—Counsel—G to N.
George and The Glassbottling Co. Ltd.,
Graham and Hurst.
The Gargantuan Co. (1953) Ltd., and Blowback, etc. etc.

First Solicitor's Managing Clerk (in loud voice):
Cosset and Green—Cosset and Green.
Anyone here from Cosset and Green?

Second Attendant (in loud voice): First call—Counsel—O to Z.
Orange and Mowbray.
Ostler Ltd. and Jones.
Onapoulos and Deep Sea Fishing Co. Ltd., etc. etc.

Second Solicitor's Managing Clerk (in loud voice):
Briggs and Moulton—Briggs and Moulton.
Anyone here from Briggs and Moulton?

Add one more attendant for the cases lettered from A to F and any number of solicitors' managing clerks, and start them all up together, and you have the Bear Garden.

"I think we're against one another," said Crabtree.

"Hullo," said Roger. "Yes, I'm in a bit of a mess, as a matter of fact. It may have to be adjourned, if we can't agree it. Will you agree to any of the interrogatories?"

"Look," said Crabtree, "I'd like to help you, but—well—if you take the first lot—I mean the first six, well five anyway—I don't personally see how . . . but no doubt I'm wrong, of course, but, if you ask me it seems to me—you see, on the pleadings it's quite clear—I mean if——"

"That's all right," said Roger, "we'd better let the Master decide."

CHAPTER EIGHT

CORROBORATION

A FEW days later Roger had an urgent call from Mr Plumb. "I've had the most extraordinary piece of information," he said. He wiped his forehead. "I hardly know what to make of it. Look at this, Mr Thursby. I took this proof myself."

He handed Roger a typewritten document. It was signed at the bottom: "Albert Thrussle." It began: "Albert Thrussle, police constable in the Carpshire Police, will state":

"Before you read it I'd better tell you how he came to see me. Yesterday Mr Glacier telephoned me and said that a policeman had called on him and he asked me if he might bring him along to my office. I said yes, of course, and they came. Mr Glacier then told the policeman to tell me what he'd told him, and after he'd told me, I made it into the form of a statement. I read it out to him. He said it was absolutely right and he signed it. He says he's quite prepared to swear to it."

"I'd better read it," said Roger.

He read:

I am a police constable in the Carpshire Police. I have been in the Force three years. I know Sergeant Warwick; I meet him sometimes in the police canteen. The other day he was drinking rather a lot of beer and we got chatting. Somehow or other we talked about cases of bribery and, after a bit, he said: "I'll tell you a thing. If anyone tries to drop you anything—d'you know what to do?" "Well, I think so," I said. "I bet you don't," he said. "Well," I said, "what is it?" He winked at me and said: "They always deny it, don't they? O.K. Take a per cent for yourself. No one the wiser. Easy as pie. I've got one on now."

213

"Well, what d'you think of it?" said Mr Plumb. "There's your corroboration for you."

"It certainly is," said Roger. "But why did he come to you, or rather, to the Glaciers?"

"I asked him that. He said he'd heard about the prosecution and he was so disgusted that anyone could behave like that he came straight along and told Mr Glacier."

"Why didn't he tell his superintendent?"

"I asked him that too. He said that he didn't like to. From what the sergeant said, the inspector must have been in it too. He was quite sure the superintendent knew nothing about it, but he was in fact on very good terms with the inspector. He knew the inspector and sergeant would just deny it, he thought the superintendent would believe them, and he was frightened of getting into trouble."

"Why isn't he frightened of getting into trouble now?"

"He says he simply had to do something and as he was frightened of going to the superintendent he came to the Glaciers."

"P'raps," said Roger, "he thought the Glaciers might do something for him out of gratitude, if it became too unpleasant in the police force. They're a grateful couple. We know that on their own story." He thought for a few moments.

"Did you happen to find out what beat P.C. Thrussle was on?"

"I didn't, as a matter of fact."

"I hope that by coincidence it didn't take in the Glorious."

"You mean?"

"Just that. Mr Glacier's moral sense is not exactly of the highest. I said I wanted what Mrs Glacier calls 'collaboration.' We've got it now with a vengeance. I hope it came of its own accord, and without any assistance from Mr Glacier. I wouldn't put it past them. One of us will have to ask them point blank. I will, if you like; it sounds a bit offensive."

"That's extremely good of you, Mr Thursby. I must confess I should feel a little hesitation in asking my own client whether he'd been—whether he'd been . . . well, whatever it is you think he may have been doing."

"I don't think one way or the other, Mr Plumb," said Roger. "But, having regard to our previous experience of the Glaciers and their ideas about the truth and what you go to lawyers for, it wouldn't be right to act on this without taking every reasonable precaution first. I'm not at all sure that I shan't make an exception and see the policeman myself. I'll have to think that one out. I suggest you bring the Glaciers to me once again as soon as possible, and I'll let you know if I want the policeman as well."

"Glacier's in London today, I know," said Mr Plumb. "I'll get his wife as well if possible—that's if you can see us."

"I'll arrange it somehow."

Mr Plumb left hurriedly.

"What *is* all this?" said Donald. "I've got to fit in Fitcham and Grant some time. You seem to like the Glaciers. Sure you wouldn't like me to offer them a bed?"

"They're more likely to offer me one," said Roger. "They own a lot of hotels, in particular the Glorious at Westlea."

"I've stayed there," said Donald, "when Consultation was running at Annington. Didn't much care for it. Too many visitors and they don't serve beer in the lounge. I'd have left, only we couldn't get in anywhere else. I'll charge them an extra con. for that."

Donald was looking at the diary as he was speaking. "All right, you can see them at six, if you like. How long are you going to be? Finish by tomorrow? D'you want me to wait, or will David do?"

"Oh—don't you wait, Donald. I don't suppose we'll be too long. If we are, I expect David can go too and I'll shut up. Tell him to give me a ring if he wants to get away."

"Thank you, sir. Oh—that'll be old Park," said Donald, as the bell rang. "You'd better get back to your room. I want to have a word with him about a fee."

Roger went back to his room, and Mr Park was admitted by the junior clerk and brought to Donald.

"How are you, Mr Park?" said Donald. "He's all ready for you."

"Remarkable," said Mr Park, "quite remarkable. The busier a set of chambers, the less you have to wait."

"Organization, sir," said Donald modestly.

"Now, I used to go to—well, I won't say where—but somewhere else—and I never had a conference on time. I didn't so much mind myself as I used to send a clerk in the end, but it's the clients, you know, they don't like it. Some people think it impresses. So busy, we have to keep you waiting. Fiddlesticks! I'll tell you what impresses. Conference fixed for two o'clock, conference held at two o'clock."

"I quite agree with you, sir," said Donald. "It's just a little matter of arranging. Would you like to go in now, sir? I think you said the clients weren't coming?"

Donald made as if to take Mr Park to Roger—and then stopped: "Oh, just one thing, as you're here, sir. I would have mentioned it to your clerk, but as you're here perhaps you won't mind. The fee in the Longworthy case, I know the other side have only got seventy-five, but I really can't let Mr Thursby do it single-handed for less than a hundred and fifty."

"A hundred and fifty?" queried Mr Park. "That's a bit steep, isn't it? I could get a leader for a good deal less."

"Of course you could, sir, and between you and me, sir, I wish you would. It's putting a lot on Mr Thursby to do this by himself. He's got a great deal on at the moment."

"Of course he has," said Mr Park, "but I want him to do this himself. Between you and me—apart from just a very few at the top—there isn't a leader to touch him. He'll be taking silk himself soon, I suppose?"

"Silk, sir?" said Donald. "I don't know anything about that, sir."

"If you did, you wouldn't tell me. Frightened of my taking my junior work away too soon, eh?"

"Well, I suppose he'll have to take it sometime, but he hasn't said a word about it to me at the moment, sir."

"I believe you," said Mr Park, "though I can't think why."

"Sir," said Donald, in a tone of injured innocence. "Well, would you like to go in, sir? That's all right about the fee, is it, sir?"

"Make it a hundred."

"I couldn't really, sir. I'm having to return work as it is. I'll tell you what, sir, for old time's sake I'll make it a hundred and thirty."

"That's a curious fee," said Mr Park.

"I thought you might say that, sir," said Donald. "All right, sir. A hundred and twenty-five. That's settled then, sir. Will you come along now, sir?"

He showed Mr Park into Roger's room.

As soon as that conference—which was about a yacht—was over, Roger had to turn his attention to the comparatively simple matter of an accident on the Kingston by-pass. By six o'clock he was ready for the Glaciers. Only Mr Glacier came this time, accompanied by Mr Plumb.

"Now, about this policeman, Mr Glacier," began Roger. . . .

"Is it not magnificent?" interrupted Mr Glacier. "From the gods it came, from the gods themselves."

Roger checked himself from saying he hoped their name wasn't Glacier.

"You asked for corroboration—and there was none—and now— how do you say?— hey presto, you have the most beautiful exquisite corroboration—and all dressed in blue. Are you not pleased, Mr Thursby?"

"Mr Glacier," said Roger, "you must forgive my asking you this question, but I'm afraid it's necessary. This is a serious matter for you, and it's also a serious matter for the sergeant and inspector— very serious indeed. Before I'm a party to putting forward your allegations, I want to be as sure as I can that they're true."

"Ah, we are back to the truth again—to the moon and the earth. I forget how we left them—brass or green cheese—flat or round."

"I'm afraid that kind of thing doesn't impress me," said Roger, "not favourably, anyhow. What I want to ask you, Mr Glacier, is, first of all, whether Constable Thrussle was a complete stranger to you before he came to see you the other day?"

"A complete stranger? As far as I know, yes. I may have seen him in the street, just as I may have seen you in the street before—but I am not aware of having seen either of you."

"Then you'd never spoken to him before?"

"Subject to the same—how do you say?—qualification, certainly not. I may have met him in a train and asked for a light, or on a country road and said 'good evening'—just as I may have said either to you, Mr Thursby, but I am not aware of it in either case. You see how careful I have become since we first met."

"So it was a surprise to you when he came to see you?"

"A complete surprise."

"And presumably to your wife too?"

"Absolutely. We looked upon it as manna from heaven. But I assume from your questions that you are wondering whether one of us put the manna there in the first place."

"Perfectly correct," said Roger. "If it's true that you bribed two policemen you might easily bribe a third."

"Logical, Mr Thursby, but fortunately not so. Why do you not send for the policeman and ask him questions? My English is not as good as his, my understanding of English ways is also not as good as his. Why not put your questions to him? After all, if he has been bribed by me we are both . . . both—what you call crooks—and it should not take long for a man of your experience to find it out."

"I had thought of seeing him, Mr Glacier, but it is not normally proper for counsel to see the witnesses in a case—except his own clients. I'm entitled to make an exception to the rule if I think there's a good reason for doing so. At the moment, in view of the advice I'm going to give you, I don't think there is. I've seen the officer's signed statement, I've heard from Mr Plumb how it was taken, and I think I must be satisfied with that."

"And you are going to advise?"

"What I originally indicated. I think Mr Plumb should go and see the Chief Constable and tell him everything quite openly, and show him the policeman's statement. What happens after that will depend entirely on the Chief Constable."

"You want me to go and see the Chief Constable?" asked Mr Plumb rather anxiously, and mopping his brow several times. "I confess I should find that rather embarrassing. Would it by any chance be possible for you to accompany me?"

Roger thought for a moment. "If you really want me to do so, I don't see any objection to it. It will be rather inconvenient, but I'll speak to Donald about it, if you like."

"I should be most grateful if you would," said Mr Plumb. "I

think it so important that a proceeding of this kind should start off on the right foot, and I might say something of which you would disapprove."

"I'm sure you wouldn't," said Roger, "but, if it'll make you any easier, I'll try to come and start the ball rolling. Of course it may not roll."

"I have a feeling," said Mr Glacier, "that it will roll."

CHAPTER NINE

TRAFFIC BLOCK

ROGER agreed to go with Mr Plumb to see the Chief Constable on the following Saturday. They were to meet independently outside the Chief Constable's house, as Roger was coming from London and Mr Plumb from the country.

"It's a shame your having to leave so early on a Saturday," said Mrs Thursby.

"I quite agree, Mother," said Roger, "but there it is—they will do these things."

"I suppose they will," said Mrs Thursby. "What things?"

"Make work for lawyers. Just as well, I suppose. If everyone were reasonable and good there'd be no need for us."

"Is the person you're going down to Westlea to see reasonable and good?"

"I'm going for two people really. Mr Plumb, I should say, was certainly good and moderately reasonable. Mr Glacier is logical, if not reasonable, but I suspect that he is pretty bad."

"I can't think why you bother to act for him then, Roger. There must be plenty of good ones to defend."

"I doubt it, Mother. Very few innocent people ever stand in the dock."

"How horrible," said Mrs Thursby. "I'm glad I don't have anything to do with it. I could never defend anyone if I weren't sure of his innocence."

"Lucky you didn't go to the Criminal Bar, Mother. You'd have felt the draught a bit. Now, I must be off. Bye-bye . . . not sure what time I'll be back. I'll ring you if I'm going to be late for dinner."

Ten minutes later he was on the way to Carpshire. It was not a very long journey, but it was a bad day for driving. Sporting events, roads up, experimental white lines being painted and the like made the traffic in places a seething mass. It did not worry Roger very much. There was plenty of time and it gave him a rest.

218

He turned the wireless on and prepared to enjoy himself for what-ever the length of the journey might be. He had just started to accelerate out of a prolonged traffic block when a small car came in fast from a side turning and would have caused a collision if Roger had not happened to have a reaction time quicker than the average mentioned in the Highway Code. The two cars stopped with half an inch between them.

"Really!" said Roger.

"So sorry," said the girl driver. "It was my fault. I'm always doing that."

"You may not be so lucky another time," said Roger.

"I really oughtn't to——" began the girl, when the sound of impatient hooters from behind made them both drive on. Ten minutes later they stopped next to each other again, but this time it was simply a traffic block. The girl noticed Roger first.

"—drive," she said.

"I beg your pardon?" said Roger.

"I was finishing the sentence," said the girl.

"How did it begin?"

"What a short memory you've got. Just as well, as a matter of fact."

Roger now began to notice that she was attractive, about thirty and with a voice he liked.

"Well, remind me please, if it isn't a nuisance."

"What I said was——"

Again hoots from behind put an end to the conversation. It was another ten minutes before it could be continued. As soon as they were stationary side by side again the girl went on: "I really oughtn't to——" But this time they did not wait for the hoots, and it was another several minutes before she was able to add "—drive."

"Why not?" said Roger.

"Well, it's like this," said the girl, and they moved on again. About a mile later Roger said:

"Like what?"

"I'll tell you," said the girl, and the traffic at once started off, this time rather faster than before and for longer. It was ten or twelve minutes before she was able to go on: "I haven't the qualities of a good driver."

Roger had time to say: "I should think you must have a lot of others to make up for it," before they went on again. Five minutes later: "—if I may say so," he added.

"Thank you," she said, and on they went.

At the next stop: "Are you going far?" asked Roger.

"I'm going to——" but, though she said the word and Roger

hoped it was Westlea, he did not really hear it. But she justified his hopes at a level crossing: "—Westlea."

"So am I."

"How curious."

"Isn't it?"

"You wouldn't have——"

Five minutes later: "—lunch with me, I suppose?"

"It ought to be the other way round, really."

"I shouldn't mind either way. But why?"

"As compensation for nearly running into you."

"I'm very grateful to you."

Prolonged hooting put at end to that part of the conversation. It was continued ten minutes later near a bridge which was being repaired. Roger had never been so pleased before to see the sign "One-way traffic ahead." He had never thought that he would have been on the look-out for any indication that was likely to produce a traffic block. It is a novel sensation for a motorist. But the girl in the car was giving him a novel sensation too.

"Have you ever picked anyone up in a traffic block before?" she asked.

"I've never even thought of it before."

"Are you going to Westlea for the week-end?"

"Well no, as a matter of fact I'm going on business."

"On a Saturday? How boring. I won't work on Saturday."

"You're going for the week-end, I suppose?"

"Well—yes. My father lives there and I go down sometimes."

"Where will you lunch with me?"

"If you really mean it—at the Glorious, I suppose. That's the best place."

"Oh——" said Roger, "isn't there anywhere else?"

"Why—don't you like it?"

"Well—I haven't been there, as a matter of fact . . . it's just—oh, well, I don't suppose it matters. My client owns the place."

"Your client? You an architect?"

"No."

"Solicitor?"

"No."

"I give it up."

The traffic moved on, and this time the high average speed it maintained was, from Roger's point of view, just too bad. "Don't see why everyone's in such a confounded hurry," he said to himself. "Traffic blocks are good for people. This craze for speed, and getting on! It's absurd and most inconvenient at the moment." It was a long time before he had another chance, but it came in the end.

"One o'clock at the Glorious, then?"

"All right, if you really mean it. You will be there, I suppose?"

"I shall be there," said Roger. "Your father's retired, I suppose?"

"Do I look as old as that?"

"No—I meant . . . I mean——" Roger collected himself before he started talking like Crabtree. "You said he lived down there, and I just assumed he'd retired. It was ridiculous, I agree."

"He's the Chief Constable, as a matter of fact," said the girl. "Don't forget there's a fifteen-mile speed limit along the Front —and he's very particular about it."

CHAPTER TEN

COLONEL MADDERLEY

ROGER duly kept his appointment with Mr Plumb outside the Chief Constable's house.

"I was afraid you might be late," said Mr Plumb. "I'm told the traffic is terrible."

"Oh, it's not too bad," said Roger. "Hope I haven't kept you waiting."

"I always like to be a few minutes early," said Mr Plumb, "so I'm used to waiting, but I've had quite a pleasant little stroll— except," he added, "that I was nearly knocked down by a car."

"Not by any chance a small grey saloon with a girl driver?" asked Roger.

"It was certainly a woman," said Mr Plumb.

"Was she all right?" asked Roger, a little too anxiously.

"All right? All right? How do you mean?"

"I mean there wasn't an accident? The car didn't hit anything —or overturn or anything?"

"No, Mr Thursby—the only thing that was nearly overturned was me."

"I'm glad it was nothing worse," said Roger.

"So am I," said Mr Plumb. "If I could recognize the woman, I'd report her to the police. It was quite disgraceful. She came from a side turning . . ."

"From a side turning?"

"From a side turning," repeated Mr Plumb, "as though she owned not only that turning and the main road but part of the pavement as well."

"Terrible," said Roger, "but you wouldn't be able to recognize her again, I gather? Too bad," he added, cheerfully.

221

"I didn't say so," said Mr Plumb. "I said *if* I could recognize the woman I'd report her. It's a small world, coincidences do happen. I might run into her somewhere."

"Then you remember what she looked like?"

"You seem to take a remarkable interest in this young woman, Mr Thursby."

"Then you saw she was young?" said Roger. "It's just in the blood, I suppose, Mr Plumb. We always cross-examine everyone when they tell us anything. Very bad form. I'm sorry."

"Not at all," said Mr Plumb, "I don't mind your asking questions in the least. On the contrary, it helps to clear my mind; I'm not very observant, you know, and it's possible this little chat of ours will have helped to make the vision on my mind less blurred. You see—I can't describe the woman at all. . . . I've no idea whether she was fair or dark, wearing a hat or not—or, indeed, anything about her, but if I see her again I may recognize her instantly. As a matter of fact, I'd started to think about the Glaciers and, if we hadn't had our little talk about it, the vision might have become too blurred to recognize again. But I have a feeling now that I shall be able to do it. Let's hope we meet her. Stranger things have happened."

"Indeed they have," said Roger. "Don't you think we might go in now?"

The Chief Constable of Carpshire, Colonel Madderley, was ready for them. "Sit down gentlemen, please. What can I do for you?"

Mr Plumb cleared his throat—the sign of a nervous advocate. Roger had done it for some little time twelve years previously and then suddenly, noticing it in other people, he found he did it himself. He stopped the habit instantly. If necessary he cleared his throat a moment or two before he got up to speak.

"Colonel Madderley," said Mr Plumb, "I act, as I told you when I made the appointment, for Mr and Mrs Glacier; and Mr Thursby is our counsel. I've asked him to be present at this interview and, indeed, to do the talking. In the special circumstances I thought it advisable. Perhaps, Mr Thursby, you wouldn't mind going on from there?"

"Certainly," said Roger. "Chief Constable, I want to make it plain at the outset that we are not asking you to treat in confidence what we tell you. As far as our clients and we are concerned, you may make whatever use you think proper of the information we give you."

"Sounds very fair," said the Chief Constable. "Will you tell me the catch now or later, or do I have to find it out for myself?"

"There's no catch, Chief Constable, I assure you," said Roger.

"Bait with no hook, eh?" said Colonel Madderley. "You're not a fisherman, I gather?"

"Not to-day anyway, Chief Constable," said Roger. "The position is this."

Roger then proceeded to tell Colonel Madderley the story told him by Mr and Mrs Glacier. As soon as he disclosed that more money had passed hands than was alleged in the charges, the Colonel's attitude changed and he became extremely interested. When this was followed by P.C. Thrussle's statement, he got up from his chair and walked up and down once or twice.

"Mr Thursby," he said eventually, "I don't trust your clients an inch. If you ask me—I don't expect you to agree—they're a couple of scoundrels. But scoundrels outside the police force are two a penny. Scoundrels inside the police force—and in particular the Carpshire police force—are very rare indeed. I'd sooner out one crooked policeman than convict fifty Glaciers. We're bound to get a bad hat in now and then, but, on the whole, the force is clean and, as long as I'm Chief Constable of Carpshire, the Carpshire force is going to stay clean."

Mr Plumb cleared his throat. The Colonel, recognizing the signs, held up his hands for silence.

"Forgive me, sir. I want to make the position plain. I wouldn't hang a dog on the word of your clients—forgive my language, and I don't expect you to agree—but it isn't just what *they* say . . . it isn't just what Thrussle says, though that's serious enough . . . it's the whole bag of tricks put together—it sounds right. I don't profess to be a clever man, gentlemen. I'm not; that's why they made me Chief Constable. But one gets a feeling in things—a sort of woman's intuition—and that's what I've got now. Don't misunderstand me—I may be quite wrong—and don't think that people in Carpshire get arrested because the Chief Constable thinks he has a woman's intuition. Not at all. When I get a feeling like this I follow it up—that's all; and if it leads nowhere, then I was wrong—that's all—and no harm done. I'm going to follow this up—and if I'm wrong I'll be damned glad. But if I'm right, we'll boot that inspector and sergeant out so far that they certainly won't be able to find their way back. Don't think I'm condemning them unheard; I'm not, but . . . well, I won't say any more at the moment about that. Now, I'll tell you what I'm going to do, gentlemen; you may think I'm acting swiftly—well, I was brought up that way . . . shoot first and explain afterwards. I'm going to get straight on to Scotland Yard and, if they agree, as no doubt they will, with your and your clients' co-operation we'll deal with master inspector and master sergeant. Now, I think you wanted to

say something, sir," and the Colonel turned towards Mr Plumb—
who had by now completely forgotten what it was.

"I'm sorry, sir," said the Colonel, "but you'll forgive me saying
that if it was worth saying it was worth remembering. I'm a blunt
man, gentlemen, as you'll find if you see much more of me."

"My clients will certainly co-operate to the full," said Roger,
"and so will Mr Plumb, I'm sure."

"It's odd the Glaciers telling you to make a clean breast of it.
That type doesn't usually. They lie like troopers, but I suppose
you advised them to do so. Damned good advice, if I may say so.
They're damned lucky." He paused momentarily. In his mind's
eye he could almost see the inspector and sergeant being flung
out of the police force. "Damned lucky," he repeated, "but I'd
sooner your clients had the laugh of us than we kept one man in
the force we couldn't trust. I don't care whether he's a flattie or a
superintendent. You've got to be able to trust them. Same in the
Army. But I won't bore you with that, gentlemen. Still, I did have a
corporal once—now, really, I mustn't. My daughter keeps me in
order when I'm off duty, but the superintendent doesn't like to.
And I don't blame him. I'd give him hell if he tried."

"Is there anything further you want of us?" asked Roger.

"Not at the moment, gentlemen, but, unless I'm very much
mistaken, there will be. As soon as I've heard from Scotland
Yard, I'll get in touch with you and let you know the plan of
campaign. I won't anticipate what they'll suggest, but I've a
very shrewd idea what it will be. Now, might I have your telephone
number, please?"

"Mr Plumb will give you his," said Roger. "Mr Plumb wanted
me to come down on this first occasion but, although I shall no
doubt be advising him, I don't think it desirable that I should
have any active part in any possible operations. Questions of giving
evidence might even arise."

"Mr Thursby," said Colonel Madderley, "you will not, I hope,
think I am being fulsome when I say that I think Mr and Mrs
Glacier—and Mr Plumb—are very lucky to have your services.
You seem, if may say so, to think two jumps ahead."

"That's very kind of you," said Roger. "I hope you don't still
think there's a concealed hook."

Colonel Madderley laughed. "How do I know?" he said. "The
fish doesn't know until it's caught him. But, make no mistake,
you'll find I struggle like hell—if there is one. Ever tried to catch a
twenty-pounder? You'd know if you had."

After a few more pleasantries, Roger and Mr Plumb left the
Chief Constable.

"Magnificent," said Mr Plumb, as they reached the street.

"Magnificent. I am most grateful to you, most grateful. I should never have put it like that—never. But, now that the ice is broken, I think I shall be able to manage quite comfortably."

"I'm sure you will," said Roger, "but keep in touch with me all the time. If necessary, ring me at home. You know my number."

"That's most kind. Now, will you do me the honour of lunching with me?"

"I should have loved to," said Roger, "but, as a matter of fact, I arranged to lunch with a friend."

"Well—perhaps you'll have a drink with me before lunch? Where are you lunching, may I ask?"

"Well, as a matter of fact," said Roger, blushing in spite of his efforts not to do so, "it's at the Glorious."

"Splendid," said Mr Plumb. "I was going to report to the clients there, anyway. I'm sure they'll want your lunch to be on the house. They'd be most ungrateful if they didn't. I suggest you bring your friend to the bar. I take it you've no objection to a glass of sherry before lunch?"

"That's most kind," said Roger uncomfortably. Able as he was at getting clients out of difficulties, he did not see any way out of his own. He hoped that either Mr Plumb wouldn't recognize his aggressor or that, by a further coincidence, there was another girl in the area who drove like . . . "Now—I wonder what her name is," he said to himself.

"It's a girl, as a matter of fact," said Roger, blushing again.

"Delighted," said Mr Plumb, "if you've no objection—and, of course, if she hasn't either."

"I'm sure she'd be very pleased. Shall we meet in the lounge?"

They drove separately to the Glorious, but arrived almost at the same time. They parked their cars and went up the steps to the hotel together.

Will she be there? wondered Roger, not certain in the circumstances whether he hoped she would or wouldn't be. He soon knew. She was. He went straight up to her with Mr Plumb. "Hullo," he said, "may I introduce—Mr Plumb, Miss Madderley." He swallowed the name Madderley so successfully that Mr Plumb did not hear it. But the girl did. In a surprised voice . . . "How——" she began, and then quickly altered it into "do you do?"

"How d'you do?" said Mr Plumb and then, as Roger had feared he might, looked curiously at the girl.

"Surely we've met somewhere before," he said.

"Then it was you," she said. "I'm terribly sorry. I nearly ran into you. I do hope it didn't give you an awful shock. There really ought to be some warning at the junction."

"There is a kerb," said Mr Plumb, recollection of his near escape and anger making him bold.

"Yes," she said, "there is, of course. I oughtn't to have gone over it. I am so sorry. I wonder why I do these things? Anyway, I'm so glad there are no bones broken."

"Miss . . . I'm afraid I didn't quite catch your name—I'm only so sorry to have to say this to a friend of Mr Thursby—but——"

"Miss Madderley," said Roger, "is a daughter of the Chief Constable of Carpshire."

"Bless my soul," said Mr Plumb. "I see. I see. Oh, I see. Well—but . . . but you didn't appear to know her father."

"I didn't until this morning," said Roger.

"I see," said Mr Plumb, "but you didn't mention you knew his daughter."

"We had other things to talk about, Mr Plumb, if you remember," said Roger. "What about that drink you promised us?"

"Of course, I'm so sorry," said Mr Plumb, and led them to the bar.

"Have you been to see my father?" said the girl.

"I'm afraid I have," said Roger and, as Mr Plumb was slightly ahead of them, added under his breath: "I know it's a bit soon."

CHAPTER ELEVEN

PAPER WORK

THE next day—Sunday—Roger went to Church. He had not done so on an ordinary Sunday for a long time.

"How nice," said his mother, "but is anything the matter?"

"Nothing unpleasant," said Roger.

After Church he spent an hour working before lunch, drafting Statements of Claim beginning with something like this:

The Plaintiff is and was at all material times the owner of a Jersey cow. The Defendant is and was at all material times the owner of a Standard motor car, index number 999 ZYX.

Somewhere in the middle of the Statement of Claim the two met. Animal lovers will be pleased to know that the penultimate paragraph showed that the cow completely recovered. The cost of convalescence, however, was considerable. This was explained in detail and a claim was made for all the expense to which the plaintiff had been put and for the inconvenience he had suffered,

Jersey milk being unobtainable in the neighbourhood and the plaintiff having to be satisfied with something less beneficial to his health, as a result of which he had lost weight. Most people today would have given a small credit for this, but not so the plaintiff. It turned out that it was most important for him to maintain his weight. He did not claim for the loss at so much a pound, but included this claim under the general heading of "damages." The total amount was unspecified—such a pity if you claimed too little —looks bad if you claim too much. "Damages" covers everything from a farthing to a million pounds or more. Nothing was claimed for the inconvenience to the cow. Unless this could be considered as coming within the last words in Roger's claim which were "further or other relief." He had asked for this in innumerable statements of claim, but he had never yet had a case in which they had done anybody any good. But it cost nothing to put them in and perhaps one day he would be glad they were included.

Having dealt satisfactorily and expeditiously with the cow and the motor car, Roger proceeded to draft a defence on behalf of a business man who was alleged to owe money to a company. Many and varied were the defences he raised. The money had never been borrowed or if it had (which was denied) it had been paid back; the Company had no power to lend money, the money if paid to the defendant at all (which was denied) was really repayment of capital which was illegal and so much the worse for the company and finally, having denied everything which was alleged against his client, he added "Save in so far as has been hereinbefore expressly admitted"—and here it may be remarked that nothing whatever had been admitted—"the defendant denies each and every allegation in the Statement of Claim contained as fully as if the same had been herein set forth and specifically traversed."

Having settled these two documents, Roger just had time before lunch to draft a letter for his solicitor to send in a case which involved carrots and linseed oil.

Then he had lunch, an hour's nap and back again to his paper work. And, of course, he must get ready for that non-jury case on Monday. What a pity he hadn't a leader in it. However, there it was—and, with luck, there wouldn't be too many Sundays on which he would have to do this again. He would be a leader himself—with time—with time for Anne.

CHAPTER TWELVE

CONFERENCES

A few days later Mr Plumb called on Roger with news of the Glacier case. He was almost cheerful.

"It's going very well, Mr Thursby, very well indeed. I've been down to see the Chief Constable again."

"Well, what's happening?"

"It's been arranged that Mr Glacier shall be provided with marked notes with which he is to try to bribe the inspector and sergeant again. So as to avoid arousing their suspicion, the prosecution is to go on just the same but, if the officers fall into the trap, it'll be dropped."

"Well," said Roger, "that's almost as good as we can get. When's the first hearing?"

"Next Friday week. I've arranged with your clerk for you to be there."

"Who's prosecuting, d'you know?"

"Well—they're not sure. But I think they're going to take in a leader."

"What's the object of that?"

"The Chief Constable says they did so in the last bribery case and he thought they'd better do the same again so as to avoid any possibility of the officers tumbling to what has happened. And I'll tell you two other things."

Roger had never seen Mr Plumb so happily excited.

"Yes?"

"They're going to have plain-clothes detectives in and round the Court throughout the proceedings, in case our client gets a chance to give them something."

"I shouldn't have thought they'd take anything like that. Still, I suppose they know what they're doing. What was the other thing you were going to tell me?"

"Most interesting. D'you know what he said to me?"

"The Chief Constable?"

"Yes. He said he'd suspected the inspector for a long time and would be damned glad to get him. They'd never had any evidence before."

"That's useful," said Roger. "If things go wrong, we may be able to use that."

"I'm afraid we can't," said Mr Plumb.

"I think we can," said Roger. "I think it'll be admissible in evidence. But let's hope it doesn't arise."

"But we can't use it, Mr Thursby," said Mr Plumb. "It was told me in confidence."

"What do you mean?" said Roger, rather crossly. "I told the Chief Constable from the start that there was no question of confidence on our side. Nor can there be on his unless he said so."

"He did say so," said Mr Plumb.

"Well—why on earth didn't you tell him there was no question of confidence either way?"

Mr Plumb brought out his handkerchief. "I'm sorry if I've done the wrong thing, Mr Thursby," he said, becoming mournful for the first time at that conference.

"It is rather aggravating," said Roger. "I thought I'd made it quite plain from the start. It's ridiculous that they should be able to use anything we say and that we can't use what they say. How did it happen?"

"It was like this," said Mr Plumb, mopping away, "it was like this. Nothing whatever had been said about confidence, I assure you, Mr Thursby. Then he told me what I've told you about his suspecting the inspector."

"Well, where does the confidence come in?" asked Roger, brightening slightly.

"After he'd said it," said Mr Plumb unhappily, "he added 'that's in confidence, of course.' "

"And what did you say?"

Mr Plumb wiped his forehead vigorously and, after a few moments of this, looked hard at the ground and, in his most doleful voice, said: "I'm afraid I said 'of course.' "

Roger sighed. "Oh, dear," he said.

"It took me by surprise," said Mr Plumb. "I never thought about it. He said 'That's in confidence, of course,' and I just said 'of course.' It's easy to be wise after the event, Mr Thursby, but I really don't know what else I could have done."

"I agree it was difficult," said Roger, "but it is a pity you didn't remind him of what we'd said in the first instance; however, there it is. It's no use crying over spilt milk. And anyway, if all goes well it won't matter."

"I'm sorry you think I did wrong, Mr Thursby. It shows how right I was to have had you there in the first instance. If you'd been there this time it would never have happened. I'm so sorry, Mr Thursby."

"Never mind," said Roger, "most people would have done the same."

"Then you don't think it amounted to negligence on my part?" said Mr Plumb. "We'd better inform our insurance company, hadn't we?"

229

"Good heavens, no," said Roger. "Of course it didn't amount to negligence. At the most it amounted to an error of judgment. Some people might even say you were quite right."

"I wish you were one of them, Mr Thursby."

"Don't take it to heart, Mr Plumb. I've done far worse things in my time."

"Thank you, Mr Thursby, that's very generous."

"Well, I'll see you on Friday week then," said Roger, "at the Magistrate's Court. One thing I must know before then. Is it agreed with the prosecution that I should withhold my cross-examination altogether? Or am I to behave just as I should in the ordinary way? That's very important. I must know that quite definitely. I'll have a word with their counsel, of course, but I'd like to know before I see him what the form is."

"You shall know," said Mr Plumb. "Oh, dear—I do hope I don't make any more mistakes."

Mr Plumb went back to his office and Roger picked up the papers for his next conference—*Streak* v. *Broad*. He had just opened them when Donald showed in his solicitor, Mr Glade, and the client—a smart gentleman of about Roger's age.

"I've asked for this conference," said Roger, "because quite frankly I don't understand this case at all. Mr Streak apparently has some claim for commission against the defendant, but I can't follow what it is and I couldn't possibly draft a Statement of Claim on these instructions."

"I shouldn't worry," said Mr Streak. "He won't defend; he can't."

"I dare say," said Roger, "but I must know what you're claiming."

"A lot of money, Mr Thursby," said Mr Streak, "and he's got it. I've seen it. And he'll pay. He'll have to."

"But what is the commission you're claiming?"

"Oh—we had a lot of deals together. Just put in anything—he'll pay."

"If I'm to draft a Statement of Claim I must know what the deals were, how they were made, what were their terms and so on. We'd better take them one by one. What was the first?"

"This is really quite unnecessary," said Mr Streak. "Let me show you something." Mr Streak opened an attaché case and brought out a number of documents. He handed one to Roger.

"What's this?" asked Roger.

"It's a photostat," said Mr Streak.

"So I see," said Roger, "but of what?"

"Of the minutes of a board meeting which was never held for a company which didn't exist."

"I don't follow," said Roger.

"D'you see who was present?" said Mr Streak. "Lord Mount, Sir Herbert Pennyfeather and the rest."

"I wish you'd tell me what this is all about," said Roger. "I'm not surprised Mr Glade's instructions are unintelligible if this is how he had to get them."

Mr Streak winked.

"That meeting was held in the imagination of Mr Broad only. That's his handwriting. He had five thousand pounds from Mrs Plant on the strength of that piece of paper. I bought it back from her for two thousand five hundred pounds—Mr Broad's money of course—and I gave it him back. But I took the precaution of having this made of it first. This is only one of them. I've got a lot more here. All forgeries. He made quite a nice bit out of it, anyway. He thinks they're all nicely burned. I saw him burn them. But when he knows we've got these, what can he do? He'll have to pay. It's a bit of cake, didn't I tell you? He'll have to pay. Just you put in anything, Mr Thursby. You won't need my help—any lawyer's jargon will do."

"D'you call blackmail lawyer's jargon?" asked Roger.

"Now," said Mr Streak, "don't misunderstand me. I only want my fair share."

"Your fair share, I should imagine," said Roger, "would be about five years, and I sincerely hope you get it one day. I'm sorry, Mr Glade, but I'm not surprised I couldn't understand these instructions. Perhaps you wouldn't mind taking Mr Streak away."

"I'm so sorry about this," said Mr Glade. "I'd no idea."

"Of course you hadn't," said Roger, "but let's get rid of Mr Streak, shall we?"

As they left Roger's chambers, Mr Streak said to Mr Glade: "But I don't understand. What did I do wrong, old boy?"

Roger sent for Donald. "Who are Glade and Bream?" he asked. "D'you know anything about them? I don't remember seeing them before."

"No," said Donald, "they're new. All right, aren't they?"

"They may be, but their client isn't. I think you'd better give them a miss in future."

"O.K., sir. Oh—you know you're going down to Westlea on Friday? I'm sorry . . . I couldn't get out of it. I did all I could."

"Oh, that's all right," said Roger. "It'll be a change to go to a police court again."

"A magistrate's court," said Donald.

"Sorry," said Roger. "They were called police courts when I first heard of them."

231

"Well, I'm glad you're not annoyed," said Donald. "I didn't expect you to take it so calmly."

"Oh, well," said Roger—but he blushed.

"Well, I'd got something to tell you to make up for it, but I needn't have troubled," said Donald.

"Oh?"

"You'll have company on the way. Who d'you think they've taken in to lead for the prosecution?"

"Not Henry?"

"Right first time. Pity you can't settle it. That's the trouble about crime. It has to go all the way."

"This one may not," said Roger. "It's out of the usual run."

"No!" said Donald.

"Yes," said Roger.

"Trust you to do a wangle," said Donald. "Blast," he added suddenly.

"What's up?"

"It doesn't matter. I forgot to back something in the one o'clock. Wangle reminded me of it. But look, sir, I tell you what. You're going to Westlea on Friday. The Annington meeting's on Saturday. Why not make a week-end of it? I'll run Conference in the three-thirty. I wasn't going to, but I will if you'll come. You've never been to a race meeting, have you?"

"Only once," said Roger. "It doesn't sound at all a bad idea. A week-end at Westlea. I've got a friend there, as a matter of fact. She might join us."

"Now I understand," said Donald. "Never known you take a brief out of Town like that before."

CHAPTER THIRTEEN

CRABTREE IN CHARGE?

HENRY and Roger drove together to Westlea in Roger's car on the day fixed for the magisterial hearing. Sally was to join them the next day.

"This is a comic outing," said Henry on the way. "The prosecution and defence conspiring together to do down a couple of prosecution witnesses."

"What troubles me a bit," said Roger, "is my cross-examination. It's been suggested by your people that I should cross-examine the inspector and sergeant on what they would expect to be Glacier's story—i.e., that no money passed. Well—I don't quite see how I can do that even if you agree to it, as no doubt you would."

"Why not?"

"It doesn't seem to me that I can put to a witness who's giving evidence on oath what I know to be a false case—even with the concurrence of the prosecution. How can I properly invite a witness to swear to something which I know to be untrue? Suppose I say—'I suggest to you that no money passed between you and Mr Glacier,' and suppose he agreed with me—after all it's my object to persuade him to do so—surely I'd be a party to his perjury? That can't be right."

"I see your point," said Henry. "Not being as scrupulous as you are, I confess I hadn't thought of it before. But you're obviously right. You can't."

"Of course I don't have to cross-examine at all—or I can just play about with them for a bit without putting my case to them. But either I must put my case to them or just ask them about their case. I can't put a false case to them."

"Right as usual," said Henry. "What a lot Grimeyboy taught you."

"It was by example then," said Roger. "You supplied the words."

"Yes, I'm quite good at supplying words," said Henry, "if I don't have to look them up. Well, that's settled then. I'll explain why you're not doing what was suggested. With regard to the rest, it'll just go its normal course, I suppose. I gather your client's pockets are going to be stuffed full of one pound notes, all marked. I can never make out why they have to mark them as well as take the numbers. I'm looking forward to meeting your Anne."

"I hope you'll like her. I don't really know her very well myself yet."

"But looking forward to doing so, I gather."

"Very much."

"I seem to sense much the same happening to you as happened to me when I met your Sally."

"Stranger things have happened."

"Good. I gather Donald's going to take us all to the races. He's a very important person on a racecourse. He goes in by the 'Owners and Trainers only.' We just go where we're told. I like these small meetings. They're much nearer to point-to-points. Friendly atmosphere about the place and not so many toughs from London."

"We represent the toughs from London this time."

Eventually they reached the Westlea Court. Mr Plumb and Mr and Mrs Glacier were already there, and Roger joined them outside the Court. Henry met his junior—a Treasury junior named

Digby—and the representative from the Director of Public Prosecutions who was instructing him. The Bench consisted of Mr Bragge, who kept a large grocery store, Mrs Thwaites, who had once represented the town as a Member of Parliament, the Chairman, Sir Henry Carstairs, who owned most of the land in the neighbourhood and had once read for the Bar, Mr Pantin, who was on the point of retiring because of old age, and Dr Spicer, who was a retired local doctor. They were already sitting, but the Glaciers' case was timed to come on later. Roger and Henry went into Court to see how matters were progressing. They arrived in time to hear Crabtree cross-examining a police surgeon. Crabtree's client was accused of being in charge of a car while under the influence of drink.

"Now, doctor," said Crabtree, "I don't want there to be any mistake about this. You've said that the defendant was unable to pass three out of the four tests through which you put him; well, it all depends upon what you mean by pass, doesn't it? Some people might think differently, mightn't they—no, doctor, that wasn't the question, what I want to ask you is this—first of all you smelled the defendant's breath and you say it smelled of alcohol; isn't it true that if you have any alcohol, however little, you smell of it—unless you've taken cloves or something, and would it surprise you to learn that my client always carries some cloves with him—his wife you know—you understand what I mean, doctor—well, if the defendant had wanted to deceive you, he could have taken one first, couldn't he——"

The doctor, having spotted an actual question, jumped in with an answer before Crabtree could continue. "Certainly, if he'd been sober enough to think of it."

"Really, doctor, don't you think that's rather offensive. I mean ——" But the doctor, who enjoyed family games, suddenly thought of a new one—Get in with your answer. Perhaps he might suggest it to the B.B.C.

"Not in the least offensive," he replied. "You said yourself he deceives his wife that way."

"Is that your answer?" said Crabtree. The doctor waited for a moment. It didn't seem possible. He was not aware that Crabtree's question was what may be termed a marking-time catch-phrase frequently used by some counsel when they are caught on the wrong foot by a witness. As Crabtree remained strangely silent, the doctor eventually answered.

"Yes, it is."

"I see," said Crabtree.

"Good," said the doctor.

The Chairman decided to intervene in the rather uneven contest, and metaphorically told the doctor to stand away from Crabtree until he'd risen to his feet.

"I think," he said, "you should confine your remarks to answering questions, doctor."

"I'm only too pleased," said the doctor," when I can find one."

"That'll do, doctor," said the Chairman, administering a caution to the rather too lively doctor, who was apparently so full of fight that he was prepared to challenge the referee.

"Now," said Crabtree, "you complain that the defendant's tongue was furry, well what I want to know is, don't lots of people have furry tongues? Look at the medicines advertised—my tongue used to be like this—picture of an ermine coat—now it is like this—picture of a sirloin of beef—you know the sort of thing, well——"

"I've never seen that particular advertisement," said the doctor. "I think it's rather good. Which particular medicine does it advertise?"

Crabtree and the Chairman came in together. "Don't ask me/him questions. You're there to answer mine/his."

"Sorry, your Worships," said the doctor, "it slipped out. I'm sorry, Mr Crabtree."

"Thank you," said Crabtree.

"Thank *you*," said the doctor.

"Next question," said the Chairman. He felt that if he didn't get the doctor out of the box soon the proceedings might get out of hand.

"Now, doctor," said Crabtree, "you could only examine his tongue if he put it out, or at any rate if he opened his mouth——"

"Correct," said the doctor. "Full marks."

"Dr Bulstrode," said the Chairman, "this is not your consulting-room, nor a music hall. Please behave yourself. You're in a court of law."

"Well, unless you forced his jaws open—and I assume you didn't do that . . . well, unless you forced——"

"No, I didn't do that," slipped in the doctor, and added—to himself— "I was a bit late that time."

"Unless you forced his jaws open and you say you didn't do that, then you must have asked him to open his mouth and put out his tongue, and he must have done so—now, doctor——"

"I know what you're going to say," said the doctor. "Well, I'm——"

"Will you kindly wait till I've formulated the question, doctor," thundered Crabtree. "This is really too bad. The question I was going to ask you was this—if he did what you told him or, if you prefer it, what you asked him—if he did that——"

"He must have understood what I said and complied with my request? I take it that is your question," said the doctor.

"Yes," said Crabtree, a little crestfallen.

"That's all right," said the doctor encouragingly. "I thought it would save a little time if I answered before you asked it. And the answer is—he was not blind drunk or unconscious—he was just wholly unfit to be in charge of a car."

"That was not the question I asked you," said Crabtree.

"I thought it was what the case was about," said the doctor. "I'm sorry if it wasn't the answer you wanted."

Roger whispered to Henry. "This is going to go on all day at this rate."

"They've had one day already," whispered Henry. "I read about it. The chap was as drunk as an owl, but there's a nice point as to whether he was in charge. Why don't you say something to him?"

"You try," said Roger. "He'll take it from you."

Henry worked his way into the seat next to Crabtree and, just after the doctor had floored him for quite a long count, he touched his arm:

"I say, old boy, why don't you let the 'drunk' go, and stick to the 'in charge'?"

"D'you really think so?" said Crabtree. "I mean to say——"

"Yes," said Henry. "I've read about it; I think you've got a jolly good run on it, but the 'drunk' is as dead as a doornail."

"Thanks so much," said Crabtree, rather relieved. "No more questions, thank you, doctor."

"But I haven't answered your last yet. I should like to."

"Oh, very well," said Crabtree.

"Would you mind repeating it?" said the doctor. It was what might be called a prize Crabtree, with hardly any beginning, no end and a sticky mess in the middle.

"Certainly not," snapped Crabtree.

"But how can I answer it if you don't?" complained the doctor.

"I didn't ask you to answer it," said Crabtree.

"But you did, really you did," said the doctor. "It began with —now, doctor, I want you to answer this question categorically, yes or no—I remember as far as that—it's the rest I've forgotten."

"Then how can you answer it?" said Crabtree, feeling that something was required of him.

"That's what I should like to know," said the doctor.

The Chairman intervened.

"Thank you, doctor," he said. "You may stand down. Is that the case for the prosecution?" he added, looking at the solicitor for the police.

"Yes, your Worships."

"Very well then. Now, Mr Crabtree, are you going to call any evidence?"

"Submit there's no evidence of 'in charge,' " said Henry.

"I submit," said Crabtree, "that there's no evidence that my client was in charge of this car at the material time."

"That's an interesting point," said the Chairman, "and we shall need the help of both you and your opponent over it. But, if you call no evidence, we shall be bound to come to the conclusion that your client was under the influence of drink at the material time. At least that's my view on the evidence so far given. I don't know about my colleagues." His colleagues nodded assent. "It seems that we're agreed on that then," said the Chairman. "So it's up to you, Mr Crabtree."

"I'm entitled, am I not," said Crabtree, after a whispered conversation with Henry, "to have a ruling on my submission before I elect whether to call evidence or not?"

"We'll consult our clerk about that," said the Chairman. There was a whispered conversation between the clerk of the Court and the Chairman. After a few minutes the Chairman said:

"Very well, Mr Crabtree, we'll hear your submission."

"If your Worships please," said Crabtree. "Now, your Worships, I submit that for a man to be in charge of a car he must be *in charge*, by which I mean that's it's no good for the prosecution to prove that he *might* have been in charge, they must prove that he *was* in charge, and it's no good for them to prove that he was in charge *before* the material time or *after* the material time, they must prove he was in charge *at* the material time. Now, what are the facts? The car was owned by my client. That's admitted. But he had a paid driver driving him. How can he be said to be in charge?"

"It all depends what 'in charge' means," said the clerk. "If you can tell your driver to drive fast or slow or to stop or to drive here or there, or not to drive at all and to hand over the wheel to you, who is in charge of the car? The driver may be driving it as long as you let him, but why aren't you in charge?"

"It would be ridiculous if that were the case," said Crabtree. "A man who knows he's unfit to drive gets someone else to drive him home—what harm has he done? What harm can he do?"

"He can tell the driver to stop and hand over the wheel," said the clerk. "And if it's his car, the driver would presumably have to obey him. The only other course open to the driver would be to drive to a policeman or to get out and find one. He surely couldn't legally refuse to stop driving. It would be a trespass, wouldn't it?"

"If what you say is right, then, a drunk man is not allowed

to be driven in his own car even if he takes no part in the driving, just because he may wake up and order the driver out of the car?"

Crabtree's unusually intelligent and intelligible replies were due to the fact that most of them were being pumped into him by Henry, who was now taking a personal interest in the case.

"Each case must depend on its own facts," said the clerk. "If the friend of a drunk man put him unconscious in his own car and drove him home, the position might very well be different. In such a case the owner of the car would not even know he was in it. I should have thought that, to be guilty of an offence while in charge of a car, a man must know that he is in charge. There must at least be some evidence that he did know. Then again, I suppose, if a man were too drunk to drive but could understand what was happening round about him, he could license someone else to drive on the express term that he could not determine the licence until he had been deposited at his home. I suppose in such a case you could say that the owner could not lawfully terminate the licence and order the driver out of the car until the journey home was over. In such a case it might well be said that the owner was not in charge. He would have temporarily parted with his right to be in charge."

"If that can be done expressly," whispered Henry. "It can be done impliedly."

Crabtree passed on the observation.

"I agree," said the Chairman, "but is that the case here? Let us consider the evidence. Your client had a paid driver. The driver in backing the car from behind another had a very slight accident and damaged a wing. Your client said: 'Here, give me the ruddy key. You can't drive. You're drunk.' At that moment—very fortunately—a policeman arrived. 'Who's in charge of this car?' he asked. 'He is,' said the chauffeur, who was still angry at being told off. 'Is that right?' asked the policeman. 'He's my ruddy driver,' said your client, 'but he's not fit to drive. He's drunk.' The evidence was that the driver was completely sober and that it was your client, if anyone, who was under the influence of drink."

"The fact that he said his driver wasn't fit to drive didn't necessarily imply that he was going to drive himself. He might have been going for the police," whispered Henry. Crabtree repeated it.

"And the statement made by the driver wasn't admitted by the defendant to be true. On the contrary, he said 'He's the driver,' " went on Henry, followed by Crabtree.

"This case," said the clerk, quite genially, "seems to be involving a certain amount of outside professional interest."

"We welcome such interest," said the Chairman, who was profoundly grateful for Henry's assistance. "Tell me, Mr Crabtree," he went on, looking at Henry, "do you say that a car need not be in the charge of anyone?"

Henry nodded.

"I do," said Crabtree.

"If I leave my car on the highway, who is in charge of it while I'm away?"

Henry shrugged his shoulders, which was correctly translated by Crabtree into: "It depends on the circumstances."

Henry whispered to Crabtree, and a moment later Crabtree said: "My client did not drive, he did not try to drive, he merely tried to prevent someone whom he thought unfit to drive from driving."

"Well, Mr Crabtree," said the Chairman, "I think we'd like to hear what your opponent has to say."

"A good deal," said a small solicitor with a fiery red moustache. "It will, in my submission," he went on, "be an encouragement to drunken drivers in the neighbourhood if the Bench finds there is no case to answer here. Here is a man obviously under the influence of drink who says to his driver, 'Give me the keys.' What for? To drive, of course."

"Why not simply to stop the driver from driving?" asked the Chairman.

"Because someone has to drive the car!"

"Why?"

"To get home. Theoretically, I agree, the request to hand over the keys could be merely to stop the man from driving, but from the practical point of view what did it really mean? 'Here, give me the keys.'"

"May it not have depended on the emphasis?" asked the clerk. "If he said—'here give *me* the keys'—that might suggest that he was going to drive. But if he said 'here *give* me the keys' that could simply mean he was going to stop him driving. I confess my note does not show where the emphasis was placed. I don't know if any of their Worships remembers."

Their Worships did not. At the time the question was asked the possible importance of the emphasis was not apparent to anyone.

"I suppose we might ask him again," queried the Chairman.

"But he's heard all this argument," said the clerk.

"I don't see why that should make any difference," said the prosecuting solicitor.

"I object," said Crabtree. "He has shown obvious bias against my client from the start, by which I mean that throughout his evidence——"

"We quite understand, Mr Crabtree," said the Chairman. "You object."

"Yes."

"All the same, unless my colleagues disagree, I think I'd like to hear the witness again."

The driver was recalled. The clerk reminded him that he was still under oath.

"Perhaps I'd better ask the question," said the clerk.

"Yes, please," said the Chairman.

"Mr Mills," said the clerk, "would you repeat to the Bench please what the defendant said to you after you'd bumped the wing."

"It wasn't my fault," said the witness.

"Never mind about that," said the clerk. "What did the defendant say immediately afterwards?"

"He said: 'Let's have the ruddy keys. You're drunk.' "

"I thought you said that he said 'Here, give me the ruddy keys.' "

"So he did."

"But you've just said he said 'Let's have the ruddy keys.' "

"So he did."

"It can't have been both—or was it perhaps both?"

"I don't understand."

"Did he say 'Let's have the ruddy keys'?"

"Yes."

"Did he say anything else?"

"Yes. 'You're drunk.' "

"Anything else?"

"No."

"Then he didn't say," went on the clerk, " 'here give me the ruddy keys.' "

"Yes he did. I've just told you so."

"You've told us that he said 'let's have the ruddy keys.' "

"That's right."

"And that he said nothing else except 'you're drunk.' "

"That's right."

"Then he didn't say 'here give me the ruddy keys.' "

"I tell you, he did."

" But 'here give me the keys' isn't the same as 'let's have the keys.' "

The witness looked blank.

"Well?" said the clerk.

"Well what?" asked the witness.

"They're not the same, are they? They're different words."

"I don't remember the *words* he said, only just *what* he said."

The clerk turned to the Chairman.

240

"We shan't get any further than that, I'm afraid, your Worship," he said.

"I should like to ask him some questions," said Crabtree.

"I shouldn't," whispered Henry.

"Very well, Mr Crabtree, what is your question?"

"I've changed my mind," said Crabtree. "No questions." There was a whisper from Henry.

"But I should like to submit," said Crabtree, "that that evidence strengthens my submission. It shows that the sense of what the defendant said was that he wanted to prevent his driver from driving."

"Well, what do you say, Mr Mountain?" the Chairman said to the prosecuting solicitor. "You surely have to prove that the defendant was in charge of the car when the police arrested him—not just that it is possible that if the police had come a little later he might then have been in charge."

"That is true, your Worship," said the solicitor, "but I submit there is at least evidence on which the Bench could decide that the defendant was in charge."

"You have to prove your case," said the Chairman.

"Not at the moment, with respect, your Worship. I only have to show that there is a case for the defendant to answer."

"Surely," said the Chairman, "if at this stage we think the prosecution has not proved its case we can say so. A jury can stop the case after the evidence for the prosecution is over, can't they? If they can, why can't we? I'll ask the clerk if you like."

He talked for a few minutes to the clerk. At the end he said: "Thank you very much. I'm not sure that I'm very much the wiser—no offence to the learned clerk. I still think that, if my colleagues and I are not satisfied that the defendant was in charge of the car when he was arrested, the case ought to be dismissed."

His colleagues nodded.

"Anything more to say, Mr Mountain?"

"It doesn't seem much use, your Worship."

"No, I don't think it would be. Let the defendant stand up."

A red-faced man stood up from where he had been sitting in front of the dock. "Luke Halliday," said the Chairman, "we do not wish our decision in this case to encourage drivers of vehicles to think that they can drink with impunity. On the contrary, this Bench takes a very severe view indeed of drivers who are found guilty of being drunk while in charge of a vehicle. Only a few weeks ago we suspended such a man's licence for seven years. We shall not hesitate to do the same again. Let no one think that drunken, wanton or even merely bad driving can take place in this area without the guilty party being in grave peril of fine, prison and,

241

perhaps most important of all, of losing his licence. But in every case the prosecution has to satisfy us by evidence that the offence has been committed. In the present case we are not satisfied on the evidence that you were in charge of the car when you were arrested. The case is dismissed." The red-faced man stood still for a moment, swaying slightly; then he spoke.

"How much?" he asked before he was led away to have it explained to him by his friends.

"I thought you did that very well," said Roger to Henry. "We'd have still been there if you hadn't."

In spite of Henry's intervention, however, their case could not start until after lunch. Before they went off to the Glorious, Roger saw Mr Glacier and Mr Plumb.

"I have arranged a magnificent lunch for you," said Mr Glacier. "I hope you will all enjoy it, particularly your—how do you call him?—your opposite number. Perhaps when he comes to cross-examine me you might remind him that the Sauce Béarnaise was specially made for him. Or does that too come under the Corruption Act?"

"It would if I weren't taking him to lunch," said Roger. "But tell me something much more important. What's happened so far?"

"As I have already told the good Mr Plumb," said Mr Glacier, "my pockets are—how do you say?—stuffed with notes—not this time taken from my safe—but from the public purse. I am to seek an opportunity of an interview with either the sergeant or inspector. And then I have my instructions. I shall do it in much the same way as it is stated that I did it before."

"Have you spoken to either of them yet?" asked Mr Plumb.

"No," said Mr Glacier, "I do not wish to be too—too obvious about it. I am learning, you see."

"D'you know," said Mr Plumb, "that there are about thirty detectives inside and outside the Court, all watching the inspector and sergeant like hawks?"

"How lucky," said Mr Glacier, "that telepathy has not been brought up to modern standards of efficiency. When it is—when by a machine I can transfer my thoughts to you—when you by a machine can suck my thoughts from me—then I think the time will have come to go to one of the other planets. Let us hope that there will be a regular service by then. I cannot think of anything worse than that people can know what I am really thinking. Then the word truth would disappear. There would unfortunately be nothing else. How boring. But I am detaining you. Please make the fullest use of the hotel services."

CHAPTER FOURTEEN

INTRODUCING MR TRENT

"I SHALL have a sherry," said Henry. "I suppose you'll stick to tomato juice, Roger."

"Thanks," said Roger. "Must keep awake somehow during your opening."

"Why bother?" said Henry. "Ah, here are our clients. I'm sure they'll be sociable and join me. Mr Lockwood, sherry for you? Mr Plumb?"

Mr Lockwood, the representative from the Director of Public Prosecutions, said that a sherry would be very nice. Mr Plumb, in his usual mournful tones, agreed and had nothing to add.

"I gather my junior's had to go off somewhere else," said Henry.

"He's left a pupil to represent him," said Roger. "A young man called Trent. Rather reminds me of myself. To look at, I mean. Hope he's not quite such an ass."

"Where is he?" said Henry.

"I told him to be here," said Roger. "Perhaps he's in the lounge. I'll go and look."

"Why should you look for my junior's pupils?" said Henry. "I'll go."

"You needn't,"said Roger. "Here he is."

Anthony Trent, aged twenty-three, bespectacled, arrived. "I hope I'm not late," he said in a rather fruity voice, which, like his appearance, seemed older than he was. "Good of you to ask me," he added. Roger glanced at Henry.

"Nice of you to come," said Henry.

"I suppose I should be here really," said Mr Trent, "as I'm the sole personal representative of Digby. I think he's awfully good, you know," he added.

"I'm sure he'd be very pleased to hear you say that," said Henry.

"Now you're pulling my leg," said Mr Trent.

"I wouldn't take such a liberty," said Henry.

"What I like about the Bar," said Mr Trent, "is the fact that as soon as you're called you're equal with everyone else. People who didn't know would be amazed if they heard me call you, a silk of some standing——"

"Thank you," interjected Henry.

"If they heard me call you just Blagrove. They'd think I was being uppish."

"Extraordinary, isn't it?" said Roger.

"Which reminds me," said Mr Trent. "This is a most extraordinary case. But there was one point I thought I ought to mention to you, Blagrove. It's this——"

"D'you think it'll keep till after lunch?" said Henry.

"Certainly, if you'd prefer it. But it is rather important. As a matter of fact, I think that everyone's missed it so far. You see, under the Prevention of Corruption Act, 1906——"

"If you don't mind, we will wait," said Henry. "And, don't forget, our opponents are here in force."

"Oh—it wouldn't matter their hearing," said Mr Trent. "It's a point which both sides appear not to have noticed."

"And it's been left to—now, I quite forget your name," said Henry.

"Trent. Tony Trent."

"It's been left to Tony Trent to discover it."

"Now you're pulling my leg again. I wasn't born yesterday, you know."

"When were you called?" asked Roger.

"Ah," said Mr Trent. "That wasn't yesterday either. Three months ago, as a matter of fact. It's amazing what one can pick up in a short time."

"Have you ever attended a conference with your lord and master?" asked Roger.

"I have, as a matter of fact," said Mr Trent.

"Just one, I imagine," said Roger.

Mr Trent looked mystified.

"You're quite right," he said. "But I expect there'll be another soon."

"I shouldn't count on it," said Roger. "Did you happen to say anything yourself at the first conference?"

"Well, as a matter of fact, I did just point out something they didn't seem to have noticed."

"They must have been pleased," said Roger.

"Well, to be quite frank," said Mr Trent, "I wasn't sure if they were."

"Didn't they thank you?" asked Henry.

"Well, not exactly."

"Shocking," said Henry.

"There you go again," said Mr Trent.

"Suppose we go and have lunch," said Henry.

"I'll join you in a moment," said Roger. "I've just seen——" and, without finishing the sentence, he left the bar. He caught Anne in the lounge.

"Hullo," he said.

"Hullo."

"It is nice to see you."

244

"And you too."

"Look, will you come to the races with us tomorrow? My clerk's got a horse running. It'll be a sort of chambers party. I'd like you to meet them—that's if you care to at all."

"I should simply love it."

"That's a sweet little hat."

"I'm so glad you like it. Shall I wear it tomorrow?"

"Please."

A pause.

"I'm afraid I must go now. I've got this case on."

"Yes, of course. Father's very worried about it."

"I like your father."

"I think he likes you."

"Does he? Does he really?"

"Yes—I'm sure he does."

"I am glad."

A pause.

"And you?"

She nodded. "I must go now. Where shall I meet you tomorrow?"

"Shall I call for you? We'll lunch at the course. About twelve do?"

"Lovely."

"I'm so glad you can come."

"So am I."

"I must go now."

"So must I."

"Must you really?"

"Yes, really."

"I should like to stay here talking to you instead of having lunch."

"So would I."

"Would you really?"

"But we can't. Anyway, it would look silly."

"I suppose it would. But I shouldn't mind."

"Nor should I really."

"Wouldn't you really?"

"No, not really."

"Really?"

"Really."

"Darling," said Roger, and hurried off to lunch. He found Mr Trent holding forth on the virtues and vices of some of the judges and silks he had come across in his three months' career.

"Now I think Swallow's really good," he was saying. "There's a top-class lawyer, if you like."

245

"How d'you recognize one?" asked Roger.

"Oh—you can tell in no time," said Mr Trent.

"I wish I could," said Henry. "You must teach me some time."

"Now," said Mr Trent, wagging his finger playfully at Henry.

"I don't know if it's the lobster cocktail," said Henry, "but I'm not sure that I don't feel a bit sick."

"If it is," said Mr Trent, "you'd have a marvellous action for damages. We'd all be witnesses. Of course Thursby's client wouldn't have to pay. They're all insured, you know."

"Is that really so?" asked Roger.

"Oh, yes," said Mr Trent. "You see, with all the possible claims by the public, all these places are insured."

"I think, Henry," said Roger, "that we ought to find that out before you actually make a claim. I'm sure you wouldn't like my client to be out of pocket over it."

"But you can really take my word for it," said Mr Trent, "they're all insured. It would be quite extraordinary if he weren't."

"But extraordinary things do happen," said Roger. "Let me see," he added, "when did you say you were born—I mean called?"

"Just three months ago to the day. Exactly twelve years five months after you. I've turned you up in the Law List. I suppose you'll be taking silk soon. Blagrove took it three years ago. I like to know these things."

"I wonder you find time to look in the Law List with all the other things you do," said Henry.

Mr Trent smiled and waved his finger at him. Roger shuddered.

Mr and Mrs Glacier kept well out of the way during lunch. Usually they had a table in the restaurant so that they could keep an eye on things. This time they lunched in their private room. But the food they ordered for their legal guests was really superb. If only it had been dinner, thought Roger, I might have been able to do justice to it. I wish tomorrow would come.

CHAPTER FIFTEEN

THE GLACIER CASE BEGINS

"May it please your Worships," said Henry, opening the case for the prosecution, "I appear in this case with my learned friend Mr Digby, and my learned friend Mr Thursby appears for the defendants."

Henry found someone pulling his coat. It was Mr Trent trying to remind him that he was representing Digby and that Henry ought to say either that he was appearing with his learned friend Mr Trent or at least with his learned friends Mr Digby and Mr Trent.

"Now look," said Henry, turning to Mr Trent. "Please keep your mouth shut throughout the whole of this case and leave me alone. If you can't be quiet, go and play in the street. And I'm not pulling your leg," he added.

Mr Trent retired hurt for a moment. And I thought he was such a nice chap, he said to himself. But I don't expect he means it. I suppose he's a bit nervous at the beginning of a case. That must be it. I'll help him by showing that I don't mind.

"That's all right, Blagrove," he whispered. "But if you want my help, I'm here."

"Shut up," said Henry.

"The defendants in this case," he went on, addressing the Bench, "are the proprietors of the Glorious Hotel of this town; and this case arises out of a prosecution in respect of certain breaches of the licensing laws which are alleged to have occurred at that hotel and for which it is alleged that the two defendants are responsible. I should say at the outset that for the purposes of this case it does not matter one way or the other whether the defendants or either of them are guilty of those offences or not. I am quite prepared to assume that they are not guilty. The only material fact is that they were in fact served with summonses charging them with licensing offences." Henry then went on to explain to the Bench in some detail the facts as alleged by the prosecution. It had been agreed between the prosecution and defence to prolong the proceedings sufficiently to ensure that there would be another day's hearing in the Magistrate's Court. This was in order to have an interval before the magistrates committed for trial, during which the Glaciers would have a further opportunity of trying to bribe the inspector and sergeant. Should the plot have proved successful, the prosecution against the Glaciers would have been withdrawn before committal. Accordingly Henry took up a rather longer time in opening the case than he would normally have taken. When he had finished he called as his first witness the inspector—Inspector Worcester. After the usual preliminary questions, Henry asked him about the licensing prosecution and finally asked him to deal with the interview when the money was handed to him. The inspector cleared his throat.

"On the 14th December last, in company with Sergeant Warwick of the Carpshire County Police, I called on the defendants at the Glorious Hotel. I was shown into their private office. Both Mr and Mrs Glacier were there. I formally asked them their names. They were in fact well known to me. I then said 'I'm afraid I have to

247

serve you each with these summonses,' and I handed them each two summonses."

"I call for the original summonses served," said Henry. Roger handed them to Henry and the usher took them from him to the witness.

"These are the four summonses," went on Inspector Worcester. "The first defendant read the summonses and then said——" The inspector referred to his notebook and was about to read out from it when Roger interposed with:

"How long after the interview were those notes made?"

"As soon as I returned to the police station," said the inspector.

"All right?" said Henry.

"If you please," said Roger.

"Go on, inspector," said Henry. "What did the first defendant say?"

"He said," continued the inspector, 'Is this really necessary?' I said: 'I'm afraid it is.' He said: 'I really don't see why. There's a perfectly good explanation.' I said: 'You will be able to tell that to the magistrates.' He said: 'But I don't like the idea of appearing in Court. The publicity's bad for the hotel.' I said: 'I'm very sorry. There is no alternative.' He said: 'But surely there are ways of—how do you say?—of arranging these things?' I said: 'I don't know of any and what do you mean by "arranging these things"?' He said: 'Oh—you know the sort of thing I mean, inspector, surely?' I said: 'I certainly don't.' He then went to a safe in his room. I said: 'What are you doing?' He said: 'I'll tell you in a moment.' Very soon afterwards he came back from the safe with a bundle of notes in his hands. I said: 'What are those for?' He said: 'To pay the fine, of course.' I said: 'You haven't been fined yet and, in any event, you can't pay it now.' He said: 'There are countries where people get fined on the spot for some things.' I said: 'This is not one of them.' He said: 'Don't these cases take a great deal of your time when you could be doing something more valuable?' I said: 'They're my duty like everything else. If it isn't one thing, it's another.' He said: 'Well, you'd do much better catching murderers and bank robbers and even some of the motorists who kill five thousand people every year.' I said: 'I do the cases that come into my hands, whatever they are, and this is one of them.' He said: 'If we're convicted how much d'you think we'll get fined?' I said: 'That's a matter for the Bench. I can't discuss it with you.' He said: 'Well, it wouldn't be much for a first offence —particularly if you give us a good character.' I said: 'I know nothing whatever against you.' That was true, your Worships."

"I hope it's all meant to be true," intervened Roger.

"I hope my learned friend will behave himself," said Henry. "Go on, inspector."

248

"He then said: 'Look, the fine wouldn't be more than this, would it?' and handed me the bundle of notes he was holding. They were one pound Treasury notes, your Worship. I said: 'I've told you I don't know what it will be.' He said: 'Well, keep them on account. You can give me back the change later.' I said: 'I can't do anything like that.' He said: 'Why not? Is it another of these red tapes I hear so much of?' I said: 'It isn't a question of red tape. I've told you already that you haven't been fined and that, if you are, I don't know how much it will be. Whatever it is must be paid to the Court and not to me.' He said: 'Well, keep it anyway. I've plenty more.' I then suspected that he might be trying to bribe me."

"No!" said Roger.

"I really must ask my learned friend to refrain from these offensive and unnecessary interruptions," said Henry. "They serve no proper purpose and they are discourteous to the Bench, the witness and to me."

"I say," Roger murmured faintly, so that only Henry could hear.

"Go on, inspector," said Henry.

"My subsequent actions were based upon my belief that the defendant was endeavouring to commit an offence against the Prevention of Corruption Act 1906. I then said to the defendant: 'What is this money for?' He said: 'For you and the sergeant.' I said: 'What d'you expect for it?' He said: 'Whatever I can get. If you can stop the summonses there's some more waiting for you. If you can't, you can make the evidence as friendly as possible.' I said: 'Very well. Thank you. I'll see what can be done.' He said: 'That's better. I thought you'd be sensible in the end. I suppose I went at it rather clumsily.' I then said: 'Yes, we do like it wrapped up a bit more.' He said: 'All right, inspector, if you get me out of this I'll wrap up the same amount again and a bit more.' I said: 'Thank you.' Shortly afterwards the sergeant and I left. We went straight to the police station and saw Superintendent Rutland. I made a statement to him and handed him the notes. In my presence he placed them in an envelope which he then sealed with sealing wax and both he and I signed our names on it."

"Is this the envelope?" asked Henry, and an envelope was handed to the witness.

"It is," said the inspector.

"How many notes are there inside it?" asked Henry.

"Twenty," said the inspector.

"Perhaps your Worships would care to open the envelope and a note can be made that it was opened in this court."

"I think perhaps I'd better open it," said the clerk. "I could then give evidence of it later if necessary."

"If you please," said Henry.

"Any objection, Mr Thursby?" asked the Chairman.

"None, your Worship," said Roger.

The clerk opened the envelope and counted out twenty one-pound notes.

"What happened next?" asked Henry.

"Acting on instructions from the superintendent, I called again on the defendants and again saw them in their office. Sergeant Warwick was with me. This was on the 27th December last. The following conversation then took place. He said: 'Well, inspector, have you any good news for me?' I said: 'I may have.' He said: 'Good. What's holding it up?' I said: 'There are formalities, you know.' He said: 'Of course—everything here is formalities. How long will they take?' I said: 'Well, I might be able to get it done in a week.' 'What's holding you back?' he asked. I just said: 'Well——' and then he said: 'Oh, of course, I see. It's I who am the slow one this time.' He then went to the safe again and got out a bundle of notes. He came back from the safe and handed me the notes, saying: 'I suppose you'll see the sergeant all right.' I said: 'Of course.' He said: 'You'll find twenty-five pounds there. I hope you think that's all right.' I said: 'Thank you, sir.' The first defendant then said: 'I can be sure this'll be the end of the matter?' I said: 'You leave it to us, sir.' We left shortly afterwards and I went straight to the superintendent again. I handed him the notes. They were placed in an envelope and sealed with sealing wax and both the superintendent and I signed the envelope."

"Is this the envelope?" asked Henry. And the same procedure was adopted with the second envelope. This one was found to contain twenty-five notes. After this had been done the inspector continued his evidence.

"Later, after the summonses in this case had been issued, I went with Superintendent Rutland to serve them on the defendants. We saw both defendants in the same office as before. The superintendent told the defendants the nature of our visit and handed each of them summonses. The second defendant said nothing. The first defendant then looked hard at me and said: 'This is infamous.' The superintendent then cautioned him and the first defendant said: 'I shall see my solicitor about this—it is infamous.' "

"Tell me, inspector," said Henry, "what part did Mrs Glacier play at these three interviews?"

"She said nothing that I remember," said the inspector.

"What was she doing when the first defendant was saying what you have told us?"

"She was standing or sitting next to him."

"But what was she doing? Was she reading or knitting or what?"

"She wasn't doing anything," said the inspector.

"Could she hear what was said?"

"She could not have failed to do so," said the inspector. "Oh . . . and I did forget to mention that the first time the male defendant went to the safe he could not find his keys, and the female defendant looked in her bag and handed them to him."

"Did she say anything?"

"Not that I can remember. She may have said: 'Oh, here they are,' but I'm not at all sure."

"Two of the summonses had been handed to her?"

"Yes."

"Charging her with licensing offences?"

"Yes."

"When Mr Glacier was saying what you've told us, did Mrs Glacier do or say anything to show that she disapproved of what he was doing?"

"Nothing at all."

"If what you say is true, the first defendant was asking you to procure the withdrawal of all four summonses——"

"I wish my learned friend wouldn't lead," said Roger.

"He has already said it," said Henry.

"With respect he has not," said Roger. "At no time did the inspector say that the first defendant referred to four summonses."

"He said the summonses," said Henry, "and that meant the four."

"It might have meant the two served on him," said Roger.

"What, and leave Mrs Glacier out in the cold?" said Henry.

"I know it's all very amusing," said Roger, "but this is a criminal prosecution and my clients are charged with a very serious offence. Both of them. I entirely agree with my learned friend that it may well be that if the defendant said what is alleged—which I do not accept for a moment—if he said that, he may well have been referring to the four summonses. My point is that my learned friend must not add anything to the evidence himself."

"Very well," said Henry, "how many summonses had been served by you in respect of the alleged licensing offences?"

"Four," said the inspector.

"What was the first defendant asking you to do?"

"To procure a withdrawal of the summonses."

"Did he say that he only meant the two served on him?"

"He did not. He just referred to the summonses."

"Did Mrs Glacier at any time by word or deed show that she

251

thought Mr Glacier was not asking you to procure the withdrawal of the summonses against her?"

"No."

"Or that she did not want her husband to pay you the money?"

"No, she did not. On the contrary, on the first occasion she gave him the keys of the safe."

"Thank you, inspector," said Henry.

Roger then got up.

"I want to make it plain," he said, "that I do not propose to cross-examine at length in this Court. Should the Bench find there is a case to answer against either Defendant, my case will be fully put to the witnesses at the Assizes. I don't want there to be any doubt about that. Now, inspector, I think you've said you've known the defendants for some time?"

"Yes, sir. Perhaps three or four years."

"And you know them to be persons of the highest character apart from these recent incidents?"

"Entirely, sir."

"It must have surprised you when they offered you money in the manner you say they did?"

"It did, sir."

"When did you first consider that an attempt was being made to corrupt you?"

"When he told me to keep the money."

"Did you not suspect it before then?"

"Yes, sir, I suspected it."

"When?"

"Well, sir, his whole attitude suggested something of the kind from the beginning but, of course, one sometimes jumps to conclusions too soon."

"May I put it this way? Almost from the beginning you smelled something?"

"Yes, sir."

"And when the scent was conclusive, you decided to trap him?"

"Yes, sir."

"You must have found that very unpleasant."

"Very, sir."

"But you have to do these things."

"Exactly, sir."

"Mr Glacier obviously considered that what you did was infamous?"

"Yes, sir."

"What do you think he considered infamous?"

"Leading him on, sir, I suppose—and then charging him."

"So you led him on?"

252

"He didn't require much leading, sir."

"I was only using your own words, inspector. You led him on?"

The inspector paused for a moment. "Yes, sir, I suppose you may put it that way . . . at a certain stage."

"But it was you who put it that way, inspector. Let's not beat about the bush. From the moment you were satisfied he was trying to corrupt you and the sergeant, you led him on?"

"Yes, sir."

"And lied to him in the process?"

"In accordance with my duty, sir."

"Then the answer is yes, you lied to him?"

"At a certain stage, yes, sir."

"How often do you lie to people to trap them into offences?"

"I didn't trap him into the offence, sir. He was already committing it. I merely had to obtain the evidence."

"All right, I'll accept that for the moment. How often have you lied to people in order to obtain evidence?"

"I couldn't say, sir. Not often."

"How often has anyone tried to bribe you before?"

"Only once, sir."

"How long have you been in the force?"

"Twenty years, sir."

"Starting as a uniformed constable?"

"Yes, sir."

"D'you mean to say no one—not even a motorist—has ever except on one occasion—expressly or impliedly tried to corrupt you?"

"There has only been one definite occasion apart from this, sir. I have had vague suggestions made before, but nothing definite enough to justify a prosecution."

"I take it, then, that you've only been concerned in one prosecution for bribery before?"

"That is so, sir."

"And is it right then that in no other case have you ever reported a case of bribery to your superior officer?"

"That is so, sir."

"Have you done work in the West End of London?"

"Yes, sir."

"There are some pretty undesirable types about there, are there not?"

"Yes, sir."

"People who run disorderly houses and the like?"

"Yes, sir."

"Have you been concerned in any prosecutions for that sort of offence?"

253

"Yes, sir."

"How often?"

"I can't say exactly, sir. A number of times."

"So many that you can't remember?"

"I wouldn't say that, sir, but on several occasions."

"A dozen or more?"

"I don't think quite as many, sir."

"Well, whatever the number, d'you mean to say that you were never offered anything by any of those gentry?"

"I was once, sir. That was the case I was referring to."

"Well, that means that you were never offered anything by a motorist, a bookmaker, a barrow boy or anyone else at any time in your career?"

"Not definitely, no, sir."

"You must have moved in a very high class of undesirables."

The inspector did not answer.

"At any rate," continued Roger, without requiring an answer, "you had to leave the motorists, barrow boys, bookmakers and the scum of the West End and come to respectable people in Westlea before you had an honest-to-God case of bribery?"

"Except on the one occasion, that is so, sir."

"A bit remarkable, isn't it?"

"I couldn't say, sir."

"But you can, can't you, inspector? Take street bookmakers and keepers of disorderly houses . . . is it not within your knowledge that they often attempt to corrupt?"

"I have heard of cases, sir."

"But only experienced one?"

"That is so, sir."

"Now, let's come to another matter—Mrs Glacier. She never said anything you can remember except possibly 'here they are'—referring to the keys?"

"That is so, sir."

"She never offered you anything or gave you anything, did she?"

"No, sir."

"When she offered the keys to her husband you didn't at that stage know that he was going to try to bribe you?"

"No, sir, not definitely. As I said, I was suspicious."

"When he first handed you the money, you said that he said it was for the fine?"

"Yes, sir."

"Well, at the time Mrs Glacier handed him the keys, there is no reason why she should not think that's what it was for?"

"I couldn't say, sir."

"But you can, inspector. As far as you could see, had anything

254

been said or done which showed Mrs Glacier that her husband was about to bribe you?"

"Nothing more than I've said, sir."

"Well, then—even you, an experienced police officer only suspected the possibility; can you suggest any reason why Mrs Glacier should even suspect that?"

"They might have discussed it before, sir."

"Of course they *might*. Anything *might* have happened, but, as far as you can tell from what you saw and heard, they had not?"

"I couldn't say, sir. I certainly never heard them discuss it."

"Didn't you really?" said Roger. "Well, then, can you tell me why Mrs Glacier is charged at all?"

"That's not my responsibility," said the inspector.

"But I presume you swore the information which led to the issue of the summonses?"

"That is true, sir, but it didn't rest with me who was to be charged. I simply swore to the facts, sir."

"Are you opposed to her being charged, then?"

"Do you mean you want my personal views, sir?"

"What on earth have the inspector's personal views got to do with it?" interposed Henry. "It will be for the Bench first and later, if the defendants are committed, for the jury to express their personal views. I don't mind in the least what the inspector thinks. The object of evidence is to ascertain facts, not views."

"Well," said Roger, "as my learned friend—and I don't blame him—feels so tender on this particular spot I won't aggravate the wound by pressing it."

"I'm not in the least tender," said Henry. "If you like to ask me as representing the prosecution why Mrs Glacier is charged, I'll gladly tell you. All I object to is the wrong person being asked the question. The Director takes full responsibility for the charges in this case. I represent him, and I am the person to ask."

"I can't cross-examine you," said Roger.

"I shouldn't even mind that on this particular point," said Henry. "It's perfectly obvious why Mrs Glacier has been charged."

"Not to the inspector," said Roger.

"He hasn't been asked that," said Henry.

"Well, I'll ask him," said Roger.

"It's got nothing to do with him," said Henry.

"I'm only trying to help," said Roger. "I gathered you wanted me to ask him."

"Gentlemen," interposed the Chairman, "I'm sure you both know what's going on, but it's a little confusing for the Bench to have this altercation during the cross-examination of a witness. Do you think perhaps you could continue it outside the Court?"

255

"I was objecting to a question being asked by my learned friend," said Henry, "and I'm afraid that unless my learned friend withdraws it I shall have to trouble the Bench to rule on my submission."

"But I thought Mr Thursby said he was not going to press the question," said the Clerk.

"I did say that," said Roger.

"Then I cannot think what the argument is about," said the Chairman.

"Can you?" whispered Roger to Henry.

He continued to cross-examine the inspector for a further half hour, and then Sergeant Warwick was called. His evidence was substantially the same as that of the inspector. Roger cross-examined him slightly, but not as fully as the inspector.

That was as far as the Bench would go that day and the case was adjourned for a week. Outside the Court Mr Glacier came up to Roger and Mr Plumb. "I must see you at once," he said.

It transpired that he had taken an opportunity of speaking to the inspector when no one else appeared to be looking—though in fact they were under the observation of detectives the whole time—and asked him if he would see him. The inspector had given him an appointment at the police station for the following Monday.

"Mr Plumb," said Roger, when they had learned this, "you must go straight to the Chief Constable and tell him. Er—perhaps you'd like me to come too."

They went straight to his house and waited till he returned.

"Right," said Colonel Madderley, when they had told him. "This is it. We'll have a microphone installed and, if he takes the money, we'll catch him with the notes on him when he comes out."

"But he might say he was going straight to the superintendent with the money," said Roger.

"Of course," said the Chief Constable. "Stupid of me. We must arrange for the Superintendent to be the first person to see him when he comes out of the room."

"And might I suggest, Chief Constable," said Roger, "that he makes an excuse for taking him into his office? Anything will do. A friendly chat or another case. Otherwise he could say he didn't want to discuss it in any place where they might be observed."

"Another bull's-eye," said the colonel. "You've missed your vocation. It shall be done. I've been watching this particular fish for months. We'll see if we can get a rise out of him this time. That's in confidence, of course."

Mr Plumb looked at Roger, who now had a very difficult decision to make. If it had been the first time the subject had been mentioned, he would have done what he had told Mr Plumb he ought to have done. But now the position was very different. Mr Plumb had already agreed to treat a similar statement in confidence. The colonel could rely on that promise to justify what was only a repetition of the statement. If Roger now stepped in and said it was not in confidence, the Chief Constable would not only be very annoyed but he might suspect double-dealing of some kind. On the other hand, if he simply said nothing he was, in effect, doing what Mr Plumb had already done. Silence in such a case must imply consent. If he was going to say at any later stage that the statement was not in confidence, he must say so now. It was all very difficult. In all the circumstances, he decided to do nothing, and he hoped more than ever that the inspector would be caught out and the prosecution of the Glaciers brought to an early end. He could foresee embarrassment and unpleasantness if this did not happen. And it did not help that he had already quite decided that, if she would have him, he was talking to his future father-in-law.

CHAPTER SIXTEEN

STATISTICS

ROGER enjoyed the next day more than he had enjoyed anything for a long time. He put the affairs of Mr and Mrs Glacier out of his mind; he decided to forget that he would have to do a day and a half's work on Sunday and that, in addition to a vast amount of paper work, he had a difficult non-jury case first in the list on Monday. This shall be a *dies non* he said to himself—or rather it shall be a Dies with a capital D. To the races with Anne. True, chambers would be there in force, but he would be able to see her alone from time to time, and anyway he would be able to see her and be near to her. This is it. Thank heaven she can't drive a car, or I'd never have met her. As he shaved he thought more and more about her. What a lovely name. What a lovely face. What a lovely voice. I wonder what Sally will think of her. I do hope she approves. She's nearly always right. Anyway, I can't help it if she doesn't.

He fetched her in his car and they met the others—Henry and Sally, Donald and his wife—in the restaurant in the members' enclosure. Donald had already drunk three-quarters of a bottle of champagne laced with brandy.

"Hullo, Roger," he said, "I feel we're going to have a good day." Roger introduced Anne and spoke for a few moments to Donald's wife.

"Two bottles of champagne," said Donald to a waiter. "No, make it a magnum. There's a feeling about a magnum like a thousand-guinea brief. This is going to be a party."

It certainly was. They all drank champagne and brandy. Before lunch was over Roger found he was holding Anne's hand. He looked at Sally. He could tell at a glance that she approved. It was all right.

After lunch they went to the paddock and on the way Sally took Roger by the arm out of earshot of the others. "Well done," she said.

"D'you mean it?"

"You know I do," said Sally. "I'm even a bit jealous. If you'd looked at me as you look at her I'd have been in heaven."

"You make me feel most uncomfortable," said Roger. "I must have been awful. I think of myself sometimes and shiver. You're terribly happy with Henry, aren't you?"

"Who wouldn't be?" said Sally. "I'm very lucky."

"So am I—I hope," said Roger. A sudden awful thought occurred to him . . . possibly he was assuming too much.

"You're all right," said Sally, reading his thoughts. "I saw the way she looked at you."

"Hullo, Thursby," said a voice. It was Mr Trent.

"Hullo," said Roger, without much enthusiasm.

"I can give you something for the first race, if you like," said Mr Trent. "I know what I'm talking about."

"That's very kind of you," said Roger, "but I don't know that we shall back anything in it."

"Well, just in case," said Mr Trent. "Capsule. It's an outsider. But you'll see."

"Thank you," said Roger, and he and Sally moved on to catch up the others. They found them at the paddock. The horses in the first race were being led round. None of them looked very enthusiastic. Roger found Henry talking to another member of the Bar whom he knew slightly—Eagally.

"My dear chap," Eagally was saying, "I work it out on scientific principles. You just can't go wrong. What I mean is this. If a thing's always happened in the past it's going to happen in the future. That's fair enough, isn't it?"

"Very fair," said Henry.

"Now, take this race," said Eagally, looking at his race-card. "There's a horse running that has never won a race. It's been out five times—not even placed. Now—and this is the point. This is a five furlong race. I look at the breeding. I find that the sire was Fair Trial, a great sire of winners up to a mile. Now for the dam. The race-card tells you the name of the dam, but that's not enough. You want to know the name of the sire of the dam. I get that from here," and he brought out a little book. "You see, most racegoers are so stupid they don't know about this. Just imagine, the race-card itself—produced by people who are supposed to know about these things—not giving you the sire of the dam. But that's how things are. Now I find that the sire of this horse's dam was Panorama, one of the greatest sires of sprinters. So, on the one hand you have Fair Trial and the other Panorama. A perfect combination for a five furlong race. But it isn't just that. I tell you, I go in for this scientifically. If you look up all the horses which have been sired by Fair Trial out of a dam by Panorama, you'll find that they all win races sooner or later and nearly always sooner."

"Suppose," said Roger, "the horse was sired by Panorama out of a dam by Fair Trial. Would that be any good?"

"My dear boy," said Eagally, "you're getting the hang of it. It'd be just as good—though, as a matter of fact, there does happen to be one exception with that particular breeding. There is a horse of that breeding which has never won a race—but, as far as I know, only one. There must be the odd exception to every rule in racing—but they're so rare you can disregard them."

"But how d'you know it's going to win this race? You'd have said the same for its fifth race, and it lost," said Sally.

"Quite true," said Eagally. "I should have said the same, and I should have backed it and lost my money. But don't forget, it's run five races now. Past statistics show that, on an average, horses of a particular combination of breeding win their first race within their first three races. Accordingly, if they don't win in the first three races, the chances of winning the fourth are greatly increased, the fifth even more, and the sixth is as near to a certainty as doesn't matter—unless it's going to turn out to be an exception to the rule. Well, as I say, you're bound to get the odd exception, but you can pay for it out of your winnings on the others."

"What's its name?" asked Roger. "Not Capsule, by any chance?"

"No, it's called Fair View. There it is. Not much to look at, I agree. But if that horse doesn't win this race or the next, I'll eat my hat."

"Is it in the next race as well, then? It'll be pretty tired, won't it?" asked Roger.

"No, I mean its next race. Anyway, I'm going to back it."

"I was told that Capsule was going to win," said Roger.

"Capsule?" said Eagally. "I'll look it up. Let me see." He referred to his little book. "By Trimbush out of a Tiberius mare. Now, this is a good example of what I mean. That's a stayer. Perfect breeding for staying. Anything from one and a half miles upwards. But not for a sprint. Oh dear, no. Of course, it's only a two-year-old and they do win sometimes, but I wouldn't touch it."

It was the general opinion of Roger's chambers that Eagally knew what he was talking about and they voted for Fair View and backed it. Then they went to the stands to watch the race.

"They're under starter's orders," said the voice over the loud-speaker, and a moment later: "They're off," it said.

Fair View cannot have heard it. As soon as the tapes went up it turned round in the opposite direction.

"Hell," said Eagally, "w.r.s.t.n.p."

"I beg your pardon?" said Sally.

"Tell you afterwards," said Eagally.

The horses came towards them with more enthusiasm than they had shown in the paddock. About two hundred yards from the finish, one horse started to emerge from the others and it eventually won by a comfortable three lengths. It was Capsule.

"So sorry," said Eagally, when the race was over. "It's just one of those things. It would happen today. It was a certainty if it had only raced. I couldn't tell it was going to do that, could I?"

"You were going to tell me what you said when it happened," said Sally. "I thought it might be a private swearword."

"Oh, you mean 'w.r.s.t.n.p.' That simply means 'whipped round at start, took no part.' I wish I knew when it was running again. It'd have to win. Couldn't lose, or my statistics are non-sense."

"Have you ever considered that possibility?" asked Henry.

On the way down from the stands to the paddock, they met Mr Trent. He was talking to Mr Justice Kingsdown, whom he had waylaid, saying: "Excuse me, judge, aren't you Mr Justice Kingsdown?"

"Yes," said the judge, who was a genial man. "I must admit that. And who are you?"

"I don't suppose you would remember me, judge," Mr Trent had said. "I was before you in chambers the other day—just as a pupil, you know. I didn't actually say anything. But I'd read all the papers. And I was quite sure you'd decide as you did."

"How comforting," said the judge. "You don't happen to be quite sure who's going to win the next race, I suppose? Horses —I imagine—are less predictable than judges—though I have known a few decisions which could be classed as rank outsiders."

At that moment Roger and his party were passing them.

"Hullo, Thursby," said Mr Trent. "The judge has just asked me for the winner of the next race. You can tell him I gave you the winner for the last. Hope you backed it."

"Hullo, Thursby," said the judge. "And Blagrove. Quite a

legal party. My daughter's somewhere about. I come to please her, you know. Doesn't mean very much to me."

"The winner of the next race," said Mr Trent, "will in all probability be Cotton Wool—but it'll be a close thing between it and Madagascar. I shall back them both, if the odds are good enough."

Eagally looked at his card. "One and three-quarter miles," he said. "Now . . . the dam of Cotton Wool is by Gold Bridge—another great sire of sprinters. That won't do for one and three-quarter miles. It does occasionally happen with a very stout-hearted sire—Whiteway was an example—but normally if the dam's by Gold Bridge you can write off the horse as a stayer. Can't think why owners and trainers enter them for races of that distance. Now let's look at Madagascar. Sire of the dam was Sir Cosmo. That's almost as bad. No, I should write those off if I were you. Now, for a race of this description I'd choose something like—let me see——" and he consulted his little book.

"What about Roman Tour? By Tourbillon out of a Tiberius mare. Stay all the way from Land's End to John o' Groats. Let's see what it did last year." He looked in another little book. "Yes—not at all bad. Quite promising and, with that breeding, it'll stay for ever—that's the horse for my money."

"Well," said Roger, "what's it to be?"

The prejudice against Mr Trent was so great that they voted for Eagally's choice. In due course they went to the stands to watch the race. Just before it started, Eagally said: "There's only one thing I ought to have mentioned. There are only six horses in this race. That may mean that the race isn't truly run—isn't run at a fast enough pace. If that happens, it enables a horse which isn't a genuine stayer to win."

"A horse like Madagascar, for instance," said Roger, "or Cotton Wool."

"Could be," said Eagally, "but let's hope there's a smart gallop. I wonder who'll make the running."

The race started and apparently no one wanted to make the running. The pace was rather like that of an underfed riding school going round Hyde Park. The crowd began to jeer and clap. But the funereal rate continued. It increased three or four furlongs from the end when two horses left the other four almost standing. They raced side by side for the last three hundred yards and made quite an exciting finish. There was no photo-finish apparatus, and the judge, after a moment's thought, awarded a dead heat—between Cotton Wool and Madagascar.

"What did I say?" said Mr Trent, as soon as he found Roger and Henry's party. "Couldn't do much better than that."

261

"Very good," said Henry. "Let's go to the paddock." In the paddock they found Mr Justice Kingsdown wandering round rather uncertainly—as though he couldn't find something he was looking for.

"Hullo, judge."

"Hullo."

A pause.

"Er—I suppose," said the judge, "you haven't seen that rather extraordinary young man about anywhere? I was just wondering——"

"He was by the stands a minute ago, judge," said Roger.

"Thank you," said the judge—and a moment or two later was seen to be moving towards the stands.

"I could have told him something for the next race," said Eagally.

"Another certainty?" asked Henry.

"Well," said Eagally, "you can't blame me for the last two races. If a horse doesn't start, it can't win, can it? And in the last race you heard what the crowd thought of the pace. If there'd been fifteen runners it would have been a different story. Now, the next race is another sprint—six furlongs this time. Now, this is where statistics come in. Fair View didn't win."

"No, we noticed that," said Henry.

"This horse is of similar breeding—I don't suppose it means anything to you—but it's by Denturius out of a Panorama mare."

"I assume it's never won," said Roger.

"You're right," said Eagally.

"But how many times has it tried?" said Henry.

"Now that's the point. Five times. Just like Fair View. Now it's statistically impossible for both horses to fail on the same day—let alone at the same meeting. It can't happen."

"Suppose," said Sally, "it w.r.n.s. or whatever the correct expression was?"

"W.r.s.," corrected Eagally. "Statistically it can't."

"But I suppose it can physically," said Roger.

"Of course it can physically," said Eagally. "Physically it could die or break an artery or fall down or throw its jockey or charge the tapes and injure itself—or even win and be disqualified on an objection. But statistically it will win. It can't help it. That's what's so extraordinary."

"Do the bookmakers know this?"

"Of course not. They only know which horses are backed most. That's all they care about. There it is, by the way. Better looking than Fair View, I should say. In pretty good condition."

"D'you think you could tell it not to w.r.s. if I back it?" said Anne.

"I tell you," said Eagally, "that it can't whip round at the start or do anything else except win. You can't go wrong with statistics. Admittedly very occasionally there's an exception. But I can count them on one hand. Which reminds me. I had one last week. Now, you couldn't have two in a fortnight. It's absolutely impossible."

"Do tell that to the horse," said Henry.

"I don't blame you for laughing," said Eagally, "but, at the end of the race—you'll see. Most chaps are a bit cautious about giving their tips—take the newspapers. 'If so-and-so can give the weight to such-and-such I think it should win. But I'm a little afraid of what's-his-name, and they say that t'other-'un is in the pink of condition.' You must admit that I tell you quite definitely that the horse will win."

"And I'm afraid," said Henry, "you must admit that so far it hasn't."

"There have been special reasons," said Eagally.

"I hope there isn't going to be one this time," said Roger.

"It's statistically impossible," said Eagally. "It's a bit of luck, really. I've never known a case where the odds were so strongly in my favour. Let's hope it'll convince you."

"I'm hoping to be convinced," said Henry. "And, to prove it, I shall put one pound to win on—what's its name?"

"Toothy Look," said Eagally. "Don't thank me now. Wait till it's won."

"Very fair," said Henry.

At that moment Donald arrived.

"Hullo," he said and then, lowering his voice to a confidential whisper, he went on: "My trainer says that Conference is bound to win if the boy can hold him in for the first mile."

"What does that mean?" said Roger.

"Look," said Donald, "it's like this. By putting a boy on him he gets a seven-pound allowance—seven pounds less weight. Easier to run with less on your back, d'you follow?"

"Yes. That's very reasonable," said Henry.

"Well, now, Conference is a little difficult for a boy to handle. He pulls like blazes, and if the boy can't hold him in he'll rush to the front and wear himself out. But if he can hold him in for a mile, he'll leave the others standing in the last two furlongs."

"Well," said Roger, "what do we do about that?"

"I'll tell you. Some bookies will give you odds during the race. I'll put you near one or two who will. If Conference is in the rear at the end of a mile, put your shirt on him. But if he's right in

263

front, leave him alone. He'll fold up in the last two furlongs and come in last. Got me?"

"Sounds plain sailing to me," said Roger.

"Which race is it, the next one?" asked Henry.

"Now, Henry," said Donald reprovingly, "the next race is six furlongs. Eight furlongs make a mile. If he's to hold him in for a mile, stands to reason race must be more than six furlongs."

"Fair enough," said Henry. "Which race is it?"

"One after next," said Donald. "Now, don't forget. What are you doing for the next race? I saw old Kingsdown at the five pound tote window."

"He must have found Mr Trent," said Roger.

"Come again," said Donald.

"Mr Trent, in addition to knowing all the law worth knowing, knows all the winners worth knowing."

"Who's Mr Trent?"

"He's the very learned pupil of my junior," said Henry. "He's worth meeting for a short time. I've no doubt he could give you a few hints."

"Pity he's not your pupil, Roger," said Donald. "We'd teach him something."

"My dear Ronald," said Roger, "if Trent were my pupil I think I should retire from the Bar." Then, in a slightly lower tone, he added: "I'm doing that anyway, I suppose."

"Don't come that one on me, Roger," said Donald. "See you later."

Soon afterwards the chambers party and Eagally went to the stands to see the next race.

"They're under starter's orders," was soon followed by "They're off" and this time Eagally's horse started with the rest.

"You see," he said, "no w.r.s. that time. It was statistically impossible. What did I tell you?"

"You said it would win," said Henry.

"You'll see," said Eagally. "There it is—nicely tucked in on the rails—lying about sixth. Doesn't matter where it is. It's going to win."

The horses charged on towards the winning post. A furlong out Toothy Look was still lying sixth.

"I wish it would hurry," said Roger.

"Don't you worry," said Eagally. "He'll make his effort any moment. But it doesn't matter whether he does or he doesn't—he can't lose."

"He seems to have a very reasonable chance of doing so at the moment," said Henry.

A hundred yards from home Toothy Look's jockey made a

very fine effort indeed. Unfortunately so did all the other jockeys, and Toothy Look duly passed the post—still sixth. But it's true to say that there was not more than a length between all six horses.

"First—number ten, second—number three, third—number eight," said the voice over the loudspeaker.

"But Toothy Look was number ten," said Sally.

"What did I tell you?" said Eagally.

"But I don't understand," said Henry. Nor did the crowd. There were groans and howls of various kinds. The race had in fact been won by the favourite, but the judge had mistaken the favourite's colours for those of Toothy Look; they were very similar.

"Toothy Look didn't win that race," said Roger.

"His number's in the frame," said Eagally, "and, as long as it's there, he won. Now, in any other race there'd be an objection of some kind, but there can't be in this one. It's statistically impossible. Just listen to the crowd. It's no good. The judge's decision is final."

And it was. As they went from the stands to the totalisator to collect their winnings, they met an extremely angry judge, talking to Mr Trent, who seemed quite calm and collected. Mr Trent had correctly informed the judge which horse would come in first—but not which horse would win. The judge had lost five pounds.

"This is quite outrageous," he said to Henry. "There should be some method of appeal. I've always been told that racing was a crook's game. Now I know it."

Five pounds is quite a lot of money to lose in that way.

"I couldn't agree with that, judge, with respect," said Mr Trent. "There's nothing crooked about it, if I may say so. The judge made a mistake. That's all. It must happen sometimes. After all, judges are only human."

"Our mistakes can be corrected," snapped the judge. "So should this judge's."

"But, judge," said Mr Trent, "surely there are occasions when a judge's decision is final and conclusive. Take, for instance——"

But the normally genial judge had had enough. Without another word he turned his back on Mr Trent and walked away.

"It's a shame," said Mr Trent. "Still, on his salary, it shouldn't hurt him all that. I'm glad to say I didn't back it myself. I had a feeling about the race. How right I was. Any of you get the first home?"

"Well," said Roger, "we backed number ten—which was rather better."

Not long afterwards, Donald came up to the party and, in a somewhat conspiratorial manner, invited them to follow him.

He led them into Tattersalls' ring and pointed out a large and beery-faced-looking man who was already saying in substance—in a loud and ugly voice—that he would lay ten to one the field bar one. Donald also pointed out a much smaller man with a pointed face, sharp nose and small moustache. He was saying—in a more staccato manner—that he also would be pleased to lay ten to one the field bar one.

"What does that mean," said Anne.

"Don't you worry what it means," said Donald. "I'll tell you later. Now——" he said, in his most confidential evening voice to Roger and Henry, "either of these two will give you a bet during the race. You'll hear them offering odds. All you've got to do when the field reaches that point—d'you see?——" and he pointed out on the course a place a little more than two furlongs from the winning post—"all you've got to do is to say, 'What'll you give on Conference?' But you'll have to be snappy, or you'll be too late. Come to think of it, you'd better do it a bit earlier. Say there——" and he pointed out a place about 150 yards before the original one. "Take whatever he offers, and put your silk gown on it," he said to Henry. "And you put your present one, Roger. You won't be needing it much longer. But, of course, only if Conference is in the rear. If he's in the lead, forget it and watch him come in last. Now—is everyone clear?"

Donald surveyed his employers and their ladies rather like a platoon sergeant giving instruction in musketry. Roger almost expected him to say "any questions." Satisfied that they knew what to do, Donald went hurriedly and erratically to see his trainer and the apprentice who was to ride Conference.

Roger and Anne, Henry and Sally and Eagally, who had become one of the party, waited where they had been told.

"You haven't told us which one is statistically bound to win this race," said Henry.

"Statistically," said Eagally, with authority, "any horse could win this race. That is why I haven't ventured to make any suggestions for it. That's one of the things I forgot to tell you. With my system, you can't back on every race. Oh, dear, no. You could certainly lose money that way."

"And would it be very rude to enquire how much you've won this season so far?" asked Roger.

"Oh—I don't keep an exact account," said Eagally. "It isn't necessary. Statistically I know that I must have won and that's all that matters."

"I should have thought it might have been worth having a check every now and then to see if the statistics had gone wrong," said Henry.

"Statistics can't go wrong," said Eagally. "You've just seen a most interesting example of that."

Not long afterwards, the horses went down to the post. Conference undoubtedly seemed to be anxious to get down to the start and indeed a good way past it. The boy on his back certainly was going to have his work cut out to hold him in.

"Hadn't we better check up with one of those bookies that they'll take a bet? Donald might have given us the wrong ones." Roger went up to the red-faced man. "Will you take a bet during the race?" he asked politely.

"What d'you think I'm something well here for?" said the bookie. "Selling sweet peas, hokey-pokey penny a lump? Eights bar," he yelled.

Roger retired.

"I don't think I cared for him much," said Roger. "I think I'll try the other one."

The sharp-nosed man, in reply to Roger's question, said: "Any particular horse?"

"Conference," said Roger.

"I'll give you a hundred to six now," said the bookie.

"I don't want to back it now," said Roger.

"How much d'you want to put on?"

Roger thought for a moment. There were four of them. "About a fiver, I suppose," he said.

"Well, you can try," said the bookie. "But it all depends what's happening. If Conference runs the other way, I'll give you a hundred pounds to a sausage."

Not at all confident that Donald's plan would work, Roger returned to the others. "We'll have to be pretty quick off the mark," he said, "or the race will be over before we've understood what they've said."

A minute later the white flag was up, and then they were off.

"Oh, dear," said Anne. And well she might. For the impatient Conference had virtually seized the reins out of the little boy's hands and was tearing for home as fast as he could go. He sprang into a two lengths lead almost at once. This he increased to three, our and, finally, to ten lengths—and by the time the vital point was reached he was still that much up.

"Tens bar," shouted the red-faced bookie.

But the chambers party did not move. Round the bend came Conference with its little passenger—who had long ceased to try to hold him—looking rather like a little apple with a coloured cap.

"What a shame," said Sally. "It looks to me as though he's going to win all the same."

By this time the jockeys on the other horses were doing everything they could to encourage their mounts to catch up Conference. They certainly made up some ground, but not enough and, in due course, as though he knew where he was going, Conference safely delivered his little apple to the winner's enclosure. Donald was there to greet him—in a state of great excitement. His trainer was equally pleased.

"Sorry I couldn't hold him in," said the little apple.

"If you win a race you're meant to win," said the trainer, "you don't have to apologize."

The chambers party came to offer Donald their congratulations.

"How much did you put on?" he asked.

They stared at him for a moment. Then Roger said: "Nothing, of course. You told us."

"Sir, sir, sir," said Donald. "But I didn't tell you not to use your loaf, did I? It was obvious he was going to win."

"You told me," said Henry, "that if he were leading at the spot you pointed out, we were not to touch him."

"Sir," said Donald, in what appeared to him to be a dignified manner, "the trouble is you boys don't understand racing."

"I think we can agree to that," said Roger.

But it had been a good day, all the same, and he had found plenty of opportunity in between the races to be with Anne alone.

Donald, too, had had an exhilarating day. He had never won a race before. His wife put him to bed.

CHAPTER SEVENTEEN

A QUESTION OF CONFIDENCE

THE next week was a particularly busy one for Roger. He was in Court every day, had a large number of conferences and had an infinite amount of paper work to do. But it all sat very lightly on him now. Towards the end of the week Mr Glacier and Mr Plumb came to see him to report progress.

"If you ask me," said Mr Glacier, "what you call a little bird must have spoken to the inspector."

"The trap didn't come off?"

"I will tell you exactly what happened," said Mr Glacier, "and," he added, "you can be sure I am speaking the truth as everything which was said was recorded by tape machine."

"Well, what happened?" said Roger.

"I duly attended the interview," said Mr Glacier, "and this is what happened. The inspector began:

" 'This is all very irregular. What is it you want to see me about?'

"I said: 'I hoped we might be able to come to an understanding.'

" 'About what?' he said.

" 'You know what about, inspector,' I said.

" 'I certainly don't,' he said, 'and I must warn you that anything you say now may be given in evidence at your trial.'

"Well, Mr Thursby, as you may have observed, I am not usually at a loss for words, but I was beginning to find myself—how do you say?—against a blank wall. It appeared obvious to me that any attempt to bribe him at that moment would have been quite hopeless. He was obviously on his guard. So I decided to play one more card—to see if at any rate I could take one trick. 'I don't mind what you give in evidence, inspector,' I said, 'so long as it is the truth. Why did you not tell the truth about the money I gave you?' He did not answer for a moment. Then: 'What do you mean?' he said. 'You know quite well what I mean, inspector,' I said. 'You know I gave you thirty pounds and thirty-five pounds, not twenty pounds and twenty-five pounds. And perhaps you would be interested to know that the whole of our conversation is now being listened to by your superintendent.' " Mr Glacier paused.

"Good Lord! What did he say?"

"Nothing," said Mr Glacier. "Not only words failed him, but blood, or whatever it is, also failed him. He fainted. Fortunately he fell to the ground with a crash. I might perhaps have saved him, but I thought that we should then miss the noise of his fall in the microphone. So I let—how do you say?—nature take its course. He was not much hurt. But, of course, gravity will have its way and the inspector is a tall man."

"What happened then?" asked Roger.

"Everything seemed to happen at once. The superintendent and Chief Constable who had been listening to the conversation rushed in to assist the inspector. At first they took no notice of me. But when they had revived the inspector and had put some plaster on the cut on his head, they appeared to notice me.

" 'Can I be of any further assistance?' I asked most politely.

" 'Kindly leave this station at once, sir, and don't come back,' said the Chief Constable.

" 'But really,' I protested, 'what have I done? Is it my fault if the inspector faints?'

" 'You have been guilty of a disgraceful breach of confidence in telling the inspector that the conversation was being overheard.'

" 'You were never going to tell him then?' I asked.

" 'Leave the station, sir,' said the Chief Constable.

"So, of course, I left and at once reported to Mr Plumb and he has brought me to you as soon as possible."

"I have spoken to the Director's office," said Mr Plumb, who had some justification for the mournful way in which he said it, "and I'm afraid they don't like us at all, not at all."

"Dear, dear," said Roger. "All is finished between us, I suppose, and the prosecution is going on as hard as ever. The armistice is over, the gloves are off, the detectives have gone back to Scotland Yard and the fight is on."

"You sound remarkably cheerful," said Mr Glacier. "I hope with reason. You will permit me to remind you once again that it is my wife and I who rot in gaol, not you."

"Well," said Roger who, for reasons wholly unconnected with Mr Glacier, was continuously cheerful, "we shall do our best to prevent that happening. And I'm bound to say that, short of having the prosecution called off, we haven't done so badly."

"You are satisfied then?" said Mr Plumb. "I must say I never thought you would be happy about the present position."

"Happier than either of you appear to be," said Roger.

"Let me remind you yet again—at the risk of repetition," began Mr Glacier, "that it is——"

"No. I won't," said Roger. "I remember perfectly. It's you who'll go to gaol if you're convicted. Quite right. So it will be. As to that, all I can say is that I think you've a very good chance of not going to gaol, but, if you do, it's entirely your own fault for giving money to policemen."

"Our little Melanie," began Mr Glacier.

"Whether it was your little Melanie or not—and I doubt whether anyone will really believe that little Melanie came into the story at all—but, even if she did, you must have known perfectly well that to give sixty-five pounds to police officers is a wrong thing to do. None the less, I think you've a very good chance of getting away with it."

"You think we will be acquitted?"

"I think it very possible. Nothing, of course, is certain, but the case has got to be proved and, apart from your word and your wife's, we have three things in our favour—and there might have been a fourth. First, there's your police constable; secondly, there's the fact that we went to the police straight away and that they set a trap for their own people; thirdly, the inspector fainted. It's quite true that the sudden knowledge that his superiors sufficiently mistrusted him to make them set a trap for him might have been such a shock to him that he lost consciousness for a moment, but, of course, it's also possible that your statement about the money, coupled with the knowledge that he was being listened to, had that effect. He, of course, will give the former explanation, but when you add the police constable's evidence to it, it'll shake the jury pretty considerably, I should say."

"What is the fourth point that you might have had?"

"Mr Plumb," said Roger, "did you tell Mr Glacier about your conversation with the Chief Constable? The one you consulted me about?"

"Yes, I did, as a matter of fact," said Mr Plumb. "Before I told you about it. Shouldn't I have?"

"Am I to understand," said Mr Glacier, "that my lawyers have some doubt whether they should tell me something they have learned in the conduct of proceedings on my behalf?"

"It was said to Mr Plumb in confidence," said Roger.

"Confidence," said Mr Glacier. "And when did I give you—how do you say?—authority to keep things secret from me?"

"Mr Plumb acted as many other solicitors would have acted. The Chief Constable said something to him and then added that it was in confidence and Mr Plumb agreed. Litigation could not be conducted if lawyers could not trust each other and say things in confidence to one another."

"First," said Mr Glacier, "the Chief Constable is not a lawyer."

"The principle is the same in this case," said Roger.

"Very well," said Mr Glacier, "I will assume that it is. Is not litigation, as you call it, proceedings between two persons over some civil dispute? Is a prosecution where one side may go to gaol or, indeed, be hanged, litigation?"

"You may be right, Mr Glacier, that litigation strictly means civil proceedings. But criminal lawyers must be able to trust one another just the same."

"I do not care two figs whether they trust one another or not. I do not mind what are the—I think you call them—the ethics of the legal profession. I who stand in danger of being sent to prison demand—yes, demand, I say—that all facts which are in my favour shall be used to help to secure my acquittal. Now I am right in thinking, am I not, that this fourth matter to which you referred is the statement to Mr Plumb that in effect the inspector was already a suspected person? I am right, am I not?" he repeated.

"Yes," said Roger, "you're quite right."

"And am I further right in thinking that, in your view, if that further fact were brought to the attention of the jury, it would raise even more our chances of being acquitted?"

"That is quite true," said Roger.

"Then," said Mr Glacier, "I demand that it be used."

"Demand is a strong word, Mr Glacier," said Roger.

"The occasion requires the use of strong words."

"I told you," said Roger, "that I reserved the right to throw up the case if it was not conducted in a proper manner."

"You, of course, have that right," said Mr Glacier, "and let me make it plain that I should be very sorry indeed if you did—how did you say?—throw it up. Indeed, I demand that unless I have done something wrong or require you to do something wrong, that you do not do so."

"I wish you wouldn't keep on using that word 'demand.' " said Roger. "I want to help you as far as I properly can, but whenever you say 'demand' I feel like pushing you out of the room. You will please assume that I will do everything that is right and proper to secure your acquittal."

"Do you not consider it right and proper that a fact which could affect the jury's verdict should be put before them? How can you have these so-called confidences in matters where a man's liberty— or, indeed, his life—the principle is the same—is at stake?"

"It is not an easy matter," said Roger.

"I see no difficulty about it at all," said Mr Glacier. "Let us suppose, for example, that you have a client charged with a crime and the counsel for the prosecution told you—in confidence—in absolute confidence—that, as a matter of fact, the prosecution knew that your client was not guilty but that, as they could not prove the case against the guilty man and the public wanted a— what is the word?—a scapegoat, they were going to try to secure a conviction against your client—supposing the charge were murder —the penalty death—suppose your client were convicted and hanged—would you think you had acted properly in keeping your learned friend's confidence or not?"

"Such a thing could never happen in this country," said Roger.

"But suppose it did—strange things do occur—would you keep the matter told you in confidence?"

Roger did not answer at once.

"No doubt you would seek to be relieved of the obligation to keep the matter in confidence, you would see your opponent and endeavour to obtain a release from him and you would have sound arguments to urge to him, but supposing all your efforts were in vain, what then? Would you keep his confidence—with a man's life at stake?"

"No," said Roger, "in a strong case like that I don't think I could. But that isn't this case. It is not a case of life or death and the statement made is nothing like so outrageous or unworthy of confidence as the one in the case you've suggested."

"One thing at a time," said Mr Glacier. "You say it is not a case of life or death. But is there any difference in what you lawyers are pleased to call principle between loss of liberty and loss of life? Who are you to say what the consequences of loss of liberty may be to me or my wife? Prison may have a—what is the word?—a permanent effect on some people, it may kill others. This is not a criticism of your prisons. I refer to loss of liberty. So first I say, how do you distinguish between death and imprisonment?"

"There is obviously a difference in fact," said Roger, "but in principle you may be right."

"Very well then. Now, as to the nature of the statement. You pride yourselves in this country on the prosecution being fair. Is it fair, do you think, to call as the main witness for the prosecution a man whom you suspect of dishonesty, to put him before the jury as a man of upright character and not to tell the defence of your suspicions? Is that fair? And, if it is not, is the statement made by the Chief Constable any more worthy of confidence than the one that I suggested?"

"Mr Glacier," said Roger, "I'm bound to say you put your point of view very ably. I shall have to think this one out. It's not at all an easy decision to have to make."

"I am quite sure," said Mr Glacier, "that you will consider the matter most carefully before coming to a decision. Should your decision be adverse to my interests, is it possible for me to consult your society or institute on the matter?"

"The Bar Council, you mean?" said Roger. "There would not be time to get a ruling of the Bar Council before the case is heard. But I would certainly speak to the Chairman about it, if you wished. Indeed, I may do so in any event. I entirely see your point of view, but the legal profession could not be carried on without rules and the rules must be kept."

"Even if the result is that innocent persons are hanged or sent to prison? Permit me to say," said Mr Glacier, "that an amendment of any such rules in a civilized community would seem to be highly desirable. But, of course, no such amendment could be made before the trial . . . you will say. You will, no doubt, send me a copy to the particular prison where I am rotting."

"I don't know why you're so convinced that you'll be convicted if we don't use the statement. I should have thought that your clear conscience would have made you more optimistic."

"Who said I had a clear conscience?" asked Mr Glacier. "You have already pointed out to me that it was wrong to give money to policemen."

Eventually it was arranged that Roger should consider what course he was proposing to adopt and that he would let Mr Plumb know when he had made up his mind.

As soon as he could, Roger went in to see Henry.

"I gather we're enemies, again," said Henry.

"So do I," said Roger. "But there's an awkward thing I want

273

to talk to you about. D'you think you could get Digby over? It's rather serious."

"O.K.," said Henry. "Are you sure you wouldn't like his able assistant Mr Trent as well?"

"I think we'll be able to manage without him somehow," said Roger. "We can always send for him if we get stuck."

So a meeting took place the next day between Henry and his junior Digby, and Roger.

"So sorry I couldn't get down last time," said Digby, "but I feel sure I was most ably represented."

"Incredibly so," said Henry.

"I shouldn't have liked you to miss Tony Trent," said Digby. "He has to be heard to be believed. I confess he fascinates me. If I had the time I could listen to him for hours. Well, what's the trouble? Your Mr Glacier, if I may so so, is a pretty good stinker."

"And a very able one," said Henry.

"He's certainly that," said Roger, "whatever else he may be . . . as to which I don't feel called on to make any admissions."

"The Chief Constable's hopping mad," said Henry.

"I don't altogether blame him," said Digby.

"I think you're being a bit unfair," said Roger. "No one had told him not to give the game away to the inspector. The Chief Constable wouldn't have minded if the inspector had been caught. What he, of course, is livid about is not catching the inspector and letting the inspector know that they'd tried to catch him. Must make it sort of awkward for him, I agree. But that isn't altogether my man's fault."

"Yes—but look at the way he did it," said Henry.

"Did what?" asked Roger.

"Look," said Henry, "if you ask me, old Glacier knew the game was up and that if he just asked the inspector why he said he'd received forty-five pounds when, in fact, he'd had sixty-five pounds the inspector would simply have denied it. So what does he do? He puts the question to him and, before he has time to answer, he fires at him point-blank about the Chief Constable and superintendent listening-in. Well—he couldn't have known it'd be such a success and that the inspector would faint, but he must have hoped that by following up the one question with the other he'd be bound to shake the inspector, and no doubt he hoped that he'd yammer for a bit. And even for the most upright inspector in the world it must be a pretty considerable shock to be told suddenly that a criminal is being used as a bait and that the conversation's being tapped. He'd no other cards to play, so he brought out that one."

274

"Well," said Roger, "we shall see, my dear fellow, we shall see. No doubt you will ask Mr Glacier the question when he gives evidence. I promise you I won't tell him what to answer."

"No need," said Henry. "He's quite capable of taking care of himself. I must say I don't blame the old Chief Constable. To blow the gaff like that was a bit steep."

Roger suddenly had a horrible thought. "I hope he doesn't think it was anything to do with me," he said.

"Well," said Henry, "I must confess I don't think he likes you very much."

"Blast and curse," said Roger. I must see Anne and explain, he thought. Confound Glacier, confound everything. Why must Anne be mixed up in it? I hope she'll believe me. Oh—good Lord!—"Where's the catch, Mr Thursby? Do you tell me now or later or do I have to find it out for myself?" "There's no catch, Chief Constable." "Bait with no hook, eh? You're not a fisherman, I imagine." Bait with no hook? Here was the hook with a vengeance. He'd never believe that Roger wasn't behind it all. Anne would believe him—he hoped—but her father would think him a scoundrel. She might marry him just the same . . . but it would be horrible for her—she was fond of her father. Blast Mr Glacier—though, to be fair, I'd never have met Anne but for him. Oh, well—I shall have to do something about it.

"I hope you told him it wasn't anything to do with me," said Roger.

"I haven't seen him yet," said Henry. "I got it from the Director."

"Well—do tell him when you get the chance," said Roger. "It's rather important to me, as a matter of fact."

"O.K.," said Henry. "I see. I'll do my best."

"Is that all you wanted me for," said Digby, "as I've got to go to Brixton to see a friend?"

"No," said Roger, "that last bit made me forget what I really wanted to see you about. But that makes it worse than ever. I really don't know what to do. Look, this is the trouble." He then told Henry and Digby what the problem was, putting all the arguments for and against the evidence being used.

"Of course," he said, "the Chief Constable shouldn't have said afterwards that it was in confidence. He ought to have said 'I'll tell you this in confidence but not otherwise.' That might have been different. But, however he did it, old Plumb said he would treat it in confidence. And if you say you're going to treat a thing in confidence, you've got to keep your word. It isn't like a contract. You don't have to have consideration for it. Moreover, if Plumb had said 'You should have said that before, you didn't say it was in confidence and I'm going to use it,' the Chief Constable would

275

probably have cried off the whole thing. So by keeping silent Plumb in effect assured the Chief Constable that the statement would be kept in confidence. Then, like a blithering idiot, he goes and tells the client. That was a breach of confidence to begin with, but he didn't realize it. But let's assume he didn't tell the client. Let's assume only Plumb and I knew it, and we'd agreed to treat it in confidence—have we the right to do so if a man may be hanged or go to gaol if we do? I'm bound to say I think Glacier's right in saying there's no distinction in principle between death and prison. My natural instinct, of course, tells me that I can't use the statement—but then, as Glacier would say, it's easy for me. I don't have to rot in gaol. What do you each think about it?"

"I don't see any difficulty," said Digby. "It was said in confidence and that's an end of it."

"What do you think, Henry?"

"I don't think it's as simple as that," said Henry. "As Roger says, it's easy enough for us. We stick to our rules and say what fine fellows we are, puff our chests out and say you can always trust a member of the Bar—good old Thursby—he'll never let you down; meantime, Mr Thursby's client is duly executed or sent to prison for life. I certainly wouldn't puff my chest out after that."

"Confidence means confidence," said Digby. "If you can't trust a member of the Bar, you might as well shut up shop. That's where it's different from business. You can rely on a reputable member of the Bar not to do a dirty trick. If you couldn't, it'd be hopeless. I don't know what you're worried about. It was said in confidence, and that's an end of it. That's what I think, anyway; I'm not a lawyer like you chaps, but I know the answer to that one."

"If the charge were murder and you were in my shoes, would you refuse to use the statement?" asked Roger.

"Of course I would," said Digby. "Shouldn't even think of using it. Fight hard but fight clean, I say."

"And you wouldn't worry if you hadn't used the statement and your client were hanged?"

"Not in the least," said Digby. "He'd have been guilty ten times over anyway if he were convicted. People make too much fuss about these things, I think. They hardly ever get to the dock if they're innocent and, if there's a chance in a million that they're innocent, they get off. Even if I happen to be defending them. No—give them a fair trial, I say, but no more. They're ninety-nine per cent guilty, but I quite agree they should have a proper trial and, if there's any loop-hole, by all means let them get away with it. But don't lean over backwards to push the guilty ones out of the dock."

"Well," said Roger, "what d'you say to *this* point of Glacier's? You say they should have a fair trial. If you have a witness who's got a previous conviction you'd tell counsel for the defence, wouldn't you?"

"Of course."

"Well—what's the difference in principle? You've got a witness whom you distrust. The defence can't know that. So, unless you tell them, the witness is put forward as a person of integrity."

"If you haven't got anything against him, he *is* a person of integrity. Suspicion isn't enough. The Chief Constable suspected the inspector. All right. But he may have been wrong. He'd no evidence. If you had to tell the defence of every witness you weren't too happy about, where would it stop? There's a limit, you know."

"Has he convinced you, Henry?" asked Roger.

"I can't say he has," said Henry. "I'm glad I'm not in your shoes. I'm hanged if I'd know what I'd do. I'm bound to say that I'm inclined to think that, when the acid test is applied, there can't be such a thing as confidence in criminal matters any more than there can be without prejudice conversations or letters. I suppose the answer is that, if anything is said in confidence in a criminal matter, the confidence must be kept if it's possible. But, in the last resort, the man in the dock comes first."

"I can only say," said Digby, "that with the greatest respect and all that I profoundly disagree. To my mind the seal of confidence is binding for ever and in all instances and there are no exceptions."

"Well, there you are, Roger," said Henry, "the Court's divided. On the whole and without a great deal of confidence—no pun intended—I agree with you, Roger, that, if you think it absolutely essential in the interest of your client to use the statement, you must use it."

"I can only repeat—with considerable confidence," said Digby, "that such a point of view, if adopted generally, would be disastrous for the legal profession."

"There I don't agree," said Roger, "because this kind of thing will only happen very, very occasionally. It's never happened to you, I suspect, and you're at the Criminal Bar. It's certainly never happened to me before, and I'll be very surprised if it happens again. Well—I'm most grateful to you both. I really have to make up my own mind."

"I'll be very rude to you," said Digby, "if you don't make it up the right way."

"I don't care two hoots about that," thought Roger . . . "but Anne's father—oh, Lord . . . Anne's father."

CHAPTER EIGHTEEN

THE MISSING WITNESS

ROGER's other work fortunately prevented him from thinking too much of his pressing personal and professional problems. Among his minor activities in Court was an appearance in the Divorce Court to do an undefended divorce case of some difficulty. It was before a new County Court judge and, as Roger's case was fairly high in the list, he went there early to see how quickly that particular judge got through his list. He was an unknown quantity. Some judges can quite comfortably dispose of twenty or thirty undefended divorce cases in one day. Others have their work cut out to deal with a dozen. It rather depends on the approach. The approach of Judge Renfrew was not known. Roger found that Crabtree was in the first case and he arrived in time to hear him saying:

"Oh—my Lord—I'm afraid I shall be in some difficulty in this case—as an essential witness, who has been subpœnæd—I can prove it, my Lord—is apparently not here and I'm not sure how much I can prove without him . . . in due course I shall ask your Lordship to take steps against the witness but, in the meantime, my Lord, I was wondering—I was wondering——" He paused for so long that Judge Renfrew said:

"You were wondering, Mr Crabtree?"

"Yes—my Lord—I was wondering——"

"Quite, Mr Crabtree—but what?"

"I was wondering, my Lord—I was wondering——"

"So am I now, Mr Crabtree."

"That's very good of your Lordship."

"Not at all, Mr Crabtree. Were you perhaps wondering if I would hear such evidence as you have, and see how far it gets us?"

"That was it exactly," said Mr Crabtree. "It is very good of your Lordship."

"Not at all, Mr Crabtree. At any rate it's stopped us both wondering. Call your evidence and we'll see how far you can take it."

Crabtree proceeded to call his evidence and, apart from proving that his client had duly married the respondent, that they had lived at various places and had no children, and that the photograph produced was a photograph of the respondent, and the signature produced was his signature—he proved practically nothing.

"And now, my Lord," said Crabtree, "I propose to prove that the missing witness was duly served with the subpœna and then I shall ask your Lordship to take steps."

"Very well, Mr Crabtree."

The process server was duly called and he duly proved that the witness had been served with the subpœna and provided with conduct money.

"And now, my Lord," said Crabtree, "I ask your Lordship to take steps."

"Yes, Mr Crabtree, what steps?" asked the judge.

"Oh, my Lord," said Crabtree, waving his arm as if to express something, "oh, my Lord——" he repeated—"steps—against the witness."

"Yes, Mr Crabtree—what steps?"

"Oh, my Lord," said Crabtree, waving his arm again—"there must be steps."

"No doubt," said the judge, "but what?"

"Oh, my Lord," said Crabtree, and waited for inspiration. After it had failed to come for the space of about ten seconds, the judge said:

"Would you like a few minutes to consider the matter and I'll take another case in the meantime?"

"That is most kind of your Lordship. It would be most helpful."

"Call the next case then, please," said the judge, "and let me know when you are ready, Mr Crabtree."

"Thank you, my Lord," said Crabtree, and went hurriedly to the Bar Library.

While Roger was waiting, Donald came up to him. "You're all right in Q.B.4 for the moment and you're quite safe in the Court of Appeal till this afternoon. You'd better wait here and I'll watch the non-jury."

"Thanks," said Roger.

Judge Renfrew had disposed of three more cases when Crabtree returned and informed his Lordship that he was now ready.

"Yes, Mr Crabtree?" said the judge.

"My Lord, if your Lordship will be good enough to look at Rayden at page 347, you will see that your Lordship can issue a warrant for the arrest of the witness."

The judge referred to the passage. "Yes, Mr Crabtree, I see the statement. Can you tell me under what rule of Court or statute the power arises?"

"Oh, my Lord," began Crabtree, "oh, my Lord——"

"Yes?" said the judge.

"Oh, my Lord," Crabtree repeated, "I'm sure it wouldn't appear in Rayden if it weren't right."

"So am I," said the judge. "It is in the highest degree improbable. But I must know the rule or the statute or whatever it is before I interfere with the liberty of the subject."

"But, my Lord, it says quite definitely here——" said Crabtree.

"I know, I know," said the judge, "but it gives no authority for the proposition and, although I don't doubt it in the least, I must know what it is."

"Well, my Lord——"

"Yes, Mr Crabtree?"

"Well, my Lord——"

"Mr Crabtree, would you like me to put the case back again for you to find out the authority?"

"That would be most kind of your Lordship."

"Very well, Mr Crabtree. Let me know when you are ready."

The judge continued with another case and several further cases, including Roger's. As he finished Roger's case, Crabtree returned and, as he had not yet been summoned by Donald, Roger waited to see what would happen.

"My Lord," said Crabtree, "I've made an exhaustive search and I'm afraid I can't actually find the authority your Lordship wants, but I'm quite sure the learned editor of Rayden would not have put it in unless——"

"So am I, Mr Crabtree, but, as I said before, I must be satisfied before I have people arrested. I see that the subpœna itself says nothing about arrest but only about forfeiting one hundred pounds."

"Yes, my Lord."

"Well, what d'you want me to do?"

"Well, of course, my Lord," said Crabtree, "if this came under the Rules of the Supreme Court, it would be quite easy to show your Lordship——"

"But it does come under the Rules of the Supreme Court, Mr Crabtree, subject to any modification by statute or the rules of this Division of the Supreme Court."

"Oh, well, in that case, my Lord, I ask your Lordship to take steps——"

"But under what Rule of the Supreme Court, Mr Crabtree?"

"I'm afraid, my Lord, I haven't the actual rule in front of me—perhaps your Lordship wouldn't mind——"

"Certainly, Mr Crabtree, I'll take another case."

The judge took several more cases and eventually Crabtree returned, looking rather dejected.

"I'm afraid, my Lord," he said, "that with such little time at my disposal I haven't been able to find——"

"Well, Mr Crabtree, wouldn't it be best if I adjourned this case for fourteen days for you to go into the matter? I should make it plain that I feel quite sure you are right in saying that, if a man deliberately disobeys a subpœna, he can be dealt with in an appropriate manner. Justice could not be administered if there weren't procedure to compel witnesses to give evidence. But I'm sure you'll understand that I must see the power under which I am acting before I deprive people of their liberty."

"Of course, my Lord," said Crabtree. "It is very good of your Lordship, and I will gratefully accept your Lordship's suggestion of a fourteen day adjournment."

"Very well," said the judge. "Adjourned for fourteen days."

Just as the judge was about to start another case, and Crabtree was about to leave the Court, a man, who had been there all the time, suddenly addressed the judge from a seat in the middle of the Court.

"May I speak?" he asked. "I didn't like to interrupt before but was it me you were talking about?"

It was the witness.

CHAPTER NINETEEN

COLONEL MADDERLEY'S OPINION

The Chief Constable of Carpshire was talking to Anne. "I'm sorry, Anne," he said. "I know how you must feel. If you're fond of him, there's nothing I can do, or would do for that matter, to stop you marrying him. And it won't alter you and me—I hope not—not as far as I'm concerned. But I can't have him in the house. I know I'm not a clever chap like he is—thank God I'm not—but I have a code. I dare say he laughs at soldiers and policemen. Blithering lot of idiots he thinks them. A lot of Blimps. All right, perhaps they are . . . and I'm one of them. But there are just certain things a chap doesn't do. And once anyone let's me down I'm finished with him. I'm not a fellow who wants revenge—I don't want my own back or anything of that sort—I just have nothing more to do with him. And that's all there is to it. I don't even say I'm in the right. If you like, he's in the right and I'm in the wrong. Be that as it may . . . when a chap does what he's done, I'm finished and that's all there is to it. I'm sorry, Anne, I really am. But that's the way it is and I'm too old to change now."

"I understand, Father,' 'said Anne. "But why d'you blame Roger for it all? I'm sure he wouldn't do anything that was disgraceful or underhand for himself or anyone else. I don't know him well, but I'm sure he's not like that."

"You don't know him well, Anne. You say so yourself. How can you tell? I judge by what a man does. It's the only way I know. Not the way he looks or what he says—but what he does. Simple, if you like, but it's the only way of judging a man that I've found any good. Your Roger could, I've no doubt, talk me into a cocked hat. He could play old Harry with me in the witness box—or in ordinary conversation if you like. I don't pretend to be any good at talking and he is—and if you ask me . . . I'm sorry to say this—he's a damned sight too good at it."

"Father," said Anne, "please."

"It's no good, Anne, and it's much better to face the facts. You and I always have. He sat in that chair you're in now. 'Where's the catch?' I said. 'There isn't one,' he said. And then, when we'd had our chat, he said: 'D'you still think there's a catch?' I trusted him, Anne, and his solicitor. The whole thing, if you ask me, was a thundering fraud. Clever, mind you—darned clever. It would take a clever chap to work that one out."

"If I could show you it wasn't Roger's fault, Father, you would change, wouldn't you?"

"My dear, dear Anne, of course I would. D'you think I like this between us—well, it isn't between us, because nothing could be—but interfering with us, hurting us both; of course I don't. But it's facts, Anne, facts. If you can show me facts are not facts, black is white and white is black—if you show it me, not by words or fine speeches but by things I can see and know—nobody will be better pleased than I shall be. But you can't do it, Anne. Facts can't lie. People can."

Later that day Anne spoke to Roger.

"I'm sure if you came to see him, you'd make him understand," she said.

"I can't during the case, Anne," he said. "He wouldn't see me anyway—and he'd be quite right at the moment. But, as soon as it's over, of course I will."

And with that they both had to be satisfied.

CHAPTER TWENTY

THE GLACIERS ON TRIAL

THE case of the Glaciers went on again the next week, but in a very different atmosphere. No co-operation this time between prosecution and defence, and no race meeting afterwards. Eventually the prosecution completed its case. Roger elected to call no evidence and both Mr and Mrs Glacier were committed for trial at the next Carpshire Assizes. They were both granted bail. Before the day of the trial they had a final conference with Roger.

"Well, Mr Thursby," said Mr Glacier, "have you made up your mind about this statement?"

"Yes," said Roger. "I have come to the conclusion that, if you require me to use it, it is my duty to do so—however much I may personally dislike doing it."

"That simplifies matters," said Mr Glacier. "I require you to use it. I am extremely sorry for any inconvenience or embarrassment in which it may involve you. It is—how would you say?—just one of those things. And now, may I ask you yet again—what do you consider our chances are of being acquitted?"

"I think they're good," said Roger. "But naturally there's no certainty about it."

"Ah, well," said Mr Glacier, "certainty is more than I could ask for, but I confess I should prefer to have certainty one way or the other."

"You would prefer to have certainty that you would be convicted," said Mr Plumb, in some amazement, "than a reasonable chance that you will be acquitted?"

"We are on bail," said Mr Glacier. "The world is a large place. Now, please don't agitate yourself, Mr Plumb," he added hastily, when he saw Mr Plumb's hand and handkerchief starting up. "I have no intention of—how do you call it?—jumping my bail."

"It wouldn't be much use if you did," said Roger. "You'd only be picked up some time and extradited."

"Do extradition treaties extend then to all countries and for all offences?" asked Mr Glacier. "It is only what you would call an academic question," he added.

"I don't know," said Roger. "I haven't looked it up."

"As a matter of fact," said Mr Glacier, "I have made some research into the subject. I have surrendered my passport, but not my British Museum library ticket. It is, I find, a good thing to consider every aspect of a case. But pray do not be alarmed, Mr Plumb. I have the utmost confidence in Mr Thursby and, of course, in your good self, and, that being so, my visits to the British Museum can be considered of no practical significance. Though, of course, I am one who thinks that knowledge is never wasted."

The case came on for trial very shortly after the conclusion of the proceedings before the magistrates. Mr Justice Kingsdown was the judge. There were two charges against each defendant. They pleaded Not Guilty, were given the usual permission to sit down, and the trial began. Henry, having informed the judge and jury that he appeared for the prosecution with his learned friend Mr Gerald Digby, and that the defendants had the advantage of being represented by his learned friend Mr Thursby, went on to tell them the facts, as alleged by the prosecution. He made no reference to the trap which had been set for the inspector and simply outlined the case as it had been before Roger and Mr Plumb went to see the Chief Constable. Before calling the evidence in support of his opening speech, Henry said this:

"Members of the jury, we pride ourselves in this country that corruption is rare and that, where we find it, we do all in our power to stamp it out. It is one of the most insidious of all evils, it is difficult to detect and, once it starts, no one knows how far it will go. No people are more likely to be tempted by corruption than the police force and it is vital that we should have a police force which is resistant to all such attempts. I venture to suggest to you, members of the jury, that—when you have heard the evidence in this case—you will come to the conclusion that it is a classic case of attempted corruption . . . by a rich man anxious to escape from the consequences of a breach of the licensing laws. Mr and Mrs Glacier no doubt find that money can buy them many things that poorer people cannot have and, in due course, I shall ask you to say that they tried to buy something which in this country is not for sale."

Henry then called the inspector to give evidence. In examination-in-chief he said very much what he said in the Magistrate's Court. Then Henry sat down and he was cross-examined by Roger.

"How is your head?" was Roger's first question.

The judge and the jury looked surprised at the question, which, of course, was Roger's intention.

"It's better, thank you," said the inspector.

"A nasty bump, I'm afraid," said Roger.

"Not too bad," said the inspector.

"I take it," said the judge, "the jury and I are going to be let into the secret some time."

"Of course, my Lord," said Roger. "You hit your head against a desk and cut it, I'm afraid?" he went on.

"Yes," said the inspector.

"That was about three weeks ago, was it not?"

"Yes."

"You were having an interview with the defendant, Mr Glacier, were you not?"

"Yes, I was."

"The man who is supposed to have tried to bribe you?"

"Yes."

"This interview was during the proceedings before the Magistrates?"

"Yes."

"A bit odd, isn't it, to interview an accused person after proceedings have started?"

"He asked for the interview."

"I dare say he did," said Roger. "But why did you give it him?"

"I wanted to know what he was going to say."

"Maybe," said Roger, "but he was represented by solicitor and counsel, and so was the prosecution. Did you ask any superior officer or anyone from the Director of Public Prosecutions Office whether there was any objection to your having the interview?"

"I told the superintendent I was having the interview."

"That isn't what I asked you. Did you ask anyone whether it would be proper for you to have the interview?"

"No."

"Have you ever done such a thing before?"

"I don't think so."

"Then why on this occasion?"

"I wanted to know what he was going to say."

"Do you mean that you thought you might get some more evidence?"

"Possibly."

"I suggest that you thought you might get some more money."

"Nothing of the kind," said the inspector indignantly.

"Why so indignant, inspector?" asked Roger. "Did you think it more likely that the defendant was coming for a proper purpose or an improper purpose?"

"I didn't know."

"Of course you didn't *know*, but did you think it more likely to be improper or proper? Here was a man who had already given you money and he asks to see you in the middle of a case. Pretty irregular, wasn't it?"

"I told him so," said the inspector.

"I know you did," said Roger, "and that's why I ask the question again. Was it more likely for a proper or improper purpose? More likely is all I ask."

The inspector hesitated for a moment. Then:

"Improper, I suppose," he answered.

"In what way improper?" asked Roger.

Again the inspector hesitated.

"May I help you?" said Roger. "Possibly he was going to try to bribe you again?"

"Possibly," said the inspector.

"They why were you so indignant a moment ago when I asked you if you thought you might get some more money?"

"I thought you meant for myself," said the inspector.

"Why did you think that?" asked Roger.

"From the way you asked the question," said the inspector.

"Any other reason?" asked Roger.

The inspector did not answer at once.

"Come, inspector," said Roger, "is it such a very difficult question? You say that you thought my question meant that you expected to get some money for yourself. Very good. Now, was there any other reason except my manner of asking the question which made you think that?"

Again there was a pause. Then the inspector said:

"What the defendant himself said, I suppose."

"And what was that?"

"He said he'd given me more than I'd put in the charge sheet."

"You mean," said Roger, "that he said to you that he had given you more money than you handed over to your superior and that you had dishonestly kept the balance for yourself? That was the effect of what he said, was it not?"

"Yes," said the inspector.

"And what was your reply?" asked Roger.

Again the inspector hesitated.

"You were very indignant with me a moment ago," said Roger. "I suppose you were very indignant with Mr Glacier and denied his wicked lies?"

As there was still no answer, Roger went on:

"Come, inspector, didn't you deny what he said?"

"No," said the inspector, "I didn't get the chance."

"Oh—why was that?" asked Roger—in an interested, enquiring tone.

"He said something else at the same time . . . and—and——"

"You fainted," put in Roger, "and banged your head?"

"Yes," said the inspector.

"What else did he say?" asked Roger.

"He said that our conversation was being listened to by the Chief Constable and the Superintendent."

"Which was the greater shock?" asked Roger.

"I don't quite understand," said the inspector.

"Was it a greater shock to be told that you'd kept some of the money or that the conversation was being tapped—or was it a combination of both?"

"I don't know," said the inspector. "I suppose it was both."

"It was true that the conversation was being tapped, wasn't it?"

"Yes."

286

"It was also true, wasn't it, inspector, that you'd kept some of the money?"

"It was not."

"On neither occasion?"

"Certainly not."

"But you didn't deny it to Mr Glacier, did you?"

"I didn't get the chance."

"You've heard the record of the conversation played over, haven't you?"

"Yes."

"There was a pause between Mr Glacier's two questions, wasn't there?"

"There was a slight pause."

"Why didn't you take advantage of it to deny the allegation?"

"It was a shock."

"You mean that?"

"Yes."

"But aren't you used to having accused persons making wicked and untrue allegations against you?"

"Sometimes."

"It's quite frequent, isn't it?"

"It does happen."

"Then why was it such a shock?"

"I can't say why exactly, but it was."

"May I suggest as a reason," said Roger, "that you were so surprised at Mr Glacier telling the whole truth about the matter?"

"No."

"Didn't you think that he would deny ever having given you any money?"

"I didn't know what he would say."

"Of course you didn't *know*, but didn't you *think* he would deny ever having given you any money? That's what you'd expect him to do, isn't it?"

"Possibly."

"Well, of course, if he denies having given you any money he can't say he's given you more than you've handed over to your superiors, can he?"

"I suppose not."

"So that, if you have been dishonest and if he's going to deny giving you any money, you're pretty safe, aren't you?"

"It didn't happen."

"I didn't ask you if it happened," said Roger. "I asked if it seemed to you a pretty safe thing for a dishonest inspector to do?"

"I don't know whether it would be safe or not. I've never considered it."

"I suggest," said Roger, "that you not only considered it but that you did it."

"I did not."

Roger then proceeded to put Mr Glacier's story about Melanie to the inspector. But he did not do it at any great length as it was a side of the story in which he did not have much faith.

Later the sergeant gave evidence, corroborating what the inspector had said in his evidence-in-chief. Roger then cross-examined him.

"You know P.C. Thrussle, do you not?" was his first question.

"Yes," said the sergeant.

"An officer of good character?"

"As far as I know."

"On quite good terms with you?" asked Roger.

"Yes—quite."

"Any reason you can think of why he should tell a lie to injure you?"

"I can't think of any."

"Do you meet him in the canteen sometimes?"

"Yes."

"Chat about this and that?"

"Yes."

"Ever speak to him about this case?"

"I told him we'd got it on."

"Anything else about it?"

"Not that I remember."

"Let me see if I can help you," said Roger. "Did you mention the amount that had been handed to the inspector?"

"I don't think so."

"Didn't you? Just try and think."

"It was only a casual conversation."

"Drinking beer at the time?"

"I do drink it. Very likely I was then."

"Tell me, sergeant, have you had any experience of bribery cases before?"

"I've had to do with one or two."

"In each case the accused person denied he'd paid any money?"

"Yes."

"That's what they usually do, isn't it?"

"I believe so."

"That's what you'd expect them to do, isn't it?"

"I suppose so."

"So that, if an officer wanted to be dishonest, he could keep part of the bribe for himself?"

288

"I suppose he could do."

"Ever heard of such a thing being done?"

"No."

"I suggest you have—and in this case too."

"What d'you mean?"

Roger explained what he meant and the sergeant denied that anything of the kind had happened.

When the sergeant's evidence was completed, the superintendent gave evidence. He told of the inspector approaching him in the first instance, of the money being handed to him by the inspector on two separate occasions, and he produced the actual notes and the envelopes which had been opened by the Magistrates' clerk. He was cross-examined by Roger about the trap set for the inspector, and he identified as correct a transcript taken from the record of the interview. He also gave evidence of finding the inspector on the ground.

"Would you have been surprised if the inspector had acted dishonestly?" asked Roger.

"Yes, I would," said the superintendent.

"Very surprised?" asked Roger.

"Yes, very."

"You were completely satisfied of his integrity?"

"Yes."

"Then why set a trap for him?"

"That was not my responsibility."

"I see," said Roger. "So you throw that on to the Chief Constable, do you?"

"All I say is that it was not my responsibility," repeated the superintendent.

"Is the Chief Constable going to be called as a witness, do you know?"

"That is not my responsibility," said the superintendent.

Roger profoundly hoped, from his own personal point of view, that the Chief Constable would not be called. But from his clients' point of view he had to try to prod the prosecution into calling him. "Is my learned friend going to call the Chief Constable?" he asked.

"Certainly not," said Henry. "My learned friend can call him himself if he wishes."

"Thank you," said Roger. "I will consider the invitation in due course."

"Mr Thursby," said the judge, "I think it would be better if you confined your cross-examination to asking questions."

"If your Lordship pleases," said Roger.

Not long afterwards the case for the prosecution was closed and

Roger opened the case for the defence. Among other things, he said:

"Members of the jury, I entirely agree with my learned friend that corruption is a deadly disease and I say at once—whether my clients like it or not—that if you are satisfied that my clients or either of them are guilty, they deserve no sympathy whatever. I also agree with my learned friend that our police force is the most reputable in all the world. We rely on them and they seldom let us down. But there must be an exception to the rule from time to time and it is my duty to suggest to you, on behalf of my clients, that this case has uncovered one of them—the case, it might be called, of The Fainting Inspector. I will deal a little later with the circumstances which led up to his unfortunate accident. At the moment I will only remind you that you are not trying the inspector, you are trying my clients and if, in all the circumstances, you are not satisfied as to their guilt, that is an end of the matter and they are entitled to be acquitted. Now, in most cases of this kind the defence can only rely upon the evidence of the man or woman charged with the offence. In this case, fortunately for the defendants, I am in a position to call before you another police officer who has nothing to gain—indeed, perhaps a good deal to lose—by giving evidence for the defendants."

Roger then went on to outline what the police constable would say and, when he had finished, he called Mr Glacier as his first witness. He took him through the whole of his story, of how grateful he was that his little Melanie had not been charged, of the circumstances in which he came to give money to the inspector, and of the amount he gave. Finally, he gave evidence of the interview with the inspector. Roger then sat down, and Henry got up.

"Are you an honest man, Mr Glacier?" he asked.

"Ah," said Mr Glacier, "what is honesty?"

"Well, what do you call it?" asked Henry.

Mr Glacier put his hands on the witness box. "This is an opportunity I have been waiting for. I have often envied the parson who, without fear of interruption or contradiction, can express his views to his congregation on all manner of subjects. Now——"

"Be quiet," said the judge, "and listen to me. You will give your evidence properly or not at all."

Mr Glacier raised his eyebrows. "I am sorry to have offended your Lordship. It was unintentional, I assure you."

"Very well, then," said the judge.

There was silence for a moment.

"Well?" said the judge. "Are you going to answer counsel's question, or not?"

"My Lord," said Mr Glacier, "how do you wish me to answer

it? I am asked—how do you say?—a metaphysical question. How can I answer it except in the same—what is the word?—the same idiom? What is honesty? It is a big—a very big question. I could talk for hours on it. I assure your Lordship I will not do so," he added hurriedly.

"I can assure you you won't," said the judge. "Mr Blagrove," he added, "it is rather a large question. Do you really need an answer? I fancy the jury can judge what is meant by honesty from the practical point of view."

"If your Lordship pleases," said Henry. "Very well, then, Mr Glacier. Whatever you yourself mean by honesty, do you count yourself an honest man—as honest as the next man?"

"That rather depends upon who he is," said Mr Glacier. "I should expect to be in a higher class than Inspector Worcester."

"Very well, then," said Henry. "Do you consider it honest to bribe the police?"

"Most assuredly not."

"It is not a thing you would do?"

"It is most certainly not."

"But you would give the police large sums of money?"

"I give the tax collector large sums of money, but I do not bribe him."

"Do you think it proper to give the police money at all?"

"I have been thinking about this," said Mr Glacier, "since these proceedings were started, and I realize now that I was wrong to give money at all. My motives might have been misunderstood—and, in fact, they have been grossly misrepresented. I shall not be so foolish again."

"Then you now consider that you acted improperly?"

"Yes. I regret it. But it was not a crime."

"It was not the crime with which you are charged," said Henry.

The judge intervened. "Mr Blagrove, if you consider that the defendants' own story discloses an offence against the Prevention of Corruption Act, why didn't the prosecution charge them with it? They are charged with giving money to procure a favour in the future. Why weren't they charged with giving money for a past favour?"

"I can tell your Lordship that at once," said Henry. "It seemed to the prosecution, rightly or wrongly, that, if the jury accepted the story put forward by the defendant—and rejected that of the police officers—it would not be right to ask for a conviction for a crime which no witness for the prosecution alleges took place."

"I understand," said the judge. "That seems eminently fair."

"If your Lordship pleases," said Henry, and continued his cross-examination. He led up to the interview during the magisterial proceedings. "Now tell me, Mr Glacier," he said, "why didn't you give the inspector the chance of answering your allegation about the money before you went on to tell him that the conversation was being tapped?"

"Oh, Mr Blagrove, if I had your knowledge of the art of cross-examination I might have acted differently," said Mr Glacier.

"Mr Glacier," said Henry, "I do not propose to let you slip out of the question in that way. I consider it a very important one. Will you kindly deal with it seriously? Will you tell my Lord and the jury what possible proper object there could have been in telling the inspector about the interview being tapped before be answered the question about the money?"

"Sometimes," said Mr Glacier, "I have heard counsel ask two questions in one sentence. Can I be blamed if I, a layman, do the same?"

"Mr Glacier, I suggest to you that you put the two questions quite deliberately—that you knew what the inspector's answer would be to the first question and that you didn't want him to give it until you'd shocked him by disclosing about the tapping of the interview?"

"What is the question, please?" asked Mr Glacier. "If I may say so, there seem to be at least two questions in that one. Even three perhaps."

"Why did you want to disclose to the inspector that the conversation was being tapped at that particular moment?"

"Why did I want to to do that?" said Mr Glacier. "I do not know that I really did want to do it. I did it. I cannot say why. It just happened. Like so many things. I repeat in all seriousness that, if I had had your training, I might have done it differently."

Henry finished his cross-examination. Roger did not re-examine, and called his next witness—Mrs Glacier. She said what was expected of her by both sides, and then the police constable was called. He stuck to his story, and though Henry tried to see if he could trace any connection between him and the Glaciers, he was unable to do so. He swore positively that the sergeant had told him that they had received altogether sixty-five pounds and were only putting forty-five pounds in the charges; that he was frightened to go to the superintendent and, not being prepared to leave the matter undisclosed, he went to the Glaciers. Finally, Roger called Mr Plumb to give evidence of his conversation with the Chief Constable. The latter was in Court and his anger was so great that he had some difficulty in refraining from making an outburst. He reserved that for later. Digby was sitting between Henry and Roger and, as Roger began to ask the questions which would lead to a disclosure of what the Chief Constable said to Mr Plumb, he started a soft *obbligato* accompaniment—"in breach of confidence, in breach of confidence, in breach of confidence."

"Shut up," said Roger.

"In breach of confidence," repeated Digby.

"I wish you'd control your little yapper," said Roger to Henry.

"In breach of confidence," repeated Digby, "and I shall go on saying it until you've finished."

"Don't be an ass," said Roger. "Do muzzle him," he said to Henry, adding, "if you don't, I shall have to ask the judge to do so."

"What is happening at the Bar?" asked the judge. "It is most inconvenient for me and the jury to have this noise going on. Please continue with the evidence, Mr Thursby."

Digby eventually subsided and a very unwilling Mr Plumb proceeded to state what the Chief Constable had said—namely, that he had suspected the inspector for a long time and would be damned glad to get him.

"How is this admissible?" asked the judge.

"My Lord," said Roger, "is it not material that a party to litigation who calls a witness to support his case does not believe in the honesty of that witness? Could not a plaintiff be asked such a question regarding his chief witness? And, if he could, is not the Chief Constable in the same position? I, of course, appreciate that the prosecution is by the Queen. But the Queen can only act through agents and, if a person who has been responsible for the conduct or initiation of the prosecution, makes such a statement regarding an important witness, it must—in my respectful submission—be material for the consideration of the jury."

"I see how you put it, but I'm not at all sure that it's right," said the judge.

"If a plaintiff or the Director of Public Prosecutions said of a witness he is calling—'he is not a trusted servant of mine'—surely that would be a matter proper for the consideration of the jury?"

"You can't call affirmative evidence to show bad character," said the judge.

"I respectfully agree," said Roger, "but the object of this evidence is to show that the prosecution, through its agent—the Chief Constable—has no belief in its case. Would it not be a proper question to ask a party to litigation who has called a witness to an important incident—'have you any belief that the incident really happened?' "

"I should have thought not," said the judge. "The belief of the plaintiff in his own witness has surely nothing to do with it. It is what the judge or jury thinks of the witness that matters. In so far as the matter goes to the credit of the witness, you must agree it is not admissible. And I must confess I can't see why the belief or disbelief of a plaintiff or Director of Public Prosecutions in the worthiness of a witness has anything to do with the matter. Obviously, if the Director knew anything specifically to the discredit of the witness, he would probably inform the defence of the matter. And, of course, the matter could be put to the witness in cross-examination."

"My Lord," said Roger, "I respectfully submit that, in a criminal prosecution at any rate, the disbelief of the prosecutor—using that term in the sense I have mentioned—in the honesty of an important witness must be a matter for the consideration of the jury."

"Well, what do you say, Mr Blagrove?" asked the judge.

"My Lord, whatever the strict legal position may be," said Henry, "I should not seek to exclude evidence which the defence desire to tender unless it is quite unarguable that it is admissible. I would respectfully agree with what has fallen from your Lordship, but, as I concede that there is an argument to be put forward in favour of the evidence being received, I do not ask your Lordship to reject the evidence."

"Very well, then," said the judge. "In these circumstances I will say nothing more—except that I have grave doubts as to its admissibility."

"As the question of admissibility has been raised," said Roger, "I think it only right to tell your Lordship that, after the Chief Constable had made the statement, he said to my client—'That's in confidence, of course,' and my client said—'of course.' Now, as your Lordship may imagine, in those circumstances it is with the greatest regret and considerable embarrassment that I have felt bound to tender the evidence. If I could have avoided doing so, I should certainly have done so, but, if it is admissible in evidence, it seems to me that the defendants are entitled to the benefit of it. I hope your Lordship will think I have taken a proper course."

"I am quite sure," said the judge, "that you have acted in accordance with your duty to your client. There can, of course, be no such thing as 'without prejudice' conversations in criminal matters and, unfortunate though the matter is, it seems to me that, if the evidence is otherwise admissible, the Chief Constable's statement about confidence cannot have the effect of excluding it. Moreover, it seems to me that in a criminal matter different considerations apply from those which obtain in civil litigation. I do not think any other course was open to you."

"I am very grateful to your Lordship," said Roger, and hoped the Chief Constable was listening. He was.

"These lawyers always stick together," he whispered to a friend in Court.

After Mr Plumb had completed his evidence, Roger addressed the jury—submitting to them that at the least the case for the prosecution had not been proved against either of his clients. Henry followed him on behalf of the prosecution and submitted that, on the contrary, the case had certainly been proved against Mr Glacier. As regards Mrs Glacier, if the jury thought she might have been under her husband's influence and was not really a willing party to the bribery, he could not ask for a conviction against her. Finally, Mr Justice Kingsdown summed up. He reminded the jury of what the charges against each of the accused were; he spoke of the gravity of such charges, and then he went on:

"Now, members of the jury, in this country it is not for a prisoner to prove his innocence but for the prosecution to prove his guilt. Now, how must they prove that guilt? They cannot prove it with complete certainty—for you could only be completely certain of a prisoner's guilt if you not only were present at the commission of a crime but plainly saw it committed. In such a case you would be witnesses, not jurors. So you will see that justice could not be administered if complete certainty were required. But what is required is that the prosecution should prove the defendants' guilt with reasonable certainty. Suspicion is not enough—even strong suspicion. Before you can convict you must be reasonably sure that the Crown has made out its case. And when I say reasonably sure, you will understand—for the reason I have explained—that you cannot be expected to be completely sure. You must be reasonably sure. So much for the measure of proof. Now, what the prosecution have to prove with that measure of proof is this."

The judge then explained the ingredients of the offence with which the defendants were charged.

"Whatever your view may be about the guilt or innocence of Mr Glacier, members of the jury," he went on, "you may well think that the case against Mrs Glacier has not been satisfactorily established. The law on the subject is as follows: there is no presumption that a wife acts under the coercion of her husband but, if the offence is committed by her in his presence, she may prove—if she can—that she was in fact acting under his coercion. If she does so she is entitled to be acquitted. The only evidence against Mrs Glacier is that she was present when the crime—if crime it was—was committed. She does not say her husband coerced her, but on the other hand it is his act that constituted the crime, and if she is liable it is only because he acted on her behalf. Now, in all the circumstances, are you reasonably sure that Mrs Glacier has committed any offence? If you are, you will, of course, find her Guilty; but you may think—it is entirely a matter for you—that it would be very dangerous on the evidence—and you are concerned with the evidence and the evidence alone—to find her Guilty of either of the charges against her. I need hardly say that, if you find Mr Glacier Not Guilty, you would, of course, find his wife Not Guilty also. But, up till now, I have dealt with the case of Mrs Glacier separately—in other words, even if you should find her husband Guilty, you may well take a different view of the case against her. I will now come to the much more difficult problem before you— the question of Mr Glacier. Counsel has quite rightly told you that you are trying him and not the inspector or the sergeant. That is absolutely true, but it will be impossible for you to come to a conclusion about the guilt or innocence of Mr Glacier without weighing up the evidence of the inspector and the sergeant. If you think they are a couple of scoundrels—that is an end to the matter. But if you are not satisfied of that, you still have to be reasonably sure that what they are saying is substantially true before you can return a verdict of Guilty. And in that connection you have to weigh up the evidence of the police constable who gave evidence for the Glaciers."

The judge then proceeded to go into the evidence in detail and, when he had done so, he said:

"Well, members of the jury, that is what these witnesses said. What do you believe to be the truth? If you are left in a state of uncertainty, the defendants are entitled to be acquitted. I have told you several times that, before you can convict, you must be reasonably sure that the truth is in the evidence given by the prosecution and not in that given by and on behalf of the defendants. What kind of an impression did the inspector and sergeant make on you? What kind of an impression did Mr Glacier make on you? Did he appear to you to be an honest man who was grateful to the police for not charging his daughter— or did he appear to you to be an extremely astute, exceptionally able man, who would be quite capable of inventing a plausible story to get himself out of his difficulties? It is of no importance what impression he made on me. What did *you* think of him? You may think possibly that that is the crux of the matter. If the story he is putting forward now is true, the inspector and sergeant are quite plainly wholly unfitted for their positions of trust. But, if it is false, then it is difficult to resist the conclusion that the evidence of the police constable called on behalf of the Glaciers is false also and—although there is no direct evidence to show that he has been induced by the Glaciers to give that false evidence—I think one must face that position, and, personally, I do not see how that inference can be resisted *if*, and only if, the evidence of Mr Glacier is untrue in the material matters. There it is, members of the jury, you are the judges, not I. I have told you the law on the subject and that you must take from me. If I am wrong in any of my directions, I can be corrected elsewhere. But the facts are for you and for you alone. If anything I have said about the facts does not commend itself to you, disregard it. It is your views which matter, not mine. I do not think there is anything further I can usefully add, members of the jury, and I will ask you to consider your verdict. I expect you would like to retire."

CHAPTER TWENTY-ONE

MR GREEN

THE jury retired, and Roger and Henry were about to leave the Court while the next case was called—when a prisoner who wanted a dock brief was put in the dock.

"Has he two pounds four shillings and sixpence?" asked the judge.

"Yes," said the clerk.

"Very well, then," said the judge. "You can choose any counsel you like."

"Ah," said the prisoner, whom Roger seemed dimly to recognize, "but not one who's engaged on a case, can I?"

"No, that's quite correct," said the judge, a little surprised. "You seem to know all about it."

"I've been caught before, my Lord," said the prisoner, and then added hastily, "about choosing counsel, I mean, my Lord. It's such a disappointment when you choose a really brainy-looking——"

"Now don't start making speeches," said the judge. "Choose someone."

"All right, my Lord," said the prisoner, "I'll have him," and pointed to Roger.

"You can't have Mr Thursby," said the judge. "He's engaged on a case."

The prisoner looked plaintively at the judge. "That's exactly what I meant, my Lord. It would be fairer if they had a label on them." He paused for a moment and looked along the line of counsel: "Some of them might have an L on them too, don't you think, my Lord?"

"Behave yourself," said the judge.

"Did I hear you say Mr Thursby?" said the prisoner.

"I told you you can't have him," snapped the judge.

Suddenly Roger realized who the prisoner was. He had aged a good deal, but Roger recognized in him a Mr Green whom he had once defended successfully at the Old Bailey while he was still a pupil. In fact, Mr Green had done most of the defending and Roger had long ago come to the conclusion that Mr Green's idea of L-plates on pupils was not at all a bad one. They should not be allowed to appear except in company with an experienced practitioner who must sit next to them.

"My Lord," said Roger, "if it isn't too long a case, I'd be prepared to take it for the prisoner."

"That's very good of you, Mr Thursby," said the judge. "Is it a long case, d'you know?" he asked. He was really addressing the clerk but Mr Green took it on himself to reply.

"Nothing long about it," he said and added, "I hope."

"Very well, then," said the judge. "Perhaps you'd like to see him now, Mr Thursby."

"If your Lordship pleases," said Roger. Before going to see his new client, he spoke to Henry. "This is a chap I did a docker for when I was a pupil of Grimeyboy. I hope he'll think I've improved."

"I gather he hasn't," said Henry.

Roger went to see Mr Green. He certainly had aged, but there was still a good deal of the old sparkle Roger had noticed twelve years before.

"Nice to see you, Mr Thursby," said Mr Green. "Nice to see you any place, but I didn't come here for the purpose."

"How are you?" said Roger. "It is a long time ago. Things not too good since then?"

"Mustn't grumble," said Mr Green. "Lose good conduct marks if you do. Let me see," and he thought for a bit. "You were toffee, weren't you?"

"That's right," said Roger, "it was a case about toffee. Glad you got off. Sorry you're here now. What's it for?"

"Oh—don't let's spoil the party," said Mr Green. "Let's talk of something pleasant. Haven't seen you for years. We can't get a pint down here, I suppose?"

"I'm afraid not," said Roger. "We'll celebrate with one when we get you off."

The old man—at any rate he now looked one—shook his head. His eyes grew a little moist. Then he brushed them with his hand in an impatient gesture. "Come, come, Mr Green," he said, "pull yourself together. It's a long lane that has no turning. If you ask me," he added, "it's going to be a ruddy long lane this time."

"What's it all about?" said Roger.

"I've lost my grip," said Mr Green. "I'm slipping. Slipped,

you might say. Nice to see you again though. Takes me back a bit. Toffee. That was good fun. We had 'em on the run, didn't we?"

"You did," said Roger. "I just followed behind you."

"Well—you've made up ground since then," said Mr Green. "See your name in the paper no end. Nice to be able to tell one's pals—'I started that young man off.' I've had several beers on that."

"Well, it's quite true," said Roger, "and you deserved them. As soon as I recognized you, I decided to accept the brief—that's, of course, if it was offered to me."

"It's a shame," said Mr Green, "that there isn't more kick in it. We could have had a high old time together—you and me. If I'd known you were going to be here—I'd never have done it. I shouldn't have, anyway. I told you I'm slipping. D'you know what I've done?"

"No," said Roger.

"I've admitted it," said Mr Green. "Can you beat it? Signed, sealed and delivered on the dotted line. I-have-been-warned-that-anything - I - say - may - be - used - in - evidence - and - I - make-this statement - voluntarily - after - having - been - cautioned - that - I - am-not-bound-to-say-anything-unless-I-wish-to-do-so. And what makes it worse is—that's quite true. I was warned. It was voluntary. No cigarettes or cups of tea. I go and make a ruddy voluntary confession. Can't think what I was up to. Tired, I suppose. I'll get four years this time. That means three nearly—if you don't grumble. Three years to wait for a pint of bitter. Hard, isn't it? Pity I'm not on bail. We could have popped across and had one."

"If you're pleading Guilty, why did you want counsel? You know the ropes as well as anyone, I should say."

"Thank you," said Mr Green. "Experience teaches. Yes, I do. But I don't know this judge. Never seen him, never read about him. I thought I'd better get a line on him. It's worth four years, but not a penny more. And suppose this chap doesn't know the scale, he might give me five or six even."

"It cuts both ways," said Roger. "He might give you eighteen months."

"Can't see it," said Mr Green. "Had three years last time. It's a good idea though. If they halved it each time instead of doubling it. I'd only get nine months next time. Only four and a half the time after. Hardly worth going in for. But what d'you think this is good for?"

"You haven't told me anything about it yet," said Roger.

"There I go again," said Mr Green. "That's what I did with you last time. Can't make bricks without straw, the labourer

is worthy of his hire, who sups with the devil needs a long spoon—
now, where had I got to? Ah—the indictment. I used to call it
in*dickt*ment until you told me how to pronounce it. I've always
remembered since then. Funny how one doesn't notice these
things. The clerk says in*dite*ment all right, but I'd never noticed
till you told me. I won quite a few bets over that. Pity there's no
beer down here. Sorry to run on. But bets always remind me of
beer. They sort of go together."

"Well, you'd better let me see it," said Roger.

"The indictment?"

"Yes."

"It's a scruffy-looking thing," said Mr Green. "Only two counts.
But they'll be enough. Not so deep as a pint mug or as wide as a
public bar—but they'll be enough—but I'll do the serving—worse
luck."

Roger looked at the charges against Mr Green, which were
in substance that he had obtained £150 by pretending that he was
running a genuine business called Glenavon Chocolate Company.

"What was the total amount involved?" asked Roger.

"It says one hundred and fifty pounds there," said Mr Green.

"I know," said Roger.

"You are inquisitive," said Mr Green. "Do I have to tell
you?"

"Not if you don't want to. But you might as well. The police
will know. And it's better if I know what we've got to meet."

"Well, as a matter of fact the business hadn't started long when
something went wrong. I'm slipping, I tell you. I sent a man a
cheque. If I'd just not paid him it'd have been all right. But I
was feeling cocky. He'd written me a rude letter threatening all
sorts of things. So I sent him a cheque."

"And it bounced?"

"So high," said Mr Green, and pointed to the ceiling. "I hadn't
an account, as a matter of fact, so you can't really blame the bank—
though it was only for ten pounds and it wouldn't have hurt them
to pay it. Still, there it is and here we are. What goes up must come
down."

"You haven't yet said how much is involved altogether."

"Only about five or six hundred pounds. Hadn't had time to
get started."

"Don't you think you could get a decent job instead of this sort
of thing?" said Roger.

"Now you've said something," said Mr Green. "That's what
I say every time. To the judge too. I'll go straight, really I will.
My Lord, if you will take a lenient view of this offence I promise
you I'll never appear in the dock again." He paused for a moment.

Then he said: "Tell me—how many times d'you think a chap can say that and still keep his self-respect?"

"It depends on the chap," said Roger. "But seriously, when you come out next time, why don't you settle down to something? After all, you're not making much of a success of this kind of thing, are you? You've had a good many beerless months in the last ten years, I should imagine."

"You're quite right," said Mr Green. "I miss my beer and I've been without a lot of it, as you say. And I've had a bad season— too many bad seasons. Yes—you're quite right. But there's one trouble—and I don't know how you can get over that."

"What is it?" said Roger.

"Well, between you and me," said Mr Green, "I don't like honest work."

"It's lucky we're not all like that."

"I certainly agree," said Mr Green. "It's very lucky indeed. Who'd run the trains and buses, who'd run Parliament, who'd run the Law Courts, the Stock Exchange, and so on and so forth? I can't really grumble, can I? I've lots of people working for me— the whole population nearly. And I get it all for nothing. Pretty good when you work it out that way."

"Depends how long you have to enjoy it," said Roger. "When were you last inside?"

"Came out ten months ago. It was a Friday. Friday the thirteenth. That's a day to let you out. I suggested that in the circumstances they should make it the day before. They said they understood my feelings entirely and suggested the day after. So we compromised and I came out on the Friday."

"Well, you'd better tell me something in your favour," said Roger. "How many honest days' work have you done in the last ten years?"

"I've just told you," said Mr Green. "I don't like it. Now, just listen. If I took a job—item—I'd have to work regular hours. Well—I just can't manage that. Then again you can't take holidays whenever you want to. You have people giving you orders. I'm not a Socialist, Mr Thursby. I don't believe that all men are equal or that everyone should have the same. Some people like being given orders. They wouldn't know how to run my business. They're happy in their little jobs. Start at nine, end at six. Half-day Saturday. Fortnight's holiday a year. Christmas and Easter extra. Sounds lovely. So it is for them what likes it. I'm not one of them and I'm too old to start now."

"Well," said Roger, "it's a change to have anyone so frank, but it won't be much use my telling the judge—that you'll do it again as soon as you come out and that you're not in the least sorry you've done it this time—only sorry you've been caught."

"You don't think that would help?" said Mr Green. "He wouldn't say—this fellow's so honest, he must have some good in him, and take off six months?"

"I doubt it," said Roger. "I doubt it very much. And the trouble is—now that you've told me that you've no intention of going straight and that you have never done so, I can't tell the judge the opposite."

"Oh—I can change all that," said Mr Green. "I could put on an act, if you'd like me to. My Lord, I know I've done wrong, but I promise you——"

Roger interrupted. "It won't do, I'm afraid," he said. "I can't deceive the judge."

"No, of course not," said Mr Green. "It was very wrong of me to suggest it. I apologize, I withdraw, least said soonest mended, no broken bones, I hope."

"Not at all," said Roger. "I'm glad we understand one another."

"What would you advise then?" asked Mr Green.

"Well, quite frankly," said Roger, "I think you'd do better not to have counsel at all."

"You advise me to make my own plea?" asked Mr Green.

"On the whole, I do," said Roger.

"Do you realize," said Mr Green, with a twinkle, "that I shall try to deceive the judge?"

"You shouldn't do so, but I can't stop you," said Roger.

"But you still advise me to make my own plea?" persisted Mr Green.

Roger did not answer at once, and Mr Green went on: "Because if that's so, you appear to be advising me to deceive the judge."

"Certainly not," said Roger. "I advise you to tell him the truth."

"What, and get an extra five years?" said Mr Green. "Is that your best advice?"

"Perhaps not," said Roger. "You'd better say nothing at all."

"But that won't do," said Mr Green. "He'll invite me to say something. And if I refuse—he'll fear the worst—and so shall I."

"I don't see what else you can do."

"Well, I do," said Mr Green. "I shall make an impassioned plea and promise that, if he exercises leniency, I'll never, never, never do it again. Never, never, never," he rattled off quickly. "Don't look so troubled. He won't be lenient and that lets me off the promise. Now, do you still advise me not to employ you?"

"I don't think there's anything I can do for you," said Roger.

"Then, as they say upstairs," said Mr Green, "the answer is Yes. But, as you know I'm going to tell a pack of lies to the judge, you're advising me to take a course which will result in the Court being deceived. How d'you get out of that one, Mr Thursby?"

"I don't know that I can," said Roger. "There's nothing whatever I can properly say in mitigation. So I'm bound to tell you that I can be no use to you. The result of that is that you'll defend yourself and I know that you'll lie in the process."

"I suppose you couldn't get up in the middle when I'm saying my piece and tell the judge it's all lies."

"Oh, good heavens no," said Roger. "I couldn't do that."

"I just wanted to be sure," said Mr Green.

"Well, then," he added, "where do we go from here? Or perhaps that's a gloomy way of putting it. I think I'll solve your difficulty by withdrawing my instructions. That's the right expression, isn't it?"

"It is," said Roger.

"Just before you go," said Mr Green, "tell me one thing for old times' sake. What's this judge like?"

"He's quite a good chap," said Roger.

"Is he nice to young counsel?" asked Mr Green.

"Yes, very. Why do you ask?" said Roger.

"I just wondered," said Mr Green. "Now I suppose we'd better both get back," he said. "Look forward to our next meeting. Hope it won't be as long again—if it's in the right place," he added.

Roger went back to Court and, at a convenient moment, Mr Green was put back in the dock. The jury in the Glacier case were still out.

"My Lord," said Roger, "the prisoner wishes to withdraw his instructions from me."

"Very well," said the judge. "Do you wish to defend yourself then?"

"No," said Mr Green, "I'd like that one," and he pointed to the white-wigged Mr Trent. The judge looked down at counsel's row and, for the first time, recognized his acquaintance of the races. "Mr—ah—Mr——" he began.

"Trent," said Mr Trent. "Anthony Trent, my Lord."

"Mr Trent, will you accept this brief?"

"I shall be very pleased, my Lord. I will go and see the prisoner at once and let your Lordship know as soon as I am ready to proceed."

The judge resisted the impulse to inform him that he would kindly be ready for the Court when the Court was ready for him. Mr Justice Kingsdown thought it most important in all proceedings, but particularly in criminal matters, that a client should not think he had done badly because of any deficiencies in his counsel. If—as he sorely wanted to do—he bounced Mr Trent up and down before the case began, it would be difficult for the prisoner to feel that he would have a satisfactory trial. So he contented himself with saying: "That is very good of you, Mr Trent."

"Not at all, my Lord," said Mr Trent. "I am only too anxious to assist the Court."

I must find out where this young man belongs, thought the judge, and pass a word to someone in his chambers. He could think of some judges—more choleric than he was—for whom Mr Trent might be fatal.

While Mr Trent was interviewing Mr Green, the jury in the Glacier case sent a note to the judge. In consequence, the defendants were put into the dock again and Roger, Henry and Digby took their places in Court.

"I have had a note from the jury," said the judge, "to this effect. 'We are agreed about the case of Mrs Glacier, but not in the case of Mr Glacier. It might help if your Lordship would repeat what you told the jury about the extent to which the case has to be proved by the prosecution.' I propose to have the jury back and comply with their request, unless either of you have any submission to make on the subject."

Henry and Roger shook their heads. So the jury came back into Court and the judge repeated to them at some length and in substantially the same words what he had said before. He added at the end: "I hope that will solve your difficulties one way or the other."

The jury retired again. The judge dealt with the next two cases, which were pleas of Guilty, and then Mr Trent returned to Court and informed the clerk that his case was a plea of Guilty too. The judge said he would take it at once.

"We must watch this," said Henry to Roger.

Mr Green was brought into the dock. The two charges were read out to him.

"Do you plead Guilty or Not Guilty?" asked the clerk.

"Unfortunately, Guilty," said Mr Green. "I should have liked to have given my young counsel a chance to show what he's made of, but I must stick to the truth and, as I'm guilty, I must plead Guilty. I'm sure your Lordship would approve of that."

"Be quiet," said the judge. "Your counsel will address me on your behalf."

"I only wanted to show willing," said Mr Green.

Counsel for the prosecution then outlined to the judge the facts of the case and then called a police officer to state the character and antecedents of Mr Green. He also read out a list of his convictions. Mr Trent said that he had no questions to ask. That's something, thought the judge, but his optimism was premature.

"Yes, Mr Trent?" he said. "Do you wish to say anything in mitigation?"

"If your Lordship pleases," began Mr Trent. "I will start by reminding your Lordship of the duties of the Court in passing sentence. First of the matters you should consider generally and then of the matters you should consider by way of mitigating the offence and then—yes—of the matters, if any, of aggravation. These remarks of mine will, of course, be entirely general and by way of what I may term preliminary submission and will not be concerned with this case in particular."

"I should prefer you to confine your remarks to this case, Mr Trent," said the judge, with as little grimness as possible.

"Oh, my Lord," said Mr Trent, "I have not made myself plain. I am so sorry. Of course my remarks will be relevant—if I may say so, they will be highly relevant—they concern every case where a judge is passing sentence and therefore they cover this case as well. They are remarks of general application."

"So I gather," said the judge, "but I have had some experience of the duties of the Court in this respect."

"I'm quite sure your Lordship has," said Mr Trent, "but I feel that it might help your Lordship in approaching this case if I brought some of the more salient matters to your Lordship's attention. Now, my Lord, in the first place your Lordship should consider the nature of the actual crime committed. Let me take an example. Supposing a man with many previous convictions is charged with a really trivial offence——"

"Mr Trent," said the judge, "I really cannot allow you to take up the time of the Court by reminding me of things I already know and which have been established for years. Pray confine your remarks to this particular case."

"Then your Lordship is bearing in mind," said Mr Trent, "that, having first considered the nature of the crime, the Court's next duty is to consider——"

"Mr Trent," interrupted the judge, with some heat, "you have not been very long at the Bar and I am afraid you have a lot to learn." The judge paused—not because he had finished but because he was saying to himself—you must tone it down, you simply must, or that wretched chap in the dock will think he's got an extra year because you didn't see eye to eye with his counsel. This gave Mr Trent the chance of saying:

"Indeed I have, my Lord. And might I say that I am most grateful to your Lordship for any instruction your Lordship sees fit to give me."

This gives me a chance, thought the judge, but, before he could say anything, Mr Trent went on:

"Of course, I'm sure your Lordship will understand that I am here to act solely in the interests of my client, as I see them, and, supposing any advice your Lordship should very kindly give me should happen not to coincide with views I have formed after mature consideration—views, I frankly admit, which may be wrong—but I can only act on what I think right, for better or worse, can I not, my Lord——"

Something burst on the Bench.

"Mr Trent, be quiet and listen to me. When you are in my Court, you will do as I say. If you object to any of my rulings, you can go to the Court of Criminal Appeal."

"Is your Lordship giving me leave to appeal?" asked Mr Trent blandly.

I can't stand much more of this, thought the judge. "There is nothing to appeal from at the moment, Mr Trent," he said with some difficulty.

"That's why I didn't follow your Lordship's observation," said Mr Trent.

Never in his career had Mr Justice Kingsdown wanted to take off his wig and throw it at counsel, and to follow it up with the glass and bottle of water which were by him—and after that to run yelling blue murder through the streets, or to sit sobbing in his private room. "This is intolerable," he said. He had not meant to say it aloud, but it slipped out.

Mr Trent looked puzzled. Then a light dawned on him. "Usher," he said in a low voice, but one that could be heard, "usher—open some windows. His Lordship is finding the heat intolerable."

"Mr Trent," said the judge, in his sternest voice, "are you intending to be funny?"

"Funny, my Lord?" said Mr Trent, "certainly not, my Lord. I heard your Lordship say that something was intolerable and I could only imagine it was the heat, my Lord."

"It was not the heat, Mr Trent—it was you," said the judge. Again he had not meant to say it aloud, but he simply could not restrain himself.

"Me, my Lord?" said Mr Trent, in a surprised voice. "I'm so very sorry, my Lord. Could your Lordship perhaps be kind enough to tell me what I have done to offend your Lordship, and then—subject, of course, to my client's interests—I will do all I can to remedy the matter."

"Mr Trent," said the judge, as calmly as possible, "you can best remedy the matter by saying as shortly as possible what there is to be said on your client's behalf in mitigation of sentence."

"But that's what I was doing, my Lord. No doubt, owing to

my inexperience, I was doing it clumsily and not probably as your Lordship, when in my position, used to do it—but I do assure your Lordship that I am trying and trying only to urge on my client's behalf the various matters which are in his favour. But, in order to do that, it is necessary—in my view—and here I am sure your Lordship will forgive me if I cross swords with your Lordship——"

"Mr Trent," said the judge, "sit down."

Mr Trent, looking puzzled, remained standing.

"Sit down, Mr Trent, sit down, sit down, sit down. If you don't, I will have you removed by the usher."

Mr Trent, quite bewildered, did as he was told.

"Arthur Green," said the judge, "the sentence of the Court is that you go to prison for eighteen months."

Mr Green seemed stunned by the sentence at first—and then he turned to his attendant warders. "Quick," he said in a whisper, "down the stairs before he changes his mind."

Mr Trent was soon able to tell his friends—and others—that he got off an old lag with eighteen months after he'd only recently come out from doing three years for a precisely similar offence. And, indeed, the leniency was entirely due to Mr Trent. Mr Justice Kingsdown had ensured that the prisoner would not think that he had received a heavier sentence because of his counsel and that, although he had refused to listen to a speech in mitigation, the sentence he passed was not one which the Court of Criminal Appeal would reduce. Indeed, had Mr Green appealed they would doubtless have increased it. But there was to be no appeal by Mr Green, who went to gaol almost singing. "And what pleases me so much," he wrote to Roger, "and what I am sure must please you, is that we were able to affect his Lordship's mind without telling any lies or making any promises."

CHAPTER TWENTY-TWO

THE VERDICT

EVENTUALLY the jury returned to Court, agreed. They acquitted Mrs Glacier, but they convicted her husband. Roger was surprised. Mr Glacier was extremely displeased. The Chief Constable was slightly—only slightly—mollified. The judge sentenced Mr Glacier to nine months' imprisonment. Roger and Mr Plumb interviewed him after he had been sentenced.

"Mr Glacier," said Roger, "I think you should appeal. In my

view the judge's summing up was wrong in law in one important respect."

"You will understand, Mr Thursby," said Mr Glacier, "that I do not place entirely the same confidence in your views. I do not mean by that that I think you conducted my defence badly. Nothing of the kind. I think your cross-examination of the inspector was—how do you say?—a masterpiece. But I should have enjoyed it more if I had been acquitted. No—I am grateful to you for your conduct of the case. But you will remember that you told me that I had a good chance of being acquitted."

"So you had," said Roger, "and the jury took long enough to arrive at their verdict."

"Not as long as nine months," said Mr Glacier. "But there," he added, "I must not yield to despair. I still have confidence in your ability. Is there really a chance of success in the Appeal Court?"

"Definitely," said Roger. "It's not altogether an easy Court, but I think you've a good point and, even if you lose there, I think there's a very good chance of your being able to get to the House of Lords. It's a point of great public importance, in my view."

"And will it take more than nine months to get to the House of Lords?" asked Mr Glacier.

"It certainly won't," said Roger, "but, even if it did, it would surely be worth your while to get rid of the conviction, even if you've served the sentence. And it's possible that, if the appeal took a long time, you'd get bail."

"I must leave it to you and Mr Plumb," said Mr Glacier. "If you think I should appeal—very well, be it so. But, may I say that I trust you will be as quick over the matter as possible?"

"We shall lose no time," said Mr Plumb mournfully. "I'm so very sorry about it. Perhaps Mr Thursby would settle a notice of appeal at once. Meanwhile Mr Glacier and I had better discuss arrangements for his business and his wife—during his . . . absence."

Roger left Mr Plumb and Mr Glacier together and then went to look for Anne. "D'you think," he asked her, very soon after he had found her, "that it would be any good my seeing your father?"

"Not at the moment," she said. "I must say . . . I see his point of view."

"You don't mean you agree with it?" he asked unhappily.

"Well—I don't know," said Anne. "I haven't really met any lawyers before, and I don't know their standards."

"That's a horrid thing to say," said Roger. "It means you think I played a dirty trick on your father. I've done nothing of the kind.

In the first place, I had no idea Glacier would give the show away at the interview with the inspector."

"You used something Father told your solicitor in confidence," said Anne.

"I couldn't help doing so. I didn't want to—but I had to. The judge said I acted perfectly properly."

"Yes, I know," said Anne. "Father told me."

"Well, doesn't that make any difference?" he asked.

"Father says you all stick together—and that's true I suppose . . . like doctors and all professional men."

"If you mean that a judge would say something was proper when it wasn't—just because he wanted to help a member of the Bar—that's absolutely untrue. He might say nothing, but he certainly wouldn't give his blessing to something he thought wrong."

"Well, I'm glad you didn't do anything improper then," said Anne. "But you can't expect me to fall on your neck and kiss you for breaking a confidence. I think it's terribly important to be able to trust people."

"So do I," said Roger. "Don't you trust me?"

"Well—ought I to after what you've just told me? Suppose I told you something in confidence now—and it became useful to you to use it for a client of yours—I shouldn't feel very safe with my confidences."

"That would be quite different," said Roger. "That would have been learned privately . . . not in the course of acting for a client. Why can't you look at it from my point of view? Suppose you were acting for someone who was charged with murder, wouldn't you feel bound to use any material you had which might show that they weren't guilty?"

"Well, that would include my private confidences," said Anne, "wouldn't it? So I'm not really safe in telling you anything."

"It couldn't happen like that," said Roger. "There's no reasonable chance that it could happen."

"But if it did, could I trust you?" asked Anne.

"If you refused to allow me to use the information, I don't suppose you could really. If you'd told me something in the strictest confidence—privately, nothing to do with any case—which later showed that a client of mine hadn't committed a crime—and if I asked you to let me use the information and you refused . . . I suppose that I should have to use it. And so would most people, I think. Which is the worse—to break your confidence or let a man whom you know to be innocent go to gaol or be hanged? Which do you think?"

Anne did not answer immediately, and Roger followed it up

with: "Well, suppose it was your problem . . . suppose you could save someone's life by breaking a confidence. Would you do it—or not?"

"Well, I must admit that the loss of a life is more important than the breaking of a promise."

"Well, then, what's the difference in principle between death and prison? Prison might kill a man. It is very likely to ruin him and his family. If he's a claustrophobic it might send him mad. What would you do? If you could save an innocent man from prison by breaking a confidence—would you do it?"

"Mr Glacier wasn't innocent."

"Oh, come, Anne, that won't do—really. He's presumed innocent until he's found guilty. He's only guilty now because the jury think he was."

"You argue very well, Roger," said Anne. "I'm not surprised you've done as well as you have."

"But what I say is right," said Roger, "it really is. Don't let it come between us—whatever your father thinks about me."

"I do see your point of view," said Anne. "I'll see what I can do with Father. But he'll be a tougher nut to crack than I was . . . but then, of course, that's rather different. I——" she trailed off.

"If only I've convinced you," said Roger.

"I think you have," said Anne, "and I must say I didn't really want to win this argument."

CHAPTER TWENTY-THREE

COURT OF CRIMINAL APPEAL

NOT long afterwards the case came before the Court of Criminal Appeal—consisting of Mr Justice Short, Mr Justice Rose and Mr Justice Mellow. In opening the case to the Court, Roger, after a few preliminary remarks, said:

"My Lords, there is only one point in this appeal—a point of law, but, in my submission, it is a very important one. This was a case where the jury took a considerable time to arrive at a verdict and, not only that, they expressly asked the judge to repeat his direction on what was the measure of proof required."

"I have yet to learn," said Mr Justice Short, "that it is a ground of appeal that the jury took a long time to find the prisoner guilty."

"It isn't," said Roger, "but if your Lordships will be good

enough to hear what the ground of appeal is, I think your Lordships will find that the fact that the jury took a long time to arrive at a verdict is at least relevant in this case—though it is in no way essential to my appeal."

"I don't know what your point is," said Mr Justice Rose, "but we've read the evidence. The jury obviously believed the evidence for the prosecution and not that for the defence. What's wrong with that?"

"Nothing, my Lord," said Roger, "if they were properly directed. I don't dispute that the jury were entitled to take the view they took if the summing-up of the learned judge was right in law."

"Hadn't you better take us to the passages you complain of?" said Mr Justice Mellow. "I'm bound to say it seemed to me a clear and admirable summing-up and not at all unfavourable to your clients."

"My Lords," said Roger, "the misdirection of which I respectfully complain consists entirely of the way in which the learned judge directed the jury as to the burden of proof."

"He said it was on the prosecution, didn't he?" asked Mr Justice Short. "That's right, isn't it?"

"Yes," said Roger, "the learned judge said it was on the prosecution but, in my submission, he directed them wrongly about the extent to which the case had to be proved. It was because that is the sole point in this case that I ventured to draw your Lordship's attention to the importance which the jury apparently attached to this question of the onus of proof. That shows that—if there had been a different direction—they might have returned a different verdict."

"If the learned judge had told the jury to acquit Mr Glacier, as he in effect told them to acquit Mrs Glacier, they might have found both of them Not Guilty, you mean?" said Mr Justice Short.

"No, my Lord, I don't mean that," said Roger.

"Well, what is your complaint?" said Mr Justice Mellow. "You concede that there's nothing wrong with the trial and nothing wrong with the summing-up, except this question of onus of proof. And the learned judge said it was on the prosecution. What more do you want? Didn't he say it often enough? Is that your complaint?"

"No, my Lord. My complaint quite simply is that, instead of saying that the jury must be satisfied beyond all reasonable doubt——"

"That's gone since *Summers'* case," said Mr Justice Mellow.

"In my submission, my Lords, it has come back since *Hepworth's* case," said Roger. "But, even if I am wrong about that, the learned judge did not follow *Summers'* or *Hepworth's* case. He told the jury they must be reasonably sure of the defendants' guilt. In my submission, that is not enough. In *Hepworth's* case this Court at least suggested that 'satisfied' is not enough."

"Well, what should he have said?" asked Mr Justice Rose. "I see that he did say that complete certainty was impossible and was not required. That's right, isn't it?"

"Yes, my Lord," said Roger.

"Well, if you can't have complete certainty," said Mr Justice Short, "what can you have but reasonable certainty?"

"That is not the expression used in *Summers'* case, my Lord," said Roger. "The word used there is 'sure' without qualification. The jury must 'feel sure.' That is repeated in *Hepworth*."

"What do you say 'sure' means?" asked Mr Justice Short.

"Frankly, I don't know," said Roger. "If 'sure' means 'sure'— it means 'completely sure,' which I agree is too high a standard. If it means something less than completely sure—how much less? I frankly don't know. But I do submit that the expression 'reasonably sure' is putting it much too low. I'm reasonably sure I brought my watch with me means there may be quite a substantial element of doubt about it. With the greatest respect, my Lord, juries seem to have understood for many, many years the expression 'satisfied beyond all reasonable doubt,' and I should have thought that it was easier to explain that expression—if it requires any explanation— than to explain what 'being sure' or 'feeling sure' means. I am sure I am addressing your Lordships. Have the jury to be as sure as that? No. Well, how far have they to be sure? If you tell a jury that they haven't to be absolutely sure but that they must be satisfied beyond all reasonable doubt—surely that tells them satisfactorily what is required?"

"I'm sure I brought my pen with me," said Mr Justice Mellow reflectively, "may mean . . . I'm beginning to have some doubt whether I brought it with me."

"I respectfully agree," said Roger.

"Reasonably sure," said Mr Justice Short, "does sound more like the balance of probabilities. Crime has to be proved with a high degree of certainty. How that is to be defined, I'm not sure; but reasonably sure does appear to me, on reflection, to be putting the standard too low."

"And," put in Mr Justice Rose, "this was—as Mr Thursby has pointed out—a case where the jury were troubled about the onus of proof. And they were told more than once—that they must be reasonably sure. That doesn't seem enough to me."

"I think we'd like to hear what your opponent has to say," said Mr Justice Short.

Henry began at once to address the Court.

"My Lords, I respectfully agree that, if this appeal had come before your Lordships twenty-five years ago, I should have found it difficult to support the learned judge's direction. But in the last ten years the Lord Chief Justice has more than once said that he thought the expression 'satisfied beyond all reasonable doubt' was only calculated to muddle a jury or, at any rate, that an explanation of it had that effect."

"It seems to have served satisfactorily for a good many years," interposed Mr Justice Mellow.

"And in *Summers*' case," went on Henry, "this Court approved the views of the Lord Chief Justice and said that that direction should not be given—and that the jury should be told that they should be satisfied of the prisoner's guilt so that they could feel sure their verdict was a right one."

"I agree that the Court said that," said Mr Justice Rose, "but was it more than a strong intimation of the Court's views? It wasn't essential to the decision, was it? Moreover, in *Hepworth's* case this Court said that *Summers*' case may have been misleading and that the expression 'beyond all reasonable doubt' would do. They also suggested that 'satisfied' might not be enough."

"That may be, my Lord," said Henry, "but there was *Kritz's* case in 1949, where this Court expressly upheld a direction by a judge that the jury must be reasonably satisfied of the prisoner's guilt. With respect, there is no difference between 'reasonably satisfied' and 'reasonably sure.' "

"How is that to be reconciled with *Hepworth*?"

"I doubt if it can be," said Henry—"although it was quoted to the Court during *Hepworth* and is mentioned in the judgment. But *Kritz's* case was a definite decision, not a mere expression of opinion and, if 'reasonably satisfied' has been held to be good, I submit that 'reasonably sure' is just as good."

"We'd better look at that decision then," said Mr Justice Short. A copy of the report was obtained for each of their Lordships, and Henry read it to them.

"That is in your favour," said Mr Justice Mellow, "but I'm bound to say for myself that I don't think it's a very satisfactory direction. But that case was a much stronger case from the prosecution's point of view than this one."

Mr Glacier listened to all these arguments, in the place specially provided for appellants in the Court—attended by two warders. He found the arguments not uninteresting, but the result of success or failure was so important to him that he wished it didn't take so long to arrive at it—provided, of course, that the result was favourable. At last, after Henry had addressed the Court at length and

Roger had replied, the judges conferred together for a little time and then Mr Justice Short proceeded to give judgment.

"The appellant in this case," he began, "was convicted at Carpshire Assizes of two offences under the Prevention of Corruption Act 1906, and sentenced to nine months' imprisonment. He appeals against the conviction. The evidence at his trial was as follows."

The judge then went into the evidence in some detail. Mr Glacier who, in the short time he had spent in prison, had learned to be able to speak without noticeably moving his lips, whispered very quietly to one of the warders: "How long does this go on for? We all know the facts. What we want to know is the decision."

"Don't worry, cock," said the warder, who, as a result of his prison experience, had become an amateur ventriloquist. "You're O.K."

"They allow the appeal, you mean?" said Mr Glacier.

"Thumbs up," said the warder.

"Can I go now, then?" asked Mr Glacier.

"Better wait till he's finished. They like you to do that."

"Certainly, if you say so," said Mr Glacier.

"Thanks, mate," said the warder.

Meanwhile, Mr Justice Short was concluding his statement as to the evidence. He then dealt with the judge's summing-up, with the return to Court of the jury and the repeated direction given to them by the judge. He then stated what the ground of appeal was and elaborated the arguments for and against it.

"Personally," he said, "with the greatest respect to the learned Lord Chief Justice, I have always thought that the expression 'satisfied beyond all reasonable doubt' was an admirable one —and it has served its purpose very well for many years. It is quite true that some judges have attempted to explain it at length and, in doing so, it is possible that they confused the jury. But I can only say for myself that, if you tried to explain the extent to which a jury has to feel sure—having told them that they do not have to be completely sure—it would be just as easy to confuse them. Whereas, if you say to a jury—'you have not to be completely satisfied as to the prisoner's guilt, but there must be no real doubt in your minds about it, or, as we put it, you must be satisfied beyond all reasonable doubt,' I should have thought a jury would have understood its duty well enough. On the other hand, if you use the expression 'sure,' I suppose you would have to say— 'you must be as sure of the prisoner's guilt as you can be sure of anything which you have not plainly seen for yourselves.' That may be putting the onus too high and *Summers*' case does not say that. But it does say that a judge should tell the jury they must feel sure. I ask myself 'how sure?' Whatever 'sure' may mean—bearing in mind that, as it does not mean 'absolutely sure,' it does not really mean what it says—because 'sure' means 'absolutely sure'—unless it is qualified by some other word—I say again, whatever the expression may mean——"

"For how long does this continue?" asked Mr Glacier.

"You'll get away in time to have lunch at the Ritz," said the warder.

"You will lunch with me, please?" said Mr Glacier.

"Can't mate, thanks," said the warder. "Got to look after some more of you blokes."

"Perhaps if I explained," said Mr Glacier.

"You'd get six months for contempt," said the warder.

"You must come and see me at my hotel then . . . the Glorious at Westlea. And bring your wife and family. I assume you have one."

"Thanks, cock," said the warder. "But once you're out you'll forget all about me."

"There you are wrong," said Mr Glacier. "I never forget a face or a friend."

"There's no need to be personal," said the warder—who had kind brown eyes but a large bulbous nose and a wart on the side of it.

"Forgive my English," said Mr Glacier. "I meant you are a friend—unless you are wrong about this appeal."

"Don't you worry," said the warder. "I don't know nothing about the law. But you get to know what's happening when you've listened as often as I have."

They stopped for a moment as the judge said: "I say again—whatever that expression may mean, it is not the expression the learned judge used in this case."

"He rests still at the same place," said Mr Glacier.

"That's nothing," said the warder. "I've heard 'em at the same place all day, and then I've known 'em to go on till the next."

"Are you talking?" said the judge suddenly to Mr Glacier.

"No, my Lord," said Mr Glacier, with the most innocent look on his face which he could produce.

"Well, someone was," said the judge.

"It was him," said the warder to Mr Glacier.

Mr Justice Short looked severely at the prisoner, and continued with his judgment.

"His name's Short," said the warder. "Makes you smile."

"Are they all like this?" asked Mr Glacier.

"Pretty well," said the warder. "But there are a few who say what the result is first, and give their reasons after. I think that's a bit fairer on a chap."

"I collaborate, as my wife would say," said Mr Glacier. "It is good to think I shall be seeing her soon. You are right, I suppose? Let me see where he is now."

"Now the expressions which the judge used . . ." Mr Justice Short was saying, "were as follows——"

"No danger of his exceeding the speed limit," said the warder. "They don't, by the way. I used to be in the police force. And I've followed one old judge all down Constitution Hill and all along Birdcage Walk—twenty miles an hour exactly. Never more."

"Perhaps he knew you were behind him," said Mr Glacier. "I should do the same in those circumstances."

"Now, I wonder," said the warder. "I'd never thought of that." He thought for a moment or two, which allowed Mr Glacier to hear Mr Justice Short say:

"Now, those expressions are not to be found in *Summers'* or *Hepworth's* case."

"But I don't think so," went on the warder. "I bet these old geysers stick to the law. It stands to reason. Dishing it out all day —wouldn't be able to do anything else."

"But, as a change, do you not think?" said Mr Glacier. "It must be so very—how do you say?—boring to keep to the law all the time."

"You wouldn't know, chum, would you?" said the warder.

"That might be described, I suppose, as a leading question," said Mr Glacier. "Whatever that expression may mean."

"Whatever that expression may mean," went on Mr Justice Short—and for a moment Mr Glacier's heart went at double time.

"I thought he had heard me again," he said, after he had recovered.

"The one that's talking can't usually hear because of his own voice," said the warder. "And the ones that aren't are so busy listening to what's wrong with what the one that's talking says that they can't hear anything else. Or else," he added, "they're asleep. With their eyes open, of course. That's one of the first things they learn on the Bench. Same as you learn to talk with your mouth shut in clink."

"How do you know they sleep?" asked Mr Glacier, "if their eyes are open?"

"By what happens when they wake up," said the warder. "They don't actually yawn and stretch themselves. But they'd like to. You can see 'em. Look at *him* now."

He pointed to Mr Justice Mellow. "Why shouldn't he have a

bit of shut eye? He's got nothing to do now," the warder added.

"Then will he not speak as well?" asked Mr Glacier.

"Show's you haven't been before, chum," said the warder. "Only one of 'em speaks. Even if they disagree. But then the one that disagrees—he keeps awake listening to all the mistakes the other two have made. There, he's waking up . . . did you see that?"

Mr Justice Mellow had taken a glass of water.

"I expect he thought it was a cup of tea," the warder added. "Given him a nasty shock, look."

They stared at Mr Justice Mellow sipping his water and imagined that they saw his Lordship give the suspicion of a jerk to his head.

"He nearly said: 'What's the weather like, dear?' " said the warder. "But he's an old one. He was able to check it. They do say that before my time one of them did say something like it, but don't take it from me. I didn't hear it myself."

"For myself," said Mr Justice Short, "I should be well satisfied to have left matters as they were before *Summers*' case. But, even accepting that case, I do not think that the direction in the present case can be upheld. Does 'reasonably sure' mean more or less than 'almost sure?' 'Almost sure' would not satisfy *Summers*' case and 'reasonably sure,' if it is a stronger expression than 'almost sure'— which I take leave to doubt—is certainly well below the standard of certainty required by 'sure.' "

"You are sure, I hope," said Mr Glacier. "Not almost sure?"

"Beyond all reasonable doubt, cock," said the warder. "It's about the only expression I know, but I've heard it so often it's stuck."

"Completely and absolutely sure?" demanded Mr Glacier.

"As sure as he'll go on for another half hour," said the warder.

"It is quite true," went on Mr Justice Short, "that in the case of *Kritz* cited by Mr Blagrove, this Court did dismiss an appeal where the judge had used the expression 'reasonably satisfied.' That case appears to us to be somewhat inconsistent with the later case of *Hepworth*, but, whether it was rightly or wrongly decided, it does not compel us to decide in this case that the repeated use of 'reasonably' by the judge was a sufficient direction."

"You seem to be right," said Mr Glacier.

"Of course I'm right," said the warder. "Have you booked your table?"

"But why does he still continue?" asked Mr Glacier. "He has said everything necessary to let me go."

"Now Mr Blagrove has argued," went on Mr Justice Short.

"He did not appear to argue as long as you," said Mr Glacier who—though now very optimistic—was becoming impatient.

"Keep cool, chum," said the warder. "He's going to say it all—whether you like it or not."

"So it seems," said Mr Glacier.

"Some of 'em say it more than once," said the warder.

"I have already gathered as much," said Mr Glacier.

Almost exactly half an hour after the warder had said that it would go on for another half hour, Mr Justice Short paused for a moment and then said: "For these reasons, we are all of opinion that the appeal must be allowed and the conviction quashed."

The judge then looked towards the prisoner. "Let him be discharged," he said.

Mr Glacier bowed to the Court.

"This way, chum," said the warder, but when he let him out below the Court to freedom and shook hands—"Good-bye, sir," he said, "and good luck."

"And good luck to you," said Mr Glacier. "We shall meet again."

"Not here, I hope, sir," said the warder.

"You may be sure beyond all reasonable doubt that it will not be here," said Mr Glacier. "Thank you for making the time pass much faster than it would otherwise have done. If only that judge would come for a drink to my hotel on a really thirsty day, after a long round of golf, I should take the place of the barman—and I should mix the drink myself. First I should fetch the ice—lovely cool ice—the basis of the beautiful drink that the judge is going to have. I should put it in the mixer with a few polite remarks about the weather and what a thirsty day it is. Then I should find that each ingredient had to be fetched from the cellar. And when I had them, I should pour them in so slowly—oh, so slowly. All the time I should make polite conversation—always about the weather—and thirst—and what a difference a long, cool drink makes; no doubt about it, I should say . . . no doubt about it. And then, when at last I had the beautiful mixture all ready and the judge's throat is in that most exquisite state of—how do you say? —of anticipation, when there is the certainty that the thirst is going to be—what is the word?—slaked . . . certainty, did I say?— perhaps I should have said reasonable certainty—then, at the last moment I should, by an unfortunate accident, drop the mixer and have to start all over again. First, of course, by clearing the mess—so very slowly."

"I think that'd be a bit unkind," said the warder. "After all, he did let you off."

"But so should I let him have his drink," said Mr Glacier, "in the end."

318

Mr Glacier met Roger and Mr Plumb in the Law Courts and thanked them for their help. "But what a lot of time and money," he said, "it has cost to arrive at the truth."

"The truth?" said Roger. "No one in Court said anything about arriving at the truth."

CHAPTER TWENTY-FOUR

SILK

FOR a variety of reasons there was unusual delay in the appointment of Q.C.'s but, not long after the successful end to the Glacier case, the Lord Chancellor intimated to Roger that he was recommending Her Majesty to appoint him one of her counsel learned in the law. In due course, the necessary ceremony took place and both Roger's mother and Anne came to see him take silk. They saw the silks, one after the other, come to the Law Courts from the House of Lords and assemble to have some photographs taken in their glory —full-bottomed wig, silk gown, Court dress, ruffle, and the rest, and then go round to most of the Courts where the ceremony of calling within the Bar took place. When each judge was told that the new Q.C.'s had arrived, he stopped the case he was trying and, one by one, he called them within the Bar.

Roger had explained to his mother a year before what it was all about, but he told her again. " 'Moving the Court,' is, in effect, making an application to the Court," he said. "And when you take silk, the judge always asks you, as a matter of courtesy, 'Do you move?'—which means, have you any application to make. To show that you are now a Q.C., he is inviting you, as a pure formality, to do something in your new capacity. Of course no one has any application to make, and you simply bow—which is the method of saying 'No.' "

"But suppose you wanted to make an application?" Mrs Thursby asked.

"You'd make it another time, Mother. This is just a ceremony. I don't know what would happen if anyone taking silk proceeded to get up, when he was asked if he moved, and launch a motion. The judge would have a fit."

"Then don't you, Roger," his mother said. "It would be very unkind."

"I won't, Mother."

In due course Roger's turn came and he duly took his place, gave the necessary bows and sat down.

"Do you move, Mr Thursby?" said the judge.

Roger bowed, went along the row, and left the Court.

The ceremony took a long time—nearly all day—but it was over at last and Roger felt a free man. They celebrated the event by having a dinner at which all members of his chambers were present.

The next day he celebrated the occasion again by taking Anne out to dinner and, after dinner, they went back to his mother's house. She had quite enough sense to go to bed early.

"Anne," said Roger, and stopped. It was not as easy to say as he had thought. Perhaps she would help him. She did.

"Mr Thursby," she said, "do you move?"

Roger moved.

SOBER AS A JUDGE

CHAPTER ONE

THE NEW JUDGE

"Judges in their private lives," said Henry, "must not only be good; they must manifestly be seen to be good."

"Isn't it enough," said Sally, "if they're not manifestly seen to be bad?"

"No," said Henry, "it is not enough."

But virtue had no terrors for Roger Thursby, whose appointment to the High Court Bench was being celebrated by himself and his wife and their great friends Henry and Sally Blagrove. In his early days at the Bar Roger had kissed a few girls in taxis and occasionally had a little too much to drink, but his career at the Bar had taken up the rest of his time. Indeed, as a result of his working habits, he had lost—thrown perhaps is the better word— he had thrown Sally to Henry, who had been only too ready to receive her. It all worked out very nicely. Henry was able but lazy and became an excellent County Court judge some years after he had married Sally. Roger went on working and working and, quite by chance, in the middle of work, caught a glimpse of Anne and married her, almost without noticing it. And now he was to have the reward of his labours and to be The Honourable Mr Justice Thursby (professionally) or The Honourable Sir Roger Thursby (privately).

"Tell me," said Anne, "why can't Roger be bad now, provided no one knows it?"

"Because," said Henry, "there's only one way of ensuring that no one knows it and that's by not doing it. Look at me, I can't even have a drink at the local or people might say I was a pub crawler. And the beer's jolly good there. However, there is one thing you must look out for. Admittedly Roger has no vices, but he has a weakness."

"And that is?"

"Well, you should know, I'm afraid," said Henry. "A tendency to pick up girls in the street."

"We were both in cars," said Anne. "That makes all the difference."

Roger had, in fact, met Anne through nearly having a collision with her. The collision would have been entirely Anne's fault but Roger had taken the initiative after that.

"For the purpose of argument," said Roger, "I am prepared to concede that I picked Anne up in the street. But that single incident does not justify an assault on my moral character as a whole."

"I never said it was more than a tendency," said Henry. "But no one could have walked down Bond Street with Roger on a bright summer day without observing that tendency."

"Does that mean that, now he's a judge, I can't walk down Bond Street with him any more?" asked Anne. "It'll be much more expensive for him if I go alone."

"Surely," said Roger, "even a judge is allowed to walk with his eyes open, and to look at the shop windows. And, if a pretty girl happens to get in between, I don't have to blink, do I, or turn the other way?"

"All I can say is," said Henry, "that I have seen glances of yours which were anything but judicial, and which, if by mischance photographed and sold to readers of *The Daily Jibe*, might not look at all well. 'Mr Justice Thursby looking round the town,' it would be called."

"Well," said Roger, "I hereby give notice that I am not going to change any of my habits. Since I married Anne I have been as good as gold. I pay my rates, I drive with care, I don't bet, I drink, but not to excess, and, if I see an attractive dress or hat, yes—or face under it—I'm going to look at it as much as I like."

"And now that we've decided that," said Sally, "what about next week-end? Are you coming to us or are we coming to you?"

"Well, it can't be next Friday," said Anne, "as I've got to go down to Father for a few days and I shall only be back on Friday. It'll take me a day to put the house straight after Roger's been on his own for three nights."

"You think it's safe to leave him after what you've heard from Henry?" said Sally.

"I shall risk it," said Anne, "and our daily woman will give me a full report on my return."

"Well, why not come down to us the week after?" said Henry. "I tell you what. Let Anne come down in the morning and sit with me in court. You come down later. There's a character I'd like Anne to meet, a Mr Saul-Bibury. He's a professional debtor and I can guarantee you your money's worth if he's there. Now, if we're not careful, we shall miss the last train. Good luck to your first case—or perhaps I should say good luck to the poor fellows who appear in front of you."

Henry and Sally caught their train, while Roger and Anne went back to their London house, and to bed.

"Where are my pyjamas?" called Roger.

Anne opened the bathroom door.

"They're in the airing cupboard, my Lord," she said, "—with great respect."

CHAPTER TWO

THE OLD BOY

THE next day Anne went to Court with Roger to hear his first case. First of all she heard him welcomed on behalf of the Bar by Anthony Trent, Q.C. Roger had known Trent for a good many years. He had first met him over a case at Westlea, a prosecution for bribery, just at the time he had met Anne. Trent was then a new boy but an incredibly bouncing one, with a self-assurance which nearly drove at least one judge to distraction. But he was extremely able, and, though his appalling self-confidence never left him, as he grew older and more experienced he supplemented it by so much learning and able advocacy that he got on at the Bar very quickly and he had just taken silk when Roger was appointed a judge.

"I can't say," said Trent, "that I'm sorry that there isn't some more senior member of the Bar to welcome your Lordship to the Bench, because I'm not. Having watched your Lordship grow up and increase in knowledge and stature since I first met your Lordship—when I was in my legal cradle—I feel that there is no one better qualified to speak as to your Lordship's attainments than I am. At the Bar your Lordship was careful, courteous and, if I may say so without disrespect, a good enough lawyer. I'm sure your Lordship will now reveal those additional qualities which the Lord Chancellor must have had in mind when recommending your Lordship for this appointment."

"Thank you, Mr Trent," said Roger. "Thank you very much. May I say that not once since we first met have your speeches ever disappointed me?"

The first case Roger had to try was an accident case. He had done a good many accident cases while he was at the Bar, though they only represented a very small portion of his practice. He had often thought them very unreal. As though the witnesses really know what happened! As though in many cases the judge could really determine where and in what proportion the blame lay! The whole occurrence was over in a second and it seemed to Roger rather unsatisfactory that whether or not a person, who was seriously injured in an accident, should recover damages should depend on such uncertainties as whether Aunt Hetty (a witness for the plaintiff) or a gentleman in the soft goods trade (a witness for the defendant) really did see the accident and can remember what they saw. And it also seemed rather unfair to Roger that, if you hit the plaintiff hard enough, he almost certainly wouldn't be able to remember what happened. Roger had formed the view that, in cases of personal injury, National Insurance should replace the present hit-or-miss form of judicial enquiry.

"After all," he said to Henry, "no one but a lunatic wants to be hurt or killed in a road accident. Why should the injured person's right to damages depend on such imponderables, whether he was careless himself or not?"

However, now that he was a judge, he had to try the cases like any other judge and make the best of it, though he had a feeling that, once he had found his feet, he might from time to time make a suggestion on the subject from the Bench.

His first case took its normal course and eventually counsel for the plaintiff called his independent witness. The witness had only been asked a few questions when counsel on the other side jumped up, protesting hotly that the witness was being asked leading questions.

"I'm sorry," said the plaintiff's counsel. "Now, Mr Jones, will you please turn to his Lordship and tell your story in your own way."

The witness complied.

"Well—it was like this," he said. "I was just going for a walk to see my young woman—we'd had a bit of a tiff the night before—you know how these things are—and I was just thinking what I could buy her to sort of make it up—you know what I mean—when I saw old Mrs Higgins on the other side of the road. She and my Dad used to be sweethearts—that was before he met my mother, you'll understand—Mr Higgins is the chemist, or at least he was before he died—they've got a son who carries on the business now——"

At that stage Roger felt that, although he had determined not to open his mouth during a case except to give judgment or unless it was absolutely necessary, there was no alternative to intervening, or the witness might go on until the afternoon without coming to the accident. So he suggested that the witness might say what he actually saw of the collision. It then transpired that Mr Jones had heard a bang, and, looking up, had seen two cars in the middle of the road in an awkward sort of embrace.

Later on the defendant gave his version of the accident and called his independent witness. He was able to give a detailed and graphic account of the accident. He had seen exactly how it all happened. He was watching both cars for several seconds (he called them minutes) before the collision. It was a pretty careful account and quite a credit to the solicitor's clerk who had taken his statement from the witness. But, unfortunately for the defendant, this witness, like the plaintiff's independent witness, had made a statement to the police almost immediately after the accident—in which he said, in almost identical language with that used by the plaintiff's witness: "I didn't really see anything." Only, the plaintiff's witness said "anything," and he said "nothing."

Roger eventually decided that each motorist was equally to blame, but on the way home with Anne he confided to her that, although he had conscientiously applied his mind to every word of the evidence and to counsel's speeches, the same result would have been achieved almost equally well by shaking up a lot of dice.

"I thought you did very well," said Anne, "and you never once made a joke."

"I couldn't think of one," said Roger.

Two days later Anne went to her father but, of course, before doing so, she told Mrs Grain, their daily woman. Mrs Grain had followed Roger's career with interest, and, almost every day from the time when he was appointed, she asked him when he was going to try a murderer.

"Poor Mr Thursby," she said, "—Sir Roger I mean, there I go again—what'll I forget next—poor Mr Thursby, having to try one of those, but they're no better than they ought to be or they wouldn't be where they are, would they—which is no more than what they deserve."

"But they might be innocent," said Roger.

"Oh, but, Mr Thursby, you wouldn't try them if they were innocent, not you, you wouldn't."

Roger tried to explain. He felt it desirable that everyone should as far as possible understand the basic principles of English justice. After he had spent some ten minutes on explanation, he said:

"Well, now, Mrs Grain, do you understand that?"

"Oh—yes, Mr Thursby, you make it ever so clear. But, all the same, you wouldn't try the innocent ones, not you, you wouldn't. It wouldn't be right, would it, not if they hadn't done anything."

Roger gave it up as a bad job.

"What'll you do tonight?" asked Anne.

"I'll go to the club, I expect," said Roger.

"You won't be lonely?"

"Of course I shall. That's what you want, isn't it?"

They kissed, and Roger left for Court.

He walked all the way. He was very happy. He knew that he would find his new job very satisfying and within his ability. And now he would have so much more time to be with Anne, whom he adored. Now they'd be able to go to concerts and theatres together. Life begins at forty-six. It took him three-quarters of an hour to walk, but it seemed only a few minutes. He went through the judges' entrance and straight to his room. His clerk was waiting for him.

"Do you know anything about nylon stockings, sir?" he asked.

"Only that they're expensive and don't last. No, I don't really."

"Well, you will, sir. The first case. I fancy they're going to invite you to see a demonstration. Where'll you have it, in here?"

"I shouldn't think so," said Roger. "If I clutter up the judges' corridor with young ladies showing off their nylons in my first week, I shan't be popular."

"That's what *you* think, sir. I can't see any objections being raised. But I'm sorry to disappoint you, sir—the demonstration's going to be on a machine."

"Then why on earth did you ask if I'd have it in here?"

"Just to see the reaction, sir. I think that's your usher—excuse me, sir."

The clerk left and came back in a moment or two and helped Roger to put on his robes. Then the usher led him to his court, and he went in, bowed to counsel, and sat down.

The visions which the mention of nylon stockings is liable to conjure up in many men's minds soon disappeared when the case was opened. It was obvious that it would be a highly technical case about gauges and deniers and even more esoteric terms, and that Roger would learn something about the way nylon stockings were made—but not how they were put on or what they looked like in position.

The case was not over when Roger rose at the end of the day and went to his room to disrobe. He was a little disappointed that Anne had gone to her father. Still, an evening at the club would be very pleasant.

Then his clerk informed him that a Major Plumstead wanted to see him. A purely personal matter.

Plumstead, thought Roger, Plumstead? But it can't be. Roger had been at school with a boy called Plumstead, and they had formed a rather odd combination. Roger, rather a prig, very disinclined to break any of the school rules and horribly inclined to admit the offence if he did. Plumstead, a wild scapegrace with all the worst schoolboy instincts—never telling the truth when a lie would serve as well, breaking every rule within reach and even some beyond it, flouting authority for the sake of doing so and brazenly denying his fault right up to the last moment. It had certainly been a queer friendship and had from time to time landed Roger in trouble. Plummer, as they called him, never tried to get Roger out of a scrape, though he never threw the blame on him unnecessarily.

"Each man for himself" was the motto, and no complaints, what-ever happened. It was probably the attraction of opposites. The anarchist in Plummer had a fascination for Roger, while Plummer could not resist Roger's virtuous instincts. Their partner-ship worked well, too, on the football field, where Plummer was scrum half and Roger fly. They knew each other's game perfectly, and would execute some extremely effective, if unothodox move-ments, which were usually a feature of any game in which they were playing. Indeed, when there was an issue as to whether one or other of them should be kept in as a punishment, any master con-cerned either kept them both in or neither. With the result that, if a school match was involved, Plummer could do almost what he liked, knowing that the virtuous Roger would do nothing. Indeed, it was partly the sight of Roger, sitting primly at his desk, not talk-ing to his neighbour when the master had gone outside for a moment, because they had been forbidden to talk, that brought out the devil in Plummer. And Roger would make things even worse because, if he were compelled to break the order so as not to be too rude to his neighbour, he would solemnly confess his fault, if, on returning, the master asked if anyone had spoken. And the crowning anguish for Plummer was when Roger refused to say to whom he had been talking, lest he should get the real culprit into trouble. On one such occasion he said quietly to himself:

"The boy stood on the burning deck."

"Did you say something, Plumstead?" asked the master.

"No, sir," said Plummer. "It was my thoughts you must have heard, sir. They must have been very loud, sir. Thoughts can be heard, sir, you know. That's why one has to be so careful, sir. As a matter of fact, sir, I heard what you were thinking the other day, sir. You were——"

"Shut up, Plumstead," said the master. There was a school match on that day.

Plumstead left school before Roger and made the Army his career. Although they met once or twice afterwards, they soon drifted apart and Roger had not seen or heard of his friend for over twenty years when his arrival was announced. He told his clerk to show him in and wondered what change the years would prove to have made. He could not know that mentally there was hardly any change at all.

"Major Plumstead, sir," said the clerk, and Plummer burst into the room.

"My dear old lordship," he said.

"Plummer," said Roger.

The clerk went out and for a split second—just time enough for the normal accident—they simply looked at one another.

"Where have I been all these years?" said Plummer eventually. "Go on, ask me that. I've known where you've been. Watched your career with interest and approval. For the plaintiff Mr Thursby, for the defendant Mr Thursby, Q.C., the judge is Mr Justice Thursby. Good for you, old boy. Only goes to show. Virtue pays. Look at me. Just a major. And out on my ear at that. Not court-martialled, old boy. Just axed. No, I haven't come looking for a job. Don't look so anxious. And I don't want a loan, either. Just come to see whether success has spoiled you. 'Fraid it won't have. Nothing could spoil you. Too good to be true. Well, how are you, old boy, after all this time?"

"Well," said Roger, "it's nice to see you, Plummer."

Plummer exploded with laughter.

"What's the joke?" said Roger.

Plummer exploded again and then, gasping for breath, looked at Roger, his eyes mutely appealing for help.

"Don't, old boy," he said. "It's impossible."

He recovered after a moment or two.

"What is it?" asked Roger. "Have I said something?"

"Don't speak," said Plummer, "or I'll have apoplexy. Write it down. Oh—my wig and toenails," and he had a further paroxysm.

"Sorry, old boy," he said, when he had finally subsided, "but you're so the same. You haven't changed, that's the trouble. You're just the same horrible, good, literal-minded little boy that I couldn't get away from in the Lower Fourth." He paused. "Oh, good Lord," he said suddenly, "is this contempt of court?"

"Sorry to disappoint you," said Roger. "I'm afraid it isn't. You can say what you like to a judge privately, so long as it isn't about a case, or his behaviour in Court."

"You don't say," said Plummer. "You don't really say. Oh dear, I'm sorry. Here we go again," and he had another outburst.

"Well, how have things gone with you—apart from the Army, I mean," said Roger eventually. "Are you married? Any children? Where do you live, and so on?"

"I'm not exactly married," said Plummer. "Had a divorce, I'm afraid. Nothing bad, you know. It was all arranged as a matter of fact. We couldn't stand each other. Still, I suppose I oughtn't to tell you all this. What about you?"

Roger told him.

"Any chance of seeing Anne?" asked Plummer. "I'd love to see who had to put up with you for life."

"I'd have taken you home tonight," said Roger, "but unfortunately Anne's down at Westlea with her father. Are you going to be in London for long?"

"All depends, old boy. I might be. Anyway, I shall be back again soon. What are you doing tonight?"

"Nothing, as a matter of fact."

"How about dinner, then, and a show, perhaps?"

"Good idea."

Plummer thought for a moment.

"No—I tell you what. I've got a little cottage about forty miles from London. Get your toothbrush and come and spend the night. I'll tell you some of my misdeeds in the past twenty years—show you some too, perhaps. It's a bit primitive, but we've got water and electric light and all that. What d'you say? I've got a car outside. Take you round to your place and then off we go. Done?"

"Done," said Roger. "I'll just ring Anne and tell her. What's the address, and are you on the telephone?"

"That's right," said Plummer, "tell Mummy. Oh dear, oh dear, oh dear."

Shortly afterwards they left the Law Courts and drove to Roger's house. Plummer certainly had a car outside the Law Courts. It was a large sports car, painted bright red. Its number was—IMA 1.

"Had to pay £5 for that," explained Plummer. "Makes it easy for the police to pick me up."

When they reached Roger's house they went in to have a drink, and Roger told Mrs Grain that he would be away for the night.

"Oh, Mr Thursby," said Mrs Grain, "will you be trying that murderer on Monday—the one what drowned his wife in soapsuds? Oh, it was terrible. I know what I'd do with him. He couldn't even just use ordinary water. Even that Mr Smith who drowned all his wives, until they stopped him, only used water. But soapsuds —it don't seem right."

"No," said Roger, "it's wrong."

"You won't let him do it again, will you, sir—not with soapsuds."

"Well, I'm not taking the case, Mrs Grain," said Roger, "otherwise I'd certainly tell him, if he were let off, that in future soapsuds were out."

"I believe you said that just to please me, sir," said Mrs Grain. "But I lie awake sometimes at night thinking of these terrible things. Just think if Mr Grain had thought of doing it to me. But he wouldn't have, not with soapsuds he wouldn't. He was that kind was Mr Grain."

Having satisfied Mrs Grain as best he could, Roger telephoned Anne and told her where he would be. They dined at Roger's club, where Plummer made a telephone call, and then they set off.

If Roger had realized what the journey was going to be like

he would have unhesitatingly refused the invitation. Plummer began by trying to go the wrong way round Trafalgar Square.

"So sorree, officer," he said, in a faked foreign accent. "We from Brazil. My friend he no speak Eenglish at all. I speakee not too good. Please to excuse. I go proper way now."

And he roared off down the Mall at fifty miles an hour.

"I say, Plummer," said Roger, "there's a limit of thirty here."

"Speedo's wrong, old boy. Registers twenty too much. You'll see, when we're on the open road."

Roger froze to his seat, thinking of the open road. But what could he do? It would be horribly rude to ask to be allowed to get out and go home. And, even if he did, Plummer would probably refuse and drive all the faster. Indeed, he ought to have thought of that before. Plummer loved baiting. The more one appeared to be worried by his antics the more Plummer would indulge in them. He must be quite nonchalant—try to pretend they were the normal thing. Even so he couldn't avoid wincing when they dashed across the lights at Grosvenor Place.

"Sorry, old boy," said Plummer. "Colour blind."

"Then how did you know they were red?" asked Roger.

"Don't," said Plummer, "or we'll have an accident."

Somehow or other they got through London without being stopped by the police. Beneath the mask of nonchalance which Roger was trying, not too successfully, to wear, he was thinking anxiously what he would say if in fact they were stopped, and he himself were questioned. Eventually he could restrain himself no longer:

"Look, old boy," he said, "I wish you'd drive a bit slower. I dare say it sounds silly to you but it wouldn't be a good thing for me to be involved in an accident."

"Sorry, old boy," said Plummer, "is that better?" and he put his foot even harder on the accelerator.

At last they came to a halt. Not entirely voluntarily. They were going through a small village where there was a pedestrian crossing. Just in time Plummer saw an old woman starting to cross one side and a couple of children the other. By some extremely skilful driving Plummer avoided them all and ended up by half uprooting the post with the flashing beacon on it.

"Near thing," he said to Roger, as he drew away from the beacon, and drove off as fast as possible. "Fortunately one's too old, and the others are too young to get my number."

"But aren't you going to report it?" said Roger.

"Don't," said Plummer, "please don't or we'll have something really bad."

"Now look," said Roger sternly, "I'm sorry to be difficult about this but you must report it, really you must. I don't even mind sharing the cost of the damage with you."

"Look, old boy," said Plummer. "Will you say you were driving?" and he laughed so loudly that he had to slow down slightly.

"I'm awfully sorry," said Roger, "I know it's terribly funny to you and you think I'm a dreadful prig and all that. Well—I am, if you like, but, if you don't report it, I shall have to. We're not at school any longer."

"Of course I shall report it, old boy," said Plummer, "but shall I say you were with me?"

"Of course," said Roger stiffly.

"I won't if you'd rather not," said Plummer.

"Naturally you must, if they ask you," said Roger.

"But suppose they don't, old boy, shall I volunteer it?"

"You must volunteer it, if you think fit," said Roger.

"Sorry you're so touchy, old boy," said Plummer. "If you're like this now——" He paused.

"Yes?" said Roger.

"Nothing, old boy. I was just wondering what you'd be like if we had a real accident."

"I should probably be dead," said Roger.

They drove in silence for a while. Then:

"I hope you're not sorry you came, old boy?" said Plummer.

Roger said nothing.

"You'll feel better when we get there. I'll mix you something special," went on Plummer.

Roger smiled.

"You used to say the same sort of thing at school. D'you remember that box of chocolates you promised me if I'd let you in the dorm window?"

"Don't tell me I never gave it to you. Here, let me feel——"

He took both hands off the wheel and started to feel in his pockets.

"I don't want it as badly as that," said Roger hurriedly. "I say —look out——"

The remark was forced out of Roger. Plummer had gone the wrong way round a roundabout, missed a cycle, gone on to the kerb, back to the road and then on to the pavement on the wrong side of the road to avoid an oncoming car and then back to the road again.

"She's a beauty to handle, isn't she?" said Plummer. "But you were saying something——"

"If I was," said Roger, "it'll wait till my heart's beating again. I'm not as young as I was thirty years ago."

"Is it only that? Then you can't be more than forty-six. Young for a judge, isn't it?"

"They make them younger than they used to. And I was lucky."

"Hope it holds out, old boy," said Plummer, as he pressed on.

Twenty minutes later they drove through some gates and up a long drive leading to a low Georgian house.

"What's this?" said Roger.

"Welcome," said Plummer.

"But you said it was a cottage."

"Just modesty, old boy."

"You must have done well for yourself."

"Oh, not so bad, old boy."

"You didn't get this out of the Army."

"You've said it, old boy. I certainly didn't. Fortunately, I've had a side line or two. Come in."

He led Roger into the house and took him to the library.

"This'll suit you best," said Plummer. "No law reports, I'm afraid, but some good, sound, boring English literature. I'll fetch the drinks. Sit down and make yourself at home."

Plummer went out and Roger, after glancing at the books, picked one out and sat down. He started to read but, after a few minutes, he fell lightly asleep. The strain of the drive had had its effect.

He was woken up by two cool hands being placed on his eyes. They were obviously not Plummer's.

"Hello, sugar," said a young female voice with a spurious American accent. "Where have you been hiding yourself?"

Roger suddenly remembered Plummer's remark: "If you're like this now . . ." and the pause at the end of it. The cool hands were still on his eyes. He had to do or say something.

"How d'you do?" he said.

"How does who do?" said the voice.

"I've no idea, I'm afraid."

"Well, guess."

"I think there's some mistake," said Roger. "I'm sure I don't know you."

"Well, I know you, sugar. Go on, guess."

"But I've really no idea. You're a friend of Plummer's, I suppose."

"Who's he?"

"Our host."

"Oh, him. More a friend of yours than mine, sugar."

"Do please take your hands away," said Roger. "I'm sure there's a mistake."

"You sound as though you wanted it to be a mistake."

"Look," said Roger, removing the cool hands with his, as

334

gently as he could. "I'm very sorry but I've never seen you before in my life."

He said that as he got his first look at the girl. And he knew it must be true. He would never have forgotten a face like that in a hurry. It was more attractive than beautiful, but whatever you called it, it wasn't a face to forget.

"You're kidding," she said. "Remember the Soft Shoe Club?"

"I've never heard of it," said Roger.

"Were you as blind as all that? You talked sober enough."

"I tell you I've never heard of the Soft or any other Shoe Club in my life and I've never been there and I've never met you before."

"Well, how d'you do, then, honey?" said the girl. "It must have been some other handsome guy, I'm sorry. Anyway, we've met now. I'm Toni."

"How d'you do?" said Roger, again wondering how long Plummer was going to be and then realizing he was very likely enjoying the scene through a peep-hole.

"And who are you, handsome, seeing that you're not the other guy?"

"I'm Roger Thursby," he said after a pause.

"That's all right," said Toni. "You don't have to apologize. It's a nice name. I love Roger."

Well, thank heaven she doesn't know who I am, thought Roger. That's something, anyway.

At that moment the young woman sat on his knee and Plummer walked in.

"Oh," he said, "I see you know each other."

"Look——" said Roger.

"I am," said Plummer. "You seem to have fixed yourself up all right. I didn't exactly mean that when I said 'make yourself at home,' but don't move, it's quite O.K. But you might introduce me."

For answer Roger lifted up the lady, plumped her down on the settee and turned on Plummer.

"Look here. What is this?" he said. "I don't know this young woman from Adam——"

"Eve, you mean," said Plummer.

"Where is the nearest station?" said Roger. "I'm leaving."

"Good ten miles walk, I'm afraid."

"Will you kindly drive me there?"

"It wouldn't be any use if I did. Last train will have gone."

"I'll go to an hotel then."

"I can't recommend any."

"I don't want your recommendation," said Roger angrily.

"Well, there's a pub which has a bed or two five miles away

335

but they'll be in bed now and won't thank you for knocking them up."

"I do hope you're not leaving on my account," said the girl. "Have I done anything? Most men like it." She draped herself over one of the chairs. Even one of Her Majesty's judges could not help observing that it was a most attractive sight.

"I'm sorry," said Roger. "There's obviously been some misunderstanding. I was a fool not to have thought of it."

"All right," said Plummer, "I'll explain in a moment or two. There's nothing to it really. When you said you'd come, I just telephoned Toni to come down with her sister. She'll be here in a moment. They won't manhandle you any more, I promise. I'll call them off. Toni—you're to leave the gentleman alone."

"Usually," said Toni, "the warning's the other way round."

"Usually," said Plummer, "we don't have the honour of entertaining one of Her Majesty's judges. Their self-control is horrible to see. Let me present Sir Roger Thursby. Miss Toni Mandeville. Her real name is Dora Stokes but we thought the other was more impressive."

"How d'you do?" said Roger.

"Toni and Gillian are at the Soft Shoe Club. They're hostesses."

"Oh," said Roger.

"I have an interest there," said Plummer. "One of my side lines. I don't suppose you'll want to visit us. Although we're highly respectable, I assure you. Duchesses come to us. You could bring your wife one day."

"Thanks," said Roger, "I'll think about it."

"I've never sat on a High Court Judge's knee before," said Toni.

"It'll be useful experience," said Plummer. "You might be called to do so as a demonstration. I see that a judge had a cabaret show or something given specially the other day to prove something or other."

"In the most unlikely event of something of the kind being necessary," said Roger, "I should call the usher."

"What a waste," said Plummer. "Now, will you forgive me a moment while I go and see what Gillian's doing? I guarantee your safety with Toni."

"Oh, very well," said Roger, and Plummer went out.

"Well," said Toni, "now what?"

Roger said nothing.

"Don't look so unhappy," said Toni. "I know you're a judge, but that isn't everything, is it? I couldn't do your job, but you couldn't do mine."

"That's true," said Roger. "Quite frankly, I'm not sure that I'd want to."

336

"That goes for me too," said Toni. "Sitting up there all day being stuffy, and then being stuffy all over again when you step down. Wouldn't suit me at all. Don't you ever let your back hair down?"

"If I had any, I'm not sure that I would," said Roger.

"You must be miserable. Don't you ever have any fun?"

"Of course we do."

"It all depends what you call fun," said Toni. "You don't look so old and you're quite good-looking, but if there were a prize for misery I'd give it to you. D'you mind my talking like this?"

"Would it make any difference if I did?" asked Roger.

"It might," said Toni. "I'm quite kind. I'd be terrified of you in Court with your wig and things, but now you look just a poor, unhappy little man. I'd love to cheer you up."

"How?" said Roger.

"That's better," said Toni, "that's the first sign of life. Well, you can give me a kiss if you like, just to show there's no ill-feeling."

Roger thought for a moment, and before he had time to answer, Toni went on:

"This is a great experience," she said. "I can see you trying out the question whether you'll kiss me or not, like you'd try a case. On the one hand, you say to yourself—she's a pretty girl and it'd be rather nice, and, on the other hand, I'm a judge and I didn't ought. That's right, isn't it?"

Roger laughed.

"You should have gone to the Bar," he said.

"Well—what is the verdict?"

"For the defendant, I'm afraid," said Roger.

"Who's that?" said Toni.

"Me," said Roger.

"That means you win, I suppose?" said Toni.

"Yes," said Roger.

"O.K.," said Toni, and came up and kissed him full on the mouth.

"By winning I meant," said Roger, when she had finished, "that I didn't kiss you."

"That's not very polite," said Toni. "Anyway, now you've had it both ways. Did you like it?" she added.

"I don't feel called upon to answer that question," said Roger.

"What happens if a witness refuses to answer in Court?" asked Toni.

"That depends," said Roger. "If it's a question he's bound to answer I can fine him or send him to prison."

"It's not the same here," said Toni. "He just gets kissed again.'"

Roger got up and backed away.

"No," he said. "I'm sorry. It just can't be done."

"It has been," said Toni.

"Look," said Roger, "you strike me, if I may say so without offence, as a very intelligent girl. Why don't you do something other than being a dance hostess?"

"Such as?"

"Secretary to a doctor or something."

"Shouldn't get paid enough. I want to cash in on my good looks while I get the chance. I can't model or act—this is about the only thing. And it's quite fun. More than with a doctor. I should know—my father's one."

"Well," said Roger, "you know your own business best, but you're very young and if you should change your mind, I—that is, my wife and I—might be able to help. We know a doctor or two."

"How sweet of you," she said. "You must be an understanding judge. If ever I'm up for anything I'd like to be in front of you. Now, don't be frightened," she added, and she came up and kissed him lightly on the forehead.

Although Roger's behaviour was neither bad nor manifestly seen to be bad, it gave him rather a shock to think that within a few days of his becoming a judge he had been kissed by a pretty stranger and had had her on his knee. But she certainly was a very pretty stranger—very, very pretty. Perhaps there was something in what Henry had said about him after all. He remembered saying to Sally many, many years previously: "Girls have a tremendous fascination for me. And, if one of them has sort of been in my arms, it does things to me afterwards. I go on thinking about it. It multiplies." Well, Toni had most certainly not been in his arms but—oh, well, there was nothing else he could have done about it.

Plummer returned a moment later.

"How are we doing?" he asked.

"My judge is doing very well," said Toni. "You'd hardly know he was one."

"Good," said Plummer. "He must be improving. But you look remarkably tidy. That suggests there's still a good bit of judge in him. But Rome wasn't built in a day. If you say he's doing well, then there must be hope for him yet."

"Would you very much mind telling me what all this is about?" asked Roger.

"That's fair enough," said Plummer. "Drink this, and I'll explain."

He handed Roger a cocktail. Then he began.

338

"D'you remember," he said, "when a man dug up Piccadilly, and it was quite a long time before they found it was a hoax?"

"I've heard of it," said Roger.

"Well, that wasn't me," said Plummer.

"I see," said Roger. "Where does that lead me to?"

"It wasn't me," said Plummer, "but it might have been. Whenever I'm bored, I do something like that."

"Well?" said Roger.

"I was bored this morning," said Plummer, "and I suddenly remembered the horrible little boy who'd been made a judge."

"You mean," said Roger, "that you like making fools of people and generally upsetting them."

"That's right," said Plummer. "Particularly their dignity. D'you remember Measles?"

He was referring to a pimply boy who had been at school with them.

Roger thought.

"Yes, he's a general now, or something?"

"That's right."

"What about him?"

"He's just the same. In looks, I mean. Pompous now, though. I took him for a ride."

"You've never grown up, Plummer," said Roger.

"No, thank God," said Plummer, "and I don't propose to."

"How did he like it here?"

"Oh, I didn't bring him down here. He'd have enjoyed the trip and loved the girls. Plenty of fun for him. None for me. No, I have other ways with generals. D'you remember Trundle?"

"The Bishop?"

"Well, he's one now. Yes, that's him. I gave him a demonstration, too."

"As far as I can see," said Roger, "you spend your time and money on trying to annoy boys who were at school with you."

"Oh—I don't limit it to them. There aren't enough who are worth while. I shouldn't have touched you, if you hadn't been a judge."

"May I take it," said Roger, "that you've now relieved your boredom and I'm finished with?"

"Part one," said Plummer. "Part two will *not* follow immediately."

"That's something," said Roger.

"But it will follow," said Plummer. "Another drink?"

CHAPTER THREE

PLUMMER IN COURT

THERE were no further incidents that night, and the next morning Plummer drove Roger to the Law Courts. Roger nearly telephoned Anne from his room, but decided that it would be better to say what he wanted to from home. His clerk informed him that he had another running down case to try and he was quite glad to have the chance of taking his mind off Plummer and Toni. But he was not able to do so for long, for there in the well of the Court sat Plummer.

Theoretically the well of the Court is meant for witnesses, barristers and solicitors and their clients, and not for sightseers, for whom there is a gallery. But, unless a court is very crowded, anyone who wishes will be allowed to sit in the well of the Court. In these circumstances Roger did not feel that he should send an usher to turn Plummer out. If he did, Plummer would only go up to the gallery and look from there. Of course, if he misbehaved, he would have to be turned out or fined or even sent to prison for contempt of court. But Roger didn't like the idea of doing anything like that at all. For all Plummer's eccentricity, he still liked the boy. That was really how he still thought of him. But what was this boy now going to do? At school he was capable of doing anything.

Roger soon found out. Every time Roger said anything, Plummer gave the faintest nod or shake of the head, indicating agreement or disagreement with Roger's observation. The movement was so slight that, unless carefully observed by someone on the look-out for it, it would not be noticed, and it was so slight that, if a complaint were made, Plummer could say with a look of innocence—which Roger knew so well:

"I'm so sorry. I was quite unaware of it. Please convey my apologies to his Lordship. One moment, usher, perhaps I have a tic and don't know it."

It was obvious that, unless Roger took action, no one else would, and in all the circumstances Roger felt that the best course was to ignore it. But, in the same way that it is very difficult to keep one's eyes away from a particularly ugly object or person, Plummer's nods and shakes had a fatal fascination for Roger.

The accident case was not quite the normal type. For this was the case of a hit-and-run driver. Almost every driver stops after an accident, but this defendant was an exception. Normally there would have been no litigation, as the insurance company would have paid up, accepting their insured's flight as satisfactory evidence that he was in the wrong. But two things prevented that course from being taken. First, the damages which would be recovered, if the plaintiff won, would be very high indeed, and secondly, in spite of the defendant's bad behaviour in driving on, it certainly looked as though the accident might, in part at least, have been due to the negligence of the plaintiff himself.

In order to support this plea the defendant called his passenger to corroborate his evidence. Part of the cross-examination of this witness was as follows:

COUNSEL: Are you a truthful person, Mr Smith?

SMITH: As much as most.

COUNSEL: Or do you mean as little?

SMITH: That's for you to say.

COUNSEL: Then you don't always tell the truth?

SMITH: No, not always. Nor does anyone.

ROGER: Don't make statements. Just answer the questions, please.

(*Plummer gave a slight nod of approval.*)

COUNSEL: You've given evidence today which, if true, would show that your friend the defendant was in no way to blame for the accident, haven't you?

SMITH: Yes.

COUNSEL: But shortly after the accident you told a very different story to the police, didn't you?

SMITH: Have I got to answer that?

ROGER: Certainly you have.

(*Again Plummer nodded.*)

SMITH: Well—yes, I did.

COUNSEL: You told them, didn't you, that you'd come by an altogether different route, and hadn't been involved in an accident at all?

SMITH: Something of the sort.

COUNSEL: Why?

SMITH: Because my friend had said so, and I had to back him up when the police asked me.

COUNSEL: Let me understand this. Are you saying that shortly after the accident your friend was asked for his account of it by the police, and that he lied about it?

SMITH: He said he hadn't had an accident.

COUNSEL: He lied about it?

SMITH: Well, if you put it that way—yes.

COUNSEL: Is there any other way to put it?

(*No answer.*)

COUNSEL: Well, now you say, do you not, that later the police came to see you?

341

SMITH: Yes.

COUNSEL: And you knew that your friend had lied about it?

SMITH: That he'd said he hadn't been in an accident—yes.

COUNSEL: That he'd lied about it?

SMITH: Well—yes.

COUNSEL: And so you lied about it, too?

SMITH: Well—I said——

COUNSEL: Never mind what you said—you lied about it?

SMITH: I suppose I did.

COUNSEL: You lied to the police?

SMITH: Yes.

ROGER: Of course, while no one can approve of telling lies to the police, there's no doubt the witness had a conflict of loyalties—which one can sympathize with (*Plummer nodded*)—if not condone (*Plummer shook his head*).

COUNSEL: With respect, my Lord, it was the passenger's duty to report the matter to the police in any event.

ROGER: Is that so? You may be right—shall we go on with the evidence?

(*Plummer nodded.*)

In the end Roger decided that both parties were equally to blame, and on his way home he again reflected that he might have produced as good a result with the toss of a coin.

As soon as he was home he telephoned Anne.

"Do you think you could come back tomorrow?" he said.

"Why? Anything particular?"

"No, not really—but I think it would be nicer if you could manage it."

"Well, I'm not sure," said Anne.

"A lovely girl has been sitting on my knee," said Roger.

"What did you say?" said Anne.

Roger repeated his remark.

"I'll come," said Anne.

CHAPTER FOUR

HOTEL DE LUXE

THAT night, after he had described his adventures to Anne, Roger spent a little time before going to sleep in asking himself whether he could have done anything else as far as Plummer was concerned. He ought, he supposed, to have jumped out of the car at Trafalgar Square, when Plummer's behaviour and his knowledge of Plummer should have warned him that worse might be in store. After that he never had a chance until they had hit the beacon post. And, if he'd insisted on leaving in the few seconds' opportunity he had then, he would have had to go to a police station and report the matter. It was true that he was no longer at school but it would have been a very difficult duty to discharge. No, it was better to have let the few seconds go—no one could blame him for that— and to be swept on by the inexorable Plummer. As for Toni— well, as for Toni—yes, it was a nicer name than Dora—as for Toni —she certainly was an attractive girl—yes, of course, there was, he supposed, too much sentimentality about girls who go wrong— which reminded him of Plummer's remark about a girl who, he said, had gone pleasantly wrong during the war—too much senti- mentality, yes, perhaps, but that shouldn't stop one from lending a helping hand when needed—thank heaven he had a sensible wife like Anne—she understood—they could help Toni together— she ought to marry some nice young man—a barrister, perhaps— they could ask one or two to drinks—that would mean Toni coming to the house quite often—well, Anne wouldn't mind that—and she was incredibly attractive—but it was a shame that she was in a club—perhaps Anne could do something—Anne was a wonderful wife—Anne—Toni—Anne—Toni—and he fell asleep. Into his dreams appeared the Lord Chief Justice:

"What's this I hear, Thursby?" he said.

"I'm sorry, Chief, she just sat down and I couldn't get her off."

"I always use a pin myself," said the Chief, and vanished.

The rest of Roger's night was uneventful, apart from one moment when he murmured "Toni," and another when Anne kicked him.

The next morning she went with Roger to Court. In the Strand a man came up to them.

"Filthy postcard?" he said. "View of the Law Courts." It was Plummer.

After they had disentangled themselves from him, Roger took Anne to his room, and asked the clerk to bring the papers in the first case.

"I'll give you an idea of what it's about. Make it easier to follow. You often miss a good deal from the back of the Court."

The clerk brought the papers and Roger looked at them.

"Good," he said, after a moment. "You should enjoy this. It's about an hotel. A chap is suing for damages on the ground that it didn't come up to expectations."

"I'm glad someone's got the nerve," said Anne. "I hope he wins. English hotels are the end."

"Not all," said Roger, "but a good one does take a bit of finding.

But you mustn't start prejudicing me with your views, or people will say it's your decision, not mine."

He sent Anne into Court and not long afterwards went in himself.

"This action," began Anthony Trent, in opening the case, "well illustrates the forbearance of the English people. They put up with almost anything in the way of discomfort, discourtesy and bad food in English hotels."

"Hear, hear," said Anne very quietly to herself.

"They occasionally grouse," went on Counsel, "they occasionally go a bit red in the face when they have been kept waiting three-quarters of an hour for lunch and are then told that everything is off except cottage pie and prunes and rice, and they occasionally swear when the hot water is cold. But, as for bringing an action for breach of contract—well, it is hardly ever heard of. The average man prefers to swallow the inferior coffee, stub his toes on the end of the too-small bed or on his wife (preferably the latter) and eat the mixture of milk powder and egg with an anchovy on top and a soggy mess of bread below, described in the high sounding menu as Canapé Ecossais—rather than risk litigation. And, as long as people will put up with what they are given, they will not be given better.

"Every now and then, however, a pioneer emerges, someone who is prepared to litigate and not count the cost, someone for whom the culinary and other insults, compared with the language on the brochure, prove too much. And my client, Mr de Blame (it is pronounced like the ordinary word, my Lord), my client is one of them.

"Last summer he was sent a brochure by the defendants, who are the owners of the Grand Hotel at Snortingbury-on-Sea. The material parts of this document I will now read to your Lordship:

" 'This is *par excellence* the hotel *de luxe* in the South of England. Here is combined superb food with gracious living in the old style. Here you will find the food fit for *gourmets* of international reputation and the service something which you have not experienced anywhere in this country since the war. Ask the chef for *Oeufs Americains à l'Orgueil*. Families specially catered for. Quiet room for those who want it, play-room for the young, television-room for all and sundry. Our terms are not low but every farthing is returned to you with interest in the happiness which we take pleasure in providing for you. Mr and Mrs Sweep, resident proprietors.'

"The defendants did not explain," went on Counsel, "how every farthing could be returned and the resident proprietors still survive, let alone how they could afford to pay interest as well. But my client, who wanted a holiday and had too often gone to hotels on

344

other people's recommendations, replied to the letter which enclosed the brochure, as follows:

" 'Dear Sir: If your hotel is really substantially in accordance with what you represent it to be, I should like a double room and private bathroom for myself and my wife for fourteen days from the 1st August. I need good food, quiet and comfort and am prepared to pay for it.'

"Mr Sweep replied that he would be delighted to accommodate my client at the inclusive charge of 45 guineas per week, and, in consequence, they arrived at the hotel on the 1st August. They left on the 3rd and issued a writ on the 1st September. My client claims that he was entitled to leave. He says that the statements made in the brochure were false and that he was compelled to take a suite of rooms at a large hotel elsewhere, as that was the only accommodation available in the first fortnight of August. He claims the difference in cost, which was considerable, and a further sum as damages for the discomfort he suffered during his forty-eight hours at the Grand Hotel, Snortingbury, and for the inconvenience in having to move."

Trent was right in describing his client as a litigant who did not count the cost. He had made this plain at the outset:

"I don't mind about money," he had told his solicitor, "but I won't be cheated. Bring them to their knees. Don't settle on any account. Don't hesitate to get in touch with me, whenever you want me. When you want money, ask for it."

The solicitor briefed Trent as leader. He explained to his client that Trent was a bit irritating but that he knew his job as well as anybody.

"In what way irritating?"

"You'll see in conference," the solicitor had said.

And Mr de Blame did see. But, as he completely trusted his solicitor's good judgment, he accepted Trent's insufferable condescension with equanimity.

"I should have thought," Trent had said, "that a gentleman of your experience would have known better than to fall for a brochure like that."

"Indeed?"

"Apart from the vulgar hyperbole, which would have been enough for most educated people, there's no such thing as *Oeufs Americains à l'Orgueil*. Did you ever have it, by the way?"

"We did not."

"You did believe it existed, though?"

"I didn't think about it."

"But you didn't suspect the whole thing was a fraud and go down to prove it?"

345

"Certainly not," Mr de Blame had said. "I wanted a luxurious and quiet holiday and that is what they offered me."

"Your letter of acceptance rather suggests that you might have had legal advice first. Why did you say, in effect, that you were going down on the strength of their representations?"

"Because I wanted them to know it. I had been had before."

"When?"

"Every time I've been to an English hotel almost."

"Then you did suspect something on this occasion. You must have, if you'd nearly always been had in the past."

"I believe people till I find them out. Naturally I knew it was possible that the language meant nothing, because I'd seen that sort of thing before, but I hoped it was different this time. And I certainly wouldn't have gone if they'd replied that my assumption was incorrect. Now, tell me, Mr Trent, is there any chance that I shall lose the action?"

"*Any* chance? There's always a chance, of course, in any action. But, if your evidence is believed, you'll win."

"And do you think I will be believed? I happen to be telling the truth, and my wife too, but naturally you don't know that for certain yet."

"I wouldn't say that you were not capable of telling an untruth if it suited you, Mr de Blame," Trent had said, "but, as far as this case goes, I should say that what you have told me is correct."

"That's very kind of you, Mr Trent."

"I'm not trying to be kind or unkind, Mr de Blame, just to let you know the position as I see it."

After the conference Mr de Blame had expressed the hope to his solicitor that Trent was as able as he was irritating.

"He certainly is."

"Then he'll go a very long way," was Mr de Blame's reply.

After Trent had finished opening the case to Roger, he called his evidence. The case took Roger several days to try. Nothing that could possibly be worth mentioning had been left out from the plaintiff's case, while the defendants called as many guests as they could to say what a high standard was maintained at their hotel.

"It is not without significance," said Trent, in his closing speech, "that one of these guests was eighty-seven, another was deaf and half blind, while the only guest who could be described as *compos corporis et mentis* was a relation by marriage of Mrs Sweep."

Eventually Roger gave judgment:

"It is, of course, well known," he said, "that every vendor of goods and services is inclined to rate his commodities at too high a worth. But every reasonable man knows that these puffs must be discounted or completely ignored. They know, too, that hotel

346

brochures are no exception to the rule. The picture of the lounge is often taken at such an angle that you might imagine that it was the length of a cricket pitch, whereas in fact two men with long arms could span it from wall to wall. An hotel proprietor is allowed to speak highly of his hotel without running the risk of an action for fraud or breach of contract, provided he does not speak of it in such a way that the ordinary reasonable man would say on learning the true facts—'this is plainly untrue'.

"It is also right that I should say, in view of some of the plaintiff's complaints and the defendant's answers thereto, that no vendor of goods is bound to advertise any disadvantages in those goods. But, as Mr Justice Darling (as he then was) observed very many years ago, in a case where a clergyman had been induced, by a travelling bucket-shop proprietor, to buy some worthless shares—'although an itinerant vendor of fish need not cry "stinking fish, stinking fish", yet, if he knows that his fish do stink, he is not entitled to cry "fresh fish, fresh fish", nor is he any the more entitled to do this if he happens to know that his customer cannot smell.'

"I am not saying," continued Roger, "that in this case Mr de Blame, the plaintiff, could not smell. I think he could. I think he suspected that Mr and Mrs Sweep might not be able to make good their representations. But, on the other hand, I am quite satisfied that he and his wife went to the Grand Hotel for a holiday and not for the purpose of experiencing an action in the Queen's Bench Division.

"Now, one of the first questions I have to decide is whether any, and if so what, meaning is to be attached to the expression *de luxe*. May any hotel, however shabby its appearance, however poor its food and accommodation, so describe itself? In my view, that must to some extent depend upon the price asked. In these days no one could expect an hotel, however described, to provide high-quality food, service and accommodation for, say, 5 guineas a week, and the use of the word *de luxe* in connection with an hotel making such a charge would not really have any effect. But when an hotel describes itself as *de luxe* and charges 45 guineas per week for two persons, I think the words do have some meaning, and that a person going to such an hotel is entitled to expect a reasonably high standard of comfort and cooking. No more than a reasonably high standard but no less. Now, the defendants in this case went a good deal further than merely describing their hotel as 'de luxe'. They said that the cooking was superb. They also said, and whether in view of the evidence it was conscious or unconscious humour I do not pause to enquire, they also said that the service was 'something that you have not experienced anywhere in this country since the war'. The plaintiff said that he had experienced it only too often. In view of the other statements in the brochure the defendants' words clearly meant that the service was really good.

"Perhaps I might mention now that the defendants say that the brochure was printed when they were not short of staff and that unfortunately, when the plaintiff arrived, they were short. But, if a brochure becomes out of date, it must be suitably amended or withdrawn. If it becomes untrue, it is no excuse to say that it was once true. A person charged with falsely describing himself as a bachelor when, in fact, he was a divorced person, might just as well say that he was a bachelor when he was born.

"The plaintiff says, and I accept, that, when they arrived at the hotel, there was apparently no porter on duty. No one appeared to take in their luggage, an untidy young lady in the reception desk pushed the visitors' book towards them without a word, and Mr Sweep himself, who was sitting next to the girl, did not raise his eyes from the crossword puzzle which he was trying to solve. The girl banged her hand down on a bell. After five minutes the plaintiff ventured to mention that nothing had happened. Mr Sweep continued with his puzzle, and the girl gave a shout which might have been 'Ernie'. As no 'Ernie' appeared, the plaintiff asked whether perhaps they could be shown to their room. The answer was that it was on the third floor and that the lift service was temporarily suspended. It is not surprising that by this time the plaintiff was comparing the statements made in the brochure somewhat unfavourably with his first impressions of the hotel. Before walking up to his room, the plaintiff spoke to Mr Sweep. He said, I suspect with more asperity in his voice than he indicated in the witness box:

" 'Are you the manager?'

"Mr Sweep said that he was, and continued with his puzzle. The plaintiff asked what was going to be done about their luggage. Mr Sweep asked the young lady if she was looking after the plaintiff. She said that she was, and Mr Sweep returned to his puzzle. I am satisfied that it was in fact twenty minutes before the luggage was taken up to the plaintiff's room. This was done complainingly by a man with tousled hair in a vest and trousers.

"Not long afterwards the plaintiff and his wife came down-stairs and went into the bar. There was a girl—munching some-thing and painting her finger-nails—behind it. The plaintiff ordered —to use his own language—'Two dry Martinis'. The plaintiff complains that that is exactly what they got, that is, two glasses containing dry Vermouth and nothing else. Now the days have, I think, long passed when a judge should ask: 'What is a dry Martini?' It would certainly be a feigned innocence on my part—

an innocence which I do not feel that the short time I have been on the Bench would in any case entitle me to assume. A dry Martini consists of gin mixed with dry Vermouth, and stirred or shaken up with ice with a squeezed piece of lemon peel put into it. The Vermouth may be French or Italian, provided it is dry, but, whatever the nationality or brand of the Vermouth, the drink is known as a dry Martini. I do not have to enquire why a drink which, for example, may consist, so far as the alcohol is concerned, solely of an English brand of gin and a French brand of Vermouth, should be called a dry Martini, although the firm of Martini e Rossi has supplied no part of its contents. But, of course, the firm of Martini e Rossi do make a dry Vermouth, and it is true that there are places where, if you ask for a dry Martini, that is all you will get. No doubt it is an admirable drink, and I am not intending to cast the slightest aspersions on the Vermouth made by the firm in question. It is of the highest quality. But if a person wants gin and Vermouth, shaken up or stirred with ice, he is entitled to be dissatisfied if he is given instead some dry Vermouth rather warm. I think Mr Trent, on behalf of the plaintiff, is fully entitled to say that an establishment which can properly describe itself as *de luxe* and which charges what I may call *de luxe* prices should know what is meant by a dry Martini.

"It is not altogether surprising that by this time the plaintiff was becoming extremely angry, and I am careful to approach the rest of his evidence with caution, for it would have taken an exceptionally good dinner, beautifully served, to have pacified him. But I am bound to say that neither Mr nor Mrs Sweep did anything whatever to pacify their guests. It may be that, as their rooms were all full and booked up for some time, they did not mind. All they did, when complaint was made about the dry Martini, was to tell the girl to put in some gin. This she did with a toss of her head—or perhaps I should have said, to prevent any misunderstanding, tossing her head, she poured some gin into the plaintiff's glass and that of his wife. The plaintiff says the gin was also warm, and I believe him.

"The next complaint is about the dinner itself, both as to its component parts and as to the manner in which it was served. I once heard a caterer, who was being asked to quote for supplying refreshments to a small society, say disparagingly, when the secretary indicated that their requirements were much more modest than the caterer had suggested: 'We call that giving them a cup of tea and throwing a bun at them.' I must say that the evidence satisfies me that that was the sort of dinner this hotel *de luxe par excellence* supplied. I think, too, that when the plaintiff said: 'A hot waitress steamed across the room hissing, "thick, clear or sardine", ' I was

349

given a fair idea of what the plaintiff had to endure. Only on one point do I find against the plaintiff in this connection. He complains that cabbage was served and that it was a soggy mess. I quite agree with the plaintiff that that *might* be a ground for complaint. But, having regard to the fact that that is the normal way of dealing with that delicious vegetable, even in restaurants of acknowledged excellence, I cannot hold that against the defendants. I do not think that their cabbage, almost tasteless and ruined as it was, was any worse than that which is normally supplied, up and down the country, by cooks and chefs of every description. I regret to say that the same abominable treatment of cabbage takes place in many homes, too. That what was served to the plaintiff was a soggy mess, I accept, but that apparently is all the Englishman expects of cabbage, even in the most exclusive restaurants and clubs. At any rate that is what he gets, and will continue to get unless and until better taste prevails.

"For the rest, I can only say that the standard prevailing at the defendants' hotel was far below the standard which had been represented to the plaintiff as existing at the Grand, however much one discounts the exaggerated description of its delights. I am satisfied that the standard at the time of the plaintiff's visit was that of a very second-rate or third-rate hotel. I am afraid that persons in the position of the defendants, and other hotel proprietors too, take advantage of the unwillingness of the public to make a fuss, let alone make such a fuss as the plaintiff has made in this case. In my opinion he has performed a public service in calling the attention of hotel proprietors to their obligations to their customers. The plaintiff is accordingly entitled to receive damages and I shall now proceed to assess them."

Roger went on to award the plaintiff £150 with costs on the High Court scale.

Mr de Blame thanked Trent and his junior cordially before leaving the Court.

"May I say," he said, "that it was a *de luxe* performance *par excellence*."

Trent thought for a moment, then:

"Thank you," he said, "I don't think I made many mistakes."

"Roger, you were quite splendid," said Anne, as they left the Court together. "I couldn't have said it better myself."

"What vegetables are we having for dinner?" asked Roger. "Cabbage?"

CHAPTER FIVE

THREE SPEECHES

ROGER's Circuit followed the usual custom of giving the new High Court judge a dinner.

"Have you thought what you're going to say tonight?" said Anne, on the morning of the day when it was to take place.

"It all depends," said Roger. "I'm no good at this sort of thing. I think I shall rely upon the inspiration of the moment. I wish Henry were going to be there."

"To tell you what to say, or to lead the applause?"

"Both," said Roger.

In the end he found it easier than he had expected. His health was proposed by the senior member of the Circuit, a very old man of nearly ninety, who never missed occasions of this kind. After a few preliminary remarks, the old man went on:

"They make them younger now. Perhaps it's a good thing. Perhaps it isn't. They last longer, of course, so the country gets more for its money, which is an advantage—I suppose. Though so much is spent by the government today that I can't think that the extra amount involved in appointing judges who are nearer to their appointment with the Great Judge would be noticed. I'm from the old school and I must confess I prefer the older type of judge.

"Roger Thursby will not, I trust—in spite of the tendency which I am told he has, to accept words at their face value— a tendency which I trust he will sometimes repress when listening to evidence—in spite of that tendency he will not, I am sure, think that I am expressing any disapproval of his appointment. Indeed, no. If one is to have whipper-snappers as judges, I couldn't think of a worthier whipper-snapper. And in ten or twelve years, or in fifteen at any rate, he will probably be a very good judge. As soon as that happens, no doubt he will retire.

"But personally I don't think you've had enough experience at—how old are you? Forty-six?—at forty-six. When I was a young man of forty-six I knew very little. I thought I knew a lot, of course. As, no doubt, does Roger Thursby. I hope he does, anyway, because if he doesn't, nobody else will.

"I think the right age for a judge to be appointed is fifty-five to sixty. At any time from then on you may be making arrangements to pack your bags and join the Heavenly Circuit. I think that's a good thing. It has a sobering effect. But at anything under fifty, you're old enough to have played yourself in and at the same time the end of the innings appears so far ahead that you don't have to worry about it. So the besetting sin of pride is allowed, if not free rein, at any rate too much, and there is probably no sin which sits more unfortunately underneath the scarlet and ermine. You cannot do justice to your fellow men if you are at any stage of a case being influenced by your own personal pride. As one gets older one understands more and one's pride recedes accordingly. I am not frightened of losing face any more, but at forty-six I certainly was.

"Well, enough of that, but don't think I've finished. Dear me no. My innings will soon be over, I shall soon be on my way back to the pavilion. But I can still see the ball, I can still make a stroke or two, and even take a wicket."

The old man paused and sipped his port.

"That was for my health, not yours," he said.

"Now, what can I say about our new young judge?" he went on. "He wasn't born when I was called to the Bar. Nothing like it. I doubt very much if his parents were married. Don't misunderstand me—I doubt if they'd met each other by then. So Roger Thursby was very much an off-chance when I was called. Well, I didn't get on as fast as he did. Everything, I think, was slower in those days. It took me ten years to earn £750 in the year. Of course, it was worth more in those days, but I fancy most people would not consider two and a half times that sum a satisfactory income today after ten years' practice. But let me tell you that I was one of the successful ones. I say that in no sense of boasting. Nor do I mean that there were not men who did not do far better. Of course there were. But in my day for a junior of reasonably average ability to have reached the £750 mark after ten years was quite good going. And you must remember that, once you reach that figure, you are likely either to go on pretty quickly or to stay at it and then to recede.

"I'm glad to say I went on. I took silk after twenty years. Our young friend here took it after, I believe, twelve, when he was about thirty-three. And thirteen years later, he's on the Bench. Well, that, I suppose, is the modern idea, but I don't agree with it at all. That isn't sour grapes. I should have hated to become a judge. That's not my type of life at all. Nothing—nothing could compensate me for losing the friendly atmosphere of the Bar. I should hate to sit up there all alone. No one to have a chat to, no one to sympathize when the old fool up there—it should be young fool now, I suppose—does something particularly stupid.

"And then again, there's another aspect of the matter. Everyone at the Bar is an advocate, and it must feel very strange having no case to press. I have known judges, I'm afraid, who remained advocates when they went on the Bench, who swiftly took sides with one litigant or the other and who ran the case as hard as they could for the side they favoured. Such men should never have become judges. They seldom give an appearance of justice and often actually do injustice. From what I hear of our young friend I don't think he suffers from that fault—I should have preferred to have been able to call it disqualification.

"Although for the purpose of proposing his health I have made the most careful enquiries into his virtues and vices, I've been unable to find any. Any vices, I mean. Except the one to which I referred earlier in my speech—of taking people too literally. Even that has an advantage. It should make counsel appearing before him choose their language carefully. And anything which may raise the standard of English at the Bar is an advantage. I regret to say that at the moment, when occasionally I go into Court, I am appalled at some of the things I hear. If counsel had addressed the Court in my young days as some do now, he would have received as serious a rebuff from some judges, as if today he appeared improperly dressed. Is it too late—I fear it is, but I shall make the plea just the same—is it too late to put in a plea for better language and better diction? I am in no way criticizing the American language for, although originally English, admittedly it is today a separate language; but must we use it in our Courts? I do hope that the younger men present today will take some notice of what I am saying. Go to the picture houses or the cinemas or whatever you call them, by all means, enjoy youselves as you will, but do not, I pray, use the language you hear there in the course of your professional duties, any more than you use the language of the public house in your own home.

"Well, I have gone on too long—tonight, I mean—I hope that my innings as a whole will continue a little yet—if only to see whether Mr Justice Thursby becomes Lord Justice Thursby— God help us—before he is fifty—and I have said little in favour of our guest of honour. There is still time for a word or two. I am quite sure that he would not have been appointed at his early age if he did not possess in a high degree those qualities which are required in one of Her Majesty's judges, modesty, integrity, knowledge of the law, understanding of human nature—phew!—what a paragon he must be—and the list isn't finished yet—next comes patience and, finally, an ability to keep quiet. And, as an example to him, that is what I shall now do. I give you the toast of Mr Justice Thursby, may be live long and happily, may he judge well and humbly."

And the old man sat down. When he had said that his criticisms were not made as a result of sour grapes, the older men in his audience knew that that was indeed true. The old man had in his earlier days been offered a High Court Judgeship more than once, had even been pressed to take it, but, for the reasons he gave during his speech, he had always refused.

When the clapping had died down, Roger was called on to respond. After the normal beginning he went on:

"Kendall Grimes was my master in the law. I learned a lot from him. But it took a year. And he was a member of the Bar. I feel that today, in little more than five minutes, I have learned from someone who has never been a judge—though we all know that he could have been one if he had wished—I have learned more about judges in those few minutes than in a whole year I learned about advocacy. Then, of course, I am older. I am not twenty-one any longer. I am—God and the proposer forgive me—forty-six. Listening to the proposer I couldn't help wishing that I could have had in my pocket some gadget on the lines of H. G. Wells' time machine, which would have enabled me to add a year or two to my age before I had to reply. I could then have begun by saying: 'I was forty-six when you began, but now I am fifty-five.' Indeed, we have all heard speeches—though certainly not tonight —where one might have said that with feeling, if not with truth.

"Most people that I know—of either sex—want to take a few years off their ages, not to add to them. But, to tell you the truth— and in a gathering such as this I see no objection to telling the truth—it is not as if we were in Court—to tell you the truth, I am very happy with my years—all forty-six of them, and my only regret is that they should seem too few to the proposer. If only my parents had known his views on the subject, I'm sure they would have done what they could to have speeded things up a bit. But I'm afraid their best efforts would not have added more than a couple of years, for, with the best will in the world, when one is in New Zealand and the other in this country—in those days at any rate—nothing more than fine words could have been achieved. And, as we know, fine words cannot even butter parsnips.

"But to return to the situation as it is, not as it might have been— not only am I entirely happy with my years, but, I confess, they seem to add to their number with extraordinary rapidity, so that—even without one of Mr Wells' gadgets—I seem to be travelling along the road of time pretty fast. But I try to keep on my proper side, to maintain a good look-out, to pay full consideration to others using the road and to stop whenever I come to a halt sign. In the words of one of our most distinguished judges—halt to me means halt.

"But I can't pretend I've always done that. There were times in my earlier days, when, though I may have paused momentarily at the red light, I went across before it changed to green. The proposer is quite right. The experience of age does teach one to be—to be careful. There are things I would do differently today if I had my time over again.

"But I can't say that I should like the opportunity, even if I were promised that I should start my career at twenty-one with the knowledge which I now have. I don't think I could bear to see the horror on the face of the judge when the white-wigged, white-faced little boy proceeded to deliver him a lecture—and a good one too—I've read Central Property and Hightrees—on the one-time doctrine of consideration. After all, I have seen my good friend Tony Trent at work—indeed I've felt him at it too. It's a joy to hear him—always has been—but one, I think, is enough. No, I don't want to go back and, of course, I can't—and I am quite happy to go forward, and I must.

"How far I go forward—in the sense referred to by the proposer of this toast—is quite another matter, and I can only hope that, if the worst should happen—and personally as an optimist I see no reason why it should—I hope that I shall bear the situation with the same fortitude as that with which the proposer of this toast has borne my unexpected advancement to the Bench. I leave you to judge what I mean by the worst.

"Now, the proposer has said that he hopes I think I know a lot. Well, I don't know a lot, but nevertheless I think that by now there must be a legal presumption that I do. I was twenty-one when I was told that I had a lot to learn. That was twenty-five years ago. Presumably, on the principle of *id certum est quod certum reddi potest*, or, if you prefer it, *omnia rite ac sollenniter*, etc., a principle, I may say, which stood me in good stead on my first day at the Bar, when I was left before the Official Referee with a brief I hadn't looked at —though it wouldn't have made the slightest difference at that stage if I'd read it through ten times—on one or other of those principles I must now be presumed in law to have learned a lot. After all, twenty-five years is a reasonable time, and am I not right in thinking that in law everything which can be done can be done in a reasonable time? At any rate, if any member of the Circuit thinks that there is a fallacy somewhere, I will be delighted to hear him on the subject in a suitable place after the adjournment.

"In case, however, I get no further opportunity of thanking you each individually, I do want now to thank you all, and particularly the proposer of this toast, for your hospitality, kindness and good wishes. I have been extremely lucky and my good fortune has pursued me up till this very moment—for how many judges have had the good fortune to have been given at my early stage on the Bench the benefit of such wisdom? I only hope that my luck may continue and that I shall have the good sense and ability to take advantage of what I have heard tonight.

355

"Could there be a finer motto for the coat of arms of a judge than *sapientia ac humilitate*? I said finer, not more modest, for most people choose their coat of arms, though seldom their epitaph. That does happen, though, and I should have expected Tony Trent to have jotted the words down on his cuff, but for the fact that, as soon as I made the suggestion, I saw the words leap into the store-house of his prodigious memory—where they will remain until he is giving instructions to his executors.

"Some time ago I suggested to a member of the Court of Appeal as a motto—*per incuriam nihil*, and now I come to think of it the two might stand together: *Sapientia ac humilitate: nil per incuriam*. The only objection is, that I doubt if the motto, as a whole, would be true of any judge. When Tony Trent becomes a judge, I should be prepared to concede the first and last, but even he wouldn't claim the middle word. As for myself, I cannot at the moment claim the right to any of them, but I shall at least have those words as targets to aim at and, if I keep aiming in the right direction, there is always a chance that I might hit something.

"I cannot hope that the members of this Circuit will always approve my judgments—for that would mean that none of them would ever appear before me—but I do hope that you will all consider that, even if my weapons are of poor quality, I shall use them to the best of my ability, and that, even if I have neither modesty, integrity nor most of the other qualities which the proposer detailed as being essential to my position—and it is rather hard that he should single out almost every quality in which I failed my forty-six plus—I hope you will consider that he and I have this one quality in common—that we know when to sit down. Thank you all very, very much."

By the custom of the Circuit there were only three speeches on these occasions. The third was normally put in the hands of an accomplished wit, who was supposed to propose the health of the Circuit, and this toast was not replied to. The committee thought it would be amusing to employ Anthony Trent, who readily obliged:

"This is becoming a habit," he began. "When the judge first sat, I welcomed him with a few well-chosen words, and now— although the honour of proposing his health has been denied me— I am at least the only other speaker. When I become a judge— or should I say if—I'm not sure what etiquette demands—but no one—not even the judge himself—would ever accuse me of false modesty—I have always said what I really thought of myself —when or if I become a judge, I hope that I shall discharge my duties on occasions such as this, at least as well as my good friend Roger Thursby.

"No one can say that I have not been one to profit by my own mistakes—for I *have* made them in the past, yes, indeed—but, if I have profited by my own, I have profited even more by the mistakes made by other people. So now, when—if and when—my turn comes, I shall know what to say and what not to say, and I hasten to add there was very little indeed that fell from the judge that was not entitled to a very high mark. His speech, if I may say so, struck just the right note and, apart from the actual phraseology and construction here and there, could hardly have been better.

"Although my duty tonight is limited to proposing the health of ourselves—and I think I may take it as no coincidence that I was chosen for this purpose—I do not think I shall be liable to a fine for Circuit misconduct if I say in all sincerity—I wish I could add humility—what personal pleasure it has been to me to see the well-deserved success our new judge promises to have. I have already appeared before him several times, and I can assure him that such errors as he made were all of a kind which are only to be expected from a newly-appointed judge, even—if I may say so —from one of more mature years. I may add that his manner was friendly but judicial, his language entirely adequate (one cannot expect every judge to have the same command of words as the late Lord Hewart), and, I am glad to assure you, infrequent. In all, he is likely to maintain the high traditions of the English Bench and to add to the renown of this Circuit, whose health it gives me the greatest pleasure to propose."

CHAPTER SIX

MR SAUL-BIBURY

ANNE was waiting up for Roger when he got home, and he told her all about the dinner.

"Did you go down well?" she asked.

"Oh, all right," said Roger. "After all, if they give a chap a dinner, they've got to pretend to listen to him, and to applaud him when—it may be because—he sits down. At any rate, I didn't make a mistake I once heard made. After a particularly witty speech a very dull fellow got up and spoke at inordinate length. Half-way through he was incautious enough to say that he wished he could have spoken in the same cheerful and witty vein as the last speaker. 'I'm with you there, sir,' said a very bored and somewhat inebriated diner."

"I'm sure you spoke well," said Anne. "I wish I could have heard you."

357

"I wish you could have heard old Hitchcock. He really was magnificent. He ought to give a course of lectures to judges. Some of them could do with it."

"You talk as though you were still at the Bar," said Anne. "Don't forget, you'd have to attend."

Roger laughed.

"How right you are. I'll probably be as bad as any of them. The trouble is, no one will tell us. If Henry had still been at the Bar, he might have. But most judges have only their powers of self-observation to guide them. And some of those I've known must either have been pretty weak in that respect or have had very odd ideas of what a judge should be. Why, the very man who said 'Justice must not only be done but it must manifestly be seen to be done' was a glaring example. Justice was, no doubt, often done in his Court, but it sometimes required more than a Bisley marksman's eye to observe it."

"Well, I'll come and listen to you and paint you a picture afterwards."

"Unvarnished?" said Roger.

"The truth, the whole truth and nothing but the truth."

"You're a darling," said Roger, and kissed her.

"I have to pinch myself sometimes," he said after a few moments. "It's odd to think that I'm really a judge. Most of the public think of us as awe-inspiring figures, completely removed from ordinary everyday affairs. It must feel very like contempt of Court to think of a judge indulging in the ordinary daily routine of life— to visualize the terrible red-robed figure getting into a bath—quite naked."

"Darling," said Anne, "you won't take yourself too seriously, will you? I think that most people must realize that there is a human being under all that clutter."

The next day had been fixed for a week-end visit to Henry and Sally.

Anne went down in the morning and looked very charming sitting next to Henry on the Bench. And Mr Saul-Bibury did not let Henry down. He was there. He was a prosperous-looking gentleman of middle age, always well-dressed and always with no money but prodigious prospects. On this particular morning his name appeared six times in Henry's list. That accounted for the attendance of two young counsel, one a very pretty girl and one a young man rather like Roger had been. In addition there were three solicitors representing three of the creditors, and a creditor in person, a Mr Crewett, who had sold Mr Saul-Bibury some chickens for which he had not been paid.

It was the first time anyone had bilked Mr Crewett. He considered himself a shrewd judge of character, and when the prosperous-looking Mr Saul-Bibury drew up in a large car and placed an order with him, to be sent to a prosperous-sounding address, he readily accepted the excuse that Mr Saul-Bibury had accidentally left his cheque book behind. As a matter of fact it was quite true. He had left his cheque book behind. And it was by accident. Mr Saul-Bibury would have been very happy to have given a cheque to Mr Crewett. He often gave cheques to his creditors, but, as none of them were ever met, it made not the slightest difference to anyone.

As soon as Mr Saul-Bibury's name was called, Mr Crewett leaped to his feet and rushed into the witness box. He had already noticed that that was the place for litigants who were not represented.

"Your Honour," he said, "I don't know much about these things, but will you please read these documents before you begin?"

He handed to the clerk a bundle of letters and some legal papers.

"Very well," said Henry. "If no one minds, I'll look at them. But I'm afraid, Mr Crewett, that I have seen letters from Mr Saul-Bibury before, and they may not shock me as much as they might shock some people."

"All I want is justice," said Mr Crewett.

"It's sometimes very difficult for creditors to get what they call justice," said Henry, "but let me see the letters."

The clerk handed the bundle to Henry, who could not resist reading it from beginning to end. It began with a letter from Mr Crewett to Mr Saul-Bibury.

Hamlet Saul-Bibury Esq.,
Hermon Lodge,
Pendlebury.
Dear Sir,
    I have pleasure in enclosing my account for the goods I supplied you last month.
    Assuring you of my best attention,

Yours faithfully,
SAMUEL CREWETT.

Mr Saul-Bibury never considered it necessary to answer at that stage.

The next letter was still in courteous terms:

    With reference to the account I delivered to you last month for £35 9s. 3d. I should be greatly obliged if you would favour me with a remittance as I am completing my quarterly stocktaking at the end of next week.
    In the hope that I may still be of service to you, I am, etc.

Mr Saul-Bibury remained unmoved at that second stage also. The third letter ran:

I am a little surprised to have had no settlement of the account I sent you two months ago in spite of my last letter, and I should be most grateful if you would effect an early settlement. Still assuring you of my best attention.

That letter was answered after about a fortnight.

Dear Mr Crewett,
Thank you so much for your last letter. I have been looking everywhere for your account, but it must have been mislaid. I am so very sorry for the delay. Would you be kind enough to send me another account at once? I am going away for some weeks, and should like to settle it before I go.

That letter was post-marked some seven or eight days after it was dated, and Mr Crewett assumed that, when he sent his account by return of post, it must have missed Mr Saul-Bibury.

In fact it did not miss Mr Saul-Bibury, who put it with the previous letters and accounts, and a good many others, into the wastepaper basket or the fire, according to the time of year.

Two months later, Mr Crewett returned to the attack.

If you are now back from your holidays, I shall be much obliged if you will settle the enclosed account, which is now long overdue.

The "if you are now back" was a fatal mistake. Mr Crewett received the following reply:

In the absence of Mr Saul-Bibury, I have opened your letter and know that Mr Saul-Bibury will be very distressed to learn on his return that your account is so long overdue. Please accept my assurance that the matter will be placed before Mr Saul-Bibury immediately on his return, when a cheque will no doubt be sent.

An illegible signature followed, which Mr Saul-Bibury very much enjoyed writing above the typewritten word "secretary."

Mr Crewett replied to the "Secretary to Hamlet Saul-Bibury" saying:

I shall be much obliged if you will let me know when you are expecting Mr Saul-Bibury to return.

After a week, Mr Saul-Bibury replied:

I have written to Mr Saul-Bibury asking him to let me have the information you requested. I also suggested, I hope with your approval, that if he receives my letter he should send me a cheque to enable me to clear your account. I asked Mr Saul-Bibury to telegraph me if he received my letter, but I regret to say that so far no wire has been received. I am afraid that this means he must have missed my letter. In this case I shall write to him at the next address he sends me.

After a few more letters of this kind Mr Crewett's patience began to be exhausted:

It is really too bad, he wrote. *These goods were supplied almost a year ago and it is quite outrageous that there has been no settlement. Unless I receive a remittance within the course of the next fourteen days I shall issue a summons in the County Court.*

Within the fourteen days a reply was received:

I am sure you will be pleased to hear that I have this day heard from Mr Saul-Bibury that he will be returning here within the next two or three weeks, or at the most a month, when your account will at once be placed before him for immediate settlement.

A month went by. Mr Crewett then wrote:

Unless I receive a remittance within seven days a summons will be issued.

Within the seven days came a letter from Mr Saul-Bibury:

Dear Mr Crewett,
I am so very sorry that settlement of your account has been delayed so long. If only I had received it before I went away it would have been paid long ago. Unfortunately my secretary has been taken suddenly ill and has had to leave me, and my accounts are, I am afraid, in complete disorder. Would you be good enough to send me a copy of your account, and I will send you a cheque?

The account was sent by return.
Three days went by. Then:

Dear Mr Crewett,
I duly received your account but as it gives no details and only says "to account rendered," I should be grateful if you would let me have the details, as you will understand that, after this long time, I have completely forgotten the transaction.

The words "after this long time" nearly choked Mr Crewett, but he sent a detailed bill by return of post, with a threat that, if it were not paid immediately, proceedings would follow.

The debt was now nearly two years old.
Within the stipulated time, Mr Saul-Bibury wrote:

Dear Mr Crewett,
I am so very sorry that payment of this account has been so long delayed, and I should like to thank you for your patience in the matter. Although I am not at all clear as to the three items of £11 3s. 7d.,

£4 6s. 9d. and £17 2s. 3d., *and believe there may be some mistake about them, it would not be reasonable to query them at this stage and accordingly I have pleasure in enclosing my cheque for* £35 9s. 3d.

Thanking you again for your forbearance,

Yours sincerely,

HAMLET SAUL-BIBURY.

Enclosed was a cheque for £35 9s. 3d. in words and £34 9s. 3d. in figures. It was dated a year ahead and unsigned. Mr Saul-Bibury had found by experience that errors of date and figures often passed unnoticed if the cheque was unsigned. The absence of signature usually struck the creditor with such force that, with a suitable oath, he put the cheque in an envelope and sent it back. When the bank pointed out the other errors it was as much the creditor's fault as that of Mr Saul-Bibury.

Mr Crewett noticed at once the lack of signature and the errors in the figures, but he missed the mistake in the year. Mr Saul-Bibury apologized profusely for the errors and sent back a letter saying that the corrected and duly signed cheque was enclosed, although it was not.

Your letter did not enclose the cheque. I am issuing a summons, wrote Mr Crewett.

Back came the cheque duly signed, with the amount in words and figures correct, but still dated a year ahead. Mr Crewett sent the cheque to his bank, with instructions to have it specially cleared. When they pointed out to him that a cheque which is dated a year ahead cannot be cleared at all until the year is over, his wrath overflowed and the spittle with which he licked the envelope sending his next letter to Mr Saul-Bibury was pretty well boiling. Mr Saul-Bibury was full of apologies and sent back a cheque for the correct amount in words and figures, with the right date and duly signed.

Mr Crewett had only had this in his possession for half an hour when a telegram followed:

Do not present cheque. Letter follows.

SAUL-BIBURY.

Mr Crewett presented the cheque immediately and it was duly returned "Orders not to pay."

At the same time he received Mr Saul-Bibury's promised letter.

Dear Mr Crewett,

I am so sorry to have had to stop this cheque but you will remember that I wrote to you that I could not quite understand three of the items totalling £32 12s. 7d. *I have now been further into the matter, and think you must have made a mistake and confused my account with someone else's. I enclose a cheque for the admitted balance in full and final settlement of your account.*

Enclosed was a cheque for £2 16s. 8d. which Mr Crewett indignantly returned under the mistaken impression that, if he accepted it, he would not have been able to recover the balance. In fact he lost nothing by returning the cheque, as even that would not have been met.

The bundle which Henry was reading also disclosed that the next step was a summons, which was duly served on Mr Saul-Bibury. To this Mr Saul-Bibury put in a long and elaborate defence which was worthy of any lawyer, and which compelled Mr Crewett to go to a local solicitor.

Now, Mr Crewett lived about a hundred and fifty miles from Mr Saul-Bibury, and he was able to issue the summons in his, Mr Crewett's, local Court. Mr Saul-Bibury promptly asked for a transfer to the Court of his own district on the ground that he would be unable to travel a hundred and fifty miles to make good his defence. With some hesitation the judge at Mr Crewett's local Court transferred the case to Pendlebury County Court and Mr Crewett had to make the long journey in order to prove his case. He had expected a long, blustering defence to be put up by Mr Saul-Bibury, and he was all ready for it. He brought up all his books, and his wife, who had been present when the original order was given, and he waited grimly for his case to be called on. When it was called, Mr Saul-Bibury was not present and Mr Crewett duly obtained judgment for £35 9s. 3d.

But it is one thing to obtain judgment for £35 9s. 3d.—another thing to obtain the money. A bailiff was sent to levy execution on the goods and chattels of Mr Saul-Bibury at Hermon Lodge. Hermon Lodge was a small but comfortably furnished cottage. It was completely furnished on the hire-purchase system, except for the television set and the carpets, which belonged to Mrs Saul-Bibury. There was a large car in the garage, but this belonged to Mr Saul-Bibury's brother-in-law (who was an invalid and unable to drive) and, which, to make assurance doubly sure, was also being acquired on the hire-purchase system.

When the failure of this method of execution was reported to Mr Crewett, he duly issued a judgment summons and, in spite of the expense involved, he made the journey to Pendlebury County Court. He was going to have his money out of Mr Saul-Bibury, even if it cost him twice as much to get it.

Now, Mr Saul-Bibury knew as much about judgment summonses as most judges, and much more than some of them. He, indeed, could have explained what a "271" was, and he knew when it was safe to ignore a summons and when he must appear in Court.

This was one of the occasions when it was necessary for him to appear. He could have obtained a doctor's illegible certificate but only to say that he was unfit for work due to "Coryza," which looks impressive on a certificate, legible or illegible, but, to anyone who knows, means a cold. But he had used that method of delay sufficiently often with Judge Blagrove. Also it meant staying at home in case a bailiff called to see how he was, and, as he had several pleasurable appointments to keep in town, he decided that he must appear.

Henry finished reading the bundle which Mr Crewett had handed in. "Very well," he said, "let the debtor be sworn."

Mr Saul-Bibury stepped blandly and smilingly into the witness box, took the oath and turned expectantly towards the advocates' row, rather like a good hotel manager welcoming guests to an expensive hotel.

"Yes, Mr Found?" said Henry. "Would you like to open the innings? I'll hear Mr Crewett later."

Mr Found, the chief local solicitor, rose ponderously. "If your Honour pleases," he said. Then he turned to the debtor.

"Well, Mr Saul-Bibury?" he said. "Have you any offer to make?"

"To your client only or to everyone?" said Mr Saul-Bibury in reply.

"To my client at the moment," said Mr Found.

Mr Saul-Bibury appeared to be deep in thought for a moment. Then he turned towards the Judge.

"I want to be fair to everyone, your Honour," he said. "At the moment I'm afraid there's only a very limited amount at my disposal. If all these summonses could be held over for three months I have every hope that they will be paid in full."

"That's what you said three months ago," said Henry.

"And three months before that," put in Mr Bridle, another of the solicitors concerned.

"That's very true," said Mr Saul-Bibury solemnly. "No one is more sorry than I am that I have had to disappoint you all. Particularly your client, Mr Found, who, I freely admit, has been rather badly treated. Perhaps, your Honour, I could make a small offer to Mr Found's client and then the other cases can be adjourned?"

"How much is the offer?"

"Well, I'm afraid it can only be described as a token offer—just an earnest of good faith, your Honour."

"Good faith!" spluttered Mr Crewett.

"How much?" said Mr Found.

"Ten shillings a month," replied Mr Saul-Bibury.

"At that rate," said Henry, "it will take five years to settle this one debt, apart from the others."

"It does seem a long time put like that," conceded Mr Saul-Bibury. "I wish I could make it more."

"What are you living on?" demanded Mr Found.

"My friends and relations," said Mr Saul-Bibury, smiling. "I'm very lucky."

"Have you no income at all?" said Mr Found.

"At the moment, no," said Mr Saul-Bibury.

"Why don't you get a decent job? There are plenty going," said Mr Found.

"What, at £10 a week?" said Mr Saul-Bibury. "How could I pay my creditors if I did? If I took a full-time job I should be unable to follow up some propositions which have been put to me and which I have no doubt whatever will in due course enable me to pay everyone."

"Yes, Mr Found," said Henry, "any further questions? No? Who's in next? Miss Paterson? Very well, then."

The pretty girl got up.

"Mr Saul-Bibury, you say you've no money, but isn't it true that you regularly dine at expensive restaurants in London?"

"Regularly?" queried Mr Saul-Bibury. "No, I wouldn't say regularly."

"Well, sometimes then?"

"Oh, yes, indeed. Last week perhaps your client saw me."

"And how were you able to do that out of no income?"

"I wasn't paying, Miss Paterson."

"Do you never pay?"

"Only when I have the money."

"And when did you last have the money?"

Mr Saul-Bibury shook his head sadly.

"When indeed?" he said. "I shall have a lot of hospitality to repay as well as my debts."

"Mr Saul-Bibury," said Miss Paterson, "isn't it correct that you go about in a large car, eat well, drink well, clothe yourself well, and live in comfort and yet pay your creditors nothing?"

"It sounds bad put like that, I agree," said Mr Saul-Bibury.

"How would you put it?" said Henry.

"It's not for me to appraise myself, is it, your Honour, with respect?"

"You don't seem to mind about your creditors at all," said Henry.

"Oh, but I do, your Honour. If I didn't mind I would just go bankrupt."

"How much have you paid your creditors in the last three years?" said Henry.

365

"In the last three years?" repeated Mr Saul-Bibury. "They've been lean years, I'm afraid. Let's hope the next three will be fat and everyone will be happy."

"Have you any offer to make to my client?" asked Miss Paterson.

"Well," said Mr Saul-Bibury, "if no one wants the ten shillings a month, your client can have it."

"Where will you get that from?"

"Indeed," said Mr Saul-Bibury, "where shall I get it from? I shall have to reduce my smoking, I suppose."

"Then you can afford to smoke?"

"Alas, no."

"But you do smoke?"

"Alas, yes."

"And drink?"

"Alas, yes."

"Where do you get the money to do it from?"

"My friends and relations."

"Then why can't you borrow the money from them to pay some of your creditors?"

"Oh, I don't get it in cash."

"Then how could you pay ten shillings a month?"

"I'm not really sure that I could."

"But you just said that you'd have to smoke less."

"To tell you the truth, at the time I said that I was thinking of the days when I'd money of my own."

"Then you can't offer even ten shillings a month?"

"No, I suppose I can't. But, as was pointed out, it would hardly be worth having anyway."

"Now, Mr Crewett," said Henry, "would you like to ask this debtor any questions?"

"Yes, your Honour," said Mr Crewett, "I should."

"Certainly," said Henry.

Mr Crewett then started to put to Mr Saul-Bibury the correspondence leading up to the judgment, but he was soon interrupted by the judge.

"I'm afraid," said Henry, "that none of this has anything to do with it. All I'm concerned with is whether the debtor could have paid the debt since judgment was obtained, not with how he put you off before then."

"But it's fraud," said Mr Crewett.

"If you think so," said Henry, "it is always open to you to go to the police. I'm not concerned with that."

"Well, it isn't justice," said Mr Crewett. "I've come a hundred and fifty miles over this and it looks as though I might just as well have stayed at home."

366

"I'm afraid," said Henry, "that is perfectly true. Unless you really can show that a debtor has means, judgment summonses are a waste of time. I'm afraid Mr Saul-Bibury is a good example of that."

"Everyone will be paid, your Honour," said Mr Saul-Bibury, "if they'll exercise a little patience. I had an appointment today, as a matter of fact, to discuss a most promising proposition but, unfortunately, I had to put it off in order to come here."

"Patience!" exclaimed Mr Crewett. "What have I been exercising for the last two and a half years?"

"I'm sorry about your case," said Mr Saul-Bibury. "I really am. The chickens were excellent, really excellent. I think I have treated you rather badly, too. But it wouldn't be right to give you a preference over my other creditors. *Pari passu* is, I think, the right expression. Share and share alike."

"But what is there to share?" asked Henry.

"Ah," said Mr Saul-Bibury. "If your Honour will adjourn these summonses for three months, I may have a surprise for you all. Nothing would give me greater pleasure."

And, as he said this, Mr Saul-Bibury beamed all round the court.

CHAPTER SEVEN

THE WEEK-END

"SURELY something can be done about a man like that," said Anne, while she and Henry were having lunch.

"Not really," said Henry. "You saw six people trying without success."

"But it's ridiculous," said Anne.

"So it is in a way," said Henry, "but it's not as simple as you think. If any creditor could prove that Mr Saul-Bibury had obtained credit from him by fraud he could, of course, be prosecuted. Presumably they can't prove fraud or he'd have been prosecuted long ago."

"Yes, but can't you make him pay? That's what they were asking you to do."

"Yes, they were asking me to send him to prison unless he paid. Of course, in the old days, before Dickens' time, he could have been put into a debtors' prison until he paid. You wouldn't want to go back to those days, would you?"

"No, of course not, but there ought to be some way of making him pay," said Anne.

"Well, if he hasn't any property of his own and you can't prove that he's had the means to pay the debt since judgment was obtained, there's nothing you can do except make him bankrupt. And that doesn't do much good."

"Well, there's something wrong with the law, then."

"I'm not so sure of that," said Henry. "You see, you're not bound to give a person credit. None of these creditors need have trusted the gentleman. Having chosen to do so they must accept the consequences. As I've said, if they could show that he'd cheated them into giving him credit they could prosecute him."

"Well, I still say it's all wrong," said Anne.

"A woman," said Henry, "is never convinced against her will. So there's not much more I can say, except that I hope you found him entertaining. He exudes goodwill, doesn't he? If that could be cashed, everyone would have been paid long ago. Tell me something quite different. You've seen Roger and me in Court now. How do we compare?"

"You talk more than he does," said Anne.

"Good," said Henry. "Tell him to keep it up. The silent judges are the best."

"Then why don't you talk less?"

"Well, it's more difficult to keep quiet in the County Court. It's what's known as an Inferior Court, as a solicitor I met at a cocktail party reminded me once. He said, rather pompously, that he thought that was unfair, as the County Court did important work. I couldn't resist saying that it was less unfair than calling solicitors members of the inferior profession. 'They do important work, too,' I said, 'and some of them are knighted.' He moved away after that. But it's quite true, really. The County Courts are much nearer to the people. Quite often litigants appear in person. Practically all judgment debtors do, for example. Well, I have to explain things to them, and I can't do that without talking, can I? Anyway, that's my story. The truth probably is that I do talk too much. But don't let Roger follow my bad example."

After lunch they went into Court again. At 4.15 p.m. Henry finished his list and he and Anne went back to his house until the time came to meet Roger's train. He arrived punctually and over dinner he told them the story of Plummer and Toni.

"I can't help liking the chap," he said, "I always did. But I'm terrified of what he'll do next."

"Practical jokers are a menace," said Henry. "He ought to be locked up."

"I know," said Roger, "but I bet you wouldn't have done any differently. However, let's hope he leaves me alone now, and turns his attention to a Cabinet Minister or something. No, I know," he added, "what about a County Court judge? I can tell him of one."

"Too small fry," said Henry, "though I can't say I'd object if he brought a couple of his girl friends along. The one he allotted to you sounds ravishing."

"I think she's probably a very decent girl," said Roger. "I'd really like to help her."

"Help who?" said Henry.

"Her," said Roger.

"Yes, I heard you," said Henry. "I was only wondering in my innocent little way if you'd be so keen on the Galahad touch if she looked like an unmade bed."

"I think I can answer that," said Sally.

"Well, of course I shouldn't," said Roger, "but what's that got to do with it? If she looked like that, she wouldn't need any help. Anne agrees with me, don't you?"

"Of course," said Anne. "I'd love to meet her."

"Would you really?" said Roger, a little surprised at the warmth with which Anne had spoken, and pleased, too.

"But I couldn't ever be left alone with her again," he added.

"Don't you trust yourself?" said Sally.

"Or don't you trust her?" said Henry.

"You know perfectly well what I mean," said Roger. "It's what you were talking about the day after I was appointed."

"You mean," said Henry, "that, if you were left alone with her, you might be manifestly seen to be bad?"

"Don't be ridiculous," said Roger.

"Don't tease him," said Anne. "I expect he's had a much harder day than you have. You've just been enjoying yourself hearing debtors cheat their creditors."

"Chambers want to give me a dinner," said Roger. "You'll come, won't you?"

"I'll come if I can," said Henry. "We might go to the Soft Shoe Club afterwards. Then I'd be able to meet Toni. Perhaps, even, I'd be allowed by Sally to help her sister."

CHAPTER EIGHT

LIBEL ON ICE

WHEN Roger sat down in Court on the following Monday he looked anxiously to see if Plummer was in the audience, and was pleased to find that he was not. The case he had to try was unusual.

369

It was a claim for damages for libel and the libel was said to be contained in an ice. Not on a piece of paper concealed in an ice cream or anything of that kind. The plaintiff complained that he was libelled by the ice itself.

The plaintiff was a local councillor, who had held various positions of importance in the borough where he lived, and the occasion of the alleged libel was a dinner which had been arranged in his honour. It was a very well organized dinner and, until the ice, the food was really superb. The caterers and the committee responsible for the dinner had both apparently set out to provide a dinner worthy of the guest of honour.

It began with smoked salmon of the finest quality; there were no little bits of dry, salty flesh with bones at the ready; a large generous portion, carefully cut, was served to each guest. It was followed by turtle soup, sole Véronique and veal done in a specially delicious way. It was no wonder that, when the ice was served, the guests were ready for something quite out of the ordinary and that nearly everyone took a large mouthful and waited for it to melt happily in the mouth. There was another reason why they might expect something special. Up to the ice all the dishes had been simply described in French, but the ice was printed in slightly larger letters and was called "Bombe à la Marcus Jones" and it need hardly be said that Marcus Jones was the guest of honour. As the guests began to eat the ice the band struck up "For he's a jolly good fellow," and all was set fair for the end of a perfect meal, apart from the coffee and liqueurs which were to follow.

The diners had been expecting something very special in the ice. They got it. It was a *pièce de résistance* with a vengeance. Whether it contained the flavour of cascara, bitter aloes, rancid butter and senna pods or a combination of one or more of these elements was not quite certain at the time, but what was quite certain was that each guest after a momentary pause—as when the barber pours boiling water over the head of his customer and, for a split second, the victim thinks it is cold—gave a gasp which almost drowned the orchestra. Some of them swallowed it because it had gone too far, others because they were made of sterner stuff than the majority, who without hesitation re-deposited what they could on their plates. Several rushed out of the room at once, and most of those who had swallowed it ran out shortly afterwards. It need hardly be said that the dinner was ruined and even the Chairman, who was renowned for his witty speeches, did not dare say anything which might make people laugh. Those of his audience who had remained were in no condition to laugh.

Mr Marcus Jones consulted his solicitor the next day. The

caterers expressed the greatest regret and reduced their charges by half. They were entirely at a loss to explain how it had happened. The ice had been made of the finest ingredients and must have been tampered with. Someone must have gone to each portion and swiftly inserted the noxious substance with a syringe. But who and why? Marcus Jones's solicitor employed detectives to find out. And eventually they found a waiter who admitted that he had been paid by the defendant to do the deed. The defendant was a member of the Committee, and there was no doubt that in the past he and Marcus Jones had been on very bad terms.

Accordingly a libel action was brought by Mr Jones against the man in question, a Mr Tester.

Mr Jones alleged in his statement of claim, among other things:

"That by procuring the ice to be so named and at the same time to be so excruciatingly unpleasant the defendant meant and was understood to mean that the plaintiff was a very nasty man, that he made people sick and was nauseating to all his friends and acquaintances, that he was not fit to associate with his fellow citizens and that he ought to be ostracized by any reasonably minded civilized community."

The defendant, though a wealthy man, conducted his own defence. In his written defence he agreed that the serving of the ice did mean that the plaintiff was all the things the plaintiff complained of, but, he said, they were true.

The plaintiff, he said, was a nauseating hypocrite, and the ice was but a poor relation of his.

Up till this point in his defence it looked as though the only question was whether the defendant could prove what was alleged against the plaintiff's character, and that the plot was admitted. But the defence ended by completely denying that the defendant had anything to do with the interference with the ice and went on to say that the plaintiff had, in fact, engineered it himself and persuaded the waiter to lie about the matter in order that he, the plaintiff, might bring this action.

It was not surprising, then, that, as soon as the case was reported in the newspapers, Roger's Court was crowded. The first part of the hearing soon developed into a slanging match between Mr Marcus Jones and Mr Tester. Two things swiftly emerged: that these gentlemen had long been enemies, and that neither of them was a particularly scrupulous person. For example, when Mr Tester put to Mr Jones that a close relation of his had had shares in a company to which the local authority had given a large contract, Mr Jones sought to parry the question by referring to similar conduct on the part of Mr Tester. At that stage Roger

371

intervened and pointed out to Mr Jones that he must answer the
questions properly.

After a day's cross-examination of the plaintiff by the defendant,
it became pretty obvious to most people that, whatever might be
uncertain in the case, it was quite certain that neither the plaintiff
nor the defendant was fit to hold public office. It was odd, thought
Roger, that reasoning beings should live like animals and indulge
quite unnecessarily in a death struggle. Their hatred of each other
made them completely unmindful of the consequence to themselves.

On the second day the plaintiff's counsel called the waiter.
After he had given his name and address he was asked to give his
account of the dinner and of anything he knew about the ice. At
that stage Roger had to ask for a question to be repeated. He had
just noticed that Plummer and Toni had come into Court. As
Plummer was perfectly capable of preparing the ice-trick himself,
Roger wondered, with a little apprehension, whether he had
anything in store for the Court that day. Roger also noticed that
Toni was looking particularly attractive. Two answers had to be
repeated to him. In rebuking himself for his misbehaviour, Roger
had the consoling thought that he was at any rate human. Much
better than those strange creatures he had sometimes read about
in fiction. But Toni really was lovely.

"Would you mind repeating the question, Mr Creamer?" Mr
Creamer obliged:

MR CREAMER: And now tell his Lordship anything you know
about the ice.

THE WAITER: About the ice?

MR CREAMER: Yes.

THE WAITER: It was served after the veal.

MR CREAMER: Yes, we all know that. What happened before
it was served?

THE WAITER: They had the veal.

MR CREAMER: Mr Turner, did you have any conversation with
the defendant, Mr Tester, before the dinner began?

THE WAITER: Any conversation?

MR CREAMER: Yes.

THE WAITER: About what?

MR CREAMER: About anything.

THE WAITER (*after a pause*): Well—I did—yes.

MR CREAMER: Where?

THE WAITER: In the street.

MR CREAMER: When?

THE WAITER: About a week before the dinner.

MR CREAMER: What was the conversation?

THE WAITER: Do I have to say?

ROGER: Do you mean that you are frightened of incriminating yourself?

THE WAITER: Of what, my Lord?

ROGER: Of getting into trouble. You don't want to answer in case it gets you into trouble, is that it?

THE WAITER: No, my Lord.

ROGER: Do you mean yes?

THE WAITER: No, my Lord.

ROGER: You mean you do want to answer?

THE WAITER: No, my Lord.

ROGER: Then you mean "no."

THE WAITER: Yes, my Lord.

ROGER: Well, Mr Creamer, what about it? The defendant is not represented, so I'd better hear what you say first. Is the witness bound to answer?

MR CREAMER: Why not, my Lord? It may be that at a later stage he will be privileged from answering. But how can it incriminate him merely to have to answer whether he was *asked* to do something by the defendant?

ROGER (*after a pause*): Very well, Mr Creamer, you may ask him if the defendant asked him to do anything, but I don't think he can be asked, if he objects, whether he agreed to do what he was asked—still less whether he did it.

MR CREAMER: If your Lordship pleases. Now, Mr Turner, did the defendant ask you to do anything?

THE WAITER: Yes. He asked me if I'd get an opportunity of squirting something in the ice.

ROGER: I gather you'd rather not answer any more questions on this subject?

THE WAITER: No, my Lord.

ROGER: You mean you don't want to answer further questions?

THE WAITER: Yes, my Lord.

ROGER: You mean—no you don't?

THE WAITER: Yes, my Lord.

ROGER: Very well, Mr Creamer, have you anything else you want to ask this witness?

MR CREAMER: Yes, my Lord, but your Lordship won't let me ask it.

So Mr Creamer sat down and Roger asked the defendant if he would like to cross-examine the waiter. He said that he would, and began at once:

DEFENDANT: Mr Turner, you're a man of bad character, aren't you?

WAITER: Do I have to answer that?

373

ROGER: Yes, I'm afraid so.

WAITER: Well, I know worse.

DEFENDANT: I dare say you do—the plaintiff, for example.

ROGER: Mr Tester, you mustn't make remarks like that. It's most improper. Ask the witness questions and don't comment on his answers, please.

DEFENDANT: I'm sorry, my Lord. Very well, Mr Turner, you know worse men than yourself. Where did you meet them—in prison?

WAITER: Do I have to answer that?

ROGER: Yes. You must understand, Mr Turner, that, while a witness is not bound to incriminate himself, he is bound to answer about any past crimes for which he has paid the penalty. Answering such questions does not incriminate you. You couldn't be charged with those offences again.

WAITER: I could get the sack.

ROGER: I'm afraid that doesn't excuse you from answering.

WAITER: I didn't want to come here to give evidence.

ROGER: I'm afraid I can't help that. You must answer the question. Will you repeat it, Mr Tester.

DEFENDANT: Have you been to prison?

WAITER: Yes.

DEFENDANT: How many times?

WAITER: Three—no, four.

DEFENDANT: Don't hurry yourself. Sure it's only four?

WAITER: Yes, quite. I went there—I ought to know.

DEFENDANT: What was the longest stretch?

WAITER: Three years.

DEFENDANT: What for?

WAITER: They called it fraud.

DEFENDANT: And what would you have called it? Business?

WAITER: Have I got to answer that?

ROGER: No, I don't think so. Any other questions, Mr Tester?

DEFENDANT: Yes, my Lord. Now, Mr Turner, you've just said that I asked you to spoil the ice. Didn't you tell me that Mr Jones himself asked you to do it?

WAITER: Have I got to answer that?

ROGER: Yes.

WAITER: Well—yes, I did.

DEFENDANT: Well, that was true, wasn't it—it was really he who asked you, not I? And he's paid you to say the opposite?

WAITER: Have I got to answer that?

ROGER: I'm not sure. I should like your help, Mr Creamer. The witness has sworn that the defendant asked him to interfere with the ice. He is now in effect asked whether that piece of evidence is

374

not perjury. Of course if his answer were 'no' it would not amount to any admission, but if his answer were 'yes' he could surely be prosecuted, could he not?

MR CREAMER: Witnesses are often asked whether their evidence is not perjured.

ROGER: Of course they are, and normally they answer indignantly that it isn't. But surely, if a witness is asked if he has not told on oath a deliberate lie on a material matter, and the judge is satisfied that his objection to answering the question is a genuine one, the objection should be allowed?

MR CREAMER: Well, my Lord, I'm in your Lordship's hands.

ROGER: Very well, Mr Turner, tell me this. Are you frightened of answering the question Mr Tester asked you because you might be prosecuted for perjury if you answered it?

WAITER: Yes, my Lord. I've had enough trouble as it is.

ROGER: Very well, then, you need not answer the question, but, in view of your evidence would the plaintiff and the defendant like to consider composing their differences? After all, whatever is the truth of this matter, no one can rely on the evidence of Mr Turner, I'm afraid. Apart from his previous convictions, he has told two distinctly opposite stories. Only one on oath, that is true, but in the witness box he has refused to deny the truth of the other statement.

MR CREAMER: I'll take my client's instructions, my Lord.

But in spite of Mr Creamer's efforts, neither the plaintiff nor the defendant would agree to give way one inch. So Roger had to hear the whole of the evidence and to arrive at a conclusion.

Before the case was over he went to a cocktail party, where a woman said to him:

"Do tell me how it is you can always tell which side is telling the truth? I should have thought it was very difficult. But you wouldn't be a judge if you couldn't, would you?"

"Wouldn't I?" said Roger, with feeling. "It's quite true that in a lot of cases, the majority, the truth does appear with reasonable certainty, and most judges, if not all of them, would decide those cases, as far as the facts are concerned, the same way. But there are cases where Judge A would believe the plaintiff and Judge B would believe the defendant, and the truth might be that they were both wrong."

"Then you actually make mistakes?" said the woman.

"I'm afraid so," said Roger.

"But that's dreadful,' said the woman. "What's the point of going to law unless the judge is going to get it right?"

"Well, we usually do," said Roger, "I hope, but we're only human, I'm afraid, and there must be some mistakes."

"Then it isn't justice," said the woman. "And what about people who are hanged and sent to prison? I'd no idea."

"Criminal law is different," said Roger. "To begin with, all serious crimes are tried by a jury. There are twelve of them. And, if they think there's any doubt about the case, they always acquit."

"But that isn't right, if the person's guilty," said the woman. "That isn't justice, either. Are many guilty people acquitted, d'you think?"

"Oh yes," said Roger incautiously, "lots. Very few others, as a matter of fact."

"D'you mean that?" said the woman.

"I'm afraid so," said Roger. "In order to prevent the injustice, to which you referred, of people being hanged or imprisoned for crimes they haven't committed, we give prisoners every reasonable chance of being acquitted."

"Then there are murderers and other criminals walking free in in the streets?"

"I'm afraid so. But, don't forget, there are quite a number of criminals who are never caught, and they're walking about the streets, too."

"Two wrongs don't make a right. Of course the police can't catch everyone. But if, when they do catch them, you let them out again—what's the good of it?"

"Well—everyone's entitled to be tried, don't you think?" said Roger.

"Certainly," said the woman, "but, if they're guilty, then they should be convicted, not let out to do it again."

"But guilt has to be proved," said Roger.

"Of course it has, and it's up to the lawyers and judges to prove it. I always had such a high opinion of English justice. You really have shaken me. What about the figure of justice on the Old Bailey? What does it stand for? Convicting the innocent and acquitting the guilty, as far as I can see."

"I never said the innocent were convicted," said Roger.

"But it must happen sometimes. You said yourself mistakes are made and that 'we're only human.' "

"Well—I suppose it does happen very occasionally."

"That's all I said," said the woman. "The innocent convicted and the guilty often acquitted. That's right, isn't it? I didn't misunderstand you about that—guilty people are often acquitted?"

"Yes," said Roger. "I apologize, but it does happen quite often."

"And you're a High Court judge and sometimes you decide cases the wrong way?"

"Yes, I'm afraid so. But they can always go to the Court of Appeal."

"And are they always right?"

"No, not always," said Roger. "But you can sometimes appeal rom them to the House of Lords."

"And are they always right?"

"Yes," said Roger. "In law they are always right."

"I don't quite know what the 'in law' means, but if they're always right, why can't we start with them? It seems much better than having a lot of judges like you—forgive my frankness—making mistakes and some more judges in the Court of Appeal making more mistakes. Why not begin in the House of Lords and make no mistakes?"

"I'm afraid that, for one thing, there aren't enough Law Lords."

"Then make some more. They're always talking about reforming the House of Lords. But I am really most disturbed by all this. As far as I can see, there isn't much point in having judges and courts at all, if they're going to make mistakes the whole time."

"We do get things right sometimes," said Roger.

"How d'you know?" said the woman. "You may be mistaken when you think you've got it right."

Roger looked round the room to see if he could find some means of escape, but, before he could find any, his assailant went on:

"Oh, there's one thing you can tell me, if you don't mind. I know it's very stupid of me—I ought to know. Can you give a weekly servant a week's notice in the middle of a week, or must the notice end with the end of a current week?"

"Well, probably——" began Roger.

"Probably!" interrupted the woman. "Probably! You're a judge, aren't you? Don't you know the law?"

"Well," began Roger apologetically, "it isn't absolutely certain, but the better view, in my opinion, is——"

"Look, what is this?" said the woman. "Have I done the wrong thing? Oughtn't I to ask a judge for his opinion? I suppose it's trade union rules. Doing a solicitor out of his six and eight."

"No, it really isn't that," said Roger. "The truth is——"

"I thought you didn't always know the truth."

"What I mean is," persisted Roger, "that it would probably be held today that a week's notice would be effective whenever it was given, but there is no definite modern authority on the subject."

"An awful lot of words to deal with a simple point," said the woman. "Anyway, what would you advise a person to do?"

"Well," said Roger, "I'd certainly advise them to give a week's notice to expire at the end of a current week."

"Come again," said the woman.

Roger repeated his remark.

377

"But I thought you said that wasn't the law—I beg your pardon, *probably* wasn't the law."

"Yes, I did."

"Well—you don't seem to have the courage of your convictions, do you? Have you been a judge long? Oh—excuse me, I must go and talk to——"

And she moved away. Roger did not very much mind that he never had the opportunity of explaining that his advice was given in order to prevent the possibility of argument; better to give a few extra days than risk an action in the County Court, however likely to win you might be, he would have said.

Next morning Roger had to make up his mind about the dispute between Mr Jones and Mr Tester. In trying to decide where the truth lay, Roger could not help remembering his conversation at the cocktail party.

Who was responsible for the interference with the ice? Mr Jones said it was Mr Tester. Mr Tester said it was Mr Jones. The waiter had said that it was each of them. The question was—what was Mr Justice Thursby going to say? There was really nothing to guide him. The waiter was a self-confessed man of bad character. The plaintiff and the defendant had each had to make damaging admissions about their past conduct. For a moment Roger did say to himself—well, does it matter anyway? No one in this case is worth twopence. But then he pulled himself together and reminded himself that, if a person came to the Courts, however undeserving he might be, he was entitled to get the best decision the court was capable of giving. He was glad that his assailant at the cocktail party could not see his mind working.

In the end Roger decided that the plaintiff had not proved his case.

"It is for the plaintiff to establish," he said, "by a preponderance of probability, that it was the defendant who was responsible for the incident. I can find nothing in the evidence to suggest that it was more likely to have been the defendant than the plaintiff. It is true that, apart from the evidence, one would have said that it was more probable that the defendant had hatched such a comparatively simple, if unusual, plot than that the plaintiff would have gone in for such an involved one. But, having had the doubtful advantage of seeing both Mr Jones and Mr Tester in the witness box, I really cannot choose between them. Unlike Mr Turner they have no criminal convictions against them but whether that is due to luck or great care it is not necessary for me to conjecture. They have chosen to wash their dirty linen in public, but that does not seem to have made it any cleaner. I do not pretend that I know where the truth lies in this case, and all I can say is that the plaintiff has not satisfied me that it lies with him. There will accordingly be judgment for the defendant but in all the circumstances I shall make no order as to costs."

Both sides left the court thoroughly dissatisfied with the decision. The only person who was reasonably satisfied was Mr Turner, the waiter, who had been paid by both parties and against whom there was not sufficient evidence to enable the police to prosecute for any offence.

After Roger had gone to his room the usher brought him a note. It was from Plummer:

"Can you remind me," it said, "whether it was tomatoes or oranges that a man once threw at the Court of Appeal?"

CHAPTER NINE

SOMETHING FOR NOTHING

A FEW days later Roger was walking to the Old Bailey for his first appearance there as judge, when he was accosted by Plummer.

"I'm not getting on your nerves, I hope," he said.

"You're a confounded nuisance," said Roger, "but I can't think what you get out of it. Anyway, it was tomatoes—and the man was sent to prison. And, I may add, he was a bad shot and they missed."

"I suppose one wants practice," said Plummer, "at that sort of thing. What's the elevation? I must work it out."

"You'll end up in gaol, you know," said Roger. "I hope I don't have to send you there."

"So do I," said Plummer. "It'd be so awkward for you. Well, I must be off. See you again soon. Shall I give your love to Toni?"

Roger did not answer at once. One sends love to all sorts of people. It is often a pure formality. It wouldn't be in writing, either. All the same, could he, a High Court judge, send his love to a dance hostess, even though her father was a doctor? Manifestly be seen to be—oh—damn! "Yes," he said.

Roger felt a little self-conscious as he took part in the ceremonial of opening the Sessions at the Old Bailey. He decided that he would take back to Anne the bunch of flowers which he was traditionally given, and then, confound it, he thought how nice it would be to give a bunch to Toni. This was multiplication with a vengeance. Of course, he wouldn't dream of doing such a thing. A little girl of twenty-three, whom he'd met once and who worked in a night club. Never heard of such a thing.

"I beg your pardon, Mr Summers?" he said to Counsel, who had apparently been addressing him.

"My Lord," said Counsel, "the facts in this case are as follows. About six months ago an advertisement appeared in a sporting newspaper to the following effect: 'Help me exploit my new system. Results guaranteed. Send £10 cash for a share. Smith, Box 1713.' The advertisement was not very different from those of many other tipsters, and no one answered it. The next week another advertisement appeared from the same source: 'Last week we backed three winners at 3 to 1, 5 to 2 and 6 to 4, and one loser (4th at 20 to 1). We only made just over £250 as we hadn't the necessary capital. Proof this paper. Send £10 for a share next week.' Mr Smith produced to the paper in question his bookmaker's account, showing that he had indeed backed the horses in question and received a cheque for the amount referred to. As a result of the advertisement a few people sent £10 each and a few more sent £5 for a half-share. They all received their money back with the following letter: 'Dear Sir, Thank you for your letter and enclosure, which I regret having to return as I was over-capitalized for the week. I hope that I may be able to let you share in the new system on a later occasion. Yours sincerely, H. Smith.' The following week the advertisement read as follows: 'We apologize to those whose money we were unable to accept. And we sympathize. Last week we backed four winners, 10 to 1, 5 to 1, 6 to 4 and even money, and NO losers. Proof this paper.' Again Mr Smith had produced to the newspaper his bookmaker's account proving his claim to be correct. In consequence of this advertisement quite a number of people sent in their money. It was all returned to them with a similar note to the first one, but adding: 'I am hoping that in the not too distant future I shall be in a position to land a really big coup at startling odds and I shall need your money for this purpose. I cannot, of course, be quite sure when this is going to be, and naturally I cannot advertise it directly or the odds may shorten.' The next week there was a similar advertisement showing the tremendous success of the system, which was again proved to the satisfaction of the newspaper in the usual way. This went on until the public were figuratively hammering at Mr Smith's Box number, and begging to be allowed to subscribe to his system and to buy a share in the gold mine. Time after time Mr Smith hardened his heart and refused to accept anyone's money. But eventually he relented and was kind enough to accept 1,000 offers, each accompanied by £10 in cash. Each of the investors waited expectantly for the registered letter which was to bring them their winnings. It was obviously pretty well a certainty. There could be no doubt about it. The sporting paper which carried the advertisement was a thoroughly reputable paper, and 'proof this paper' meant what it said. There was no reason why a system which had succeeded week after week should suddenly fail. So each waited for the registered letter. And, when it never came, they looked in the paper to see what the advertisement would say. It said nothing, because there was no advertisement. They started to write to Mr Smith at the Box number, to enquire what had happened, but they had no answer. Then they wrote to the newspaper, which at once started to make enquiries for Mr Smith. But he was not to be found—neither he nor the £10,000 which had been sent him. The address which he had given to the newspaper was an accommodation address belonging to a newsagent. All the newsagent could say was that a bearded man with dark glasses used to call for the letters. So the newspaper made enquiries from Mr Smith's bookmaker. They had no answer from that source either. They then made enquiries about the bookmaker and they found that it was a small limited company which had been formed a few months before Mr Smith had started to insert his advertisements. It didn't take the investigators long to realize that Mr Smith had been his own bookmaker and sent himself his winning accounts. The police were informed and they made a search for Mr Smith. Eventually they found him, and here he is, my Lord. He has pleaded guilty to ten counts of obtaining money by false pretences, but the total amount involved is, as I told your Lordship, £10,000."

Counsel then called the police officer in charge of the case, who gave a short account of the prisoner's past history, and Roger then asked Mr Smith if he had anything to say in mitigation of sentence.

"Although it is a first offence," Roger said, "you will have to go to prison. The question is, for how long?"

"My Lord," said the prisoner, "if it weren't for people's greed, things like this would never happen. Everyone wants something for nothing, and then they grumble when they don't get it." He paused.

"Anything else?" said Roger.

"Well, my Lord," he added, "I did send them back their money each time—except the last."

"But you wouldn't have made anything like so much if you hadn't. It was worth it, wasn't it?" said Roger.

"I don't know, my Lord," said the prisoner. "That depends on you."

CHAPTER TEN

THE MOTOR MOWER

IF ROGER had known that Plummer was preparing a further assault on him, he would have felt less comfortable when he sat for the first time as Judge in Chambers. The 'Judge in Chambers' has to deal mostly with the various applications which are made in the course of an action. While Roger was dealing with a number of such matters, Plummer was talking to Toni.

"I think perhaps," he said, "that we should use you again."

"That suits me fine," said Toni. "I like my judge. Can't see too much of him. Pity he's married."

"Good," said Plummer. "I must see how to bring the young people together."

While Plummer was considering this problem, Roger was beginning to hear an application in a case about a motor mower.

"This is an appeal from a decision of Master Banger, my Lord," began Mr Twine of Counsel. "The learned Master refused to order the plaintiff to deliver particulars of his statement of claim."

"What is the action about?" said Roger.

"It's a claim for damages in respect of the sale of a motor mowing machine which my clients, the defendants, sold to the plaintiff, my Lord. He complains that it makes all sorts of odd and sometimes vulgar patterns on his lawn. We want particulars of each oddity and vulgarity relied upon."

"Can't the machine be adjusted?" asked Roger. "It seems a bit absurd to have litigation on the subject."

"Exactly what my clients said and say," said Mr Twine.

"Really!" said Mr Twine's opponent, Mr Groaner. "I'm amazed at my friend saying that. We've begged and begged the defendants to come and adjust the machine."

"Each time my clients have called," replied Mr Twine, "there's been nobody in."

"Well," said Roger, "is it too late now? Mightn't it be better for an appointment to be made now, so that there need be no oddities or vulgarities on the plaintiff's lawn in the future, rather than for an enquiry of doubtful value being made into the oddities and vulgarities of the past? Though I must confess," he added, "I'm a little intrigued to know what they were."

"My Lord," said Mr Groaner, "I can satisfy your Lordship's curiosity. Here are some photographs."

"This is an application for particulars," said Mr Twine, "his

Lordship isn't trying the action. I don't know what the photographs have got to do with it."

"Well, they might constitute the particulars, mightn't they?" said Roger.

"If my learned friend will limit his complaints to the photographs, I should be quite satisfied, my Lord."

"Well, Mr Groaner," said Roger, "are you prepared to rely solely on the photographs?"

"Not at this stage, my Lord," said Mr Groaner.

"My learned friend wants it both ways," complained Mr Twine. "He won't limit his particulars to the photographs and at the same time he wants to prejudice your Lordship by showing them to you. My clients have no knowledge of them whatever—they may have been taken anywhere as far as my clients know. They ought to have been asked to be present when they were taken."

"They were," said Mr Groaner.

"They were not," said Mr Twine.

"Well," said Roger, "you can't both be right. Anyway, let me see the photographs."

Mr Groaner handed them to Roger, and the clerk leaned slightly to one side so that he could see them too.

"They are rather extraordinary," said Roger, "but I'm not quite clear where the vulgarity comes in."

"Well, my Lord," said Mr Groaner, "if your Lordship takes photograph number one and holds it upside down——"

"Really," commented Mr Twine, "perhaps my friend has an X-ray apparatus as well."

"If your Lordship will be good enough to look at photograph number one upside down . . ." repeated Mr Groaner.

"No, I don't think so," said Roger, restraining his natural curiosity very creditably. "I should probably miss the point anyway. However, Mr Groaner, if you won't limit your complaints to what is shown on the photographs, why shouldn't you give particulars of everything you do complain about?"

"My Lord," said Mr. Groaner, "surely I can't be expected to say in what position every blade of grass lay after the machine had been over it? That was the Master's view, my Lord, and he is, if I may say so, a very experienced Master."

"I'm afraid," said Roger, "that I've always deprecated the threatening of new judges in chambers with the names and experience of Masters."

"Oh, my Lord, I wasn't doing anything of the sort. I shouldn't dream of——"

"Very well," said Roger, "I must have misunderstood you. The appeal will be allowed and the particulars as asked for must be delivered in fourteen days. Unless, of course, both parties are sensible enough to put their heads together and settle the whole dispute by putting the machine right."

"But who's to pay the costs, my Lord?" asked Mr Groaner.

"Who's to pay them when the action's been fought, Mr Groaner?" said Roger. "It may be the plaintiff or it may be the defendant, or it may be both of them, but, whoever it is, the costs will then be ten times as much as they are now."

Roger completed the order, and Mr Twine and Mr Groaner gave place to Mr Bone and Mr Streak. Outside the judge's room Mr Twine, flushed with victory, ventured his opinion to Mr Groaner that Roger was going to be jolly good, with which opinion Mr Groaner, smarting with defeat, profoundly disagreed.

CHAPTER ELEVEN

THE SOFT SHOE CLUB

ROGER had always found time very kind to him when he walked down Bond Street. That is to say that, after his eyes had strayed in the way to which Henry had referred, although a feeling of regret that he could not follow his inclinations sometimes assailed him, it did not last long, and within a few minutes or at the most half an hour or so, it was all over. So, when some months had passed without his seeing Toni again, the various emotions which she had stirred in him had pretty well died down. Then, one day, a judge, who was much older than he was but whom he knew quite well, asked him to come and see him in his room.

"Ah, Roger," said Mr Justice Breeze, "nice of you to come."

Mr Justice Breeze was a very cheerful bachelor. He did not pretend to be a good lawyer nor, indeed, a particularly good judge, but he dealt out rough and ready justice with robust good humour. When at the Bar he had been almost irresistible to juries. His smiling red face and his down-to-earth, boisterous speeches, full of colloquialisms, jollied the jury along with him. When he went on the Bench he retained very much the same manner, though he toned it down a little. Counsel in his Court knew that it was no use relying on the finer points. Mr Justice Breeze was going to take the broad view and he intensely disliked technical points.

"That's a mean little point, Mr Jones," he would say. "You know what I'd like to tell you to do with that. Abandon it. Hasn't your client any merits? I'm sure such a jovial looking man must have some. Take fresh instructions, Mr Jones," he would add.

384

"Tell your client not to skulk in the nasty, mean little street he's wandered down and to come out into the broad, open highway of justice."

He often got his way, though not always, but, when he did, he was frequently reversed in the Court of Appeal. Not that he cared. He had given a decision which was just in his view, and if the lawyers above him chose to alter it, that was their business.

"I was upheld again the other day," he once remarked to a friend. "I must be losing my grip."

Why he had remained a bachelor sometimes puzzled even him. He was a normal man, with normal instincts, but he had never had a love affair, unhappy or otherwise. Marriage had simply passed him by. At one time, in his younger days, he had been very much in demand by mothers of eligible daughters. He had been a double Blue, was ruggedly good-looking and was obviously doing well at the Bar. But it just never happened. Possibly he was too bluff and too hearty. The broad, open highway of justice was all right in the Courts, but at home technicalities and refinements have their place.

"I've had an invitation," said Breeze, "and I wondered if you and your wife would care to come with me. I'm not much used to these places."

"Oh?" said Roger enquiringly. "It's very nice of you."

"I'll tell you what it is. A girl, a dancer or something, broke or sprained her ankle at one of these clubs and she's brought an action against her employers. She claims that the floor was unusually slippery and various other things about the platform where she had to perform, and so on. They want me to see the place. They offered me an evening's entertainment and asked if I'd like to bring a friend or a couple of friends. Well, in view of my celibate state and the gossip column reporters, I thought I'd take a couple of friends. We can choose any night. What about it?"

Roger did not answer for a moment. He was puzzled. Here was a judge trying a case between the proprietors of a club and an employee and the judge was actually going to accept hospitality from the owners of the club. It seemed odd to Roger, very odd indeed. If a judge accepted a favour from one party to litigation either side might think he had been influenced by the fact. If he decided for the person who did him the service the other party might feel aggrieved; if he decided the other way it might be thought that the judge had deliberately decided against the person doing him the favour, to show how fair he was.

Breeze apparently sensed what Roger was thinking.

"Don't look so puzzled," he said. "Both sides want me to come. Counsel for the plaintiff was quite upset when I suggested that I

385

couldn't very well accept hospitality from the defendants. He begged me to come and said that, if I didn't, I shouldn't be able to follow the plaintiff's case properly. I saw them in my private room. They're going to be there too, and both of them pressed me to come. Apparently they both agree that, unless one sees the place as it is when guests are there and so on, you can't see the point of the case. Well, I don't suppose I shall see the point anyway, if it's as difficult as that, but I don't mind trying on the terms suggested. Might be quite amusing. Haven't been to one of those places for years."

"Well, it's very nice of you," said Roger. "I think Anne and I would love it. Is there much in the case? Is it a permanent injury?"

"Oh, no," said Breeze. "It's not really serious."

"Well, it's very odd spending so much money on the case. Anyway, why didn't they bring it in the County Court?"

"I asked them that," said Breeze, "and, what's more, I warned them of the consequences of trying the action in the High Court. Neither side seemed to mind in the least."

"Are their counsel any good?" asked Roger.

"Oh, yes, both of them. They know what they're up to. That's why I didn't say any more."

"Well, I must just ask Anne, but I'm sure we'd love it. What's the name of the club, by the way?"

"Some odd name. I forget. No, I've got it. The Soft Shoe Club. Heaven knows what that means."

"Plummer!" said Roger.

"What's that?"

Roger thought for a moment. Then all he said was:

"I know the chap who runs it. He was at school with me."

He had been about to warn Breeze about Plummer's activities, and then he suddenly realized that, if he did so, he might be prejudicing the judge who was trying the action by giving him private information unknown to either side. Unless, therefore, Plummer really started to do something, he decided he would say nothing about him, at any rate until after the action had been decided. Having got over that hurdle Roger realized, not without some pleasure, that he would be seeing Toni again.

When he got home that evening he said to Anne:

"We've had an invitation."

"Oh?"

"To go to the Soft Shoe Club."

"What!" said Anne. "You're not serious?"

"It's quite all right," said Roger. "Plummer didn't ask me."

He then told Anne how the invitation arose.

386

"It would be quite fun, wouldn't it?" he said almost casually.

Anne hesitated for a moment. She was going to agree to the suggestion and the only question in her mind was in what form she should do so. If she said—"Yes, of course we'll go," that would at once indicate to Roger that she wasn't really keen on the idea herself but would go to please him. If she just said—"All right," or "Yes, certainly," it would have much the same effect. On the other hand, if she said, with obvious enthusiasm, "Yes, let's, it'll be great fun to break out for a bit," it would not be true. She was not a jealous woman, but she had not been altogether sorry when Roger had ceased to mention Toni's name. She was not in the least frightened that Roger would lose his head if he saw her again; they were entirely happy in every sense of the word and nothing could come between them; moreover, as Roger had more than once explained to her, there were certain things—quite a number —which a judge mustn't do; and Roger, who had always been virtuous to the point of priggishness, was not going to fling over the traces now; fling over the traces! What a ridiculous thought; he wouldn't even do anything mildly silly; what more natural than that he should want to see Toni again? She was apparently a most attractive girl. Anyway it would be a good thing for her to see what she was up against. Up against! How ridiculous. She really must take hold of herself. And perhaps it would be better to see this Toni, not to have to wonder—to wonder—but the moment was up; if she let it go on any longer Roger would assume that she didn't want to go.

"What a lovely idea," she said. "It'll be fun to break out for once."

"You're wonderful, Anne," said Roger. "What a bit of luck you're such a bad driver."

So a day was fixed for the party and, when it arrived, Roger went to Court in a very happy frame of mind. What an incredibly lucky man he was. A High Court judge at the age of forty-six and a perfect wife whom he adored. And today he was going to see again the most attractive girl he had ever met—apart from Anne, of course.

Roger was always courteous on the Bench, but he was particularly friendly that day.

"He's going to be like Hathaway," said one counsel to another. He was referring to a judge who was so extremely good-natured that he almost apologized in his judgments to the party against whom he decided. He certainly said everything nice he could about someone who was going to lose his case. It was not long before the Bar realized this and counsel for the plaintiff, for example, would hear with much regret Hathaway J. say, early in his judgment:

387

"Now, the plaintiff is plainly an honest man, and I have no doubt whatever but that he came here to tell me what in his heart he believes to be the truth."

That preamble meant that in due course Hathaway J. was going to reject everything the plaintiff said in favour of what the defendant said. Or, if the case depended on a point of law, Mr X would know the game was up if the judgment contained sentences like this:

"Now, Mr X has argued with great skill and determination that the words used could not in law amount to a warranty. I am most grateful to Mr X for the great help he has given me and, if it is not impertinent of me to say so, his argument on the matter was as powerful and clear an argument as I have heard for a long time."

If Mr X appeared for the plaintiff, he would at once start to endorse his brief with "Judgment for the Defendant."

Even when addressing a hardened criminal before sentence, he would use words of apology. On one occasion, for example, he said:

"George Smith, you have, I am afraid, been convicted by the jury of what I cannot avoid describing as a most serious crime. Moreover, it is unfortunately the case that you already have several convictions for the same kind of crime, and the present offence was committed very shortly after your release from your last sentence. I am sure you will understand that it is my duty to protect the public from——" (he was going to say "people like you" but, realizing the offence this might give, he changed it just in time to) "from being knocked down and robbed. I am sure you will appreciate that. One must be able to walk down the road without fear of being attacked, in what some people might describe as a somewhat cowardly way, from behind with a bludgeon. In all the circumstances and bearing in mind everything that your learned counsel has said—if he will allow me to say so—so very ably on your behalf, the least sentence that I can pass on you for this offence is twelve years' imprisonment."

"Twelve years!" said the prisoner dumbly.

"I'm afraid so," said Hathaway J.

"But I only got half a crown off her."

"But wasn't that mere chance? I suspect that you would have taken more if she'd had more. And you did hit her over the head with a bludgeon, you know, didn't you? No, I'm afraid I can't alter my decision."

"I'll appeal."

"Of course you can appeal and——" but the next words stuck in Hathaway's throat. He had been about to say that no one would be more pleased than he if the Court of Criminal Appeal reduced the sentence, when he realized that the prisoner deserved every day of his sentence for a cruel and wicked crime. So Hathaway J. contented himself with substituting for words a friendly smile, as the prisoner was taken away.

"Cor," he said to one of the warders, "give me old Bouncing Bill any day."

He was referring to a judge who delivered long and fierce homilies to criminals on whom he was about to pass judgment, but followed up the words with an exceptionally light sentence.

"This," he had been heard to say, "is one of the worst cases I have known. I repeat, one of the worst cases I have ever known. It has no redeeming features whatever. You are a coward and a bully and you are extremely lucky that you are not charged with murder. That is no fault of yours. The man you struck might well have died. He owes his life to no mercy shown by you. There was no provocation of any kind and you haven't even the excuse that you were drunk. You have made things worse by pleading not guilty and putting up a perjured defence of an alibi, which the jury rightly rejected. If it were not for your previous good character, I should sentence you to imprisonment for life."

At this stage those who did not know Bouncing Bill expected a sentence of anything from five to fifteen years, though five would have seemed a bathos.

"As it is," the judge went on, "the least sentence I can pass upon you for a dastardly crime like this is twelve"—(the prisoner went white)—"months imprisonment." (The prisoner fainted.)

"Cor," repeated Mr Smith, after having been sentenced by Hathaway J., "you don't have to listen to the words, but you have to do the sentence. Twelve years for half a crown!"

"Lucky it wasn't five bob, chum," said the warder.

Roger rose from Court in the same good spirits in which he started the day. It seemed a long time between 4.30 p.m. when he left the Law Courts and 9.30 p.m., the time they were to meet at the Soft Shoe Club. But, by reading bits in the evening papers which he never normally read, and some of the advertisements, Roger helped to make it pass and he was delighted when he looked at the clock and saw that it was time to start.

"You'll make yourself sore," said Anne, after Roger's electric razor had seemed to her to be buzzing for hours.

"Is that all right?" asked Roger, presenting his smooth face for inspection.

"Beautiful, darling."

"But you didn't feel it," said Roger.

Anne took his face in both her hands.

389

"You could kiss anyone with that face," she said, as she let him go.

"I've no intention of kissing anyone," said Roger.

"Not even me?" asked Anne.

It was a gala night at the Club. According to the parties it had been a gala night when the accident took place. There was a special floor show and there seemed to be a legal flavour about a good deal of it. Even the first crooner, a girl with a lazy, husky voice, sang a song about Love Limited, a company which had only issued two shares, one for me and one for you. She dealt at some length with the memorandum and articles of association of the company. There was a line which ended in "Wore 'em" in order to rhyme with quorum, and a quorum consisted of two, that is to say, me and you, and the lady added that she didn't *care* if at a meeting the quorum filled the only *chair*.

Then came a troupe of girls dressed in barristers' wigs and bands and very little else, who sang a chorus the words of which, mercifully, Roger thought, could not be heard. And then another girl came and sang a song, the last line of each verse of which was: "But I'm no judge." Needless to say, she turned to the judges' table whenever she said it.

It was just after this turn that Toni came up to their table, looking dazzling. Roger introduced her to Anne and to Breeze, who, after she had gone, asked Roger:

"Was she at school with you, too?"

Roger explained, without going into detail, how he had met her.

"You seem to get around a bit," said Breeze. "That's the advantage of being married. You can do all sorts of things that I can't."

"I thought it was the other way round," said Roger.

During the evening counsel on each side explained to Breeze how, according to their respective views of the case, the accident had happened. While they were doing so, Roger danced with Toni. He had already danced twice with Anne.

"So you really are a judge," said Toni, as they danced. "I thought Plummer might have been pulling a fast one on me. I'll pull one on him one of these days."

"No, I am a judge, I'm afraid," said Roger.

"Don't apologize," said Toni. "Someone has to be. It does cramp your style a bit, though," she added.

"Well," said Roger, "I suppose it does. But that's just as well."

At that moment a photographer took a picture of them.

"There's one for my album," said Toni. "Will you sign it for me?"

"I'm afraid not," said Roger.

"Frightened I might forge your signature later?"

"Of course not."

"Well, what is it? You're almost as stern as you are on the Bench—worse, really. I came to Court the other day and saw you. When you seem to look at people in the Court—the public, I mean—are you really looking at them? I thought you looked straight at me."

"I did," said Roger.

"Were you pleased I came?"

"Yes, of course."

"Why?"

"Oh, I don't know. It's nice to have the look of the Court improved by someone like you coming in."

"Then any pretty girl would have done?"

"I didn't say so," said Roger.

Toni waited a moment before going on, and then:

"Isn't that the sort of answer some witnesses give?" she asked.

Roger laughed.

"Quite right, but how do you know?"

"One learns quite a lot in this job. But oughtn't you to have been thinking about the case, not about people in the Court?"

"I was," said Roger, "but that doesn't prevent one noticing people coming in and out."

"Tell me something else," said Toni. "Sending people to prison; what does it feel like?"

"Well, I haven't sent many, so far, but I can't say that I felt very much at the time. It's just one's job. Like an undertaker's. Of course, if we can avoid sending people to prison most of us do."

"Makes you enjoy your lunch or dinner better?"

"No, that isn't a fair way of putting it at all. We do try to do the right thing. I dare say we fail sometimes, or often if you like, but we do try. I certainly wouldn't give a man another chance because I should enjoy dancing with you more in the evening if I did."

"How do you enjoy it?"

"Very much."

"Will you come again?"

"I shouldn't think so," said Roger, "but that isn't because I haven't enjoyed it. It's just one of the disadvantages of my job."

"Then," said Toni, "if you weren't a judge would you come and dance with me more often?"

"Certainly, if I weren't married."

"But you are."

"I know. Very happily."

"Then being a judge has nothing to do with it."

"Well, it's both," said Roger. "A judge shouldn't be seen

391

regularly at night clubs and, apart from that, you're much too attractive for a married man to see a lot of."

"What a shame," said Toni. "I wore this dress for you."

"It's charming," said Roger. "If ever you think of changing your job, and you want an introduction to a doctor, Anne and I will be very pleased to help you."

"Anne and you?"

"Yes—Anne and I."

"And, if I became a doctor's receptionist, would I see more of you then?"

"Well, you'd see me if I came to the doctor."

"What complaint do you think you're most likely to suffer from? Then I'll know the sort of doctor to choose."

"I'm very well at the moment."

"What do judges mostly suffer from? Jaundice?"

When the dance was over, Toni went with Roger back to his table.

"You know," she announced to them all, "it didn't really feel any different from dancing with anyone else."

"If you'd been dancing with me," said Breeze, "it would have felt different all right."

"In what way?" asked Toni.

"Well," said Breeze, "I used to play forward at Rugger, and everyone says that I dance like it."

"I'd love to find out," said Toni.

Breeze got up.

"At your own risk, young woman," he said, "you may. But no damages, mind you, if I kick your shin and stand on your toes."

"I'm sure you dance beautifully," said Toni.

"Well," said Breeze, "something learned is something gained. Come along." And he and Toni took the floor. At that moment one of the counsel engaged in the case asked Anne to dance, and Roger was left to himself. He sought out Plummer.

"What's all this in aid of?" he asked him.

"Her Majesty's judges," said Plummer.

"You've something up your sleeve," said Roger. "What is it?"

"You're not in Court now," said Plummer. "I can refuse to answer here. But I'll tell you, if you like."

"Well?" said Roger.

"You won't pass it on, old boy, of course."

"Provided there's nothing illegal about it, I won't," said Roger. "But if there is, I may have to."

"No," said Plummer, "there's nothing illegal, as far as I can see. But I don't want everyone to do the same thing. So keep it to yourself."

"Well," said Roger, "what's it all about?"

"D'you know how much it costs to advertise for three minutes on commercial T.V.?"

"No," said Roger, "but I know it's a lot."

"And half a page in a daily paper, that's a pretty good price, too."

"Well?"

"The law is cheaper, my dear boy, that's all."

"What d'you mean?" said Roger. "Is this action just a fake to get advertisement?"

"No and yes," said Plummer. "Of course it's not a fake. That would mean perjury, contempt of Court, conspiracy and I don't know what. No conscientious objection to any of 'em, old boy, but very inconvenient to be found out. Oh dear no, the action's genuine enough. The poor girl sprained her ankle all right. So I suddenly had a bright idea. Make a case of it. There are always a few celebrities here. Call them as witnesses. If you can, get the judge to come and see the place in action. Keep the evidence as interesting as possible. I sent her to a good firm of solicitors. Of course I'll pay her costs, win or lose, and she'll get any damages she recovers. The whole thing won't cost me more than £600, and, properly managed, I'll get more than five times that in advertising. The papers tomorrow will have some quite nice photographs, and when the case comes on again there'll be more and lots of publicity. The girl may give an interview on T.V. and so forth and so on. Now, what's wrong with that?"

Roger thought for a moment.

"It might be said to be an abuse of the process of the Court," he said, after a pause.

"Why?" said Plummer. "The girl sprained her ankle, didn't she? She did it while doing her job. I may be responsible or I may not. Why shouldn't she sue me, and, if she does, why should I pay unless the Court says I'm liable? And why shouldn't a decent employer pay his employee's costs? It's quite true that that isn't the real object of the exercise. But then what about libel actions? They're brought to advertise sometimes, aren't they?"

"I see your point," said Roger. "You ought to have gone to the Bar instead of the Army."

"Don't," said Plummer. "I might have become like you, or old boneshaker. Look at him there. There's one person who's glad the action was brought. I'll have to give Toni a new pair of shoes—and a new back, too, I should think."

Breeze J. certainly appeared to be enjoying himself, though it looked as though he could have done with more room for manœuvre.

"And if we serve it up with just a little bit of embroidery here and there," continued Plummer, "well, there's no harm in that."

"Embroidery?" queried Roger.

"Well," said Plummer, "all I mean is that we shan't ask the witnesses to be as boring as possible. Pop in anything that'll look good in the papers. We're lucky in the judge, too. He's always good news value. We might have had you."

"Oh, no," said Roger. "I should have refused to try it, as I know you."

"Suppose we knew all the judges, what would happen then?"

"Well, if it were absolutely necessary, they'd appoint a Commissioner specially to try the case. You couldn't know every barrister who'd be competent to try it."

"Shouldn't want to, old boy," said Plummer. "But it's a good way of getting out of being tried by a particular judge. Ask him to tea."

"He might not come," said Roger.

"Oh, dear," said Plummer. "You don't change, do you? In words of one syllable, let me explain. There are ways and means of asking a particular judge to tea. And I don't necessarily mean tea. It might be supper or drinks or what have you. One can usually find someone who knows someone who knows someone who knows the chap you want. Then just arrange it."

He stopped for a moment.

"If I were up at the Old Bailey," he went on, "there are certainly one or two judges I'd ask to tea."

"You'd better start," said Roger. "It looks as though you'll find yourself there one day."

"Can I call you to give evidence of good character?" said Plummer.

Eventually the evening ended and there was unanimity among the judges about the success of the evening at the Soft Shoe Club.

"I could do with a few more cases like this," said Breeze to Roger as they left. "What's that young lady's name?"

Roger told him.

"It's really 'Dora Stokes,' " he added.

"You seem to know a lot about her. Known her long?"

"No," said Roger, "I just happened to meet her through Plummer."

"You happened to have been extremely lucky," said Breeze.

On the way home Anne asked Roger what he thought of Toni on closer acquaintance.

"She's too attractive," said Roger, "but somehow I don't think I shall be finding her a job as a doctor's receptionist. I think she's quite capable of looking after herself."

Meanwhile Plummer was questioning Toni.

394

"What have you arranged with your judge?" he asked.

"Well," said Toni, "I think I've handled the situation quite competently. But actually one can't rush the man."

"Well, keep at him," said Plummer. "I can't think why his virtue still annoys me so much. But it does. And you're the answer. Now, if we can get him to take you out one evening all by yourself, we'd be getting somewhere."

"A girl like me," said Toni, "always gets her judge."

CHAPTER TWELVE

THE CASE OF THE TWO USHERS

WHETHER it was meeting Toni again or mere coincidence, the Lord Chief Justice again appeared in Roger's dreams that night, and this time for much longer.

"I was telling you," the Chief said, "that I always use a pin myself. I remember once, I was sitting in the Court of Criminal Appeal when the same thing happened to all of us. It caused quite a sensation. There were five of us at the time. There'd been a disagreement on the first hearing, and I'd ordered a rehearing with a court of five. Well, Counsel for the appellant, a very young man who required encouragement (you know how they get it in our Court), opened the appeal by saying rather tentatively that he had a rather unusual application to make.

" 'Don't let that worry you, Mr Crape,' I said in my bluff, hearty manner. 'We like new suggestions in this Court. Helps to keep us on our toes, stops us becoming too hidebound. Let's hear your unusual application.' And the next thing we knew was that we each of us had a girl on his knee. Naturally, as I had encouraged the young man, I did not want to rebuff him too hastily. It wouldn't have been fair. So I contented myself with saying:

" 'Exactly what is this in aid of, Mr Crape?'

" 'Your Lordships,' said Mr Crape.

"I waited a moment or two but, as he remained silent, I said:

" 'Yes—Mr Crape, go on.'

" 'Go on yourself,' said the young lady on my knee.

" 'Silence,' said the usher.

"Now, that raised a nice point which, so far as I know, has never been decided in any of the books. It has been plainly laid down that an usher may not silence the judge, not even if he goes on far too long or makes a series of incredibly bad jokes. That was decided as long ago as The Queen against Willgo and Blanket. In that case an usher, whose son was at the Bar and was being prevented from arguing a case by the constant interruptions of the judge, pretended to see someone in the gallery creating a disturbance whenever the judge intervened. He did this so often that eventually the judge had to send for another usher to keep the first usher quiet. But unfortunately the new usher was an uncle by marriage of the young barrister, and he, too, began to see disturbances at the back of the gallery. So, according to the report:

"THE JUDGE: But, really, Mr Spink, that argument has been raised——

"1ST USHER: Silence in Court.

"THE JUDGE: Be quiet.

"2ND USHER: Silence.

"THE JUDGE: You, too.

"1ST USHER: Silence.

"THE JUDGE: This is really too bad.

"2ND USHER: Silence.

"Both ushers were indicted for contempt of Court, the matter being too serious to be dealt with summarily. But the difficulty was to obtain an usher at the Central Criminal Court. Although there was no actual trade union of ushers, they all stood together and refused to take part in the proceedings. Eventually the only solution was for a spare judge to act as usher. They chose a County Court judge whose presence could be most easily spared from the Bench, and the experiment was so successful that they made his deputy a judge and kept the judge on as usher, the duties of which he discharged admirably. Which makes one wonder whether it wouldn't be a good idea to repeat the process. There are one or two judges who would really make much better ushers and it would save the Court of Appeal a lot of trouble. But let me continue with The Queen against Willgo and Blanket. The judge there directed the jury as follows:

" 'Gentlemen of the Jury' (there were no ladies in those days—on the jury, I mean), 'some of you may think that I have gone on too long' (a murmured 'never' from the judge-usher), 'but justice could not be administered in this country if judges were prevented from going on for as long as they liked. You are not bound to listen. You have sworn to try the case according to the evidence, not the judge's version of it. Moreover, I'm sure you will understand that, if ushers were allowed to silence judges every time they made a mistake, or went on too long, or unnecessarily interrupted, the vocation of usher would be almost as important as that of the judge and the country could not bear the expense of the additional salary which would be demanded. Indeed, the usher would very soon be more important than the judge, and the ranks of the ushers would be filled by promotion from the House of Lords. Then they would start to acquire new titles. "One of Her Majesty's Ushers learned in the Law," for example, though Q.U. looks odd and is a little difficult to say. So you see, gentlemen of the jury, the thing won't work. And it is your duty to convict these two men Willgo and Blanket if you are satisfied that they really intended to silence the judge. Of course, if you believe that they thought there was some disturbance in the gallery each time they said "silence," you will acquit them. But, though it is entirely a matter for you, gentlemen of the jury, and you will completely disregard my opinion, if you think I have unwittingly expressed one, in preference for your own, the coincidences which are involved, if the story told on behalf of the prisoners is right, are surely beyond human belief. We have the record of what the learned judge was trying to say. Almost every other word was punctuated by one or other usher with a stern "silence." Was that word uttered because of some disturbance in the gallery, or because of a very intelligible (albeit lamentable) desire to help the young barrister whose relatives they were? And it may not be altogether without significance, gentlemen of the jury, to point out to you that, the case itself not involving any reference to murder or brutality of any kind, nor any matrimonial misconduct nor even casual immorality, the gallery was empty at the time. Of course, gentlemen of the jury, it is possible, not, you may think, likely, but possible, that each usher, looking up at the empty gallery, genuinely imagined that he saw or heard some disturbance there, but that each should make so many mistakes, and only when the judge was speaking and never when counsel was speaking, is surely beyond the bounds of even your credulity. But, I repeat, although no sane person could possibly believe the story told on behalf of the accused, it is for you to form your own opinion, unaffected by anything I have said on the matter. Will you kindly consider your verdict. It should not take you long.'

"The jury, without leaving the box, returned a verdict of not guilty. The cheering which broke out was immediately suppressed by the jury itself, which, unknown to the prosecution, consisted entirely of ushers. But, although the two accused in that case were acquitted, the summing up of the judge has stood the test of years and has never been unfavourably commented on. It can, therefore, be taken as settled law that an usher may not silence the judge himself. But unfortunately in that case there was no lady on the knee of the judge. Now, there can be no doubt that the decision that an usher may not silence the judge implicitly prevents him from silencing any appendage of the judge. Should his boots be squeaking, for example, or his deaf-aid make noises, it will be as much contempt for an usher to cry 'silence' as it would be to silence the Judge's sneeze, cough or laughter. But what about a living entity which, though nearly as close to the judge as his clothes, has a separate existence? A suggestion that at once occurred to me was that, if the noise from the lady was deliberately provoked by the judge—by a pinch, for example, or a tickle—the noise could be said in law to be the judge's, on the principle of *qui facit per aliam facit per se*. Personally, I should have been prepared to hold that it would be contempt by an usher to repress a lady's squeak, if it had been deliberately provoked by the judge. But what shall we say of what I may call an independent squeak by the lady, not judicially provoked? That is a far more difficult matter. On the whole, however, I would say, speaking for myself and not without hesitation, and recognizing that another judge might come to an entirely different conclusion—speaking for myself, I would have been prepared to say that there was sufficient identification of the judge with the lady, *if the Judge placed her on his knee himself*, to make a silencing of the lady equivalent to a silencing of the judge and to constitute contempt. But that, of course, didn't decide the question, because in that case we had not brought the ladies with us. They had, as it were, been wished on us by counsel. And that raised a further difficulty. I must confess—between you and me— and I'm sure you won't let it go any further—that the young lady on my knee was very personable, very personable indeed, and, apart from the fact that there was an audience, I'm bound to say that the situation was not without its intriguing side. And so the question arose—did it make any difference whether the judge liked the experience or not? For example, I could see my brother, Scales, who was a pronounced anti-feminist, writhing with fury, while my brother Twine seemed to be enjoying himself (if I may use the vernacular) no end. I may describe myself as being somewhere between the two. As I have said, I found the young lady attractive and the situation not without its reward but, on the other hand, I had to uphold the dignity of my position, and I did not find that altogether easy. Now, it was my young lady who squeaked. No one except me knew that it was my fault and that, by an almost unconscious act of mischief, I had—very gently, of course—used a pin. Obviously I couldn't admit it to the usher. Therefore, the squeak must be assumed in law not to have been judicially provoked. We solved the difficulty in that case by declaring the Court closed, and the rest of the proceedings were heard *in camera*. You will, of course, understand that that does not mean that pictures were taken."

CHAPTER THIRTEEN

THE CASE OF MR MOWLER

A FEW days later Roger was asked to sit in the Court of Criminal Appeal. That Court has sometimes been the subject matter of criticism both by the Bar and in Parliament. Roger himself had had experience of it in his earlier days at the Bar which made him determined that, if ever he became a judge and sat in that Court, he would not treat counsel as he himself had been treated on one occasion. But he had sense enough to realize that a good many judges must have said that at the Bar and failed to appreciate that, in due course, they gave a perfect performance themselves of the conduct they had previously deplored. As the late Mr Justice Salter once remarked:

"When I was at the Bar I'm bound to say that I found some judges extraordinarily wooden-headed. I had to say the same thing over and over again to them. And, now I'm on the Bench, I can't understand why counsel are always repeating themselves."

Roger soon found that one of the difficulties with which the Court of Criminal Appeal has to contend is the low standard of representation which often occurs, and another, the very large number of cases with which they have to deal, the vast majority of them being entirely without merit. Judges, being human, may after much experience of this, tend to expect cases to have no merit. Moreover, like the lady whom Roger had encountered at the cocktail party, they consider it just as much an injustice for a plainly guilty man to be acquitted as for a possibly innocent man to be convicted.

The Court normally consists of three judges and the procedure is for one of the three to go thoroughly into each case before the Court sits. One of the cases with which Roger had to deal arose in a rather curious way.

The Honourable Mrs X was a lady who liked beautiful clothes and gay parties, and betting on horses. She liked her husband, too, but he was not always able to keep her provided with the money which she needed to indulge her various tastes. Ladies of that kind often have accounts with one or more bookmakers and from time to time they have to ask the bookmaker to give them a little more time to pay losing bets. The bookmaker nearly always obliges, and usually gets paid in the end. He seldom has to report clients of this kind as defaulters. The point about these ladies is that there is seldom a moment when they will not find a windfall of £50 extraordinarily useful. If they have no pressing commitments, the purchase of a new hat and a pair of shoes makes a morning pass very pleasantly.

A search through the list of clients of any big bookmaker will inevitably disclose the names and addresses of some ladies in this category. Mr Mowler had at one time been employed by Messrs Vulgans, who were bookmakers in a very big way. The Hon. Mrs X was one of their clients and they had paid her a considerable sum of money over the years. She had paid them considerably more. One day the Hon. Mrs X received the following letter from Mr Mowler:

Dear Madam,

I was until recently employed by Messrs Vulgans where I had charge of your account. I have now left to set up business on my own account and hope that you may care to let me have some of your investments. I can assure you of the best possible odds and of every consideration in the conduct of your account.

At that stage the Hon. Mrs X nearly threw the letter away. It was one of a pattern she knew well, and she had no desire at all to open a new account with another bookmaker. But her eye could not help noting further down in the letter the figure of £50, which was in slightly larger type than the rest of the letter. So she read on:

Whether or not you open an account with me, there is, however, a matter I feel I must mention, as it has been rather on my conscience for some time. You may remember that you backed the winner of the Oaks last June. Your actual stake was £5. By some mischance, the responsibility for which was entirely mine, I worked out the amount due to you at Starting Price odds, whereas you had in fact placed your commission at Totalisator odds. The result was that you were paid an amount which was some £50 less than the amount to which you were entitled—the actual sum due to you being £103 3s. 0d. whereas you were paid only £52 10s. 0d. I did not notice the mistake until some time afterwards and I then found, to my dismay, that I had made the same mistake with a number of clients. One or two of them had complained and the matter had been adjusted, but the others, like you, had apparently not noticed the error. I need hardly say that my employers were extremely annoyed with me over the mistakes which were brought to light by the complaints, and I'm afraid that, when I discovered the other mistakes, I hadn't the courage to own up. But I did make a note of those clients who had been let down, being determined that, if ever I was able to do so, I should make it up to them. I am delighted to say that that time has now arrived. My business has prospered so well that I am now in a position to make full restitution to everyone. And I should make it plain, lest you think this is just a catchpenny, that there are no conditions attached to my offer at all, and that, if you do not choose to become my client, I shall pay you just the same. I left my late employers in rather a hurry and unfortunately the list of names and addresses got mislaid and I was unable to find it. I am, therefore, relying on my memory but I feel reasonably certain that in your case it is accurate. If, therefore, you will be good enough to sign the form below and confirm that the money is due to you I shall be pleased to send you my cheque (or cash if you prefer it) for £50 13s. od. If, thereafter, you choose to become a client of this firm I shall be pleased to open a credit account immediately with a daily limit of £50 (weekly £250) and your code name will be VENDOR.

With apologies for the mistake, and in the hope of receiving your forgiveness and future commissions,

Yours sincerely,

ARTHUR MOWLER.

Below was a form:

I confirm that last June I placed with Messrs Vulgans a winning bet of £5 on the Oaks Stakes at totalisator odds and that by mistake I was paid only at starting price odds. Please send me £50 13s. od. in accordance with your letter.

(Signed) Name:
Address:
Date:

PS.—I shall naturally be grateful if you will refrain from drawing the attention of Messrs Vulgans to this letter, and I am afraid that I cannot undertake to pay you if you do. I am sure you will understand this.

Mr Mowler prepared similar letters for despatch to a number of other ladies, who appeared to him to have the necessary qualifications. The amounts were slightly different in each case, and he did not send the other letters until he tried the effect on the Hon. Mrs X.

Now, when Mr Mowler wrote these letters he knew quite well that none of the ladies in question had made winning bets on the Oaks. They had either not backed anything at all or they had lost. He also knew that, though regular backers may easily forget whether they have or have not backed horses in all sorts of races, they will not forget having backed the winner of the Derby or the Oaks. They might forget the exact amount of their winnings or losses, but, if they have backed the winner, they will remember it very well, and will from time to time during that current racing year, and it may well be for a year or two thereafter, tell their friends that they backed it.

The average person, who backs horses, has two qualities, stupidity and greed. Stupidity, because he is going to lose in the end, greed because he wants something for nothing. There are, of course, some kind, unselfish and intelligent backers of horses, but there are not many, and, as Mr Mowler rightly guessed from a careful perusal of her account before he left Messrs Vulgans, the Hon. Mrs X was not one of them.

When she got the letter she realized at once that a mistake, as she thought, had been made. She knew quite well that she had not backed the winner of the Oaks. But within a quarter of an hour of the receipt of the letter she had not only convinced herself that she had backed the winner, but she actually remembered wondering why the amount she had received was so small and deciding that she must remember to query it. Within twenty minutes, she had filled in the form and within half an hour it was in the post on its way back to Mr Mowler.

The Hon. Mrs X worked it out that she ought to get a reply by the Friday. That would be very convenient for Sandown. But no reply came by the Friday or Saturday, and she was just beginning to wonder whether it was a hoax when Mr Mowler himself telephoned to know when she would be in alone. The Hon. Mrs X was delighted to make an appointment during the day, when her husband would be at the office. She had not mentioned the matter to him, as she knew him to be a man of the most ridiculous integrity, who would never have agreed to her signing the form. She knew that, though she might convince herself that she had won on the Oaks, she would never convince him. So she waited expectantly by herself for Mr Mowler, and at the appointed time two gentlemen arrived.

"Mr Mowler," she said, holding out her hand. "I'm afraid not, ma'am," said one of the two—not taking the proffered hand. "We've come to see you about him. May we come in? We're from the Criminal Investigation Department of Scotland Yard."

The Hon. Mrs X went white for a moment, but she soon recovered herself and asked the gentlemen in and invited them to sit down.

"Yes," she said. "What is it you want?"

"Is this your signature, ma'am?" said the first man, bringing out the form she had signed and torn off from the bottom of Mr Mowler's letter.

"Let me see," she said, and took the form in her hand.

The first man kept his hand on it at the same time. After a pause:

"Yes," she said. "I think it is."

"Think, ma'am?" said the first man. "Have you any doubt about it, ma'am? If you have, I must ask you to be kind enough to give me some specimens of——"

But Mrs X interrupted:

"Yes, it is my signature. What about it? Is it a fraud? Are you looking for Mr Mowler?"

"We've seen Mr Mowler, ma'am," was the reply, "but you'll forgive me not answering the first part of your question for the moment."

Mrs X began to have a horrible feeling in the pit of her stomach.

"Now, ma'am," the man went on, "you say in that form that you had a winning bet on the Oaks with Messrs Vulgans." He stopped.

"Yes," answered Mrs X—when she could stand the silence no longer.

"You knew that by making that statement you would receive £50 13s. od.?"

"I haven't had it."

"No, ma'am, you haven't, but you hoped that by making that statement you would get it?"

"Well, what if I did?" asked Mrs X. "That's what the letter suggested I should do, didn't it?"

"Yes, ma'am, it did—if the statement was true. Was it true, ma'am? Did you back the winner of the Oaks?"

Mrs X did not answer for a moment.

"How did you place your bets, ma'am? By telephone?"

"Yes—except on the course."

"Did you back the winner of the Oaks by telephone then, or on the course?"

There was no answer.

"Surely, ma'am, you remember if you went to the Oaks?"

Yes, thought Mrs X, it's hopeless to lie about that. "No—I didn't go to the Oaks."

"Then you backed the winner by telephone?"

"I suppose so."

"I should tell you, ma'am, that we've just come from Messrs Vulgans, where we have inspected your account."

Mrs X said nothing, until the silence made her say—"Well?"

"And we find, ma'am, that you did not back the winner of the Oaks."

"Then—then—I must have made a mistake," said Mrs X.

"A mistake which would have cost Mr Mowler £50 13s. od."

She hated the way he always put in the thirteen shillings; why not just say £50? There was something so like the steam-roller of the law when he said the thirteen shillings just as deliberately as the £50.

"I'm afraid I must now warn you, ma'am, that anything you now say will be taken down in writing and may be given in evidence at your trial."

"My trial?" exclaimed Mrs X with deep anxiety in her voice. "What for?"

"They call it fraud, ma'am, to make an untrue statement in order to get money, ma'am."

"But it was a mistake—I'd forgotten."

"That's what they all say, I'm afraid, ma'am. But don't be too upset, ma'am, the jury sometimes believe them."

"The jury? Am I going to be tried before a jury?"

"Well, you go before a magistrate first, ma'am, and then you get what's called committed for trial to the Sessions or Assizes, ma'am. But, of course, you'll be able to have solicitor and counsel to defend you, ma'am. And I shouldn't be too upset, ma'am. A lot of guilty people get off."

"But I'm not guilty," said Mrs X, not very convincingly.

"Then you've all the more chance, haven't you, ma'am? Now, I'm afraid we must be on our way, ma'am. We'll see ourselves out. Thank you so much, ma'am. So very sorry to have had to trouble you."

They left and the Hon. Mrs X burst into tears. If only I'd thrown the beastly thing in the wastepaper basket. The lives of a good many people like Mrs X contain a good many "if onlys". Most people have their fair share of them in childhood, but the weaker sort carry on with them for most of their lives. Whether it's a kiss, a bet, an angry word, a letter, that extra glass—or a little form asking for £50 13s. od.—if only I hadn't, if only, if only——

What was she to do? She would have to tell her husband. But it would be as dreadful for him as for her. It was at a time like this that people see things in their proper perspective. She did love her husband. He wasn't just a convenience. But what was she do to? She knew she was guilty. Those policemen and lawyers would tie her up in no time. She could hear her weak little protest of "mistake" getting fainter and fainter until it became an admission of guilt and a plea for mercy. But there would be no mercy for her—even if they didn't send her to prison, it would be in all the papers:

"Appearing to feel her position acutely, the Hon. Mrs X held her face in her hands as the judge pronounced sentence."

I wish I were dead, she thought—and said.

It was just at that stage that Mr Mowler telephoned. He seemed anxious:

"Mrs X," he said, "have two C.I.D. officers just been round to see you?"

"Yes," said Mrs X tearfully, "they have."

Mr Mowler noted that his timing was just about as perfect as he could have hoped.

"I'm terribly sorry," he went on. "It must have been very distressing for you."

Hope started to rise in Mrs X. She never considered why he should be telephoning. She only knew that he sounded kind.

"I must see what I can do," he said, and then stopped for a moment. "Look," he went on, "is anyone with you? Because this is rather confidential."

"No—there's no one."

"Well—I'm terribly sorry about this. I am really. I never meant them to act so soon—with you, that is. I must see what I can do." He paused, as though thinking. "Now, let me see," he went on. "The trouble is that, once you start these fellows off, there's no holding them. I'd better tell you what happened. You see, I've had so many fraudulent claims made on me that I just had to turn the whole thing over to my accountants and the police. Cost me a pretty penny, I can tell you. These accountants charge the earth. But I never meant them to get on to you so quickly. I'm sure that in your case it was just a mistake."

"Oh, it was—it was!" said Mrs X.

"I'd stake my oath on that," said Mr Mowler. "I know you aren't the sort of lady to do a chap down."

"No, of course I wouldn't. I am grateful to you for seeing it like that."

"The trouble is to stop these johnnies carrying on. They won't take any notice of me. The law's slow enough, but once you put your penny in the slot and the machine starts, it goes on and on—just like a steam-roller, and no one can stop it, not even the judges themselves." He stopped again for a moment. "But we've got to do something in your case. We can't have nice ladies like you dragged through the Courts. When's the prosecution starting—did he say?"

"He said something about a magistrate's court or Sessions or Assizes, but he didn't say when."

"Humph—look, I've an idea—but you'll have to back me up."

"Yes?"

"Suppose I tell them you did have the bet after all?"

"But they've been to Vulgans, and saw that I didn't."

"Yes, but I could say that I took it myself and didn't book it up—hoping it would lose or something like that. They're bound to believe me, as I've nothing to gain."

"Would you really say that for me?"

"Well—as I see it, it's the only way. It's a bit of a risk for me, of course, but——" he paused again. Then: "I tell you what—you help me and I'll help you."

405

"What can I do?"

"Well, I told you about my accountant's charges, they're too dreadful for words. It's almost better to pay the tax. Costs you more to get advice how to avoid it. But you don't want to hear my troubles. Now—look—I can see a way out for both of us. You give me a hand with my accountant's charges, and I'll tell the police I've made a mistake. Then you needn't feel it's all on one side."

"How much?" asked Mrs X cautiously.

"Well, it's up to you, isn't it? I don't expect anything. Certainly not more than, say, ten per cent of what I've got to pay. Yes— how about that?—you let me have fifty guineas."

"Fifty guineas!" said Mrs X.

"Look," said Mr Mowler, "I think we'd better wash the whole thing out. You obviously think I'm trying to sting you, when I was only trying to help. No—we'll just let things take their course. I can manage all right."

"No—please, Mr Mowler," said Mrs X, very anxiously indeed. "I'd like to help—really I would."

"That's very nice of you, I'm sure," said Mr Mowler. "But you only say that because you're excited. No, I don't really see why I should risk getting into trouble with the police just because you've got a nice voice on the telephone. No, Mrs X, I think we'll leave things as they are," and Mr Mowler rang off.

After a few frantic attempts to re-engage him, Mrs X started to walk sadly away from the telephone. A few seconds later it rang again.

"Is that Hammersmith 7835?" said Mr Mowler.

"No," said Mrs X. "This is Mrs X. Isn't that Mr Mowler?"

"Well," conceded Mr Mowler grudgingly, "it is. But we'd finished our conversation. I was trying to get another number. We must have been still connected. Good-bye again."

"Don't ring off, Mr Mowler, please," said Mrs X, desperately.

"Why not?" said Mr Mowler. "What is there to say?"

"I'd like to help," said Mrs X. "Really I would."

"How can I know it's true?" said Mr Mowler. "After all, you did sign the form, didn't you? I'm afraid I'm disappointed in you Mrs X, very disappointed. I was sorry to begin with, but now I think I was wrong to be."

"No, really—really—really, I promise," said Mrs X. "Where can I give you the money? Please let me, I do mean it."

"Well, look," said Mr Mowler. "You mustn't blame me if I don't altogether trust you, but you do sound genuine at the moment. Now, I tell you what. You go straight to your bank and get out— how much did you say you *wanted* to give me?"

"Seventy pounds," said Mrs X.

"All right," said Mr Mowler, "that's a fair deal. Take an envelope with you to the bank and get seventy one-pound notes. Put them in the envelope. Turn to the right when you come out of the bank and, when you've taken twelve paces, drop the envelope, I shall pick it up and give it to you, and you can give it to me back again. Now, where is the bank?"

Mrs X told him.

"All right—in half an hour."

"Wouldn't tomorrow do?" asked Mrs X.

"Of course," said Mr Mowler, "any time. Next week—next month—next year, but I thought you wanted me to get on to the police today."

"I'll come at once," said Mrs X.

Mrs X's bank manager required a little persuasion to let her have the £70 in view of the state of her account, but he did so in the end, and within a very few minutes the money was in the safe keeping of Mr Mowler.

"You'll let me know about the police, won't you?" she whispered as she gave him the envelope.

Mr Mowler winked.

"Trust me," he said.

Nothing happened for a few days, and then Mr Mowler telephoned.

"Look," he said, "I've run into a snag. It's my fault. Trying to be too clever."

"Oh—what is it?" said Mrs X anxiously.

"Well, I went to one of the C.I.D. officers you saw and said what you and I agreed, but he didn't seem to think much of it. Then, very stupidly—I can't think what made me do it—I slipped a couple of fivers into his hand. Now I'm probably going to be charged with bribery. I'm seeing my solicitor and counsel this afternoon."

"But what about my case?" asked Mrs X.

"Coming up in a fortnight, I think they said."

"But can't you stop it? They must believe you."

"There's no must about it," said Mr Mowler. "And I'm afraid I've too many worries of my own now to worry about yours. D'you know my solicitor wants £80 on account. I can't think about other people's affairs while I've got my own."

"Look, Mr Mowler, I'll let you have £80 if you'll go on helping me."

"All right," said Mr Mowler, "I'll try. Meet me at the bank as before. Half an hour."

"I shall have to borrow the money," said Mrs X.

"Come off it," said Mr Mowler. "A lady like you."

"It's quite true," said Mrs X. "The bank won't let me have any more."

"All right," said Mr Mowler. "The same drill. Where do we meet?"

"I'll have to think," said Mrs X. "Can I ring you?"

"I'll ring you in ten minutes," said Mr Mowler, "and I'm afraid I shan't be able to wait after that."

He rang off and Mrs X hurriedly considered whether she should pawn some jewellery or beg from a friend.

It was only after she had adopted both expedients several times, and paid Mr Mowler £350, that it suddenly dawned on her that Mr Mowler might be leading her up the garden. There had been no further signs from the police—if they were police—she had never seen their warrant cards—no mention in the papers of any bribery case, and, once the thought occurred to her, it developed as swiftly as her belief that she had backed the winner of the Oaks. She went straight to her husband with the necessary tears.

"You blithering idiot," he said consolingly, and went to the police.

The next time Mr Mowler picked up the little envelope and handed it to Mrs X, and received it back again, he had not gone more than a few paces when he felt a hand on his shoulder.

"We're police officers. What is in that envelope?"

"Hell," said Mr Mowler, "I might have known it was too good to be true. If only I'd stopped before."

They arrested Mr Mowler, but they could not find his two confederates who had pretended to be C.I.D. officers. Mr Mowler expressed complete ignorance of their existence.

"You've only Mrs X's word for their existence, and she isn't too particular what she says," he said.

"She didn't invent *them*," said the inspector, who was in charge of the matter.

"Well, perhaps it *was* two of your chaps," volunteered Mr Mowler hopefully. "After all, she had committed a crime—attempting to obtain money by false pretences. You ought to have been after her even if you weren't."

"Come on, Mowler, you're for it anyway," said the inspector. "If you'll help us land your pals we'll put in a good word for you when the matter of sentence arises."

"Not a very tactful approach, inspector," said Mr Mowler, "even if they were my pals—which they were not—d'you think I'd give them away to save my own skin? Not on your life. Haven't sunk as low as that."

"And how low d'you call blackmail?" asked the inspector.

"Blackmail!" said Mr Mowler—"you can't charge me with blackmail. Where are the threats?"

"If our lawyers can't make what you've been doing into blackmail I'll agree for once that the law's an ass," said the inspector.

"Well—how are they going to do it? I haven't made any threats. Nor did anyone else. Even my pals, as you call them, they only asked questions. Very sensible ones, too, if I may say so."

But when they brought Mr Mowler to trial, in addition to charges of fraud there were three charges of blackmail against him, namely that he and certain persons unknown demanded with menaces and with intent to steal £70, £80 and £200 from Mrs X contrary to Section 30 of the Larceny Act, 1916.

"Who thought that one out?" said Mr Mowler. "Anyway, I'd nothing to do with the other chaps. So you can't bring in what they said. It isn't evidence."

But the judge at the trial ruled otherwise and it was pointed out that, if Mr Mowler knew nothing about the supposed C.I.D. officers it was odd that, when he telephoned Mrs X, just after they had left, he had asked whether they had called on her. When Mr Mowler saw the significance of this, he promptly denied that he had been the first to mention the C.I.D. officers. He said that Mrs X had mentioned them first, and added:

"Why believe her rather than me? We know she's prepared to tell a lie—if it's made worth her while."

In fact Mr Mowler defended himself with great perseverance and ability. And he hadn't the embarrassment, which some barrister defending him might have had, of believing the client to be guilty. He knew he was, and was not in the least embarrassed in denying it.

"Members of the jury," he said in his final address, "you will, I hope, overlook any deficiencies in my address to you. I have not the training and experience of my learned friend."

"Don't call counsel your 'learned friend,'" said the judge.

"Now I've forgotten what I was going to say," said Mr Mowler —quick to try to obtain the sympathy of the lay jury for the layman. "You see, members of the jury, I've made a mistake already. It's very difficult for an ignorant inexperienced person, unlearned in the ways of the law, to compete with the expert. But I must do my best—or it will go hard with my client. Is that all right, my Lord?"

"You won't find that trying to be funny or impertinent will do you any good with the jury," said the judge. "You've chosen to defend yourself. You could have had counsel allotted to you, if you'd wanted."

"But think what counsel, my Lord. Would you care to be defended by one of them, my Lord?"

"Don't be insolent," said the judge, "and continue with your address."

Mr Mowler looked for sympathy to the jury.

"I'm sorry, my Lord," he said. "I'm sorry, members of the jury—I'm doing my best. It isn't easy—when you're fighting for your life—for that's what it is. You've never been in prison, members of the jury, but wouldn't you prefer death to fifteen years' imprisonment—and that's the penalty for the crimes I'm charged with."

"That's the *maximim* penalty," said the judge.

"There I am again," said Mr Mowler. "Alway putting my foot in it. But, if you convict me, members of the jury, d'you think his Lordship's attitude suggests anything less than the maximum? Did he interrupt counsel's speech like he interrupts me?"

"Counsel did not make false or unfair assertions, nor was he alternately insolent and impertinent. If he had been, he would be treated the same way."

"To resume, members of the jury," continued Mr Mowler, as it were, wearily, "I was saying, when I caused his Lordship displeasure for the I don't-know-how-manyeth-time—I was saying—now I've forgotten again."

"If you dealt with the facts, instead of keeping off them and making stupid or impertinent remarks, you might do better," said the judge.

"Perhaps you'd make my speech for me, my Lord," said Mr Mowler—who knew that, as soon as he came to deal with the facts, he was in difficulties, but who hoped that, by baiting the judge, he might get sufficient sympathy from the jury to procure his acquittal on the more serious charge.

"Does that mean you've finished?" asked the judge.

Mr Mowler made a mute appeal with his head and eyes to the jury, and then said:

"Is that what your Lordship really thinks?"

"How dare you speak to me like that!" said the judge. "When this case is over I may deal with you for contempt of Court."

"That makes it all the easier for me to address the jury," said Mr Mowler, "doesn't it? 'Never mind what they do. I'll put you inside in due course.' Why bother about a trial? I thought this was a court of justice. Have they taken the figure down from up top? If they haven't, they ought to."

"Now, look," said the judge, "I don't want to have to do this, but I must, if you force me. If you persist in being rude, instead of addressing the jury about the facts of the case, I shall postpone this case until next sessions and discharge this jury from giving a verdict."

"Will *you* be here, then?" asked Mr Mowler.

The judge had now to carry out his threat or, in effect, admit defeat and give Mr Mowler free rein.

"Very well," said the judge, "I'm extremely sorry, members of the jury, that your time has been wasted, but it is impossible for a trial to be properly conducted like this."

"Who's fault's that?" put in Mr Mowler.

"Take the prisoner below," said the judge, and went on to discharge the jury in his absence.

At the next sessions, Mr Mowler was not so fortunate, for the presiding judge was Mr Justice Hathaway. Mr Mowler had rightly judged that his only chance in all the circumstances was to get the judge at loggerheads with the jury, and the only way to do that was to goad him into being unfair or at any rate giving an appearance of unfairness. It is fairly easy for the prisoner in person to obtain sympathy, if he goes the right way about it. There is the poor little man, with the whole of the law ranged against him, and, if the judge is against him too, there is only the jury left. It may well be that Mr Mowler had overdone it, and had not succeeded in his efforts. But, however that may be, it was a hopeless task to do the same with Mr Justice Hathaway, who responded, to every attempt by by Mr Mowler to provoke him, with a kindly remark—which made the judge the object of sympathy rather than the prisoner. However, Mr Mowler was nothing if not persistent, and he had another card to play. He knew that sympathy is always against a black-mailer. He started his speech to the jury like this:

"Members of the jury," he said, "I'm not sure that I'm really in a condition to address you properly. I've been in prison an extra two months for nothing—unconvicted, unsentenced—just because the other judge didn't like me to address the jury in my own way. It isn't justice to interrupt a prisoner when he's addressing the jury, but he did it all the time, and when he found the jury were taking some notice and would probably have acquitted me, he sent me to the cells and told the jury to go home. Why should I be tried twice? Is it fair?"

Mr Justice Hathaway said nothing. So Mr Mowler turned directly to him:

"Is it fair, my Lord?"

Mr Justice Hathaway still said nothing.

"I'm speaking to you, my Lord," said Mr Mowler. "I know I'm only the prisoner, but haven't I the right to have the assistance of the Court?"

"Of course," said the judge. "I'm so sorry. I thought it was a rhetorical question."

"I don't understand long words, my Lord, I'm not educated like your Lordship and my learned friends of the Bar."

"That's all right," said the judge. "You're doing very well. I wish everyone were as well defended."

"I'm not doing well at all, and you know it," said Mr. Mowler.

"Mr Mowler," said the judge, "I'm sure we understand one another. I think yours is one of the most brilliant efforts I have ever seen. You ought to have gone to the Bar."

Mr Mowler looked wearily at the jury.

"I don't know which is worse," he said, "threats or sarcasm."

"I assure you there was no sarcasm intended," said the judge. "If I gave you a different impression, I apologize. Yours is one of the most brilliant performances I have seen. If you deal with the facts as well as you have dealt with what I may call preliminary matters, you should make a profound impression on the jury, and, I may say, on me."

Mr Mowler realized that he was fighting a losing battle. No one could get angry with Mr Justice Hathaway, and to be rude to him was like hitting a child. As a last resort, but without much hope, he tried slightly different tactics.

"His Lordship," he said, "is as kind and good a judge as I could wish to appear before, but, members of the jury, you mustn't be deceived by the gentle glance and the kindly word. It's his Lordship's duty to get me convicted if he possibly can, and his method is—until I'm convicted—to use the velvet glove. You'd think butter wouldn't melt in his mouth. But just wait till you've found me guilty. Then you'll see. He'll send me down for the count, I tell you—imprisonment for life, that's what I'm up against, and don't you forget it. Now you may think, members of the jury, that though I don't pretend that what I've done was right, Mrs X got no more than she deserved. She, with all her money—all her education—all her chances—was quite prepared to tell a lie to get money out of someone whom she wouldn't smile at across the street. Oh—I know all about the Welfare State and no class distinctions, but you've seen the lady in the witness box—you know the type. At least I hope you do. Well—did she get more than she deserved? I didn't go for some poor little defenceless country girl. I shouldn't expect any sympathy if I had. I went for someone who'd no business to be tempted. But she fell for it, like a kitten after a reel of cotton. If anyone ought to be in the dock, it's she. She tried to obtain money by false pretences all right. That's one thing there's no doubt about. Isn't such a person what you might call fair game? I'm no Robin Hood. I don't pretend I was going to give the money to hospitals, and all that. But if ever a person ought to have been shown up for what she was, it's Mrs X. What right has she to hold her head high in society, when she told a lie to get £50? But *she's* allowed to be called Mrs X. Is that fair? Why should I get all the stick? Well now, you may say, 'that's all very well, what can we do about it? We don't like Mrs X, but the prisoner did have the money off her, and he did tell her a lot of taradiddles to get it.' All right, members of the jury, I did, and I'm not saying you couldn't convict me of obtaining by false pretences. Mind you, I'd prefer you not to, but I'm not saying you can't. But it's this other charge I'm really fighting. And the only bit of evidence against me is that I'm supposed to have spoken about the C.I.D. to her first. Well, I say I didn't. And why shouldn't you believe me rather than her? And, if there's a doubt in your mind, I'm entitled to it. So that's what I ask you to do. Wash out the blackmail charge, and, if you convict me on the other, you can always recommend me to mercy, if you think fit. And I suggest that a couple of looks at Mrs X should make you want to think fit. That's all, members of the jury, thank you for being so patient—and your Lordship."

But in spite of his struggles, the jury convicted Mr Mowler on all counts, and Mr Justice Hathaway sentenced him apologetically to a total of twelve years' imprisonment.

It was from that sentence that he appealed to the Court of Criminal Appeal, and it fell to Roger, in the first instance, to consider the appeal. After he had read the transcript of the evidence at the trial, he went to Mr Justice Breeze, who was to be one of the other judges.

"I'm only a new boy," said Roger, "but it seems rather a lot to me. He's only been to prison once before."

"Blackmail is always expensive," said Breeze.

"I realize that, of course," said Roger, "and it's a bad case. Similar letters to several other ladies were found at his address, and no doubt they'd have received his attention in due course. But the maximum for each offence was only five years."

"Apart from that are there any redeeming features?"

"Only his age—thirty-eight—if that can be called a redeeming feature, and the fact that he's only been to prison once before."

"For false pretences, I suppose?"

"Yes, he got six months."

"Humph. He's gone up in the weights. Six months to twelve years. All the same Hathaway's a pretty good handicapper."

"I don't understand the language," said Roger, "but I suppose the metaphor is something to do with horses."

"You're coming on, Roger. Tell me, have you ever had any vices? Your wife must find you a very dull fellow."

"I break out and go to the cinema occasionally," said Roger.

"'U' certificate, I suppose?"

"Of course, unless I have an adult with me. But what d'you think of this? Mrs X certainly deserved what she got, I suppose, but then they're the only people that can be blackmailed."

"How true. Chaps like you are unassailable, unless, of course, you're framed in some way—snapped with a girl on your knee— or something."

"What did you say!" said Roger.

"Unless you're framed, I said. You haven't been, I suppose? But no one would want to. It's extraordinary that no criminals or litigants, however bad or mad, try to get their own back on the judges they've appeared before."

"It's a pretty good compliment, I suppose, to our impartiality."

"You won't let it make you pompous, I hope," said Breeze. "That's a failing some of us have suffered from."

"Not you, anyway."

"Thank you. No, I have some other failings. Breeze by name and breeze by nature, they say. Well, it's true, I suppose. And I must say I don't give a fig for what people say. You'd be horrified at the things I do. The other day I went to Brighton races. Did you see the picture in the *Daily Journal*? I was in the paddock. 'Is he as good a judge of horseflesh as he is of people?' Well, I could have given them the answer on that occasion. No, decidedly no. I backed three losers."

"Do you often go racing?" asked Roger.

"Once or twice a year. Why not? Helps me to understand my fellow men better. Now, when I get a case about trainers and jockeys, I know what they're talking about. You'd have to start from scratch."

"Well—I have been on a race-course." said Roger.

"Dear, dear," said Breeze. "Disguised, I suppose?"

"Oh, I didn't mean since I was appointed," said Roger.

"Oh, well," said Breeze, "so long as you're happy, it doesn't matter. Have you always been so solemn, or are you weighed-down by the responsibilities of your appointment?"

"No," said Roger, "it's not that. I've always been like this really. Fortunately my wife doesn't seem to mind."

Breeze thought for a moment.

"Women are wonderful," he said. "How have I managed to do without one?"

"There's still time," said Roger. "But what about Mrs X?"

"No, I don't think I should care for her."

"But what about the twelve years?" persisted Roger. "Is it all right, d'you think?"

"Sorry, I was thinking about something else. Twelve years is a lot. I'm not sure. I see he pleaded not guilty, and fought all the way. Has he helped the police at all?"

"No. Won't give the names of his friends."

"Well, I must say that's the only good thing you've said about him so far. Blackmailers usually haven't many redeeming features, but that's certainly one. You can be quite sure they've asked him often enough."

"Of course," said Roger, "it was his case that they were nothing to do with him. So he couldn't very well give their names and addresses."

"Yes, I see. Well, from what you tell me it's a really bad case. Carefully thought out. The victim threatened by bogus policemen, squeezed and squeezed unmercifully. And other victims all ready to be dealt with. I'll think about it."

In due course the application for leave to appeal came on for hearing and Mr Mowler was allowed to appear before the Court and speak on his own behalf. He found the three judges in scarlet more awe-inspiring than he had expected. While in prison he had spoken airily of the way he was going to speak to them, if they did not look like reducing his sentence.

"They can't do any more to you," he said to an old hand. "Might as well get something for your money."

"They can add a bit."

"What, to twelve years?"

"My boy," said the old hand, "when you've been in this business as long as I have, you'll know that there's nothing they can't do. You take my advice and speak oily. It pays."

"What, with them?"

"I once had three years knocked off. But I wouldn't have, if I'd gone about it your way. Now, you'd have attacked the judge I was appealing from. A perishing so-and-so you'd have called him. And so he was. I called him that too, and some more, but to myself. When I was up before them redskins I said I wouldn't have wanted to be tried by a better or finer judge but I did feel that though I deserved the sentence, if they took a bit off, it'd help me to go straight when I came out, really it would. I was getting on in years and ten years was an awful long time at my age. So they made it seven. So don't forget, when you're up there. Make it oily."

And, in the circumstances, Mr Mowler found it easier to take the advice he had been given than he would have found it to behave as he had behaved at his trial.

"My Lords," he said towards the end of his address, "would it make any difference if I gave the names of the men who were in with me?"

Breeze whispered to Roger.

"I was going to suggest knocking something off until he said that. I told you blackmailers had no redeeming qualities."

He looked at Mr Mowler.

"It is always open to you to help the police if you choose to do so and the Home Secretary can, if he wishes, consider whether such help as you may give justifies remission of sentence. As far as this Court is concerned, we do not make bargains with appellants. If you'd wanted to help the police you could have done so long ago. Is there anything else you want to say?"

"Twelve years is a terrible long time," said Mr Mowler.

"Blackmail," replied the judge, "is nearly always a very serious crime but sometimes the blackmailer has drifted or been tempted into blackmail. In your case, it was a carefully and ingeniously prepared plot. You deliberately set out to procure someone to commit a crime in order that you might batten on her and, if you had not been caught, it is plain that the other persons whose names and addresses were found at your home would have received the letters you had already prepared. Did you ever consider the effect on Mrs X or her family of your extortion? Some people are driven to suicide by people like you."

"She shouldn't have signed the form, my Lord, then nothing would have happened to her."

"You shouldn't have sent it to her," said Roger. "Then nothing would have happened to you."

And the appeal was dismissed.

"Make it oily!" said Mr Mowler, as they took him down to the cells. "I wish I could have made it boiling oily."

CHAPTER FOURTEEN

ORANGES

I'M GLAD you didn't reduce that sentence," said Anne.

"You sound as though you might have been caught by him," said Roger.

"Well, out of consideration for you, I shouldn't have been. But there are an awful lot of silly women around, who'd sign anything almost for £50."

"But isn't that the only point in his favour?" said Roger. "He'd only catch worthless people."

"I wouldn't say worthless," said Anne. "There are a lot of otherwise quite decent people who smuggle things through the customs."

"I'm glad you said 'otherwise,' " said Roger. "I dislike that sort of thing."

"What are you doing tomorrow?"

"I'm sitting in a Divisional Court with old Breeze."

"I see he gave that girl £150."

"Yes," said Roger. "Plummer did pretty well out of that."

"Did you expect him to give more?"

"No, it wasn't that," said Roger, "but his club got terrific advertisement out of it. Pretty well worth it."

"He hasn't been badgering you recently. D'you think he's been trying someone else?"

"I hope so," said Roger. "I've had my fair share. Oh, by the way," he added, "I won't be in to dinner tomorrow. Harrison is up for the night and wants me to dine with him."

"Harrison? I thought for the moment that you were going to say that you were dining with Toni."

Roger blushed.

"Why on earth should you think that?" he said.

"No idea," said Anne. "Silly of me."

But she would have felt, at the least, a little worried if she had heard Toni tell Plummer that morning that she was dining with her judge that night.

Next day, when Roger and Breeze entered their Court, Plummer was sitting three rows behind counsel. He bowed slightly as they sat down.

"I know that face," whispered Breeze to Roger.

"Don't take any notice of him," said Roger, and explained Plummer's little habits in Court.

The case before them arose out of an arbitration.

"There used to be a man who stood outside the Law Courts," said Breeze, shortly after the case had begun, "who carried a board with 'arbitrate, don't litigate,' on it. He was a friend to the lawyers, if ever there was one. This case is a good example. It took seven days before the arbitrator. Counsel were employed on both sides. It came to the High Court, up to the Court of Appeal, back to the arbitrator for another three days. And now here we have it again. If it had been an ordinary case brought in the ordinary way it wouldn't have cost half the money. Litigation's bad enough, but arbitration's ten times worse."

'Except, perhaps, my Lord," put in counsel, "for real trade arbitrations."

"You mean," said Breeze, "when an expert just looks at the goods and says these are up to sample or they're not. Yes, I agree, that's better than all of us put together. But it's the only kind of arbitration that is. Well, we'd better get on, I suppose."

Counsel continued his speech. Every now and then Roger and Breeze interrupted with a comment or a question. To which counsel would often reply:

"With respect, no, my Lord," or "with respect, my Lord, I would say etc., etc."

Eventually Breeze said:

"By 'with respect,' Mr Cling, you mean, don't you, 'surely you're not serious when you say that?' "

" 'With respect' is shorter, my Lord," said counsel.

"A good point," said Breeze. "Pity you haven't a few more like that. As far as I can see, your client, who contracted to supply oranges, supplied orange juice. Why isn't he liable in damages?"

"The terms of the contract, my Lord."

"The contract said oranges."

"It said a good deal more than that, my Lord—with respect."

Breeze laughed.

"I wish your client had your merits, Mr Cling," he said. He turned to Roger and whispered:

"I like this chap. D'you know him?"

"A bit," said Roger. "He's good, don't you think?"

"He won't let me blow him out of Court, if that's what you mean. Yes, Mr Cling, you were explaining how the law of this country permits a man who contracts to deliver oranges to deliver orange juice instead, and get away with it."

"It wasn't all orange juice, my Lord. There were some oranges."

"Only about a tenth of the total quantity. If you came back from the greengrocer with one orange out of ten, what d'you think your wife would say to you if you explained that the other nine had leaked through the bag?"

"Fortunately, my Lord," said Mr Cling, "or unfortunately, I am in your Lordship's happy position, and it couldn't happen to me."

"Well, if you had a wife, what d'you suppose she'd say? She'd send you back for the other nine, wouldn't she?"

"But in that case, my Lord, there would have been no special contract between me and the greengrocer."

"Special contract!" said Breeze. "They bought oranges. You might just as well say that a contract to deliver butter can be fulfilled by the delivery of soap."

"With respect, no, my Lord. If your Lordship said milk and cheese, that would be a closer analogy."

"All right, Mr Cling, I'll accept your suggestion. A contract to supply milk. The milk has turned to cheese on delivery. Cannot the buyer complain?"

"No doubt he will complain, my Lord, but whether successfully or not will depend upon the terms of the contract."

"Well, if I buy milk, I expect milk, not cheese, and if I buy oranges I expect oranges, not orange juice." He leaned towards Roger.

"Wake up," he said. "What d'you think? Don't leave it all to me."

"I think it depends on the terms of the contract," said Roger.

"You ruddy lawyers, you're all the same," whispered Breeze.

"My brother seems to think cheese will do," said Breeze. "We'd better hear what your opponent has to say."

Meanwhile Plummer, finding that his approbation or disapprobation was having no observable effect, wrote a note on a piece of paper and asked the usher to give it to Roger.

"Toni will be coming into Court any moment," it read.

Roger screwed up the piece of paper, put it in the pocket of his gown and tried not to look in Plummer's direction. Half an hour later Breeze was just saying to Mr Cling's opponent:

"Apparently your client was unwise enough—unwise enough——" he stopped.

He had suddenly noticed Toni come into Court.

"Unwise enough," he went on, "to make a contract under which he had to take the oranges even if they arrived as orange juice."

"Contracts must be read reasonably, my Lord."

"Would you repeat that, please," said Breeze.

Counsel obliged.

"Are you saying that my brother Thursby is reading it unreasonably?"

"With respect, yes, my Lord."

Breeze again leaned towards Roger.

"Well, stand up for yourself," he said.

"The contract," said Roger, "makes express provision for oranges going bad. It makes a special allowance. That your clients have had."

"But no one expected the consignment to go as bad as this one."

"I dare say," said Roger, "but as they have provided for the contingency of oranges going bad, I don't see how your clients can get any more relief than is expressly provided for by the contract. *Expressum facit cessare tacitum.*"

"Do talk English," whispered Breeze.

"Where express words are used there is no room for implication," said Roger.

Breeze laughed.

"I didn't mean it," he whispered, "but you did it very nicely. Well, I think that will do for the day," he added aloud, and both judges rose and left the Court.

"Well, I suppose you're right about the oranges," he said to Roger, as they walked along the judges' corridor together. "But, by Jove, she's a pretty girl."

CHAPTER FIFTEEN

THE TRUTH

ALTHOUGH Anne would have trusted Roger completely even if he had not been a judge, she would have been horrified to hear Toni confide to Plummer on the morning after Roger's dinner with Harrison that she was doing very nicely with her judge.

"Did he give you a good dinner?" asked Plummer.

"Lovely," said Toni, "and he took me somewhere where no one would be likely to recognize us."

"Wise man," said Plummer. "But you know, I don't want things carried too far."

"But I'm enjoying myself," protested Toni. "I like my judge. He's so human."

"That's what I meant," said Plummer. "I'd like to wipe some of the superiority off his face, but I don't want any real trouble. And his wife is charming."

"Yes," said Toni, "she is nice. But it's all very well for you to blow hot and cold. One doesn't get a judge on one's hands every day."

"Well," said Plummer, "if he comes a cropper, it'll be his own fault, I suppose. He shouldn't have taken on the job unless he was prepared to abide by the rules."

Meanwhile Roger was concerned with a very different problem. It was in Court. When he was at the Bar he had been used to many kinds of witnesses, but he knew that there is in fact no limit to their variety. As a judge he was prepared for any kind, but on this occasion, a man, who was called to give evidence, gave him rather more trouble than usual and made him think more than he had done before about the whole question of witnesses and giving evidence.

There was nothing particularly interesting about the case itself. It was a claim for damages for breach of contract. The contract had been made by word of mouth only and there was a dispute between the parties as to what exactly was said when it was made. To support the defendant's version of the interview, his counsel, Mr Steaming, called a man named Jones. Mr Jones went into the witness box.

"What is your full name?" asked the associate.

"Andrew Penitent Jones."

"Take the book in your right hand and repeat after me," said the associate. "I swear by Almighty God."

Without touching the Bible Mr Jones said: "I will do my best to tell the truth."

"No," said the associate, "you must repeat the words I say, and kindly take the Bible in your right hand."

Roger tapped his desk with a pencil and the associate turned away from the witness to speak to the judge.

"Perhaps he wants to affirm," whispered Roger.

"Very good, my Lord," said the associate, and then spoke to the witness again.

"If you have no religious belief, you may affirm instead of taking the oath," he said.

"I have a deep religious belief," said Mr. Jones. "I am a practising member of the Church of England."

"Very well then, sir," said the associate, "will you kindly take the Bible in your right hand and repeat the words of the oath after me."

"I'm afraid not," said Mr Jones, "but I will do my best to tell the truth."

"Mr Jones," intervened Roger, 'I'm afraid you must take the oath. What is your objection to doing so?"

"Well, my Lord, first of all the Bible tells us not to swear by anything. Secondly, it's much too difficult. If I did take an oath to tell the truth, I couldn't possibly break it."

"No one wants you to," said Roger.

"I dare say they don't, my Lord," said Mr Jones, "but what is the truth? I may think something to be the truth but I may be wrong."

"Obviously," said Roger, "you can only do your best. I assure you that you'll come to no harm if you do your honest best to tell the truth."

"But, my Lord," said Mr Jones, "your Lordship is no doubt very important, but you are not God. I may not come to any harm here, but can you speak for elsewhere?"

"Mr Jones," said Roger, "I appreciate your scruples and, if you give your evidence as carefully as you have considered the words of the oath, you will no doubt be an excellent witness, but in a civilized country one has to have forms and they must be complied with. If there were a different form of oath for every person the administration of justice would be impossible."

"I don't see why, my Lord. You could provide penalties for telling deliberate lies. Then it wouldn't matter what words the witness said."

"I'm sorry," said Roger, "but, while I sympathize with your point of view, I can't take up much more time arguing with you. I'm afraid I must ask you to take the oath."

"If I agree to swear, my Lord, may I add the words: 'to the best of my ability'?"

"I'm afraid not," said Roger.

"But how can I possibly swear by God that what I am about to say is the truth, the whole truth and nothing but the truth, when I know very well I may be mistaken?"

"Nothing in the world is certain, Mr Jones," said Roger. "You can only swear what you believe to be the truth. That is what the oath means."

"That isn't what it says, my Lord," said Mr Jones. "May I put that in—and say: 'I'll swear to tell what I believe to be the truth'?"

"No," said Roger, "you must take the oath or affirm in the ordinary form."

"Why should I, my Lord?" protested Mr Jones. "It's against my conscience to do so. It's really against my conscience to swear at all, but, if I can arrange things with my conscience on that matter, I should have thought you could have arranged things on the other. It's not much I'm asking, my Lord. I only want to say what you say the oath means."

"I'm sorry," said Roger. "You may affirm if you wish. But this is a Court of Law and in a Court of Law the law's forms must be observed."

"But if you bring the Almighty into a Court of Law, my Lord, hasn't He any say in the matter? All the judges in the world can't speak for Him."

"Now, Mr Jones," said Roger. "I've listened to you most patiently, but I must now ask you to take the oath."

"In it's ordinary form, my Lord?"

"Yes."

"May I add something under my breath?"

"No."

"May I make a mental reservation?"

"Yes, you may do that."

"Well, really, my Lord," said Mr Jones, "it seems that the law isn't interested in the religious side of it at all, although it brings it in to frighten people. Apparently you wouldn't mind if I took the oath—like children tell stories—with my fingers crossed, so long as I say the words."

"I'm afraid I can't allow you any further latitude," said Roger. "Will you kindly take the oath or affirm."

"And if I refuse?"

"Then I'm afraid I shall have to commit you to prison."

"For how long?"

"Until you have purged your contempt."

"How could I do that, my Lord, without taking the oath or affirming?"

"I'm not sure that you could."

"Then I might be in prison for life just because I wanted to add the only words to the oath which would make it an honest thing for me to say."

"We'll deal with that problem if it arises," said Roger. "I hope it won't." He looked at the clock. "Mr Steaming," he said, after a moment's thought. "I shall rise now for the luncheon adjournment, and I can only hope that during the interval the witness will reconsider the position."

During the adjournment Roger decided to consult one of the older judges. He realized that Mr Jones might very well insist on being sent to prison and, if possible, he wanted to avoid that situation, which could do no good to anyone and indeed might delay and prejudice the fair trial of the action. The only judge available was the oldest Queen's Bench judge, Mr Justice Pantin. He had been a judge for over thirty years at the time Roger consulted him and he was in his eighty-eighth year.

From time to time journalists had suggested that he should retire but he took no notice of their suggestions, and it was fairly plain that, unless Parliament imposed a retiring age for High Court judges, he would go on until he died. Fortunately he was in full possession of his faculties and tried his cases well. He had, however, in his later years tended to become verbose, and, though he still did justice, he was inclined to take a long time about it. In ordinary conversation he was rather worse and would sometimes take a prodigious time to come to the point. On the way to the point he would find so many interesting side-roads to go down that, unless reminded by someone who knew him well, he would sometimes forget what he was leading up to.

"Ah," he would say, "that reminds me of a case I once heard before Chief Justice Manners. It was a most interesting affair—unique, I should say. He was a great judge, you know. I'm not saying that his appointment was popular. It wasn't. Too much politics about it. But he proved them wrong and pretty quickly too. I was at the Bar with him, you know, and a nicer opponent you couldn't have. But a fighter, if ever there was one. You had to be awake the whole time. He rather reminded me of Coles—as an advocate, I mean. He had a deeper voice, though. But a most imposing presence. When he defied a jury to convict his client, they must really have felt they'd get into serious trouble if they did. Now, where was I?" He would then be gently reminded that he was about to tell his listener of a case which Manners C.J. had tried, and off he would start again, but it was quite an event if the case was reached within a quarter of an hour.

In spite of this reputation, Roger felt that his great experience

423

in dealing with witnesses might be of help, and he took the risk—a considerable one—of missing his lunch altogether.

"Well, my boy, what can I do for you?" he said, as Roger came into his room. Roger told him his problem. "Ah, my boy," said the old judge, "a good many of us don't think enough about witnesses. I didn't at first. You've never been in the witness box, I suppose?"

Roger confessed that he had not.

"Well, of course it wouldn't be much of an ordeal for us, though, if some of us talked as much in the box as we do on the Bench, we certainly ought to get into trouble. Well, I have given evidence. A good many years ago. I can't say that I was nervous, but then I'd been at the Bar for years then. I knew the form. I wasn't in a strange place. How many of us think of the fluttering little heart in the breast of some witnesses? He looks all right, he stands up all right, his colour's all right. So we assume he is all right. Have you ever considered the self-control that might be necessary to produce that effect?"

"I can't say that I have," said Roger.

"Well, you should, my boy. The case may be vital to the man. Just think of the anxiety lest he should say something wrong. Think of the possibility of his mind going a complete blank. Of course we all know the type that wants a chair and a glass of water. Then we're all of us, I think, pretty humane, whether the witness is putting on an act or not. But it's when there's no chair or glass of water asked for that we don't always realize the strain the witness may be undergoing. It must be a very alarming experience to give evidence in Court for the first time, even if you've nothing to gain or lose by the case. But I was telling you about when I gave evidence. It was about a compromise. I was called to prove that there had been a compromise or was it the other way about? But, wait a moment, what was it you were asking me?"

Roger repeated his problem.

"I see," said Mr Justice Pantin. "I'm sorry. I'm afraid I do tend to run on. But, oddly enough, not, I think, in my judgments. I'm rather like an actor with St Vitus' dance who can control it when he's on the stage but never when he's off. Which reminds me. Did you ever see—now, there I go. I'll try and control it this time. Yes, I see your difficulty. There's a lot to be said for altering the form of oath. But there are still people who are affected by the solemnity of the words. The invocation of the Almighty still influences some people. Not just the fear of a prosecution for perjury, but the fact that they are swearing by God. But for a lot of people it would be just as good to say 'I promise to tell the truth.' They'd tell as much truth after that—or as little—as they would after the present form. But that doesn't help you with your case. Of course

424

a lot of us would just pack him off to Brixton until he became a little less refined in his ideas. But I agree with you—it's worth taking a lot of trouble to avoid that. Let me think." The old man thought for about a minute. "If I were you," he said, "I'd point out again that the words 'the truth, the whole truth,' etc., can only mean 'what I believe to be the truth.' Tell him he's quite right in saying that none of us know the truth for absolute certainty about anything and that you take the responsibility of telling him as a judge that the words he says are not to be interpreted literally."

"And suppose he falls back on his objection to swearing at all?"

"Let your yea be yea and your nay, nay," said Mr Justice Pantin. "Yes—well, if he says that, I should let him affirm."

"I've told him he may do that."

"Well, tell him again," said Mr. Justice Pantin. "That deals with one of his troubles. But if he won't swear and he won't affirm, well, in the end you'll have to send him off to Brixton. But with your persuasive manner I'm sure you'll win."

Roger thanked his adviser and, after a further chat about other matters, he went back to Court. Mr Jones came into the witness box. Roger began:

"Now, Mr Jones, I've been thinking over what you've said to me——"

"My Lord," began counsel for the defendant. Mr Steaming was a rather irritating counsel. He was inclined to interrupt the judge and hardly ever for any good reason. During the course of the case Roger had suffered him fairly patiently, but he had had at last to ask him to refrain from interrupting.

"Mr Steaming," said Roger, "it must be obvious to you that this witness is causing considerable difficulty. I shall be obliged if you will wait until I have finished."

"But, my Lord, I thought——" went on Mr Steaming.

"Really," said Roger. "This is too bad. I am, I hope, being as patient as possible, but it's difficult enough to make this witness understand the right point of view without interruption. It is impossible with."

"I only wanted to say, my Lord——" said Mr Steaming.

"I dare say you did, Mr Steaming," said Roger, now thoroughly irritated, "but why can't it wait?"

"Because, my Lord," said Mr Steaming, "I only wanted to say I'd called Mr Jones by accident. I don't really want him as a witness at all."

CHAPTER SIXTEEN

THE JUNGLE

ROGER had always remembered the first time his voice was heard in Court. That was one advantage of being appointed a judge so young; his early days were not so long ago. So he was particularly sympathetic towards young men who had been left behind by their masters to hold the fort. Whenever possible, he would accede to such an application as:

"Would your Lordship allow the cross-examination of this witness to stand over until my learned friend Mr Snail returns?"

But on one occasion the application was so fiercely opposed by counsel on the other side that Roger felt he must refuse it.

"B-but," began the young man. "I d-don't know what to ask."

"Never mind," said Roger. "Suppose I suggest something to begin with."

"That's very g-good of your Lordship."

So Roger started the young man's cross-examination, and was soon making such progress that counsel on the other side began to wish devoutly that he had agreed to wait till the young man's master returned.

Indeed, eventually he said:

"My Lord, if your Lordship will forgive me, I think I was perhaps rather hasty and unfair to my learned friend when I said that I didn't agree for his cross-examination to stand over. If your Lordship will allow me, I should now like to accede to his application."

"Now, I wonder," said Roger, "why you've changed your mind. I'm not asking too many questions myself, am I, by any chance?"

"Oh—no, my Lord," said counsel, "it was just that I felt it might be better if the cross-examination stood over."

"What do you say, Mr Purse?" said Roger to the young man. "Now that you're warming to it, would you like to go on or not?"

"I think perhaps my learned leader would prefer—my Lord——"

"Very well," said Roger. "As you ask me and as your application is no longer opposed, I might say, is now supported by your ever considerate opponent, I'll agree to it."

There was a pretty girl sitting in the back of the court. Roger wondered if it was the young man's sister or girl friend. He remembered how once—but he must get on with the case in hand, not reminisce to himself now.

One morning Roger had experience of a new type of counsel. Mr Meldon had only recently been called to the bar but he was a little over thirty. It very soon became apparent that, before being a barrister, he had been a high pressure salesman, and he obviously thought that there was no reason why he should not make good use of his past experience in presenting his cases. After all, he had worn down hard-headed business men and cautious housewives, why not judges too?

"My Lord," he began in opening his case to Roger. "This is a claim which will cause your Lordship no difficulty at all. Of that I can assure your Lordship. I have two witnesses who will only have to be seen to be believed. They are both persons of the strictest integrity and their memories are extremely good. Your Lordship will be able to rely with confidence on every word they say."

"Hardly worth fighting the case," murmured his opponent to a neighbour.

"I've no doubt," said Mr Meldon, "that my learned friend thinks that he has some very good witnesses too, but the proof of the pudding is, if I may say so, my Lord, in the eating, and your Lordship will find that, when you compare the witnesses on each side, you will find that those called on behalf of the plaintiff are very much superior to those called on behalf of the defendant."

Roger could not resist intervening with:

"Do you mean to look at, Mr Meldon?"

Nothing daunted, Mr Meldon replied:

"In appearance, learning, diction and last but by no means least, I hope, my Lord, in honesty."

"What are their vital statistics?" whispered his opponent but loud enough to be heard.

Mr Meldon ignored the interruption.

"Wouldn't it be better if you told me something about the case, Mr Meldon, rather than enlarge on the beauties of your witnesses?" said Roger.

"Yes, indeed, my Lord, I was coming to the case. Now your Lordship has in the past tried numerous cases on various subjects. Some of the cases have been plain, some fairly plain and some far from plain. But I venture to say to your Lordship that this case that I am presenting to your Lordship is the plainest case that your Lordship has ever tried. Plain, if I may say so, beyond a peradventure."

"You may not say so," said Roger gently.

"I beg your Lordship's pardon," said the puzzled Mr Meldon, who was not used to the customer intervening at this early stage.

"Your duty and your only right," said Roger, "is to make submissions to the Court. You are not allowed to give me the benefit of your own opinion, however valuable."

"If your Lordship pleases," said Mr Meldon slightly abashed

and completely unaware of the respect in which he had offended. However, he soon recovered.

"Well, my Lord," he said, "your Lordship will find that the plaintiff is entitled to succeed in this case beyond any doubt of any kind whatsoever."

"Wouldn't it be more helpful, from your point of view, in order to arrive at that desirable result, to tell me what the case is about?" said Roger.

"Of course, my Lord. I shall, of course, do so, but at the moment I am trying to condition your Lordship."

Roger had read of people biting their lips until the blood came, and he now for the first time realized that it might actually happen. But he had to keep on biting for some time.

"That's very kind of you, Mr Meldon," he said eventually, "but normally in these courts counsel opening a case tells the judge what it is about before he does anything else."

"Thank you, my Lord," said Mr Meldon. "Then the pep talk comes later?"

Roger nearly drew blood again.

"Suppose you tell me what the claim is for," he said, as soon as he was able to speak.

"Certainly, my Lord. My clients who are reputable members of a reputable trade sold the defendant a motor car."

"What is their trade, Mr Meldon?" asked Roger.

Mr. Meldon looked puzzled.

"I've just told your Lordship," he said, "the motor car trade."

"Thank you," said Roger. "I see."

"The car was, I need hardly say, in perfect condition, and had only been registered the previous year. A new car of the same make would have cost £1,000. My clients only charged £350."

"Are they a benevolent institution?" said Roger; "£350 for a £1,000 car?"

"I'm glad your Lordship has noticed that," said Mr Meldon. "That's a point I want to bring out. My clients' business has always been conducted on those lines, a very small margin of profit so as to have a quick turnover and an ever-increasing goodwill. If your Lordship went to my clients' showrooms——"

"I don't think," said Roger, "this is the time or place to try to sell me one of their cars."

"Oh—my Lord," said Mr Meldon. "I shouldn't dream of doing any such thing, though if I may say so, your Lordship could go further and fare worse."

"Never mind where I'm going," said Roger. "What about this car that the plaintiff sold to the defendant? Didn't it go? Did the plaintiff pay for it? What are your clients now suing for?"

428

"Ah, my Lord," said Mr Meldon. "I can well understand that your Lordship is impatient to hear the details. But they will be no worse for being waited for. What's good keeps, my Lord."

"Mr Meldon," said Roger firmly but still kindly, "you have not been very long at the Bar and I think you'll find things easier if you take a hint from the Bench now and then and do what the judge asks you to do."

"My Lord, I shall be delighted," said Mr Meldon. "It is not as though my clients have anything to hide or anything to be ashamed of. They have, as I've told your Lordship, an unanswerable case."

"Well, please let me hear it," said Roger. "What are you suing for?"

"Your Lordship will already have seen," began Mr Meldon.

"Mr Meldon, I'm sorry to keep on interrupting you, but I have seen nothing so far," said Roger. "I never look at the pleadings until I am referred to them by counsel. And I'm bound to say I'm beginning to doubt if we will ever reach that stage."

"Oh, we will indeed, my Lord, and your Lordship will find the pleadings very rich, very rich indeed."

Roger sighed and waited.

"Now, my Lord, the defendant took away the car—would he have done that if he had not been satisfied?—and he gave the plaintiff a cheque, and, my Lord, I have the cheque here. It is present in court and I'm going to make it an exhibit."

Mr Meldon paused in order to get what he considered the right dramatic effect. He was leading up to his climax.

"My Lord," he said in a somewhat hushed voice, "that cheque— that cheque was—was—DISHONOURED."

Mr Meldon stopped, as though waiting for applause.

After a moment Roger said, in a very matter-of-fact voice:

"So you're suing on the dishonoured cheque? Is that the case?"

"My Lord," said Mr Meldon, feeling that Roger had not appreciated the full force of his words, "The cheque was DISHONOURED."

"So I assume," said Roger. "Your clients couldn't have sued on it, if it had been paid."

"Nor would they have done so," said Mr Meldon. "That is not the way they carry on their business."

Roger had recourse to his lip again and, when he had recovered, he asked:

"Why was the cheque dishonoured?"

"Your Lordship may well ask," said Mr Meldon.

"Well, I do ask," said Roger, "and I should really like to know the answer."

"My Lord," said Mr Meldon, "I hold in my hand the cheque.

429

It is signed by the defendant. It was DISHONOURED by the defendant," and he held up the cheque in his hand.

"Yes, you've told me all that. Why was it dishonoured?"

"Because, my Lord," said Mr Meldon, "because the defendant has the impudence to say that it was obtained by fraud."

"I see," said Roger.

"In order to evade his just liabilities the defendant does not scruple to make this wicked allegation against my highly respectable clients. They have come to meet this charge and I venture to say to your Lordship, that that charge will be found to be as worthless as is apparently the defendant's signature on the cheque."

"What is the alleged fraud?" asked Roger.

"The defendant says that this car was manufactured twenty years ago."

"Well, was it?" asked Roger.

"Some very good cars indeed were manufactured twenty years ago," said Mr Meldon. "Indeed some people in the trade think that the quality of those cars is superior to many which are being made today."

"I dare say," said Roger, "but do I gather from that, that you admit that the car was in fact manufactured twenty years ago?"

"Yes, that is quite correct, my Lord."

"I think I see now what the case is going to be about. The defendant says that your clients represented that the car was made last year, whereas, in fact, it was made twenty years ago. Is that right, Mr Meldon?"

"That is, indeed, what the defendant says, my Lord, but what in fact happened is that my clients said that the car was first REGISTERED last year. They said nothing as to when it was manufactured."

"So that's the issue, is it?" said Roger. "Tell me, what happened to the car between its manufacture and its first registration?"

"It was used in the Army, my Lord, and then sold by auction by the Ministry of Supply. I need hardly tell your Lordship of the care with which the car was likely to be used when being driven in the Army. It was a COMMANDING OFFICER'S car, my Lord. I need say no more."

"Good," said Mr Meldon's opponent under his breath.

"Why didn't the registration book show that the car, although first registered last year, was ex-Army stock?"

"My Lord, I'm instructed that registration books should show the fact, but they do not always do so."

"I see," said Roger. "So that, if one's buying a second-hand car, the date of the first registration does not necessarily mean that the car was new on that date?"

"Usually it does, my Lord, but not always."

"Well, if this case does nothing else," said Roger, "I hope it will put the public on their guard about that matter. I suppose the actual date of manufacture can easily be ascertained by looking at the engine or chassis number?"

"Yes, my Lord. Most dealers have a book which shows them the year of manufacture for one or other of those numbers."

"So your clients knew that the car was an old one?"

"Yes, my Lord."

"Did they tell that to the defendant?"

"Oh, my Lord," said Mr Meldon with a deprecating gesture of his hands, "the vendor need not decry his own goods, need he?"

"But I thought you said that the car might be all the better for being made twenty years ago," said Roger.

"Ah, my Lord," said Mr Meldon virtuously, "my clients are not the sort of people to take advantage of a point like that."

"So the long and short of it is," said Roger, "that your clients told the defendant that the car was first registered last year, that the defendant thought that meant the car was one year old and that when he found it wasn't, he claimed that he had been tricked."

"Yes, my Lord," said Mr Meldon. "Absurd isn't it?"

"I don't see anything absurd in it," said Roger.

"But, my Lord, look at the price my clients charged. The defendant couldn't have expected a nearly new car for that."

"Well, Mr Meldon," said Roger. "You yourself pointed out to me that your clients prided themselves on making a very low margin of profit. May they not have said that to the defendant?"

"If they did, my Lord, it was true."

"I dare say, but that may have satisfied the defendant's curiosity as to why such a low price was charged for such a new car."

"Anyway, my Lord, it was a very good car. The defendant drove away in it himself."

"That was something," said Roger. "Did he by any chance ring up shortly afterwards and say the car had broken down?"

Mr Meldon looked astonished.

"My Lord," he said in a surprised tone. "How did your Lordship know?"

"I didn't," said Roger, "but I have had some experience of these cases."

"But that, of course, has nothing to do with it, my Lord. A car has to break down some time. And, after all, this one was twenty years old. We must all break down some time, my Lord."

"Whenever we were first registered," said Roger.

Eventually the plaintiff's counsel was prevailed upon by Roger to produce his beautiful witnesses. Before he did so, Roger asked

431

Mr Meldon's opponent, Mr Brent, whether it wasn't really for the defendant to call his evidence first, in view of the fact that the drawing and dishonouring of the cheque were admitted.

"Yes, my Lord," said Mr Brent, "your Lordship is, of course, right. I may tell your Lordship, though, that I mentioned this to my learned friend before he opened the case. Whereupon he said he wanted to tell the judge what the plaintiff's case was. I then said that, if he opened the case, he'd have to call his witnesses first. He said that that was what he had every intention of doing. He then started to describe the beauty of his witnesses, but I was in a better position to duck than your Lordship."

"Very well," said Roger.

So Mr Meldon called his witnesses. First he called a typical car salesman with an Air Force moustache, and a spurious Oxford-B.B.C.-Guards accent. Among other questions Mr Meldon asked him:

"Tell me, Mr Plaster, have you ever in the course of your career described a car to a customer in language which was not entirely justified?"

"Good heavens, no, sir," was the reply. "I wouldn't keep my job for a moment if I did."

"Are the cars you sell always worth what the customer pays for them or more?"

"Oh, certainly, sir. I'd be prepared to swear to that."

"You are swearing to it," said Roger.

"Quite, my Lord."

"And it's true?" asked Roger.

"Oh, yes, my Lord."

"That you've never sold a customer a car which was not worth what he paid for it?"

"Well, my Lord, there may have been something wrong with the car which I didn't know about."

"And have customers sometimes complained that there was something wrong with cars you have sold them?"

"Oh, my Lord, customers are always complaining. Most of them don't understand cars," said the witness.

"That must make it much easier to sell cars to them," said Roger.

"Oh, no, my Lord," said the witness. "Much harder. They can't see what bargains they are getting."

Later Mr Meldon called his second witness, a Mr Prince. He was of a very different order.

"Look," he said in cross-examination, "the car trade is rather like driving in London. Each man for himself and no quarter asked or given. It's a jungle."

"And what particular animal are you?" asked Mr Brent.

432

"It all depends," said Mr Prince. "At the moment I'd like to be a monkey, safe up in the trees and throwing nuts at you."

"And how would you describe yourself when you're selling a car? A snake? A crocodile?"

"No, sir, thank you. I do very well as I am. Homo sap something, I think they call it. I don't know where the sap comes in."

"He comes into your showrooms, doesn't he?"

Mr Prince smiled.

"Yes, sir. Not one every minute, as I should like," he said, "but enough to give me an honest living."

"An honest living?" queried Mr Brent. "You'd say anything, wouldn't you, to sell a car?"

"To tell you the truth, sir, words don't mean a thing. When I buy a car, I go by the car, not by what's said about it."

"Quite, Mr Prince, but people outside the trade are not so fortunate. They don't know what to look for."

"And if they did," volunteered Mr Prince, "they mightn't find it, I can tell you."

"You're being very frank," said Roger. "Why?"

"Well, my Lord," said Mr Prince, "I've sworn to tell the truth, and it's a new experience."

"You like it then?" asked Roger.

"I like it here all right," said the witness, "but it wouldn't be any good in my business. Go broke in no time."

"Well, Mr Prince," said Roger, "it's very refreshing to hear so frank a witness. Perhaps you can help me over this case. It's going to be said by the defendant that he was told this car was manufactured about a year ago. Did you tell him that?"

"It wasn't necessary, my Lord. We couldn't keep him off the car. You see, my Lord, we advertised it as 'first registered last year.' And so it was. Then we put: 'New price £1,000. Our price £350.' It would have been cruelty not to sell him the car. He'd set his heart on it."

"Did he ask why it was being sold so cheaply?"

"I expect so, my Lord. They usually do."

"And what was he told?" asked Mr Brent.

"The usual, I expect, but I don't remember exactly. Have too many cases like this."

"By 'the usual' you mean that you worked on small profits and quick returns?"

"That's right."

"But that wasn't a true answer, was it?" asked Roger. "The car was being sold at that price because it was a very old car."

"Well the price was worked out by what we'd paid for it, and, as a matter of fact, it's quite true we do work on a very small margin of profit. If we can make £5 over a car quick, it's better than waiting to make £10. That's the way we look at it."

"So that, when you tell customers that you work on a low margin of profit, that's actually true?" said Roger.

"Yes, so it is, my Lord," said Mr Prince, slightly surprised. "Now, I'm not saying that's why we say it, my Lord, but it just happens that way. Rather like in driving. Every now and then a taxi-driver says 'after you.' But that's when he hasn't a fare and wants to dawdle."

The case went on and Roger eventually decided that the defendant had been told not simply that the car had been registered the year before but that it had been made the year before. So he found against the plaintiffs. Mr Meldon had failed to make a sale.

Outside the court he offered his sympathy to Mr Prince.

"Oh, that's all right, old chap," said Mr Prince, "you did your best, but it's the same here as in the trade. It doesn't pay to tell the truth. I'll know better another time. I couldn't sell you a new Vauxhall, second-hand, could I, first registered next year?"

CHAPTER SEVENTEEN

THE TROJAN KITCHEN

FROM time to time a High Court Judge is asked to sit in the Court of Appeal, when, for example, one of the Lords Justices is ill or performing some other duty, and it was not long before Roger was asked to do this. He sat with Lords Justices Crewe and Soulsby and they heard appeals from County Courts.

One of the first of these was an appeal from Henry and, for a moment, Roger felt a little odd at the thought. Roger, although not Henry's pupil, had probably learned more from Henry in his early days than from anyone else. And now here he was in a position to say:

"With the greatest respect to the learned judge, although his language is far from clear, I cannot think that he meant that."

However, he soon got used to the idea and, as it turned out, he never had to use such an expression about any part of Henry's judgment.

The case had arisen as a result of trouble between a landlord and a tenant. Although, no doubt, practitioners in the County Court see many such cases, it is remarkable how comparatively few there are. After all, for many people it is difficult not to be, if not irritated, at the least inconvenienced by the footsteps, wireless noises, parties and babies of the friends who live upstairs. If they are not friends, the irritation and inconvenience must be far worse, and, if they are on the worst possible terms with their downstairs neighbours, it is difficult to know how the latter can bear it and keep their sanity.

But they do. Up and down the country they manage to live somehow, without recourse to the Courts or nervous breakdowns. It is only a very small percentage of cases which find their way to the Courts, but every Court where the housing situation is acute (and this applies to most Courts) has a fair number of them.

The case which eventually came before Judge Blagrove and then before the Court of Appeal arose in this way. Mr Stream was the tenant of a small house with two floors and he had lived there for many years with his wife and growing family. When the children grew up and left to get married, the house seemed rather big for them and, with the permission of his landlord, Mr Stream sublet the upper floor to Mr and Mrs Bulge. The Bulges were very anxious to find a place and, although Mr Stream was unable to give them a proper kitchen, it was agreed that they should make do with a sort of kitchenette which Mr Bulge constructed on the upper landing. It was also agreed that the bathroom and lavatory should be shared by the two families.

Things went very well at first and Mr Stream found the Bulges' rent quite useful. But one day there was some altercation between Mrs Bulge and Mrs Stream which, though unimportant in itself, was the origin of the trouble. Within a week of this episode each side was asking the other to turn its wireless down. Within a month Mrs Stream was asking Mrs Bulge to walk more quietly up the stairs. Within two or three months it was difficult for the Bulges to move about upstairs without Mr or Mrs Stream banging with a broom on their ceiling. This was answered by the Bulges with deliberate thumps.

It was six months before the police had to be called the first time. Things were quieter for a few weeks after that, but then one evening, both sides, having consumed a certain amount of alcohol, a quantity which ordinarily would have made the parties mellow and happily ready for bed, happened to arrive home at the same time. They glared at each other and then Mr and Mrs Bulge, after thumping up the stairs, turned on their wireless.

Mr Stream shouted up to Mr Bulge to turn the wireless down. Mr Bulge asked Mr Stream if he'd like to come up and do it himself, and eventually, after a few further pleasantries, hostilities began. The police were called again.

After quiet had been restored the policeman asked what it was all about, whereupon both sides started to explain at once.

"Just a moment," said the policeman, "I think I'd better see you separately."

"It'll be all lies she tells you," volunteered Mrs Bulge.

"That's all right," said the policeman, "I'll listen to yours afterwards—your story, I mean."

So the policeman interviewed Mr and Mrs Stream first.

"Well—they had the wireless on loud, so I asked them quite friendly to turn it up——"

"Down, you mean," put in the policeman.

"Just a manner of speaking—and he threatened to murder me. I'd like to see him try. He hasn't the guts."

"Then you weren't frightened he'd really try?"

"I'd like to see him. I could hit him if he did, couldn't I? That'd be self defence."

"I shouldn't get mixed up in a fight," said the policeman, "you never know where it's going to end."

"Well—what can we do? We can't stand any more of this."

"Well," said the policeman, "if I were you I'd see a solicitor. Mind you, I'm not saying it'll be any good, but, if they really are a nuisance, you might be able to get an order for possession against them. But I can't tell you if you will. That's up to the lawyers."

"D'you know one?"

"Well," said the policeman, "there's a chap called Digby opposite the police station. Quite a good chap and he won't skin you, like some of them. I'd go and see him."

After a little further talk, the policeman went up to the Bulges and heard their side of the story.

"It's nag, nag, nag all the time. We don't get any peace at all," said Mrs Bulge.

"They even pinch our letters," said Mr Bulge.

"Ah," said the policeman. "That's bad, if you can prove it, but can you?"

"Well, we haven't seen them at it. They're too cunning for that. But how is it there's no letter when I go down in the morning, and half an hour later there's one on the mat? It can't grow there, though from the way they live downstairs I shouldn't be surprised if something started to grow there."

"Well—what happened tonight?"

"Well, they started screaming and shouting, and if you hadn't come," said Mr Bulge meaningly, "I think someone might have got hurt."

"Well, I shouldn't get mixed up in a fight," advised the policeman. "Don't start anything you can't finish is our motto at the station."

"Well, what about the letters? There must be a law about that."

"Well, if I were you, I should consult a solicitor about it. There's one just round the corner from the police station in Flint Street—name of Bromley."

"Come to think, there's one opposite the police station, isn't there?" said Mr Bulge.

"Yes, there is," said the policeman slowly, "but if I were you I'd go to the one in Flint Street—Mr Digby's a bit busy at the moment. Now d'you think I can go back to the station without being called out again?"

"It's not our fault," said Mrs Bulge. "We keep ourselves to ourselves."

"I know, mum, just how it is," said the policeman, and went back to the station.

The next day the Streams consulted Mr Digby, who listened to them courteously and at length. In consequence a summons was issued in the Pendlebury County Court for possession of the Bulges' rooms on the ground of nuisance. The details were long and varied:

1. Threatening to murder Mr Stream.
2. Using abusive and obscene language towards Mr and Mrs Stream.
3. Deliberately playing the wireless too loud late at night.
4. Banging doors.
5. Deliberately hammering on the floor.
6. Moving furniture late at night.
7. Cutting the washing line in the garden just after Mrs Stream had put her washing out.
8. Taking the Streams' milk.
9. Assault.
10. Leaving the front door open.
11. Slamming the front door.
12. Preventing the Streams from using the lavatory.

As soon as the Bulges received the summons they went round to Mr Bromley. He was a quiet, modest little man who did not like appearing in Court, and invariably instructed counsel if it were possible. On this occasion he arranged that Mr and Mrs Bulge should have what he called the advantage of being represented by a young man called Docket. Mr Docket's enthusiasm considerably outweighed his experience, but he had the necessary wig, robes and voice to appear in the Pendlebury County Court, and he was able to pay the fare there.

The day of the hearing arrived and Mr Docket made the journey from London by train. In the train he read his brief over again, and made more marks on it, underlining this passage, noting a query here and there, and generally putting the finishing touches to his work, like an artist with a picture. By the time he arrived at the Court everything was ready for an impassioned assault upon the Streams.

In the robing room he met Mr Digby, his opponent. Mr Digby was a solicitor of many years' experience who did a great deal of advocacy himself. He was known as the local Solicitor-General. After they had had a chat for a few minutes, Mr Docket expressed the view that he was sorry for anyone whose case was in the list after theirs. Mr Digby asked him why.

"Why?" said Mr Docket, in a surprised tone. "Why? Because we'll take three hours at least, probably all day. Lucky we're at the head of the list."

"D'you know why we're so high in the list?" said Mr Digby.

"A mistake, I suppose."

"Not at all. D'you know this judge?"

"I can't say that I do," said Mr Docket. "What's he like?"

"Very nice, but he has a way with nuisance cases."

"What d'you mean?" asked Mr Docket.

"Shall I tell you exactly what'll happen in our case?"

"If you can do so without giving away professional secrets, I'd be most grateful."

"No secrets at all. You'll see for yourself in a moment. Our case is where it is because the clerk thinks it'll take about five minutes."

"Five minutes!" said Mr Docket. "It'll take you half an hour to open it, I should have thought."

"So?" said Mr Digby. "Shall I go on?"

"Well?" said Mr Docket.

"After I've opened the case for about two of your thirty minutes, the old boy will say:

" 'Mr Docket and Mr Digby—don't you think this is the sort of case where the parties might put their heads together?' What he means by this is that the parties should have their heads banged together. I quite agree with him as a matter of fact."

"Well, I don't," said Mr Docket with some heat. "I think your clients have behaved disgracefully, if my instructions are right."

"My dear boy," said Mr Digby, "if you'll forgive my relying on my superiority in age and forgetting my inferiority in profession, don't be angry with me. If my instructions are right, your clients ought to be turned out of the house tomorrow."

"I quite agree with you, *if* they're right. But, by the time I've cross-examined your Mr Stream, I fancy you won't be so sure of your client's instructions."

"I'm afraid it doesn't require your cross-examination to produce that effect. In this sort of case it's very rare for either side to have correct instructions. But I was telling you what will happen —shall I go on?"

"Please."

"Well, whatever either of us says—unless there's something really serious or unusual—he'll suggest an adjournment—'Just to see how things go on. Would you like me to say a word to each of your clients?' went on Mr Digby, giving a very good imitation of Henry's manner and voice. 'Certainly. Now, Mr and Mrs Stream—Mr and Mrs Bulge—you each of you have my deepest sympathy in having to live with people you don't like. But in these days of housing shortage we just have to make the best of these things. Now, you both go away and try to see the good in each other. Of course if things don't improve, Mr Bulge, I may have to make an order against you or, if it's your fault, Mr Stream, I may have to dismiss the action with costs. Expensive business, going to law. Counsel and solicitors have to be paid, you know.' "

"Does he always go on like that?" asked Mr Docket.

"Nearly always in nuisance cases on the first hearing. Of course, if it comes back to him he tries it."

"Well, I'm going to make him try it today."

"Go ahead, my dear boy," said Mr Digby, "I like to see enthusiasm."

Soon afterwards, the case was called on and Mr Digby had not been speaking for more than a few minutes when the judge duly interrupted, and the next dialogue was as follows:

HENRY: Mr Digby, I've been looking at the allegations in this action. Don't you and Mr—er—Mr Docket think this is perhaps a case where you might put your heads together?

DIGBY: I should be very happy to take instructions on the point, your Honour.

HENRY: And you, Mr Docket?

DOCKET: My clients want the action heard today, your Honour.

HENRY: Quite so, Mr Docket, quite so. But have they considered the possibilities? Of course, I'm not expressing an opinion one way or the other—I don't know anything about the case— but, if I were satisfied—I say *if* I were satisfied that, for instance, your client had without sufficient provocation threatened to murder the plaintiff, I should take a very grave view of the matter.

DOCKET: My clients have a perfect explanation of that matter, your Honour.

HENRY: Quite so, Mr Docket, quite so—but just suppose for a moment that I don't accept that explanation—I'm not expressing any view at present naturally—I don't know who's in the right—

though in this type of case it is not uncommon for it to be six of one and half a dozen of the other—suppose I don't accept the explanation—it would be most awkward for your clients if I made an order against them. *They* haven't anything to lose by an adjournment. If the plaintiff doesn't mind, I don't see why your clients should.

DOCKET: There are the letters, your Honour.

HENRY: Oh—your counterclaim. How many letters do your clients have in a week?

DOCKET: I'm not sure, your Honour.

HENRY: I rather suspect they don't have enough to make it worth while risking having an order for possession made against them. Surely with a little goodwill on both sides something can be arranged and we can see how things go?

DOCKET (*doggedly*): I should prefer to have the action tried, your Honour.

HENRY: Very well, then, Mr Docket. No doubt you have your instructions and must abide by them. Call your evidence, Mr Digby.

So the case proceeded, and after two and a half hours Henry gave judgment as follows:

"It is a great pity," he said, "that my advice was not accepted two and a half hours ago. There is nothing whatever to choose between either of the parties, as I rather suspected from the start. Both claim and counterclaim will be dismissed, and each side will bear its own costs."

But it was not from that decision that the case went to the Court of Appeal. Mr and Mrs Stream went home very unhappily, and, as soon as it was opening time, Mr Stream went out to drown his sorrows. In the public house he met a solicitor's clerk. They got talking and Mr Stream confided his troubles to the stranger. Over the third pint, Mr Stream was given some advice which he decided to act upon as soon as possible.

He went home and told his wife about it. The next thing that happened was that the Bulges came home triumphant, banged their way up the stairs and turned the radio on. After all, they had only lost their claim about their letters. The real fight they had won. As they did not receive the usual response to the noise they were making, Mr Bulge came out on to the landing and, pretending to hear some noise from below, shouted down:

"Stop that ruddy noise, will you?"

He could only just be heard above the blaring of their own radio, and Mr Bulge thought he must have misheard the reply that seemed to come from below. For what Mr Stream had in fact said was:

"Sorry, old man."

Quite certain that he was mistaken, Mr Bulge yelled down even louder:

"Stop that ruddy noise."

But this time there was no doubt about the reply, because Mr Stream came out of his room and, instead of the usual expletives, he said:

"So sorry, old man."

Mr Bulge was very much taken aback. The only reply he could think of was:

"Well, do something about it then," and he went back to his own room, and grumbled even more than usual about the people down below.

But the next morning, which was a Sunday, there was another surprise for the Bulges. About noon there was a knock on the door and there was Mr Stream. Mr Bulge said aggressively:

"What d'you want?"

"I only came up about the noise last night," began Mr Stream apologetically.

"We'll make as much noise as we ruddy well like," said Bulge. "Take us to Court, would you?"

"No," said Mr Stream, with unaccustomed mildness, "you've got me wrong. I wanted to say I was sorry about the noise *we* were making. To tell you the truth, I was in a bit of a two and eight. Lucky not to have been picked up by the old grasshopper."

Mr Bulge was so surprised that he could only say:

"Oh!" And then added grudgingly, rather like a judge granting an adjournment which it is personally inconvenient for him to grant: "Very well."

Mr Stream went away and Mr Bulge asked his wife whether she thought Mr Stream was going round the bend. If she did, there was confirmation for her view during the next fortnight. For whatever the Bulges did or said the Streams behaved with an incredible meekness, and started to go out of their way to try to do favours for the Bulges. It was not long before this method of attack had its effect, and the parties started to smile at each other when they met. And the Bulges no longer stamped up the stairs—they walked up them. One thing led to another and it was not long before they were having drinks together. After several sessions anyone who met them would have thought that they had always been bosom friends.

It was when the relationship had been pretty well cemented that one day Mr Stream made his finest gesture of all.

"It must be pretty awkward," he said, "for your old woman cooking up on the landing. How would it be if you shared our kitchen? Of course, I'd have to ask the missus, but she and your missus seem to get along all right."

"Well, that's very kind of you, old man," said Mr Bulge, and spoke to his wife about it. Within a week it had been agreed that the rent should be increased by sixpence, and that the Bulges should share the Streams' kitchen.

Mrs Stream did find it a bit irksome after many years of having her own kitchen to share it with that—with the lady upstairs. But she controlled herself and made the best of it. So for at least two months after the new arrangement (which had been confirmed by the presentation to the Bulges, at the expense of the Streams, of a brand-new rent book) things went well. But after that time Mr and Mrs Stream started to make remarks to each other or to themselves which the Bulges could and were intended to hear. At first, in view of the new relationship, they thought they must have misheard and took no notice, but that could not go on for long. It only required one retort from Mrs Bulge to a sarcastic aside from Mrs Stream about the dirt that some people carried around with them, to set the smouldering embers ablaze. Once more the rows began, but, within a week from the first real one, Mr Stream had served on the Bulges a notice to quit.

"Here's what I think of that," said Mr Bulge, and tore it up into little pieces and threw it down the stairs.

"You've had it anyway," said Mr Stream.

"So have you," said Mr Bulge. "Take me to Court again! Don't make me laugh."

But Mr Stream did take Mr Bulge to Court again, and this time there was a difference, because the summons said nothing about noise or misbehaviour or anything as offensive as that. It was a mild little affair, the summons. Or so Mr Bulge thought, until he took it to his solicitor.

"Oh, dear," said Mr Bromley, "you have got yourself into a mess."

"We ain't done nothing," said Mr Bulge.

"Oh, but you have, Mr Bulge, you have indeed. You've made a new tenancy agreement with Mr Stream, under which you share the kitchen."

"They suggested it," said Mr Bulge.

"No doubt they did," said Mr Bromley, "no doubt they did. But you agreed to it, and, once you did that, you lost the protection of the Rent Act. You didn't know, I suppose, that a landlord who shares his kitchen with his tenant can get the tenant out, whenever he likes, if he gives him notice to quit?"

"The dirty——" began Mr Bulge.

"I quite understand your feelings," said Mr Bromley. "It was

442

a very dirty trick, but strong words are no good—we've got to see what we can do to get you out of it. I'll send the papers to counsel at once."

In consequence Mr Docket again met Mr Digby at the Pendlebury County Court. When they first met in the robing room, Mr Docket gave the solicitor a very curt "good morning."

"It's nothing to do with me," said Mr Digby, "I never suggested it to them. They met a solicitor's clerk in a pub and he put them up to it. You say anything you like about it in Court. I quite agree with you. But how are you going to get out of it?"

"I say it's fraud," said Mr Docket.

"I know you do in the defence," said Mr Digby, "but how are you going to prove it?"

"Well, if this isn't fraud, I don't know what is," said Mr Docket.

However, Henry, after a patient hearing, decided that, although in a sense the Bulges had been tricked into making the new agreement, it did not amount to fraud in law, and regretfully he made an order for possession against the Bulges.

It was from that decision that the Bulges appealed, and Roger and the two Lords Justices had yet another case which dealt with the strange story of the shared kitchen. For strange it seems to some people that the Courts expressly, and Parliament impliedly, have decided that, as long as a landlord only shares a bathroom or a lavatory with a tenant, the tenant is fully protected by the Rent Acts. And, indeed, if he only has a partial use of the kitchen, such as for boiling water occasionally, he is still protected. But, once he has the right to use the kitchen equally with his landlord, he has apparently lost the protection of the Rent Acts. The exact principle upon which it has been decided that the sharing of a bath or a lavatory is different from the sharing of a kitchen is a little difficult for some people to follow, except, of course, that the bathroom and lavatory are not used at the same time by both landlord and tenant. But then, normally, neither is the gas stove or sink. However, that is the law, as the Bulges found to their cost, and there is no getting away from it. The only escape available to the Bulges was if they could show that they had, in the legal sense, been cheated into making the new agreement by which they shared the kitchen.

Mr Docket, who appeared for the Bulges, soon found that addressing the Court of Appeal was very different from appearing in a County Court. He had only just started when he received a fast ball from Lord Justice Crewe.

"But, Mr Docket," he said, "the judge has negatived fraud. Surely that's an end of the matter? It's purely a question of fact, isn't it?"

443

"I suppose," said Roger, observing that Mr Docket did not seem in a condition to deal with the delivery, "that you would say, Mr Docket, that the learned judge did say that the defendants had— to use his own words—been tricked into making the new agreement."

"Yes, my Lord," said Mr Docket eagerly, thankful to have found a friend so early.

"And you'd go on to say, I suppose," said Roger, "that, although the learned judge has negatived fraud, that decision is inconsistent with his finding that the defendants were tricked?"

"Yes, indeed, my Lord," said Mr Docket.

"But," said Lord Justice Crewe, looking at Mr Docket, but talking at Roger, "the actual words of the learned judge were— 'in a sense tricked'—were they not?"

"Yes, my Lord," said Mr Docket less hopefully, and glancing towards Roger in the hope that he would find whatever was the best answer.

"Well, Mr Docket," went on the Lord Justice, but this time actually looking at Roger, "the learned judge plainly knew what are the ingredients necessary to prove fraud, and he came to the conclusion that they were not established. Was he doing more in using the words you mention than saying in more elegant language that it was what might be termed colloquially 'a dirty trick'?"

"Well, my Lord," said Mr Docket, "I submit——" and he paused sufficiently long to show Roger that he had no idea what to submit.

"Yes, Mr Docket," said Roger, "you say, I suppose, that a learned judge of the experience and learning of Judge Blagrove, if I may say so, chooses his language carefully. He did not say that it was a dirty trick, but that the defendants had been tricked."

"In a sense, Mr Docket," put in Lord Justice Crewe.

"Yes, in a sense," conceded Roger. "But tricked. Tricked," he repeated. "And I'm bound to say that, for my part, I agree with the learned judge. The defendants *were* tricked. The whole behaviour of the plaintiffs was a lie—an acted lie. Their pretence that they liked the defendants, for example, was not that as much a fraudulent representation as an ordinary deliberate lie? Is that what you say, Mr Docket?"

"Yes, indeed, my Lord," said Mr Docket.

"But, Mr Docket, really," said Lord Justice Crewe, "can you rely on that? Was it in your defence?"

"Well, my Lord," began Mr Docket unhappily, for it was not in his clients' written defence, but, before he could finish, Roger intervened with:

444

"But in the County Court it doesn't have to be, does it? You can rely on any defence at the trial, whatever may be in the written defence."

Roger leaned across to Lord Justice Crewe: "I believe it's Order 9 Rule 8," he whispered.

"I dare say," said Lord Justice Crewe testily. He did not expect a fairly new puisne judge to talk as much as Roger was talking.

"You were saying, Mr Docket," went on Roger, "that, if a man tells a lie, he can just as easily live a lie. A deaf and dumb man can tell a lie. A tic-tac man at a racecourse can certainly tell a lie with his hands. In this case it was not just the actions of the defendants. It was the words as well. Is it conceivable that Mrs Bulge would have agreed to have shared a kitchen with a person who disliked her? You say it isn't, Mr Docket?"

"Yes, my Lord, I do."

"And you add, I suppose, that it was by pretending that they were reconciled and that the Streams really liked the Bulges, when the truth was that they intended to get them out of the house as soon as they could, that the plaintiffs tricked the defendants into making the new agreement? Why isn't that just as much fraud vitiating the new agreement as if they told some other lie about it? I fancy that, if the evidence were examined, a very large number of untruths told by the plaintiffs would emerge. Every time Mr and Mrs Stream made a conciliatory statement or gesture, it was untrue and it was made fraudulently."

"What," said Lord Justice Crewe, "did the learned judge say to that point, Mr Docket, when you put it to him—no doubt as forcefully as you are putting it to us?"

"He was against me, my Lord."

"Yes, yes, we know that. But was it really put to him in the form you are now putting it to us? My brother Thursby was not able to lead you at the County Court."

"My Lord, I did submit the whole thing was a fraud," said Mr Docket.

"And presumably," said Roger, "by 'the whole thing' you must have meant the behaviour and language of the defendants from first to last?"

"Yes, my Lord," said Mr Docket.

"And did the learned judge give any indication that he did not so understand it?"

"No, my Lord."

"And did the learned judge," said Lord Justice Crewe, "give any indication that he did understand it in the way you are putting it to us?"

"Your answer to that, Mr Docket," said Roger, "is, I suppose, the use of the words 'in a sense tricked.' How, you ask, could the learned judge suppose that the defendants had in a sense been tricked unless it was because of the words and behaviour of the plaintiffs for the weeks preceding the new agreement?"

"Yes, that's what I say," said Mr Docket.

Lord Justice Crewe leaned towards the other Lord Justice.

"You're very quiet," he whispered. "What's your view about it all?"

"I'm thinking," replied Lord Justice Soulsby.

"Good exercise," whispered Lord Justice Crewe, 'but what about? Forgive me," he added aloud, and motioned to Roger to come and talk to him and the other Lord Justice. Roger got up and went and stood between his two senior brethren. They talked in undertones.

"Well, is Thursby right?" asked Lord Justice Crewe.

"I must say," said Lord Justice Soulsby, "that Blagrove doesn't seem to have considered this point at all. He seems to have looked for some ordinary untrue statement before the new agreement, but he doesn't seem to have dealt with the possibility that the whole set-up—words and music—was untrue. I suppose he could have found that it was just a coincidence, and that the parties had genuinely got on better together."

"He doesn't seem to have dealt with that aspect at all. Won't it have to go back for a new trial?"

Meanwhile, Mr Docket was being encouraged by the London agent of Mr Bromley, a Mr Marrow.

"Stick to it," he said, "you're doing fine."

"Thank you," said Mr Docket.

"Don't sit down till Thursby's said everything he can think of. He's making a jolly good judge. He'll be in the Court of Appeal in his own right soon, if he isn't careful."

At this stage Roger went back to his own seat.

"We think," said Lord Justice Crewe, "that in view of Mr Docket's powerful submission, we should like to hear what his opponent has to say."

Eventually the appeal was allowed, the order for possession was set aside and a new trial ordered—"if," added Lord Justice Crewe, "the parties really wish to continue this litigation. They have already had three hearings in Court. Might I suggest to their respective advisers that the parties might now try and forget the past, go back to the old arrangement of kitchens, and really try to behave as they did for a couple of months just before and just after the new arrangement was made. Whatever the truth about the case may be, we are all sure that the most certain chance of happiness lies in that direction, and not in a further hearing in the County Court with a possible further appeal to this Court."

"I don't see why he should have added that," said Roger, when Henry and Sally next visited them. "You wouldn't go wrong twice in the same case."

"Thank you, Roger," said Henry. "You've always been such a comfort to me."

"I hope you think we were right to upset you," said Roger.

"Don't apologize," said Henry, "but, as a matter of fact, I do. It's an obvious point. Can't think how I missed it. Must be old age."

At that moment the telephone rang. Roger answered it. It was Plummer.

"I've got some good news for you, old boy," he said. "D'you remember a boy called Barrow? We used to call him 'Wheelbarrow.'"

"Yes," said Roger. "He's an M.P. What about him? And why is he good news?"

"Well, I've just heard that he's going to be the new Minister of Transport. So I'm going to help him make the wheels go round."

"Poor fellow," said Roger. "Now I suppose you'll be leaving me alone."

"Cross my heart," said Plummer. "That's if the papers are right. Anyway, I'm getting a bit tired of you. Have to be too careful. I think you're jolly good, by the way. A credit to the old school. Heard from Toni lately?"

"No," said Roger, "I haven't. Why d'you ask?"

"I just wondered," said Plummer. "Bye-bye. I've got to think up something to launch the new Minister."

Roger reported the conversation to Henry, Sally and Anne.

"I must say it's a bit of a relief," he said, "but after my first outing there wasn't much he could do."

"What about Toni," said Henry, "you've never had to find her that doctor's job?"

"No," said Roger, "I'm afraid she's slipping out of our life."

The telephone rang again.

"It's your turn, Anne," said Roger.

Anne went to answer it and was back in a few moments.

"It's Toni," she said. "She wondered if you could introduce her to a doctor."

"We've come just at the right moment," said Henry. "Shall we lock him up for you?" he asked Anne.

"It's very odd," said Roger, as he went to the telephone.

"I do hope you don't mind my troubling you," said Toni.

"No, of course not."

"Well, you did say that, if I ever wanted a change, you might introduce me to a job as a doctor's receptionist."

"Yes," said Roger, "I will, if you like."

"That's very sweet of you," said Toni. "I'll tell you why it is. You see, I'm just going to get engaged."

"My best wishes," said Roger.

"And we—Charles and I—thought it would be better if I were described as a doctor's receptionist or something, rather than a dance hostess."

"I see," said Roger. "Then it's only a very temporary job you want?"

"Oh very," said Toni.

"Well—please congratulate the lucky man for me," said Roger.

"You know him," said Toni.

Roger hesitated for a moment.

"Do I?" he said.

"Yes, very well indeed."

"You don't mean to say," he began.

"I do," said Toni. "How will you like me as a sister in law? That would be a fair description, wouldn't it?"

After a little further conversation, Roger went back to the others.

"What d'you think?" he said. "Toni's going to marry Charlie Breeze. She's a fast worker. I didn't even know they'd been seeing each other. She let Plummer think it was me."

"A case," said Henry, "of a judge not manifestly being seen to be done."